The Sugarloaf Bakery

ROSEMARY WHITTAKER

Also by Rosemary Whittaker

A Sugarloaf Christmas
A Sugarloaf Easter
A Sugarloaf Surprise
A Sugarloaf Summer
A Tale of Two Christmases
A Boxful of Christmas
The Cinnamon Snail
Sunshine State
The Wattle Birds
The Feijoa Tree
The Villa Mimosa
Making The Effort

Stopwatch Publications

First printing in this edition, 2024

ISBN-13: 978-1-922651-52-5

This book is a work of fiction. Names, characters, places, and incidents are the product of the author's imagination or are used fictitiously. Any resemblance to actual events, locales, or persons, living or dead, is coincidental.

Published by Rosemary Whittaker
www.rosemarywhittaker.com

Cover designs by 100 Covers.

A SWEET ROMANTIC COMEDY

A Sugarloaf Valentine

ROSEMARY WHITTAKER

Chapter One

'And these are the cupcakes,' says Mr Mason. 'Cupcakes are an extremely important part of our business. Can you remember that, Lily, or should I write it down?'

I look at the cakes, wondering whether they contain some magical property of which I wasn't previously aware.

'Absolutely!' I say when it becomes obvious he's expecting an answer. 'Cupcakes!'

He doesn't seem convinced. 'We'll go over it all again after lunch.'

'I think I have it!' I say in alarm, but he's turned away to adjust the thickness of the bread slicer.

My new employer seems to have a poor opinion of me, although I'm not sure why. He only met me a few hours ago. He's entitled to form his own judgement, but he doesn't have much to go on.

I've correctly identified the names of all the cookies and cakes, mastered the complexities of the old-fashioned till, and even laughed at some of his jokes. I haven't commented on the ridiculous overall he's given me to wear, and I arrived at work this morning with my hair neatly tied back as instructed.

But he still seems pessimistic about my future in the baked goods sales environment. If I'd been anticipating a meteoric rise from shopgirl to store manager, his manner indicates I should lower my sights.

I'm not too bothered. This is a stopgap for a few months while I search for a job in my own field. I won't tell him that. It's better for him to think of me as a keen member of his flour-based product emporium, anxious for the honour of the bakery and deeply ambitious for my future within it.

I may never know what I've done to merit such pessimism. Mr Mason isn't the chattiest of employers. All I can do is radiate as much enthusiasm as possible and hope he revises his opinion of me.

He flips the sign on the door from *Open* to *Closed*. 'You have half an hour for lunch. Make sure you're back on time.'

I'm tempted to ask why a food-based business closes during what must be one of the best times to sell its products. I restrain myself. It's not my concern whether he makes a profit. I'm here to exchange sugar-filled treats for cold hard cash or the electronic version of it and to try not to misidentify the cupcakes.

Half an hour is an annoying length for a lunch break. There isn't enough time to walk home for some of Mum's leek and potato soup. She always makes it when it snows, and it's my favourite. She and Dad will soon be tucking into large portions of soup, with crusty bread and cheese from the local farm shop. I hope she's saved some for me.

There's plenty of bread available here. I've been too busy to think about being hungry until now, but the sight of the glossy loaves with their crisp crusts makes my stomach rumble.

'Are staff members allowed to eat the products for lunch?' I ask.

'You mean the cakes?' says Mr Mason.

'I mean the bread, although the cakes look good too. Not the cupcakes, of course!' I add, remembering his obvious attachment to them.

He frowns. 'Our products are for the customers, not the staff.'

'You mean I have to buy them?'

This appears to be a new concept to him. 'You aren't a customer.'

'But I could be,' I point out.

'Our products are for customers only,' he repeats.

I wonder what he would do if I came into the bakery on my day off, minus my fetching tabard, demanding to purchase an assortment of delicious cakes. Would I be treated as a customer or thrown out and put on some sort of list?

Even better, I could borrow Dad's balaclava and Ben's old combat trousers, burst in, hand Mr Mason a bag for life, and demand he fill it with as many vanilla slices and croissants as it will hold.

He tries to usher me out of the shop. He obviously doesn't consider me a fit and proper person to be left alone in such a tempting environment.

'Can you wait for a minute while I get my coat?' I say. 'It's cold outside.'

He gives an exasperated sigh, but I ignore him. It can't be part of The Sugarloaf Bakery's official policy to insist the staff risks hypothermia. There's a limit to the keenness I'm willing to demonstrate.

I zip up my jacket and pull on my knitted hat, and he locks the door behind us.

'Don't be late,' he says, and I suppress an urge to salute.

I watch him trudge off along the street. What am I supposed to do now? I could go to the Red Lion at the end of the high street. They have a roaring fire, and the landlord serves an excellent mulled wine in the winter. I regretfully decide against it. It might not create the right impression to turn up for my afternoon's labours smelling like a character from Charles Dickens.

I'll have to go home, after all. It's a ten-minute walk, so I can spend exactly ten minutes in the bosom of my loving family before facing the walk back. There will only be time for a coffee.

I set off in the same direction as my employer, feeling like the pageboy in Good King Wenceslas. Either Mr Mason's footprints don't possess the same magical quality as the King's or I'm treading in the wrong ones because my feet remain obstinately cold.

I walk briskly along the pavement, slowing down to negotiate the icier parts. I don't want a broken leg to end my fledgling career in the bakery business before it's even begun.

'Lily?' says Mum as I burst into the kitchen. 'I didn't expect to see you until this evening. Is everything all right?'

I collapse onto a chair. 'This is my lunch hour – lunch half hour, to be precise. Mr Mason didn't want to leave me alone in his precious shop, so I had to come home.'

'I'll have to get moving,' she says.

'Some coffee would be great if you have any.'

'There's some coffee in the pot,' she says. 'You can start with that while I make you a sandwich.'

'I thought you might have made soup,' I say, taking the mug she hands me and curling my frozen fingers around it.

'I was just about to,' she says. 'It's a pity you didn't tell me you were coming home, but I'll know tomorrow.'

I look at my watch. 'I have four minutes left.'

'Nonsense!' she says. 'Your father will take you back to work.'

She opens the kitchen door. 'Martin, start the car and get it warmed up! We'll need you in about ten minutes' time.'

'There's no need for Dad to go out in all this snow,' I say.

Mum looks affronted. 'Of course, there is. He *wants* to!'

I'm not convinced, but the offer of a lift is too good to turn down. Mum hands me a cheese and pickle sandwich, which I eat at top speed.

I finish my coffee in two gulps. 'Thanks, Mum. You're a lifesaver.'

Dad appears at the door. 'Are you ready, Lily? Your chariot awaits.'

I love my parents. They're always there when I need them, no questions asked. Neither of them has said a word about me losing my job in London last week. Instead, each of them called me to say I absolutely must come home.

They both made a different excuse. Mum said Dad's sciatica was playing up, and she needed some help in the garden. Dad said Mum has been a bit down recently and it would be a great favour if I would keep her company for a few weeks.

As far as I'm aware, Dad has never had sciatica. Also, the garden is currently under a foot of snow and absolutely no plants are visible. Dad's excuse was even worse. Mum has never been down in her life. She's the most relentlessly positive person I know. But I appreciated their joint effort to help me save face, so I agreed to come home while I looked around for a new job.

I arrived yesterday afternoon to be met by Mum's delighted announcement that she had secured me a temporary job at The Sugarloaf Bakery while I'm here.

'But you mustn't tell Mr Mason it's temporary,' she instructed me. 'He's looking for a full-time employee. He wants to train them from scratch.'

I felt guilty about getting the job under false pretences, but after a morning of being trained from scratch, that feeling is wearing off. I now feel I'm doing the workforce a huge favour by keeping this particular job off the market.

Mum hands me my woolly hat. 'Off you go, love. You don't want to be late back on your very first day.'

That's exactly what I want. I'd be delighted to be so late that Mr Mason has no choice but to fire me. But I need the money, and work around here is scarce. Also, it was lovely of Mum to rush around and find me a job before I even got home. I'll stick with it for now and do my best to live up to Mr Mason's exacting standards. Who knows, with diligence and application, I may one day reach the dizzy heights of employee of the month.

Chapter Two

Mr Mason returns from lunch in a better mood. I don't know what's changed. Maybe his wife had leek and potato soup waiting for him. Or maybe he's had time to appreciate the quality of the staff member who has so undeservedly fallen into his lap. Whatever it is, he greets me with a pleasant smile and hopes I enjoyed my break.

'Yes, thank you,' I say warily.

This change of mood might be a trap. He may be trying to catch me off guard before launching into an interrogation about the relative prices of eclairs and apple slices, with particular emphasis on the rules surrounding discounts for cream-based products after four thirty.

Perhaps he'll set me homework – a short essay on the difference between an Eccles cake and a Banbury cake. Extra points will be awarded for topological charts showing the relevant geographical areas of the country. Your work to be handed in tomorrow morning to your head of department. That would be Mr Mason. There are only two of us working here. I wonder whether this makes me the assistant manager, but I have too much sense to ask.

'Did you go home?' he asks.

Is there a binding rule in my terms of employment forbidding junior members of staff from straying more than fifty metres from the premises during business hours in case of an unexpected baked goods emergency? I must remember to check my contract.

He looks at me in mild surprise, perhaps wondering whether it was a mistake to employ someone who has trouble with the most basic of questions.

'Yes!' I say with enormous enthusiasm.

He looks even more surprised. 'I understand you are staying with your parents?'

'Yes!' I say again. I can't think what else to add.

'Your mother is a very nice woman,' he says.

'She really is.'

He takes off his coat and slips on a full-length apron bearing the slogan *Here to Serve*.

'She visited my wife in the hospital last year,' he says. 'Brenda was delighted to see her.'

I remember now that Mum volunteers each week as a hospital visitor.

'It was particularly helpful as I was away from home that week,' he says. 'My mother had a fall.'

'I'm sorry to hear that,' I say. 'I hope she's alright now.'

He lowers his voice to a respectful whisper. 'She's in a better place.'

'I'm so sorry,' I whisper back.

There's a long silence while he inspects a tray of oatmeal cookies. He looks up from them at last.

'Southampton,' he murmurs. 'I managed to get her into an excellent nursing home there.'

I'm not sure Southampton qualifies as a better place, but who am I to argue?

'Well,' he says more briskly, 'we can't stand around chatting all day. We have work to do before the afternoon rush begins.'

'What time does the rush usually start?' I ask.

'Any time now. Do you feel ready to serve an actual customer?'

We only had a few people in this morning, and Mr Mason insisted on serving them himself. He didn't want to risk losing his long-standing clientele by allowing me to sell them a sesame seed roll when they'd asked for poppy seed.

I pull on my tabard and prepare for battle. 'I'll do my best.'

'Remember the rules of customer service I taught you, and you won't go far wrong. Would you like to tell me what they are?'

I can think of few things I'd like less. But he's my boss, so I plaster on my most charming smile and rattle off the rules. Most of them are absolutely ridiculous, especially the one about we should greet and say goodbye to our customers, but I pretend to take them seriously.

'Very good,' he says when I've finished. 'Very good indeed.'

I'm not sure I like his amazed expression. A cynic might think it betrayed a lack of faith in my abilities as a purveyor of diabetes-inducing delicacies.

Before he can quiz me further on the complexities of the apricot as opposed to the apple slice, we're interrupted by the jangle of the doorbell. I instinctively straighten my shoulders as I turn to face the customer. My heart sinks when I realise it's Mum. What's she doing here? I'm not a kindergarten child taking part in her first nativity play. As far as I know, the wise men didn't bring doughnuts for the baby.

Her face lights up when she sees me. 'Hello, darling! How's it going?'

'Fine, thanks,' I mutter. 'What are you doing here?'

With any luck, she's here to announce a family member has been gruesomely dismembered in a freak accident, or the house has burned down, and I need to leave work immediately. This hope is shattered when she beams at me.

'I'm here for a cottage loaf. Your father and Ben finished off the last one with their soup. There'll be nothing to make toast with tomorrow if I don't buy more. Breakfast is the most important meal of the day, especially in this weather. You rushed out without eating anything this morning. That won't happen again, even if it means I have to get up at five a.m.'

Mr Mason looks puzzled. 'Why would you have to do that?'

'It's a figure of speech,' she says. 'It isn't so vital now Lily is working in a bakery.'

'Our products are for customers only,' I say helpfully.

Mr Mason has the grace to look a little embarrassed. 'That is usually the case. But you didn't tell me you had missed your breakfast.'

'It's because she was so keen not to be late on her first day,' says Mum.

I try to look like someone whose every waking thought is for the reputation and financial success of my chosen profession. I'm not sure I succeed.

'How is she getting on?' asks Mum, sounding like a proud parent hoping to be shown her daughter's finger painting of a Chelsea bun.

'Very nicely,' says Mr Mason. 'Lily has already mastered our basic range, and she has a good understanding of the till. She's picked it all up far more quickly than the last girl who worked here.'

I wonder how anyone could struggle with the names of a few pastries and remembering a few buttons. Still, it's nice to shine by comparison. And it may explain his less than welcoming attitude to me when I arrived.

'I'm sure you'll work very well together,' says Mum. 'Lily has always been a quick learner.'

'Not everyone is cut out for a career in retail,' he says. 'It can be very demanding.'

I barely manage to stop myself from rolling my eyes. I've spent the last year in London working as an office manager. But that's the peril of returning home. People see you as the child you used to be and treat you accordingly. At least, Mum does.

'I'm after a cottage loaf,' she says, scanning the racks behind me.

Mr Mason gives me an encouraging smile. 'Perhaps we should ask Lily to deal with that.'

I point to a loaf. 'I believe that's the one you usually have.'

'Perfect!' she says. 'You clever girl.'

I could have pointed to a currant bun and she'd have said the same thing. She's always been like this. She sees the best in everyone and encourages it. If there is no best, she sees it anyway, and somehow, it magically appears. I don't know how she does it.

I put the loaf in a paper bag and hand it to her.

'You're a pro already,' she says. 'Are you going to ring it up as well?'

I look at Mr Mason, who considers. 'I think you may be ready.'

I try not to giggle as I enter the price. I take the note Mum hands me and count out her change.

'Wonderful!' she says. 'I'll see you at home, darling. Have a lovely afternoon, Mr Mason.'

He actually escorts her to the door and gives what looks like a half bow as she leaves. I hope I'm not supposed to drop a curtsey each time anyone comes in. It wasn't part of my initial training.

The afternoon passes slowly, with no sign of the rush Mr Mason predicted. I wonder whether my presence has jinxed it. If so, I'll soon be out of a job.

He doesn't seem to notice anything amiss. He hovers over me as I serve the trickle of customers. His disapproving look gradually fades when he realises I probably won't plunge the bakery into bankruptcy on my first day.

I take a surreptitious look at my watch. Half past four. Only one more hour to go. It's already growing dark, and it's started to snow again. I'm not looking forward to my walk home, but I am looking forward to the end of my shift.

At five o'clock, Mr Mason instructs me to cover the trays of cookies.

'I doubt we'll sell any more of these today,' he says, 'but a few last-minute customers may pop in for a loaf of bread on their way home.'

The bell jangles, and he looks pleased. 'What did I say?'

I'm bending down covering the cookies with red checked cloths and don't look up. I've served everyone this afternoon. He can manage this one by himself. I finish the cookies and move on to the coconut slices. I'm about to ask Mr Mason whether we have any more covers when the customer speaks.

I freeze. I'd know that voice anywhere. I haven't heard it for nearly a year, but it's as familiar to me as my own heartbeat.

It can't be. It absolutely can't be. He isn't supposed to be anywhere near here. He's in Manchester. Mum told me all about his wonderful new job with Hewlett Packard when I was home for Christmas. I'm not sure how far Manchester is from Honeywell, but it definitely isn't commuting distance.

I keep my head down and concentrate on the coconut slices. It's vital they're covered correctly or something awful will happen to them. I forget what, but I learned all about it this morning.

I decide to stay down here until he's gone. It may not even be him. Lots of people have similar deep, gravelly voices.

'Lily?' says Mr Mason's voice. 'We have a customer.'

There's nothing for it. I slowly straighten up and find myself staring straight into Stephen Parker's eyes.

Chapter Three

For a moment, neither of us speaks, then his face breaks into a smile. 'Lily, it is you! What are you doing here?'

I stare at him, unable to formulate a coherent answer. I'm acutely aware of Mr Mason watching us. As far as he's concerned, Stephen is just another customer. My mind flips frantically through the list of directions for dealing with our clientele. None of the rules tell you how to greet a customer who appears without warning and reminds the staff member how completely they broke her heart a year ago.

'Hi, Stephen,' I begin.

I'm aware my voice is half an octave higher than usual. I lower it to a more appropriate level. 'I work here. What are you doing here?'

Mr Mason gives me a disapproving look.

I try again. 'I didn't know you were back in Honeywell. Mum mentioned you're living in Manchester now.'

'I'm home for a quick visit,' he says.

'To see your family?'

Mr Mason looks even more annoyed. I'm not sure why. I haven't asked anything personal. I merely enquired about the customer's family, which is a polite and appropriate thing to do. It falls under rule number four – inquire in a pleasant yet discreet manner about your customer's day. That's exactly what I've done. I haven't suggested Stephen's family is the lynchpin of the local drug trade or that they smuggle in exotic pets from the Far East.

Stephen gives me an awkward smile. 'Actually, I'm visiting my girlfriend.'

I feel as though he's thrown one of our extra dense wholegrain rolls at my head. This shouldn't be a surprise. We broke up a year ago. Of course, he's been seeing other people.

'That's nice,' I say in a strangled voice. 'Does she live locally?'

He shuffles his feet. 'She lives in Little Compton.'

'What's her name?'

'Isabella,' he says. 'Isabella Campbell.'

Mr Mason comes to my rescue. 'You and your friend must have a lot to catch up on, Lily, but we close in fifteen minutes. He may be in a hurry.'

Stephen clears his throat. 'I only came in to ask … but it was a stupid idea. I'll come back another time.'

'Not at all,' says Mr Mason courteously. 'We would love to help you in any way we can. Isn't that right, Lily?'

I hardly hear him. A flood of memories is washing over me, threatening to drown me. Stephen and me walking hand in hand along the riverbank. Stephen telling me I was the most beautiful woman he'd ever met. Stephen telling me he didn't want to see me anymore …

'Lily?' says Mr Mason.

I return to the present with a jolt. 'Oh, yes! What Mr Mason said.'

Stephen grins. He knows perfectly well I haven't been listening. I only hope he doesn't realise why.

'I popped in to see whether you might do me a box of cookies next week,' he says. 'It's Valentine's Day, and I thought it might be a nice gesture …'

He trails off, looking embarrassed.

'We'd be only too happy to help,' says Mr Mason. 'We have a fine selection from which to choose.'

Stephen glances at me, then away again. 'I was hoping to personalise them.'

'In what way?' says Mr Mason.

Stephen looks even more embarrassed. 'Could you ice some letters on them or something?'

Mr Mason looks baffled. 'What sort of letters?'

I can't stand any more of this. Usually, I'm all for watching a vaudeville act, particularly if it means I don't have to work. But this one is getting painful.

'I imagine Stephen means the letters of his girlfriend's name,' I say.

Stephen looks relieved. 'Something like that. Or some sort of message.'

I can think of several messages I'd like to ice on the cookies, but none that wouldn't result in my instant dismissal.

'This is my first day,' I tell Stephen. 'I don't know whether we offer this service.'

Mr Mason is wearing the look of a dog whose toy bone has been hidden from him. He knows it's somewhere, but he's not sure where to start.

'Is this a service we offer?' I prompt him.

'I've never been asked that before,' he says. His eye falls on me, and his face clears. 'I'm sure Lily would love to oblige.'

Stephen looks horrified. 'I wouldn't dream of putting her to all that trouble.'

'No trouble at all,' says Mr Mason. 'She'll be delighted to help you in whatever way she can.'

'Delighted,' I echo feebly.

'Did you say Valentine's Day?' Mr Mason goes on. 'That's most fortuitous. Martha always delivers a batch of heart-shaped cookies on the thirteenth. I'll make a note to put some aside, and Lily can ice them however you like. It's a very good idea. We could offer them at other times of the year too – Christmas and Easter and ...'

Halloween, I think viciously. I could do wonders with a bag of bright red icing.

'What's the message?' I ask Stephen.

'Message?'

'I need to know what message you want on the cookies. Unless you'd prefer me to make up my own.'

I'm pleased to see his ears turn a delicate pink. He looks at his watch. 'You're about to close. I'll have a think about it and come back when I've decided.'

Mr Mason looks disappointed not to have secured the order and started laying the foundations for our amazing new service.

'I'll pop in again tomorrow,' says Stephen.

'We'll be ready and waiting,' I promise with a touch of malice in my tone.

He won't come back. When he walked in today, I thought for one ecstatic moment he must have heard I was home and rushed over to see me. But it's clear he had no idea I was here and would have avoided the place entirely if he had known. Besides, he has a girlfriend. And not just any girlfriend – a girlfriend for whom he has come home especially for Valentine's Day, and to whom he plans to present romantic cookies with a personalised message.

My stomach does a flip as I wonder what the message was supposed to be. It had better not be a proposal. Customer service is all well and good, but if Mr Mason thinks I'm going to ice an impassioned declaration of love onto his vile cookies, he's sorely mistaken. I'd sooner quit my job and stay unemployed for the rest of my life.

In the unlikely event Stephen does come back to the bakery, I should put some boundaries in place – things I am and am not prepared to write on the stupid heart-shaped cookies.

Have a very pleasant day would be acceptable.

Make me the happiest man in the world by agreeing to be my wife would not.

'Perhaps we should pack up for the evening,' says Mr Mason. 'I need to show Lily what to do. It's a complicated process.'

Stephen catches my eye and smiles. I almost smile back, but I manage to stop myself. He doesn't deserve a smile. Not only did he dump me and break my heart, but he didn't have the grace to stay single for a mere twelve months.

'See you tomorrow,' he says, and I nod. I won't be seeing him again, but it's best to preserve the polite fiction.

Mr Mason jerks his head imperceptibly towards the inspirational list of rules on the wall.

I sigh. This has been a long day, and it's gone from bad to worse. Still, I don't want to go home and tell Mum I couldn't handle this job for even one day. So, I grit my teeth and force a rictus grin.

'Thank you for visiting us at The Sugarloaf Bakery. I hope your experience was everything you hoped for.'

Chapter Four

My walk home takes longer than it did at lunchtime. For one thing, I'm not racing back to spend ten minutes with my family before returning to the bakery. For another, it's more difficult walking in the dark. The pavements have been cleared with varying degrees of proficiency. Most people have dug out a path to their gate and piled the snow in random heaps along the pavement. I have to use the torch on my phone to navigate my way around them. Otherwise, I might pitch headfirst into one of them and not be discovered until spring.

Mum is in the kitchen when I arrive home. She's stirring something on the stove. It smells delicious.

She greets me with a delighted smile. 'I was getting worried. I was about to send your father out to look for you.'

'I came as quickly as I could. We're supposed to close at half-past five, but Mr Mason insisted on teaching me to close up properly.'

She holds out a spoon. 'Taste that!'

I open my mouth automatically. 'It's scalding!'

'What did you expect?' she says. 'It came straight out of the pan. It's chicken chasseur. What do you think?'

I pour myself a glass of water and take a gulp. 'It's delicious, as long as you aren't serving it with bread. I won't be able to look another loaf in the eye for a long while.'

'I'm making mashed potatoes,' she says soothingly. 'You must be doing well if Mr Mason allowed you to close up the shop. He probably hopes you'll do it all by yourself soon and give him an afternoon off. He isn't getting any younger.'

She brightens. 'He may be looking for someone to take over from him when he retires.'

'Let's not get carried away,' I say. 'It was kind of you to get me the job, but it's strictly temporary.'

She looks disappointed. 'It would be lovely to have you living in the village permanently. Your father would be delighted.'

Mum and Dad always do this. They don't like to put pressure on me on their own account, so they project their own wishes onto the other one.

'I'm an office manager,' I say patiently. 'I need to be where the work is.'

She picks up the potato masher. 'I know. But we plan to make the most of it while you're here.'

I leave her pounding the potatoes and humming *Sweet Potato Pie* and go upstairs to clean up before dinner. My legs are aching, and my lower back feels as though someone has been kicking it at regular intervals throughout the day. I'd love to have a hot bath, but there isn't time.

Instead, I take a shower with Mum's familiar rose-scented soap. She's used it for as long as I can remember, and it always makes me feel safe and secure. I'm convinced the smell of the bakery has got into my pores, and I'm determined to wash it off. It's a pleasant enough smell, sugary and fruity with a hint of vanilla, but I'd prefer not to be a walking advert for Mr Mason's products.

I wander back to my bedroom and put on my pyjamas. It makes me feel even more like the child who used to live here, but I don't care. It's so lovely to be home. I've been battered by the events of the past week. Everyone knew layoffs were coming, but I thought I was doing so well. However, as my manager told me very kindly, last in, first out. She's promised me an excellent reference, so hopefully it won't be too long before I find a new job.

In the meantime, I'll enjoy being home. I know how lucky I am that Mum and Dad will always welcome me with open arms, no matter what. Not for the first time, I'm grateful to have such lovely parents. Even my brother Ben isn't too bad – in small doses.

He's also temporarily back home. In his case, it's because he's broken up with his girlfriend and moved out of the flat they rent. Mum told me last night she's sure they'll patch it up because they're both such wonderful people. Until then, it's lovely for her and Dad to have the whole family under one roof. I don't know what's going on between Ben and Mia, but if relentless positivity can get them back together, Mum will provide that in spades.

I haven't unpacked yet. Mum emptied the wardrobe for me, but there was no need. I've only brought one case. I didn't want to make things too easy for myself. If she had her way, I would move in permanently, and she would look after me exactly as she used to. It's a tempting prospect, but it isn't what I want. I need my own life, which means I have to find employment fairly quickly. But there's no harm in enjoying a few weeks at home in the meantime.

My bedroom hasn't changed at all since I was about thirteen. Dad and I spent an entire weekend painting it pink and carefully stencilling butterflies all over the walls. It stayed like that until I went to university. I expected my parents to change it at some point, but they haven't, either because they've been too busy or because they want me to feel I always have a place to which I can return.

Ben's bedroom is also untouched. It's a violent shade of purple with a black ceiling. He was going through his goth phase when it was decorated. I wonder how he feels about sleeping in it after spending two years in his and Mia's delicately minimalist flat. Perhaps it will encourage him to seek a reconciliation sooner rather than later.

I put on my fluffy dressing gown and wander downstairs to help Mum.

'You look lovely and comfortable,' she says when she sees me. 'Can you set the table? Ben's always home by six thirty, and Dad's doing something or other in the garage. Give him a call when you've finished.'

Ben arrives ten minutes later. 'How's life in the fast lane?' he asks me.

'Fine, thank you,' I say with dignity.

'She's already managing the till!' says Mum.

Ben raises an eyebrow. 'Maths was never your strong suit, Lily. I hope you haven't bankrupted the business.'

'I'll have you know I've served several customers in an exemplary manner,' I say. 'Mr Mason can't think what he'd do without me.'

I may be shading the truth slightly here, but Ben doesn't need to know that. I doubt he ever goes into the Sugarloaf.

Dad comes in, and we sit down to dinner.

'An extra-large helping for Lily,' says Mum, handing me a plate. 'New jobs are always exhausting.'

'How did it go this afternoon?' asks Dad. 'Your mother says you're picking it up remarkably quickly.'

I ignore Ben's sardonic smile. 'It isn't exactly rocket science. I unload the boxes when they're delivered, and I put everything on the correct shelves. I serve the customers and give them their change. And I cover the cakes with cloths at the end of the day.'

'Richard Branson would be proud,' says Ben. 'Leave some mashed potato for the rest of us.'

'There's plenty more in the pan,' says Mum. 'Let your sister have as much as she needs.'

'Do you make all your bread on site?' Dad asks me.

'We don't make any of it,' I say. 'I don't know why. There's a huge kitchen behind the bakery, but Mr Mason has everything delivered.'

'He used to make a lot of his own bread and cakes,' says Mum. 'The bakery was quite a thriving business until a year or two ago. But he's approaching retirement, and I think it's become too much for him. He doesn't have many customers these days. I often wonder how long the bakery will stay open.'

It isn't until we're eating crumble and custard that I mention Stephen's name. Mum's bound to know what he's up to. She probably also knows this Isabella woman.

'The other reason I was late back this evening was because Stephen Parker came in as we were closing,' I say, without looking up from my bowl.

There's a pause before Mum answers. 'I heard he was home. His father's been in the hospital recently. The family has been quite worried about him.'

I hear the note of concern in her voice, but I'm determined not to betray myself. It was bad enough when Stephen and I broke up. I stayed in bed for an entire week, only emerging for meals. Mum was wonderful, but I know how stressful she found the whole thing. I don't want her to start worrying about me again.

'He told me he was here to see his new girlfriend,' I say in a casual tone.

There's a collective intake of breath around the table. Dad quickly covers it with a cough.

Mum lays a hand on mine. 'I'm so sorry, Lily.'

'Don't be! She sounds very nice.'

She gives me a doubtful look. 'That's good. Did you and Stephen have a pleasant chat?'

I consider how best to answer this. I suppose our interaction fell under the umbrella of pleasant chats. At least, I didn't launch myself over the counter at him and push his face into the mini pavlovas.

'That's right,' I say.

'What's his girlfriend's name?' asks Ben.

I pretend to search my memory. 'Irene, is it? Iris? I can't quite remember.'

'What does she do?' he asks.

'I'm not sure.'

'Where does she live?' asks Dad.

'Somewhere around here,' I say.

'How long have they been together?' asks Mum.

'I don't know.'

Ben helps himself to the last of the crumble. 'It's been great learning about Irene, or maybe Iris. I almost feel as though I know her.'

There's a knock at the front door, and I jump up in relief. 'I'll get it!'

'Who can it be at this time?' says Mum.

It doesn't matter when the knock comes. She always says the exact same thing. I've never known the time at which she thinks it's appropriate for someone to arrive on the doorstep.

'It's probably someone collecting for something,' says Dad. This is his invariable answer to her comment, although I can't remember anyone ever turning up on our doorstep waving a charity tin.

I hope it isn't Mr Mason, come to tell me I've forgotten some crucial part of the closing-up process and must return to the bakery at once to rectify it.

The knock comes again. It couldn't be … of course not. But it's faintly possible. He knows where I live.

I open the door a crack and peer out. The figure on the doorstep is too tall to be Mr Mason, but not tall enough to be Stephen.

'Aren't you going to let me in?' says a familiar voice.

I fling open the door to see my friend Jack smiling at me. I throw my arms around him and give him an enormous hug. 'I thought you were collecting for something!'

He looks puzzled. 'Anything in particular?'

'Oh, you know. Charity, or a new sewage plant for the village.'

'Now we've established I'm not after your money, will you let me in?' he asks plaintively.

'Of course! I'm so pleased to see you. I was going to call you this weekend.'

I usher him into the hall and take his coat. 'Come on through. We're finishing dinner.'

He follows me into the kitchen. 'Hello, Ben. Hello, Mr and Mrs Carson.'

Mum jumps up to hug him. 'Jack, how lovely! Sit down, and I'll find you something to eat. Ben, put that spoon down right now! Jack wants some crumble.'

'I'm fine, thanks,' says Jack. 'I had dinner before I came here. My mother called to let me know Ben and Lily were both home. It seemed too good an opportunity to miss, so I thought I'd drop around to see them before they disappeared again.'

'I'll make us all some coffee,' says Dad. 'You young ones go through and make yourself comfortable. You must want to catch up with all the news.'

'Ben and I should clean up first,' I say.

Mum flaps her hands at me. 'Your father and I will do all that. Off you go!'

She shoos us into the living room like a mother hen directing her disorganised chicks.

'I think I left something in my car,' says Ben. 'I'll be back in a minute.'

He disappears, leaving me alone with Jack.

'It's so nice to see you,' I say. 'It must be nearly six months since we last met.'

'About that,' he says. 'I keep meaning to get up to London, but time gets away from me. I hoped to see you at Christmas, but my parents booked us all into a huge house in Cornwall. Amy and Mike were there with the children, which kept us all busy.'

He gives me a sympathetic look. 'I heard about your job. I'm sorry.'

'That was quick. Who told you?'

'Your mum told Mr Dobinson, who told his wife, who told my mum. You know how it is.'

'I do indeed. It's the worst of a place this size. No one's business is ever private.'

'It's also the best of a place this size,' he says. 'You're never alone.'

'I suppose you've heard where I'm working?'

'The Sugarloaf, isn't it?' he says.

'That's the place. I get to wear a hideous flowered tabard and curtsey to all the customers.'

His eyes widen. 'This I must see! Standards have obviously gone up since I was last in there.'

'I'm doing my best to drag them down,' I assure him.

I wonder whether to mention Stephen's visit but decide against it. There's no point. Jack must be absolutely fed up with talking about Stephen and our breakup. He came to see me every day during that awful week. He told me terrible jokes and took me out for coffee and played endless games of snap, the only game I could manage. I'll always be grateful for that, but I don't want to put a strain on our friendship by starting it all again.

Dad brings in the coffee, and Jack and I chat with him and Mum for half an hour.

Ben comes in after a while. 'Sorry about that. I needed to make a phone call.'

I wonder whether he was calling Mia. I hope this isn't a permanent split. I like her far more than any of his previous girlfriends, but it's none of my business.

'It's been great seeing you all,' says Jack. 'I have an early start tomorrow, so I should get going.'

'So has Lily,' says Mum. 'I want her to have a proper breakfast before work.'

I walk Jack to the door.

'Are you free for lunch at the weekend?' he asks.

'That would be lovely. I'm not sure which day I'm working. I'll ask Mr Mason tomorrow. He can't make me work the entire weekend.'

'If he does, I'll disguise myself as a delivery driver and sneak you away on a pallet,' he promises.

He turns at the gate and waves. 'Call me!'

He sets off down the street with his familiar, loping stride. I watch until he's out of sight before closing the front door. Despite what Mum seems to think, working in a bakery is not my dream job. But now I have something to look forward to. Jack is one of my favourite people in the world. Just knowing he's around makes the prospect of the next few weeks far more bearable.

Chapter Five

I arrive at work early the next day. I don't want to give Mr Mason any cause for complaint.

He almost smiles when he sees me. 'Good morning, Lily. Ready for another busy day?'

'Absolutely,' I say. 'It was interesting to learn so much yesterday.'

He looks pleased. 'I'm glad to hear that. It isn't everyone who appreciates what goes into running a small to middle-sized business such as this.'

Middle-sized is stretching it a little. Honeywell is a village with fewer than one thousand inhabitants. The row of shops comprises a tiny barber that almost always seems to be closed, a corner shop that functions as both post office and mini supermarket, a newsagent, and this bakery. Our much-vaunted afternoon rush yesterday consisted of four customers. The first one came in to ask where the nearest bus stop was, the second was Mum, and the third asked if we had any day-old pound cake we were throwing out because she wanted to make a trifle.

The other customer was Stephen. He definitely won't come back as long as I'm here. I'll be home longer than he is, which means our already small-sized business will have its takings reduced even further.

Mr Mason keeps a close eye on me as I remove the tray cloths from the slices and unpack the pallets of bread and rolls.

He nods approvingly when I've finished. 'Would you like me to refresh your till training?'

'I think I'm fine,' I say. 'I'll let you know if I forget what the buttons do.'

The doorbell jangles, making me jump. It's a hideous noise, somewhere between a yodel and a strangled squawk. I'm hoping to persuade Mr Mason to change it for something more melodious. If I get a new job fairly quickly, I could present it to him as a parting gift to ease the pain of losing such a valuable member of staff.

A middle-aged woman comes in, wheeling a tartan shopping trolley. A small dog trots in behind her, and Mr Mason's eyes widen in horror.

'Shoo!' he exclaims, clapping his hands loudly.

'Don't speak to Bernard like that!' says the woman. 'He doesn't like it.'

Mr Mason looks even more horrified. 'Do you know this dog?'

The woman closes the door. 'Of course, I know him! You don't imagine a stray dog has wandered in off the street?'

Judging by the look on Mr Mason's face, this is exactly what he imagines.

I take a quick look at the second list he's stuck on the wall. This one details the rights and responsibilities of our valued customers. It begins with explaining the circumstances under which they may request a refund – all of which strictly preclude any sampling of the goods. It finishes with a stern sentence to the effect that abuse of the staff will not be tolerated, and the proprietor will not hesitate to call the authorities should any occur.

Somewhere in the middle of the list is a rule stating no animals of any kind are permitted in the bakery for reasons of hygiene. It should say dogs. What other animals are likely to be brought in by their doting owners, especially in weather like this, when all decent, god-fearing rabbits, parrots and boa constrictors are safely in their warm houses?

'I'm afraid we don't allow dogs on the premises,' I tell her.

She turns pink with annoyance. 'Why not?'

This wasn't part of my training. Mr Mason led me to believe that all rules are instantly and graciously accepted by our customers.

'This is a place where food is served, madam!' he says.

She doesn't flinch. 'Why do you think I'm here? I'm not posting a parcel.'

'The post office is two shops along,' I say helpfully.

She withers me with a glance. 'I'm perfectly aware where the post office is, young lady. It was a figure of speech.'

She points to a garishly iced doughnut. 'I'll take that one.'

I pick up the tongs, but Mr Mason forestalls me. 'Don't move, Lily!'

I stop obediently, holding the tongs poised midway between the counter and the doughnuts. This is quite exciting. Who would have thought there was scope for so much drama in a small to mid-sized bakery?

'What are you waiting for?' snaps the woman. 'I don't have all day.'

Mr Mason has regained his composure. 'As I said before, it is impossible for us to serve food with an animal on the premises. I could lose my licence.'

She snorts. 'Listen to you! What are you – Harrods?'

He stands his ground. 'No, madam, I am the proprietor of The Sugarloaf Bakery. As such, I must refuse to allow any but service animals into the bakery on the grounds of hygiene.'

She wavers, obviously torn between wanting to storm out and wanting to buy the bright pink doughnut.

'He had a bath last night,' she says, but I can tell she's giving way.

Mr Mason assumes the stance of Custer at Little Bighorn. 'I must insist,' he tells her.

'But Bernard hasn't had time to choose his cake,' she says.

I turn my involuntary snort of laughter into a cough. 'Isn't the doughnut for him?'

She gives me a withering look. 'Not at all. He doesn't like strawberry.'

'What flavour does he like?'

She glances at the cakes. 'He's very fond of raspberry slices. They don't contain chocolate, do they? Dogs can't eat chocolate.'

I doubt our raspberry slice is on any list of canine nutritious snacks. However, Mr Mason is turning an alarming shade of purple, so it's probably time to bring this to a close.

'There's no chocolate in these,' I assure her. 'But should he be eating cakes at all?'

She gives me a withering look. 'Please don't tell me how to look after my dog. I only give him a small piece.'

'Fine,' I say. 'Are you paying by cash or card?'

'Cash,' she says suspiciously.

'That's fine. If you take Freddy outside, I'll bring your cakes out along with your change.'

She hesitates, considering whether I'm likely to snatch her money and lock the bakery door. She decides to take the risk. She hands me a five-pound note and takes Bernard outside, where the pair of them peer at me suspiciously through the glass while I ring through the sale.

I carry the bag of pastries out to her and wait while she scrutinises the receipt and carefully counts the change to make sure I haven't pulled a fast one. She nods curtly and sets off down the street in the direction of the barbers. Maybe Freddy is due for a haircut and a shave.

I go inside, where I'm pleased to see Mr Mason's face has returned to its usual colour.

'Lily, you were wonderful!' he exclaims.

'Thank you,' I say.

'I mean it! If I allow one customer to break the rules, it's the thin end of the wedge. It never occurred to me to serve her outside. When I next see your mother, I will make sure to mention what an aptitude you've shown for the business.'

I'm not sure whether to be amused or offended. Serving a cantankerous woman with a couple of cakes hardly makes me the bakery equivalent of Lee Iacocca. Also, I'm a little old to have my every move relayed to my parents. Still, I won't be here for long, and it's nice he seems so pleased.

A few more customers trickle in over the next two hours. Mr Mason doesn't attempt to serve them. He leaves it all to me. After my triumph with Bernard's raspberry slice, I'm not surprised. If things continue at this pace, I'll be assistant manager by Easter.

It's a shame custom is so slow. I'd prefer to be kept busy while I'm here. It may not be the most scintillating of occupations, but I quickly grow bored with staring out of the window at the shoppers on the high street, very few of whom seem to notice we're here. They go from the newsagents to the corner shop without glancing into our window, where Mr Mason has tastefully arranged an eye-catching selection of French Fancies.

I look at my watch and realise it's only ten minutes until our lunch break. I've promised Mum I'll go home for lunch, but I hope it doesn't become a regular thing. It wouldn't be so bad in the spring and summer, but it's a miserable walk through the slush and ice at this time of year. And ten minutes in my parents' bright, warm kitchen is worse than not going at all. It's a tantalising glimpse into another world – a world full of fresh coffee and home-made soup and uncritical adoration. A world, in short, that I left behind me when I left childhood.

I don't really want to return there, but it's oddly tempting. Adulthood is all very well and good, but it's considerably more painful than childhood. It doesn't seem that way when things are going well, but when heartbreak hits, it's all too easy to look back with regret.

As if on cue, the door opens, and the cause of my biggest ever heartbreak appears. I wasn't expecting him to come within a million miles of the place today. I can't imagine why he's returned when he knows I'm working here. Are there no other bakeries within a short driving distance to which he can take his annoying custom?

He looks pleased to see me. 'Hi, Lily. Is now a good time?'

There's no appropriate answer to this. Now definitely isn't a good time, but that's because no time is a good time to see him. How does he not understand that?

Mr Mason is fussing around at the far end of the counter, removing the last of yesterday's chocolate muffins and refilling the tray. I don't dare to be rude to a customer in front of him. It's a pity Stephen hasn't tried to bring a dog in with him so I could throw him out. His family doesn't have one because his mother is allergic to almost everything, but he could easily have picked up a stray on his walk over here. It's yet more evidence of his general thoughtlessness.

'We're about to close for lunch,' I say. This isn't rudeness. It's the exact truth.

Stephen looks disappointed. 'I didn't know bakeries shut at lunchtime.'

'Ours does,' I say. 'What can I help you with?'

I expect him to say he wants a split pan loaf or some wholegrain rolls. It is lunchtime, after all. But, to my surprise, he returns to the subject of cookies. I thought he might have had the decency to stay away from them entirely, but he doesn't. He seems obsessed with them.

Does he even know his girlfriend likes cookies? She may have a severe wheat allergy or be diabetic and have forgotten to tell him. In a way, it could be a kindness on my part to ensure this ridiculous idea doesn't happen.

'I was actually hoping to talk to you, Lily,' he says hesitantly.

'About the cookies?'

He glances at Mr Mason. 'Not exactly.'

My heart skips a beat. Not exactly? Does that mean he no longer wants the cookies? There could be plenty of reasons for that apart from the health-related ones I've come up with. Isabella may have texted him to say she's run off with the master of the local fox hunt and never wants to see him again.

To be fair, I don't know for sure she's into fox hunting. But it seems a strong possibility in the sort of person who agrees to start dating someone who couldn't remain single for one short year after breaking up with the love of his life.

Also, she lives in the Manor House. I've never been inside it, but I've driven past plenty of times. It's a huge house set in its own grounds, with paddocks and horses and a duck pond. If her family can afford to live there, she can definitely buy her own cookies. There's no need for Stephen to waste his money.

My mind has been too full of gymkhanas and hunt balls to pay attention to what else Stephen might be saying. I give myself a mental shake and return to the subject at hand. 'You could come back after lunch.'

'I'm afraid I can't keep the shop open any longer,' says Mr Mason. 'I have somewhere I need to be. And staff members can't remain on the premises over the lunch period for health and safety reasons.'

These regulations must exist solely in his mind. What does he think I plan to do – run amok around the shelves of pastries, hurling cream doughnuts at the walls? After an early start and dealing with Bernard and his owner, I honestly don't have the energy.

'Can I buy you lunch at the pub?' Stephen asks abruptly.

I'm too startled to answer. It sounds as though what he has to say to me will take some time, which could be good or bad, depending on what it is.

'I only have half an hour,' I tell him.

'That's enough time for a sandwich and a drink,' he says. 'You need something to warm you up in this weather.'

'A coffee would be nice,' I say for Mr Mason's benefit. A triple brandy would be more warming, but I doubt he would approve.

Mr Mason shepherds us both outside, where he appears to wrestle with himself for a moment before speaking.

'You were here later than I expected last night, Lily. And it may take us longer than usual to close up tonight while you're learning the ropes. Perhaps you would like to take a slightly lengthier lunch break today in lieu.'

If Stephen wants to talk about our relationship and possibly discuss resuming it, I'd like to spend as long as possible with him. On the other hand, I have no intention of sitting there listening to him prattle on about horsey girl. Either way, the prospect of some flexibility around my future lunch breaks is too good to pass up.

'That's very kind of you, Mr Mason,' I say, rather touched at his suggestion.

'Shall we say forty-five minutes?' he says. 'Just for today, you understand?'

'I'll be here on time,' I promise.

'We should make a start,' says Stephen.

Mr Mason looks as though he's already regretting his generous offer, but that's too bad. I set off as quickly as possible in the direction of the pub before he can change his mind.

Chapter Six

It only takes us five minutes to reach the Red Lion. The pub is just as I remember it – all exposed beams and flagstones, with a huge roaring fire at the far end.

'Are you still drinking red wine?' Stephen asks me.

'I can't,' I say regretfully. 'Mr Mason wouldn't approve of me drinking at work.'

'You aren't at work right now,' he says. 'Besides, if he gave you an hour for lunch, like any halfway decent employer, it would all have left your system by the time you got back to the bakery.'

'I'd like a glass of mulled wine,' I decide. 'But make sure it's not too large.'

'Would you like a sandwich too? I can ask Ted to hurry it up.'

'That would be nice. Is there a menu somewhere?'

He pulls out his wallet. 'There's no time! You have to be back at the bakery, remember? I know what you like.'

He disappears into the crowd around the bar. I ought to feel annoyed. The days of men ordering for women and returning with a small port and lemon are long over. But it's nice to think he remembers my likes and dislikes, even after a year apart and with one or possibly several new girlfriends in between. I wonder whether he orders for Isabella, and if so, what she has. She probably eats nothing but game pie and roast pheasant washed down with champagne.

I've built up a fairly complete picture of her, which I'm sure is accurate. I know her type. I grew up with them. I didn't meet them at school because Ben and I took the bus each day to the comprehensive school in the next town. But I saw the Range Rovers setting off from our village each morning towards The Grange, an exclusive private school several miles in the other direction. It's a boarding school, but it takes day pupils too. I expect Isabella went there. I bet she was Head Girl. I can see her now, tall and lanky, giving her end-of-year speech in her Barbour and green wellies.

Stephen returns before I can flesh out this picture any further. He's carrying two plates, which he sets down on the table next to me. 'I'll go and get our drinks.'

I peel back the edge of the nearest sandwich. It's my favourite, Emmenthal and lettuce, and I see he's remembered to ask for extra pickles. My eyes sting. He knows me so well. Why did he throw it all away?

He reappears, carrying two glasses of mulled wine. 'Are you alright, Lily?'

I blink hard. 'I'm fine. It's just the effect of coming in from the cold and sitting by the warm fire.'

He takes a bite of his sandwich. 'It's awful out there. It took me a long time to get the car out this morning.'

'When are you going back to Manchester?' I ask.

Maybe he'll be snowed in and unable to leave the village. That may or may not be a good thing, depending on what he wants to talk about today. I allow my mind to drift off into rosy visions of him telling me what a hideous mistake this new relationship has been, and how he realises his future is with me and no one else.

If so, I'm prepared to ice the cookies as a farewell gift. *Goodbye, Isabella. Sorry it didn't work out. See you around.*

If finances are tight, he could go for *Ciao!* which would have the benefit of being both non-fattening and economical. It's also probably the sort of thing she says to all her horsey friends.

'I'm here until the sixteenth,' he says. 'You aren't eating your sandwich. Did I order the wrong one?'

'Not at all. This is my favourite. You even remembered the extra pickles.'

He smiles. 'How could I forget your obsession with ordering pickles with everything?'

I take a bite. How was I to know he would remember? He's been happy enough to forget everything else. We haven't been in contact since that dreadful day he told me he couldn't see a future for us, so it was best for us to move on with our separate lives.

He's clearly done that, and so have I. At least, I've managed to get through each day, trying not to think about the fact he smashed my heart into tiny pieces with no warning. I've been mature and sensible and concentrated on working hard and advancing my career. I'd still be doing that if not for the downturn in the economy and my company having to tighten its belt.

It isn't my fault I've been forced to take a step backwards, living with my parents and working in a job I'll never grow to love. It's hardly your average thirty-year-old's dream, but I'm aware how lucky I am to have had something to fall back on. I wasn't the only one who was made redundant, and some of the other employees had families to support rather than an immediate offer of accommodation and as much home-made soup as they could manage.

Stephen breaks the silence. 'Are you sure you're ok?'

'Sorry, I was miles away. It's been a busy few days.'

'I can imagine. What brought you home? The last time I heard, you were living in London and working as an office manager.'

I take a slug of my mulled wine and almost choke. 'What do they put in this?'

Stephen tastes his. 'It's quite strong, isn't it? But you need it in this weather. It's antifreeze for your veins.'

I recklessly tip the rest of the wine down my throat. The worst Mr Mason can do is to fire me for drunkenness, which wouldn't break my heart. Speaking of broken hearts, I want to know what Stephen has to say to me.

'My company was downsizing,' I say, 'and I got caught in the crossfire. Is that what you wanted to talk to me about?'

'Not really,' he says. 'But I'm sorry it happened.'

'I'm sure I'll find something else soon.'

'Of course, you will. In the meantime, your parents must be enjoying having you home.'

'They are,' I say. 'It was Mum who got me this job. She's secretly hoping I'll discover a latent passion for retail and move here permanently.'

'Would you ever consider it?' he asks. 'You could apply to your old firm. I know they're small, but at least they're local.'

My heart skips a beat, and I choose my words carefully.

'I wouldn't rule anything out. I only took the job in London because it came up at a good time for me personally.'

I don't elaborate further. He knows exactly when I took the job and why. Anyway, he's moved away too, so that's irrelevant.

He finishes his mulled wine. 'I'm living in Manchester at the moment.'

'I know. Mum told me. I expect your mother told her.'

Silence hangs between us. Does he sense the unspoken implication that he should have told me himself? Probably not. Stephen has always been a practical person. When he makes a decision, he sticks to it. It would never have occurred to him to contact me and risk opening up the whole messy situation again.

'I only have ten minutes before I have to leave,' I say.

He shuffles his feet, looking like a small boy caught in mischief. 'I wanted to make sure you were ok.'

I don't know what he's asking. Does he mean ok with our breakup? It's a little late to ask me that. And he must know I'm unlikely to tell him the truth after all this time, especially as he appears to have moved on.

'I'm fine,' I say.

He looks relieved. 'That's good. It was horribly awkward when I came in yesterday, and I wanted to apologise.'

He leans forward and lowers his voice so the people at the next table can't hear. 'I couldn't stop thinking about it all evening. The look on your face when I told you about Isabella has been haunting me ever since.'

I stiffen. What look on my face? I'm pretty sure it only conveyed mild pleasure at seeing an old friend and polite inquiry as to the reason for his return to the village.

'I'm not sure what you mean,' I say. 'Did you think I was upset about something?'

'Well, yes. You looked pretty upset when I mentioned my new girlfriend. If I'd known you were in the village, and I'd be likely to bump into you, I'd have let you know. But I had no idea we were going to meet like that.'

I give him a cool stare. 'I may have been surprised to see you, but that's all. Why should I care that you're seeing someone else? You and I broke up a long time ago, and neither of us feels the slightest interest in the other one's life.'

'I wouldn't go that far,' he says, looking embarrassed.

I sweep on as though I haven't heard him. 'I'm happy you're seeing someone else. As a matter of fact, so am I.'

He looks surprised. 'I didn't know that. My mum passes on all the gossip from your mum, but she hasn't mentioned anything.'

I force myself to meet his eye. 'That's because my parents don't know yet.'

'That makes sense. I take it this is a new relationship?'

'Very new,' I say. 'But I think it could be extremely serious.'

He smiles. 'Despite being very new?'

I try to look dignified. 'It isn't all that new, but we haven't been together as long as you and I were. That's all I meant.'

He looks even more amused. 'I'm glad to hear it, or there would have been quite a bit of crossover.'

I'm starting to feel angry. It's insulting that he thinks I might be upset about his new girlfriend. It's even more insulting that he's brought me to the pub to persuade me to admit to it while he offers me sympathy. I don't need sympathy from Stephen Parker. I don't need sympathy from anyone.

'No crossover at all,' I say. 'But I started seeing him fairly soon after we broke up. It was casual at first, but now we're more serious. I expect I'll tell my parents about it while I'm here.'

'Did you meet him in London?' he asks.

My brother is quite correct to say I can't do maths, especially not in my head and while under pressure. How soon after breaking up with Stephen did I move away? And when did I say I met this man? My brain appears to have frozen.

'I met him the week before I left,' I say. 'He comes up to London quite often, and I see him whenever I'm down here.'

'So, he's a local,' he says. 'Do I know him?'

'I don't think so. In fact, I'm sure you don't.'

My head is spinning, although whether with the deception or the mulled wine, I'm not sure. I need to bring this conversation to an end before I dig myself in any deeper. All Stephen needs to know is that I couldn't care less about him or his stupid new relationship, and I'm blissfully happy in my wonderful new one.

'I have to go,' I say abruptly. 'Mr Mason will be upset if I'm late, especially after he's extended my lunchtime. Thanks for the sandwich. It was nice catching up with you. Maybe I'll see you around.'

He pushes back his chair. 'I'll walk with you. I'm going to the bakery, anyway.'

'You are?'

'I still have those cookies to order. I thought it would be a bit tactless if you were the one who had to ice them. But now I know you're fine …'

'You can order anything you want,' I say. 'I'll be happy to help.'

We step outside, and I gasp as the freezing air burns a trail inside my lungs.

Stephen takes my arm. 'We should hurry. You only have three minutes. By the way, does this new man of yours have a name?'

My first instinct is to tell him to mind his own business. But that isn't what someone who is happily getting on with her own life would do.

'Yes, he does,' I say, almost tripping over a pile of snow by the gate.

He steadies me. 'I'm glad to hear it. It can be inconvenient going through life answering to, "Oi, you!" Are you planning to tell me what it is?'

A selection of names flashes through my mind. They race past so quickly that I'm unable to grab hold of one. Algernon, Cary, Albert, Marmaduke … I wonder why my subconscious is throwing up characters from a black and white movie. Surely, I can think of one nice, age-appropriate name?

'Jack!' I say when the silence threatens to become embarrassing. I clear my throat and add more calmly, 'His name is Jack.'

'Jack,' he repeats. 'It's certainly better than, "Oi, you!" Well, I'm home for another ten days. I look forward to meeting him.'

Chapter Seven

Mr Mason is looking at his watch when I burst in. But I've made it with thirty seconds to spare, so he can't complain.

'I'm glad you came back to see us today,' he tells Stephen. 'I've been giving your request a lot of thought.'

Stephen looks taken aback, and I almost feel sorry for him. When he set out to procure his girlfriend a Valentine treat, he didn't have the faintest idea he would find himself enmeshed in a web consisting of his ex-girlfriend, her new 'boyfriend', and the possibility his request would lead to the entire overhaul of a long-established business. That's his problem. Everyone knows the theory of the butterfly's wing and the tsunami. It may teach him to think more carefully about his actions in the future.

Mr Mason pulls out a tatty notebook and opens it to a fresh page. He beams at Stephen. 'Perhaps you could give me some details about your girlfriend.'

Stephen looks at me, then away again. I have a fleeting impulse to help him out, but I squash it. I wouldn't mind hearing a few details about my rival. Not my rival – my unlucky successor.

Stephen fixes his gaze on a tray of meringues. 'Well … er ... she's twenty-eight. She's about five foot eight and slim with beautiful curly hair. She likes horses …'

I knew it! I said she was horsey. And true to shallow, predictable male form, he's gone for someone younger this time around. Only two years younger, admittedly, but it's the principle of the thing. It shows the direction in which he's heading. If he goes two years younger with each successive girlfriend, then by the time he's fifty he'll be giving Leonardo DiCaprio a run for his money.

The hair preference stings a little. As a child, I longed for curly hair. But my hair was ramrod straight and only got straighter as I grew up. Stephen always told me he preferred straight hair. Clearly, he was lying. All the time we were together, he was secretly wishing I was tall and thin with a mass of curls, and that I liked horses, instead of jumping in terror every time one of them makes that weird snorting noise.

I could fix two of the differences between me and his new girlfriend with the aid of a skilled hairdresser and a trained therapist, but the third is completely out of my grasp. I could never reach the dizzy heights of this Isabella stick insect woman, and there's no point trying. I've been shopping in the petite section of every store since the age of eighteen, when I finally accepted I must have been absent the day they handed out height genes.

I'd prefer not to hear any more. If we give him enough encouragement, Stephen may blurt out Isabella's bra size, and I'm not prepared for that.

'We only need to know what message Mr Parker would like us to ice on the cookies,' I tell Mr Mason.

'Quite so,' he says. 'Have you had any thoughts about that yet, Mr Parker?'

Stephen pulls a piece of paper from his pocket and smooths it out. 'I thought perhaps *Happy Valentine's Day Isabella.*'

He needed a piece of paper to remember that? It seems the kind of message which, with a little effort, he could have retained in his head until he'd put in the order. I wonder how long it took him to write it. Did he sit up for hours last night, chewing the stub of a pencil and trying out all the possible variations?

'That's a lot of cookies,' I point out. 'Twenty-six, in fact.'

Stephen counts the letters. 'You're right! Very impressive. How did you do that?'

I don't tell him that I too went through all the possible permutations of his likely message last night. He isn't known for his creativity, so this one seemed the most likely choice.

I shrug, trying to convey the impression of being some kind of maths genius – the Good Will Hunting of the bakery business. 'It's actually twenty-seven if you include the apostrophe.'

He narrows his eyes at me. 'We can leave out the punctuation for now.'

'That's up to you. You're the customer.'

'Quite right,' says Mr Mason approvingly. 'So, have we agreed on the wording?'

'Have we?' I ask Stephen.

He gives me an uncertain look. 'Now you mention it, twenty-six cookies *is* rather a lot.'

'Twenty-seven if we're preserving the punctuation,' I remind him.

He frowns. 'Perhaps it should be something a little shorter.'

'That's entirely up to you,' I say. 'We're here to provide a service.'

He looks at our display of cookies. 'How big will they be? Are the heart-shaped ones the same size as these, or are they more bite-size?'

Mr Mason considers. 'I believe our Valentine's cookies are similar to these.'

I'm starting to enjoy myself. 'Are we able to order custom sized cookies from our supplier?' I ask Mr Mason.

Stephen doesn't appear to think I'm taking this whole business seriously. 'There's no need to do that. I can make it shorter.'

'I don't mind phoning the supplier to find out,' I say. 'There's also the problem of packing them. We don't have any boxes large enough to lay out the cookies in a long message. It might be better if I put them into one of our regular cake boxes, all jumbled up. That way, your girlfriend could have fun deciphering the message before she eats them – like a type of edible crossword.'

'There's no need,' Stephen says shortly. 'Just give me eight cookies spelling her name.'

'Certainly,' I say with a professional smile. 'Are you sure her name is exactly eight letters long?'

He looks even more annoyed. 'Of course, I'm sure.'

I pretend to count on my fingers. 'That seems to be correct. And how are we spelling it? Is it the usual way, or is there a twist?'

His lips tighten. 'The usual way.'

'I thought there might be a *Z* instead of an *S*, or an extra *L*,' I say innocently.

Stephen turns to Mr Mason. 'I'll pick them up on the morning of the fourteenth if that suits you.'

He barely waits for Mr Mason's reply before turning and leaving the shop.

To my surprise, Mr Mason looks delighted. 'Very good, Lily! You handled that beautifully. It wouldn't have occurred to me to ask all those questions, but you're right. It's important to get the details correct, especially if we hope to add this service to our repertoire. I'll check that Martha plans to deliver enough cookies on the thirteenth. You can ice them when they arrive and box them up. If you can hold the fort for a minute, I'll call her now.'

He disappears into the back room, and I pull out my phone and text Jack. I don't dare call him because Mr Mason has oddly batlike hearing, and I can't think of a suitable excuse if he asks who I'm speaking to.

I can't say it's our bread suppliers. It may lead him to believe I'm planning to set up a rival guerrilla operation to poach his business, although I doubt that Honeywell is a prime location for pop-up stores. And all the other shop fronts on the high street are currently occupied, if not precisely thriving.

I decide not to give Jack too many details over the phone. Mr Mason is unlikely to have set up a staff messaging intercept, but it isn't a risk I'm willing to take. Besides, I don't know who might have access to Jack's phone. It would be easier to tell him in person. So, I send him a quick text. *Great to see you last night. Are we still on for lunch this weekend?*

I don't expect to hear back quickly. Like me, he's at work. But he replies almost at once. *Saturday or Sunday?*

I slip my phone into my pocket and gently knock on the office door.

Mr Mason peers out. 'Is there a problem?'

'I have a quick question.'

'Have you left a customer waiting in the shop?' he asks.

'No, and I'd hear the bell if anyone came in. I wanted to ask whether I'll be working this weekend.'

'Let me consult my rota,' he says.

He slides back inside the office and closes the door behind him. I wait outside, wondering what all the secrecy is about. It's an office. It isn't NASA mission control.

He emerges a minute later, holding a sheet of paper. He lays it on the counter and points to a carefully ruled chart. 'This is our staff rota. Do you see the title at the top?'

I suppress a smile. As an office manager in a large company, I had to produce spreadsheets showing the leave allocation for more than a thousand members of staff in four different countries. But I try to remember this is as important to Mr Mason as those spreadsheets were to my employer.

Mum told me last night that he's owned this bakery for thirty years. He left school at sixteen and started working here, and he saved enough to buy the business when the previous owner retired. It's nice to see someone fulfilling a lifelong dream, even if it isn't one I fully understand.

We study the paper together. He's written our two names across the top. Down the left-hand side are the days of the week.

He peers at the chart. 'Ah, yes, we are both here on Saturday. It's one of our busiest days, and we can't afford to be understaffed.'

'Does that mean I'm free on Sunday?' I ask.

He points to the chart. 'As you can see, only I am working that day. The bakery opens at seven at the weekends, but we close at lunchtime on Sundays, so I handle that shift myself.'

My heart sinks at the thought of getting up at the crack of dawn on Saturday, but at least I'll have the whole of Sunday off. I check the chart again and see I'm not in on Wednesday. That should break up the week a little.

I wait until Mr Mason returns to his office before texting Jack again. *Working Saturday. Free Sunday.*

He replies almost at once. *Sounds good. I'll book us a table somewhere and send you the details.*

Lunch with Jack sounds great. It's been ages since we caught up, and I'm looking forward to it. There's the slight added complication that I've recently announced he's my boyfriend, and apparently we're very serious. But that can't be helped. Stephen didn't leave me with much choice.

I'm sure Jack will understand. At least, I hope he will. I don't allow myself to consider what will happen if he says no. The idea of having to tell Stephen I made a mistake, and I'm not actually seeing Jack, is too much to bear. I could try to persuade him he misunderstood what I said to him at the pub. What I meant was that Jack and I were starting a business together and were partners strictly in that sense.

It wouldn't work. Stephen isn't stupid. He would know I'd lied, and he'd know why. He would be horribly sympathetic and understanding, and I couldn't bear that. I'd prefer to pack up and return to London and take my chances of finding a new job when I get there. Mum and Dad would be upset, but that would be better than the humiliation of Stephen's sympathy. Even worse, his amusement.

I decide to keep it as a backup plan if things go really wrong. With any luck, Jack won't make too much of a fuss, especially when I explain the circumstances. It's the sort of miniscule favour friends do for each other all the time. I'd do it for him if he asked me. Anyway, there's no point worrying about it now. I'll just have to wait until Sunday and see how he reacts.

Chapter Eight

I sleep until ten o'clock on Sunday morning, then go downstairs to see where everyone is. I wasn't going to bother with breakfast, but Mum insists.

'Now, Lily, what do we always say about breakfast?'

'It's the curse of the modern age?'

She clicks her tongue at me. 'It's the most important meal of the day. Everyone says so.'

'The cereal companies say so,' I tell her.

It's no good. She already has the pans out. 'Would you like a full English breakfast or something light, like porridge?'

Only Mum could describe porridge as a light breakfast, particularly the way she makes it, with plenty of brown sugar and cream.

'Could I have a partial English breakfast?' I say.

She looks confused. 'I don't know what that is.'

'Eggs, mushrooms and tomatoes without the other things. Think of it as an Isle of Wight breakfast – small, yet part of the entire country.'

She's even more puzzled. 'No bacon or sausages?'

'That's right.'

'But you'd like some of my fried bread?' she says. 'You always have that when I make you a cooked breakfast.'

I waver. Mum makes the best fried bread in the world – golden and crispy and the perfect foil for bacon and sausages.

I shake my head regretfully. 'Just scrambled eggs with tomatoes and mushrooms, please. Jack and I will be eating in a couple of hours, and I need to have an appetite.'

Mum seems relieved I'm not facing the peril of going for more than two hours without a meal.

'I'll make you some toast too, just in case,' she says. 'Toast isn't filling at all. You won't even notice you're eating it. I have some lovely Oxford marmalade in the larder.'

I know better than to offer to cook my own breakfast. Mum considers both her children to exist in some precarious universe where they can barely manage to feed themselves or wash their own clothes. She stopped worrying about Ben so much when he moved in with Mia, but now he's back under his parents' roof, she refuses to let him lift a finger. As far as I'm concerned, it's very bad for him. It's probably bad for me too, but there's nothing I can do about that.

I make the coffee while she scrambles the eggs. No one scrambles eggs as well as Mum. I've never been able to discover the secret of making them as light and fluffy as hers. I've asked her several times to teach me, but I suspect she deliberately leaves out some essential part of the process so she can continue her unbroken reign as Breakfast Queen.

She hands me a plate piled high with toast. 'This will keep you going.'

I take the smallest piece and spread butter on it. Even Mum's toast is perfect. It's hot and crunchy and never seems to get damp and tough, no matter how long it sits in the toast rack.

Ben appears in his dressing gown. 'Fantastic! I haven't missed breakfast.'

'Not at all,' says Mum. 'What can I get you? I have everything here for a proper cooked breakfast.'

'I'm fine with toast,' he says, helping himself to the largest piece and smothering it with butter.

'You can't just have that,' she says, distressed. 'You must have something warming on a day like this.'

Ben crams the toast into his mouth and reaches for another piece. 'If you absolutely insist.'

She tips an entire packet of sausages into the pan. 'Quite right. A growing boy can't exist on a couple of pieces of toast in the morning.'

'Ben is thirty-two,' I say. 'He probably stopped growing a while ago.'

He smirks at me. 'Just because you only made it to five foot two doesn't mean the rest of us did.'

'Lily is the perfect size,' says Mum soothingly. 'She takes after her Grandma Rose. She was petite, too. She doesn't want to be six feet tall like you, Ben.'

Actually, I wouldn't mind. It would be nice to see over people's heads in crowds and reach high shelves without a stepladder. The only advantage I've ever found from my height is fitting comfortably into aeroplane seats. As I only fly once every few years, it doesn't seem an adequate trade-off for everything else.

I spend so long thinking about this that I don't remember my lunch date with Jack until half an hour before he's due to arrive. I shouldn't call it a lunch date, not in light of the news I have to break to him. What should I call it instead

– our lunch engagement? That's far worse. Why does the English language insist on attaching such romantic terms to the simple act of sharing roast beef and Yorkshire pudding?

I finally decide on lunch appointment. It has a detached, professional feel to it. I try not to think about my last lunch appointment. Marnie, my manager, insisted I order the most expensive items on the menu before telling me in a hushed tone the company no longer required my services.

Hopefully, Jack won't react in a similar way when I tell him what I've done. I couldn't bear to lose our friendship. I've known him ever since I started sixth form college at the age of sixteen. He and Ben were in the year above me, which meant I'd already seen him several times in passing. But I met him properly when I started college, and our somewhat unlikely friendship developed.

I was shy and lacking in confidence, whereas he was at the centre of everything that was going on. But somehow, we hit it off, and we've been friends ever since. We've seen each other through failed exams and failed relationships and excruciatingly awful jobs. We know the best and the worst about each other, and we still like to hang out. It's the best kind of friendship, and I wouldn't knowingly do anything to put it in jeopardy. I may have told Stephen the tiniest of white lies about the actual nature of our friendship, but I didn't plan to do it, so it doesn't really count.

I run upstairs to take a shower. I wash my hair, then wrap it in Mum's favourite primrose yellow towel. I stare at myself in my bedroom mirror, trying to imagine myself with a mass of curly hair. Would Stephen have stayed with me if my hair had been different? It seems unlikely, particularly if this was the look I'd chosen. I look like a demented poodle.

The doorbell rings, bringing me back to reality. I hastily switch on Mum's extra powerful hairdryer. It immediately turns my hair into candyfloss. I switch it from cyclone to gentle breeze and restore my hair to some semblance of order. Then I pull on a pair of jeans and my warmest sweater and run downstairs.

I find Jack in the kitchen, politely refusing the slice of toast Mum is doing her best to thrust into his hands.

'You don't know how long they'll keep you waiting for your table,' she says. 'Why not take it with you?'

We leave her staring forlornly at the piece of toast and wave goodbye to Dad, who's oiling the hinge on the garage door and showing no signs of sciatica.

Jack starts the car. 'I'm glad you appeared when you did, or your mum would have started force-feeding me leftovers. No one ever goes hungry in your house, do they? I used to love coming over for dinner when we were younger. She always insisted on giving me third helpings.'

I settle into my seat. 'As far as I remember, you never raised any objection.'

'I was a teenage boy,' he says. 'I needed to keep up my energy for being cool.'

'You were incredibly cool,' I admit. 'I remember you and Ben doing wheelies on your BMX bikes for the benefit of all the local girls. I can't think how any of them managed to resist.'

'It's a mystery, isn't it?' he agrees. 'I couldn't understand it then, and I can't understand it now.'

He swings the car off the main road and along a gravel drive and pulls up outside The Wild Horse. 'I hope you're hungry.'

I follow him towards the main entrance. 'I thought we'd be going to a pub. This place looks terribly upmarket. I'm not dressed for it.'

'I'm sure they'll lend you a jacket and tie if need be,' he says.

I stay two steps behind him as he approaches the front desk. 'Table for two. Name of Fisher.'

Thankfully, the man doesn't bat an eyelid at the sight of my old jeans and wild hair. He leads us across the vestibule and into a small dining room, where I'm thankful to see people wearing a variety of outfits.

Two elderly women in tweed suits and brogues are talking earnestly together over their soup, while a harassed looking couple is sitting in the corner with their two young children. The little girl is dressed as Red Riding Hood. The little boy has made an even more daring fashion choice. He's dressed head to toe in a Spider-Man suit, including the hood, but he's chosen to accessorise it with a pink tutu and sparkly tiara.

Jack gives him an approving look. 'That outfit could have missed the mark, but he's managed to make it work.'

The server shows us to a table by the window and hands us both a menu.

'This one's on me,' says Jack before I can speak.

'Don't be ridiculous,' I say. 'I haven't seen you for ages. I plan to get this one.'

'You can get the next one. I chose this place. I'm paying.'

'The thing is,' I tell him, 'there may not be a next one.'

His brow furrows. 'You aren't going back to London at once?'

'I don't think so. But I may have to.'

He closes his menu. 'Let's order, and you can tell me all about it.'

He orders a steak with fondant potatoes, while I choose the salmon. I love it, and Mum only rarely cooks it because Dad is allergic to fish.

'And to drink?' asks the server.

'I think we'll need some wine,' says Jack. 'What do you think, Lily?'

I force a smile. 'At the very least. You may need something stronger by the time the meal's finished.'

He doesn't look too bothered. 'Let's start with the wine and see how we go.'

Thankfully, the server returns almost immediately with our drinks. I down half of mine in one gulp, and Jack looks concerned.

'Has something happened, Lily? Your Mum didn't mention anything.'

'Nothing too awful,' I say. 'At least, I hope you'll agree. It's just something I've done that I wish I hadn't.'

'I'm intrigued,' he says. 'Do you want to tell me now or wait until the food arrives?'

I finish my wine, and he waves to the server and points to my glass.

'Why don't you tell me what it is and get it over with?' he says. 'You won't enjoy your dinner otherwise, and it would be a shame to waste a perfectly good piece of salmon.'

He's right. There's no sense in putting this off any longer. If he's going to be angry with me, I may as well find out now and pack my suitcase as soon as I get home.

I take a deep breath, trying to think where to start. 'You already know I came home because I lost my job.'

He nods. 'I imagine you were pretty upset about that.'

'I wasn't too thrilled, but these things happen. And I was lucky to have somewhere to go while I picked up the pieces.'

'True,' he says. 'Your parents are great.'

'They are. I know how fortunate I am. Mum got me the job in the bakery before I arrived home.'

'What's the problem?' he asks gently. 'Do you hate it that much?'

'I don't hate it at all. I'm not saying it's my dream job, but it's absolutely fine. Mr Mason is nice enough, and I'm not exactly rushed off my feet. We have very few customers.'

'So, what's the problem?' he prompts me again.

'The problem is one particular customer.'

He stops smiling. 'What do you mean? Is someone stalking you?'

'I'm talking about Stephen,' I say.

'Stephen's stalking you?'

'No, he isn't. But he came into the shop on my first afternoon and took me by surprise.'

'You didn't know he was home?' he says.

'No, I didn't. And he didn't know I was home or that I was working in the bakery. It was pretty awkward.'

'I imagine it was,' he says. 'But you were bound to bump into him sooner or later. You both have parents who live in the village, so it's inevitable you'll be home at the same time. Did you see him at Christmas?'

Our meals arrive, and I feel suddenly hungry. I take a forkful of salmon. 'This is really good. No, he wasn't home for Christmas. He went skiing or something.'

'I see. How long is he back for?'

I stab one of the new potatoes viciously with my fork. 'I'm not exactly sure. But he's come home for Valentine's Day.'

Jack looks up from his steak. 'He happens to be home over Valentine's Day, or he's come home for Valentine's Day?'

'The second one.' I roll my potato moodily through the dill sauce and stuff it into my mouth.

He gives me a sympathetic look. 'I think I know what's coming.'

I nod. 'Mum told me he was visiting his Dad. But Stephen said he was here to see his new girlfriend.'

'I suppose it was inevitable sometime,' he says. 'It's been a year.'

'We don't know he waited a year,' I say. 'For all I know, he may have started seeing this woman the day after he broke up with me.'

He takes a sip of his wine. 'That's possible. But I don't see what difference that makes, so long as he wasn't seeing her while he was with you. Once you'd broken up, you were both free agents.'

'I know that!' I say. 'I understand how relationships work.'

He doesn't react to my snippy tone. 'What's this really about? Is it that he's seeing someone new, or is something else going on?'

I stare out of the window, trying to compose myself. 'It was all such a shock. I knew he was bound to start seeing other people at some point. But I didn't count on him waltzing into my place of work and demanding I write stupid messages for her all over our heart-shaped cookies.'

His lips twitch, but to his credit, he doesn't laugh. He reaches over and gives my hand a sympathetic squeeze. 'I'm not sure anyone ever expects that. It's like the Spanish Inquisition.'

I smile. 'In Stephen's defence, he had no idea I was working there. He thought he'd be seeing Mr Mason.'

'I don't know Mr Mason very well,' says Jack, 'but he isn't my idea of Cupid. However, appearances are deceptive, and who are we to judge?'

'Mr Mason was terribly confused,' I say. 'You'd have thought Stephen had stormed in demanding we turned the bakery into a gambling den.'

'It's lucky you were there,' says Jack.

I stop laughing. 'I didn't feel lucky. I felt like tipping a box of cookies over Stephen's head.'

'So, what happened?'

I finish my salmon and push away my plate. 'You'll be proud to hear I acted like the true professional I am. I suggested that Stephen go away and think about the message he'd like to write. I wanted to get rid of him. I honestly didn't expect to see him again.'

Jack looks dumbfounded. 'Are you saying he came in a second time?'

'The very next day.'

'I was right in my first supposition,' he says. 'You do have a stalker. Would you like me to alert the authorities?'

'Not yet, but I'll let you know. I haven't told you the reason he came back. He asked me out to lunch because he wanted to talk to me.'

Jack gives me a quick look but doesn't say anything.

'At first, I thought … but it wasn't that.' My face burns with the remembrance of that humiliating lunch.

'You don't have to tell me,' he says.

'Actually, I do. It's more complicated than icing cookies.'

I sneak a look at him and see he's looking amused. 'I mean it, Jack. You won't be smiling by the time I've finished.'

The server arrives to take our plates. 'Would you like to see the dessert menu?'

Jack looks at my flushed face. 'Perhaps in a minute.'

I wait until the server has left before speaking again. 'Stephen wanted to talk to me because he thought I was really upset about this Irene woman.'

He raises an eyebrow. 'Irene?'

I don't have to pretend to Jack that I've forgotten her name. 'Sorry, her name is Isabella. Anyway, Stephen wanted to check I was ok about it all.'

'Which you weren't,' he interrupts, keeping his eyes fixed on me.

'But he had no right to assume that!' I say hotly. 'I don't know where he got the idea I was upset. I was extremely polite to him, and I agreed to ice the cookies. What else did he want me to do – offer to be Isabella's bridesmaid or act as godmother to their firstborn son?'

Jack looks startled. 'They're getting married?'

'No!' I must have spoken more loudly than I intended because several heads swivel to look at us. I give the Spider-Man ballerina a thumbs up before continuing.

'Of course, they aren't getting married. At least, he didn't mention it. All he wanted was a Valentine's Day present for her. He isn't the most imaginative person I know, so I'm surprised he managed to come up with the idea of cookies. The first year we were together, he gave me a book on databases for Valentine's Day because he knew I was struggling with my IT qualification.'

Jack makes a small sound. I decide to interpret it as a cough. 'How thoughtful of him,' he says.

'Wasn't it? I'd spent the previous three months knitting him this amazing Icelandic sweater because he really liked the ones on that Danish show. You can't imagine how bad I felt about my lack of effort when I received my romantic computing book.'

'What did he get you the following year?' he asks. 'A slide rule?'

'He booked us a mini break in the Lake District,' I admit.

'It's nice to know he's capable of learning from his mistakes.'

I don't answer. It was a lovely thought, and we had a great time. But he broke up with me a week later, so it obviously didn't mean as much to him as it did to me.

Jack senses my mood and changes the subject. 'You were talking about having lunch with him so he could check you were ok. That isn't too bad. It's not as though he told you he'd put his Icelandic sweater on eBay or had always hated your taste in shoes.'

'He may as well have done. He thought I was upset because he was seeing someone else. You can imagine how that felt.'

'I can,' he agrees. 'What did you say?'

'I told him he was completely wrong. I wasn't remotely upset. I told him we'd broken up a long time ago, and I never gave him a thought.'

'Good for you,' he says. 'I'm guessing he didn't believe you?'

There's no point avoiding the subject any longer. He has to know some time.

'He didn't seem convinced,' I say, 'which was extremely arrogant of him. He kept giving me sympathetic looks. Honestly, Jack, I couldn't bear it. I wanted him to know I was fine without him. So, I …'

'You what?'

'I said he must have been mistaken about how I felt because I was seeing someone else too,' I say in a rush.

'Good for you!' he says.

'I'm glad you think so. But that wasn't all. He kept asking questions about my new boyfriend. I tried to change the subject, but it was no good.'

Jack looks delighted. 'Why am I never there when anything interesting is happening? Did you tell him you were dating a supermodel who moonlights as a professional boxer? Even better, a famous actor? Extra points if you said you were seeing one of the Hemsworth brothers!'

'I wish,' I say gloomily. 'But you know me. I can't think on my feet.'

'I'm disappointed. You made up some boring boyfriend instead?'

I give him a sideways glance. 'Not quite.'

His eyes are alight with laughter as he waits for the rest of the story. Time to wipe the smile off his face and possibly end our friendship for ever.

'Jack,' I say as calmly as possible, 'I told him it was you.'

Chapter Nine

There's a long silence. I don't dare look at him while he digests what I've just told him. I dig my fingernails into my palms and wait for the explosion. It comes at last, but it's an explosion of laughter rather than anger. It's a relief, but I can't help feeling offended that he finds the idea of dating me so funny.

He wipes his eyes at last. 'Please tell me you're joking!'

'I'm not joking at all,' I say rather huffily. 'Yours was the first name I could think of. I told you I wasn't any good at thinking on my feet.'

'I suppose I should be flattered,' he says.

'Not really. It was only because I'd seen you the previous evening.'

'It's lucky you didn't see Mr Mason,' he says.

Whatever reaction I'd expected, it wasn't this. I'd anticipated he might be angry, although not too angry, because that isn't him. He's one of the calmest people I know. He would have every right to feel annoyed at me for dragging him into my power game with Stephen. But I didn't expect him to find the whole thing so hilarious.

He grins at me. 'Sorry, Lily. You took me by surprise, that's all.'

I laugh in spite of myself. 'I took myself by surprise. It was out before I knew it. He was sitting there looking smug and trying to commiserate with me. I wanted to make him stop.'

'I can understand that,' he says. 'So, where does that leave me?'

'Nowhere,' I say, surprised. 'I needed to tell you in case you bumped into Stephen, but that's all. He'll be going back to Manchester soon. I'll probably never see him again.'

'Will you tell him we've broken up?' he asks after a moment.

'I won't need to. I've already told you he and I aren't in contact. I haven't heard from him since we broke up.'

'So, he'll think we're still dating?' he says.

'I hadn't thought about that. It doesn't really matter. The only person who's likely to mention anything about me is his mother, because she knows my mum.'

'What does your family think about this?' he asks.

'They don't know anything about it, and I intend it to stay that way. Can you imagine their reaction?'

He looks hurt. 'I'm not sure I like being kept a secret from your nearest and dearest. It makes me feel so used.'

'I didn't mean it like that!' I say. 'Oh, you're teasing me.'

'Possibly. So, this is solely between you and Stephen?'

He no longer looks amused. I don't really blame him. It's a stupid situation, and I had no right to drag him into it.

'He isn't likely to spread it around,' I say. 'He was never one to gossip, and he's made it clear my life is of no interest to him.'

I try to keep the bitterness out of my tone, but Jack isn't fooled.

'He probably thought it was for the best,' he says. 'It didn't end too happily, did it? He isn't stupid. He must have known you didn't want to break up. What would have been gained by him staying in contact with you? It would only have given you false hope.'

I glower at him. 'It wouldn't have given me anything of the kind. I'm absolutely fine about our breakup. It's simply common courtesy to stay in touch when you've been together for so long.'

'You're probably right,' he says. 'Anyway, there's no point going over it all again. Whether or not he ought to have stayed in touch, he didn't. And now he's seeing someone else, and he thinks you are too.'

His familiar look of devilment returns. 'Did you tell him it was me?'

'You're the only Jack I know.'

'You know that,' he says patiently. 'But does he? Shocking though it is for either of us to realise, I'm not the only Jack in the world. There are plenty of us about. Did you specifically say Jack Fisher?'

I try to remember. 'It was all a bit of a rush, but I'm fairly sure I only said his name was Jack.'

I suddenly realise what he's saying. 'How stupid of me! I've been worrying about telling you all week, but there was no need. I could be dating any old Jack. Why didn't I think of that before? You're off the hook.'

'What if I don't want to be off the hook?' he says.

'You must! I'm only sorry I dragged you into this. Let's forget about it now and order dessert.'

He lifts a hand. 'Of course, I want to be dragged into this. It sounds like fun. And I definitely don't want you dating 'any old Jack'. We know nothing about him. We certainly don't know his intentions. He could be after your money or your job at the bakery.'

'He's welcome to either of them,' I say. 'Fine, I'll pretend it's you if it makes you feel better. But it doesn't matter either way. I only said it to shut Stephen up, and I achieved my aim. He couldn't get out of the bakery fast enough as soon as he'd ordered his cookies. Speaking of cookies, I want to see the dessert menu.'

Jack waves to the server, who brings them over.

I study mine carefully. 'I ought to choose something we sell at work so I can make notes on how to improve our products. But I want the sticky toffee pudding or the caramel sundae. I'm not sure which. Do you have a coin I can flip?'

'No, and I wouldn't give it to you anyway,' says Jack. 'That's no way to make a decision. Choose the one you really want.'

'That's the point,' I say. 'I don't know which one I want. They both look good.'

'There's bound to be one you want more,' he insists. 'Close your eyes and think about something completely different.'

I close my eyes obediently and think about Stephen. I'd forgotten how handsome he is and what a devastatingly attractive smile he has.

Jack's voice interrupts me. 'Open your eyes, Lily. What would you like for dessert?'

'Caramel sundae,' I say without thinking. 'Oh!'

He gives me a smug look. 'That wasn't so difficult, was it?'

'It was. I hate decisions. But it seemed to work. Is that how you make all your choices?'

'Sometimes,' he says. 'I usually know what I want, so I don't have to think about it. But it's a useful tactic when I can't decide. The trick is to let your mind go completely blank before choosing.'

'You told me to think of something entirely different,' I say, hoping he won't ask me what I thought about.

'That works too,' he says. 'At least, for dessert. I wouldn't use this method for anything important.'

'Like which job to take or whether to start a new relationship?'

He looks surprised. 'Possibly the job thing if I was offered two equally good opportunities. But never the other one.'

He smiles at my puzzled expression. 'Love isn't a decision you make with the flip of a coin or by closing your eyes. You just know.'

He's right. I knew the moment I saw Stephen that this was the man I wanted to spend the rest of my life with. That's never changed. It probably never will. But I don't want to admit this to Jack. I've spent the past year telling myself Stephen was a huge mistake, and we were never meant to be, but I never really believed it. When it comes to love, the heart knows exactly what it wants. It's simply that in my case, it isn't allowed to have it. At least, not yet.

I didn't expect to bump into Stephen again. I didn't even want to. But a chain of circumstances over which I had no control brought me home. And he happened to come home at the same time. Not only that, but he also walked into the place where I work on my very first day. Surely, that must mean something. It can't be a coincidence.

For the first time since Stephen and I broke up, I feel a tiny flicker of hope. This may not be the end of our story. Isabella is a slight problem, but not necessarily a permanent one. She may be nothing more than a slight roadblock in the path of true love. She and Stephen may not even be exclusive. I should have asked him more about their relationship when we had lunch together, but I didn't want to. I was too focused on disabusing him of the impression I was still hung up on him.

Perhaps it was a mistake to tell him about Jack. It momentarily soothed my pride, but it may have put him off the idea of us getting back together.

'Somehow, I sense you're no longer with me,' says Jack. 'Do you still want that caramel sundae?'

I come back to the present and smile at him. 'Try to stop me! And thank you for my lesson on decision-making.'

'One caramel sundae, and one sticky toffee pudding, please,' he tells the server.

He catches my eye and bursts out laughing. 'You're wondering whether you should have chosen the sticky toffee pudding, aren't you?'

I want to deny it, but I can't. He knows me too well.

'Maybe a little,' I say. 'But you can't go through life changing your mind all the time. I'll stick with my first choice.'

'There's nothing wrong with trying new things,' he says.

'Does that mean you're going to let me have some of your sticky toffee pudding?'

He grins. 'I walked into that one, didn't I? Fine, we'll split them and compare notes.'

We spend the rest of the meal chatting about everything that's happened to us during the past six months. I discuss my job and my worries about finding a new one. It's difficult to talk to Mum and Dad about it because I know how much they worry. But it's familiar and comforting talking to Jack. We've been friends for so long that we've developed a kind of shorthand. We seem to have an instinctive feeling for what the other one is trying to say.

When at last we can eat no more, Jack pays the bill and collects our coats.

'What now?' he says. 'Should we go for an extremely long hike to walk off our meal?'

'We could do that,' I say. 'Or we could go to my house and spend the afternoon slumped on the sofa watching a movie.'

He closes his eyes and appears to go into a trance. He opens his eyes dramatically and looks at me. 'The second one! My goodness, it really does work. I had no idea which I was going to choose until the words were out of my mouth.'

It starts to snow as we drive home, and I give silent thanks for his decision. I'm barely even a fair-weather walker. The merest hint of bad weather always sends me scurrying inside.

He parks on the drive, and I jump out and make for the warmth of the house as quickly as possible. Before I reach the front door, Mum throws it open, beaming from ear to ear.

'You're back, at last!' she says. 'Ben's told us the news!'

'What news?' I say.

She flings her arms around me. 'Your father and I couldn't be more thrilled, Lily. It's absolutely wonderful!'

She lets me go and makes a dart towards Jack, enfolding him in an enormous hug.

'Welcome to the family!'

Chapter Ten

There's a stunned silence. Jack is the first one to break it. 'Thank you very much, Mrs Carson,' he says politely.

'No, not thank you very much!' I say. 'What are you talking about, Mum?'

She pats my head. 'Don't let's stand out here in the cold any longer. You'll catch your death. Come in, come in, both of you!'

She slips her arm around my waist and leads me into the house before I can make a break for it. I'm not sure what this is about. Whatever it is, it can't be good.

Jack follows us. I give him a frantic look of enquiry, and he flashes me a mischievous grin.

We find Dad sitting in the living room, reading the Sunday newspaper. He jumps to his feet when we arrive. 'Marvellous news! Your mother and I are delighted, Lily.'

He claps Jack on the back. 'Well done!'

I drop into an armchair. 'Would someone mind telling me what's going on?'

Mum points to the sofa. 'Lily, come and sit here with Jack.'

'Go and sit over there!' she tells Dad. 'And take your newspaper with you.'

He obediently picks up his paper and moves to the armchair facing mine.

Mum pats the sofa invitingly. 'You sit here, Lily. And you too, Jack. We want to hear all about it.'

Jack immediately places himself at one end of the sofa. 'Come and sit with me, Lily.'

'I'm perfectly fine here, thanks,' I say shortly.

Mum's behaving as though she knows about our so-called relationship. But that's absolutely impossible. I haven't said anything, and Jack has only just found out. Which only leaves Stephen, and I told him very clearly that Mum doesn't know.

Stephen couldn't possibly have told her. For one thing, he isn't a gossip. For another, she's been here ever since I left. She was making roast lamb for her and Dad, and she never leaves the kitchen for more than five minutes when she's doing a roast.

'Don't be silly, darling,' says Mum. 'You know I prefer the armchair. It's exactly the right shape for me.'

She never sits in this chair. She rarely sits down anyway, but she always says her legs are too short for it. Is she planning to announce she has sciatica too?

She hovers next to me until I give up and grumpily sit on the sofa, as far away from Jack as possible. It's only a two-seater, so I can't avoid him entirely.

Mum sits down and watches the pair of us closely. She seems to be expecting us to perform some sort of trick, with Jack as the ventriloquist and me as his puppet, grinning at everyone and talking about *gottles of gear*.

'That's much better,' she says. 'Now you can tell us all about it.'

She gives me a roguish smile. 'And while you're at it, perhaps you can tell me why we had to hear the news from Ben.'

What does Ben have to do with this? I have to be careful here. I don't want to blurt out the whole story of lying to Stephen, along with the reason why I did it, only to find that Mum is referring to something else entirely.

'What has Ben said?' I ask.

'Now, you mustn't be cross with your brother,' says Mum. 'He wasn't to know you'd been keeping everyone in the dark. Even your parents,' she adds severely.

This could go on for a while if she doesn't get to the point.

'What did he say?' I repeat.

She clasps her hands. 'He happened to bump into Stephen this afternoon, who told him about you and Jack. There's no need to be shy. I can't think why you didn't tell us yourself.'

'What about us?' I ask.

'That you're courting!' she says excitedly.

'Courting?' I say in a tone of disgust.

'That isn't what the young people call it nowadays, Alice,' says Dad. 'Sorry, Lily, I think your mother means stepping out together.'

I give a snort of laughter. Jack is quicker. 'Or wooing,' he says seriously.

Mum looks delighted. 'I haven't heard that one for a long time. It's nice to hear some of the old phrases coming back.'

'Like sick,' Dad chips in. 'When we were young, it meant being ill.'

Time to bring this conversation to a halt. I have no wish to discuss all the words my parents' generation find confusing.

'Jack and I are not courting,' I say firmly. 'Neither are we stepping out or wooing or spooning or parking or going steady.'

I turn to Jack for confirmation. He gives me a reproving look. 'Perhaps we no longer use that terminology, Lily, but I'm sure you understand what your parents are trying to say.'

'Yes, but –' I'm interrupted by the doorbell.

'Now, who can that be at this time?' says Mum.

'Probably someone collecting for something,' I say before Dad can speak. 'Why don't you go and see?'

She jumps up. 'I suppose I ought to. I'll only be a second.'

Dad jumps up too. 'I'll come with you, in case …'

They leave the room, shutting the door carefully behind them. There's no time to ponder the end of Dad's sentence, although I'm intrigued. In case the unexpected caller does what – tries to recruit Mum into a cult? But there's no time to speculate. I need to speak to Jack before they return.

'What do you think you're doing?' I whisper. I don't dare raise my voice in case Mum hasn't answered the front door but has gone to get a glass to press against the wall.

Jack slips his arm around my shoulders. 'What do you mean?'

I return his arm to its proper place. 'Don't play dumb with me, Jack Fisher. You know exactly what I mean. Why didn't you tell them we aren't seeing each other?'

'You mean wooing,' he corrects me.

'Stop it! This isn't the time to play games.'

'I don't agree. It seems the perfect time to me,' he says.

'You can play it by yourself!' I snap. 'It's bad enough having to lie to Stephen. I'm not doing it to Mum and Dad too. Besides, there's no need.'

'I disagree,' he says calmly. 'Think about it, Lily. Your mum says that Stephen told Ben, which means the news is out. You can tell your parents the truth and swear them to secrecy, but you don't know who else Stephen might have told. He's probably mentioned it to his girlfriend, and she won't have seen the need to keep it to herself. This sort of news gets about. It's inevitable in a small village like Honeywell.'

'If anyone mentions it, we'll have to deny it,' I say.

'We can do that,' he says. 'But that means denying it to Stephen too. If you don't, he'll only hear about it from someone else, which makes it far weirder.'

I open my mouth to argue, then close it again. He's right. I was stupid to believe I could tell Stephen about my mythical romance and not expect it to spread any further. Especially in a place like Honeywell.

I've backed myself into a corner here. Either I deny it to no one, or I deny it to everyone, which includes Stephen. I couldn't bear that. He'd know I lied to him. What's worse, he'd know exactly why. It's the very thing I was trying to avoid when I told him the lie in the first place.

But if I don't want him to know the truth, I can't tell anyone else, which includes Mum and Dad. Mum would be absolutely unable to keep it to herself. She'd let it slip within the first twenty-four hours. I wonder whether there's a train to London this afternoon. That would be the simplest solution.

'What's it to be?' asks Jack. 'You need to make up your mind before your parents come back.'

I can't think what's keeping them. Even if, for the first time in our lives, it was a charity collector at the door, how long does it take to drop a couple of pound coins into the tin? Maybe it really is a cult trying to recruit Mum. Even now, a couple of smartly dressed young men may be handing her flowers and convincing her of the benefits of selling all her worldly possessions and going on the road with them.

The door opens a crack, and Dad clears his throat. 'Is it all right if we come in?'

'Of course, it is!' I say more loudly than I intended. 'This is your house.'

Maybe it won't be for much longer. At this very moment, Mum could be signing a deed of transferral. But they may as well enjoy it for as long as they can.

Dad opens the door more fully and gives us an embarrassed glance. What was he was expecting – me to be pulling on my sweater inside out, while Jack hastily buttoned his shirt?

Mum appears behind him. 'Everything all right?'

'Wonderful,' says Jack in a dreamy voice, and she looks delighted.

'Who was that?' I ask.

'It was Ben!' she says. 'He'd forgotten his front door key again. Honestly, that boy would forget his head if it wasn't screwed on.'

'Even that's a matter for debate,' I say waspishly.

She ignores me. 'He'll be down in a minute. I know he'll want to see you both.'

This feeling is very much not mutual, but there's no point in saying that to Mum. She would never believe it.

She and Dad sit down again and look at us expectantly.

'What?' I say.

'You were about to tell us why we were the last to find out,' Mum says. 'You surely didn't think we would disapprove?'

Now is the time to tell the truth and get it over with. It's the sensible thing to do. It's the adult thing to do. It's the right thing to do.

I take a deep breath. 'We were planning to tell you all about it while I was home. We just wanted to find the right time.'

Jack takes my hand. 'It isn't the sort of thing you announce any old how.'

'Quite so,' says Dad. 'The important thing is that you've found each other.'

'I don't believe I was lost,' I say.

'Well …' says Mum. She catches my eye and stops. 'This is all so exciting. Ben is thrilled too.'

'What's Ben thrilled about?' says a voice in the doorway.

'Here he is!' exclaims Mum. 'We're talking about Lily and Jack's news. Don't worry. It's all out in the open now. You were only the tiniest bit premature.'

'That explains a lot,' I mutter to Jack. 'I always thought he was dropped on his head as a baby.'

Ben drops onto the sofa between us. 'Room for a little one?'

'Get off!' I yell.

He looks concerned. 'Sorry, I forgot! You want to cuddle up to Jack.'

'No, I don't!' I catch Jack's eye. 'I mean, maybe later. Anyway, you can cuddle up to Jack for a while. I'm going to put the kettle on.'

'I'll come with you,' says Jack.

'Don't bother.' I make a dart for the door, but he's close behind me.

I wait until we're in the kitchen. 'Are you enjoying this?'

'I am, as a matter of fact.' He reaches out and tucks a strand of hair behind my ear. 'You have such beautiful hair, Lily. I couldn't take my eyes off it over lunch.'

I stare at him, dumbfounded, then see he's grinning.

I lower my voice to a throaty murmur. 'You must tell me what you use on your hair. I want to run my fingers through it and tear it right off your head.'

He gently touches my cheek. 'Your skin is so soft. It's like the old saddle of my BMX bike.'

I feel a bubble of laughter rising inside me. I can play this game as long as he can. I consider what else to compliment. I'm about to say something about his muscles but stop myself. He does actually have a very nice physique. If I comment on his body, he may get entirely the wrong idea.

'I've always admired your ears,' I say. 'They're a perfect shape – like a seashell.'

'What kind of a seashell?' he enquires.

'A clam?' I say wildly. 'Depending on what a clam actually looks like. I've only ever eaten them in chowder.'

'A clam?' he says with a look of disgust.

'Not a clam,' I correct myself. 'One of those twirly ones. Or an oyster. Yes, that's it, an oyster! Have you ever thought of having one of your ears pierced? I could give you a pearl to wear in it.'

'If that's what you want, I'll have it done tomorrow,' he promises. 'Anything for you, my darling.'

'Well, isn't this adorable?' says an amused voice. Jack and I spring apart as Ben walks into the kitchen.

'What are you doing here?' I say.

'I came to see why the kettle was taking so long to boil,' he says. 'I should have guessed. Time loses all meaning when you're in love.'

'Yes, it does,' I say defiantly.

'Adorable,' says Ben. 'Mum and Dad are delighted.'

'As I'm sure are you,' I say sweetly.

'How could you doubt it?' He hesitates. 'Just don't …'

'Don't what?' I ask suspiciously.

'Oh, nothing. I wondered, that's all. Forget it.' He ruffles my hair and leaves the room.

'What was that about?' I ask Jack. 'Why was he being so weird?'

'No weirder than usual,' he says.

'True. And at least he didn't pull any of that, "How dare you date my sister?" nonsense.'

Jack pulls me towards him. 'Where were we when your brother so rudely interrupted us? I think we'd fully covered the all-round attractiveness of my ears. Shall I move on to your lips?'

'Absolutely not!' I say, releasing myself from his grip. 'You don't need to do this when other people aren't here. In fact, you barely need to do it when they are.'

'Spoilsport,' he complains. 'Well, if I have to put my wooing on hold for now, the least you can do is show me where your mum keeps the tea bags.'

Chapter Eleven

Jack refuses Mum's invitation to stay for dinner. 'I wish I could, but I promised my mum I would go over tonight to reprogram her TV. I don't know what she does to it.'

Mum looks disappointed. 'We were looking forward to having you here this evening and hearing all about how you and Lily got together.'

I almost choke when she says this. Since deciding to stick to my story about Jack, I haven't had an opportunity to talk to him and agree upon the finer points of our narrative. Left to himself, I dread to think what he would come up with. He combines an extremely fertile imagination with an over-developed sense of humour.

I'll have to keep a close eye on him over the next week. Once Stephen is safely in Manchester, we can abandon the pretence, which will be a relief.

I don't know how I'll handle telling my parents about our breakup. Mum will be devastated. Dad, too. I knew they both liked Jack, but I wasn't prepared for their wild excitement when they heard we were together.

I don't really understand it. It isn't as though they didn't like Stephen. It would have been surprising if they hadn't. There's absolutely nothing not to like – apart from his taste in women. One woman, I correct myself. He obviously showed excellent judgement when he chose me. I still don't know what was going on with him when he decided to call it a day with us, but it was an aberration, and one that could very easily be fixed.

I've inadvertently made things more difficult for myself by this charade with Jack. Stephen's a very decent guy. I never seriously suspected he cheated on me with Isabella. He isn't like that. He's scrupulously honest and kind and would never deliberately hurt anyone. When he broke up with me, it was because he thought it was the best thing for both of us. He was completely wrong as far as I was concerned, but he did what he believed was right.

It's a pity I moved to London almost straight afterwards. It might have been better to stay in the area for a while in case he changed his mind. As it was, I left him alone, and everyone knows that nature abhors a vacuum.

I wonder how quickly nature filled that particular one and with how many contenders. It's unlikely that Isabella is the first person he's dated since he and I broke up. I hope she knows that. There's nothing more tedious than someone who thinks they're the centre of someone else's universe, when in fact they're barely even a star at the outer edge of their solar system.

'Can we have a quick chat before you go?' I ask Jack in a low voice.

Mum overhears. 'How sweet! You remember young love, Martin? We couldn't bear to say goodnight to each other, could we? Don't mind us, you two. We'll make ourselves scarce. Come on, Martin, I need you to help me with something in the kitchen.'

She never allows Dad to help in the kitchen. She's convinced he'll burn the entire house to the ground if he attempts to make so much as a cup of tea. I have no idea why. Dad is perfectly capable of cooking for himself whenever she's away, and he appears to enjoy it. But Mum likes to have one part of the house to call her own, and in which to show off her expertise. There's nothing wrong with that, and it seems to work for them both.

In return, dad refuses to let her fix the sink when it gets blocked, and he wouldn't dream of asking her to change a tyre on their old Civic. I suspect Mum is equally capable of doing both these things, but I've given up trying to convince either of them of this.

To their credit, they insisted Ben and I learned to cook and run a house and perform basic DIY and car maintenance. It's simply that when either of us is home, they revert to treating us as young children again and doing everything for us. Ben doesn't seem to mind. I'd hate it on a long-term basis, but it's lovely for the odd week.

I wonder where Jack will fit into this set up. Will Mum see him as the teenage boy she used to know and force feed him cake and offer to mend his torn jeans after a spill from his BMX? Or will she treat him as an adult, as she did Stephen? To be fair, it would be difficult for anyone to treat Stephen as anything less than an adult, even Mum. He exudes grownup-ness. I can't imagine him as a child. His family moved to our village three years ago, so none of us met him until he was an adult.

Jack is nothing like Stephen in that way. He's transitioned to adult life perfectly capably, but he's retained his infectious sense of humour and refusal to allow life to get him down. I wonder what Stephen would think of him if they met properly. They bumped into each other a couple of times while Stephen and

I were together, but Jack was working away quite a bit and I was completely taken up with my relationship.

Stephen would probably like Jack because there's nothing about him to dislike. He's fun, kind, smart, and great company. But when I try to imagine the pair of them being friends, my brain gets stuck. I'm not sure why.

Jack would be bound to love Stephen. Jack likes everyone until they give him a reason not to do so. The only negative thing he knows about Stephen is that he broke up with me, and Jack is far too reasonable to hold that against him. He was hugely supportive during that first awful week, but I don't remember him saying a bad word about Stephen, which was probably a good thing. For all he knew, the breakup was only temporary.

None of this is relevant, anyway. With any luck, they won't meet for the next ten days. After that, Stephen will be gone. I don't know whether I'm looking forward to it or dreading it. If he insists on sticking with the horrible Isabella, I'm looking forward to it. But if he shows any sign of regretting his rash choice, I'd prefer him to stick around for a while.

Which brings me to the problem of having told him I'm in a committed relationship. Stephen would never make a move on a woman who was seeing someone else, even if Isabella were suddenly to disappear off the face of the earth. That isn't likely, so I try to think of what else might happen to her. Maybe her horse will throw her, and she'll have to spend the next six months in traction. That's no good either. Stephen is far too noble to dump someone when they're cocooned in plaster from head to toe.

The best thing would be for her to meet someone else. She's bound to have lots of braying, horsey types from which to choose. She may even have been secretly in love with one of them since childhood, in which case it would be a kindness to hope she gets her very own happily ever after.

'Lily?' Jack's voice breaks into my reverie.

'What?' I say.

'You wanted to talk to me? Isn't that why your parents have so tactfully left the room?'

His eyes narrow. 'At least, that's what I thought. Are you actually intending to make out with me? Your parents would be delighted.'

'Don't be so ridiculous. I told you we only need to keep up the pretence when strictly necessary.'

'I know you did, but I wasn't sure how seriously you were taking your method acting.'

I laugh. 'Not that seriously.'

'I'm disappointed,' he says. 'What did you want to talk to me about? I have to leave soon. I promised Mum I'd be with her about half an hour ago, and she worries.'

'I thought we should get our story straight,' I say. 'How we met, and all that.'

'You were dissecting a tadpole in Mrs Cornwall's biology class,' he says soulfully. 'A shaft of sunlight came in through the laboratory window and lit up your face. I knew then my life would never be the same again.'

I can't help giggling. 'I didn't do biology in the sixth form. I gave it up when I left high school.'

He looks shocked. 'Are you sure? Then it must have been somebody else I fell instantly in love with.'

'Very likely. We don't have time to talk about this properly right now. Can we meet after work one day this week and sort out the details?'

'Good idea,' he says. 'In the meantime, we can talk on the phone and text each other constantly. I'll be counting the minutes until I see you.'

The door handle rattles, and I hear Dad clear his throat again.

'If that cough of his gets any worse, he ought to see a doctor,' says Jack. He runs a finger down my cheek.

'What are you doing?' I hiss.

'I told you,' he murmurs. 'Method acting.'

Dad puts his head around the door. 'I'm sorry. I thought you must have finished …'

'For now,' says Jack. 'I'll call you tonight, Lily.'

'Not if I call you first,' I say in a sickly voice.

Mum appears in the doorway. 'Your mother rang to ask if you're still with us, Jack? She says she was expecting you, and she's a bit worried.'

'I'm just leaving.' He hesitates. 'You didn't, by any chance, happen to mention …?'

Mum looks shocked. 'Of course not! You must be dying to tell her all about it when you see her.'

'Or not,' I say.

Mum looks surprised, and I hurry on. 'It's up to Jack when he wants to make this public. In the meantime, we'd both appreciate you not mentioning it to anyone.'

'I understand,' she says, slipping her arm through Dad's. 'It's a very precious period, that time between confessing your feelings to each other and sharing your joy with the whole world. I wouldn't do anything to jeopardise it.'

I hope she means this. Her natural inclination is to share absolutely everything with everyone she meets, which would be a disaster. I can warn Ben tonight. He isn't one to gossip, anyway. He may mention it to Mia if they're in contact, but she and I don't know any of the same people, so we should be safe. If anyone will be a problem, it's Mum, but there's nothing I can do about that.

Jack lets go of me. 'I'm afraid I have to tear myself away.'

'Like an Elastoplast,' I say.

'What a romantic image! Nice to see you again, Mr and Mrs Carson. I'll see you again soon.'

'Although you did tell me you had a very busy couple of weeks ahead,' I say in a warning tone.

He touches my cheek. 'I'm never too busy for priorities.'

'How lovely!' says Mum.

She accompanies him to the front door, chattering all the way about new relationships and young love and what she and Martin always used to say to each other. As soon as Jack has left, I slip upstairs. I don't want to face any more questions until we've had a chance to talk.

'Lily?' says Mum as I pass her. 'Don't you want to stay and chat?'

'I'm a bit tired,' I say.

As I round the bend of the stairs, I hear her say to Dad, 'She's probably gone upstairs to play some music. Don't you remember how she …?'

I close the bedroom door thankfully and throw myself onto my bed. It's exhausting having a fake boyfriend. I haven't had one before, but they seem to be far more tiring than the regular kind.

Jack, on the other hand, doesn't appear to find it exhausting at all. He seems to regard the whole thing as an amusement laid on especially for his benefit. That's fair enough. I'd prefer that to him being angry about the whole thing.

I should have known I could rely on him. He's never let me down yet, and I don't expect he ever will. If we get through this without it turning into a complete and utter disaster, I'll owe him a huge favour.

I close my eyes and stop thinking about Jack. The more important issue is Stephen. I managed to salvage my pride by telling him this lie, so he no longer feels sorry for me. But he's bound to consider me off-limits now, which is the last thing I want. If he discovers he isn't as committed to this new relationship as he thought, I need him to consider me as very much on limits. Or within limits, or something.

This will take careful planning. I have to find a way to show him I was being truthful about being in a relationship with Jack, while also demonstrating that I may have rushed into it too quickly, just as he may have done with Isabella. I can't make a play for him while I'm supposed to be with Jack. Even if I could, I wouldn't. Stephen has to make up his own mind about what he wants. If this new relationship turns out to be what he's looking for, there's nothing to be done about it. I'll have to accept the inevitable and return to London, after fake dumping Jack.

There's still a slim chance that Stephen regrets breaking up with me too hastily. In which case, it would be better for all parties concerned to find out the truth as soon as possible. Maybe Isabella and Jack would get along? I banish this thought as soon as it occurs to me. They definitely wouldn't. Jack has never gone for hunting, shooting, fishing types. He's too down-to-earth and has far too strong a sense of humour.

I'm not sure what his current type is. It's been a while since we've exchanged relationship news. I must remember to ask him when I see him this week. Anyway, I'm reasonably certain this Isabella won't fit the bill.

When Mum calls me for dinner an hour later, I still haven't decided how to handle things with Stephen. I'll have to steer a middle course between making him think I'm madly in love with Jack and making him think I'm a heartless woman who's using him as a toy.

Bur there's nothing more I can do until I see Jack again, so I head downstairs for Mum's macaroni cheese, hoping she and Dad haven't decided to bring out their wedding album for the five hundredth time.

Chapter Twelve

I'm not too thrilled at the idea of going into work on Monday morning. It's been lovely having a day off, even if it turned out to be slightly more stressful than I anticipated.

A hideous noise rouses me from my sleep. I sit up and stare around wildly. It can't be my alarm. That's set to a soothing melody, which starts quietly and gradually increases in volume until I switch it off.

Mum comes rushing into the bedroom. 'Are you all right, Lily?'

'What's going on?' I say. 'Is there a fire?'

'The smoke alarm would have gone off if there had been.' She makes a dart for my bedside table. 'It's your phone!'

She jabs at it ineffectually before handing it to me. 'You'll have to do it. It's a different model to mine.'

This is hardly surprising, as she insists on using an old Nokia pushbutton phone. Ben and I have tried to buy her a new one several times, but she always refuses.

'Why would I want one of those? This one works perfectly well whenever I need to make a phone call. Dad showed me how to send a text the other day, but it didn't go well. I won't be trying that again. It came out as gibberish, and goodness knows who received it. Dad tried to find out, but it hadn't gone to anyone in my address book. I'll stick with this one, thank you. It suits me fine. I know you and Ben love yours, but according to Dad, you could start a nuclear war with one of those things. I don't know how you cope with the stress!'

I switch off the alarm. 'Sorry about that. I hope it didn't wake you. I must have knocked the settings somehow.'

Ben puts his head around the door. 'Hardly the behaviour of a good guest.'

I glare at him. 'Did you download that chainsaw alarm onto my phone?'

'I thought you'd like it.' he says. 'The other one doesn't appear to wake you up properly. I lay there for ages on Saturday morning waiting for you to turn it off. Beethoven's all very well in his place, but not when I'm trying to have a lie in.'

I put on my dressing gown and follow him downstairs, plotting a hideous revenge. I wonder how much it would cost to buy a police siren alarm tone and install it on Ben's phone – preferably somewhere it wouldn't be immediately visible.

He gives me a cheery wave. 'Must get going. Some of us have proper jobs. See you tonight.'

Mum puts a plate of toast in front of me. 'He didn't mean that,' she says soothingly. 'Working in a bakery is a very important job. It's the heart of a village. At least, it was before the arrival of supermarkets, and it still is. Think of all the old folk who can't drive. They depend on the corner store and the post office and the bakery. They couldn't manage without you. You're performing an essential service.'

I tip almost half a pot of jam onto my toast. It's Ben's favourite, so I consider it my personal duty to deprive him of it. My ears are still ringing from that hideous alarm.

'If people don't drive, they can get their groceries delivered,' I say through a mouth full of toast.

Mum hands me a cup of coffee. 'I suppose so, but it isn't very personal. At least they can enjoy a chat while you serve them. You may be the only person they get to talk to all day.'

I feel sorry for anyone if I'm the only person they talk to. But I decide to adjust my attitude while I'm working at the Sugarloaf. I have to be there whether I like it or not, and it wouldn't harm me to spread a little cheer when required.

I smile to myself at the thought of becoming known as the village sunbeam. People will start coming from miles around, driving past a host of other bakeries to be served by the girl with the personal touch. I'll be a sort of Florence Nightingale of shop assistants. We may become so successful that Mr Mason can open up a chain across the country and put Starbucks out of business.

He could promote me to work in the head office, where I'd never have to look another jam doughnut in the face. I'd certainly never have to ice weird calligraphy letters onto romantically themed cookies.

By a natural progression of thought, I remember Stephen. I doubt he'll come into the bakery again after I annoyed him last week. He'll stay away until the morning of Valentine's Day. It's likely he'll ask someone else to collect his order for him. His mother, perhaps, although I hope not. I've always found her rather intimidating. She and Mum get on very well together, so she must have some good points, but she's always struck me as a less personable version of Stephen.

It would be excruciatingly embarrassing if she came in demanding her son's ex-girlfriend hand over a gift for his new one.

I look at the calendar with sudden hope. Maybe Valentine's Day falls on a Wednesday or a Sunday this year. My heart sinks when I see it's on a Friday.

I finish my toast and drop the empty jam jar into the recycling before Mum realises she needs to buy some more.

I arrive outside the Sugarloaf at exactly the same time as Mr Mason.

'Good morning, Lily,' he greets me. 'Did you have a pleasant day off yesterday?'

'Very nice, thank you,' I say, hoping he won't ask me what I did. If he does, I'll say I had lunch with an old friend and hope he leaves it at that. I wonder how he would react if I came out with the story of breaking the news to Jack that he was now my serious, albeit temporary, boyfriend, followed by Ben blabbing the whole thing to Mum and Dad, and Mum practically starting to organise the wedding. I wouldn't be surprised if she appears later to order the cake.

Will Mr Mason make me ice it? If so, it won't be recognisable as a cake. I could pretend I've gone for a snow scene – our front garden after a week of snow, followed by a thaw, followed by another blizzard. I could have a figure representing Dad pulling the weeds if his sciatica has finally cleared up. And another of Mum at the garden gate chatting to all the passers-by. I could ice a message across the lawn – *Better luck next time, Isabella!*

Mr Mason gives me an odd look. 'Are you alright, Lily?'

'Fine, thanks.' I follow him into the shop and start to remove the tray cloths.

He watches me approvingly. 'You're really getting the hang of this.'

I mentally roll my eyes. How difficult do he and Mum think this job is? Put another way, just how incompetent do they think I am?

I remember in time my resolution to become the shining light of Honeywell and look out of the window, hoping to spot elderly shoppers I can entice into the store to enjoy my sparkling repartee. No one seems to be about, which is hardly surprising at nine o'clock on a Monday morning. I'd be in bed if I possibly could. It's bitterly cold, the snow has melted to a freezing slush, and there's a chill wind.

I wonder whether it's ever occurred to Mr Mason to offer to deliver. I may mention it to him later, although I don't want to overwhelm him. He's only recently got to grips with our new cookie decorating service.

The morning passes slowly. A few customers drift in and out. To my disappointment, none of them are elderly. But it's perfectly possible to be lonely at any age, so I do my best to engage them in meaningful discussion. Unfortunately, no one is in a chatty mood, and all my pleasantries about the British climate and the current exchange rate are wasted.

I feel a flicker of excitement around eleven thirty when I see Bernard the cavoodle walking along the street with his owner. I prepare myself for another standoff and reiteration of the food hygiene rules under which we operate, but the woman walks straight past the bakery, despite Bernard's frantic tugging at his lead. I hope his raspberry slice didn't disagree with him.

Only one more hour until lunchtime. I look around the bakery for something to do. I could rearrange the macaron display for the hundredth time, but there are only so many ways you can arrange coloured discs.

Yesterday, I arranged them by colour from dark to light. I was pleased with the result until an annoying customer came in and bought four of the light pink macarons we optimistically label as strawberry. They look like the bottles of penicillin Mum gave me when I suffered from tonsillitis as a child.

If the customer had ordered one of each flavour, it would have kept my display symmetrical. I thought of suggesting it, but Mr Mason was there, so I didn't dare.

I could arrange them into attractive shapes if I had the slightest skill at art. I've always fancied myself as one of those artistic baristas who make the most incredible shapes on your cappuccino foam. But I can barely manage to draw a recognisable stick person, let alone produce a highly detailed and instantly recognisable picture of the Mona Lisa meeting the Dalai Lama on a Ferris wheel.

Still, I'm bored enough to have a go. I pull on my disposable gloves and pick up a circular display tray. Ten minutes later, I've given up all thoughts of emulating Rembrandt and settled for a smiley face using two chocolate and six raspberry macarons. I hope no one comes in today and buys one of the chocolate ones or I may have turn it into a pirate.

The bell jangles, and I turn to greet the customer, hoping Bernard's owner has had a change of heart. I've been looking forward to mediating another standoff between her and Mr Mason. But it's a young woman with fair, curly hair peeking out from under the hood of an old and exceptionally battered duffle coat.

She greets me with a cheerful smile. 'It's freezing out there!'

'It's nice and warm in here,' I say. 'Welcome to The Sugarloaf Bakery. How can I help you?'

I realise a moment too late that I'm supposed to say, 'How may I help you?' It's one of Mr Mason's pet peeves. But unless this woman turns out to be the linguistics professor from the local university, I may still get the sale.

'I'm after a doughnut,' she says. 'Unless, by any chance, you sell coffee? I didn't get one this morning, and I'm desperate for some caffeine.'

'Sorry,' I say sympathetically. 'We don't sell any drinks. I'm the same. It takes at least two cups of coffee for my brain to kick into gear.'

She looks disappointed. 'Just the doughnut, then. The biggest one you have! If I can't have caffeine, I'll have to rely on carbs.'

I point to our selection. 'Those are the iced rings. Our filled doughnuts are in that tray. They're bigger, but they aren't iced.'

She considers the options. 'I'll take one of each.'

I slip the largest of the jam doughnuts into a bag and add the chocolate ring doughnut she indicates.

She reaches for her purse. 'Thanks. You're a life saver.'

She taps her card on the reader and takes an enormous bite of chocolate doughnut while she waits. 'This has to go through. I'm not returning these without a fight.'

'I'm not allowed to fight the customers,' I tell her. 'My boss made that extremely clear when I started last week. He's a stickler for rules.'

'Are you new here?' she asks.

'Not to the village itself. I grew up here, and I've worked in the area for years. I moved to London last year, but I lost my job and had to come home for a few weeks while I look for another one.'

I hand her the card, but she doesn't leave. She finishes the chocolate doughnut and pulls the jam doughnut from the bag. 'That must have been tough. I've always wanted to work in London, but our family business is here, so it hasn't been possible.'

'What's the business?' I ask, watching in fascination as she crams half the doughnut into her mouth without getting any jam on her face as I inevitably would. Clearly, this isn't her first rodeo.

'Farming,' she says indistinctly. 'My family's been doing it for generations. I mostly work in the office, doing the accounts, but I get called on occasionally to deliver the odd lamb when things are frantic. I quite enjoy it.'

She makes short work of the second half of the doughnut and wipes her mouth. 'That was absolutely delicious! I didn't have time for breakfast today, and I was starting to wilt.'

'You came to the right place,' I say. 'Can I get you anything else?'

'I'm fine, thanks. I'm meeting my boyfriend for lunch in a few minutes, so I should save some room. We're going to the Red Lion, and they make the best steak and kidney pudding for miles around.'

My respect for her increases. I can demolish doughnuts with the best of them, but I wouldn't be talking cheerfully about lunch straight afterwards. She may not have been in the office today. For all I know, she's been out since six a.m. pulling mangle wurzels from the frozen ground and rescuing cows from snow drifts, or whatever it is farmers spend their mornings doing.

She hands me the empty paper bag. 'Do you mind throwing this away? My boyfriend hates even the threat of crumbs in his precious car.'

I laugh. 'I used to date someone like that. I accidentally dropped a bag of salt and vinegar crisps on the floor once, then stood on it when I was getting out. I thought he was going to cry.'

She peers out at the street. 'Here he is. Right on time, as always. That's another of his pet hates – crumbs and unpunctuality.'

'My boyfriend was exactly the same,' I say. 'Perhaps the two things go together. Does he also …?'

My voice trails off as I catch sight of the car pulling up to the kerb. Surely, there can't be two bright yellow Mazdas in Honeywell. That would be too much of a coincidence.

I take an automatic step back, although there's no need. The driver can't see into the shop from where he's parked. Our tasteful display of rainbow-coloured meringues takes up most of the window.

'It was nice to meet you,' says the woman. 'I'll know where to come in the future when I need my sugar fix.'

I don't answer for a moment. Can this really be Isabella – the annoying, stuck up, horsey snob? It seems highly unlikely. But it's definitely Stephen's car, so unless he's juggling a bewildering variety of tall, blonde paramours, this must be her.

The car horn beeps, and the possible Isabella looks annoyed. 'Just for that, he can wait.'

'He may be in a hurry,' I suggest.

'That's his problem! I don't answer car horns. My mum taught me early on that if someone wants to see you, they can jolly well come and get you.'

That's exactly the sort of thing families like hers teach you. My mother would jump out of her chair at the first indication someone wanted her. She hates keeping anyone waiting. Maybe that's why it never occurred to me to tell Stephen where to go when he used to beep his horn at me.

I feel a grudging admiration for this woman. On the other hand, I understand why Stephen arranged to meet her outside the shop rather than come in.

'We're about to close for lunch,' I say on a note of inspiration. 'My boss is very particular about closing on time.'

'Your sign says twelve thirty,' she says, and I groan inwardly. That's the worst of these expensive private schools – they teach you both literacy and numeracy. Why couldn't she have gone to the local comprehensive?

The horn sounds again, and she folds her arms. 'That does it. If he wants me to have lunch with him, he can come in and get me. If need be, I'll buy some more doughnuts to keep your boss happy.'

I manage a weak smile. She turns her back to the shop window and pretends to study our appetising selection of mini apple crumbles. I'm curious to see which of them wins this battle of wills. I secretly want it to be Isabella. When I was with

Stephen, I didn't win a single one. To tell the truth, I barely tried. But if Stephen wins, it means he won't come into the shop, and I won't have to see him and his new girlfriend together.

Mr Mason comes bustling out of the office. 'Have you started closing up for lunch, Lily? You know we open again at one o'clock sharp.'

He sees Isabella. 'I beg your pardon. I didn't realise we had a customer. Please, take your time.'

Isabella gives him a charming smile. 'I'm trying to decide between an apple and a blackcurrant crumble. They both look delicious. Your assistant has been incredibly helpful.'

Before he can speak, a car door slams, and Stephen emerges onto the pavement. He opens the bakery door but doesn't come inside.

Isabella doesn't turn around, although she must be aware he's there.

Mr Mason recognises Stephen. 'Good morning, Mr Parker! How nice to see you back so soon. Is there anything we can help you with? Any special orders, or are you here to amend your previous order?'

He looks startled as I make a wild throat slashing gesture. I point to Isabella and lay a finger on my lips.

'Are you ready, Isabella?' says Stephen curtly.

She turns her head. 'Oh, are you here already? I wasn't expecting you so soon.'

He looks annoyed. 'We agreed to meet outside the shops at twelve thirty.'

'So we did,' she says coolly. 'But I was hungry, so I popped into the bakery. Are you a regular here?'

'Not at all,' he says with a glance at me that clearly says this state of affairs will continue as long as I'm working here.

'So, why do you have a special order?' she asks.

Stephen opens his mouth, then shuts it without speaking. Mr Mason still looks puzzled.

'It's for your mother, isn't it?' I improvise wildly. 'Doesn't she get her bread from us each week?'

Stephen gives me a grateful look. 'I believe she does. We really need to go. We have a table booked.'

Isabella smiles at me. 'Thanks for all your help. I expect I'll see you the next time my blood sugar gets low. I didn't catch your name.'

'Lily.' I watch her for any sign she recognises it.

She looks at me more closely, then back at Stephen, who looks profoundly embarrassed.

A slow smile creeps over her face. 'I know that name. Are you the Lily that Stephen used to date?'

She doesn't look remotely put out. I'd have found it difficult to bump into one of Stephen's exes when we were together. But she obviously doesn't see me as any kind of threat, even wearing my baggy flowered smock, with my hair attractively pulled back under a hairnet.

She holds out her hand. 'Nice to meet you, Lily. I'm Isabella.'

She laughs. 'We should have known we were talking about the same man.'

Mr Mason jangles his keys and coughs. 'If there's nothing else, we are about to close.'

'Of course,' says Stephen with a look of relief.

I pull off my hair net, pick up my coat and follow them outside. Mr Mason carefully locks up and sets off down the street at a brisk trot.

'He's in a hurry,' says Isabella.

'You shouldn't have kept him waiting,' says Stephen.

She shrugs. 'He can reopen a few minutes later if he wants. Do you really only get half an hour for lunch, Lily?'

'I do, so I should go. It's a ten-minute walk home.'

'You poor thing!' she says. 'That's absolutely ridiculous. Why don't you come to the pub with us?'

'No!' Stephen and I say simultaneously.

'It's very kind of you,' I add, 'but I won't gate crash your lunch. Besides, my mum's expecting me. But I hope you enjoy your steak and kidney pudding.'

She looks disappointed. 'That's a pity. Another time, perhaps.'

Judging by Stephen's expression, he won't be arranging to pick her up again within ten miles of here.

'Perhaps,' I say and set off as quickly as I can down the high street. As I turn to cross the road, I see them driving off in the direction of the pub.

I walk home in a daze. That was unexpected. If I hadn't found out who she was, I'd have thought she was really nice. I liked her amused eyes and quick sense of humour. Even more, I admired her refusal to dance to anyone else's tune.

In any other situation, she's someone I'd have liked to be friends with. As it is, I'll probably never see her again. Stephen will make sure of that. Just in case, I resolve to meet up with Jack as quickly as possible so we can get our stories straight.

Chapter Thirteen

I meet Jack for a drink after work on Wednesday. I would have preferred to see him sooner, but he said it was the earliest he could manage. I arrive a few minutes before him and buy the first round.

He rushes in a few minutes later. 'Hey, Lily, sorry we couldn't meet any earlier. I had a work thing on Monday night, and I had to meet a friend yesterday. Did you have a good day?'

I feel a flash of disappointment. Surely his girlfriend ought to be more of a priority than meeting some random friend, and certainly when she's in the middle of a crisis.

I check myself, remembering I'm not his actual girlfriend. Also, he's doing me a huge favour when he probably has a hundred other things he'd prefer to be doing. He lives in this area and has a life here, whereas I made the decision to leave.

I'm ashamed of my selfishness. I do this with my parents too, assuming they wait in some sort of limbo for my visits. I don't seriously expect that. I'm not that selfish, but I'm always taken by surprise when things change while I'm away. I resolve to find out more about what Jack's been up to over the past six months – once we've talked about our romance and got our stories straight.

'Lily?' he says, and I realise I was supposed to answer.

'I'm still here,' I say.

He looks amused. 'I know. I can hear you breathing. That sounded suspiciously like a deep sigh. What's up?'

'Nothing, apart from this stupid mess I've got myself into. And you, too.'

He laughs. 'You haven't got me into any kind of mess. I'm having fun.'

'I'm glad one of us is,' I say gloomily, then quickly add. 'I'm extremely grateful to you for agreeing to go along with it. I should never have done such a stupid thing in the first place.'

'Don't beat yourself up about it,' he says. 'What's done is done, and no one's being harmed by it.'

'Except you.'

'I told you. I'm having fun. Work's a bit dull at the moment, and this gives me something to do. Plenty of people dress up in medieval costumes and rush around enacting battles and learning how to use spinning wheels and whatever. This isn't too different.'

I blink. Is he comparing me to some old woman in medieval times? I decide not to pursue this.

'There's Mum and Dad too,' I say. 'They'll be devastated when we break up, even if they don't find out I lied to them.'

'They'll be fine,' he reassures me. 'I'm fine as a fake boyfriend, but they'd absolutely hate having me as a son-in-law.'

'That's not true! They love you.'

'They love everyone,' he says. 'But they wouldn't want you to stay with someone who isn't a good fit for you.'

I'm not sure what he means. They weren't at all surprised when they heard Jack and I had got together, which must mean they think we're a good fit.

'Lily?' he says. 'Are you still with me?'

'I was thinking about what you said about my parents. They'll be upset when I tell them. I need to think of a plausible reason to break up with you.'

'I could give you several,' he says. 'If you prefer, I could make up some truly terrible secrets about myself that will leave you with no choice but to dump me at once and run back to London.'

'They wouldn't believe me,' I say. 'They already know what a nice guy you are. And you don't deserve that. I'll think of something and hope for the best. You have to live here when I've left. I don't want to trash your reputation.'

'Some women like bad boys,' he says. 'I may be inundated with beautiful women trying to tame me. In the meantime, I'll put up with you. Speaking of being a good boyfriend, your birthday is coming up. What would you like to do for it?'

I groan. 'Nothing at all. I want to forget all about it. I feel guilty enough about all this without allowing people to make a fuss of me.'

'So, you should,' he says severely. 'You should be ashamed of yourself. But can I point out that your parents will expect your amazing new boyfriend to arrange something incredible for the love of his life on her special day?'

'You could say you're working,' I suggest.

'They'd only expect us to do something another day. I'm afraid you're stuck with me for your birthday celebration. You'll have to make the best of it.'

There's no one with whom I'd rather spend my birthday, but I feel increasingly guilty about all this. It was lovely of Jack to agree so readily to this complete farce. Maybe he's telling the truth and is having fun. But there has to be a limit to what I ask of him.

'We'll find something or other to do that night,' I say. 'But I'm paying.'

'McDonald's, it is!' he says. 'I'll start getting myself into training.'

'I think I can run to somewhere a little more special than that. I have my redundancy money, and my parents absolutely refuse to take rent from me. Where would you like to go?'

He considers. 'If we're talking hypothetically, there's an amazing new place called The Oasis all the critics are raving about. It would be cool to say we'd tried it.'

'Let's do it!' I say. 'Don't worry about the cost. I'd love to take you there to say thank you for being so great about all this.'

He bursts out laughing. 'Are you kidding? It isn't the price, although I imagine you'd need a mortgage just to buy one of their starters. That place is booked out for about a year ahead. You could probably get in if you were a cabinet minister or a film star. But the likes of us have to go on a waiting list and still risk being turned down when we arrive, in case we jeopardise one of their precious Michelin stars.'

'That's a shame,' I say, deflated. 'I'd have loved to take you there. We can put our names down anyway, and I can come home when we finally get in.'

'Maybe,' he says, with less enthusiasm than I would have expected. 'Anyway, we'll have to choose somewhere else this year. Does your family have anything planned?'

'Not that I'm aware of. Mum loves birthdays, so I expect she'll want to go out for lunch. It's lucky it falls on a Sunday, so I don't have to work.'

Jack picks up our glasses. 'This is my round. Same again?'

'Thanks.'

He heads towards the bar, and I think about Sunday. It will be lovely to spend the evening with Jack. I hope he didn't have anything else planned. Perhaps we can't go to The Oasis, but there must be somewhere almost as nice. He deserves it, and as he pointed out, Mum and Dad will expect it. Whatever he thinks, they'll be sad to lose him. Who wouldn't want their daughter to meet someone like Jack? He's kind and generous and hard working – every parent's dream.

I'll wait to tell them until Stephen's gone back to Manchester, but I don't want the news of our breakup getting around the village too quickly. If Stephen's mother hears it and relays it to him, he may put two and two together and make some ridiculous and completely unwarranted number.

I'll have to leave it for a respectable period before announcing it. I may find myself a new job soon. If so, I can tell my parents I don't want to turn down the job, and Jack doesn't want to move. It's simply a matter of competing priorities.

Jack returns with the drinks. 'You look very serious. What are you thinking about?'

'Our breakup,' I say.

He hands me a glass. 'I can understand that. It must be hard to let go of such a catch. Personally, I don't think I could do it.'

'Especially such a modest one,' I agree. 'We'll cross that bridge when we come to it. At least, I will.'

'And I'll be at home licking my wounds,' he says. 'But I'll enjoy it while it lasts.'

I pull out a notebook and pencil. 'Shall we get to work while I'm sober enough to spell correctly?'

'Great idea,' he says. 'We must get our entire backstory correct. Every single detail. We can't risk even the tiniest mistake.'

'I don't think we need to worry too much,' I say. 'A rough outline will do.'

'Not at all,' he insists. 'Even the smallest discrepancy could ruin everything. I need to know the colour of your second favourite duvet cover and your favourite brand of toothpaste – assuming I'm in a position to know that. Do I spend the night at yours when I visit London? Do you use sheets and blankets instead of a duvet? It's an absolute minefield. You'll need several more notebooks.'

I can't believe how seriously he's taking this. This is a side of him I've never seen before.

'Jack,' I begin, then catch sight of his face. 'You're winding me up. I should have known.'

'You should indeed. I think we can get away with a broad outline. We know each other pretty well, which makes it easier. All the rest – those delightful, romantic details which make falling in love so special – can come later.'

I take a gulp of my drink. 'I'll need several more of these before you get any delightful, personal details from me.'

'I'm disappointed,' he says. 'I'd hoped we were taking our relationship to a whole new level. You may come around when you see how open and vulnerable I'm prepared to make myself. My favourite brand of toothpaste is Colgate, extra minty. And when I was eight, I told my parents it was my sister who had eaten the last slice of chocolate cake, when in fact it was me. I even watched them send her to her room for an hour without lifting a finger to save her. I only hope you can continue to love me after such shocking revelations.'

I open the notebook. 'I'll try to remember you were very young and forget the rest. It won't be easy, but if this relationship is worth fighting for, I'm prepared to do my part.'

'Me too,' he says cheerfully. 'I already know about the time you told your parents you had a special advanced history class on a Saturday so you could meet that boy they didn't approve of, and I'm still willing to be your boyfriend. So, we're off to an excellent start.'

He picks up his glass and inspects the dregs. 'I'll need another of these in a minute. But first, let's drink a toast.'

I pick up my glass. 'What shall we drink to?'

'To everlasting love,' he suggests.

'Let's not get carried away.'

'What, then?'

'To friendship,' I say. 'It may not be as romantic as true love, but it lasts a lot longer.'

'Fine,' he says. 'I'll drink to friendship! And to my best friend putting away that ridiculous notebook, taking out her purse, and organising the next round.'

Chapter Fourteen

I wake the following morning with a throbbing headache. At least, Mum wakes me.

'Up you get, sleepyhead!' she trills as she opens my door.

I groan, roll over, and pull the pillow over my head. 'Go away. It's far too early.'

She snaps on the bedroom light. 'It's seven o'clock. You need some breakfast before you go to work.'

I resist the urge to hurl the pillow at her. It's kind of her to get up specially to make me breakfast. I've tried several times to persuade her there's no need, but she's determined.

She looks at me with concern. 'Oh, dear. You do look rough. Do you think you're going down with something? Shall I call Mr Mason?'

I swing my legs off the bed. 'No, don't do that. I'm a bit … dehydrated.'

There's a loud guffaw. Ben is walking down the landing and has overheard us. 'Dehydrated? More like hungover.'

I debate throwing the pillow at him, but it might hit Mum. I content myself with glaring at him instead. 'I'm starting to understand why Mia left you.'

He turns on his heel and stalks off. Mum gives me a shocked look. 'What a terrible thing to say, Lily.'

She's right. That was completely uncalled for.

'I'll go and apologise,' I say, pushing my feet into my slippers.

She lowers her voice. 'I'd wait until he's eaten. You know what your brother's like in the morning.'

I do indeed. Ben has been a byword for the perils of low blood sugar for as long as I can remember. He's a pleasant, easy-going guy, but if you catch him before a meal, you take your life into your own hands. Which is still no excuse for what I said to him.

I pick up my towel. 'I'll take a shower and see you downstairs.'

Ben is already at the breakfast table when I come in. He doesn't look up. I touch his shoulder as I pass. 'I'm sorry, Ben. I didn't mean it.'

He nods in acknowledgement but doesn't speak. Mum bustles in with a dish of bacon and eggs.

'There you go, sweetheart,' she says to Ben. 'You'll feel much better once you've got that inside you.'

'I was planning on having toast,' he says. 'I'm in a hurry. I can take it with me if I don't finish it.'

'Good idea,' says Mum. 'I'll bring it through.'

She disappears, and I remember my jam eating marathon yesterday. I was hoping Ben would ask for toast today and be upset to discover his favourite plum jam had all gone. But that was before I behaved like an idiot and spoke to him so unkindly.

'Why not have the bacon and eggs now they're ready?' I say. 'It's much better for you in the morning than toast.'

'No, it isn't,' he counters.

That's Ben all over. If you want him to do something, suggest he does the opposite, and you end up with your preferred outcome. I should have extolled the virtues of simple carbohydrates. That would have had him reaching for the eggs in no time.

'Yes, it is,' I say. 'I was reading an article about eating protein in the morning. Apparently, it helps you to stay full longer.'

'Go ahead,' he says.

'I don't have time. I'm already running late. Why don't you eat this, and I'll take the toast to go?'

'Because I'm having the toast,' he says. 'Mum can make some more for you. Better still, why don't you make it yourself?'

I bite back a sharp retort. I don't want to upset him any further. 'Maybe I will. You could try honey on your toast for once. I read this article where –'

'People who eat honey live an average of ten years longer?' he interrupts. 'I'm sure you did, but I'll take my chances.'

Mum comes through with the toast, and Ben grabs a handful of slices. 'Thanks, Mum. Do we have any plum jam?'

She looks worried. 'I opened the cupboard to get it for you, but I couldn't find it. Your father must have put it somewhere ridiculous, as usual.'

I cram a piece of bacon into my mouth and finish my coffee. 'I have to go. Mr Mason wants to show me the ordering procedure this morning.'

Mum claps her hands. 'Oh, Lily, how marvellous! He must think a lot of you if he's showing you the ropes so soon.'

I leave the room, but not quickly enough to avoid hearing Ben's derisive snort.

I arrive at work a minute before Mr Mason and wait outside the shop, feeling smug. For all he knows, I've been waiting here for hours, eager to crack the mysteries of the bakery business.

He comes trudging up the street exactly on time. He looks tired, which is unusual. I don't know him well enough to ask whether anything is wrong. Mum would, but she gets away with talking about the most personal of issues to people she barely knows. They seem to sense her boundless store of goodwill towards humanity and respond to her. I haven't inherited that trait from her, and neither has Ben. We're more like Dad – slightly reserved until we get to know someone.

Mr Mason and I go about our morning tasks in silence. Once we've set up the shop, and he's confident no burglars have been in during the night to throw a custard slice and lemon muffin rave, he disappears into his office, leaving me in charge.

I have mixed feelings about this. I'm terrified of doing something wrong. But I enjoy the feeling of power it gives me and spend a while amusing myself by pretending I own the business and have the right to reject unpleasant customers with dogs. Not Bernard, though. He has a cheeky glint in his eye I rather like.

But I could refuse to allow his owner inside. I could insist she waited in the street and sent Bernard in with a note. I could also ban any tall, dark-haired men making unreasonable requests that we alter our perfectly good products to fit in with some ridiculous Hallmark holiday.

The door opens, and I look up expectantly. I'm surprised to see Isabella.

She smiles when she sees me. 'I'm glad it's you. I came in on Sunday morning, and your boss served me. He was most put out that I didn't know the difference between a ciabatta and a baguette. My mum asked me to pick one of those long loaf things, and I thought he'd be bound to know what I meant.'

'I had no idea we sold baguettes,' I confess.

'I don't think you do. He seemed to think I was making fun of his bakery. I almost asked for a sourdough focaccia, but I thought better of it.'

I can't help warming to her. She may be dating my ex-boyfriend, but that isn't technically a crime or even a moral failing.

'Are you here to buy another long loaf?' I ask. 'Or are you after our doughnuts?'

Her eyes light up. 'Now, there's an idea. I had breakfast almost an hour ago, so it could count as elevenses.'

She looks around the shop. 'It must be fun working here, eating as many cakes as you want.'

'The staff isn't allowed to eat the products,' I say. 'It may seem small and unimportant at first, but it quickly leads to further abuses, and very soon the bottom line is affected.'

She gives a snort of laughter. 'Does he really say that?'

'That, and many other things. You wouldn't believe what a complicated business it is running an outfit like this, nor how many rules we have.'

'It's good to expand my education,' she says. 'But I think I'll stick to accounts. I didn't come in for anything special today. I wanted to ask whether you'd like to have lunch sometime.'

She laughs at my startled look. 'Not to discuss Stephen – although it would be fun to compare notes. I thought it would be nice to get to know you. Loads of my friends have moved away from the village, and I don't know many people around here.'

I stare at her, my mind racing. There must be more to this request than appears on the surface. Why would anyone choose to get to know their boyfriend's ex-girlfriend? It's clear she doesn't see me as a threat, and it's equally clear why. But it's less obvious why she would want to spend any more time with me than she has to.

She watches me, an enquiring look on her face. 'Only if you'd like to. You don't need to decide now. Give me your phone.'

I don't move. Why is this complete stranger demanding my phone? Is this show of friendliness a pretext to get my phone away from me and check whether Stephen and I are still in contact?

She seems to read my thoughts. 'Here's my phone. Put your number into it, and I'll send you a text. That way, we'll have each other's details.'

'Oh, yes. Good idea.' I take her phone and type my number into it, then hand it back.

'Great!' she says, tapping the keys.

My phone pings, and I reach for it, wondering who could be texting me during work hours.

I am not a mad stalker!

I look up at her and see she's laughing. 'Message me sometime if you'd like to get lunch. It's awful that you only get half an hour, but we could go to the pub. If you let me know what you'd like to eat, I could order it before you arrive.'

I nod, bewildered by the speed at which events have overtaken me. I wonder whether Stephen knows she's here. Is this his idea? I'm sure it isn't. He seemed uncomfortable being in the same place with us on Monday. The last thing he'd want would be to engineer another meeting between us, especially one involving alcohol.

'See you around,' she says and turns to leave.

On a sudden impulse, I say. 'I'm free today if that works for you.'

'Fantastic!' she says with what sounds like genuine enthusiasm. 'I'll meet you at the Red Lion at twelve thirty. The menu's online, so choose what you want and message me ahead of time. This one's on me, so feel free to go for the lobster.'

She waves and disappears. I watch her walk along the high street, not sure what to make of it all. No one asks to meet their boyfriend's ex-girlfriend without an ulterior motive. I have no idea what it is, but I suppose I'm about to find out.

Chapter Fifteen

I arrive out of breath a few minutes after twelve thirty and find Isabella waiting for me.

She greets me with a huge smile. 'You made it!'

'Did you think I wouldn't?' I ask, accepting the glass of mulled wine she hands me and deciding Mr Mason will have to take his chances on my accuracy with the till this afternoon.

'I thought the old curmudgeon might demand you work right through lunch,' she says.

'He isn't a curmudgeon,' I say. 'He's just fussy.'

She takes a gulp of her wine. 'Anyone who allows his staff half an hour for lunch counts as a curmudgeon in my book.'

'He only takes half an hour himself,' I point out.

'That's his business,' she says. 'I can't think why you work there.'

Our food arrives, which saves me having to answer. How much does she know about me? Has Stephen told her everything or nothing? He may consider me to be so far in his past that I don't count at all.

'I told you when we first met that I lost my job in London,' I say.

'I know you did. But that doesn't explain why you're working in a bakery.' She crams several chips into her mouth and chews rapidly.

I feel a wave of annoyance. Of course, someone like this can't understand why regular people need to work for a living. She probably doesn't work full time in her family business but goes in for a few hours whenever she feels like it. It's probably a tax break for them. Even the concept of having a family business shows she hasn't the faintest idea of how ordinary people live.

'It's a temporary thing,' I say at last. 'I'm looking for a new job in London.'

'What do you do?' she asks.

So, she and Stephen haven't discussed me. I'm not sure whether to be pleased or annoyed.

'I'm an office manager,' I say.

'Do you enjoy it?'

I pause with a forkful of fried cod halfway to my mouth, not sure how to answer. Most people say things like, 'That must be interesting,' or, 'That sounds like fun.' They take it for granted that I enjoy it.

'It pays well,' I say, 'and there's a good career structure.'

'But do you enjoy it?' she persists.

Why is she asking all these questions? She can't be interested in the life of a woman she's only just met. Is Stephen behind this, after all? Has he asked her to dig out all the information she can about me and my new life? Does that mean he's still interested in me and what I get up to?

My wave of euphoria dies as quickly as it arrived. This has nothing to do with Stephen. He isn't sneaky like that. If he wanted to know something, he would ask me directly. For another thing, he's seeing Isabella now. He wouldn't use her like that, and she wouldn't allow it. Reluctant though I am to admit it, she seems smart. She would see straight through him if he tried it. So, she must be asking for another reason, although I can't for the life of me imagine what it is.

I decide to hedge until I've worked out her motivation. 'I enjoy my job. It's interesting and varied.'

'More so than working at the bakery?' There's a definite note of amusement in her voice that raises my hackles.

'Beggars can't be choosers,' I say. 'We don't all have family money to fall back on.'

She regards me with what looks like fascination. 'Is that what you think? That I come from family money?'

I didn't expect such a direct attack. I hoped she might have taken the hint and backed off.

'I assumed you did,' I say. 'Stephen told me his new girlfriend lived in the Manor House in Little Compton. It's a pretty swish place.'

'It is,' she says, 'but we live at the Lodge. It's the house near the gates. You can see it from the road.'

'Who lives in the main house?' I ask.

'Our cousins. Dad's older brother owns the farm. That's how it goes in farming families.'

My hackles rise at the thought of Ben inheriting our family business, simply because he's the oldest. Not that we have a family business, but the point still stands.

'That seems incredibly unfair,' I say.

'I can see how you'd think so,' she agrees, 'but it's the way it's usually done in farming. Otherwise, all the farms would be broken up, which wouldn't work at all. I don't think Dad minds too much. We get to live in the Lodge, and we don't have any of the worries associated with running the farm. Dad only works part time now, whereas I doubt my uncle will ever retire. None of his children want to go into farming, so I suppose the farm will have to be sold when he dies.'

I finish the rest of my fish and chips in silence. I may have rushed to judgement a little too quickly. But even if her family aren't massive landowners, that doesn't mean I have to like her.

'Where did you go to school?' I ask.

'The Grange.'

Ha! I knew she must have gone to the Grange!

Something of what I'm thinking must show on my face because she smiles.

'We were pretty lucky. My parents could never have afforded it, but my uncle chipped in, and I had a partial scholarship.'

'My brother and I went to Bournefield Comp,' I say, watching her for any sign of derision.

She sighs. 'I wanted to go there. All my friends from primary school did. But my parents thought it was too good an opportunity to miss.'

'What was it like at The Grange?'

'It was fine. There's something to enjoy in most places if you put your mind to it.'

'Like the bakery?' I say, and she laughs.

'I expect so. What are your three favourite things about working there?'

I frown in concentration. How am I meant to come up with even one nice thing to say about the Sugarloaf? But Isabella looks expectant, and I don't want to disappoint her.

'It's an easy walking distance from my parents' house,' I say with a burst of inspiration.

She gives me an encouraging smile. 'That's a good one. I expect you had a long commute in London?'

'I did. Over an hour. It's alright in the summer, but not so much fun in the winter.'

'What else?' she says.

'You sound like my mother,' I grumble. 'Fine, I quite like chatting with the customers. In my last job, I was stuck in a tiny cubicle well away from the main offices, and I never got to see anyone except during meetings.'

'There you go!' she says.

I give her a reluctant smile. 'I'll admit it isn't as bad as it could have been if that makes you happy.'

'I tell you what would make me happy – some of Ted's treacle tart and custard. Just the thing for a chilly day.'

'I have to be back at work in twelve minutes,' I protest.

'No problem,' she says. 'I pre-ordered it. Here it is!'

Sure enough, I see a server approaching us carrying two steaming bowls. I look at the golden, syrupy tart and thick yellow custard and give in.

'You're going to lose me my job,' I say, picking up my spoon.

She waits until I've taken my first mouthful before asking. 'What are you doing this weekend?'

'I'm working on Saturday. It's my birthday on Sunday, so I'll be going out for dinner.'

'With your boyfriend?' she asks.

I can't remember whether I've talked to her about Jack. Stephen may have mentioned him to reassure her that she shouldn't be concerned about my presence in the village. Not that she seems in the slightest bit threatened. Looking at the pair of us, I can kind of see why.

'Uh huh,' I mumble, pretending to be deeply interested in getting the perfect ratio of custard to treacle tart onto my spoon.

'That's nice,' she says. 'How long have you been seeing him?'

I try to remember what I told Stephen about my wonderful new relationship. I ought to write myself a timeline and memorise it. I didn't expect anyone to find out about it, let alone interrogate me at every opportunity about the intricate details.

'Nearly a year,' I say.

'So, you met soon after you and Stephen broke up?'

What is it with this woman and her questions? She has Stephen, and I don't. Isn't that enough for her?

I decide to carry the battle into her territory. 'How long have you and Stephen been seeing each other?'

'About three or four months,' she says.

What does she mean by 'about?' How does she not know how long she's been seeing him? I knew to the day how long he and I were together. If I can give the date of my fictional relationship to within a week, she ought to remember the exact date she started seeing Stephen.

'Not long,' I say, relieved to find he didn't go straight from me to her.

'Not at all,' she agrees. 'It's early days with us. We're still getting to know each other. We only met at the end of September, and he moved to Manchester after Christmas.'

'But he came all the way down here to visit you for Valentine's Day. That must mean he's serious.'

She laughs. 'He came home to see his parents for a couple of weeks. His father hasn't been well. The trip happened to coincide with Valentine's Day. I don't think he's romantic enough to have made a special trip.'

I debate whether to tell her he took me away to the Lake District last Valentine's Day. I don't need to mention that he broke up with me straight afterwards. It isn't relevant.

'He's not the most romantic person I've ever met,' I say. 'But he has a kind heart, which is more important.'

'Possibly,' she says. 'But wouldn't you rather have both?'

'In a perfect world. But you can't have everything. If you hold out for perfection, you may end up with nothing.'

'True, but he'd better have something nice planned for Valentine's Day,' she says cheerfully. 'Men can be so lazy.'

I think of the cookies he's ordered and wonder whether that counts as romantic in her book. Especially when iced by her predecessor. I almost warn her not to get her hopes up but stop myself. The cookies may be part of a larger overall plan – an *amuse-bouche* before the actual celebration begins, like the twelve days of Christmas.

For all I know, he's planning to whisk her away for a day of amazing romantic treats. He may have booked a couple's treatment at a spa, followed by hot air ballooning over the New Forest, accompanied at a discreet distance by a fighter jet escort. After which, he'll whisk her away in a limousine to a country hotel for a five-course meal with champagne to be eaten in their luxury suite next to a rose-petal covered four poster bed.

I wrench my thoughts away from the movie playing in my head. I'm not going there.

'What's he like, this new boyfriend of yours?' she asks.

I'm tempted to tell her to mind her own business, but I don't have the heart. She looks eager and interested, like a puppy. This could be an excellent opportunity to practise getting my story straight before I have to tell it to anyone who matters, by which I mean Stephen.

'Erm, five foot ten, brown hair –' I begin.

She laughs. 'I don't mean what does he look like? What's he like as a person?'

This one is trickier to answer. When you talk about someone you barely know, you have to use your brain. When you talk about someone you know almost as well as yourself, you simply feel them without needing to put their essence into words. Still, I should try.

'He's lovely,' I begin, then stop. She's looking for something more specific than that. A rose is lovely. A sunset is lovely.

I try again. 'He's the kindest man I've ever met.'

Should I say except for Stephen? I don't want to sound as though I'm denigrating him to his new girlfriend. I decide not to refer to Stephen. It's a potential mine field, and I don't trust myself to talk about him with believable indifference. It would be the height of humiliation if my voice were to wobble when I mentioned his name.

'He makes me laugh more than anyone I know,' I say, smiling at the memory of Jack's face when he's teasing me.

She sighs. 'That's so important. I could forgive almost anything in a man who makes me laugh.'

Does Stephen make her laugh? If so, he must show her a different side of himself to the one he showed me. I loved Stephen deeply. I still do. But his sense of humour was never his overriding quality. He had plenty of good points to make up for it. He was charming and intelligent and driven, and when I was with him, he made me feel as though I was the only other person in the world. He gave me his entire focus, and I felt I was the only thing that mattered to him.

Does he make Isabella feel that way? He must do. She isn't the sort of person who would settle for anything less. I remember with admiration how she forced him to come into the bakery to collect her.

But we aren't talking about Stephen. We're talking about Jack. It's impossible to describe him to someone who's never met him. How can I put into words his zest for life, his infectious laugh, the way he looks at the world in a slightly different way to me but still closely enough for us to connect, so that I end up seeing things from a new and exciting perspective?

How can I explain the way he takes me seriously but makes me believe there's never anything that can't be fixed? I think of the way his grey-green eyes light up when he's interested or amused, his ready smile, his ability to make everyone around him feel comfortable in their own skin.

I look up and meet Isabella's interested gaze. 'He's great,' I say.

'He sounds it,' she says, and we both laugh.

'It's more difficult than you'd think to describe someone you know so well,' I say.

'I wasn't trying to be nosy,' she says. 'I'm just interested in people. By the way, where is this paragon taking you for your birthday dinner?'

Jack's last suggestion was McDonald's, but it might be better not to mention that.

'I expect we'll find somewhere,' I say. 'Jack was telling me he wants to go to The Oasis, but they're booked up for months ahead, as well as being hideously expensive.'

Her face lights up. 'Does he really want to eat there? I might be able to help you. My uncle's friend is the head chef, and he often does my uncle a favour. Would you like me to see whether I can get you a table for Sunday night?'

I gape at her, stunned. Jack would love that. It would be great to take him somewhere special to thank him for taking part in this ridiculous charade.

'If that's a serious offer, I'd love to take you up on it,' I say. 'But it's such short notice.'

'I can't promise anything,' she warns me. 'I'll do what I can and let you know.'

'I have to go now, or I'll be fired,' I say. 'I can't tell you how grateful I am. It's fine if you can't get us a table. I'm sure we'll find somewhere else.'

'I'll call now,' she says, pulling out her phone. 'Don't worry. I usually manage to get what I want. Perseverance is the key.'

She may be right. She certainly managed to get my boyfriend. I pull myself up short. She did nothing of the kind. She happened to meet someone who was single, and she started a relationship with him. I'm finding it increasingly difficult to feel resentment towards her.

It wasn't Stephen's fault, either. I may not like the way things have turned out, but it's time I stopped behaving like a petulant child over the whole thing.

I give her a quick wave and head for the door, thinking of Jack. I shouldn't get my hopes up too much, but I can't help feeling excited. I won't tell him where we're going. Jack is rarely lost for words, and I'd like to enjoy surprising him.

Chapter Sixteen

Mum asks me that evening what I'd like to do for my birthday.

'Dad and I thought we might take you to Massimo's for dinner,' she says. 'But that was before we knew about you and Jack. I'm sure the pair of you are looking forward to a nice romantic evening together.'

I give her an uncomfortable smile. 'We're planning to have dinner on Sunday.'

'Of course, you are,' she says with a beaming smile. 'You never forget the first birthday you spend with the love of your life.'

I lift a hand in protest. 'Let's not get carried away. Jack isn't the love of my life, and I'm definitely not his. We're casually dating, that's all. It probably won't work out between us.'

She tips her head on one side. 'I don't think so. You're absolutely perfect for each other. Dad and I were saying that only last night. Neither of us could understand why we hadn't thought of it before.'

'Don't say that to Jack,' I warn her. 'You'll terrify him!'

'I wouldn't be so daft. I'm saying it to you.'

'And I'm telling you that you're way ahead of yourself,' I say. 'Honestly, Mum. It's nothing. I don't want you and Dad getting upset if it doesn't work out.'

She hands me some cutlery. 'Set the table, please. And don't be so ridiculous. This has nothing to do with me and Dad. All we want is for you to be happy. If Jack isn't the right person for you, that's fine.'

At least I've warned her I don't see this as anything serious. It would look odd if I pushed the subject any further. People in the first flush of a new relationship aren't usually expecting it to end.

'We can do something as a family during the day,' I say. 'Maybe we could go out to lunch.'

'If you're sure,' she says. 'Why don't you find out what Jack wants to do first?'

I remember Isabella and her approach to relationships.

'It isn't important what Jack wants to do,' I say. 'It's my birthday, and I want to have lunch with my family. I'm sure Jack will cope without me until the evening.'

'Unless he'd like to come with us?' she says.

Usually, I'd be happy for Jack to join us for a family lunch, but not this year. I can't bear a repeat of last Sunday evening, with my parents watching me and Jack as though we were interesting specimens at a zoo and they a couple of anthropologists making notes on our mating behaviours.

'It will be nice to spend some time with you and Dad,' I say. 'Ben too, if he wants to come along.'

'As long as you don't say anything unkind about him and Mia,' she warns me.

'I won't,' I promise. 'Is she likely to be around? We could invite her too.'

'Now, there's an idea,' she says. 'I wonder why I didn't think of it before. I'll suggest it to Ben.'

I lay the table, then return to the kitchen to see what I can do to help. Mum doesn't allow me to do anything important, but she lets me stir the sauce.

'The trick is to stir it slowly, but constantly,' she says. 'If you do it too fast, it will splash. If you do it too slowly, you risk it catching on the bottom of the pan.'

'I'll do my best,' I promise.

I stir the sauce for a few minutes before asking. 'Did you and Dad say the same thing about me and Stephen when we were together? That we were perfect for each other, I mean.'

Is it my imagination, or does Mum's face turn pink? Maybe it's the heat of the stove.

'I'm not sure we had that exact conversation,' she says, not looking at me directly.

'Why not?' I ask. 'Didn't you like him?'

She looks shocked. 'Naturally, we liked him! He's a lovely young man.'

'It sounds as though there's a 'but' in there somewhere.'

She switches off the potatoes, which are threatening to boil over. 'It's just that it wasn't as immediately obvious to us why you two were together. But Stephen made you happy, which was all we cared about. So, it comes to the same thing.'

'He did make me happy,' I say. 'He still would.'

Her eyes are sympathetic as she considers me. 'But that's all over now. You broke up a long time ago, and you told us he's seeing someone else.'

She brightens. 'You've found someone new too, and he seems to make you very happy. You aren't still thinking of Stephen?'

'Of course not!' I say rather too vehemently, and she gives me a worried look.

'Not at all,' I say more calmly. 'I was only wondering why you weren't as enthusiastic about Stephen as you are about Jack. It doesn't matter.'

'Things work out the way they're meant to,' she says. 'I've always said that. And that's what happened with you and Jack. Now, if only Ben and Mia would start talking again, I'm sure they could work everything out. However, it's none of my business, and I don't intend to interfere.'

'Except for inviting Mia to my birthday lunch,' I tease her.

'That's different,' she says.

I let it drop. At least she isn't focusing on the many perfections of Jack and the rather fewer perfections of Stephen. I always felt she was slightly uncomfortable around Stephen, although I never knew why. If he and I had stayed together, she would have had more opportunity to get to know him. I'm confident she would have come to love him as much, if not more, than Jack.

The rest of the week passes quickly. I'm busy at work, although not with customers. Mr Mason insists on teaching me the intricacies of his bookkeeping method, which seems to have come straight out of some *Business for Beginners* course from the 1950s. He uses ruled ledgers and favours the double entry method of bookkeeping. I try to persuade him all this would be far easier on a computer, but he gives me a worried look.

'I've heard terrible tales about people losing all their information on computers. I couldn't risk it.'

'Nowadays, everything gets saved automatically to the cloud,' I assure him.

'What sort of cloud?' he says.

'It isn't an actual cloud. It's just an expression. Your information wouldn't only be on your computer. It would be saved on someone else's server.'

He looks even more confused. 'Who would be serving it?'

Too late, I realise this was the wrong word to use to explain the intricacies of data storage to someone whose only thought is of serving his customers.

'It doesn't matter,' I say. 'I'm quite happy to accept whatever method you prefer.'

'The old methods are best,' he says. 'Everyone chases after the newfangled ways of doing things, but they always come back to where it all started.'

By this reasoning, he ought to be inscribing his accounts on papyrus by the flickering light of a tallow candle. I'm about to comment but remember in time my resolve to be a little ray of sunshine around the workplace.

'I should sort out the out-of-date cream cakes,' I say.

'Good idea,' he says. 'We can't have our customers eating anything that might give them food poisoning.'

I'd be more than prepared to risk it, but I know better than to raise the subject again. The last time I mentioned taking the out-of-date cakes home, he reacted as though I'd suggested spreading cholera throughout the village.

I'm surprised and touched at closing time when he appears holding a cake.

'Your mother told me it's your birthday tomorrow,' he says. 'I wanted to give you something to show my appreciation of all your hard work. I didn't know what you'd like, but this seemed appropriate.'

I take the cake he hands me, trying not to laugh. He's obviously been inspired by Stephen's request because he's used the tip of a knife to scratch *Happy Birthday Lily* into the vanilla frosting. At least, I think that's what it says. Several of the letters have run into each other, and his writing is spidery at the best of times. For all I know, he meant to write *You're Fired.*

'Thank you very much, Mr Mason,' I say. 'I very much appreciate having this job.'

He looks pleased. 'Off you go. Enjoy your day tomorrow. Give my kindest regards to your mother.'

I set off down the street, clutching my cake. It's surprisingly heavy, and I wonder what it's filled with. We don't sell family size cakes. We order them in if our customers request it. He must have put in a special order for this one, which was kind of him.

'What have you got there?' says Mum as I walk in.

I lay the box on the table. 'Mr Mason gave me a cake.'

She looks at it in dismay. 'But I spent all afternoon making your favourite coffee and walnut cake.'

I switch on the kettle. 'I should hope so! Nothing beats your coffee and walnut cake. But there's nothing wrong with having two.'

'I suppose so,' she says. 'What flavour is this one?'

I peer at it again. 'I have no idea. It has vanilla icing, but it could be anything underneath. It's extremely heavy. Maybe it's not a cake at all. He may have iced a gold bar for me as a delightful surprise.'

'I wouldn't think so,' says Mum. 'He can't be making much money out of that shop.'

'Have you decided where you'd like to go tomorrow?' I ask, abandoning the subject of my cake and its possible contents.

'Let's go to Massimo's for lunch,' she says. 'We've never been there, and we hear good things.'

'That sounds lovely,' I say. 'I won't go hungry tomorrow.'

'Do you know where Jack's taking you yet?' she asks with interest.

'Actually, I'm taking Jack,' I say. 'But it's a secret. I'll tell you when I get home.'

She looks surprised. 'I hope he's paying.'

I'm about to tell her this one is on me, but I stop myself in time. It would involve an explanation I'm not prepared to give. Better to allow her to think this is a romantic meal and Jack is paying. She's hardly likely to demand the receipt when he drops me home.

My phone rings after dinner. I look at the screen and see Jack's name. 'I'll be back in a minute.'

Mum and Dad exchange glances that say only too clearly they think I need privacy to murmur sweet nothings down the phone line. Not the phone line, exactly. My words of love will bounce straight up to a satellite whizzing around somewhere above the atmosphere, then beam down to Jack as if by magic. Mr Mason would be horribly confused.

'Hi, Jack,' I say as soon as I'm out of earshot. 'I've booked us a table for tomorrow evening.'

'So have I,' he says. 'Isn't it the part of a loving boyfriend to make birthday arrangements?'

'Usually, it would be. But as you are neither loving nor a boyfriend, we can dispense with formalities. I'd rather go to my restaurant if you don't mind.'

'You don't know where I've booked,' he says. 'I know I promised you McDonald's, but I discovered in the interim that Burger King has a special two-for-one deal on onion rings this weekend only.'

'Tempting though that sounds, I'd prefer to stick with my original arrangements. Do you mind picking me up? I could borrow Mum's car, but …'

'No, you couldn't,' he interrupts. 'Have you no romance in your soul? I'll be there on time, wearing my smartest outfit. I expect your father will want a word with me about manly things before we leave. Does he own a shot gun?'

I giggle. 'I think Ben has his old BB gun somewhere around. Will that do?'

'I suppose it will have to. Speaking of being on time, can you be precise?'

I think rapidly. 'Our table is booked for eight o'clock. It's half an hour's drive from here, and we'll want a drink first. How about seven o'clock? I'll see you then.'

'Is that it?' he asks. 'No loving words, no promises of eternal faithfulness? I'm not sure your heart is entirely in this relationship.'

'You're my very favourite Jack in the entire world,' I say. 'Will that do?'

He sighs. 'It's a start. I'm off to write a sonnet about your beauty. Dare I hope you'll be doing the same?'

'I'll write you a limerick about your ears. It's the best I can offer.'

He sighs again. 'Beggars can't be choosers. I bet you can't find a rhyme for seashell.'

'Challenge accepted,' I say. 'See you tomorrow. Don't be late!'

'Listen to the pair of us!' he says. 'We're like an old married couple.'

And he rings off before I can answer.

Chapter Seventeen

Jack arrives exactly on time on Sunday evening. I've already decided not to rush out to the car as I used to do with Stephen. I'm taking a leaf out of Isabella's book from now on. If Jack beeps his horn at me, he can stay out there and freeze to death.

But he comes to the front door, carrying a bunch of flowers. 'Happy Birthday, Lily!'

'Thanks,' I say. 'Are these for me? They're lovely.'

He holds them away from me. 'They're for your father.'

'Dad?' I say, puzzled.

'Of course. McCall's book of dating etiquette says you should always obtain the good opinion of the father if the course of wooing is to run smoothly.'

'In which case, give them to Mum,' I say. 'She loves flowers.'

Mum appears behind me. 'Hello, Jack! Don't stand out there in the cold. Why haven't you asked him in, Lily?'

I step aside to let Jack pass. 'He's brought you some flowers,' I say maliciously.

'How thoughtful! I'll fetch a vase.' She disappears towards the kitchen.

Jack's eyes are alight with laughter. 'You don't plan to make this easy for me, do you?'

'You're having a little too much fun with this. It's time I did too.'

I inspect the flowers more closely. 'These aren't lilies. Everyone brings me lilies. They seem to think it's funny.'

'They're daisies,' he says. 'Your favourite flower. You were misnamed.'

'I've often thought that,' I agree. 'Although if my parents had named me Daisy, my favourite flowers would probably have been lilies.'

Mum comes back with the vase. 'Let me put these in some water.'

I relent towards Jack. It was thoughtful of him to remember my favourite flowers. 'Actually, I think they're for me.'

Mum smiles. 'I'd already guessed that. You mustn't mind Lily teasing you, Jack. She does it to us all.'

She bustles off towards the kitchen with the daisies.

Jack laughs. 'She has the measure of you.'

I'm surprised. I've always thought my sarcasm bounced off Mum unnoticed. It's unsettling to think she may have been less oblivious than I realised and just decided to let it pass.

'We should get going,' I say.

Jack looks disappointed. 'What – no interrogation from your father? No instructions as to the only proper way to treat his daughter?'

'If anything, they believe you're doing me a favour.'

'Don't give me that,' he says. 'They think the sun shines out of you and Ben. Neither of you can do anything wrong.'

I reach for my coat. 'So, now you're telling me I'm a spoiled brat?'

'Oddly enough, I'm not. Quite the opposite, in fact. You and Ben have turned out fine despite it all – or because of it.'

'We're very lucky to have such great parents,' I say, following him to the door. 'Although I personally think they're batting one for two. I turned out great. Ben, not so much.'

Mum reappears, holding the vase of daisies. 'I'll take these up to your bedroom, Lily. You can see them before you go to sleep, and they'll be the first thing you see when you wake up in the morning, so you can think of Jack.'

As soon as we're out on the drive, I mime throwing up.

Jack waits patiently until I've finished. 'I'm hurt. This early in our relationship, we should be thinking of each other all the time.'

He opens my car door, and I climb inside. A horrible thought strikes me. I wait until we're driving out of the village before voicing it.

'I was thinking about what my mum said about putting the flowers in my bedroom so I can think of you. You don't think they'll expect us to spend the night together at some point?'

'No idea,' he says. 'Do your boyfriends usually sleep over at your parents' house?'

'Oh yes!' I say airily. 'At one point, I considered asking Dad to put in a revolving bedroom door to make things easier.'

'I wasn't trying to be offensive,' he says.

'I didn't think you were. Stephen is the only one who's ever stayed over, and it was pretty awkward. Everyone was so hideously polite and unconcerned. I tried to avoid it after that.'

'There you are,' he says. 'Your parents won't want you to be uncomfortable.'

'But you have your own place. Will they expect me to stay over there?'

'No one expects anything,' he says a little shortly. 'Your life is your own concern, Lily. You know that. There's a junction coming up. Which way do I turn?'

I direct him towards Banford, wondering at what point he'll realise where we're headed. Hopefully, not for a while. I'd like to surprise him. He's amazing at selecting thoughtful and unusual gifts, and it's my turn to reciprocate.

We chat about nothing in particular as we drive through the forest. I glance at him when we're three minutes away from the restaurant. He doesn't look excited, although he must have twigged where we're going.

'Left at that junction,' I say, pointing. 'Then take the second left and we're there.'

He slows down as we reach the end of the long driveway that leads to The Oasis. 'Now where?'

'Down there! Didn't you realise where I was taking you?'

He noses the car down the driveway. 'This is where we're going?'

I grin at him. 'Surprise!'

He pulls up outside the restaurant and turns to look at me. 'You can't be serious?'

'Perfectly. You told me you wanted to eat here. Don't say you've changed your mind?'

He seems dazed. 'Not at all, but I'm still not sure you're serious. When we started heading in this direction about ten minutes ago, I thought it was an elaborate joke. I suspected you'd discovered a fast-food place in the vicinity and were taking me there instead.'

'That would be a horrible thing to do,' I say. 'You don't really think I'd do that?'

'Not really,' he says. 'But how … I mean, how is it possible …?'

'Isabella got us the table.'

'Isabella?' he says. 'Horsey, unpleasant Isabella? The Isabella who stole your ex-boyfriend?'

I wish I hadn't expressed my opinions quite so freely, especially about someone I'd never met.

'I've got to know her a bit this week,' I say with as much dignity as I can muster. 'She's quite nice. I told her you wanted to come here, and she said her family knows the head chef and she could get us a table. The details don't matter. The important thing is that we're eating here. I hope it's everything you dreamed of.'

Before I realise what he's doing, he leans over and kisses my cheek. 'Thank you, Lily. You're the best.'

I mumble something in reply. Jack isn't usually so demonstrative. He always hugs me when he sees me, but I'm not sure he's ever kissed me. Not that this was an actual kiss, at least not a boyfriendly kiss. Then again, he isn't my boyfriend, so that makes sense.

'Our table is booked for eight o'clock,' I say awkwardly. 'We've arrived in good time. Let's go inside. There's plenty of time for you to buy me a birthday drink before dinner.'

Chapter Eighteen

I don't know what I expected when I walked into The Oasis, but it wasn't this. I thought there would be gold fittings and chandeliers and servers scurrying around in white jackets and bowties. Instead, this is low key and casual. At first, I'm not sure we've come to the right place.

A man wearing a trendy sports jacket and chinos comes over to greet us. 'Good evening, and welcome to The Oasis. May I have your name, please?'

'I booked it in your name,' I tell Jack.

He looks surprised. 'Jack Fisher,' he says. 'We were hoping to have a drink first.'

'The bar is over there,' says the man. 'Let me know when you're ready to be seated. May I take your coats?'

We walk over to the bar, where a young woman is polishing glasses.

'What's it to be?' asks Jack. 'Champagne? Or would you prefer a pint of Guinness?'

'Champagne sounds lovely, thank you.'

'It's my fiancée's birthday,' he tells the woman, who smiles.

'Happy birthday. I'm sure you'll enjoy your evening.'

She pours us both a glass of champagne and disappears.

'Why did you say it was my birthday?' I ask.

'I was under the impression it was.'

'But you know how much I hate strangers knowing that.'

'I do,' he agrees.

'So, why?'

'Why did you tell your mother those daisies were for her?' he counters.

I give a reluctant smile. 'Point taken. That makes us even. Actually, it doesn't. Why did you also tell her I was your fiancée?'

He gives me a soulful look. 'I may have been jumping the gun a little. I was planning to propose to you over dinner tonight, but now you've spoiled the surprise.'

My mouth falls open before I see his expression. I relax. 'Of course, you were. I shall inspect my desert carefully, so I don't break my teeth on the diamond ring.'

'Zirconium,' he corrects me.

I giggle. 'Can you imagine Mum's face if I came home with a ring on my finger?'

'I was worried she might be expecting it,' he says. 'Especially when she hears where I've brought you tonight. Why did you put the table in my name? You know women are allowed to go to restaurants on their own these days?'

'I'm aware. Isabella asked me which name I wanted to use for the reservation when she called, and I thought it was better to give her yours. There's a tiny chance she might mention it to Stephen, and it could get back to my mum. She'd be horrified if she thought you hadn't arranged this evening for me. You know how old-fashioned she is.'

He nods and raises his glass. 'What shall we drink to? Your birthday, but what else? True love and happily-ever-afters?'

I clink my glass against his. 'To friendship.'

He smiles. 'I'll drink to that.'

We finish our champagne, and the server shows us to our table. I stifle a giggle as he spreads the napkin in my lap for me. Jack looks even more horrified when the server does the same for him.

'Do you think he's worried about our table manners?' I ask when the server has left.

'I expect it's because they serve lots of splashy food,' he says. 'It's probably their thing.'

He inspects the menu. 'You see? I was right. Consommé, turtle broth, mushroom tart.'

'Mushroom tart isn't runny,' I say.

'It might be the way they cook it,' he says. 'The only way to get a Michelin star is to have a unique selling point. This chef has probably gone for runniness.'

'Even the bread?' I say.

'I expect they dip it into some sort of liquid before serving it. Some exclusive brand of water that costs ten pounds a glass.'

'Which reminds me,' I say. 'This dinner is on me.'

'But it's your birthday!' he objects.

'As you insist on telling all and sundry. But you got the last one, and I want to get this one. I was excited to surprise you.'

He squeezes my hand. 'You certainly did that.'

I almost pull my hand away, then stop. It's a friendly gesture, like kissing me on the cheek. It isn't intimate to squeeze someone's hand in public, but it's the sort of gesture that would make Mum and Dad give each other a meaningful look and a knowing smile.

The server shows no sign of being overcome by the romance of it all. He's too busy greeting the couple who've just come in. He takes the woman's coat. As her hood falls back, the light catches her fair, curly hair. It can't be! But there's no mistaking the broad shoulders and dark wavy hair of the man she's with. What are they doing here?

'Is something wrong?' asks Jack.

His eyes follow mine, and his face assumes an impassive expression. 'I didn't realise you'd asked anyone to join us.'

'I haven't!' I say. 'I have no idea what they're doing here. Isabella didn't mention it when she called to tell me about the reservation.'

I lift my menu, trying to shield my face. 'Don't keep looking in their direction. They'll see us.'

Jack's face relaxes. 'Lily, there are eight tables, and the dining room is only fractionally larger than your parents' living room. Short of diving under the table, I think we'll be seen.'

I chance another look towards the doorway. As luck would have it, Stephen has turned to inspect the room. His eyes meet mine, and I stare at him, unable to move.

Isabella's face lights up when she sees me. 'You made it! I'm so glad. Are you having a lovely time?'

'Yes, thank you,' I say through stiff lips.

She gives Jack a tiny wave. 'Don't worry, we aren't here to gate crash your special evening. When I asked Uncle Henry if he could enquire about a table for two, he thought I said two tables. I was going to call and cancel, but then I remembered how lovely it was here. Stephen and I will sit on the other side of the room. You won't even know we're here.'

Stephen lays a hand on her shoulder. 'This isn't a good idea. You should have mentioned it to me beforehand.'

Her face falls. 'You're right. We should leave. We can get a table at The Wild Horse. I'll let Michael know we won't be staying.'

I breathe a sigh of relief. 'Sorry about that,' I begin.

Jack is quicker. He holds out his hand to Stephen. 'Nice to see you again. There's no need for you to leave. In fact, why don't you join us?'

Chapter Nineteen

I'm not sure which of us looks more horrified, Stephen or me. I give a strangled squeak, while he makes a sort of growling sound, which he turns into a cough.

'It's kind of you,' he says, 'but we wouldn't dream of it.'

'Nonsense,' says Jack. 'You and I have never had the chance to talk properly, Stephen, and this is a great opportunity to get to know Isabella.'

I glare at him. What does he think he's doing? It's bad enough that we've run into my old boyfriend with his new girlfriend without spending the entire evening with them. What happened to being British and pretending the other people don't exist?

Isabella looks doubtful. 'It could be fun, but it's Lily's birthday. It's a special night for you two. You don't want anyone gate crashing it.'

'Exactly!' says Stephen in a relieved tone.

I'm about to agree with him when I realise he thinks I can't bear to have anyone else around on my romantic date. He may even, heaven forbid, imagine Jack is planning to propose to me tonight. After all, I told him I was in an extremely serious, albeit surprisingly new, relationship.

He can't really think that. Jack would hardly have asked him and Isabella to join us if this was what he planned. On the other hand, some people invite an entire baseball stadium to witness their over-the-top proposals. Only inviting two onlookers seems quite modest by comparison.

'It's a great idea,' I say in an unconcerned tone, trying to look as though I don't care if the server pushes all eight of the dining tables together and covers them with a parachute before sitting down to eat with us.

'I knew you'd agree,' says Jack.

'If you're sure,' says Isabella. 'Maybe they can move us to a larger table.'

'We don't want to put them to so much trouble,' says Stephen, but in the tone of a man who knows he's lost.

I wonder whether his objection is to spending time with me, or whether he wanted to be alone with Isabella. He may have been looking forward to a lovely romantic evening of whispering sweet nothings into her ear. Jack's suggestion has put a spoke in that wheel, I think with satisfaction.

Isabella disappears to speak to the server, leaving the three of us staring at each other in silence.

Jack is the first to break it. 'Have you been here before?' he asks Stephen.

Stephen doesn't appear to be paying attention. I'd like to believe he's distracted by my beauty and rendered tongue-tied by bitter regrets about what he's carelessly thrown away, but he just looks annoyed. I recognise that look only too well from the odd evening we fell out, when he remained monosyllabic until I apologised.

I can't imagine Isabella apologising when she's done nothing wrong. Her mother will have taught her a hundred ways to deal with that sort of situation, most of them involving ordering a taxi and putting it on her date's account.

My mother would be more likely to advise me to smooth over troubled waters because she hates atmospheres and sees no need for them. She may be right. She and Dad have had a long and happy marriage. But I can't help hoping Isabella doesn't allow Stephen to get away with half the things I did.

Stephen seems to come back to reality with a start and realise he's being spoken to. 'This is the first time I've been here. Isabella assures me it's very nice. Good food, and all that.'

Jack seems to find this amusing. 'I believe it's been well reviewed.'

The server returns and directs us to a table near to the fireplace. 'I hope you find this table to your satisfaction.'

Stephen pulls out Isabella's chair for her, and Jack promptly does the same for me. I suppress an urge to giggle and give him a demure smile. The server brings our menus.

Isabella picks hers up. 'Have you decided what to order?'

'Not even close,' says Jack. 'We were busy arguing –' he catches my eye – 'I mean discussing whose turn it was to pay.'

'It's Lily's birthday,' says Stephen. 'Surely, you weren't expecting her to pay for her own birthday meal?'

'That's what I told her!' says Jack. 'But you know Lily, as stubborn as a mule.'

'I can't say I'd noticed,' says Stephen.

I give Jack a smug look. 'You see? Not everyone has such a low opinion of me as you do.'

'How can you say that when you know I consider you to be the pinnacle of perfection?'

He thinks for a moment, then adds, 'Darling.'

I can't give him a withering look in front of Isabella and Stephen, but once we're alone in the car, all bets are off.

'Sweet!' says Isabella. 'I'm still waiting for someone who thinks I'm perfect.'

I can't help asking, 'Doesn't Stephen?'

She laughs. 'He doesn't give any sign of it.'

Stephen flushes. 'This is a ridiculous conversation. No one's perfect. It's silly to pretend they are.'

'Don't tell Jack that,' says Isabella. 'It's nice to see someone so much in love.'

I catch Stephen's eye and look away. I have no idea what he's thinking, and I'm not about to ask. At least he doesn't find Isabella perfect. He was clearly aware of most of my faults, but that never bothered me. It showed he loved me despite them. Unconditional love is rare to find, and that's what he gave me.

I didn't see any faults in him. I still don't. He must have some, but it's never been obvious to me what they are. The only fault I could ever discover in him was that he didn't want to be with me any longer. That wasn't even a fault, more of an unfortunate choice he may or may not regret. It's impossible to read Stephen when he doesn't want you to.

Isabella doesn't seem perturbed by the idea of her boyfriend not worshipping the ground she walks on. She appears to find the subject more fascinating than upsetting.

'Do you feel the same way about Jack?' she asks me. 'Do you think he's perfect, too?'

I give a snort of laughter. 'Not remotely!'

I grin at Jack, who gives me a saintly smile in return.

'Don't look like that,' I tell him. 'You have plenty of faults. And despite what you say, you know I do too.'

He laughs. 'Maybe a couple of very tiny ones, but they're vastly outweighed by the good points.'

'The same with you,' I say.

'This is all fascinating,' says Stephen, 'but we should order.'

'You're right,' I say. 'Everything looks so good that I want to try it all. Do you have any recommendations, Isabella?'

'They do a tasting plate,' she says. 'We could order that for the table.'

'Not for me, thanks,' says Stephen. 'I think I'll have the pheasant.'

I'd forgotten he isn't keen on sharing food. It's one of his foibles. I can hardly call it a fault. He was always happy for me to order anything I wanted, as long as I didn't eat off his plate.

'I'm quite keen to try the Beef Wellington,' says Isabella. 'Uncle Henry says it's the best he's ever tasted. You two could share the tasting menu,' she says to me.

The thought of sharing a host of dishes with Jack under Stephen's disapproving eye is too much to contemplate. It would give an air of intimacy I'm keen to avoid. Knowing Jack, he would insist on us nibbling a bread stick from opposite ends just to embarrass me.

'I'm having the venison,' I say. 'It looks fantastic.'

Jack is clearly aware of what has been going through my mind. 'Are you sure, Lily? It would be so romantic.'

'Perfectly sure,' I say. 'What are you having?'

'The trout,' he decides. 'I'll enjoy it in lonely splendour.'

Isabella opens the menu again. 'They do a wonderful chocolate soufflé for two, but you have to order it in advance. It takes about an hour.'

'Marvellous!' says Jack. 'Lily and I will have that. How about you and Stephen?'

'I never eat dessert,' says Stephen.

This is true. He's rigidly disciplined about his eating habits. He runs five miles each morning and goes to the gym three times a week. But this is a special occasion.

'Can't you make an exception for once?' I say. 'How often do you get to eat at a place like this?'

'Quite right,' says Isabella. 'Don't be such a stick in the mud, Stephen.'

He looks embarrassed. 'I'll order something after the meal if I have room.'

'Why don't you order the chocolate soufflé?' I suggest to Isabella. 'I bet you could finish it all by yourself. If not, Jack is sure to volunteer. I've never seen him refuse a dessert.'

'Quite right,' agrees Jack. 'It's a shame to let something delicious go to waste. Think of all the starving people at Weight Watchers.'

'I'll do that,' says Isabella. 'Stephen can have some if he likes, but I'll manage fine without him.'

Does she mean this literally or metaphorically? Hopefully, the latter. She's so sorted and independent, and Stephen has always struck me as the sort of man who needs someone to need him. I'm not getting that vibe off Isabella at all. This may be wishful thinking, but I hope not.

As soon as the server has taken our order, Isabella returns to the previous subject. She seems fascinated by this discussion of our failings. I can't think why.

'Lily, you were about to tell us about Jack's faults,' she says. 'I'm all ears.'

I look at Jack, who doesn't appear bothered.

'He's always late for everything,' I say with a sidelong glance at Stephen. I know how much he hates unpunctuality.

'I'm late for everything too!' exclaims Isabella. 'That isn't a fault! It's a quirk.'

'It's an annoying one,' says Stephen.

She doesn't take any notice. 'What else?'

'He finds almost everything funny,' I say.

'Again, not a fault,' she says. 'You'll have to do better than that, Lily.'

'And he's the untidiest man I've ever met,' I finish.

Isabella looks at Jack with interest. 'Were we separated at birth?'

'My mother's never mentioned it,' he says. 'But I suppose anything's possible.'

I watch them laughing and feel a twinge of annoyance. There's no reason for this. It's no surprise the pair of them get on well together. They seem similar in lots of ways. I wonder whether Jack finds her attractive. Too bad if he does. She's going out with Stephen.

'In the light of these terrible revelations, would you care to revise your statement about Lily having no faults?' she asks him.

I brace myself for I'm not sure what. Jack gives me an affectionate smile. 'Not at all. She's the closest thing to an angel that ever walked this earth.'

'Sweet!' says Isabella again.

'I realise you're saying that to be polite,' says Stephen. 'But are you honestly telling us there's nothing about Lily you'd change if you could?'

I feel an odd mixture of emotions. I don't want Jack to say anything negative about me to Stephen. But this is a great opportunity to find out why Stephen dumped me. If it was for some specific fault, it would be helpful to know so I could work on it.

Jack shakes his head. 'I stand by my original statement. Lily is pretty much perfect in every way. Any imperfections she has are a part of her. Wanting her to get rid of them would be wanting her to be an entirely different person. I'll stick with the one I have.'

Stephen doesn't look as touched by Jack's speech as I feel.

'That's all very well at the beginning of a relationship,' he says. 'Everyone starts with a rosy view of the other person. But as time goes on, it's important to be honest about the other person's faults, and your own. Otherwise, you're sticking your head in the sand.'

'Honesty is important in a relationship,' I say. 'But communication is equally important. How can anyone work on themselves and fix things if the other person doesn't communicate?'

The table has fallen silent, and I realise I may have given myself away. 'Hypothetically,' I add.

Stephen is looking at me with an expression I can't quite read.

Jack is the first to answer. 'Why would anyone fix themselves to please another person? If you aren't a good fit, it's best to accept it and move on. You're bound to find someone else who suits you.'

'Plenty more fish in the sea,' agrees Isabella.

She may be right, but I don't want another fish. I want the first one I caught, the one with whom I spent two years, and with whom I planned to spend the rest of my life. He's sitting across the table from me, almost within reach, possibly thinking the same thing about me. I'm desperate to send him some coded message only he and I can decipher, but my brain has frozen, and I can't think of anything. All I can do is stare at him helplessly, willing him to understand.

The silence is broken by the server carrying several silver domes. He seems to know by instinct which one belongs to each diner.

He smiles around at the four of us. 'Enjoy your meal!'

Chapter Twenty

It's a relief to have something to do instead of continuing this uncomfortable conversation. Even though I had lunch with Mum and Dad, I'm pretty hungry, and this food is a work of art. The presentation is simple but as beautiful to look at as it is to eat. I can see why this place has a Michelin star.

Contrary to Jack's earlier speculations, the meat isn't liquid, and neither are the potatoes and vegetables. There's a redcurrant reduction that could just about count, but that's all.

'This is amazing,' says Jack. 'I haven't tasted anything this good since Lily made me toast and jam on Christmas morning.'

'Did you come home for Christmas this year?' Stephen asks me.

'Yes, Mum would never have forgiven me if I hadn't.'

'I expect she'd have managed,' he says.

I lay down my knife and fork. 'What do you mean?'

He looked surprised. 'Nothing. But she can't expect to have you home every Christmas for the rest of your life.'

'I don't see why not. It's a special time of the year for her. She and Dad always made Christmas wonderful for us when we were small. I don't think it's much of a sacrifice for us to repay the favour.'

'But you can't do it forever,' he says. 'What happens if you meet someone who also wants to spend Christmas Day with their family?'

'There's nothing to stop them.'

He smiles. 'And what if you have children? Won't you all want to be together for Christmas Day?'

He turns to Jack. 'Where did you spend Christmas this year?'

I realised too late the trap into which Jack is about to fall. I give his ankle a vicious kick, but he's already answering.

'My parents rented a house in Cornwall. It worked out pretty well for us all. My sister was there with her husband and children, and one of my cousins came with her boyfriend, so we had a big family Christmas.'

'Christmas was ages ago,' I say in a futile effort to change the subject. 'We're closer to Easter now. What are you doing for Easter this year, Isabella?'

'Hang on a minute,' says Stephen with a puzzled frown. 'You said you came home for Christmas, Lily.'

'That's right. Anyway …'

'But Jack was in Cornwall,' he says. His frown deepens. 'How could Lily be making you toast and jam on Christmas morning? Cornwall is hours away.'

'To people deeply in love, time and space is but a concept …' begins Jack.

'Don't take any notice of him,' I tell Stephen. 'Jack didn't mean Christmas Day itself. When we realised we couldn't spend the holidays together, we had our own Christmas Day the previous week.'

'What a great idea!' says Isabella. 'You and I should do that next year, Stephen. You can never have too many Christmases.'

He doesn't look convinced. I change the subject before he can return to his bizarre calendar obsession.

'What did you do this Christmas, Isabella? Mum mentioned that Stephen went skiing. Did you go with him?'

She pulls a face. 'Perish the thought! All I want to do at Christmas is to stay warm. I can never understand why people voluntarily spend a week sliding down mountains, only to take a cable car back up.'

'I think it sounds fun,' I say.

Skiing isn't on my bucket list, but if Isabella doesn't like it, it's a great way to differentiate myself from her in Stephen's eyes. It will show him that if he fancies going again next year, I'd be happy to join him. Not on Christmas Day itself, though. I'd prefer to spend that with my family.

'Lily?' says Jack.

I drag my thoughts away from visions of gliding down snow-covered mountains with Stephen, our arms wrapped around each other. Can people ski like that? I've never skied, so I'm not entirely sure. Perhaps one of them could ski backwards?

'Yes?' I say.

'Isabella asked what you and I are doing for Valentine's Day,' he says.

'Nothing,' I say before realising it's a perfectly natural question. Jack and I are supposed to be deeply in love. Of course, we'll want to do something for Valentine's Day.

'She's joking,' he tells Isabella. 'Lily knows perfectly well I'm planning a romantic surprise for her. She's very excited.'

'I can't sleep,' I say.

'How about you?' Jack asks Stephen. 'Do you have anything exciting planned?'

'He'd better have!' says Isabella.

Stephen looks uncomfortable. 'I'm sure we'll find something appropriate for the occasion.'

I can't resist saying, 'You told me you'd come home specially to see your new girlfriend. That was pretty romantic of you. By the way, how's your dad doing?'

'Fine, thanks,' he says shortly.

'What did you and Stephen do when you were together?' Isabella asks me.

'Not much. I'm sure he'll be more thoughtful with you.'

I'm pleased to see him look annoyed. I haven't quite forgiven him for the database book. And that weekend away in the lakes doesn't count now that I know he was planning to break up with me.

The soufflés arrive, and Jack's eyes light up. 'My favourite! If I didn't love you so much, Lily, you wouldn't get any of this.'

I pick up my spoon. 'Likewise.'

I'm not sure how to eat the souffle. I've shared plenty of food with Jack in my time – greasy kebabs at three in the morning after a night out, pizza and ice cream after break ups. But that feels very different to sharing the same dessert with Stephen watching us.

Am I supposed to start at one end of the dish and Jack at the other and meet in the middle? Is the dessert a metaphor for a loving relationship? Even worse, are we supposed to feed each other? The thought makes me feel hot with embarrassment.

'I'll put my portion onto a plate,' I tell Jack.

'If you must,' he says, 'although you're ruining the mood. I'll watch very closely to make sure you don't take more than your share.'

Isabella is already halfway through her own soufflé.

'Are you sure you don't want any?' she asks Stephen. 'It's delicious.'

She offers him a spoonful, and he gives her a faintly revolted look. 'No, thank you. I've had more than enough to eat.'

She doesn't look perturbed. 'I've never understood how anyone can have had enough to eat when something like this is on offer. It takes up almost no room.'

He doesn't answer. Not the first time, I wonder what drew the two of them together. Isabella is pretty, and she's easy to spend time with, but somehow, I thought Stephen would be looking for more than that. What do I know? I thought he and I were happy together, and apparently we weren't.

Isabella lays down her spoon and surveys her plate with satisfaction. 'I give up, but I managed three quarters of it. Would anyone like the rest?'

I shake my head regretfully. 'I couldn't eat another mouthful.'

Jack pulls the dish towards him. 'I, on the other hand, could eat several more of these.'

'Too bad they take an hour,' says Isabella. 'You'll know next time you come.'

'At these prices, I doubt there'll be a next time,' he says. 'Especially as it would be Lily's turn to pay, and she's notoriously mean.'

He knows full well I can't comment, but I add this to the list of things I plan to discuss with him on the way home.

We finish the meal with coffee and liqueurs.

'Only a small one for me,' says Jack. 'I have to drive Lily home, and her mother will never forgive me if we end up in a snowdrift or worse.'

Stephen looks at his watch. 'We should really get home, Isabella.'

She pushes back her chair. 'I think I'll go to the ladies before we leave.'

'I'll settle the bill,' he says.

'Half the bill,' I say.

He looks at me with some of the old warmth in his eyes. 'Not at all. Consider it my birthday gift to you.'

'That's kind of you,' says Jack before I can speak. 'But this happens to be my birthday gift to Lily. I'm afraid I must insist.'

I wait until Stephen has walked over to the desk before nudging Jack. 'What did you do that for? He offered to buy me dinner. What's wrong with that?'

'You aren't his girlfriend,' he says flatly.

'I'm not yours either.'

'I'm aware of that. But you seem to forget he has a girlfriend. She's the one he should be buying dinner for, not you.'

'It was simply a nice gesture from one old friend to another,' I say.

'Fine, let's leave it at that. Anyway, I'm buying your dinner. It's your birthday, and I'm your fake boyfriend, so you don't have any choice.'

He strides off towards the desk before I can answer.

When we get outside, I see Stephen's Mazda parked close to the entrance. My feet want to turn towards it. I want to climb in as I always did and have Stephen drive me home. This all feels so wrong. He shouldn't be here with Isabella. He should be here with me. And there were several times this evening when I was sure he felt the same.

We say good night and walk across the gravel towards Jack's car. Something makes me turn and look back, and my heart contracts with pain as I see Stephen and Isabella locked together in the light streaming out of the doorway. He's kissing her more passionately than I ever remember him kissing me, and she's responding with equal enthusiasm. So much for him feeling the same way I do.

Jack hasn't noticed them. I follow him to the car and, on a ridiculous impulse, grab his shoulders and spin him to face me.

Before he can speak, I pull him towards me and kiss him. He pulls away, but I press myself closer to him. His lips part. I don't know whether he's trying to say something or responding to my kiss, and I don't care. All I care about is that Stephen knows how completely over him I am.

Jack's arms go around me, which prevents me from turning to see whether Stephen and Isabella have noticed us. It feels surprisingly natural to kiss Jack. I've never imagined kissing him before, but it somehow feels exactly how I knew it would. The smell of him is so familiar, the woody cologne he's worn for as long as I can remember, mixed with the faint coconut smell of his shampoo. His lips are warm, and I can taste the Benedictine he ordered after dinner.

He lifts a hand to cup my face and pulls me closer. 'Lily,' he murmurs, his voice seeming to come from a long way away.

'Mmm?' I don't want to talk right now. I just want to keep on kissing him.

An engine roars, and we spring apart as the Mazda turns in a tight circle and sweeps past us, spraying us with gravel. It disappears into the night, and I stare after it, my mind in a whirl.

'Lily?' says Jack again.

I turn back to him, almost surprised to find he's still there. 'Yes?'

He looks down the drive at the retreating Mazda, then at me. He opens the car door. 'Nothing. Are you ready to go home?'

Chapter Twenty-One

We drive most of the way home in silence. I'm not sure what happened back there. I kissed Jack on a stupid impulse I now regret. The only reason I enjoyed it was that it showed Stephen how little I cared about seeing him kiss Isabella. I would never have done it if I'd had time to think.

I'm also puzzled by Stephen doing something like that where he must have known Jack and I would see him. He isn't one for public demonstrations of affection. He was uncomfortable even holding my hand in public.

Was the display for my benefit – an attempt to show he doesn't care I'm dating someone else? It's an enticing thought, but it doesn't stand up to scrutiny. He couldn't have faked that kind of passion. He seemed utterly lost in the moment, as did she.

I imagine he also saw me kissing Jack, and that wasn't real. But the fact remains that Isabella is his actual girlfriend, whereas Jack is my fake boyfriend. Stephen has no motivation to stay with her if he doesn't want to. He could have come to me at any point and asked for another chance, and I'm reasonably sure he knows I would have agreed.

The unpalatable fact is that he must feel something for Isabella, and I've spent the entire evening cherishing unfounded hopes. I assumed because they bickered, and she contradicted him, that their relationship must be rocky. But perhaps that's their thing. Stephen may prefer someone who stands up to him. He's such a strong, decided character. I always thought he wanted an easy-going girlfriend who didn't challenge him. It appears I was wrong.

I file this away for future reference, although it seems likely there will be no future for us. If I was more like Isabella, I might have been able to keep his interest. I don't pursue this line of thought. I may still be hopelessly in love with Stephen but pretending to be someone I'm not could never work.

The best I can hope for is that she's a diversion for him – someone he met when he was feeling directionless and at a loose end. Much against my wishes, I like her, but I can't believe she's the kind of person he'll stay with long term.

My more immediate problem is Jack. I need to explain without hurting his feelings that I only kissed him to annoy Stephen. I won't put it like that. It's hurtful and unnecessary. I'll tell him it was a necessary part of the ruse. He and I had shown no signs of physical attraction during a romantic birthday meal, and I didn't want to raise Stephen's suspicions. It's a plausible and not too unkind explanation for what Jack must see as pretty bizarre behaviour.

An unpleasant thought strikes me. Jack kissed me back, and not in the amused way which might have been expected from someone enjoying this ridiculous situation. He kissed me in a way I'd expect from someone in a genuine relationship. He may have been acting, but if so, he did an excellent job of it.

I also did an excellent job of pretending I was enjoying it, but that was different. I was a prey to a range of conflicting emotions that he wasn't. I was on edge after an evening watching the man I love choosing to be with someone else. To add insult to injury, he kissed her right in front of me. Is it any wonder I retaliated in kind?

Jack doesn't have that excuse. He isn't in love with an ex-girlfriend, and he isn't hoping against hope she will see the error of their ways and ask to try again. I sneak a look at him out of the side of my eye. His expression is as calm as ever as he concentrates on the road. He doesn't look upset or annoyed. Then again, he never does. But I can't shake the nagging suspicion that's taken root in my mind. If I'm right, this whole charade is the unkindest thing I could have done.

I have to let him know as kindly as possible that my feelings for him are those of a friend. I kissed him solely for Stephen's benefit, not for my own, and certainly not for his. Yet again, I regret the stupid impulse that led me to set off down this road. Would it have been so bad if Stephen thought I was single?

What's wrong with being single, anyway? It's better than jumping in and out of any old relationship through fear of being alone. If Stephen was having second thoughts about ending things with me, it would have made things far less complicated all around if he'd thought I was unattached. It's too late to say anything now without making myself look even more of a fool, but I resolve to be more sensible in the future. It's unlikely such a situation will arise again, but it's as well to be prepared.

In the meantime, I need to clear the air with Jack and make sure he realises the game he and I are playing is nothing more than that.

'Jack,' I begin.

He turns his head to look at me, the usual smile absent from his eyes.

'I owe you a huge apology,' I say.

'Why is that?' he asks.

I try to adopt a light tone. 'You know what I mean, or do all your friends lunge at you and kiss you without warning?'

'Not on a regular basis,' he says. I still can't tell what he's thinking or whether he's annoyed.

'I'm glad to hear it,' I say in a tone of mock severity.

'What are you saying, Lily?'

'I'm trying to apologise. I had no right to do that. The thing was …'

'I'm quite aware what the thing was.'

I flush. 'Yes, well, I wanted to make our relationship look more realistic.'

'Is that so?' he says. 'To whom?'

'To Stephen! Who else?'

'It could have been to any number of people.'

'I don't know what you mean. You know perfectly well I'm trying to show Stephen I'm fine.'

'I wasn't sure what you were doing,' he says. 'You could have been showing Isabella she was welcome to Stephen or proving to yourself you don't care. You could even have been trying to show me something.'

This is the perfect opportunity to clear the air once and for all. 'There's nothing I need to show you!' I say.

'That's good.'

He isn't making this easy for me. I try again. 'While we're on the subject, I should clarify that I don't … I could never … just in case you …'

He swings the car into our street and pulls up outside my parents' house. He switches off the engine. 'Lily, there may have been some misunderstanding between us.'

'I think there has,' I say guiltily. 'I'm sorry, Jack. I didn't mean things to end up like this.'

He doesn't seem to hear me. He takes my hand. My first impulse is to pull it away. I don't want to add to his pain or appear to give him encouragement.

He looks deep into my eyes with no glimmer of his usual smile. 'Lily, I already have a girlfriend. I thought you knew.'

I'm not sure how long the silence lasts before I break it. It feels like several minutes, but it may be only a couple of seconds. 'You do?'

'I'm sorry,' he says. 'I was certain I'd mentioned her to you.'

'I think I'd have remembered it.'

It's a relief to see the old smile on his face. 'Who knows? You're extremely forgetful.'

'Tell me all about her,' I say. 'What's her name? How long have you been together? Where does she live? What does she do?'

He grins. 'It might be quicker if I forwarded you her resume.'

'It might be quicker if you answered my questions,' I say.

He shrugs. 'Her name is Carolyn. We've been seeing each other for six months. She lives in Weymouth, and she's an accountant.'

'She isn't a local?'

His eyes crinkle. 'Is that a deal breaker, as far as you're concerned?'

'I wondered whether I knew her, that's all.'

'I doubt it,' he says.

'Where did you meet?'

He hesitates. 'At a work thing.'

'You said she's an accountant,' I say, confused. 'You work in forestry. How could you work together?'

'What is this, a BBC detective series?' he complains.

'It's a natural enough question.'

'I suppose it is. I don't mean we met at work. I should have said I was down there for a conference, and I met her one evening at the hotel bar.'

'So, she's an alcoholic!' I say.

He smiles. 'Naturally. After being friends with you for so long, I wanted to find someone who could hold their drink.'

'You mean someone who wouldn't jump you purely on the strength of one glass of champagne and a small brandy?'

His smile widens. 'Exactly so. Not that I have any deep-seated objection to someone jumping me, just…'

'… not me?' I finish for him.

I know it's ridiculous, but I can't help a slight feeling of hurt that our kiss this evening meant nothing to him. I'm being irrational. It's just difficult to discover the two most important men in my life are taken up with other women. It adds to my current feeling of loneliness and isolation.

'I didn't say that,' he says, squeezing my hand again.

He sees my expression. 'Don't look like that. You're absolutely gorgeous, and you know it.'

'Not as gorgeous as Isabella,' I say dolefully.

'You're just as pretty,' he says. 'But the pair of you are very different.'

I sigh. The biggest difference I can see between us, apart from her long legs, blonde curly hair, and self-confidence, is that she has Stephen, and I don't. But there's no point in going over all that again, especially with Jack, who's been so patient with me about this whole thing.

'When will I meet this Carolyn?' I say. 'Will she be visiting soon?'

'I'm not sure. She's pretty busy at work, and so am I.'

'What about Valentine's Day?' I persist. 'You must be planning to see each other then. It's your first Valentine's Day together.'

'It isn't that big of a deal,' he says. 'Besides, there will be plenty of other Valentine's days.'

'Not with that attitude,' I say. 'You ought to do something special. I know how it feels when your boyfriend doesn't make an effort.'

'I'll think about it,' he promises.

'I feel I owe you a double apology for tonight's shenanigans.'

He laughs. 'Is that what they were? I wasn't sure.'

'What would you call them?'

He considers. 'Tomfoolery, hijinks, skylarking, pranks …'

'I suppose I should expect that from a man who refers to dating as wooing,' I say. 'Regardless, I'm so sorry. I would never have kissed you if I'd known you had a girlfriend. I hope you know that.'

'Of course, I do. That's why I told you about her. I didn't want things to go too far.'

'You were worried I had feelings for you?' I say, surprised.

'I wasn't sure,' he says. 'You seemed extremely enthusiastic about that kissing business.'

'So were you!' I say, stung. 'That's why we're having this conversation. I was worried you might have got the wrong idea and thought this was something more than it was.'

He lets go of my hand and switches on the engine. 'A comedy of errors all around. I'm glad we cleared up our mutual misunderstanding. Oh, I almost forgot.'

He reaches into the glove compartment and pulls out a small parcel. 'I meant to give you this earlier. Happy birthday, Lily!'

I take it from him but don't open it. I'm still dazed by the twists and turns this evening has taken.

'You don't have to open it now,' he says. 'You should go inside before your mother wonders what we're doing out here.'

He leans over and kisses my cheek. 'Thanks for an amazing evening. I still can't believe you arranged it for me.'

I smile. 'You're welcome. I'm sorry we ended up eating with Stephen and Isabella.'

'That's fine,' he says. 'It isn't as though you and I are an actual couple.'

Why does he keep saying that? It's as though he thinks I haven't yet got the message.

'Are you alright with carrying on with the pretence for another few days?' I ask. 'Or would your girlfriend be upset?'

'Not in the slightest. She isn't like that. I would never have agreed to this whole thing if I'd thought it would upset her.'

I give him a doubtful look. 'Fine, but the minute Stephen goes back to Manchester, you and I are breaking up.'

'I'll look forward to it,' he says. 'I'll go home now and start working on a script.'

I close the car door, and he drives away, leaving me standing there, wondering what just happened.

Chapter Twenty-Two

I don't sleep much when I finally get to bed. It's probably all the rich food I ate at The Oasis. I can't help thinking about Jack. Why didn't he tell me about his girlfriend sooner? If he'd mentioned her from the beginning, I would never have allowed him to go through with this stupid charade.

Knowing Jack, that's why he didn't mention it. He loves anything ridiculous, and few things are more ridiculous than what I asked him to do. I hope he hasn't been laughing at me behind my back. Of course, he hasn't. Jack laughs with people, never at them.

However, this whole situation is excruciatingly embarrassing, and most unfair on Jack's girlfriend. I know how much I'd have hated it if Stephen had agreed to such a ridiculous request while we were together.

I toss and turn until the early hours, when I fall into a light doze, punctuated with feverish dreams. I'm almost relieved when my alarm goes off. Thankfully, it's my usual gentle music. I've been careful to keep my phone on my person at all times since Ben thought it would be amusing for me to be woken by a chainsaw each morning.

Mum is even more chipper than usual when I arrive downstairs. 'Hello, darling. How does it feel to be thirty-one?'

'Pretty much the same as being thirty,' I say, rubbing my eyes and trying to locate the kettle. 'Only with slightly more of a headache.'

'Sit down, and I'll make you some coffee,' she says. 'Did you and Jack celebrate too enthusiastically last night?'

'What?' I say suspiciously.

'It's fine,' she says. 'If you can't drink a little too much on your birthday, when can you?'

I relax. For a moment there, I couldn't think what she meant.

She makes me a cup of coffee while I try to prepare myself for the day ahead. My work isn't taxing, but I need to maintain a cheerful appearance for the customers. Mr Mason won't be impressed if I turn up looking as though I haven't slept for a week.

'What pretty earrings you're wearing,' says Mum. 'I haven't seen them before.'

'Jack gave them to me for my birthday.'

'How sweet!' she says. 'I don't have my glasses. Are they pink, sparkly hearts?'

'Almost,' I say, lifting a hand and gently touching one of them. 'They're cupcakes.'

She looks disappointed. 'Hearts would have been more romantic.'

'He knows how important cupcakes are to me,' I say. 'I think they're lovely. Speaking of cakes, did you try the one I brought home from the bakery on Saturday?'

'Your father had a slice last night after dinner,' she says.

'That's good. What flavour was it?'

'I didn't think to ask him. He said it was very nice. Would you like some for breakfast?'

I give an involuntary shudder. 'Please, no! But Mr Mason is bound to ask whether I enjoyed it. He'll think I'm very ungrateful if I say I haven't even tried it.'

Mum reaches up to the top shelf. 'Let's have a look.'

We inspect the contents of the tin. The cake is a beige-pink colour and offers no clues as to its flavour.

'The icing is white, so it must be vanilla,' I say.

Mum scoops out a little of the icing. She licks her finger. 'I don't think it's vanilla.'

She picks up a teaspoon and scoops up some more. 'It's definitely not vanilla. I'm not sure what it is. Why don't you try it and see?'

I groan. I'm not at my best in the early morning. I can usually manage some toast, but I prefer to save my cake tasting sessions for later. Why isn't Ben here? He can eat anything, at any time.

I reach for a spoon. 'Pass me the tin.'

Two teaspoons later, I'm as baffled as Mum. 'It's definitely not vanilla, but I have no idea what it is.'

'Banana?' she suggests without conviction.

'I don't think so. Maybe it's white chocolate?'

'Why chocolate isn't usually tangy, is it?' she says. 'Is it cream cheese?'

'Definitely not! At least, I hope not. It has some sort of fruity taste, which you'd hope cream cheese wouldn't. Let's try the cake itself. That might give us a clue.'

Mum cuts us both a thin slice, and we dig in. I close my eyes as I chew, trying to imagine I'm at a wine tasting session. I wish I was.

'It's light-bodied, with a fruity bouquet, citrus top notes, and a nutty finish,' I pronounce at last.

Mum looks puzzled. 'Do you mean strawberry or lemon?'

I laugh. 'I don't know what I mean. I can rule out chocolate, coffee, and vanilla, but that's all. It could be anything.'

She takes another bite. 'It's quite a pleasant flavour. Perhaps he meant it to be a surprise.'

I put my plate in the sink. 'That's possible, but it isn't how bakeries usually operate. Customers expect us to know what our products taste like. Never mind. At least, I can tell him I've tried it.'

'Don't be late for work,' she says.

I skid to a halt outside the Sugarloaf as Mr Mason turns the corner. He looks pleased to see me. 'I'm glad you're here on time, Lily.'

'I'm always on time,' I say with a saintly smile.

'I suppose so.' He seems preoccupied as he opens the door.

'Thank you for the lovely birthday cake,' I say.

He looks at me as though he doesn't know what I'm talking about. 'Birthday cake? Ah, quite!'

I reach for my flowered tabard. 'Are you all right, Mr Mason?'

He gives me a harassed frown. 'As a matter of fact …'

I look at him in alarm. He isn't really ill, is he?

'Can I get you anything?' I say. 'A cup of coffee or a –'

I almost said cake, but he doesn't appreciate jokes about the staff eating the stock.

He passes a hand over his brow. 'No, thank you, Lily. My wife is rather unwell today.'

'I'm sorry to hear that,' I say. 'Should you be here?'

'What choice do I have?' he says. 'The village depends on our presence. It would never do to close the bakery unexpectedly.'

'I could look after the shop,' I suggest.

'You?' he says. 'All by yourself?'

'Why not? There's nothing too complicated for me to remember.'

He peers over his spectacles at me, and I correct myself. 'What I mean is, you've trained me very well. I know how to open up in the morning and close in the evening. I can use the till, and I know how the ordering system works if we run out of anything. Honestly, Mr Mason, I'll be fine. I think you should go home and look after your wife. If you give me your phone number, I can call you if I have any questions.'

He visibly wavers. 'It's an enormous risk, but if you really feel able to cope.'

'More than able!' I almost push him towards the door. 'I promise nothing will go wrong. If I can't get you on the phone, I'll call my mother. She could be here in five minutes, and I know she'd love to help.'

His worried frown disappears. 'What a good idea. It's not that I don't trust you, Lily. You've been a most conscientious employee. But it's no use expecting an old head on young shoulders.'

'Of course not,' I say soothingly. I can't resist adding, 'Mum has an old head on old shoulders, at least middle-aged shoulders.'

He gives me a reproving look. 'Your mother is a wonderful woman.'

'She is,' I say. 'You can rest easy knowing she'll come straight here if I need her.'

After a little more fussing and insisting on showing me one more time how to process refunds on the till, he disappears. I haven't had to issue any refunds so far, but it could happen. It's entirely possible that Bernard's owner will return at some point, telling me Bernard has cut his tongue on a raspberry pip, and she expects us to pay the vet's bill. I wonder if she'd be prepared to take the balance in doughnuts and cream slices. We always have plenty of those left over.

I busy myself for the next ten minutes uncovering the trays of cakes and unpacking the pallets of bread the lorry delivered this morning. I'm tempted to rearrange the cakes more attractively, making the brighter ones visible in order catch the eye of hungry customers. I decide against it. Mr Mason has assured me many times that his system is honed by long experience in the bakery trade. It doesn't appear to be a system that brings him much profit, but that's his own business.

I can't help feeling excited at being left alone in charge of the bakery. It's hardly a hub of activity, but if any crisis arises, it will be up to me to deal with it. Whatever happens, I have no intention of calling Mum. Ben would never let me hear the last of it. Neither would Jack, and I don't feel up to his merciless teasing right now.

I feel uncomfortable thinking about him at all. Last night was an absolute disaster from start to finish. I was so excited at the thought of our evening together. I was delighted to surprise him and looking forward to the usual evening of jokes and easy conversation, born of our long and uncomplicated friendship.

None of that worked out as I planned. First, there was the unexpected arrival of Isabella and Stephen, followed by Jack's inexplicable decision to invite them to join us. It probably didn't seem a big deal to him. He and I weren't on a date. We were having dinner together as so many times before. And, as he said, he always likes meeting new people.

I, on the other hand, found it extraordinarily difficult. Sitting opposite Stephen in a nice restaurant brought back memories of all the evenings we'd spent together in happier times. I'm surprised Jack didn't realise how painful it would be for me. It isn't like him to be so insensitive. His mind must have been elsewhere. Maybe he was wishing he was there with Carolyn instead of me.

I expect he was. They're in the first flush of a new relationship, when all you can think about is the other person, and you're counting the minutes until you see them again. It's odd he hasn't mentioned her before. There's no reason for him to keep his relationship a secret. He never has before, and neither have I. We always discuss our new loves and give advice and condole with each other when things don't work out.

It's obvious now that he didn't discuss his girlfriend with me because he thought I was developing feelings for him, which is ridiculous. He must know I'm still in love with Stephen. But I can't think of any other reason for his reticence. Our conversation last night certainly showed he was worried I had a crush on him.

It's so strange that we both came to the same conclusion about each other based on one stupid kiss. It isn't as though either of us enjoyed it. At least, not much. I was so caught up in the emotion of seeing Stephen and Isabella that I barely had time to think about what I was doing.

As for Jack, it's natural for most men to go along with it when someone kisses them, assuming they aren't utterly repulsed by that person. I hope Jack isn't utterly repulsed by me. And he happens to be an extremely good kisser, so it made it easier for me to pretend. But that's all. I wouldn't have done it if he'd told me he wasn't single. So, in a way, this whole thing was entirely his fault.

Chapter Twenty-Three

The morning passes at a snail's pace. The excitement of pretending to be a prominent local business owner quickly passes off. It's started to rain in a half-hearted, miserable sort of way. I wish it would make up its mind. I'm not too keen on rain, but a good hard downpour would wash away the grimy piles of snow dotted along the pavements. Fresh snow is exciting and magical, but snow which has melted and refrozen several times and now sits in grubby heaps is depressing.

People drift in and out through the morning, and I serve them without catastrophe. I haven't decided whether to close at lunchtime. What if I slip and break my leg on the way home? They would be no one to run the bakery this afternoon. It might not mean much in terms of sales, but Mr Mason is relying on me. This business is his baby, and I've promised to look after it.

I'm beginning to understand why he always seems so harried and anxious. It must be difficult if you don't have someone to pick up the slack when things go wrong. It's a bit like a relationship, assuming it's a good one. You know that whatever happens, someone else has your back and will do whatever it takes to support you, just as you would for them.

Hopefully, Mr Mason feels he can rely on me not to do any real damage while he's gone. I hope his wife is all right. I'll let Mum know about her this evening. She's always good at chatting with people and finding out what they need.

I've just decided not to take the risk of leaving the bakery for lunch when the door opens. Somewhat to my surprise, Isabella walks in. The last time I saw her, she was … but I've promised myself not to think about that. Still, I can't help feeling embarrassed at having to face her again so soon. I'm pleased she hasn't brought Stephen with her.

She doesn't appear to share my embarrassment. 'How's it going? You're about to close, aren't you? I thought I'd stop by and see whether you'd like to have lunch.'

'I can't,' I say. 'Mr Mason had to go home, and he left me in charge.'

Her eyebrows rise in fake astonishment. 'You've been promoted to assistant manager already?'

'Hardly! It's only for today, and you wouldn't believe how difficult it was to convince him he wouldn't come in tomorrow to find the place a heap of smouldering ruins.'

'How exciting!' she says. 'Can I light the match? I've always fancied myself as an arsonist.'

'Don't even joke about it! It would break the poor man's heart. He loves this place. It's been his life's work.'

'I can understand that,' she says. 'But if he isn't here, you can take a full hour.'

This thought had already occurred to me, but I dismissed it at once. Mum always tells me that ethics are what you do when no one is there to see you. I've taken on this job, and I'll see it through to the bitter end – no shirking, no bending of the rules.

'I've decided not to close for lunch,' I say. 'I know it sounds silly, but I'm worried something might prevent me from coming back. I'll feel happier if I don't take any unnecessary risks.'

'Fine, I'll stay here,' she says. 'You can take your lunch break without leaving the premises.'

'I wasn't planning on taking a lunch break at all,' I say. 'As you can see, I'm not exactly rushed off my feet working here.'

She turns the sign on the door from *Open* to *Closed* and takes off her coat. 'Everyone needs a lunch break.'

She looks at our displays. 'What shall we have?'

'I'm not allowed to eat the products,' I remind her, but she waves a dismissive hand.

'That's a ridiculous rule. He won't miss a cake or two.'

'It will be a lot more than that if you're here,' I say, pulling out my purse. 'Mr Mason will return to find half the stock gone.'

She picks up a tray of brownies and inspects them. 'I have a healthy appetite, that's all.'

'So does a boa constrictor,' I say. 'Choose what you want, but I'm paying for it. You bought lunch last time, remember?'

'Fine,' she says. 'But I always tell Stephen I'm not a cheap date.'

She wanders over to the cabinet at the far end of the counter. 'I didn't notice these last time I was here. Are they meat pies?'

'So we claim. I've never tried one, but the customers seem to enjoy them. Go ahead.'

'I'll have the steak and mushroom,' she says. 'How about you?'

'I'll try the chicken and leek,' I say, reaching for the tongs. 'I don't know where we can eat these. There aren't any chairs in here.'

I pay for the pies and point her towards Mr Mason's office, which is the only available space to sit.

'Don't get crumbs anywhere,' I warn her. 'I don't want him to know we were in here.'

'I'll eat quickly,' she says. 'I've always found that's the best way to avoid crumbs.'

I watch in awe as she disposes of the pie in three large bites. 'How do you stay so thin?'

She laughs. 'Genetics, I think. My mum says I have a tapeworm.'

'Do you?'

She carefully folds the paper bag. 'I have no idea. I don't think anyone's ever checked.'

I finish my own pie more slowly, trying not to drop any crumbs. 'And what would your tapeworm like for dessert?'

She chooses a large eclair and a couple of my carefully arranged macarons. I'll have to arrange them into a new pattern this afternoon.

I select a chocolate chip cookie and lean against the counter to eat it.

'Is that all you want?' she asks.

'We don't all have your expandable stomach.'

'True, but if I only had room for one thing, it wouldn't be a boring cookie.'

I stop with the cookie halfway to my mouth. So much has happened this week that I'd forgotten about Stephen and the original reason he came to the bakery.

'Cookies aren't boring,' I say. 'We sell lots of lovely flavours. I'm sure you'd enjoy them.'

She crams both the macarons into her mouth at once. 'Cookies are what you choose when there's nothing else more exciting on offer.'

'I don't agree,' I say. 'Cookies aren't the most exciting product, but I love them. They're reliable and consistent and comforting.'

She takes a huge bite of her eclair. 'Is that what you're looking for in your baked goods? I'm not. I like new flavours and unexpected tastes, and I always enjoy trying things I haven't come across before.'

'In which case, you'd probably enjoy my birthday cake,' I say in sudden recollection. 'Mum and I had some this morning, and we couldn't decide what flavour it was.'

Her eyes light up. 'It sounds amazing! I'd love to try it if you can spare me a slice.'

'You can have as much as you like,' I say. 'It's the cake Mr Mason gave me. Mum made my usual coffee and walnut cake.'

She finishes her eclair. 'What do you mean, your usual? Do you have the same birthday cake every single year?'

'Of course. Doesn't everybody?'

She looks horrified. 'I doubt it. Don't you ever want to try something different?'

'Not really. I did as a child, but by the time I was about ten, I realised I liked Mum's coffee and walnut cake best.'

'You and I are very different,' she says.

I'm not sure how to take this. Of course, we are. No two people are alike. Is she making a point about Stephen? I scrutinise her face, but she shows no sign of hostility.

'I suppose we are,' I say. 'Are you using our baked goods preferences as a metaphor for life?'

'Not really,' she says. 'But I wish I'd thought of it. My uncle made me go on an incredibly boring course when I started working for him. We had to do this weird personality test. Everyone took it, but the questions were ridiculous. I didn't fancy being pigeonholed by some paper pusher, so I didn't answer any of them honestly.'

'I had to do one of those when I started my last job,' I say. 'It didn't occur to me to be anything less than honest. Your way sounds more fun.'

She grins. 'I filled in all the questions as though I was a serial killer. I wanted to see what results I'd get.'

I give a snort of laughter. 'Did it warn your manager you were a psychopath?'

'Unfortunately, not,' she says. 'I'd have loved to see my uncle's face when he got my assessment. It said I was focused and results-oriented and showed meticulous attention to detail.'

'The test sounds pretty accurate to me,' I say. 'Those results are exactly what you'd expect from a serial killer. They'd have to be all those things if they wanted to be successful in their chosen career.'

'You make an excellent point,' she says. 'Maybe there's something in these tests after all. What did yours say?'

'Nothing very exciting, as far as I remember. It said I was conscientious and liked routine and was prone to worry about my mistakes.'

'All of which is pretty obvious from meeting you,' she says. 'I could have saved them loads of money if they'd asked me first.'

'Is that what you thought of me when we first met?' I ask.

'Among other things,' she says. 'You were anxious not to overstay your half hour for lunch, which shows you're conscientious. And you'd managed to work in this bakery for a week without chewing your own arm off with boredom, which shows you like routine.'

'That makes me sound dull,' I say.

'I don't think so. It's only a tiny part of who you are. The rest of it can't be measured with their stupid tests.'

She considers me carefully. 'You're very kind. You look after that old fusspot you work with, whereas he'd drive me mad in a day. You have a great sense of humour, and you're obviously intelligent or you wouldn't have passed all those exams. I'm sure there's more, but I don't know you very well yet.'

I'm rather touched by this. She seems sincere.

'What about you?' I say. 'What would the test have said about you if you weren't pretending to be Hannibal Lecter?'

'Goodness knows! I don't really care. I'm comfortable with who I am, which is all that matters.'

'You always seem so confident,' I say. 'It must be nice to feel that way. I rarely do.'

'You should,' she says. 'You have a lot going for you. Look at you – good qualifications, lovely family, fantastic boyfriend …'

I turn away so she doesn't see my expression. I'd forgotten about Jack. At least, I'd forgotten he was supposed to be my boyfriend. Ever since I heard about Carolyn, I've tried not to think about him at all. Each new person added to this deception makes me feel more guilty. And Carolyn is now a part of it, even if she doesn't know it.

Isabella doesn't deserve to be a part of it either. She's been nothing but nice to me since we met.

'I'm very lucky,' I mumble. 'But you have a good job too, and your family sounds nice. And you also have a fantastic boyfriend.'

'True,' she says, but she doesn't sound convinced. 'That's actually what I wanted to talk to you about today.'

'Your family?'

'I'm talking about Stephen.'

He's the last person I expected to be discussing today. I can't read her face, and my heart contracts in fear. Has she realised I'm still in love with him and come to warn me off? I don't think I can face any more humiliation, not until I've processed what happened between me and Jack last night.

'Stephen?' I say in a strangled voice.

'That's the one,' she says. 'Do you mind?'

I shake my head. If she has something to say, she may as well say it and get it over with. It won't make it any better to wait.

Her face is uncharacteristically serious. 'I hope you don't think it's cheeky of me to discuss him with his ex-girlfriend. It wouldn't have occurred to me if I hadn't seen how happy you are with Jack.'

I'm tempted to give a hollow laugh but restrain myself. If only she knew.

'Is anything wrong?' I ask.

'I'm not quite sure. Stephen's a great guy, and we get on really well. But I'm starting to wonder –'

She breaks off and stares out the window. 'He's very attractive, isn't he? I mean physically. That's the first thing I noticed about him.'

'He is,' I say cautiously.

She smiles. 'I have no complaints about that side of our relationship.'

'I know. I saw you both last night.'

She raises an eyebrow. 'There's the pot calling the kettle black! We saw you too.'

I can't help feeling pleased my plan worked. So, that was why Stephen drove off so quickly.

'You know how it is,' I say, trying to sound casual.

'I do, indeed. As I say, Stephen is a very attractive man. But I've been wondering lately how well suited we are. I haven't thought about it much because it's early days. But then we had dinner with you and Jack last night …'

'And?' I prompt her, hoping she says that seeing me and Stephen together made her realise that he and I are far better suited than they are.

'I was watching the pair of you,' she goes on. 'You looked so comfortable together. You practically finish each other's sentences, and you laugh at all the same things. Stephen and I don't laugh much. I do, but he doesn't. Last night made me question things more seriously. I want what you and Jack have, and I'm not sure I'll find that with Stephen.'

I have no idea what to say. I thought the pair of them were madly in love. They gave a good impression of it last night, at least the end of the night. I wonder how I can find out what Stephen thinks about their relationship.

'Have you talked to him about this?' I say.

'Not really. It's a casual thing. We've only been together a few months, and we don't see each other very often. Some relationships are worth working on, like yours and Jack's. I'm not sure this is one of them.'

I don't know why she's talking to me like this. It isn't, as I feared, because she thinks I'm after Stephen. In which case, what does she want? Does she want me to talk her into giving it some more time? That's the last thing I want to do. But I no longer want to break them up by any means possible.

'You told me you wanted some advice,' I say. 'About what, exactly?'

'About the best way to break up with him,' she says. 'You know him a lot better than I do, Lily. I don't want to hurt him more than I need to. I thought you might have some idea of how to do it gently.'

I stare at her, dumbfounded. Is the love of my life's current girlfriend seriously asking me how to go about breaking up with him?

'You know he's the one who broke up with me?' I say.

'I didn't. He hasn't talked much about you and him, and it wasn't my business to ask. Have I upset you? I didn't mean to.'

'You haven't upset me,' I say, surprised to find this is true. This is a bizarre situation, but I feel oddly detached from it all.

'I have to say I'm surprised,' she says. 'It never occurred to me that you hadn't broken up with him.'

'Why is that?' I ask with a painful jolt as I remember the events of a year ago.

'Because I've seen you with Jack. He's the complete opposite of Stephen. You and Jack have such an amazing relationship. I assumed you must have realised Stephen would never make you happy and broken up with him.'

A bewildering variety of emotions is sweeping through me. I can't untangle them, particularly not with Isabella standing right here. How can I tell her that Stephen is the perfect man for me in every possible way, and Jack and I are completely unsuited for each other? It's impossible without admitting I've been lying to everyone all week.

She seems convinced Jack is my soulmate, so she would take a fair bit of convincing. The only way would be to tell her about Carolyn. For some reason, I can't bear to do that, not until I've come to terms with having made such a complete fool of myself with Jack.

I need time on my own to get my thoughts in order and decide what I ought to do.

'I should open the bakery again,' I tell her. 'Can we talk about this later?'

'No problem,' she says. 'I have to go into work this afternoon, but I finish at five. Shall I come back at closing time? Maybe we can go for a drink.'

Going for a drink with Isabella is the last thing I want to do, but I can text her some excuse.

'I look forward to it,' I say untruthfully, wondering what Mum would say about my ethics if she could hear me now.

Isabella switches the sign on the door back to *Open* and waves goodbye. I watch her walk down the street and wonder what I'll say to her the next time we meet. It seems to be in my power to break up Stephen's new relationship, which is not at all what I expected when I met him last week. The only issue left to decide is exactly how and when.

Chapter Twenty-Four

Jack calls as I'm closing the bakery. 'How's it going?' he asks.

'Not too bad,' I say in a guarded tone.

'Do you fancy meeting up tonight?'

I was hoping to avoid him until I'd come to terms with the crashing fool I made of myself last night. But seeing him would give me the perfect excuse not to talk to Isabella tonight. I decide she's the more pressing of my two problems, and therefore the one I'd most like to avoid.

'I'm free around seven,' I say. 'I'm just closing up. Mr Mason left me in charge today.'

He whistles. 'Impressive stuff! I said you'd climb the greasy pole if you stuck to it.'

'How can I climb it if I'm stuck to it?'

'Don't be such a pedant,' he says. 'Are you up for a drink tonight? We could go to the Red Lion. That way, neither of us has to drive.'

If I have to face any kind of postmortem, I'm determined to do it with a drink in my hand. I'll use it to give myself some Dutch courage. If things get too bad, I can throw it in Jack's face and make a run for it. I'm not much of a drinker, but since coming home and embroiling myself in such a ridiculous set of circumstances, I've been thankful not to live in Prohibition times.

'Sounds good to me,' I say. 'See you there at seven?'

'I'll be there bang on time,' he says. 'Which probably means a quarter past.'

'I wouldn't expect anything less,' I say and ring off.

I finish closing up and call Mr Mason to ask how his wife is and reassure him nothing awful has happened to his shop. He doesn't answer, but I leave him a message telling him I'm happy to work alone tomorrow. After this, I text Isabella to tell her I'm not free tonight, after all, but I'll let her know when I am.

I arrive home feeling exhausted. Mum greets me at the door. 'You look pale. Is last night catching up with you?'

It is, but not in the way she means. I have the unpleasant sensation that several freight trains are rushing towards me at once, and I'm not sure which way to leap to avoid them all.

'I've had a busy day,' I say. 'Mr Mason's wife is ill, and he left me in charge of the shop.'

It's amusing to see the way her face struggles with conflicting expressions – sympathy for Mr Mason and pride that her little girl has managed the bakery all by herself.

Sympathy wins. 'That poor man! I'll pop around this evening and see if there's anything I can do.'

'Do you know what it is?' I ask.

'She has chronic bronchitis. January and February are always terrible months for her.'

'Poor thing,' I say. 'If you see Mr Mason tonight, let him know I'm happy to keep running the bakery for him.'

'Of course,' she says. 'Your dinner is almost ready, and then you should have a nice early night. You look exhausted. Did you have lots of customers?'

'The usual amount,' I say, 'but that's not why I'm tired. I didn't sleep well. I'm meeting Jack tonight, but I won't be home too late.'

She shakes her head indulgently. 'Oh, you young things. I can't keep up with you. Your father and I were the same at your age.'

I sincerely hope not. I'd like to think I'm the first one in our family to have messed things up to quite this extent.

Ben is absent for dinner. When I ask where he is, Mum looks delighted. 'Mia asked him over for dinner this evening. It's a good sign, don't you think? She wouldn't have asked him if she thought there was no hope for them.'

'It's a great sign,' I say. I really hope she and Ben manage to work it out. There's no point in us both being alone and miserable.

I reach the pub at seven o'clock. Jack can be as early or as late as he likes. I don't really mind. It's one of the things that makes him Jack. I remember he said to Isabella that he likes me because of my flaws, not despite them. That was such a sweet thing to say. I hope he meant it.

Somewhat to my surprise, he's already there when I arrive.

I join him at the bar. 'I assume your watch is broken?'

'This is me turning over a new leaf,' he says. 'I took on board what you said about my pathological lateness.'

'Don't say that!' I say, stricken. 'I was thinking that your lateness is one of your most endearing qualities.'

The corner of his mouth lifts. 'You're a difficult woman to please, Lily Carson. First, you tell me you don't like something about me. As soon as I change it, you ask me to change back.'

'I shouldn't have mentioned it at all,' I say. 'I felt backed into a corner, that's all. It would have looked strange if I'd said you were absolutely perfect. Stephen would have smelled a rat.'

'I see,' he says. 'What are you drinking?'

I wait until we're sitting at a table before asking, 'How does Carolyn feel about your lack of punctuality?'

'Carolyn?' he says vaguely. His brow clears. 'Sorry, I was miles away.'

He takes a reflective sip of his drink. 'I don't know. She's never mentioned it.'

'Which means it doesn't bother her,' I say. 'Are you going to tell me some more about her? I'm bursting with curiosity. All you've told me is that she lives in Weymouth, and you met at a bar. That wouldn't help me pick her out of a crowd.'

'What do you want to know?'

'Everything!' I say with as much enthusiasm as I can muster. 'How old is she? What does she look like? What does she like doing in her spare time? Can you see yourself staying with her forever?'

He lifts a hand. 'Slow down! This isn't a police interrogation.'

'Sorry.' I settle into my seat and wait for him to answer.

He takes a surprisingly long time to speak. He doesn't seem eager to talk about her. He may not want to jinx a promising new relationship by saying too much about it. Or he may be having doubts and doesn't want to discuss them.

'Jack, this is me,' I say when he doesn't break the silence. 'You can talk to me about anything. You know that. You've told me about your other girlfriends. Why not this one?'

'I don't mind talking about her,' he says. 'You just asked so many questions, I didn't know where to start. Let's see, she's a year or so younger than me. She's a similar height and colouring to you. She likes doing the same things I do. What was the last question? Oh, yes. Do I see myself staying with her forever?'

He downs the rest of his drink in one gulp. 'To be honest, Lily, I'm not sure. I'd like to think so, but I don't honestly feel it's likely.'

'Oh, well,' I say, sounding like Mum. 'Time will tell.'

'Indeed, it will,' he says with the flicker of a smile. 'What will be, will be. What goes around, comes around. We all have to go with the flow.'

'How wise you've grown since I last saw you,' I say. 'Seriously, Jack, I hope it works out for you if that's what you want.'

'It is what I want,' he says. 'But I have no idea what she wants.'

'Ask her! It seems the simplest answer.'

'Do you really think that?' he says, his expression unusually intense.

'Of course.'

I pick up our glasses. 'And now, I have something to tell you. I'll get us a refill first. This could take a while.'

I return with our drinks and sit down. 'I told you I was in charge today. Isabella dropped by to ask me to go to lunch, but I'd already decided not to close the bakery. So, she ended up having lunch with me at work.'

'Poor Mr Mason,' he comments.

'Mr Mason is fine,' I say. 'What the eye doesn't see, the heart doesn't grieve after.'

He grins. 'Aren't we full of platitudes today?'

'I think they're sayings.'

'Whatever,' he says. 'Get on with the story. What happened over lunch? Did the pair of you eat all the stock, so there was nothing left to sell this afternoon?'

'We tried,' I admit. 'But not that. You'll never guess what she told me?'

I lower my voice, although no one can hear. The pub is packed, as it always is on a winter's evening. There's far too much noise for anyone to listen in to anyone else's conversation.

'She told me she's thinking of breaking up with Stephen!' I lean back in my chair and watch his reaction to this bombshell.

'Is that right?' he says. 'I can't say I'm surprised.'

I jerk upright. 'I was! They were all over each other last night.'

'So were we,' he reminds me. 'And that meant nothing.'

'True, but we're in a very weird situation.'

'You're telling me,' he says.

'And I've already told you I would never have kissed you if I'd known you had a girlfriend. You know me better than that.'

'I do,' he says. 'I'm simply pointing out that one person kissing another isn't proof they're madly in love.'

'I don't see what else it can mean,' I say stubbornly.

He smiles. 'I don't suppose you do. You see things in black and white, don't you?'

'Another of the many things you love about me?'

He doesn't rise to the bait. 'I can think of plenty of reasons why a person would kiss someone in that way. They might feel they ought to, or they might want other people to see them, or they might be trying to breathe some life into a flagging relationship.'

'Which do you think was their reason?' I ask.

'The last one,' he says without hesitation. 'I've only just met them, but it was obvious within the first five minutes they didn't make sense as a couple. They're so different.'

'Opposites attract,' I say. I feel impelled to remind him of this because Stephen and I are opposites, yet we maintained a successful relationship for quite a while. Maybe we will again.

'Not that sort of opposite,' he says. 'Some differences are fine. An introvert can be happy with an extrovert, for example. But that isn't the sort of thing we're talking about.'

I'm surprised by his certainty. He barely knows Stephen, and he only met Isabella for the first time last night, and under rather unusual circumstances. It isn't like him to make snap judgements about anyone, let alone dismiss an entire relationship without ascertaining all the facts.

'What makes you so sure they aren't suited for each other?' I say.

I'm secretly hoping he says that, having observed me with Stephen, he can see us being very happy together.

'It's difficult to put into words,' he says. 'They have different outlooks on life. It's not that he's quiet, and she's bubbly, or he likes skiing, and she doesn't. It's more fundamental than that. They see things so differently, and they want different things out of life. A relationship like that never lasts.'

I'm pleased to think he expects Stephen to be free soon. If he is, what's to stop the pair of us trying again? I almost broach the subject, but it seems ghoulish to be picking over the bones of someone else's relationship with a view to making a move myself.

'What about you and Carolyn?' I say. 'Are you a case of opposites attracting, or are you one of those disgustingly over-compatible couples who wear matching sweaters and share an email address?'

'Never that!' he says with a horrified look. 'As for the rest of it, I'm not sure. All I know is we get on well, and we share the same values. Also, we laugh a lot.'

'That's a good one,' I agree. 'Although it isn't a complete deal breaker if everything else is right.'

'What did you tell Isabella?' he asks.

'About Stephen? I didn't say much at the time, but I texted her this afternoon to say it might be kinder not to break up with him right before Valentine's Day.'

'Is it any better to do it right after?' he says.

'I'm not sure. Neither option is great. Stephen broke up with me the week after Valentine's Day, and it was awful. It felt as though everything about that day had been fake. There was I, enjoying our lovely romantic trip, while he was secretly plotting to get rid of me straight afterwards.'

Jack's lips twitch. 'It all sounds very dramatic. It wasn't a murder mystery.'

His face lights up. 'Maybe it was. Is that why he took you up there – he thought it was a good place to hide a body? You had a narrow escape, Lily. I wonder why he changed his mind.'

'You aren't being very kind to someone who had their heart broken,' I complain.

'I'm sorry. I got carried away with the drama of it all. It was thoughtful of you to advise Isabella against doing that. You're a kind person, Lily.'

Speaking of being kind, would you like another drink?' I say, a little embarrassed by the sincerity in his voice.

He glances at his phone. 'I won't, thanks. I should get going. There are a couple of things I need to do.'

He helps me on with my coat, and I follow him to the door, wondering what these unspecified things are, and why he doesn't mention them. He probably wants to go home and call Carolyn. Of course, he does. It must be difficult to keep a long-distance relationship going, especially in the early days.

We step outside into the frosty night and start to walk down the high street together. A motorbike backfires behind us, and I swing around in alarm.

Jack takes my arm. 'It's fine. Just a motorbike.'

I don't answer. Even in the dark, I'm almost sure I recognised the couple going into the pub. The man had his arm around the woman's shoulders, and they were laughing together.

So, Isabella has taken my advice not to break up with Stephen right now. Was what she said to me today only a passing whim? Has she thought it over and decided Stephen's good points far outweigh the bad ones?

If so, where does that leave me? I gave up on Stephen entirely when I came home and heard about Isabella. Then we had dinner, and I wondered just how compatible they really were. But that was followed by seeing him kiss her, which confused me further.

I no longer know what to think. All I can hope is that things resolve themselves sooner rather than later. I can't take much more of this uncertainty.

Chapter Twenty-Five

I wake early on Valentine's Day and slip downstairs as quietly as possible to avoid Mum. I'm not in the mood for cheery conversation today. I pour myself a cup of coffee, pull on my coat and boots, and leave the house. I decide to walk the long way to work. I want to clear my head before I have to see Stephen and give him Isabella's cookies. It will be painful, but it may give me the closure I need and allow me to move on once and for all.

I thought Stephen was the love of my life, but it seems I was wrong. I fell madly in love with him and wanted to spend the rest of my life with him, but he didn't feel the same. When that happens, the only thing left to do is accept it with as much grace as possible and move on, hoping the heartbreak will gradually disappear. That's what I have to do now.

I walk several times around the village, warming up as I go. Yesterday's snowfall is white and unblemished, and the village looks like the illustration on a chocolate box. I walk past a row of thatched cottages and admire the way the snow has settled on the roofs, obliterating the thatch. They look like gingerbread houses with beautifully iced roofs, just like the cookies I iced yesterday evening before the bakery closed. The houses are far more symmetrical than my creations. Still, I did my best. As Mum always tells me, no one can do more than that.

Mr Mason arrives a minute after me and opens up the shop. We've fallen into a routine, which I find helpful today. I don't want to think about anything in too much detail. I want to get through the day, go home, and take a long, hot bath while I attempt to make plans for my immediate future.

'Did you put those cookies into a box for Mr Parker?' Mr Mason asks me.

'Over there,' I say. 'I expect he'll be in to collect them soon.'

He nods but looks distracted. 'I wonder whether you would mind looking after the shop for a couple of hours, Lily. My wife wasn't feeling too good this morning, and I'm a little concerned about her.'

'Of course,' I say. 'Take all the time you need. I can look after the bakery for the entire day if you like.'

He gives me a relieved smile. 'It's such a comfort having you here, my dear. I wouldn't have trusted the last girl to stay alone in the shop for even five minutes.'

Not for the first time, I wonder what this girl was like. Mr Mason has never been explicit, but from the occasional dark hints he's dropped, I picture her as somewhere between Typhoid Mary and Jack the Ripper.

'You should take your wife one of those,' I say, pointing to the heart-shaped cookies sitting on the counter. 'It's Valentine's Day, after all.'

'Do you know, I think I will?' He selects the largest one and puts it into a bag.

'Would you like me to ice a message on it?' I say.

He considers this. 'Perhaps her initials?'

I fill the icing bag with pink frosting. 'I'm afraid I don't know your wife's first name.'

'Daisy,' he says. 'Daisy Mason.'

'That's a pretty name,' I say. 'Daisies are my favourite flower.'

He looks pleased as he watches me pipe an uneven *DM* onto the cookie. I finish with a pink flourish and put it into a box, so the writing doesn't smudge.

He sets off up the street, clutching his striped bakery box as though it's the crown jewels. I hope his wife likes it. I hope the pair of them have a lovely Valentine's Day. Just because I've been dreading this day doesn't mean that other people shouldn't enjoy it. It's a celebration of love, and there isn't enough of that in the world.

I arrange the heart-shaped cookies more attractively on their tray and wait for the influx of loved-up customers. But either people have organised their Valentine's Day well in advance or Honeywell is one of the most unromantic villages in England, because an hour passes with no customers. I pass the time by rearranging the macarons into what, by narrowing my eyes and standing well back, might just about resemble a Cupid's heart.

I'm about to start taking inventory when a car pulls up outside. My heart contracts when I see it's Stephen. I take a deep breath and prepare to face him for what may be the last time.

He opens the bakery door and looks around. 'Good. You're alone.'

'Mr Mason's been called away.'

'I'm glad,' he says, coming up to the counter.

I reach for his box of cookies. 'Here they are. I've done my best with them. They haven't been iced to a professional standard, but you aren't paying professional prices.'

I try to smile as I hold out the box to him.

He doesn't take it. 'I came in to ask you to do me some more.'

He wants me to redo the cookies without even seeing them? I feel a flash of annoyance that he assumes my work isn't good enough.

He reads my expression. 'I'm sure they're lovely.'

'I wouldn't go that far,' I say. 'But it's a little offensive to assume I've messed up without looking at them.'

'I wouldn't dream of making such an assumption,' he says. 'I'm not managing this very well, am I?'

'Why do you need more? Do you have several more secret girlfriends hidden around the village I ought to know about?'

'No secret girlfriends,' he says, 'but I'd still like you to ice me one last batch of cookies.'

I reach for the icing bag again. 'I have no idea what you're talking about, but let's get on with it. I can't write a long message. We only have –' I quickly count the remaining cookies – 'six left. That's Isabella's fault for having such a long name.'

He smiles. 'I only need four.'

I select the most symmetrical cookies. 'Here I am, icing bag at the ready. What do you want them to say?'

'Can you write an *L* on the first one?' he says.

I obediently trace the letter *L* onto the first cookie. 'Now what?'

'The next one is *I*,' he says.

I squeeze the bag to make sure there aren't any bubbles and trace a wobbly *I* onto the cookie. 'I'm almost out of icing, but I should have enough for two more.'

'The third letter is also an *L*,' he says.

I obediently start to pipe another *L* onto the cookie, then stop. What's going on here? Four cookies, and the first three letters are *LIL* … There can't be that many four-letter words in the English language starting with L.

My mind races through the possibilities, but I can only come up with three – lilt, lilo, and lily.

There's no reason for Stephen to write the word lilt on a row of cookies. Maybe he's writing lilo because he's planning to take Isabella on a tropical vacation, and this is his way of telling her what to pack. I imagine them bobbing merrily on the waves on his-and-hers flotation devices, but I know I'm being ridiculous. Which only leaves …

I raise my eyes to his, hardly daring to believe what's happening. He's smiling down at me with the expression I remember so well, the expression he used to wear before he smashed my heart into a million pieces.

I can't speak, but my eyes ask a question.

He nods. 'The last letter is *Y*.'

I don't pick up the icing bag. 'But why, Stephen?'

'Because I've been a complete idiot,' he says. 'I threw away the best thing that ever happened to me, and I'm hoping it's not too late. Please say it isn't, Lily. I know you've been seeing this Jack guy, but that isn't serious.'

I stare at him, my heart pounding. I can't believe this is finally happening. I've hoped against hope all year that Stephen would change his mind and come back to me. And now he has, just as I dreamed he would.

Everything I've ever wanted is standing in front of me. All I have to do is reach out and take it. All I have to do is pick up the icing bag and ice that final *Y*, and everything will return to the way it used to be.

Stephen leans towards me. 'Lily?'

Even the way he says my name is the same it used to be – gentle, loving, and playful. A shiver goes down my spine as I remember he always said my name like that right before he kissed me.

I look down at the cookies, then at Stephen. This is all happening too fast. He isn't giving me time to think.

'Lily?' he says again. 'Perhaps I should tell you I broke up with Isabella last night.'

I don't want to say anything that might betray her confidence. But it's important for me to know the truth.

'Are you sure you broke up with her?' I say.

'What a ridiculous question. Of course, I'm sure. We had a long talk last night, and we agreed it was best for both of us.'

'She didn't break up with you?' I say.

'Oh, I see what you mean. No, I've been thinking about it for a while. We weren't as well suited as I first thought. Certainly, not as well suited as you and I were, and still are.'

He told me when we broke up that we weren't compatible on a long-term basis. But dating someone incompatible may have helped him to realise his mistake. I can't hold that against him forever. Everyone's allowed to make mistakes. I've made plenty in my time, one in particular since I arrived home last week.

'So, you've changed your mind about us being compatible?' I say.

'I'm so sorry, Lily. I don't know what I was thinking. It took me a while to realise the truth, but we got there in the end.'

'*You* got there in the end,' I correct him. 'I never thought we were incompatible.'

'Either way. The important thing is that we both realise how we feel. There's no mistake that can't be put right if we want it enough.'

'What about Isabella?' I say.

'What about her?'

'Was she devastated?' I already know the answer to this, but I'm interested to hear his take on it.

'She didn't say so,' he says.

'But you must know,' I insist. 'You broke up with her out of the blue. Surely, you'd expect her to be upset?'

He has the grace to turn pink, but he doesn't lose his composure. 'She may be sad in the short term, but she'll realise I acted for the best. If she and I aren't compatible, we shouldn't take it any further.'

'Is that what you told yourself when we broke up?'

He considers. 'I think so. It seemed unkind to continue with a relationship I wasn't sure about.'

He has a point. It's irrelevant that I didn't agree with his decision. No one owes anyone else a relationship. If one party decides it isn't what they want, they have a perfect right to say so.

'Are you going to check up on her?' I ask. 'Right before Valentine's Day is a pretty rough time to break up with someone.'

'I know,' he admits. 'I thought about waiting until after the day itself, but it seemed worse to spend the day with her, pretending everything was fine, and drop the bombshell straight afterwards.'

The conclusion he arrived at is the opposite of the advice I gave Isabella. But there are no absolute rights and wrongs in these situations. The important thing is that he thought about it and tried to do the right thing. It helps to restore my trust in him as the decent person I've always known him to be.

'I hope you check to see she's ok,' I say. 'Breakups are always difficult.'

I try not to speak in an accusing tone, but his face flickers. 'I know, and I'm sorry for how I treated you. That's one of the things I came to tell you today.'

'What was the other thing?' I ask. I know what it is, but I want to hear him say it. I've dreamed of having this conversation with him all year, and I refuse to be deprived of it.

He reaches for my hand. 'I wanted to tell you I still love you and ask if we can try again. I should never have let you go, Lily. I see that now. But it doesn't have to be too late.'

'You're aware I already have a boyfriend?' I say, moving my hand away.

He gives me a quizzical look. 'I'm aware that you say you have.'

'What's that supposed to mean? You've met Jack. You've had dinner with him, for goodness' sake. You saw us –'

I break off. That kiss wasn't my finest hour, and I've been trying to forget it ever since it happened.

'I know what I saw,' he says calmly. 'What I don't know is whether I was meant to see it.'

'Not at all! We were caught up in the moment.'

He doesn't look convinced. 'If you say so, but none of it rings true to me. Be honest with me, Lily. Are you and Jack really in a relationship?'

How dare he assume I would do anything so petty and ridiculous as faking a relationship to get back at him for dating someone else? It wasn't like that at all. At least, it was more complicated than that.

'You don't think someone like Jack could fall for someone like me?' I say.

'Quite the reverse. I don't think someone like you could fall for someone like him.'

I feel defensive on Jack's behalf. 'Why not? He's a great guy. He's smart and fun and easy to spend time with and –'

'I'm sure he is,' he says before I can enumerate any more of Jack's wonderful qualities. 'But that's not the point. You and he don't belong together. Anyone can see that.'

'Isabella couldn't! She told me we made a wonderful couple. In fact –' I break off. Stephen doesn't need to know it's one of the reasons she planned to break up with him.

'That's because she doesn't know you as well as I do,' he says.

His expression softens. 'Maybe no one does. I'm sure this Jack guy is everything you say he is. That doesn't mean the pair of you are romantically compatible.'

I want to argue further, but I remember Carolyn. There's no point in making a futile argument about me and Jack belonging together when I'm perfectly aware he's my fake boyfriend. Stephen has guessed the truth without much difficulty. I should have known he would.

But I'm not going down without a fight.

'You didn't think we were so well suited when we were together,' I say. 'It's only now I'm with someone else that you realise it.'

'No, it isn't,' he says. 'I've been thinking about it for some time. I almost contacted you in the autumn, but then I met Isabella, and I wondered whether I was wrong about you and me. She was so different to you in every way, and it was tempting to see whether she might suit me better. But I soon realised my mistake. No one has ever suited me as well as you, Lily. No one ever will.'

My heart gives a small flutter. That's a pretty romantic thing for anyone to say. And I know how much Stephen hates admitting he's been wrong. It must have taken courage for him to come here and admit it today.

There's still the small matter of Jack, but it will be a relief for him to hear Stephen and I are back together. We can stop playing this stupid game, and he can concentrate on his wonderful new relationship with Carolyn.

'I can't give you an answer right now,' I say. 'Whatever you may think about Jack, he's the person I've been seeing. He and I need to talk before I do anything else.'

The bell jangles, and there's a rush of icy air as the door opens. This had better not be Bernard's owner, here to complain he's thrown up the pineapple macaron she bought him yesterday, and she intends to bill us for the carpet cleaning.

But it isn't her, and neither is it Mr Mason, returning to his post. To my surprise, I see Jack standing in the doorway, holding a brightly wrapped parcel.

Chapter Twenty-Six

He closes the door and turns to face me. My brain is whirling too madly for me to speak. He looks at my flushed face, then down at the cookies lying on the counter.

'Lilo?' he says. 'Are you going on holiday, Stephen?'

I give a choke of laughter. 'That's what I said! At least, I thought it.'

Jack's mouth twitches. 'Of course, you did.'

'You're just the man we need,' says Stephen. 'Lily wants to talk to you.'

'Is that right?' says Jack. He turns to me. 'I think I can guess why. But go ahead.'

It's ridiculous to feel this surge of guilt. He'll be relieved to put this whole charade to bed once and for all. From the looks of it, he's heading off to visit Carolyn after this. I may as well tell him what's happening and get it over with.

'Stephen thinks you and I are only pretending to be a couple!' I blurt out.

I can't think what makes me begin with this. I meant to tell him calmly and quietly that Stephen has asked if we can give things another go. After long and mature consideration, that's what I'm doing. After two minutes' consideration? Two seconds? It isn't relevant. It's the right decision, so I don't need to spend time agonising over it.

'And what do you think about that?' says Jack.

I don't know what he means. What does it matter what I think? We both know Stephen is right. He's seen straight through our ridiculous pretence. I don't know why I thought he wouldn't. I'm lucky it didn't annoy him and stop him from asking me for another chance.

'I'm not sure what you mean,' I say.

Jack doesn't drop his gaze from mine. 'I'm not interested in what Stephen thinks about our relationship. I want to know what you think about it.'

I draw him to one side, murmuring in a low voice so Stephen can't hear.

'What are you doing? He's right. You and I have only been pretending to have a relationship. We don't need to do that anymore. Have you forgotten you have an actual girlfriend, as well as a pretend one?'

'You mean Caitlin?' he says.

'You told me her name was Carolyn,' I say.

His eyes light with sudden laughter. 'Did I? That's because it's the name her parents gave her when she was born. But when she was five, she decided to change it because she didn't think it suited her. Naturally, I call her by her preferred name.'

My mind is racing, trying to remember the conversations he and I have had about this girlfriend. There haven't been many. He didn't even mention her existence until the night we had dinner at The Oasis.

What has he told me about her? They share the same values and enjoy doing the same things, and they laugh a lot. What else? She's a year younger than him and about my height and colouring. He'd love to think they'll stay together, but he doesn't think it's likely. That's strange in itself. If he likes her so much, and they have so much in common and so much fun, why can't he see himself staying with her long term? It must be because he thinks she doesn't feel the same way. There can't be any other explanation.

Jack is smiling at me in the way he always does when he isn't sure how I'll react.

Stephen clears his throat. 'Are you ready, Lily?'

I turn to face him. 'Why did you think Jack and I were pretending?'

'Is it important?' he asks.

'I need to know. I can't explain why, but it will give me closure.'

'Fine, although I don't see the point.'

He thinks for a moment. 'It's all pretty simple. I didn't question it when you first told me about your new boyfriend. Nothing was more natural than for you to have moved on. I was happy for you. But when I thought about it later, I wondered why you seemed so upset when I told you about Isabella.'

'You didn't just tell me about her. You asked me to ice her some cookies,' I remind him.

'True,' he agrees. 'It was an awkward situation all around. So, I put it out of my mind. But when we had dinner on Sunday evening, I knew for sure.'

'You did?' I rummage through my memory, trying to discover what gave us away.

He smiles. 'Come on, Lily. It's clear Jack isn't the right man for you. I started thinking back to our relationship and the sort of things we used to do together and the discussions we had about serious subjects. It was obvious you and Jack would never do any of those things. All you did was laugh and make jokes.'

'You mean we enjoyed ourselves?'

He shakes his head. 'That's fine as far as it goes. But I know you better than you know yourself, Lily. You're looking for more than that from a long-term relationship. You don't want to waste your time messing around with a lightweight.'

Jack starts to speak, but I lift a hand to stop him. 'Perhaps you know me as well as you say, Stephen, but maybe Jack does too.'

'As a friend,' says Stephen. His eyes soften. 'But he'll never know you as I know you. Which means he'll never love you as I do because he'll never understand the real you.'

The silence lengthens as I think about this. Is Stephen right to say he knows me better than I know myself? He's told me this me before, and I've accepted it as a sign that he and I are soul mates.

Jack is watching me intently, his face no longer amused.

'What's in the parcel?' I ask suddenly.

He looks down at the box he's holding as though he's not sure how it got there. 'Something I thought you might like.'

'Can I open it now?' I say, and he hands it to me.

I lay the parcel on the counter, smiling at the over-the-top wrapping paper, covered with silver cupids and bright pink hearts.

'Is this all they sell at the post office?' I ask.

His eyes dance. 'I had to go online to find that wrapping paper. It took me a while, I can tell you. Most of it was tasteful and discreet. But I got there in the end.'

I pull the paper away, trying not to tear it more than I have to. Inside is a vivid pink box. It looks familiar.

'Is this one of ours?' I ask.

Jack grins. 'I'm afraid so. I had to buy quite a few cookies before your boss would give me this. It took me a long time to paint it this tasteful shade of bubble-gum pink. But I knew you'd want something subtle.'

I inspect it more closely. 'The silver glitter is an especially classy touch. You used a fair bit of glue, I see.'

'The post office only sells one size,' he says. 'It seemed a waste not to use it all.'

I lift the lid and look inside. 'Cookies?'

'Valentine's cookies,' he corrects me.

'You realise I work in a bakery?'

'I do, but so what? It occurred to me that customers would be coming in all day to buy things for the people they love, and I wanted you to have something too.'

'Are these our cookies?' I ask.

'That's right. I wanted to do my bit to boost the local economy and make sure you kept your job.'

'It's hardly my dream job,' I object.

'But it's local,' he says.

I pick up the nearest cookie. 'What happened to this one? Did you ice it yourself?'

He frowns. 'This must be how Picasso felt when uneducated people commented on his paintings. It's a picture. Perhaps it isn't as sophisticated as your beautiful calligraphy, but I did my best.'

I peer at it more closely. 'Is that a wine glass?'

He looks pleased. 'Not just any wineglass. It's the one I gave you for your university graduation. It was Waterford Crystal, and it cost me a week's wages. You broke it a week later when we came home after an evening out and didn't dare put the lights on because of your grumpy landlord.'

'This one is even nicer,' I assure him.

I pick up the next cookie. 'Is this a mountain or a traffic cone?'

'It's a tent!' he says. 'Don't you remember that time we went camping and neither of us knew how to put up our tents? There was a thunderstorm during the night, and they collapsed on top of us.'

'And we had to take the overnight train home,' I say. 'Thank goodness the bar was open!'

He points to the next cookie. 'That's the train. I've smudged the windows a bit, but you get the general idea.'

I pick up the third one. 'Is this a snake? No, it's a rollercoaster!'

'That one took me a long time,' he says. 'The blobs of blue icing are us. I think I caught our likeness very well.'

'What's the pink blob?'

'It's the candyfloss you insisted on eating. I warned you, but you refused to listen.'

'I'm sorry I was sick on you,' I say. 'You didn't put that on a cookie too?'

'I'm not so heartless,' he says.

I look at the white shape on the next cookie. 'Is that an ice skate?'

'Got it in one! You insisted on taking me, much against my better judgement. You'll notice there's a bandage around the edge of the cookie.'

I turn to Stephen, laughing. 'I sprained my ankle really badly. We had to sit in Accident and Emergency half the night. All they had in the vending machines was cheese crackers and Dr Pepper.'

He doesn't smile. 'That sounds stressful.'

'It was one of the best nights of my life,' I assure him. 'I've never laughed so much.'

I look at the last two cookies. 'That multi-coloured one has to be trivial pursuit.'

'Drunken trivial pursuit,' says Jack. 'It's the best kind.'

I pick up the final cookie. 'I'm not sure what this is?'

Jack leans over to see. 'That's you wearing your new red dress, the one you wore to The Oasis.'

'And that must be you making a rare appearance in your smart grey suit,' I say. 'What are we doing?'

One corner of his mouth turns up. 'You're kissing me.'

'It looks more like you're kissing me,' I say.

'Does it matter? It's one of my very favourite memories with you. It belongs with the rest of them.'

I lay the cookie back in its box and turn to Stephen. 'I'm really sorry, but there's been some misunderstanding. I'm not sure why you think Jack and I aren't in a relationship, but I'm afraid you're wrong. He and I are in exactly the sort of relationship I've always wanted and never had.'

'Because he decorated a few cookies for you?' he says. 'You were about to say yes to me before Jack came in. I know you were.'

'Maybe I was, but it would have been the biggest mistake of my life. And it isn't because of the cookies. At least, not entirely, although they helped me see things more clearly.'

'This is ridiculous,' he says. 'You aren't over me any more than I'm over you.'

'Maybe I wasn't fully over you,' I say slowly. 'But the person I wasn't over was someone I never knew. And he didn't know me at all. Even when you came in here today, wanting to get back together, you expected me to ice my own name on those cookies. Jack took the time and trouble to do it himself, which shows he knows me better than you ever will.'

Stephen doesn't speak, and I feel a pang of guilt. I've never wanted to hurt him, and I still don't. But that doesn't mean I want to spend the rest of my life with him.

'If that's the way you feel,' he says at last, 'there's nothing more to be said. You have to do whatever's best for you, Lily. All I can do is wish you well.'

He nods to Jack and turns to leave the shop.

'Don't forget the cookies you ordered,' I say. 'You've already paid for them.'

'You keep them,' he says.

I watch him stride along the pavement and climb into his car. I can't believe what I've done. I've spent an entire year waiting and hoping for Stephen to come back to me. When he finally did, I sent him away again. I wonder for a moment whether I've done the right thing, but in my heart of hearts, I know I have. And I know exactly why.

I turn to face Jack. 'You've spent the past two weeks being my fake boyfriend, even while you thought I was in love with someone else. Do you think you could ever consider being my real boyfriend?'

He shakes his head. 'I'm not sure, Lily. This is awfully sudden. I need some time to process all these emotions and get some kind of – what did you call it – closure?'

I'm too disappointed to speak, so I just nod.

He grins. 'Sometimes, I think you don't know me at all.'

He takes a step towards me and brushes a finger over my cheek before tilting my face up to his.

'Lily, I've been in love with you for years. I've almost told you many times, but I was too afraid of losing you. Then you met Stephen, and I thought I'd lost you forever. I was going to tell you how I felt after you kissed me on your birthday, but then I realised you'd only done it to make Stephen jealous. It seemed that no matter what happened, you would always be in love with him, and there would be no chance for me.'

Tears are pricking the back of my eyes, but I'm too happy to cry. I look up into my best friend's face. 'So, what happens now?'

'This!' he says with decision and kisses me.

It feels like only five seconds later, but it could be five minutes, or five hours, when the doorbell jangles. I jump and try to pull away from Jack.

'Leave it,' he murmurs. 'Let the answerphone get it.'

'It's the shop bell. I'm supposed to be working.'

I turn around, expecting to see Mr Mason. He'll probably fire me on the spot for flagrant misconduct. At this moment, I don't much care, but it would be a shame for my career at the Sugarloaf to end this way.

It isn't Mr Mason. It's his arch enemy, the woman with the cavoodle. She's standing in the doorway, looking at us as though we've tried to force feed Bernard a chocolate brownie.

I smooth down my hair. 'Good morning. Can I help you?'

Bernard ambles in behind her and gives me an idiotic grin.

'I can't let your dog into the shop,' I say. 'My boss isn't here, but I know he wouldn't be pleased.'

'Is that so?' she says snidely. 'And I doubt he'd be pleased to hear his employee spends all her time canoodling while he's away.'

Jack looks delighted. 'Canoodling! I'll have to add that one to the list.'

'It's hardly all my time,' I tell the woman. 'And it's Valentine's Day,' I add in an attempt to soften her heart.

It doesn't have the required effect. She makes a harrumphing sound. 'That's no excuse. All this talk of health and safety, yet I walk in to find this sort of thing going on! I'll make very sure your boss hears of it when he gets back.'

I can't think of anything to say. Hopefully, I can persuade Mr Mason to take a lenient view of the situation, but he may take her complaint seriously.

Jack is quicker. He picks up Stephen's box of cookies and hands it to her with a courtly bow.

'In the spirit of St. Valentine, perhaps you would accept this as a complimentary gift for one of our bakery's most valued customers.'

She takes the box and peers inside as though she expects it to contain a hand grenade. She squints at the cookies. 'What do these say – I S A …?'

'They're completely random letters,' Jack assures her. 'My girlfriend has made up several boxes of these. Any words or proper names you may form are entirely coincidental. But you can imagine what fun our customers will have with them.'

'Hmmm,' she says.

'I'm sure Bernard will enjoy them,' I add. 'He loves our cookies, and there's no chocolate in them.'

Bernard is yapping excitedly, leaping up and down to catch a glimpse of the contents of this mystery box.

The woman pats his head. 'In a moment, Bernie. Mummy will give you a lovely treat as soon as we get home.'

She tucks the box firmly under her arm. 'I'll let it go this time. But I don't wish to see this sort of behaviour when I come in here to buy my cakes.'

'It will never happen again,' I assure her.

'Don't count on it,' Jack mutters.

We watch the woman walk down the high street, with Bernard frisking around her in anticipation of the treat he's been promised. As soon as she's out of sight, Jack walks over to the shop door and switches the sign from *Open* to *Closed.*

'You can't do that!' I say. 'Mr Mason might lose valuable business.'

'I'll buy up his entire stock, if need be,' he promises. 'But I'm sick and tired of all these interruptions.'

I try to remember my staff training, the list of rules on the wall, my flowered tabard, and even the unflattering hairnet I now remember I'm still wearing. But it's no good. All I can think of is that I'm finally alone with the man who has loved me for years, patiently waiting for me to realise I love him too.

Jack pulls me into his arms, and this time I don't resist. The look on his face makes my heart pound.

'Happy Valentine's Day, Lily,' he says, bending his head towards mine.

I slip my arms around his neck and look deep into his eyes, a wave of happiness washing over me.

'Thank you for visiting us at The Sugarloaf Bakery today,' I whisper. 'I hope your experience was everything you hoped for.'

A Sweet Romantic Comedy

A Sugarloaf Mix-Up

ROSEMARY WHITTAKER

Chapter One

Mum's voice floats up the stairs for the third time in five minutes. 'You'll be late, Abby!'

'No, I won't!' I shout. 'My interview isn't for another half an hour.'

I peer over the banisters. As I expected, Mum is standing in the hall, looking up at me.

'I'll be down in a minute,' I tell her.

I return to my bedroom and look at myself in the mirror. This feels worse than getting ready for a first date. I scan myself from head to toe in case I've missed anything major. I had a dream last night where I turned up for my interview with my hair neatly brushed and my blouse ironed. It wasn't until the interviewer, who looked like a cross between my old French teacher and Winston Churchill, gave me an odd look that I realised I'd left my skirt on the train on the way there.

I look down at my legs, which I'm happy to see are appropriately covered in navy blue trousers. I check that I'm wearing matching shoes and decide it's the best I can do. This interview shouldn't depend on me dressing like a server at a five-star restaurant. If I get the job, I'll spend the next twelve months in a white overall with my hair tucked under a cap. But Mum's right to say I need to make a good first impression. I don't know how many other people may have applied.

None of them will be as keen as I am. Being offered this position would mean I could leave my current awful job in Reading and move to Honeywell to be nearer to my parents while Dad recovers from his stroke. I almost put that on my application, but decided it wasn't professional.

I won't mention it today unless I'm asked. It would look too much like blackmail. I tell myself yet again there's no reason for them not to employ me. I'm qualified and have plenty of experience. I'd be an asset to their business.

Mum is waiting in the hall, looking more nervous than I feel. 'You look lovely, Abby. I'm sure you'll get it. I have a good feeling.'

Mum and her good feelings! If even a tenth of them were accurate, we'd be living in a mansion and taking holidays abroad several times a year. And Dad wouldn't be needing any more treatment.

This isn't a productive path to go down. Dad is ill, and we all have to cope with it however we can. But it would make things a lot easier if I lived locally.

'I'll give it my best shot,' I say as cheerfully as possible. 'I'm wearing my lucky earrings. The ones you and Dad gave me for Christmas.'

Mum peers at my ears. 'I'd forgotten about those. Dad chose them for you because he liked the colour. I didn't know they were your lucky earrings.'

'They will be if I get this job. Shall I say goodbye to him?'

'You'd better not,' she says. 'He was asleep when I looked in, but he told me to wish you luck and say how proud of you he is.'

I doubt this is true. Dad hasn't been able to speak more than a few words since his stroke. But I realise Mum is speaking for both of them, and she's saying what she knows he would have told me if he could.

'That's lovely,' I say. 'If he wakes up before I get back, tell him I'll do my best. He always said that was all anyone could do.'

Mum sighs, then smiles. 'He's quite right. I'm sorry I can't drive you, but I don't like to leave him alone.'

'I'll be fine,' I reassure her. 'Don't tell Dad I've taken his car. You know how he is about letting other people anywhere near it. He'll be driving again soon, and I don't want him checking it from head to toe for scratches.'

'I wouldn't let you drive it if I didn't think you'd take care of it,' she says. 'Off you go now. I'll be thinking of you.'

I swing the car out of the driveway and set off towards the high street. I would usually walk such a short distance, but it's been drizzling all morning. It's stopped for now, but I wouldn't put it past the rain to start again the minute I'm too far from the house to turn back. I've also straightened my hair for the occasion, and ten minutes in the rain would turn it back into its usual curly state. I don't know who decided straight hair was more professional than wavy, nor when the edict went out, but it makes things far more difficult.

Having spent almost an hour on achieving the effect, it would be a shame for my new employers to miss out on the full glory of my freshly straightened hair. My possible new employers, I remind myself. I mustn't get ahead of myself, no matter how confident Mum is, or how confident she pretends to be.

She's so keen for me to get this job. It would be wonderful for her to have someone else to help her out and give her the occasional hour to herself. The local nurses are great, but they're constantly rushed off their feet with an unreasonable workload. Dad is now officially convalescent, so he needs physical therapy and rehabilitation rather than urgent medical treatment.

It shocked me when I arrived home last night to see how grey and worn Mum was looking. I've done what I can to help since Dad had his stroke. But I work long hours, and the train ride home takes nearly three hours, so everything has fallen on Mum.

I park behind the shops and take a few deep breaths to compose myself. I look at my reflection in the mirror, happy to see I'm still interview ready. I check to see whether any mysterious substance has become lodged in my teeth, then decide I can't procrastinate any longer.

I carefully lock the car. Dad can't speak clearly at the moment, but he understands everything we say to him. The occupational therapist says anything that stimulates his brain is valuable, so we should talk to him as much as possible. But I doubt that includes informing him his pride and joy has been stolen. I don't want to be the one to explain that his car has disappeared and is even now on its way to the local chop shop.

I walk along the high street, careful to avoid any puddles that might take it into their heads to jump out at me as I pass. The village has changed since I was a girl. The old-fashioned sweet shop has been replaced by a barber's shop, and the post office has been absorbed into the mini supermarket. The gift shop next to the bakery has entirely disappeared. I stop outside the bakery and look in at the window, where I'm greeted by an intriguing view of my head surrounded by floating meringues.

A young woman with fair, curly hair is sitting at one of the cafe tables. She looks up and smiles when I open the door. 'Welcome to The Sugarloaf Bakery. How can I help you today?'

Chapter Two

I had a speech all prepared, but I can't remember a word of it. Something about being delighted to be considered as a viable member of the Sugarloaf team and looking forward to making an already successful business even more amazing.

Luckily for me, the woman speaks first. 'How are you today?'

Now is the time for my professional smile and polished speech of introduction, but my tongue won't cooperate. It feels as though it's swollen to twice its usual size and has no intention of ever forming words again. I glance down at my legs to check my trousers haven't disappeared during the short walk from the car.

The woman's smile widens. 'Would you like an eclair? I'm about ready for one.'

I blink. 'An eclair?'

'This *is* a bakery,' she points out.

'I'm not a customer,' I say.

'I know you aren't. Neither am I.'

Does this woman even work here? Maybe she's wandered in off the street and has the staff neatly tied up in the back room while she empties the till. I consider backing away very slowly and telling her I was after some stamps, but I've remembered where the post office is, and I'm sorry to have bothered her. How long would it take for the police to arrive? It's a rural area, so probably a while. They'll have more pressing countryside crimes to take care of first, like tractor vandalism or egg theft.

The possible burglar looks amused. 'If eclairs aren't your thing, how about a cream doughnut? Everyone likes cream doughnuts.'

Should I accept this offer to keep her off her guard? What if she's spiked them? A light soporific isn't outside the bounds of possibility. Even now, the rest of the staff members may be snoring lightly, oblivious to the crime taking place on their premises.

'I'll join you,' she says. She walks over to the counter, picks up two trays of cakes, and holds them out to me. 'Choose your poison.'

I take a step backwards and put my hands behind my back.

She laughs. 'Not the most amusing joke when you're trying to sell food! Lily is always telling me off for saying that sort of thing in front of the customers.'

Lily? That's the name of the person who set up this meeting. Maybe this woman isn't an intruder after all. Meanwhile, I'm not making the greatest impression. Time for a reset.

'I'm Abby,' I say. 'I'm here for an interview. I'm supposed to meet someone called Lily. Is she here?'

The woman puts down the trays and holds out her hand. 'I'm Isabella, Lily's business partner. She should be here any minute. You're a little early.'

'I like to be early for things,' I say. This isn't strictly true, but it's the sort of thing a prospective employer likes to hear.

'I'm the complete opposite,' she says. 'This is the first job I've ever arrived on time. Nothing less than the lure of coffee and cakes gets me out of bed on a winter morning. Speaking of which, where did we land on the question of eclairs versus doughnuts? I'd be interested to hear your professional opinion.'

Is this my actual interview? If so, my answer may be a deal breaker. She may be allergic to choux pastry or have been swindled out of her life savings by a doughnut salesperson.

'Let's sit down while you're thinking about it,' she says.

I follow her to a table by the window. She nods towards the coffee machine at the far end of the counter. 'Can you work one of those?'

'I've used that model before,' I say. 'I worked as a barista during college.'

She picks up an eclair and takes a bite. 'Great. We're off to a good start.'

Have I got this wrong? The advertisement clearly asked for a pastry chef. Do they want someone to make coffee instead? My heart contracts with disappointment. I'll have to tell Mum I won't be moving home, and she'll need to look after Dad all by herself. I can't bear to think of her face falling before she forces a smile and says it doesn't matter. She's doing fine all by herself.

Isabella swallows her mouthful of cake. 'Are you ok?'

'There's been some mistake,' I say. 'I answered the advertisement for a pastry chef, not a barista.'

'I know you did. I asked whether you could work the machine because I thought you might like some coffee with your cake. I can do it otherwise.'

'I'd love a coffee,' I say. 'Shall I make one for you too?'

'If you don't mind. I'm a coffee fiend, and I've only had three cups this morning.' She doesn't appear to be joking.

'What would you like?' I say.

'Cappuccino, please. Extra-large.' She finishes her eclair and bites into a doughnut.

I make us both a cappuccino and she takes a sip. 'This is great. If your baking is as good as your coffee making, this is a lucky day for us. You aren't eating anything. Don't you like cake?'

I love cake. Who doesn't? But no one has ever greeted me with plates of cakes at an interview, and I'm not sure of the etiquette. What if I squeeze too hard and end up with cream all over my shirt? But I don't want to appear rude, so I pick up a doughnut and take a cautious bite.

Isabella watches me expectantly. 'What do you think?'

This is a potential minefield. I don't know who made the doughnuts. For all I know, Isabella may have made them herself and be expecting a compliment. Or she may have a supplier she isn't happy with and want to know whether I can tell a great doughnut from a mediocre one.

Her face gives no sign of what she's thinking. I could land myself in hot water either way, so I may as well be honest.

'They aren't bad,' I say. 'They're a little blander than I'd like, and the ratio of cream to dough isn't optimal.'

I wait for the tears to spring to her eyes as she tells me she made these using the recipe her great-great grandmother created when she cooked for the Tsar of Russia, then passed onto her daughter on her deathbed.

She regards me thoughtfully. 'How about the eclairs?'

I don't know what she thinks of my previous answer, and her face isn't giving anything away. If this really is a treasured family recipe, either something has got lost in the translation or the Tsar wasn't too fussy about his pastries.

I throw caution to the winds. The worst she can do is throw me out, in which case I'll offer to come in and sweep the floors each evening. I need to move back to Honeywell for a year. I can't leave Mum to handle everything by herself.

I bite into an eclair. 'It's a little dry. It can be tricky making choux pastry, but these seem to have been left in the oven too long. It's a common mistake, especially when you're baking in bulk.'

'I see,' she says. 'Would you like to try a meringue?'

Will this interview comprise me tasting every single product in the shop to test my tolerance for sugar? A blood glucose test would be simpler.

'Is there a problem with your meringues?' I ask.

'Not at all,' she says. 'They're fantastic. But you don't seem keen on our eclairs and doughnuts. I'd like to offer you something you might actually enjoy.'

'The cakes are fine,' I say. 'You asked for my professional opinion, and I gave it. Can I ask who made them?'

'Our supplier delivered them.'

I relax. Unless the supplier is some near and dear relation, I probably haven't offended her family honour.

'Do you have everything delivered?' I say.

'Most of it,' she says. 'How much do you know about our bakery? Are you a local?'

'I grew up here, and I remember coming to this bakery as a child. I left for catering college when I was eighteen and didn't come back. I spent a while working in a hotel in Switzerland, and I've been living in Reading for the past few years.'

'I grew up in this area too,' she says. 'Oddly enough, I didn't discover this place until a couple of years ago.'

She gives a mischievous grin. 'Strange, really. I thought I knew all the best places to get cake for miles around.'

'My mum told me it went downhill for a while,' I say. 'She mentioned some new buyers had taken over and completely renovated the place. She'd pretty much stopped coming here, but she often stops in now for her bread. She enjoys being able to buy things locally. My Dad hasn't been well, and it isn't always easy for her to leave him to drive to the supermarket.'

'What does she think of our new cafe?' she asks.

'She hasn't tried it yet. She said you've only recently opened it. I'm sure she'll come in soon.'

'Unless you put her off by telling her our cakes are dry,' says Isabella.

'I wouldn't dream of it!'

She laughs. 'I'm kidding. We've only just got the bakery up and running again. We've been incredibly busy with the renovations. We were lucky the gift shop didn't renew their lease last year. We took over their premises, knocked the two buildings into one, and turned the gift shop into a cafe. You wouldn't believe the amount of work it took to get all the planning permissions. After that, we had the builders in for months, so we were living in a cloud of dust, which isn't great when you're selling food. Lily had the brilliant idea of starting a delivery business until the building work was done, and that kept us afloat until it was all sorted.'

She looks around the cafe. 'Now it's time for phase two. That's where you come in.'

'I'd love to be involved,' I say. 'Start-ups are always exciting. You get the chance to put your stamp on the whole thing.'

'That's what we think,' she says. 'But neither of us are chefs. Lily was an office manager before she worked here, and I worked in accounts. We have the business side of things pretty well covered, and now we need someone to work their magic in the bakery. What do you say? Are you up for it?'

I blink in surprise. 'Do you mean I've got the job?'

She nods. 'Your resume is excellent, you make a great cappuccino, and you told me the truth about our cakes. That's good enough for me.'

'What about your partner? Doesn't she need to meet me too?'

'Of course,' she says. 'Neither of us does anything without the other one's say-so. But Lily won't object. She has enough on her mind right now without second guessing any of my decisions.'

She turns her head to look out of the window. 'Here she is, right on time, as usual. Let's hear what she has to say.'

Chapter Three

The door opens, and a woman walks in. She's about the same age as me, with straight blonde hair. She and Isabella could be in a commercial for the before and after photos of some hair product.

One application of Smooth Easy and you'll never have to worry about straightening your unruly hair again.

Lily looks exhausted, which is probably because she's pregnant. She sinks into the nearest chair with a sigh of relief.

'How many times do I have to tell you not to turn that sign around?' she asks Isabella. 'I met Mrs Ogilvie in the car park, and she was most put out. She said she wanted to buy a wholegrain loaf, but the bakery was closed, so she was going to the supermarket instead. She wasn't sure she'd be back at all if we couldn't stick to our advertised opening hours.'

'She's all talk,' says Isabella. 'She likes our lemon meringue tarts far too much to desert us.'

'It's bad for business,' says Lily.

She catches sight of me. 'Hello, are you Abby?'

I hold out my hand. 'I am. Nice to meet you, and congratulations! I assume this job is to cover your maternity leave?'

'That's right. Have you and Isabella been having a chat?'

Her eyes fall on our table, and she laughs. 'I needn't have asked. I hope she offered you one of those. Her manners tend to disappear when she sees cake.'

Isabella looks affronted. 'Any cake consumption is purely in the interests of research.'

Lily raises an eyebrow. 'Which of you was doing the actual research? The reason we aren't yet in profit, Abby, is because my business partner here insists on eating most of the stock.'

'You're hardly one to talk,' says Isabella. 'Nothing has been safe around here since you found out you were pregnant.'

Lily sighs. 'It's true. As soon as I got over my morning sickness, I developed the worst sugar cravings imaginable. Jack says if the baby isn't born looking like a cupcake, it won't be from lack of effort on my part.'

'There are worse things to look like than a cupcake,' I say consolingly.

'Very true,' says Isabella. 'Bran muffins or hoagies would be far uglier.'

'Do you know whether it's a boy or a girl?' I ask Lily.

'We decided we'd prefer it to be a surprise,' she says. 'Isabella wasn't happy. She hates waiting for anything.'

'I'm planning to name the baby,' says Isabella. 'Lily is considering boring names that wouldn't do our business any good. I'm thinking about Croissantine for a girl and Bagelbert for a boy.'

'Or Ryely,' I suggest. 'That would work for either sex.'

She looks pleased. 'I knew I'd enjoy working with you.'

'There was no actual need for you to come in today,' she tells Lily. 'I've given Abby an exhaustive interview and found her to be sound on all aspects of baked goods. She also makes an excellent cappuccino.'

'Would you like me to leave while you discuss this?' I say awkwardly.

'No need,' says Isabella. 'Abby also agrees with me that our doughnuts are bland, and the eclairs are dry.'

Lily smiles. 'I notice it hasn't stopped you from eating an entire plateful.'

'I've already told you,' says Isabella. 'That was research.'

'Your resume is impressive,' Lily tells me. 'I've been wondering why you want to work at a small bakery with no proven track record.'

'Her father's ill,' interrupts Isabella. 'She wants to move home for a while.'

'I didn't say that!' I protest. I'd hate for Lily to think I've been spinning Isabella some sob story to get the job.

'You didn't have to,' says Isabella. 'Of course, you want to come home if your father's ill. Will you be living with your parents?'

'If I get the job,' I say. 'But I'm not trying to use that to –'

'I know you aren't,' says Lily.

'No one thought you were,' agrees Isabella. 'I didn't offer you the job because your father was ill. I offered it because I thought you'd fit in well around here.'

I look at Lily, who laughs. 'Who am I to argue? I won't be here for long anyway. If Isabella would like to work with you, that's good enough for me. It's only for a year. Possibly less. I haven't yet decided when I'll be returning to work. Is that alright with you?'

'More than alright!' I say joyfully. 'I can't believe I've got the job. Don't you have other candidates to interview?'

'Not really,' says Isabella. 'At least, none with similar resumes to yours. Come through to the office, and I'll get started on the paperwork.'

'We'll need to contact your referees,' says Lily. 'Assuming they all check out, when can you start?'

'Almost at once,' I say. 'I'm on a zero-hour contract in my current job.'

'I hate those!' says Isabella. 'They're simply an excuse not to treat your staff properly. The only good thing about them is that you don't have to work a notice period. It serves your employer right.'

I follow her to the office, where she takes some further details and tells me she'll be in touch.

I leave her filling in forms and go to find Lily, who's busy refilling the depleted cake trays.

She gives me a guilty smile when I appear. 'I thought I should check to see whether you and Isabella were right. I agree, these doughnuts are bland. I look forward to seeing what you come up with.'

'I'll do my best,' I promise.

The door opens, and a woman comes in with a small dog in tow. She gives me a suspicious look, but I beam back at her. I don't care what the customers here are like. I've got the job!

I almost skip back to the car. Mum will be delighted. Dad will too if he understands. I hope he does. I hope he'll be pleased I'm around a bit more, even if he doesn't know exactly why.

I park his car in the garage and walk around to the kitchen, where I find Mum making a pot of tea.

'Is there enough for me?' I ask. 'Interviewing is thirsty work.'

She spins around, almost dropping the tea pot. 'I didn't hear the car. How did it go?'

I was planning to tease her, to look sad and shake my head as though I'd messed things up. Looking at her anxious face, I don't have the heart. She seems to have aged ten years during the past few months.

I give her a hug. 'You're looking at the newest team member of The Sugarloaf Bakery!'

She makes a sound somewhere between a scream and a sob. 'I can't believe it! You're coming home?'

'For a while, at least. This job is only temporary. It depends how long my new boss decides to take off for her maternity leave.'

She wipes her eyes. 'It will be so good to have you here. And your employer has no idea what's about to hit her. She may not want to come back to work for a while.'

'You make it sound as though children are a chore,' I complain.

'Not at all,' she says. 'But they're extremely hard work. Do we know for sure she's only having the one?'

'I think she'd have mentioned if she was having twins.'

She doesn't look convinced. 'Margaret Wilson had no idea she was having twins until out they popped. The doctors were most surprised. They said she wasn't nearly big enough.'

'I expect that was before they had scans,' I say.

'Medical science doesn't know everything,' says Mum. 'I'm going to keep my fingers crossed it's triplets. I'll finish making the tea while you tell your dad the good news.'

I move towards the door, then stop. 'Is there any point? He won't understand.'

She turns to face me, her hands on her hips. 'I don't want to hear any more talk like that. Your father may not understand everything we say to him, but he's improving every day. You have some exciting news, and he is a much-valued member of our family. Off you go now and tell him all about it. And don't you dare leave out a single detail!'

Chapter Four

I find Dad in the living room sitting in his usual chair. Mum has turned it to face the garden, and Dad is looking out at what used to be his favourite place. A fox sometimes comes in the evening and stands on the patio watching us, disappearing as soon as we make the slightest movement. Dad has christened him Foxy Loxy.

'Looking for Foxy Loxy?' I say. 'He doesn't usually arrive until dusk.'

Dad gives no sign he's aware of my presence. But Mum is right. We need to behave as though he understands everything we say to him and include him in everything that's going on.

'I've been for a job interview,' I say. 'It was at The Sugarloaf Bakery, the one on the high street. You and Mum used to send me there for croissants on Saturday mornings. I hardly recognised the place. It changed hands a couple of years ago, and the new owners have expanded and rebuilt. They've added a cafe where the old gift shop used to be. It's lovely. I'll take you up there when you're more mobile.'

Mum comes in with the tea tray and sets it down between us. 'Is Abby telling you all about her morning?'

Dad doesn't reply, but he blinks a couple of times. I feel a little hurt that he responds to Mum and not to me, but it makes sense. She's with him all the time, whereas I'm only here for a few hours each week.

'Have you told him?' whispers Mum.

'I was about to,' I murmur back. I raise my voice. 'They offered me the job, and I said yes. So, I'll be moving back home in a few days. Just when you thought you'd got rid of me!'

I don't know why I expect Dad to react to a feeble joke when he hasn't even acknowledged my presence. I give Mum a helpless look, and she pats my arm.

'Isn't that lovely, Geoffrey?' she says. 'Abby says she's coming back to live with us for a few months. You'll be able to have lots of lovely talks together.'

She pours us a cup of tea and picks up Dad's cup. I hate seeing this sign of his utter dependence and inability to care for himself. It reminds me of how close we came to losing him. Dad was such a strong, capable man, always busy around the house and garden. Now he's sitting there while Mum gives him his cooled tea out of what looks like a child's sippy cup.

She doesn't seem to notice my discomfiture. She must be used to all the small indignities that make up Dad's life. I doubt he is.

She sips her own tea while she helps him drink his, all the while keeping up a steady flow of chatter.

'It will be lovely having Abby home, won't it, love? It will give you a new face to look at instead of being stuck with me all day. She and I can do a little gardening if she has time. It's got out of hand since you've been … unwell.'

For the first time, there's a slight break in her voice. I glance at her quickly, but she gives me an encouraging smile and jerks her head towards Dad.

'Of course, I will!' I say a little too loudly. 'I'm not great at gardening, but I'll have a go if someone tells me what needs doing. Do you remember the time I was about four when Mum was working in the garden and wanted to give me something to do? She found that bucket I used to take to the beach and filled it with water so I could water the flowers. As soon as she took her eye off me, I added a scoop of compost and "washed" all the downstairs windows with mud.'

Dad doesn't react, although he and Mum have been telling me that story ever since it happened. Mum behaves as though it's the most uproarious thing she's ever heard.

She wipes her eyes at last. 'Lunch will be ready soon. You two have a nice chat while I serve up.'

I jump to my feet. 'I'll finish lunch while you stay and chat with Dad. That's what I'm here for.'

Mum looks dubious, which is a little insulting.

'I went to a catering college,' I remind her. 'You can trust me not to burn the soup.'

'Of course, you did. But you're a pastry chef. I have nothing in the fridge for dessert.'

'I've had enough of that to last me all week,' I assure her. 'I had to taste half the products in the shop this morning and give my expert opinion. The new owners are most enthusiastic about their products. I hope I can live up to their expectations, especially as one of them is eating for two.'

I catch Mum's eye and grin. 'Or three or four.'

'Get along with you and your nonsense,' she says. 'That's Lily Carson, isn't it? I know her mother slightly. She brought me a meal when your father was in hospital. She's terribly excited about becoming a grandmother. It's her first.'

She gives me a meaningful look, but I don't rise to the bait. She's been convinced every single one of my boyfriends is *the one*, which I've taken to mean the one who might give her the grandchildren she's always dreamed of. Except for Jake Harrison in year twelve. Mum would have been horrified to be connected with him or his family in any way. She had several pointed conversations with me that year about paying attention during my health education classes and not skipping any of them.

I wash up after lunch and say goodbye to Dad, who's sitting by the garden window again and shows no sign of hearing me. I tell him I'm going back to Reading to collect my things, and I'll be home again in a couple of days.

I say goodbye to Mum, who looks almost tearful as she hugs me.

'I'll be back before the weekend,' I promise.

'I know,' she says. 'But I'm so delighted you're coming home, I'm frightened something will happen to stop it.'

'Nothing will,' I say. 'I'll take extra care when crossing the road, and I'll wrap up warmly if it gets cold. My taxi's only a minute away. I have to go.'

I give her another hug, and she goes back to the living room to sit with Dad. How does she stay so patient and hopeful when the man she married has completely disappeared, and she doesn't know who he'll be when he finally returns?

She must love him very much to put her life on hold like this and watch all her dreams for their retirement fade away. I resolve to spend as little time as possible in Reading. Honeywell is my home for the foreseeable future. The sooner I get back here and make a start on my new life, the better.

Chapter Five

My flatmate Emily is out when I arrive, and I don't see her all evening. When she arrives home in the early hours, she's in no condition to talk about anything.

I leave the house the following morning and walk to the North Street Bakery to see my manager. As I told Isabella, I'm only on a zero-hour contract, but she'll be contacting Matt for a reference, so I need to keep him sweet.

Liam looks surprised when I walk in. 'Hi, Abby, I didn't think you were working today. You aren't on the roster.'

'I'm not,' I say. 'I'm here to see Matt. Is he in?'

'He's in his office. He seems in a bad mood.'

'When isn't he?' I say.

I head upstairs to Matt's office. It's at the back of the building, next to what he euphemistically describes as the *Staff Relaxation Room.* It contains two chairs of the type we used to sit on in primary school. There's a small table that originally had four legs but lost one in some unspecified accident. It now wobbles quietly in the corner, muttering to itself about days gone by when tables had to stand on their own four feet. There's a rusty sink in the other corner, and a microwave with a frayed cord that looks as though it belongs in a museum.

I tap at the door of Matt's office and wait. Our beloved boss is somewhat mercurial, depending on what he got up to the previous evening. There's no answer, so I tap again.

'Who is it?' a voice barks.

'It's Abby.'

'Abby who?'

This isn't the time for knock-knock jokes, so I suppress an impulse to say, 'Abby wanting to see you!' and put my head around the door.

'Hi, Matt. Do you have a minute?'

Obviously, it's been a heavy night. He blinks at me in bemusement. 'I thought it was someone called Abby.'

'That's me,' I say.

'Oh, that's right. I had it in my head you were called Bridget.'

I almost ask what connection these two names have for him, but I doubt I want to know.

'I'm here to let you know I'm moving,' I say.

He frowns. 'What does that have to do with me? You don't get paid for personal days. Read your contract.'

'You never gave me one,' I remind him.

'That's because you didn't need one!' he says triumphantly. 'You're a casual, right? That means you work when I say you do, and you don't work when I say you don't.'

'Fine,' I say. 'But that works both ways. I don't work when I say I don't.'

'You what?'

I try again. 'I'm moving away. My father's been ill, and I'm going home for a while. My parents live in the New Forest, so I can't work here anymore.'

'The New Forest isn't that far,' he says.

'Are you offering to pay for my petrol?'

His face turns purple. 'Are you mad? I have no responsibility to sort out my employees' travel!'

'I realise that,' I say. 'I'm letting you know I won't be available for any more shifts. I could have called, but I thought it would be more polite to tell you in person.'

He gives me a blank look. Politeness isn't a word anyone would associate with this man. No wonder he has trouble comprehending my meaning.

I press on. 'I've found a new job in my parents' village. They'll be contacting you for a reference. I was wondering …'

I don't finish the sentence. He must follow what I'm saying.

He gives a guffaw. 'You've got a cheek letting me down without a moment's notice, then expecting me to give you a reference.'

'It's a normal request,' I say. 'Can you let them know I've worked here for the past couple of years and done a good job?'

'I'll tell them you can't read,' he says. 'So, they'll have to spell out to you exactly what is and isn't in your contract. Otherwise, you'll be trying to trick them into paying your accommodation and electricity bill.'

'I've already looked at the contract,' I say. 'I'm happy with my terms and conditions.'

I don't add that the Sugarloaf is paying me almost twice as much as he does, and my new employers offer sick leave and pension. I really want that reference.

He notices my presence again. 'Are you still here? I'll say you worked here for a while and managed not to burn the place down entirely. Will that do?'

'Thanks,' I say. 'Goodbye, then.'

He makes a dismissive gesture. 'Bye, Bridget.'

I go downstairs to the bakery and say goodbye to Liam. He's far more sympathetic about Dad and sends my parents his best wishes.

'Let me know if any other openings come up at your new place,' he says. 'I can't wait to get out of this dump. I don't know how you've stood it for so long.'

'It's a mystery,' I say and leave the place with far more of a spring in my step than when I arrived.

I arrive home to find Emily emerging from the depths of sleep. She's pale and puffy-eyed and makes a shushing gesture when she sees me.

'Whatever you were about to say, don't! Not unless the flat is literally on fire.'

'You've been here all morning,' I say. 'Wouldn't you have noticed?'

'I'm in no state to notice anything.'

I switch on the kettle. 'I'll make you a coffee, if you can bear the noise.'

'That would be nice,' she says. 'I'll go into the other room so I don't have to listen to that awful gurgling and hissing.'

It must have been a rough night. Emily has a much harder head than me. She can drink most people under the table, and frequently does. She stays out until the early hours and rolls in unable to see straight. She still leaves for her job at an investment firm at seven o'clock the following morning, perfectly groomed and with a serene expression on her face, to wrestle with the enigma that is stocks and shares.

Maybe she's getting old. I've felt that way ever since the awful day a week before Christmas when Mum called in tears from the hospital to say Dad had been rushed there in an ambulance, and she had no idea what was wrong.

I push the memory away. It doesn't help to dwell on all the what-ifs. What would have happened if Mum hadn't come home unexpectedly from her shopping trip and found him unconscious? What if the ambulance hadn't been nearby when she called? I've been through these scenarios repeatedly, and it doesn't do any good.

She did come home and find him, and they got him to hospital in time to stabilise him and start treatment. For all our sakes, I have to let go of my morbid imaginings and hold on to the idea he's going to make a full recovery. He will if Mum has anything to do with it. She's been amazing since it happened. I could never have coped half as well.

I take the coffee to the living room, where I find Emily stretched out on the sofa with her eyes closed.

'Never again,' she says as I hand her a mug.

'I've heard that before.'

'This time, I mean it. I have to make some changes.'

'I've heard that before too.'

She tucks her legs under her and takes a sip of coffee. 'This is perfect. No one makes coffee like you, Abby. What would I do without you?'

There's an awkward silence while I think about how to tell her she'll be making her own coffee from now on. And those cinnamon rolls I always bake on Saturday mornings.

'I'm glad it's helping,' I say. 'I need to talk to you when you're feeling better.'

'Talk to me now.' She settles herself more comfortably into the cushions and looks at me expectantly.

I decide to rip off the band-aid. 'I got the job.'

She looks blank, so I elaborate. 'The job I interviewed for yesterday. The bakery in Honeywell where my parents live.'

Her face clears. 'I remember now. They offered it to you?'

'On the spot,' I say.

I can't help feeling proud. Two years of working for Matt has sapped my confidence in my abilities. I can't imagine how I stayed there so long. Actually, I can, but that's no longer relevant.

'That's wonderful!' she says. 'When do you start?'

'Almost at once. They said I could go in on Monday for my orientation if I'm free. I'm only waiting for my references to come through.'

She grins. 'Did you have to ask Greasy Matt for a reference? How did that go?'

'About as well as I could have hoped. He didn't throw anything. He seemed happy enough once I'd assured him I wasn't expecting him to pay for the move. The reference will probably be for someone named Bridget, but my new employers seem pretty understanding. I'll do my best to explain to them.'

'I told you I'd be your back-up referee,' she says.

'You're an investment banker,' I point out, in case that fact has slipped her mind after her recent Bacchanalian orgy.

'No one thing defines me, babe,' she says with a grin. 'For all anyone knows, you could have been single-handedly organising the catering for our events for years.'

'I'm sorry I'm not giving you more notice,' I say. 'I'll pay you a month's rent in lieu.'

'Don't worry,' she says. 'I expect I'll find someone pretty quickly. Victoria at work asked me only the other day whether I knew of anyone looking for a flat share. She and I would get along fine. She's quiet and doesn't seem to go out much, but she's very nice.

'You could do with a bit of quiet,' I say.

She shrugs. 'You're pretty quiet, but we've worked out fine. We've each done our own thing. I've gone clubbing and met interesting people, and you've had –'

She breaks off, looking guilty.

'Paul,' I say. 'It's fine. You can say his name.'

'I didn't know if it was too soon. You were pretty cut up about it. I wasn't sure how long it would take you to get over him.'

'I'm not quite there,' I admit. 'But I'm getting there. Besides, Paul would never have understood why I needed to go back home. He didn't even like it when I visited my parents for the weekend when he wasn't working.'

She pulls a face. 'Not a good sign.'

I feel impelled to defend him. 'He put in such long hours, it was understandable that he wanted to see me on his rare days off. I tried to visit my parents when he was working or travelling, but things changed after Dad had his stroke. I had to go home whenever I could, and it was hard on Paul.'

She doesn't say anything. She must know there's no point. We've had this conversation a million times since the breakup, and we never get anywhere.

I tell her about my interview, and she laughs at Isabella's cake fixation.

'I wish my interviews were like that. All I ever get is a cup of machine coffee while I go through their fantasy share portfolio, tell them their investment strategy has been created by an idiot, then discover they developed it themselves and are extremely proud of it.'

'At least you're paid in line with your abilities,' I say. 'I have to fight Matt for my wages. The staff schedules go missing, and he has no recollection of me working the hours I claim. That's something I won't miss in my new job.'

'It was your choice to stay there,' she says. 'You wanted to be near Paul, or you could have found somewhere better.'

She's right, but she's putting an unsympathetic spin on it. Paul kept talking about us moving in together, so it seemed ridiculous to change my job before he'd decided where he'd like us to live. That took longer than I expected. Things kept getting in the way, and he couldn't get himself into the right headspace for making big decisions.

That's all in the past anyway. He met someone else and fell in love. It happens. His new partner owns a large house on the edge of the city, so they didn't even have to look for somewhere to rent.

It's left me free to look for a job nearer to my parents, although I didn't expect to find one in the village itself. I would have been happy to travel a reasonable distance, but this couldn't be more perfect. I can walk to work each day, spend plenty of time with Mum and Dad, and make sure she gets a break. It would be difficult to conduct a long-distance relationship at the same time. If Paul and I had to break up, this is the silver lining.

Emily must have followed at least some of my thought processes, but she doesn't comment.

'It's all worked out for the best,' I say in as cheerful a tone as I can manage.

'What are we doing toasting your new life in coffee?' she asks. 'We need something stronger.'

I raise an eyebrow. 'A few minutes ago, you were slumped on that sofa, vowing never to drink again. I think this Victoria woman has the right idea. I haven't met her, but I imagine she'll be good for you. She'll make sure you eat properly and get to bed on time and generally lead an abstemious life. The next time I see you, I won't recognise you.'

Emily looks horrified. 'You make it sound as though I'm becoming a nun.'

'That's extreme, but we shouldn't rule anything out. With Victoria's gentle influence and good example always before you, who knows?'

She sits bolt upright. 'On second thoughts, I don't need a roommate. I can afford this flat by myself. I'll turn the spare bedroom into a …'

'Meditation room?' I suggest. 'Place of spiritual retreat and fasting? Indoor Zen garden?'

She groans and pushes herself off the sofa. 'I was going to get us a bottle of Sauvignon Blanc out of the fridge because I don't have any champagne. But now I need something stronger. I'm fetching the overproof rum.'

'Not the overproof rum?' I say in mock alarm. 'The bottle your father gave you for special occasions and made you promise not to drink in anything less than a full-blown crisis? The one he refers to as the skull blaster?'

'That's the one. What's more, we're finishing the entire bottle.'

She turns in the doorway and looks back at me. 'This may not be a full-blown crisis, but it's a huge step for you, Abby, and it's about time. Things are going to work out well for you. I have a good feeling about it.'

Chapter Six

I'm glad one of us has so much confidence. By the time we've drunk several glasses of rum, I've developed a severe case of cold feet. Yet again, there are so many what-ifs. What if this doesn't work out well? I'll have given in my notice at a perfectly good job for nothing. Maybe not a perfectly good job, or even a good one, but still a job.

What if I don't even start at the Sugarloaf? Isabella may read the first few lines of my reference and decide this Bridget woman isn't worth the trouble if all she does is demand payments to which she isn't entitled. Even worse, she may decide to call Matt directly.

The chances of him being sober enough to remember who I am are slim. The chances of him deciding to tell her about the time he thinks I nearly burned down his bakery are much higher. It was my first day, and he'd had trouble lighting the oven that morning. So, he poured in some methylated spirits in order to, in his words, 'Liven things up a bit.'

Being Matt, he got distracted by something or nothing and wandered off, leaving me to fire up the oven when I arrived. The resulting explosion was quite a shock. My eyebrows have never been the same. Instead of grovelling and offering me a week's pay and time off to recover, Matt shouted that only a fool lights an oven without first checking for alien substances. I was too scared to argue. It was my first week in Reading. I'd moved there to be near to Paul, and I couldn't bear anything to ruin that idyll.

Matt's version of the story isn't one I want getting back to my new employers until I have the chance to explain what really happened. I should have mentioned it at my interview, but it isn't easy to work into a conversation organically. 'I must tell you how I almost lost my eyebrows. You'll absolutely roar!'

The obvious next question would be why I didn't leave the place at once and never look back. That would inevitably lead to discussions of Paul, which isn't a good idea. I was telling Emily the absolute truth when I said I was nearly over him, but the memory of his face pops into my mind at odd times and makes me cry.

Hopefully, Matt won't remember to put that story into my reference. I make a mental note to inspect the oven at the Sugarloaf for any noxious substances before lighting it. Once singed, twice shy. I sleep fitfully and dream of exploding ovens and burned cakes.

I make one last check of the flat after breakfast to make sure I haven't forgotten anything, then head to the station. I reach Honeywell after lunch. I didn't tell Mum which train I was taking. She would only have felt guilty she couldn't leave Dad to come and meet me.

I take a taxi to the house and lug my cases up the drive. I walk around to the back door, knowing Mum is likely to be in the kitchen. Dad often naps after lunch, and I don't want to wake him up by ringing the front doorbell.

I find Mum washing up. She flings her arms around me when I walk in and gives me a soapy hug. 'I wasn't expecting you this early. Did everything go all right in Reading?'

'Fine,' I say, dropping into a chair. 'I gave in my notice at work and told Emily I was leaving. I offered to pay her a month's rent, but she wouldn't hear of it.'

'She'll miss you,' she says.

'I'll miss her too. She's been a fantastic flatmate. She was the best thing about living in Reading.'

Mum looks doubtful. 'Did you see anyone else while you were there?'

I know who she means, but I have no intention of discussing Paul with her. There's nothing to say. She barely knew him. He never had time to visit Honeywell, and my parents only met him briefly a couple of times when they were visiting me. As far as they're concerned, he and I dated for two years, then broke up with no hard feelings on either side.

I didn't go into the details of Paul's new relationship when I told them we were no longer together. What would have been the point? That part of my life belongs in Reading, not here. I have a confused feeling that if I don't mention Paul's name in Honeywell, he won't gain a foothold here. I'll be able to start a whole new life in a place where I don't imagine I see his face on every street corner or find myself eating at restaurants he and I visited together.

I hadn't envisaged this move home as a new adventure until Emily mentioned it. I'd been thinking of it as a necessary hiatus, a sort of corridor between two different parts of my life – the one in which I've lived for the past two years, and the one in which I hope to live in the future. Emily has made me see it through fresh eyes. This period can be important too, even if it's only a year. I'd like to enjoy it and try new things, as well as supporting Mum and Dad through his illness. There's no point in wasting time treading water.

'Have you had lunch?' asks Mum.

'I had a sandwich on the train. I'll be fine until this evening. I'll say hello to Dad, then unpack my suitcases and think about dinner. How does spaghetti bolognaise work for you? I know Dad loves it.'

'You can't cook the dinner,' she says. 'You've had a tiring journey.'

'I haven't come from the North Pole,' I say. 'Do we have the ingredients or should I pick them up this afternoon? Even better, why don't I sit with Dad while you drive to the supermarket? You can take your time and have a cup of coffee afterwards.'

She squeezes my hand. 'That's so thoughtful of you, Abby. I'd love to do that. We have a delivery each week, but the fruit and veg aren't as good as when I choose them myself.'

She hesitates. 'It's lovely to have you home, and I'm grateful you're here, but that doesn't mean I expect you to do my job for me. Dad and I have a routine, and we're doing fine. You're starting a new job, and you'll be busy with that. Hopefully, you'll meet some nice people and have a social life too. It's enough for me just knowing you're around.'

'But you deserve a break too,' I say. 'Dad would be the first to tell you that if he could –'

I break off and clear my throat. 'You know what I mean. The doctors say it may take a while for him to recover. We don't want you burning yourself out before he's well. For now, let me take some of the slack.'

I can see she wants to argue further, but she doesn't have the energy.

'Off you go!' I say. 'You know the supermarket cafe always runs out of Florentines by late afternoon.'

She collects her coat and says goodbye to Dad. A minute later, I hear her car pull off the driveway.

I spend the next hour sitting with Dad doing a jigsaw. At least, I do the jigsaw and chat with him while he watches me. I talk to him about the Sugarloaf and how nice it is to be home. He doesn't speak, but he nods once or twice. Yet again, I'm filled with admiration for how Mum is able to talk to him. She doesn't ask many questions. She chats about little things she's done that day or tells him about the garden. I try to follow suit. I'll have more to talk about once I start my job.

Isabella texts mid-afternoon to say my references are fine, and she'll see me at nine o'clock on Monday morning. My entire body expands with relief. I hadn't realised how nervous I was about that reference. It would have felt like the height of cruelty to have this job dangled in front of my nose, only to have it whisked away again.

Chapter Seven

Mum arrives home looking brighter than I've seen her in a long time.

'I bumped into Meg Peters,' she says. 'We were standing next to each other at the checkout, so we had coffee together. It was wonderful to get some time to myself and do something normal.'

'That's great,' I say. 'But we need to find you something more exciting to do than going to the supermarket. We'll talk about it over dinner. I'll get started on that while you chat to Dad.'

We eat dinner at six o'clock. Dad gets tired early these days, and it takes Mum a while to help him get ready for bed. The nurse no longer comes in twice a day, which Mum says is a good sign. This may be true, but it means a lot more work for her, which is a shame. I hope she'll delegate some of these jobs to me while I'm here.

She feeds Dad his spaghetti, keeping up an endless flow of small talk all the while. I try to join in, but it will take practise. Emily and I rarely ate our meals together. She worked long hours and had an active social life, whereas I tried to be in bed at a reasonable hour because of my five a.m. starts.

I haven't yet asked Isabella how early she wants me to arrive. Hopefully, she won't waltz in at nine o'clock every morning, criticise everything I've done, tell me she doesn't know why she's paying me when a trained monkey could do a better job for half the money, then demand I make her a coffee, into which she pours some suspicious liquid from a hip flask before disappearing into her office for the rest of the morning. Maybe she will. It's difficult to tell what an employer is like from one brief interview when you're both on your best behaviour. But even if she's as awful as Matt, the job is local. I'll hang onto that.

Mum stops feeding Dad and takes a bite of her own food. 'This is delicious! Isn't it delicious, Geoffrey? Your father always likes bolognaise, Abby. He ate it every night when we went to Rome. I couldn't get him to try anything else. They had lovely risottos and pizzas, and I even had squid one night, but I couldn't persuade him to join me. Still, it's a great thing to know what you like.'

'I have a recipe for butternut squash risotto I'll make for you,' I promise. 'It was Emily's favourite whenever she was tired. She said she loved having a meal she didn't have to chew.'

'That sounds lovely,' she says. 'But you mustn't feel obliged to cook every evening. I'm hoping you'll make some friends and go out with them.'

She shoots me a sidelong glance, and it's obvious what's coming next. 'It's been a while since you broke up with Paul. You must want to get out there again and …'

She pauses, and I wait in fascinated horror for her to finish this thought. Get out and what?

'Mingle,' she says when I don't speak.

I give a snort of laughter. 'Mingle? Honestly, Mum!'

She looks defensive. 'That's what they say, isn't it? *Single and ready to mingle.*'

'Maybe a few decades ago. Besides, how do you know I'm ready to mingle?'

She sighs. 'Aren't you? It's been nearly three months since …'

'Three months isn't long to get over a two-year relationship.'

She looks worried. 'I hate to see you wasting your life like this.'

'I'm not wasting my life. I've found a new job, and I've moved to a new place.'

'I know,' she says. 'It's a big step forward. I hated you working at that awful place. I understood why you stayed there while you were seeing Paul, and the pair of you weren't sure where you were going to live. But you didn't make a move after you broke up. Why was that?'

I've asked myself the same question a thousand times. At first, it was because I couldn't take in what had happened. I'd built my entire future around Paul, and I couldn't imagine making plans that didn't involve him. By the time I accepted it, I'd lost the ability to make plans.

I shrug. 'Inertia, I suppose. I'd spent two years of my life going in one direction, and it seemed impossible to imagine going in a different one.'

She gives me a sympathetic smile. 'I understand, but now you've been forced into making a change, you may as well make the most of it.'

She's right. It's pretty much what I've been thinking ever since I realised my time back in Honeywell doesn't have to be a hiatus. It can be a part of my life in its own right.

'What do you suggest?' I say.

'I've had a few ideas.'

'Such as?' I ask suspiciously.

'I was talking to Karen McDaniel the other day. She said her son has recently broken up with his girlfriend and is at a bit of a loose end.'

I have to put a stop to this line of thinking. 'That isn't happening.'

'You haven't even met him!' she protests.

'I don't need to. I mean it, Mum. If I get even the faintest sniff of you trying to set me up with any of your friends' sons, I'll move out.'

'You wouldn't!' she says.

'Probably not. But I'll spend all my time playing music in my room and refusing to come out.'

'Like you did when you were a teenager?' she says.

'Exactly, and I'll throw in some tantrums for extra effect. I refuse to be set up by you and your friends. Is that clear?'

'It was only an idea,' she says. 'There are plenty of other ways to meet people. How about an evening class?'

'What sort of an evening class?'

'I'm not sure, but I know people meet each other there. Moira's daughter went to a class on car maintenance, and she ended up living with the instructor.'

'I'm perfectly able to change my oil and the odd tyre,' I say. 'Anyway, I don't have a car to maintain. I didn't need one in Reading, and I doubt I'll need one here. I can always borrow yours or Dad's.'

Dad shifts in his seat and turns his head to look at me.

'I mean yours!' I tell Mum. 'No one but Dad is allowed to touch his car. I know that.'

Is that a smile on Dad's face? It's hard to tell because one side of his mouth is still a little droopy. But I could swear he looks amused.

Mum doesn't notice. 'If you don't want to go to an evening class, perhaps you could run one? Cooking classes are popular these days. Sharon Matthews runs a basic cookery course for beginners up at the church hall. She says she's inundated with divorced men who don't know how to cook.'

'That's another hard pass,' I say. 'I don't need a manbaby who's never bothered with basic life skills and was happy to leave it all up to his poor wife.'

'That's true,' she says. 'How about the classified ads?'

'The what?' I say.

'Oh, you know. The ones in the newspapers. They used to call them the lonely-hearts columns. You write a bit about yourself and talk about the person you're hoping to meet. Then people contact you, and you go out for coffee.'

'Which century are we living in?' I say. 'People don't advertise in the newspapers anymore.'

'That isn't true,' she says. 'Pamela Redfern got a beautiful pair of winter boots from the local paper only last week. They were barely worn.'

'Which would be fine if I were looking for winter boots,' I say. 'But not for a person.'

She sighs. 'I'm only trying to help.'

'I know you are, but I'm not advertising in the local newspapers. Or the national ones, for that matter.'

'There's nothing for it, then,' she says. 'You'll have to go on the apps.'

I almost choke on my spaghetti. 'The apps?'

She gives me a helpful slap on the back. 'Don't eat so fast, love. All the young people are doing it. Suzanne Downer says her daughter is out with a different man every night.'

'I don't want to be out with a different man every night,' I say.

'But that's the point,' she says. 'You choose how many people you want to meet. I can find out which app Suzanne's daughter uses.'

'There's no need, thank you. If I want to use a dating app, I can find one for myself. I'm surprised you even know about them, let alone approve of them.'

She smiles. 'Our generation isn't as old-fashioned as you appear to believe. It seems an excellent idea to me. You work such long hours, and you don't know many people around here. Why not make a few nice friends if you can?'

I ignore the *nice friends* part. I dread to imagine what sort of man I might encounter if I put that on my dating profile. Probably, someone who lives with his mother and knits his own yoghurt. His idea of a romantic evening would be me cooking him dinner before watching him paint his collection of Star Wars figurines.

But Mum's right that it would be nice to meet some new people. I'm not ready for anything serious yet. My breakup with Paul is too recent. But there will be plenty of people in the area in a similar position. As long as I make it clear upfront that I'm not looking for a permanent commitment, I should be fine.

I gather up the plates. 'I'll think about it, but only on the condition you leave me alone and let me get on with it in my own way. I don't want to arrive home to discover one of your friends' sons has just *happened* to drop around with a cup of sugar. Neither do I want to log onto a dating app, only to find I already have a profile, complete with face-tuned picture. Agreed?'

Mum seems unfazed by my attitude. 'I wouldn't dream of interfering in your life. You know that. You're an adult, and what you get up to is your own business.'

She rarely gives in this easily. Maybe she's too busy to interfere at the moment. I decide to give her the benefit of the doubt.

'I'm glad we're on the same page,' I say. 'I've made strawberry mousse for dessert. That's one of Dad's favourites, isn't it?'

She looks pleased. 'And mine!'

'That's good to know,' I say. 'If I get even the smallest hint of you trying to meddle in my love life, I'm cutting off supplies!'

Chapter Eight

I arrive at the Sugarloaf early on Monday morning. I want to make a good impression on my first day. It's one thing to have got the job. It's quite another to keep it. Hopefully, Lily will take an entire year's maternity leave. If she's considering doing that, I need to show her the business is in safe hands for as long as she wants to leave it.

I'm secretly hoping to make myself so indispensable that she and Isabella decide to keep me on as a permanent employee. Neither of them seems particularly interested in the practical side of the business. I'm determined to do an excellent job and prove myself indispensable to the smooth running of the place.

Isabella looks pleased to see me. 'I was about to take a coffee break, and it's always nice to have someone to chat to.'

'What about the customers?' I ask, remembering Lily's annoyance when Isabella closed the shop last week to interview me.

'Hopefully, we won't have any in the next half hour,' she says.

I can't help laughing. 'That may not be the best attitude for a fledgling business.'

'I know,' she says. 'But I've been here for an hour already. I'm exhausted.'

'I'll make you a coffee,' I say. 'I can serve any customers that come in. I'm used to that. I was supposed to be the head baker at my last place, but the manager was slightly … erratic, so we all did a bit of everything.'

'I spoke to him on the phone,' she says. 'He seemed a bit weird.'

'That's putting it mildly. What did he say about me?'

'He didn't say anything about you, but he had a lot to say about someone called Bridget. She sounds awful.'

'That's me!' I say.

She looks pleased. 'I thought it must be. Did you really try to make him pay for a company car and your flat?'

'Of course not!'

'That's a pity,' she says. 'He sounded as though he deserved it.'

'If you realised I was Bridget,' I say, 'why did you give me the job? Did Matt say nice things about me too?'

'I'm sorry to disappoint you, but no.'

'Then, why?'

She shrugs. 'I liked you when you came in for interview. So did Lily. I wasn't prepared to take the word of someone who operates his business with zero-hour contracts and can't be bothered to learn his employees' names.'

Our conversation is interrupted by the arrival of a customer. It's the same woman I saw last week, the one who gave me the disapproving look. I'm not sure why. I was only holding the door open for her. Now is the time to charm her and show Isabella what an asset to the bakery I can be.

'Good morning!' I say with my friendliest smile. 'How may I help you today?'

The woman ignores me and looks at Isabella. 'Have you fixed the coffee machine yet?'

Isabella jumps to her feet. 'Good morning, Mrs Ogilvie. Yes, it's in perfect working order again. Would you like your usual?'

She bends to pat the small dog who has trotted in behind Mrs Ogilvie. 'And how are you this morning, Bernie? Have you been for a nice walk? Is it time for your biscuit?'

The dog gives her an idiotic grin and sits down next to his owner.

'What a beautiful dog,' I say, bending to scratch his head. He immediately flings himself onto his back and looks up at me hopefully.

'There you go,' says Isabella, handing him a biscuit in the shape of a bone. He crunches it busily.

She straightens up. 'Mrs Ogilvie, this is our new staff member, Abby. She'll be standing in for Lily while she goes off on maternity leave.'

Mrs Ogilvie gives me a hard stare. 'I saw you the other day.'

'That's right,' I say. 'I'd been interviewing for the job. I started work this morning. You're my very first customer.'

She doesn't look impressed.

'And Bernie,' I add.

Her face softens. 'I hope you like dogs. The last owner didn't. He used to keep us standing outside the shop in all weathers. I'm glad the current owners have seen sense.'

'I love dogs,' I say truthfully. 'And this one seems a sweetheart.'

Her face relaxes into what, with a little imagination, might be interpreted as a smile. 'He's a very good dog. He's clever too. My vet says he's never seen such an intelligent dog. He said if I'd started training him earlier, Bernie could easily have been on the films.'

'What a pity,' says Isabella. 'I'd love to meet a real live film star.'

Mrs Ogilvie gives her a disapproving look. 'I would never have considered it. Bernie wouldn't have enjoyed it at all. He would have had to mix with all sorts of strange people, and he's fussy about who he spends time with.'

Bernie rolls onto his back again and gives a huge yawn.

Isabella ghosts me a wink. 'The vet said something else about Bernie, didn't he, Mrs Ogilvie?'

I'm surprised to see Mrs Ogilvie's cheeks turn pink. 'He said it wasn't good for Bernie to eat quite so much cake. It's a shame because he's so fond of it.'

'So, Lily and I looked up some recipes online and started making him healthy treats,' Isabella tells me. 'He's been a most enthusiastic taste tester. We settled on a couple of recipes, and now they're one of our best sellers.'

She turns to Mrs Ogilvie. 'Abby is a trained pastry chef. Maybe she'll come up with some new flavours while she's working here.'

This isn't exactly what I trained for. I imagine Monsieur Blanchet's face if he found out one of his ex-students was baking biscuits for spoiled dogs. But he never has to know, and there's something oddly engaging about Bernie.

'I'll do my best,' I promise, and Mrs Ogilvie's face relaxes even further.

'He doesn't like cheese,' she says. 'It gives him a runny tummy. And I hope you are aware that dogs can't have chocolate. He likes basil and rosemary. The vet says he has a refined palate. Lily makes some beef and coriander biscuits he's very fond of.'

'They pair well with a nice Beaujolais,' Isabella murmurs in my ear.

I change my snort of laughter into an unconvincing cough.

'I'll do my best to come up with something nice,' I promise, and Mrs Ogilvie gives me an almost approving look.

I spend the rest of the morning going through the ordering system with Isabella and acquainting myself with the bakery kitchen. It's old fashioned but functional. She asks whether I need to order new equipment, and I tell her we're fine for now.

'As long as the ovens work well,' I add.

I tell her about my adventure in the North Street Bakery, and she shrieks with laughter.

'I can't understand why you stayed there for even five minutes,' she says, wiping her eyes. 'And to think I was worried your employer would be devastated when you handed in your notice and would try to make you an offer you couldn't refuse.'

'He did,' I say. 'Several times over the past two years. But I had no trouble refusing.'

She pulls a face. 'I'm not surprised, but I am disgusted. Say the word, and we'll send him something unpleasant in the mail.'

She looks at the clock. 'I was expecting Lily to be here by now. I wonder whether Jack's car has broken down again. He usually gives her a lift in the mornings.'

'How long have they been together?' I say.

'Nearly three years. But they've been friends since they were teens.'

I sigh. 'I'd love a relationship like that. I don't think I've ever been friends with anyone before I've dated them.'

'It is pretty special,' she agrees. 'So, we've established you weren't dating the luscious Matt, despite him giving you every opportunity. We've also established you didn't leave the bakery the moment you nearly lost your eyebrows. I'm guessing you had another good reason to be living in that area?'

'As it happens, I did. How did you know?'

She considers. 'I think I must be naturally nosy. You can tell me to mind my own business. Lily tells me that all the time.'

I'm usually reticent about my private life, but Isabella is easy to talk to. She's so friendly and eager. She reminds me of Bernie. I wonder whether she taste tested his biscuit recipes too.

'I don't mind telling you,' I say. 'I was seeing someone while I was there. He was the reason I didn't leave my old bakery. It was around the corner from his flat, which meant I could see him more often than I would have otherwise. He worked long hours, and he travelled a lot. I knew what his life was like when we got together. He didn't hide it from me, and I chose to be with him regardless.'

'But it didn't work out?' she says.

'No, but not because he was working long hours. He met someone else.'

'I'm surprised he had time,' she comments.

'Me too. It would have been more understandable if it was someone he worked with, but it wasn't. I'm not sure where they met, but by the time he told me about her, they were about to move in together.

'That tells me as much about him as I need to know,' she says.

I open my mouth to defend Paul, then stop. I don't know why I feel so defensive of someone who has treated me, by any objective standard, extremely badly. Maybe it's because I'm embarrassed I fell for his spiel for so long and ignored all the signs he no longer wanted to be with me. In many ways, I felt worse about that than I did about losing him. Breakups happen, but they're far more bearable when you're able to keep your dignity, which I very much didn't. It's time that changed.

'I don't want to talk about him,' I say. 'Not because I'm pining for him but because I don't want to give him any more headspace.'

'Good for you,' she says. 'How do you plan to meet people while you're living here?'

'You sound like my mum. She's been discussing how to get me back on the dating scene.'

'Who calls it the dating scene?' she says.

'My mother does. Next, you're going to ask me whether I'm *going on the apps*.'

She looks delighted. 'Is that what she said? She must be pretty cool. I doubt my mother would even know what that meant.'

'She made several other suggestions first,' I admit. 'Starting with a lonely-hearts ad.'

'If you decide to do that,' she says, 'you absolutely have to let me help you write it! But your mum's right. You've moved to a new area where you don't know many people, you've broken up with your boyfriend, and you're a free agent. There's no harm in using a dating app to meet people. It's what I do.'

I'm surprised to hear this. Isabella is exceptionally pretty. She's tall and slim, and she has that indefinable air of confidence which people find attractive even if technically you're fairly average.

'I'd have thought someone like you would find it easy to meet people without resorting to that,' I say.

She laughs. 'You have an odd idea about dating apps. They aren't for losers who can't find anyone else. Plenty of people use them, including me. I've met some really nice guys as well as the odd loser. No one special as yet, but I haven't given up hope.'

'Maybe I'll give it a go,' I say. 'Which one do you use?'

'*LuvLocatr*,' she says. 'If you decide to use it too, we could go on double dates together!'

'I wouldn't mind,' I say. 'I'm a little out of practice, and I've never used one of those apps.'

'No problem,' she says. 'It's really easy. I'll help you set up your profile, and you can get going right away. Someone like you will be fighting people off. You aren't working on Sunday. If you don't have several dates lined up by then, I promise I'll eat five of our doughnuts in a row. You can choose the flavour.'

Chapter Nine

My first week at the Sugarloaf passes surprisingly quickly in comparison with my first week at the North Street Bakery, where, besides having my eyebrows reshaped for free, I had to contend with a supplier who refused to deal directly with Matt, and a cockroach infestation.

The Sugarloaf Bakery is run along different lines. Not only does the staff refrain from throwing things, but the baking equipment is functional, and my bosses speak to me as though I'm a human being. It's a little bewildering after two years of Matt, and I wonder for the thousandth time what it was about Paul that made me think he was worth putting up with that life. He knew what Matt was like because I complained about him often enough, but he never suggested a change. He told me I should focus on the positives, rather than the negatives. My work was close to his flat, and it was a steady income, which many people would be grateful for.

I can't blame Paul for my decisions. It wasn't his responsibility to make my life better; it was mine. And I chose not to improve things. That was on me. But I won't make that mistake again, no matter how good looking someone may be.

I quickly fall into a routine. Isabella is easy to work with, which is a tremendous relief after Matt. Lily comes in most days, but she often leaves early. She tells me she expected her replacement to take longer to get used to the job, which is why she arranged for several weeks' crossover.

'I'm not doing anything I haven't done before,' I tell her. 'But it's a far nicer environment in which to do it.'

She looks pleased. 'I thought you'd enjoy working with Isabella. I'm going to miss her when I go off on maternity leave.'

'I expect you'll find plenty to do instead.'

'My mum says I have no idea what's about to hit me,' she says. 'She told me she felt as though she'd been run over by a train for the first few months, and she lost all track of time. And I was supposedly a delightful baby. Maybe she was talking about my brother, Ben.'

'What does he do?' I ask.

'He works for a computer company. He lives about ten miles away with his girlfriend, Mia. They've been together for a while now. I keep telling him they should have a baby soon, so the cousins can be close in age, but he only laughs.'

'It's nice that your mum is local,' I say. 'Will she be helpful?'

'She will. If anything, she'll be too helpful. She's convinced she's the only one who knows how to do things properly, and she says nothing gets done unless she does it herself. She seems to think I'm about twelve years old and won't know what to do with a baby if she isn't there to supervise.'

'What about your partner?' I ask.

She rolls her eyes. 'Jack thinks it's funny to wind her up. He asked her last night if babies sleep through the night as soon as they get home from the hospital. She nearly hit the roof. She spent ages explaining to him that babies need feeding every couple of hours in the early months. He listened carefully, then asked whether they can sit up unaided from birth.'

'Your poor Mum,' I say. 'It would serve him right if she moved in with you.'

'He wouldn't mind,' she says. 'They get on really well. He loves my dad too.'

'How does Jack feel about becoming a father?'

'He can't wait. He's read lots of books. I expect he'll be very hands on.'

I think of Paul, who told me he wasn't sure he wanted children because they demand so much of you for so many years.

'Jack will be excellent,' says Lily. 'I know he will. He's completely prepared, although he's terrible in our childbirth classes. To be fair, they are pretty awful. They're run by some relation of one of Mum's friends. She gave us a voucher for them and insisted we go each week. Jack loves to wind up the instructor by asking ridiculous questions. I'm always expecting her to throw him out. In his defence, Morag takes it all terribly seriously, and she talks a lot of nonsense. She insists we all source crystals and stare at them if the discomfort gets too much.'

'Discomfort?' I say, amused. 'I've heard other words for it.'

'So have I,' she says. 'But Morag doesn't allow any negativity in her classes. She uses words like twinge and ache. I'm pretty sure I'll be demanding all the pain relief they have once the contractions start. I mean the twinges.'

'I would too,' I say. 'I don't see the point in suffering any more than you have to.'

She laughs. 'Isabella says if she ever has a baby, she's going to demand an epidural before labour even starts. And she wants to keep it in for at least a week afterwards, just in case. Jack told Morag during our last class that he may need an epidural too. She gave me a pitying look but didn't say anything. When she showed us the actual process of birth, she used a legwarmer.'

'A what?' I say.

She waves her hands in explanation. 'Those things people used in the eighties when they were exercising. Jane Fonda had quite a collection. My mum did all her video tapes. She was always telling me it was important to feel the burn.'

'But what do they have to do with childbirth?' I say. 'Do you use them if your feet get cold?'

'That would make some sense,' she says. 'But you aren't even close. Morag pulled out a lifelike doll from her bag, like Mary Poppins. I half expected her to pull out a lampshade next and tell us it was vital the lights were kept low during the birth. She told us the baby's name was Gabriel, and she pushed him through this red and green striped legwarmer. I expect she got it for Christmas thirty years ago and thought it would be perfect for these classes.'

'It sounds … educational,' I say.

'That's one way of describing it! Jack's face was a picture. I wish I'd had my phone with me. But we aren't allowed any electronic equipment in class, even if it's switched off. It does something or other to the spiritual vibrations. I'll never forget the look on Jack's face when Gabriel's face popped out of the legwarmer. He told me if I was planning on having such an ugly baby, I could think again.'

'I thought all babies looked like Winston Churchill,' I say. 'And their parents are still supposed to think they're beautiful.'

'I'm with Jack on this one,' she says. 'Winston Churchill would have been fine, but Gabriel was another matter entirely. He looked like something out of *The Exorcist.* He had those creepy eyes that follow you around the room.'

She laughs. 'Isabella is most put out I didn't get a picture of him. She's terrified Morag is going to retire before she gets the chance to meet her and Gabriel. She's been muttering about IVF and single parenthood before it's too late. Jack drew her a picture of baby Gabriel to make up for it, but it didn't do him justice. Still, Morag seems to like him, which is the main thing.'

I breathe a silent thanks that I'm not the one who's pregnant. I had no idea what was involved in what I'd always assumed was a straightforward process. I'd like to have children one day, but Lily isn't filling me with enthusiasm.

She sees my face. 'Sorry, Abby. I talk about this a lot. It's all rather scary, being my first one. But I try not to worry about it too much. My mum says I'm going to be fine, and she's always right.'

'Will she be at the birth with you?'

'She wanted to be, but I'd prefer to keep it to me and Jack and the midwife if possible. Morag gave us all her card last week and told us she's a trained Doula and would be happy to be a part of any or all of our birthing experiences. I noticed she didn't offer a card to Jack, but he insisted on taking one anyway. He keeps waving it at me and saying he's going to call her at the first sign of me making a fuss. He's also insisting we call the baby Gabriel if it's a boy.'

'And Gabriella, if it's a girl, I suppose?' I say.

She shakes her head. 'No, he's dead set on Morag. Between him and Isabella, I have no idea what the poor baby will end up being called. Isabella wants to name it after a cake because babies are sweet, and so are cakes. Also, she thinks it would be good for business. I've only just talked her down from *Sugarloaf Carson Fisher*.'

The bakery door opens and a group of women comes in and settles down at the largest table in the cafe. Lily greets them and takes their order.

'They come here each week,' she tells me. 'They play poker.'

I look at the women with increased respect. 'So, you're running a gambling den? Do the authorities know?'

'They play for cake,' she says. 'They stay here for a couple of hours, and the loser picks up the tab. It's a great idea. They get through a surprising amount of food while they're here. Isabella is hoping to be asked to join them one of these days.'

Isabella comes out of the office. 'Did I hear my name? What have you two been talking about?'

'I've been hearing all about Gabriel,' I say, and her face lights up.

'I love Gabriel! I think he should become our shop mascot.'

'But I don't,' says Lily. 'And neither does Abby. So, it's two against one.'

'I don't want to get in the middle of this,' I say. 'You can sort it out between you. I have to say he sounds creepy.'

'Nonsense,' says Isabella. 'He sounds adorable. Speaking of babies, have you set up any dates yet?'

'I'm having coffee with someone on Sunday afternoon,' I say.

I hold out my phone to Lily, who stares at the screen. 'He looks ok. What do you think, Isabella?'

Isabella takes the phone and studies it carefully. 'He looks fine. He's about the right age, and he's good-looking. He has his own car and flat, so he isn't living with his parents.'

'I'm living with mine,' I point out.

'That's different. I doubt his father has had a stroke. If he has, I'll reconsider. He looks nice. I hope it goes well.'

'Aren't you planning to hide around the corner and keep an eye on me?' I say 'My mum would love to, but she can't leave my dad.'

'I'd be happy to,' she says. 'But you're old enough to go on a date without a chaperone. You know the rules. Meet in a public place, let someone know where you are, don't tell him where you live or work until you know him a lot better …'

'Mum sent me a list of rules last night,' I say. 'It included all those, plus several more. I'll be fine.'

'I'll be in early on Monday morning,' says Isabella. 'I want all the details.'

I smile at her excited face. 'You're looking forward to this far more than I am.'

'I have so little in my life,' she says. 'All I do is work, work, work.'

'And sample the products,' says Lily.

'Lily and I plan to live through you vicariously,' Isabella warns me. 'Take a notebook with you and jot down every single thing he says and does. Better still, record it.'

'Or don't,' adds Lily. 'You could just go and have a good time instead.'

'I'll do my best,' I promise.

There's a shout of *Full House!* from the table in the corner and a roar of laughter.

One of the women waves at me. 'Another round of coffees, please, and a selection of cakes. Vera's paying!'

Chapter Ten

I set out for my coffee date in good time on Sunday. Coffee meeting? Coffee assignation? I'd prefer not to call it a date. It's an exploratory consumption of caffeine with someone who may or may not turn out to be the love of my life and the father of my future children. At least, that's what Mum seems to think.

She fusses around me before I leave. 'Are you sure about this, Abby? I don't like the thought of you meeting a total stranger all by yourself.'

'You were the one who wanted me to do this,' I say. 'Don't tell me you've changed your mind?'

'No, but it all seems so odd to me.'

I give her a hug. 'I'll be fine. You know where I'm going, and you have a photo of the person I'm meeting. If he doesn't look like his picture, I'll turn around and come straight back home.'

She still looks anxious. 'I'd have preferred you to put an ad in the newspaper.'

'No one my age reads newspapers,' I say. 'Except occasionally online. If I'd put an ad in the online edition, it would have been the same as using a dating app.'

She doesn't look convinced. 'Don't tell this man anything about yourself. That's most important. And get as much information about him as possible. Mavis Sotherby has promised to look him up for you when you get home. If there's anything dodgy about him, she'll ferret it out in an instant.'

'Who's Mavis Sotherby?' I ask. 'A private detective?'

'Don't be so silly, love. Where would I find a private detective? Mavis is the founder of the Honeywell Silver Surfers. They meet in the village hall every Wednesday, and she gives talks about how to use the internet. Some of the older members can't even use email when they arrive, but Mavis and her team soon sort them out.'

I imagine a group of women with blue rinses and determined expressions bullying bewildered octogenarian technophobes into installing a firewall. Maybe Mavis and her team carry out elaborate heists like Vanessa Redgrave in *Mission Impossible*. Or they're Honeywell's answer to *Ocean's Eleven*. The village seems well supplied with active groups of pensioners who might be glad of a little adventure. The Sugarloaf poker players could supply upfront funds for a cut of the future profits.

'Abby?' says Mum.

I tear my thoughts away from this vision of Honeywell's criminal underbelly. 'I was listening to everything you said. Mavis Sotherby!'

'That's right,' she says, smoothing down a wrinkle in my top. 'She wants you to get as much out of this man as you can. Not just his name and address, but more personal things too. The more specific information we have, the better. She can't do much with generic details but give her the faintest sniff of an unusual hobby or a genetic abnormality and she'll have him! That woman can do wonders as long as she has something to work with.'

'Got it,' I say. 'The moment he tells me he's a keen member of the Hampshire Naked Hang-gliding Club, I'll let Mavis know.'

Mum doesn't blink. 'That's exactly the sort of thing that would help. Although if he tells you something like that, I hope you'd have the sense not to get involved.'

'There's no pleasing you,' I grumble. 'You used to say being with Paul had made me prematurely middle aged. Now I have the chance to meet someone with a fascinating hobby, you aren't interested.'

She smiles. 'You'd better get going. And I need to go and make sure Dad's looking his best. The Occupational Therapist is coming this afternoon, and I like him to look smart. He was always so neat.'

I offer to take Dad's car in case she needs hers, but she refuses. 'It isn't a good idea to turn up for your first meeting driving a restored Daimler. He may think you have money.'

'What if he turns up in one?' I ask, and she brightens.

'That would be wonderful. It would show he was solvent.'

I muse on her double standards as I drive into town. According to Mum, I have to turn this guy inside out and extract his full life history while refusing to confirm anything more than my name and county of residence. He has to prove he's financially independent and a good catch, while I have to conceal any and all information about my own circumstances.

This could be a silent coffee date, especially if Harry pursues the same tactics. I imagine us sitting opposite each other, sipping our coffee and sizing up our opponent like Kasparov and Karpov in a Grandmaster chess match. I expect they had to do it without the coffee. Neither of them would want to leave the game to visit the bathroom in case the other one moved the pieces while they were away.

I arrive a few minutes before the appointed time, wondering whether Harry will be there before me. Would that be a power move, or would it show he's someone who hates to be kept waiting, like Paul? It's been so long since I went on a first date that I'm not sure. Hopefully, Mavis Sotherby will tell me later.

I don't see anyone who looks like the picture in Harry's profile, so I order myself a coffee and settle down to wait. Maybe we should have arranged a code to help us recognise each other. I could have brought a drawing of a cheesecake, and he could have brought a photo of his latest sky dive. I give an involuntary shudder and try to think of something else. There are people who could carry off that sort of picture with style, but they're few and far between. Even then, I'd prefer to get to know them first.

'Abby?'

A man stops by my table and inspects me closely. I'm not sure why. I put a recent photo of myself on the app – no filters, no duck pout. Plenty of people upload old or ridiculously flattering photos of themselves, but I can't see the point. The person you're meeting will see the real you as soon as they arrive, so why bother? I'm not enthused enough by the idea of online dating to bother to play games.

I'm pleased to see Harry looks like his photo too. It's an encouraging start. Maybe I can get a few surreptitious camera shots of him from various angles when he isn't looking. I may as well give Mavis plenty to work with.

'Have you been here long?' asks Harry, looking at my coffee.

Is this a faux pas on my part? Have I broken some unwritten dating etiquette by not waiting for my date to arrive? But I needed the caffeine, and there was no guarantee he would turn up.

'About half an hour,' I say.

'I looked in about ten minutes ago,' he says. 'I didn't see you here.'

I should have told the truth. There's nothing wrong with ordering yourself a coffee while you wait for someone to arrive.

'I must have been in the toilet,' I say without thinking. 'I have an upset stomach.'

He raises an eyebrow. 'I'll get myself a coffee. Back in a minute.'

I debate abandoning my drink and making a run for it while he's at the counter. Why did I say that? Who talks about upset stomachs on a first date, especially when it isn't true? Still, it's a perfect opportunity to cut this short if I'm not enjoying myself. Even the most committed seeker after love is unlikely to argue when their date doubles over in apparent pain and says she has to leave.

Harry returns with his coffee. 'Are you feeling better now?'

For a moment, I can't think what he's talking about.

He makes a vague gesture somewhere around his mid-region. 'Your stomach. You said it was upset.'

I didn't expect him to pursue this. He isn't a doctor. He's an accountant, at least he is if his profile is accurate. Mum always says it isn't polite to talk about bodily functions in mixed company. Although, to be fair to Harry, I was the one who brought up the subject. Maybe he thinks hypochondria is one of my hobbies, and he's giving me a chance to expound on it for a while before cutting in with his own stories of forced landings in slurry pits in the middle of a field, stark naked and miles from civilisation.

'It's a simple yes or no question,' he says with a half-smile.

This date could not have started any more badly. That isn't strictly true, but I'd rather not imagine how it could be worse. I can either tell him my upset stomach is a thing of the past or I can tell him the truth. Either way, I'll look like an absolute fool. I decide the truth is marginally less embarrassing.

'I'm sorry,' I say. 'I only arrived a few minutes earlier than you. When you asked how long I'd been here, I didn't know whether I ought to have ordered coffee without you, so I made up an excuse.'

I half expect him to make an angry speech about honesty and trust being an essential prerequisite to online dating. People put themselves on the line and make themselves vulnerable. The least their dates can do is take that seriously and treat them with respect.

Instead, he looks amused. 'That's a first. Most people make up far better lies about themselves.'

'They do?'

'Yeah, I've been doing this for a while, and I've learned it takes at least three dates before you discover even a small part of the truth about anyone. That's the way it goes. We're all meeting perfect strangers, and who wants to spill their guts to a stranger?'

'Don't you search for them online before you arrive?' I ask.

'When I can be bothered. It doesn't tell you much. It rules out people with a criminal history, but that's about all. Most of the stuff we put online about ourselves is heavily edited. Look at anyone's Facebook page. Who leads that sort of glossy life? No one I know.'

I think of the Insta-perfect lives many of my friends seem to live. 'That's true. I don't use social media much.'

His smile widens. 'You're high on actual life?'

'Not really. I was with someone for a while who didn't approve of it, and I lost the habit.'

'That isn't good,' he says. 'Do you always do what other people want?'

'Not remotely!' I say, annoyed.

He doesn't seem to notice. 'I wouldn't come off social media because someone told me to.'

'He didn't tell me to!' I say. 'He didn't use it himself, and he worked a lot, so he liked me to be fully present when we were together. Like I say, I lost the habit.'

'And you're making up for it now?'

'You mean what we're doing here? That's different. It isn't social media. It's social …' I trail off, unsure what I'm trying to say.

'It's all the same thing,' he says. 'It's people trying to project a certain image of themselves to others.'

'Everyone on this dating app appears to lead pretty perfect lives,' I say. 'But that doesn't mean they're lying. They're presenting the best version of themselves. If you were an Olympic gold medallist, and you also painted bad water colours of your friends' pets, which one would you put in your profile?'

'The pets,' he says without hesitation. 'Anyone can win medals if they try hard enough. It doesn't make for the most interesting dinner conversation. Painting your friend's pet iguana, on the other hand …'

I'm not sure he's right about anyone being able to win a gold medal. If I spent twenty years training for ten hours a day, I still wouldn't be able to run more than a mile without collapsing with a stitch. I could also never learn to do the butterfly stroke. I'm not built for it. More importantly, I wouldn't want to.

'Do you have any interesting hobbies?' I ask, praying that any answer he gives isn't prefixed with the word naked.

'It depends on what you call interesting,' he says. 'I renovate old cars and sell them.'

He sees my face and laughs. 'And you clearly don't. What do you do in your spare time?'

I should have prepared some answers to this. It's an obvious enough question. Most people would have come up with something impressive, whether or not it was true. I'm starting to realise my heart may not be in this as much as it should be.

'I haven't had time for hobbies over the past couple of years,' I say. 'I've been busy at work.'

'You work at The Sugarloaf Bakery, don't you?' he says.

I stare at him in horror. He seemed so normal. It's a shock to discover he's a mad stalker. Will I have to change my name and move to a different city? A new country, even? Wild thoughts of plastic surgery flit through my mind as I continue to stare at him.

'Don't look like that,' he says. 'Your name's on the bakery website. It's the first thing that comes up when you search for your name and this area.'

I'll be having words with Isabella tomorrow. She knew I was starting online dating. She ought to have had more sense than to make me so easily discoverable.

Harry follows my train of thought. 'If someone wants to track you down, there are far easier ways than that. It's the downside of everyone living their lives online.'

He's right. No one is anonymous these days, at least not without going into witness protection, which seems a little extreme at this point in time. Besides, if what Mum says is correct, Mavis Sotherby would have me tracked down by teatime.

'I've only recently started working there,' I say. 'It's temporary cover for someone who's taking a few months off.'

'Maternity leave,' he says and laughs at my expression. 'It was right there on the website.'

He looks at his watch. 'I'm afraid I have to go. We have a family thing on tonight.'

Is this a rescue call? Not a call, exactly, but a pre-prepared excuse to leave if things aren't going well.

Again, he seems to know what I'm thinking, which is uncanny. Either that, or I have an unusually expressive face.

'I really do have a family thing,' he says.

'No problem,' I say. 'So, what … I mean, how do these things work?'

'You *are* new at this,' he says. 'When I meet someone for the first time, we discuss at the end of the date whether we'd like to see each other again.'

'Ok,' I say.

He smiles. 'I find it best to be honest. I've enjoyed meeting you, but I'm not feeling a connection. How about you?'

'The same. But it felt rude to come out and say it.'

'Not at all,' he says. 'When you've been doing this for as long as I have, you realise it's easier. It saves a lot of awkwardness and hurt feelings.'

'What if I'd fallen madly in love with you and wanted to see you again?' I ask.

'I'd have given you the same answer. But as kindly as possible. No one owes anyone their time or anything else. It took me a while to realise that, but it's good advice. I suggest you take it.'

He stands and holds out his hand. 'Best of luck.'

'You too,' I say. 'Do you have any other advice for me before you leave? As you can see, I'm a complete novice at all this.'

'Honestly? Be yourself. People will find out who you are in the end. When they do, they'll either like who you are or they won't. Why prolong the inevitable?'

'I'll bear that in mind,' I promise.

I watch him go, then order myself another coffee. That wasn't quite what I was expecting. I thought it would be far more intense and adversarial, but Harry didn't seem interested in playing games. Hopefully, everyone else I meet will be the same. I'm grateful to him for making it so easy for me. I resolve to follow his advice during future dates, assuming I have any further matches.

I sit for a while longer, looking through my old Instagram account, the one I had before I met Paul. I haven't used it for years. Harry is right that people are doing their best to present the most flattering version of themselves – the most photogenic, the glossiest and most polished. There are very few untidy kitchens or unflattering haircuts. That's natural, but I must remember that what I see on this dating app isn't likely to be the full picture, or anything close to it. In the same way, I have no intention of revealing much of the real me until I know someone well.

I set off towards the carpark, wondering whether Mum will be disappointed that nothing has come of this first date. She's so keen for everything to work out for me. I suspect this has a lot to do with the fact that the man with whom she fell in love has temporarily left her, and she isn't sure when he's coming back.

I decide to give her the most positive version of my date. I met a nice man, and we had a pleasant conversation. We won't be meeting again, but it's got me back into the dating pool, and it wasn't as painful as I expected.

I won't be requiring Mavis Sotherby's services this time, but it's good to know she's on standby. There's no knowing who I may meet next. I'll make sure Mum has her on speed dial, just in case.

Chapter Eleven

Isabella is waiting for me when I arrive on Monday morning. She's holding a mug of cappuccino in one hand and a jam tart in the other.

'How did it go?' she asks eagerly.

'It was great,' I say with a dreamy smile. 'The wedding is next Friday. I'm hoping you'll let me have the day off even though it's short notice.'

'Sorry,' she says, 'but Lily has a hospital appointment. You'll have to reschedule.'

I hang up my coat and pull on my overall. 'That's fine. I didn't like him much, but it seemed a wonderful opportunity to get out of working in this dump.'

'I was about to offer to make you a coffee,' she says. 'Just for that, you can make your own.'

I pick up a jam doughnut and take a defiant bite. 'I've had one, thanks. Anyway, I don't have time. I have to mix the dough for the rolls.'

She follows me into the kitchen and plumps herself down next to the mixer.

'The dough can wait, or the customers can buy yesterday's bread. They'll never notice. I want all the details.'

'There aren't many,' I say. 'I met a nice man who gave me a few tips on online dating. We had a pleasant chat, but we've decided not to see each other again. I'm sure that had nothing to do with the fact I told him I had diarrhoea.'

Isabella almost chokes on her tart. 'You didn't?'

'It seemed less embarrassing than telling him I'd arrived five minutes before him and ordered my own coffee.'

I explain the details, and she rocks with laughter. 'What will you do with your next date – threaten to throw up all over him?'

'Maybe. I don't like to plan these things ahead of time. Dates should be spontaneous and unpredictable.'

She takes a swig of coffee and regards me with fascination. 'I can see that. It's going to be fun hearing all about your dating journey.'

'What about yours?' I say. 'You said you were using the same app.'

'I am, but I'm taking a break right now. I've been busy with my other job. I do the accounts for my family business and help out around the farm. Now that Lily has cut down her hours here, I've been stretched a bit thin. Most evenings, all I want to do is collapse in front of the TV. That's why I encouraged you to join the app. I can live vicariously through you.'

'I wouldn't get your hopes up,' I warn her. 'I'll try a couple more dates, but I don't think it's for me. If you're so busy, could you afford to employ someone else part time?'

'I hadn't thought about that,' she says. 'Do you mean to help with the baking or work in the shop?'

'Either, although working in the shop might make more sense. I've been filling in for Lily, which means I don't have as much time to progress the baking side of the business as I'd like. Still, it's up to you.'

She jumps down. 'That's the bell. It's probably Mrs Ogilvie. She and Bernie come in for coffee most Monday mornings.'

'I'm surprised to hear that. She seems to find so much to disapprove of. You'd think she would spend as little time here as possible.'

'I think she's lonely,' she says. 'She comes in several times a week and tells us what we're doing wrong. It's her way of interacting with people. She's been doing it for so long that she doesn't know any other way. It doesn't hurt us, and it gives her pleasure. Besides, I get to say hello to Bernie.'

She goes through to the shop while I set up the mixer. She's right. There's no harm in offering a lonely person somewhere to sit and talk, even if they're not exactly a beam of sunshine around the place. And Isabella is sunny enough for several people. I wonder why she's single. It must be by choice. She's pretty and bubbly and easy going. I imagine every man swipes right on her the moment they see her.

Will anyone else swipe right on me? Harry may be the only one, which is why his message was the first to appear on my screen. It's a depressing thought. I'm not enthused about the whole idea of online dating, but I don't want to fail at it. I'd prefer to quit on my own terms.

I pull out my phone and study my options. There are several pictures I haven't seen before. I skim through the profiles, which aren't too awful. At least, they aren't as bad as some I read last week.

One in particular stood out as an example of what not to do if you want to date an actual human being. He started by listing every movie he'd watched this year, but with no hint as to whether he'd enjoyed them. He said he was a Leo, so he needed a lot of attention. He finished by saying he only dated women who owned their own homes because he needed a second bedroom for his drum kit. I thought he must be a wind-up merchant, but Isabella assured me she'd seen much worse.

On an impulse, I swipe right on all the new profiles. My phone pings, and I'm pleased to see I already have two matches. I message them asking whether they'd like to meet for coffee some time, then go into the shop. As Isabella predicted, Mrs Ogilvie is here, sipping coffee with a pursed mouth and looking around as though hoping to find some aspect of the décor she can criticise.

I greet her politely and ask how Bernie is. He gives me his trademark goofy grin and wags his tail.

'He hasn't been at all well,' she says.

'I'm sorry to hear that.'

She narrows her eyes at me. 'And I know what the problem is. He's been feeling off colour ever since I gave him one of your dog biscuits last Friday. I have no idea what you put in them, but they didn't agree with him.'

'I used the same recipe as always,' I say. 'Are you sure that's what it was? Did you take him to the vet?'

She turns pink. 'I didn't need to. I know when something has disagreed with my dog. He has an extremely sensitive stomach.'

I look at Bernie, who has rolled onto his back and is lazily watching a fly crawl up the table leg.

'He seems to have recovered now,' I say. 'What were his symptoms?'

'He just wasn't himself,' she says. 'It can't have been the trifle. He loves that.'

'He had a taste of your trifle?' I say, surprised.

'How much did he have?' asks Isabella.

Mrs Ogilvie frowns. 'A small helping.'

Isabella gives her a quizzical look.

Mrs Ogilvie sighs. 'And then he finished mine.'

'I think you have your answer,' says Isabella. 'Dogs shouldn't be eating trifle. I knew it wasn't the biscuits. Abby is a wonderful baker. I've seen the latest batch she made. I was tempted to eat one myself.'

She picks up a biscuit from the bowl on the counter. 'Would Bernie like to try one now? We could do with a taste tester.'

Bernie sits up at once, looking so hopeful that I can't help laughing.

'I put a little extra basil in these,' I say. 'I'd be interested to see what he thinks. It isn't often we get a dog in here with such a discriminating palate.'

Mrs Ogilvie hands Bernie the biscuit. 'Would you like a nibble, darling? Don't eat it too fast.'

Bernie interprets this instruction as, 'Please demolish it in two bites!' He crunches it noisily and with evident enjoyment before giving Isabella another hopeful look.

She scratches his head. 'You aren't allowed too many treats. Perhaps Mummy would like to take a few of these biscuits home with her for another day?'

To my astonishment, Mrs Ogilvie meekly pulls out her purse and hands Isabella her card. She tucks the biscuits into her bag, says goodbye, and she and Bernie set off up the high street together.

'That was amazing,' I tell Isabella. 'You're not just a dog whisperer. You're also a Mrs Ogilvie whisperer.'

She laughs. 'She's fine if you handle her properly. She used to come in here to complain about everything, but now she's one of our best customers.'

'I'm glad she doesn't think I poisoned her dog,' I say. 'I like Bernie.'

'She once accused Lily of sending him into a three-day depression by looking at him oddly,' she says. 'Don't take any notice. She'll come around.'

I'm glad to get home on time after work. I've promised Mum I'll make dinner before she goes out to her book club. She hasn't been for months, and I've persuaded her to give it another try.

She greets me with a huge smile. 'Dad's had a wonderful day. We did a jigsaw together and looked at a few gardening books. I suggested you and he should watch something nice this evening. I showed him a few DVDs, and he chose *Brief Encounter*. He's always loved that movie.'

I sling my bag onto the bottom stair. 'I remember how much you enjoyed it. You and I used to make toffee and watch it when I was about thirteen.'

I don't add that I always wondered what she saw in it. As far as I could tell, it was a movie about two indecisive people who couldn't make up their minds what they wanted to do. Perhaps I'll see it differently now I'm no longer looking at it through judgemental teenage eyes.

We eat dinner together as usual. I've made a cheese and onion quiche, which was always one of Dad's favourites. I hope it still is.

Mum scarcely seems to notice what she's eating. There's a glow about her I haven't seen since Dad was taken ill. It's about time she started getting out again and doing things for herself. She was always so active and sociable. Honeywell is a small village, but it's never seemed that way to her. She's always found plenty with which to occupy herself, and she often complains there isn't enough time in the day to do everything.

Since December, her life has grown smaller. I hadn't appreciated until now exactly how small. I resolve to do everything I can to help her expand it again. Now the initial crisis is past, she can allow others to step in. It's a much better use of my time than going out on endless dates with people I have no interest in meeting.

I wave her goodbye, assure her for the umpteenth time that I have her number on speed dial, along with the non-emergency health number and the hospital ward. I promise to call an ambulance at the first sign of trouble and to give Dad his emergency medication while I wait.

Despite all this, I almost have to push her out of the door. 'Everything will be fine, Mum. I promise. Go and enjoy yourself.'

'Perhaps I'd better …' she says.

'No, you shouldn't. If you don't get going, they'll start without you. And it's one of your favourites this week.'

She wavers. 'I do like that Mr Rochester. He's very manly. He reminds me of David Niven.'

Now isn't the time for me to delve into that thought process, so I give her an encouraging smile. 'There you go, then. If you hang around here any longer, Dad and I won't have time to finish our film.'

'I hope he manages it alright,' she says. 'You may have to remind him who some of the characters are. He got confused about that even before his stroke.'

I remember how Dad used to push his chair back so Mum couldn't see him before nodding off, only waking at intervals to ask who the characters were.

'I'll remind him,' I promise. 'Don't forget how many times I've seen it.'

I watch her climb into her car and drive away. I wait a minute longer in case she loses her nerve and circles back to the house. Thankfully, she doesn't.

I find Dad staring out of the window as usual. It's dark outside, so he can't be looking at the garden.

I close the curtains and turn to face him. 'Mum says you want to watch *Brief Encounter* this evening.'

He gives the tiniest shake of his head, and I feel a rush of relief. Dad is still in there somewhere.

'That's what I thought,' I say. 'And I expect you've seen the rest of these films a hundred times. Let's have a look at my phone and see what you might like.'

I open an app and scroll through the films, reading out their titles and watching his face closely. When we reach *Psycho*, he blinks twice.

'You'd like to watch this one?' I ask, and he nods.

'That suits me,' I say. 'We should have enough time to finish it before Mum comes home. In the meantime, I'll put *Brief Encounter* into the DVD player and leave the case on the table where she can see it. There's no need for her to know you've let me watch something that will give me nightmares.'

He makes a small noise that sounds like a laugh.

I squeeze his hand. 'Mum's left the coffee ready for me to make, but I'm not in a coffee mood tonight. I'd prefer a beer. How about you?'

I don't wait for him to answer but go to the kitchen and take two beers out of the fridge. I pop them open and carry them to the living room.

'Tap my arm when you want some,' I say. 'No need to bother with that sippy cup thing. We'll manage fine.'

I pick up the handset and switch on the TV. 'Here we go. Warn me when the scary bits are coming up, and I'll hide behind the sofa.'

Chapter Twelve

Isabella is as good as her word. She advertises for a part-time position in the bakery. We have several applications, and she and Lily whittle down the list to two – a student taking a year off before university, and a young man in his twenties, who's studying at the local catering college.

Somewhat to my surprise, Isabella asks for my opinion.

'It's your business!' I protest, but she doesn't take any notice.

'You'll have to work with them too,' she says. 'It's important we all get along.'

'In which case, I vote for Alice,' I say. 'She's keen to learn the bakery business from the ground up. She can help you in the shop, but she could also be useful to me in the kitchen when we have a rush on. The Sugarloaf is doing well since you reopened. The cafe is a hit, and most people take something home with them. Now is the time to take advantage of that and expand as much as we can. The guy you interviewed yesterday was nice enough, but he obviously had no intention of getting his hands dirty. He wants to serve behind the counter and make coffee, but that's all.'

'I agree with you,' says Isabella. 'I'll call Alice and see whether she's interested.'

I'm delighted to think I may have more time to build up the baking side of the business. It's what I'm trained for. I'm happy to help in any way that's needed, but it makes sense for me to use my expertise. I may even persuade Alice to take some of my early shifts. I like to eat breakfast with Mum and Dad before leaving for the day.

I've cancelled my subscription with *LuvLocatr*. It seems more trouble than it's worth. It still has two weeks to run, and Isabella persuades me to make full use of it.

'If only so I can enjoy it all second hand,' she says. 'I love hearing about other people's dating failures. They make me feel so much better about myself.'

I don't waste sympathy on her. I suspect she's more than capable of meeting people if she wants to, although there's no reason why she should. She's working two jobs and trying to build up a business. No wonder she doesn't have time for anything else.

I allow her to talk me into setting up a couple more meetings before my subscription runs out.

'Two dates won't kill you,' she says. 'And it would mean so much to me.'

She gives me a plaintive smile, and I laugh. 'Your manipulative tactics don't work on me. I'll meet these guys, but only because I've paid for a full month. And because my mother will be disappointed if I give up without trying.'

This is true. Mum asks me almost every day whether I'm meeting anyone that evening.

'Why is this so important to you?' I demand when she asks me again the following morning. 'You've only just got me home, and now you're doing your best to get rid of me.'

Her face clouds. 'That isn't true, and you know it. But I'm aware of what you've given up in coming home to help us out. I don't want you to be lonely on top of everything else.'

She couldn't be further from the truth. I've had more fun working at The Sugarloaf Bakery these past two weeks than during the whole of my time in Reading. I put up with Matt and a sub-optimal work environment for far too long, simply for a man. And not just any man. One who had no intention of committing to me but was obviously waiting until someone better came along.

I'm never going to let that happen again, which may be why I've decided not to continue with *LuvLocatr*. I don't feel in a position to trust anyone in a hurry, particularly strangers I've only just met. But I'd rather not explain all this to Mum, who's anxious enough about her current life without me adding to it.

I give her a quick hug. 'You're just upset Mavis Sotherby won't get to do her stuff. I have to run now. It's our "get a free coffee with every cake" hour at the cafe this morning. Last week, we had people queueing out of the door, and there was nearly a fight for the last table. Umbrellas were waved threateningly at one point. Honeywell seems like a sleepy little village, but there's a dark undercurrent of elderly mafia. You should come along. I'll make sure you get a seat as a friend of the management.'

She looks regretful. 'Oh, Abby, I'd love to, but the physio is coming this morning, and I have to be here. Maybe next week. Dad's been doing so well since you came home. He's much brighter in himself, and he smiles a lot more. It's so nice for him to have another face to see each day.'

I'm pleased to hear this. I've certainly detected a change in him, but some of that will be due to the passage of time and the natural process of recovery. I can't ascribe too much of it to my presence. Mum is the heroine, not me. She's worked patiently with the professionals and kept her hopes up during these past few months. She deserves any credit that's going.

'I'll be home around six,' I say, 'but I'm going out again later. You'll be delighted to hear I have not one but two dates lined up for tonight.'

She looks shocked. 'Not at the same time?'

'Absolutely not!' I say. 'This is a respectable dating site. I'm meeting one of them at seven for coffee and the other at eight for decaf coffee. Otherwise, I won't sleep, and tomorrow is sourdough day, which means an early start. I'll give you all the details before I leave in case Mavis Sotherby wants to hide behind a pillar or plant a voice recorder in a nearby yucca.'

Isabella is interested to hear about my plans for the evening. 'That's adventurous of you, but aren't you worried your first date will overrun, and the next one will arrive early and see you with someone else?'

I give her a patronising smile. 'You're such a novice. For one thing, I'm meeting them at different cafes. For another, if the first one is late, I'll get up and leave. I'm not interested in getting to know someone who can't be bothered to turn up on time for our first meeting.'

She looks impressed. 'Quite right. My mother always told me never to wait for dinner or a man.'

She reaches for a madeleine. 'Do you have time to whip up another batch of chocolate chip cookies? It's happy hour at ten, and I'm expecting a rush.'

'You could start issuing tickets,' I suggest.

'I wanted to buy one of those red velvet ropes,' she says. 'We could cordon off the tables at the far end of the cafe. Having a VIP area would add to our reputation for exclusivity. People would come from miles around just to say they'd sat there. We might even get celebrities. I hear Harry Styles is partial to a bit of jam roly poly.'

'What did Lily say about the rope?' I ask as I pull on my hairnet.

'Oh, you know Lily,' she says. 'She's terribly conservative. It's one of the reasons I hired you. You and I can make a lot of changes while her mind is on other things.'

I laugh. 'I wouldn't know what to say to a celebrity.'

'"Have a scone!" would be a good icebreaker,' she says. 'We can talk about it another time. Right now, we have work to do. Those cookies won't bake themselves, and it's already nine o'clock. We have exactly one hour to avert a riot.'

Chapter Thirteen

By the time I finish work, all I want to do is take a long, hot bath and collapse in front of the TV. I wouldn't even mind watching *Brief Encounter* if that's what it takes. I miss the days when I would arrive home from a night out to find Mum glued to the movie, with Dad dozing in his chair or teasing her by asking at intervals if the film was a remake of *Close Encounters*.

Life was so predictable and uncomplicated in those days. I often wonder why none of us realised and appreciated it. Even if Dad exceeds our wildest expectations and makes a complete recovery, nothing will ever be the same. The memory of that phone call will never leave me. And Mum will never again live in a world where she can come home without expecting anything awful to have happened while she was away.

We're far luckier than many people. We have the chance to pick up the threads of our own lives and weave them into a new and acceptable pattern. But I can't help wishing I didn't have to do any weaving at all. I'd like to be back where we were two years ago, when my life was rosy and full of promise, and my future with Paul felt assured.

This dating thing is part of my attempt to make sure I keep moving forward and accept I can't move backwards. But it feels exhausting after a long day of baking, making coffee, and watching Isabella adjudicate the happy hour scrimmage.

I help Mum cook dinner, then sit with Dad and tell him about my plans for the evening. This is another thing that reminds me of how much has changed. In the past, I would never have dreamed of discussing my social life with my parents, and I never mentioned casual boyfriends. Mum and Dad only got to meet someone when I'd been with them for at least a year, which means they only really met Paul. Even that didn't go as well as I'd hoped. Paul was polite but busy, and I could tell Mum and Dad thought he should have made more of an effort.

They knew better than to say this to me. Emily was the only person I allowed to say mean things about Paul. I doubt I'd have been able to stop her if I'd tried, so I didn't bother. Her outraged invective was a comfort when I couldn't find my own words to talk to myself about how I felt.

I say goodbye to Mum and Dad and set off for the same cafe where I met Harry last week. There are plenty of cafes in our nearest town, but not all of them are suitable for this sort of meeting. I want somewhere large enough for us to remain anonymous. I don't want anyone overhearing our painful attempts at getting to know each other. It's bad enough having to go through it myself without seeing other people's suppressed smiles as we talk about our hobbies and jobs, and, if things get really sticky, our favourite colours.

I order myself a coffee while I wait for Mike to arrive. I wonder why I was so ambivalent last week about the idea of ordering for myself. It's far easier and saves the embarrassment of one of us offering to pay and the other one feeling they ought to arrange a second date to keep things even.

Mike arrives exactly at seven o'clock, which is a mark in his favour. He greets me pleasantly and waves to the server. He doesn't ask about the state of my digestive processes, and I don't volunteer any unnecessary information. I'm getting better at this.

'So, Abby, what do you do?' he asks.

I've already realised it won't be possible to hide my profession from anyone with half a brain and an internet connection. It doesn't matter. I don't have to tell him where I live or give him the pin code for my bank card or my grandmother's maiden name.

'I work at a bakery near here,' I say.

He looks surprised. 'Are you sure?'

'Pretty sure. At least, I walk up there each day and serve the customers, and the owners put money into my account at the end of the week.'

He doesn't smile. 'I read your profile, and it said banker.'

'Either it's been hacked, or you can't read too well.'

He pulls out his phone. 'Let's have a look.'

Is this guy for real? Is he going to mansplain my job to me after having only known me for two seconds? Not mansplain exactly but try to catch me out and prove I can't type accurately.

'Is this a problem for you?' I say.

He looks up from the screen. 'Maybe not. It depends on whether you made a mistake typing or were lying on your profile to big yourself up.'

I can't speak for a moment, which is lucky. It gives me time to plan an answer and choke down the sort of response that would have me thrown out of the cafe for outraging public decency.

I reach over and take his phone from him. I feel an impulse to drop it into his coffee, but that may not be the best idea. I lay it on the table, its screen facing downwards. 'Are you telling me a baker isn't good enough for you?'

He has the grace to flush. 'No, but I don't want anyone who plays stupid games.'

'I get that, but it's a pretty serious accusation to make. Are you sure this is a road you want to go down?'

I'm not sure why I'm giving him a chance. I should get up and walk out without a backward glance. But it's raining, and I'm not due at the next cafe for another forty-five minutes.

He picks up his phone. 'I'm simply checking whether this was a mistake or a deliberate deception.'

That does it. I'd rather stand in the pouring rain for the next hour than spend one more second with this man.

I point towards a table at the far end of the cafe where two women are standing up to leave. 'That table is free. You can do your "checking" over there. We're done here.'

The server approaches with Mike's coffee.

'Can you put it over there, please?' I say. 'This is my table, and I don't want company.'

Mike pushes back his chair. 'You're overreacting. If I find it was a typo, I'll be happy to continue with our date.'

I pick up my book and open it to the bookmarked page. 'Not a date. A lucky escape.' I start reading, ignoring his aggrieved snort.

Thankfully, he doesn't make a scene. He follows the server and sits down. I wait for a minute, then sneak a look at him. He's staring at his screen, a crestfallen expression on his face. He sees me watching him and turns his chair away.

I pretend to read for a few minutes longer while I finish my coffee. I have to walk past Mike's table as I leave, but he doesn't look up. This was a waste of time. The only good thing is that I'll have a story to tell Isabella in the morning.

I wander around the shopping centre until it's time to meet Marcus. Hopefully, he's not a talker, and we can keep this short and sweet. It doesn't even need to be sweet. Right now, I'd settle for him not accusing me of lying.

He's already there when I arrive. I recognise him at once. He's wearing the same blue sweater as in his profile. Is that his version of a red rose and a rolled-up newspaper? I remind myself this isn't a spy novel, which is a pity because Mavis Sotherby would have a field day.

I walk over to greet him. He stands and shakes my hand. 'Can I get you a coffee?'

'That's kind of you, but I'll get it,' I say, walking to the counter before he can argue.

I take the number the server hands me and sit down.

'How did you know what I wanted?' asks Marcus.

'I'm so sorry,' I stammer. 'I thought you'd already ordered.'

'Why would I do that when you hadn't arrived?'

I swallow hard. 'It's quite common on these sorts of dates to order for yourself if the other person hasn't turned up.'

He frowns. 'It's the first I've heard of it. If you ask me, it's rude.'

I haven't asked him, but he seems the sort to give his opinion anyway. He has an abrupt way of speaking and a decisive air that reminds me of someone I once dated who was in the army.

'Would you like me to go back and add something to my order?' I say.

'Don't bother,' he says, waving to a nearby server. 'Excuse me, I'd like a latte when you have a moment.'

He darts a look at me. 'She's already ordered for herself.'

That's told me! Perhaps he's right, and Harry was wrong. It may have been a gauche thing to do. It's yet another reason for me to discontinue using this app. I have neither the time nor the energy to bother learning a stack of unwritten and meaningless rules. I did enough of that in primary school.

Marcus' order arrives, and we face each other over the coffee cups.

'What do you do for work?' I ask to get the conversation flowing. I already know he's an investment analyst, but I'm not sure what else to say. This date has got off to a rocky start, but we haven't quite reached the stage of discussing our favourite section of the Dulux chart.

'I'm an analyst,' he says.

This is a good start. He hasn't told me a barefaced lie right out of the gate. My standards have slipped since I started doing this.

'Do you enjoy it?' I enquire when he shows no sign of asking me the same question.

'It's fine. The money's great, which is more than you can say about your job.'

I blink. 'What?'

He shrugs. 'You're a baker. That can't pay much.'

I don't know whether to be outraged at his rudeness or relieved he's at least able to read.

'Did you mean to be so offensive?' I manage at last.

He raises an eyebrow. 'It's hardly news that an investment analyst earns more than someone working in a shop.'

'If that's so important to you, why did you meet me?' I say. 'My job is right there in my profile. It doesn't say banker, despite what some people appear to believe.'

He doesn't miss a beat. 'I know what it says. I almost didn't swipe, but you're a good-looking girl, so I thought I'd take a shot. I'm telling you upfront that I don't intend to be anyone's meal ticket. If someone wants to be with me, they'd better be earning well or be prepared to up their game.'

I snatch up my bag. 'My "game" is fine, thank you very much. You may earn well, but I'd be astounded if anyone wanted to share your millions with you. Not if it meant being in the same room with you for more than five minutes, and I've already exceeded that.'

'You should calm down,' he says. 'Men don't like it when women get hysterical. I certainly don't.'

'Then you definitely won't like this!'

I pick up the rest of my coffee and tip it into his lap. It's a pity it isn't boiling hot.

I beckon to the server. 'I'm afraid my friend here has had a bit of an accident. I wonder if you could bring him a cloth.'

Marcus hasn't moved. His face is frozen with shock. I don't know why he seems surprised. This can't be the first drink he's had poured over him.

'It's nothing to be ashamed of,' I tell him sweetly. 'It happens to lots of people.'

Without giving him time to reply, I sweep past him and out of the cafe.

Chapter Fourteen

I walk past the shops towards the car park, half horrified with myself and half tempted to burst into hysterical laughter. I've never done anything like that before. I can't think what possessed me. All I had to do was maintain my dignity, tell Marcus I wasn't feeling the connection, and leave. Instead, I threw all Harry's advice to the winds and behaved like an absolute idiot. It's a good thing I'm through with internet dating. I'm not cut out for it.

Isabella will be delighted when she hears what I've done. It's exactly the sort of thing her mother would have told her to do. At least, I expect it is. I've heard many stories about the advice her mother has given her over the years. It's left me with a strong desire to meet her as soon as possible.

I pass Bendine's and remember I promised Mum I'd pick up some navy blue thread the next time I was in town. She wants to mend a pair of Dad's favourite trousers. They weren't expensive, and I would usually suggest she buy some new ones. But I understand why she wants to hold on to this pair and try to fix them.

I locate the racks of thread and examine the dark blue reels. How many shades of navy blue can there be? I try to visualise the exact shade of Dad's trousers, but I can't. I select a reel of bright navy and another rather closer to black. One of them ought to match.

I stand in line to pay, annoyance bubbling up inside me. It was fun to give into my impulse and dump my coffee into Marcus' lap. But the elation has subsided now, and I'm feeling increasingly upset. Both of my dates tonight have objected to my job. Mike, because I tried to trick him into thinking I was a banker, which is far more prestigious than a baker. Marcus, because I don't earn enough, which means I don't have enough ambition.

Part of this annoyance is directed at myself. I've never been driven to reach the pinnacle of my profession and become the next Raymond Blanc. But I've spent the past two years treading water and ignoring all thoughts of career progression because of a man who always put himself first.

I'm living back home now because my circumstances have changed. There's nowhere I'd rather be and nothing more important at this point in my life than spending time with my parents. If that means working in a tiny village bakery for a relatively low wage, so be it. How dare anyone try to put me down for that?

By the time I reach the counter, I'm fizzing with rage. I'd like to buy a bottle of blackcurrant juice and return to the second cafe to see whether Marcus has left. It would make a lovely pattern on his white shirt. As for Mike and his insistence on catching me out, words fail me.

I slam down the reels of cotton and tap my card. I remember this isn't the assistant's problem and thank her as politely as I can when she hands me the bag. I walk towards the door, fighting a rising feeling of anger. Why did I come here tonight when I didn't even want to? Why am I allowing complete strangers to judge me and make me feel bad about myself?

I walk around a display of brightly coloured wools without looking where I'm going. Someone cannons into me, and I stagger and almost fall. My bag goes flying, and the cotton reels tumble out onto the floor. One of them rolls under a cabinet. I can't see where the other one has gone until I hear an ominous crunch.

'I'm so sorry!' says a voice.

I glare at the man who bumped into me. 'What do you think you're doing? Why does no one look where they're going? First, you crash into me, and now you've ruined my reel of cotton.'

'I'm so sorry,' he says again. 'To be fair, we both crashed into each other. You were moving pretty fast. You came around that display before I had time to react.'

'Of course, it was my fault!' I shout. 'I knocked your purchases all over the floor, then stood on them with my stupid great boot.'

He looks amused, which infuriates me further. 'I'm wearing trainers.'

'I don't care! You've ruined my stuff. My mum really needed that cotton.'

I half expect him to lose his temper too. I'm acting like a child, and I know it. He would be well within his rights to shout back at me, tell me to get a grip, and storm off.

'It was obviously important to you,' he says. 'Can you show me what you bought, and I'll replace it for you?'

I instantly deflate. It's one thing to argue with someone who's yelling back at you. It's quite another to shout at someone you know perfectly well is blameless for your situation.

'Don't bother,' I say sulkily. 'I'll get it myself.'

'Can I at least pay half?' he says. 'That seems fair.'

'Fair?' I hear my voice rising. I know I'm being unreasonable, but I'm powerless to stop myself. 'Why are you talking about fair? Nothing is fair about life. Absolutely nothing!'

To my fury, I feel tears spring to my eyes and turn away before this complete stranger can see me cry. What must he think of me banging into him and yelling at him about a couple of reels of thread? But he's the third man I've met tonight who's annoyed me, and I don't seem able to control myself. Time to go home.

I stuff the empty paper bag into my pocket. 'Excuse me,' I say, and try to push past him.

He doesn't move. 'If you won't let me buy you some more cotton, will you at least let me buy you a coffee?'

'Why?' I'm aware of how rude I sound, but I'm past caring.

'Because you look as though you need one,' he says. 'And because you're clearly having a bad day, and I thought you might like someone to shout at a bit more.'

This unexpected kindness makes me cry in earnest. What am I doing, standing in the middle of Bendine's, sobbing all over a complete stranger? I want to refuse, but I can't go home like this. Mum would know in an instant something was wrong, however cheerful I tried to appear. If I have to stay here, it would be nice to have someone to talk to whom I don't need to impress. He isn't one of my dates, so I'm not trying to put on a façade for him. I never have to see him again.

'Is it a deal?' he asks.

'If you must.'

I don't want to sound too enthusiastic and give him any ideas, although it's unlikely he has any. My face gets hideously blotchy when I cry, and I'm pretty sure my mascara is running.

'I could do with a drink myself,' he says. 'I've had a long day, and I hate shopping. There's a place down there.'

I follow him towards the cafe, and he points to a table. 'That one's free if we hurry. What are you drinking?'

'A latte, please.'

I reach for my purse, but he stops me. 'This is a penance, remember?'

I'm too tired to argue, so I sit down and wait for him to return. I pull a mirror out of my bag and inspect my face. It's even worse than I imagined, but I don't care. I wipe my eyes with a tissue and remove a streak of eyeshadow from my cheek. That will have to do.

He returns to the table carrying two mugs. 'Yours is the one with the pretty pattern on top.'

I look at the foam on my latte. 'What's it supposed to be?'

'No idea. A squirrel, perhaps? That feathery bit could be its tail.'

'I think it's an aeroplane,' I say. 'A pre-war model.'

'You may be right. The barista was making so much effort I didn't like to ask.'

'Thank you for the coffee,' I say, taking a sip. 'I'm sorry I was rude to you.'

'You were upset,' he says. 'I didn't take it personally. Do you want to talk about it?'

'Not really. I don't know why I reacted like that, but it's not your problem.'

I take another sip of coffee. 'What's wrong with being a baker?' I burst out. 'It's a perfectly legitimate job.'

He looks surprised. 'It is. As a matter of fact …'

'Maybe it doesn't pay too well,' I say, hardly hearing him. 'But there are more important things in life than money, and most of them are out of our control. Besides, people need bakers! They may not notice us often, but they would if we all disappeared.'

'I don't disagree,' he says. 'I …'

'It isn't only bread!' I press on, unheeding. 'I make cakes too, and biscuits, tarts, slices. Last year, I made a wedding cake for an elderly couple who were getting married, and she cried when she saw it.'

I realise too late how that must sound. 'Because it was so beautiful, not because I messed it up.'

He grins. 'I'm glad to hear it. I don't know who you're arguing with, but it isn't me. I'm a baker myself.'

I feel oddly disappointed that someone who seemed so nice should think this was a good time to make fun of me.

'No, you aren't!' I say.

'I'm the head baker at The Slice in Parford. Do you know it?'

'I've never heard of it. Are you making it up?'

'I'm afraid not.' He pulls out his phone and starts scrolling through it.

'You're the second person who's done that to me tonight,' I say.

He shrugs. 'You seem so sure my bakery doesn't exist that I'm starting to wonder whether it's all been a bad dream. No, here it is.'

He pushes his phone towards me and shows me a website that says *Slice Bakery*.

'That's us,' he says. 'How about you? Where do you work?'

Is this the time to tell him I've made a mistake, and I'm actually a banker? He seems ok, but so do most con men. They have to, or no one would ever allow themselves to be conned.

'You don't have to tell me,' he says when I don't speak. 'In fact, I'd rather you didn't. I like your air of mystery.'

'Misery?' I say.

He laughs. 'I said mystery. But speaking of misery, you're welcome to talk about it. We'll probably never see each other again. We've already established that you're using being a baker as your cover story. Are you working for the government on some top-secret mission involving a lot of cotton thread?'

I laugh despite myself. 'Such as?'

'How should I know? You're the spy.'

'I might be trying to catch someone attempting to steal the crown jewels,' I suggest.

He nods. 'That sounds plausible. I know that rich countries like Switzerland use lasers because I've seen Mission Impossible. But this country is in a recession. Our government is always talking about cutbacks. This is probably one of them.'

It's impossible to dislike this man. I hold out my hand. 'I'm Abby.'

'Our woman in Hampshire?' he says, shaking my hand.

'Not our woman anywhere. At least, not in that sense. I work at The Sugarloaf Bakery in Honeywell.'

'I'm sure that makes excellent cover for whatever you're really up to,' he says. 'Who would suspect someone of conducting a covert surveillance operation out of a newly renovated bakery?'

'Do you know it?' I say.

'Of course. It's my business to know all our rivals. It's been interesting watching what the new owners have done with the place. Are they making it pay?'

'You have a cheek accusing me of being a spy!' I say.

'Professional curiosity. My name's Chris, by the way. You can't have been working there for long. They've only recently opened again after the refit.'

'I started a couple of weeks ago,' I say. 'I'm enjoying it.'

'Where were you working before?'

'At a horrible bakery in Reading. You won't have heard of it. I wish I hadn't.'

'How did you hear about the Sugarloaf?' he asks.

'I grew up in this area. My parents are still here. That's why I moved back. My father's been ill.'

He gives a sympathetic nod. 'I'm sorry to hear that. How's he doing?'

'He had a major stroke before Christmas. He was lucky to get to hospital in time and have all the right treatment, but it's going to be a long process.'

'And you came home to help out.' It's a statement, not a question, so I don't feel the need to answer.

'I can understand why you lost it tonight,' he goes on. 'I'm surprised you didn't pick up a cotton reel and stuff it down my throat.'

'That's kind of you, considering I had a complete meltdown over something so trivial.'

'Nothing's trivial when you're dealing with something like this,' he says. 'I was the same when my mum was diagnosed with cancer. A guy in the shop gave me Diet Coke when I asked for Pepsi, and I threw it on the ground and stormed out.'

My eyes fill with tears again, and I look away from him. Why is it that you can cope when the entire world seems against you, but you crumble when someone is nice to you?

He touches my hand gently. 'It's fine, Abby. Nothing will be normal for a while. You may as well prepare for that.'

'Did your mother …?' I can't finish the question.

'She's been in remission for ten years,' he says. 'We know how lucky we are, but it doesn't make it any easier while you're going through it. Don't be too hard on yourself. If you need to throw the odd can of soda, go ahead. Just try not to hit anyone.'

I give a reluctant smile. 'I poured a cup of coffee on someone right before I met you.'

He grins. 'I got off lightly, then. Why did you do that?'

'He told me to calm down.'

'I'd say he was asking for it. That's a pretty awful thing to say even when things are going fine. Did he know your father wasn't well?'

'We hadn't got that far,' I say. 'It was a blind date. Well, a dating app date. We'd only talked for five minutes when he told me that bakers don't earn much, and I shouldn't plan to mooch off a high-earning alpha male like himself.'

He whistles. 'You were most restrained in limiting it to a cup of coffee. I hope it was extremely hot?'

'Sadly not, but that was probably for the best. I have enough on my plate at the moment without coping with lawsuits.'

'I'm sorry that happened,' he says. 'It's none of my business, but do you think now is a good time to be doing this? From what I hear, these dating apps are a minefield at the best of times.'

'I agree. I only joined because my mother was so anxious about me coming home. She feels guilty because she thinks she's destroyed my wonderful social life in Reading. If only she knew! I paid for a month's trial, and I've already cancelled my account. But my co-worker insisted I get as much value as possible for my money, so I set up a final couple of dates. It wasn't the greatest idea.'

I remember Mike. I'd forgotten him in all the excitement of the coffee throwing. 'I met someone else earlier tonight. He was sure I'd written banker on my profile, and he felt short changed by my actual job.'

'Hence your rant about bakers,' he says. 'That makes a lot more sense now.'

'I don't know why I was so sensitive about it. I love my job, and I've never regretted choosing it.'

'Me neither,' he says. 'I couldn't bear to work in an office doing the same thing all day. I like plenty of variety.'

'Me too, although there is such a thing as too much variety. I almost lost my eyebrows on my first day at my previous job.'

'This I must hear!' he says.

A server stops by our table. 'I'm afraid we're about to close.'

'Now I'll never know what happened,' says Chris.

'You said you liked mysteries,' I remind him. 'Thank you for rescuing me. I'm glad you were there.'

'It was nothing,' he says. 'Plenty of people had to do the same for me when I was going through a similar thing.'

We walk to the door, and I turn to say goodbye. 'Thanks again.'

He hesitates. 'Is there any chance you'd like to meet up again sometime? I really enjoyed talking to you, and I still don't know what happened to your eyebrows.'

I'm too surprised to answer.

'I shouldn't have asked,' he says quickly. 'It feels as though I'm taking advantage of you when you're vulnerable. Forget it.'

'How do you know I'm single?' I ask.

'Is your husband about to appear and knock my teeth out? That would serve me right, wouldn't it? I assumed you wouldn't be using a dating app if you weren't single, but that's pretty narrowminded of me.'

I study his face. I like his friendly grin and calm demeanour. I decide to take a chance. How much worse could this man be than the people I've met tonight?

'Why don't you give me your phone number?' I say. 'I can call you when I'm ready.'

He looks pleased. 'If you're sure. You could always drop by the bakery sometime and make sure I'm exactly who I say I am. Here's my number. It would be great to go out some time, but it's fine if you decide not to. You're going through a difficult time, and you should call all the shots.'

He looks down at me, his grey eyes more serious. 'You're going to be ok, Abby. I know it doesn't feel like it right now, but you are.'

My throat constricts. 'How can you know that for sure?'

'Because that's how it works. Things happen to us out of the blue, things we're convinced we'll never cope with. But we do, partly because we have to, and partly because we want to. Don't underestimate your resilience. You're stronger than you give yourself credit for. We all are. But we have to learn to allow other people to help us. There's always someone around anxious to lend us a hand if we let them.'

I can't think of anything to say. I'm sure he's right, but it's difficult to feel that way when you're in the middle of the situation.

He seems to understand. 'It was great meeting you, Abby. If I don't see you again, take care.'

Chapter Fifteen

I arrive at work a few minutes late the following morning. I apologise profusely to Lily, who's unloading a box of chocolate chips.

'I'm so sorry. It won't happen again. I can work late tonight to make up for it.'

'You're only five minutes late,' she says. 'Isabella is usually much later than that.'

'She owns the bakery. It isn't the same thing.'

'She's a part owner,' she says. 'To be accurate, neither of us owns it. If we went bust tomorrow, the bank would take everything.'

'I could call the bank and apologise for being late,' I say, and she laughs.

'That won't be necessary unless you make a habit of it. Is everything alright at home? Should you even be here today?'

I pull on my overall. 'Everything's fine, thanks. This was on me. I didn't sleep well last night, and I overslept my alarm.'

'I did that all the time when I first started working here,' she says. 'If it hadn't been for my mum, I'd have been fired during my first week. My brother used to download ringtones for my alarm. One of them was a fire engine.'

'I must ask him where he got it from,' I say. 'My mum would wake me up every day if I asked her, but it wouldn't be fair. She often gets up with my dad in the night, and I like her to get as much sleep as she can.'

Lily looks sympathetic. 'It must be tough for her. For you both.'

'It's toughest for Dad,' I say. 'Although I'm not sure how much he's aware of what's happened to him. That's the worst thing about it. He was always so strong and decisive, and he took care of everyone else. I can't imagine how it feels to have all that taken away from you and have to depend on other people for even your basic needs. If he knows what's going on, he'll hate it. I sometimes hope he doesn't, but not really.'

'I can hardly imagine,' she says. 'If you ever need to come in late or leave early, let us know. We can cover you for a while. The baby's not due for ten more weeks, and it's good for me to stay active. At least, that's what my midwife says. My mum doesn't agree. If she had her way, I'd lie on the sofa all day eating chocolate and never lifting a finger. I can't think why. My dad says she didn't slow down at all with either of us, and she was rushing around as usual soon afterwards. But she's always been protective of her children.'

'Mum's a bit like that with me,' I say. 'I mean, she used to be. She doesn't have the time nowadays. She worries about every single thing I do, but she has no energy to do anything about it. I'll know she's getting better once she starts interfering in my life again. Who would have thought I'd be looking forward to that?'

The shop door opens and Isabella bursts in. 'I'm not too late, am I?'

She makes a dive for the coffee machine. 'Anyone else want one?'

Lily and I shake our heads. Isabella pulls off her coat and looks from Lily to me. 'Don't tell me I've missed the debrief! That's not fair. I got here as quickly as I could, considering I overslept both my alarms.'

The door opens before I can answer. A man comes in and closes it carefully behind him.

'Hello, Mr Mason,' says Lily. 'How nice to see you. What can we get for you today?'

The man looks puzzled, as though this is an odd question for anyone to pose to someone who wanders into a shop.

'I'm not sure,' he says.

'No problem,' says Lily. 'Take your time.'

'Hello, Mr Mason,' says Isabella, appearing from behind the coffee machine and making him jump.

'Good morning … er …'

'Isabella,' she prompts him. 'Have you met our newest member of staff?'

He peers at me. 'I don't think …'

'This is Abby,' says Lily. 'Abby, this is Mr Mason. He owned the bakery for many years until he retired and we took it over.'

I shake his hand. 'It's lovely to meet you. It must feel strange to see how much the place has changed.'

'Hardly at all!' interrupts Isabella with a warning glance at me.

'But the cafe is new,' I say. 'And you told me no one has used the kitchen for a while.'

'It was used for many years,' says Mr Mason. 'It was only during my last couple of years here that I decided it would be easier to order things in.'

'It worked very well,' says Lily. 'I learned everything I know from Mr Mason. He was an excellent teacher.'

Mr Mason looks pleased. 'You were a quick learner, my dear. It was a pleasure to work with you. And how is your mother?'

Isabella draws me away from the counter, leaving Lily to update Mr Mason on her family details.

'Never mind all that,' she says. 'How did last night go?'

I'd almost forgotten last night, which is surprising. I'm exhausted from lack of sleep and my mad dash to work. I wasn't expecting to be fired on the spot for my lateness, but Lily and Isabella have been so kind and supportive that I don't want to let them down. If I hadn't found this job, I'd have had to look further afield, which would have been far less convenient. It would have been odd if I'd ended up working at The Slice.

'It was weird,' I say at last.

'Good weird or bad weird?' she asks.

I'm not sure how to answer. The first part of the evening was awful, but it was redeemed by Chris's kindness.

'Mixed weird,' I say.

Her eyes sparkle. 'My favourite sort of weird. Sit down and tell me what happened. Lily and Mr Mason will be ages. He's a bit of a talker when he gets going, and she's too kind for her own good.'

The shop door opens again, and Isabella sighs. 'No rest for the wicked.'

'It's awful, isn't it?' I agree. 'It's almost as though we aren't here to drink coffee and discuss my love life all day.'

She rolls her eyes at me and walks over to the counter, where Mr Mason and Lily are still deep in conversation.

'Hello, Mrs Ogilvie!' she says loudly.

Mr Mason spins around. He sees Mrs Ogilvie and Bernie and his face freezes.

'Madam!' he begins.

'It's alright, Mr Mason,' says Lily. 'We allow dogs in here if they're quiet and well behaved.'

Mrs Ogilvie gives him a smug look. Bernie has already trotted over to his usual table. He sits expectantly next to the chair and gives an experimental bark.

'Shhh, darling!' says Mrs Ogilvie. 'Mummy is choosing you a nice biscuit.'

Mr Mason looks even more horrified. 'This is a food area,' he tells Lily.

'I know,' she says in a soothing voice. 'We're careful to keep animals out of the food preparation areas. We've passed all our health and safety inspections, and they're happy with the precautions we've put in place.'

He shakes his head. 'You're making a grave mistake, my dear. A very grave mistake.'

'I always think it's a shame when businesses can't move with the times,' says Mrs Ogilvie.

'Can I get you a nice cup of coffee, Mr Mason?' says Isabella. 'On the house, of course. I'm so pleased you've come in today. We've been wanting to show you around and ask your advice on a few things.'

Mrs Ogilvie snorts. 'Nothing to do with customer service, I hope. That's one area in which this establishment has always been sadly lacking.'

Isabella ignores her. She shepherds Mr Mason towards a table at the far end of the cafe and beckons to Lily to join him.

'I'll bring you both a coffee,' she says. 'And some of those nice caramel slices you like. I'm glad you've come in, Mr Mason. Lily shouldn't be on her feet too much, but you know what she's like. She's a hard worker.'

'She is indeed,' says Mr Mason. 'I would be delighted to stay for a coffee.'

Lily pulls a face at Isabella as she passes. 'I'm supposed to be sorting the spices this morning. I noticed our stocks were getting low.'

'Abby can do that,' says Isabella. 'Put your feet up for a few minutes. You look exhausted. If you don't talk to him, Mrs Ogilvie will, and we don't want a fight breaking out in our prim and proper little establishment.'

Chapter Sixteen

She waits until Lily and Mr Mason are settled with their drinks before dragging me into the kitchen.

'I'm not waiting any longer!' she says. 'I want to know how last night went. Don't keep me in suspense. How was it weird?'

Most of last night is hazy. I barely remember the earlier part, and the drive home was a blur. I was exhausted by the time I got back. I only had time to assure Mum I'd enjoyed my evening and met some nice people before falling into bed.

I was so wiped out that I expected to crash the moment my head hit the pillow. Instead, I lay awake half the night thinking about the bizarre situation in which I've found myself. Six months ago, I was about to move in with Paul and look for a better job wherever he and I decided to live. I expected to visit Mum and Dad each month, as I always had, and help them plan their retirement. They had so many wonderful ideas for trips away, and they wanted to remodel the house and garden so they could stay there as they got older.

Instead, I've left the city entirely and moved back to my childhood home, where my mother is worn to shreds looking after my father, and he's a shadow of the man he used to be.

I've also lost Paul, the one constant in my life. Even if by some miracle he realised what he'd thrown away, I wouldn't want him back, but it still hurts. It would have been different if he'd asked for space to consider his future. But he didn't. He considered his future without talking to me, and he did it while seeing another woman. No relationship could survive that.

Still, it's yet another loss to add to the long list of losses I've suffered over the past few months. I hadn't thought about it that way until last night. I'm still not sure what happened, but it had nothing to do with meeting a couple of jerks.

People meet jerks every day, and they don't react by hurling coffee and screaming at complete strangers in the haberdashery section of their local department store.

I didn't want to talk to Isabella about any of this until I'd got my head clearer, but she's so eager to hear about last night that I can't refuse. I decide to give her edited highlights.

'The first guy turned up on time,' I begin.

'That's a good sign,' she says.

'I thought so, but it all went downhill from there. He'd got it into his head that I was a banker, not a baker.'

She grins. 'It's a simple mistake to make when you're skimming through someone's profile. Like genealogists and geologists, or barristers and baristas.'

I wait until she's finished amusing herself. 'It wouldn't have been a problem if he hadn't got on his high horse about a possible deception and insisted on demonstrating how I'd set out to trick him.'

Her eyes gleam. 'Are you serious? What did he do?'

'Pulled out his phone and started searching through the app to prove he was right.'

'He sounds dreamy,' she says. 'I love a man who can't bear to be wrong. What did you do?'

'Told him the date was over and he could conduct his detective work from a different table.'

'I'm disappointed,' she says. 'I would have expected something far more drastic.'

'I was saving that for the next one.'

'Tell me at once!' she commands. 'Before any more customers arrive.'

'There isn't much to tell. The next one was at least literate. He knew what I did for a living.'

'Thank goodness for that,' she says.

'Not so fast! He didn't approve of my life choices. But my photo was enough to make him overlook my being a low earner, as long as I understood I wasn't getting a sniff of his money and needed to pull my socks up and find myself a better career if I wanted a shot with him.'

She gives a shriek of laughter. 'That can't be true! You're making it up.'

'Not even a bit. It's lucky he's a top earner because he'll be able to afford his dry cleaning bill. He was wearing an expensive suit, and unfortunately he got coffee all over it.'

She looks at me in awe. 'When you say unfortunately …?'

I shrug. 'My hand isn't always as steady as it might be.'

She wipes her eyes. 'I'm going back on that app today. I had no idea it was so much fun.'

'It didn't feel like fun,' I say. 'It was all pretty stressful. I got out of there as quickly as possible before he could sue me for assault.'

'He'll probably report you to *LuvLocatr*,' she says.

'I doubt it. That sort of man doesn't like to admit someone made him look like an idiot in public. I don't care if he does. I've cancelled my subscription. It isn't for me.'

'I understand,' she says. 'I hope you didn't feel pushed into it because I was so keen for you to join.'

'Not as keen as my mother,' I say. 'Don't worry about it. I've tried it, and it's not for me. No harm done, but I'd prefer to meet someone more organically.'

I don't mention Chris. I'm not sure whether screaming at someone in the middle of a store counts as organic. Besides, I haven't decided whether to meet him again. Until I have, I don't want to talk about it with Isabella. I don't want her or anyone else feeling sorry for me.

The shop bell rings, and she gives a dramatic sigh. 'I hate it when people expect me to do some work around here!'

She goes into the shop, and I sort through the store cupboard to make sure I have enough dried cherries for this afternoon's batch of cookies.

Isabella reappears, holding a paper bag. 'This is for you.'

'Who's it from?'

'I don't know. They'd disappeared by the time I got there. Lily says a boy handed it to her and left. It has your name on it. Are you expecting a delivery?'

'I don't think so.' I open the bag and peer inside. I give a choke of laughter when I see an array of cotton reels ranging in shade from palest blue to deepest midnight.

Isabella peers over my shoulder. 'Why are you ordering thread?'

'It's a long story,' I say.

'The best stories always are.' She perches on the edge of the sink and looks expectant.

I can see I have no choice. She isn't leaving until she gets an explanation, and I have work to do. As well as running low on spices, we're almost out of dog biscuits. We don't have any coriander, so mixed herbs will have to do.

I give Isabella a run-down of my meeting with Chris. She listens with rapt attention until I've finished.

'That's the most romantic thing I've ever heard,' she says.

'Were you listening to anything I told you or thinking about a batch of meringues?' I say. 'Chris and I only met because he wasn't looking where he was going, and I shouted at him.'

'If that was all, I'd agree with you,' she says. 'But it wasn't. He didn't shout back or tell you it was your own fault. He realised something was wrong, and he did something about it. How you didn't fall in love with him on the spot and propose is beyond me.'

'I can give you his address,' I say. 'His work address, at any rate. You can pretend to be a customer and accidentally drop something on the floor and hope he steps on it.'

'Lightning never strikes twice,' she says sadly. 'He would just think I was clumsy. Anyway, I've missed my chance. He's obviously interested in you.'

'No, he isn't,' I say. 'He's being polite. He ruined my stuff, and he's doing the decent thing and replacing it.'

She reaches for the bag and inspects the contents. 'You lost two reels of cotton. He's sent you seven … eight … nine! That's more than being polite, Abby, and you know it. What does the note say?'

She pulls a piece of paper from the bag and unfolds it.

I snatch it from her. 'Give that to me!'

'Why does it matter?' she asks. 'You said he was only being polite. It probably says,

'Dear Ms Edwards, I would like to take this opportunity to apologise for my appalling behaviour last night. I will of course be moving to the Antipodes forthwith to spare you the risk of running into me again and being reminded of my disgraceful manners.

Sincerely something or other.'

Chris,' I say, skimming the note without allowing her to see it.

'What does it say?' she demands.

I smile as I read it out loud.

'Dear Abby, I've been thinking about your father's trousers all night. I won't be able to rest until I've made reparation. The woman in the shop says this is all the blue cotton they sell. If none of them match, let me know, and I'll go to Harrods on Saturday and demand they find exactly what you want. It was nice meeting you last night. Hope you're feeling better.

Chris.'

'Why wasn't I in Bendine's last night?' mourns Isabella. 'I think I'll go there this evening. I have a pair of trousers I tore helping my uncle free one of his sheep from a barbed wire fence. I can hang around the haberdashery department looking helpless and hope for the best.'

Lily comes into the kitchen. 'What's taking you so long? I'm having lunch with Jack today, so I need to get going.'

'I'm trying to persuade Abby to give someone a chance,' says Isabella.

Lily looks pleased. 'Have you met someone on the dating site?'

'She met someone when she was running away from the dating site,' says Isabella.

'It's complicated,' I say when Lily looks puzzled. 'I'll come and mind the shop while you have lunch.'

Isabella follows us into the shop. 'I'm fine to stay here until Lily gets back. You carry on with whatever it is you were doing, Abby. But you are going to give this Chris a chance, aren't you?'

'I don't know,' I say. 'It might be better to wait until I'm feeling a bit more settled. There are only so many screaming fits you can direct at one person.'

'Direct them at me,' she says. 'I don't mind. You can scream at me as often as you like as long as you give this guy a call. I have a good feeling about him.'

I laugh at her eager face. 'Only if you drop the subject and let me do it in my own time.'

'I could do it for you if you like,' she offers. 'It wouldn't be any trouble. I could text him, or I could speak to him if you prefer.'

She puts on a throaty voice. 'Hey, Chris, this is Abby from the other night. I thought we could get together sometime to discuss haberdashery and … notions.'

'Don't you dare!' I say. 'But you clearly have nothing going on in your life right now, which is sad and pathetic. If it means so much to you, I'll give him a call.'

Chapter Seventeen

I call Chris on my walk home from work. I didn't want to call him from the bakery in case Isabella overheard and jumped in with another impression of me. I hope the first one wasn't accurate. I don't want to sound as though I have a permanent case of laryngitis.

If I wait to speak to him until I get home, I risk Mum overhearing. She wouldn't mean to, but it's a small house, and she's developed batlike hearing since Dad has been ill. So, my walk home seems the best time. The worst that can happen is that random passers-by may hear me, and I can cope with that.

Chris probably won't answer. Now isn't the most convenient time to call someone. Most people will be on their way home from work. I almost send him a text, but I decide it's the coward's way out. I want to thank him properly for the bag of cotton reels.

I'm ridiculously touched by the gesture and the fact he didn't stay and insist on seeing me. From what Lily said, it wasn't him anyway. She described the messenger as a boy, and Chris is about my age. We aren't exactly decrepit, but people in their early thirties aren't generally described as boys and girls.

I hope my call doesn't go to voicemail. I hate it when that happens. The owner of the phone has plenty of time to think about their outgoing message before recording it, whereas I'm always caught off balance and end up stammering and forgetting what I wanted to say. If Chris doesn't answer after three rings, I'll hang up and try again another time.

I punch the numbers and start walking.

He answers on the second ring. 'Hello?'

'It's Abby,' I say.

He sounds pleased. 'Hi, Abby. I wasn't expecting to hear from you so soon.'

Does that mean he was hoping not to hear from me at all? I feel my cheeks flame as I realise he was probably being polite to a distressed stranger the other night and had no intention of keeping up contact. Have I made things awkward for him by calling? He may even be with his girlfriend. I remember he was the one who asked to see me again. If he has a girlfriend, that's on him, not me.

'Abby?' he says. 'Are you there?'

'I was calling to thank you for your gift. It was very thoughtful of you.'

I can hear the tension in my voice. He seems to hear it too.

'No problem at all. I hope you didn't mind me sending it. You told me where you work. I didn't look it up or anything creepy like that.'

I relax. 'I didn't think you had. My mum will be delighted. She was disappointed when I told her I'd forgotten to pick up the thread. I'm not sure what she'll do with the rest of it, but knowing my mum, she'll find something. Anyway, it was very kind of you. It was also kind of you to rescue me last night. I hope I didn't spoil your evening.'

'Not at all,' he says.

That doesn't help much. It would be far more helpful if he mentioned that I'd made him late to see his girlfriend for dinner, but he'd explained it all to her, and she understood. Or that his boyfriend had cancelled their plans at the last moment, so he'd been free to scrape me off the floor and put me back together.

He doesn't speak. The ball is in my court. I take a deep breath. 'You mentioned you'd like to see me again …'

'That's right,' he says.

'But you didn't mention it again in your note,' I say, feeling my cheeks turn pink. I'm so bad at this.

'Of course not,' he says. 'I told you to call if you wanted to. The gift today was nothing to do with putting pressure on you.'

'I didn't think it was. I'll start again. I enjoyed meeting you, and I'd love to see you again sometime.'

I wait for him to let me down gently and say his circumstances have changed in the hours since we met, and he and his entire extended family are now moving to Bermuda.

'That sounds great,' he says. 'Would you like to have dinner this week?'

'I'm free on Wednesday evening.'

'Me too,' he says. 'Is there anywhere in particular you'd like to go? Do you have any dietary restrictions or preferences?'

'Parsnips and redcurrants,' I say. 'Other than that, I'm flexible.'

'That's a shame,' he says. 'I was about to suggest that new root vegetable and berry place on the bypass. Obviously, that's out now. How about *The Wild Horse*? I've eaten there a couple of times, and the food is pretty good.'

'I've never been there,' I say. 'Shall we meet there about seven thirty?'

'Great. I'll book us a table. I'll be the one wearing waders.'

'Waders?' I say, puzzled.

'It seems a sensible precaution considering your coffee throwing proclivities.'

I laugh. 'I can't promise anything. But if we steer away from the subject of gold digging and deliberate spelling mistakes, we should be fine.'

I walk the rest of the way home with a lighter step. Chris sounded exactly as I remembered him. If nothing else, we'll have a pleasant meal together, which is exactly what I need after my experience on *LuvLocatr*. It's nice he wants to see me again after last night. I was hugely embarrassed by the whole thing, but at least I won't have to put on a façade when I meet him again. If he's seen me at my tear-stained, coffee hurling worst and still wants to have dinner with me, he must like me a little.

I swing in at the front gate in a much lighter mood than when I left this morning. As I expected, Mum is in the kitchen, cooking dinner.

'How was your day?' she says.

I take the wooden spoon from her and stir the cheese sauce. 'Great, thanks. I've brought some reels of thread. I hope at least one of them matches Dad's trousers.'

She takes the bag. 'Oh, Abby! Did you get them on your way home? You shouldn't have done that. It's half an hour each way on the bus.'

'I got it at lunchtime,' I say, feeling guilty for not mentioning that Chris bought it, not me. I can't face a lengthy explanation about everything that happened last night, so I'll have to take the credit for it.

'I'll mend them tonight,' she says. 'They're Dad's favourite pair, and it seemed such a shame when they were torn. You didn't need to buy all these colours. Any dark blue would have done. I hope you've kept the receipt.'

I mumble something and change the subject. 'Are you going to your book club this week?'

'I'd like to,' she says. 'But only if you don't have anything booked. I thought you'd have plans for most evenings.'

'I've cancelled my subscription,' I say. 'I'm not enjoying it.'

'What a pity. Alison Phillips says her daughter has a whale of a time with her app. She doesn't have to be home any night unless she wants to.'

'I have one last meeting set up before my subscription runs out,' I say, shading the truth slightly. I don't want her asking me how I met Chris, which she definitely will if I say I didn't meet him on *LuvLocatr*.

Her face lights up. 'Where are you going?'

'We're having dinner at *The Wild Horse*.'

'Dad and I went there on our last anniversary,' she says. 'It's lovely. But I thought you were supposed to meet people for coffee first.'

'There aren't any hard and fast rules,' I say. 'People often suggest that because it's short and in a public place. If you aren't enjoying it, you can finish your coffee and say goodbye. It's more difficult if you arrange something that takes all evening, although it must make it easier for Mavis Sotherby. Those quick half hour meets can't possibly give her enough time to gather the information she needs.'

She laughs. 'I wish I'd never mentioned her to you. Are you sure about having dinner with this man? As you say, it's an entire evening.'

'Not if I eat quickly or tell him I only enjoy starters. Anyway, I've met him before. We had coffee together.'

She looks pleased. 'So, this is a second date? How exciting! He must be keen if he wants to see you again so soon.'

I can't help smiling. 'Who knows? But I'm looking forward to seeing him again.'

Chapter Eighteen

I arrive at *The Wild Horse* a few minutes before the agreed time. I look around for Chris but can't see him. I debate whether to order myself a drink. He appears before I can decide.

'Hi, Abby. I hope I'm not late.'

He looks the same as I remember him, and my nervousness vanishes. He's just the sort of person I'd like to have a meal with, friendly and easy going. I don't need any complications in my life at the moment, and Chris seems as uncomplicated as they come.

'You're right on time,' I say. 'Can I buy you a drink?'

'Thanks,' he says. 'But dinner is on me. I'm still doing penance, remember?'

He ignores all my protests, so I give in and order us both drinks. We sit at the bar and chat until a server comes to say our table is ready. He hands us our menus and leaves.

I scan mine. 'Do you have any recommendations?'

Chris shakes his head. 'Not really, and I wouldn't tell you if I had.'

'Why not?'

'Because it's much more fun to choose for yourself,' he says. 'If I recommended something, you might feel obliged to order it.'

'Unless it was the parsnip soup with redcurrant jelly.'

'That's back on the menu?' he says. 'I'm definitely having that!'

The server appears, and we order. Chris chooses the lamb, and I go for the mushroom risotto. It's always been one of my favourites. I enjoy seeing the twists various chefs put on it.

As I expected, Chris is easy to talk to. He tells me about his childhood in Shropshire before his family moved to this area. His family sounds like fun. He has two older sisters and says they still treat him like the little brother they used to push around the garden in a wheelbarrow.

'It wasn't as altruistic as it sounds,' he says. 'Mostly, it was an excuse to tip me out into patches of mud when my parents weren't looking. It was their favourite game to see how dirty they could make me before my mum stopped them.'

'That sounds fun,' I say. 'I'm an only child, so I had to get muddy all by myself.'

'That's so sad,' he says. 'Let me know if you ever want a ride in a wheelbarrow. There's a great stretch of marsh behind the gas works.'

'When did you decide to become a pastry chef?' I ask.

'I didn't,' he says. 'I failed one of my A-levels and couldn't get into the course I wanted. My parents suggested I take a year off to think about things. I started working part-time at my local bakery and enjoyed it. I did another couple of years there full-time, then went to catering college to learn how to do it properly. How about you?'

'I always knew I wanted to work in hospitality,' I say. 'I dreamed of being the head chef in a busy restaurant, with everyone running around in a mad panic and grovelling to me. I'd probably watched too many cooking programmes.'

'I can see it now,' he says. '*To Hell and Back with Abby.*'

'I wanted to own my own restaurant,' I say. 'But after three months' work experience in London, I decided it wasn't for me. Being constantly shouted at while working ridiculous hours and being paid a pittance isn't as much fun as you might think.'

'You surprise me,' he says. 'So, you switched to something less frantic?'

'Partly, but I also found I preferred the baking side of the business.'

'I've never dated a pastry chef before,' he says. 'I don't know whether we'll compete with each other or have lots to talk about.'

'You're getting a little ahead of yourself,' I say. 'You aren't dating one now.'

I'm amused to see his ears turn pink.

'I didn't phrase that well,' he says. 'Let's say I haven't been on a date with a pastry chef before. Will that do?'

I feel ashamed of my churlishness. 'I was only joking. I know what you mean. When you meet someone in a different line of work, you always have something to fall back on when things get sticky. When you both have the same job, there's nothing new to talk about.'

'What would you like to talk about instead?' he says.

'What's your favourite colour?' I say with a bland smile.

He doesn't miss a beat. 'Mauve. How about you?'

'Chartreuse. Or heliotrope.'

'You win,' he says. 'Do you really like chartreuse?'

'I hate it! It's the colour of migraines. But I wanted to sound more knowledgeable about colours than you.'

'So, you're competitive as well as having a violent temper?' he says.

'Violent temper?'

'That's what I've heard,' he says. 'The word on the street is that you had to leave *LuvLocatr* before you were thrown off.'

'I was the one who told you I was cancelling my account,' I say. 'Don't pretend you heard it elsewhere.'

He pulls a face. 'I'm sorry to tell you someone filmed it on their phone and put it on TikTok. You've gone viral!'

I stare at him, horrified. This is the last thing I need. Mum and Dad don't use social media themselves, but Mavis Sotherby is sure to see it and come rushing around to show them.

'Abby, I was joking,' he says. 'Of course, no one filmed it. Why would they? People dumping coffee into someone's lap is pretty normal these days. You'll have to find a new angle if you want the publicity. An ice cream sundae over their head or a brick through their windscreen might do it. A common or garden latte wouldn't get you more than about five views.'

I laugh in relief. 'You're right, but I still feel ashamed of myself. He was pretty rude, but I overreacted. I'm glad I've come off the app. I wasn't enjoying it, and I suspect I might be tempted to do it again.'

'It's why I've never tried online dating,' he says.

'You seem pretty easy-going to me,' I say, but he shakes his head.

'That's because I'm trying to impress you. I have a much darker side too. When I was five, I stole some apples from our neighbour's garden. When I wasn't caught, I went back and did it again.'

'That's nothing,' I say. 'When I was nine, I climbed over the fence to get into my school playground one evening. Even when I was caught, I went back and did it again.'

He gives a shout of laughter. 'You're the original bad girl. I'll never measure up. Still, if I hang around with you for a while, I may get some tips.'

'I'll make you a list for next time we have dinner,' I say. 'So far, you've bought me a cup of coffee, nine reels of cotton, and now dinner. I want to redress the balance.'

'I wasn't planning on paying for our meal,' he says, surprised. 'I usually get my date to pretend to choke, then I berate the management for negligence before taking her outside to get some fresh air. That's when we make a run for it.'

'I've already decided to have the Cointreau mousse for dessert,' I say. 'That won't have lumps in it if it's properly made. I'm afraid you're stuck with the bill for this one.'

He doesn't seem too put out. We finish our meal, and he pays without trying to create a diversion.

He walks me to my car. 'I'm so glad you called, Abby. I had a great evening. And I'm glad your competitive spirit means we'll be seeing each other again.'

'I'll look out for a place that does half-price specials and let you know,' I say.

He hesitates before leaning towards me and kissing me gently on the lips. 'I'll look forward to it.'

I climb into my car and drive away, acutely aware that he's standing there watching me. That was barely even a kiss, but I'm surprised to find my legs are unsteady and my heart is beating much faster than usual. I drive home, thinking of Chris and the way his eyes crinkle when he's amused. I can hardly believe I wasn't planning to call him. Thank goodness for Isabella and her interfering ways.

Chapter Nineteen

I don't expect to hear from Chris for the next few days. All the articles I've read since joining *LuvLocatr* say that men need down time after the first date, a chance to regroup and take stock before initiating the next contact.

Mum says the same thing. She asks about my date while we're making breakfast the following morning, and I give her a brief rundown of the menu.

'That's all very interesting,' she says when I've finished detailing the culinary delights of *The Wild Horse*. 'But that isn't what I'm asking, and you know it. How did you get on with Chris?'

'We had a great time,' I say. 'He's a really nice guy. You and Dad would like him.'

She looks pleased. 'I'm so glad. Are you seeing him again soon?'

'I don't know. He texted to ask whether I'd got home safely, and I thanked him for a lovely evening, but that was all.'

I'm surprised to find myself talking to her in so much detail. I usually keep her at arm's length from my dating life. Either Chris is a special case or it's impossible to hide things from the people with whom you live.

'I hope he calls you soon,' says Mum.

'Or I could call him,' I say.

She looks shocked. 'Don't do that, Abby! Men don't like to be rushed.'

'Is that some of Mavis Sotherby's advice?' I say. 'We're in the twenty-first century now. I was the one who asked him out.'

'That's all the more reason he should ask you out the next time,' she says. 'You mustn't look desperate.'

'Definitely not! Maybe I should ignore the first few calls from him. There's no sense in making myself cheap.'

'Now you're being silly,' she chides me. 'I'm not as old-fashioned as you think. I just want him to value you. I'm not sure Paul did.'

I'm taken aback to hear her speak so frankly about Paul. She's always been so restrained when he's mentioned. She's told me I'm an adult and must make my own decisions, and she and Dad will support them whatever they are. It's disconcerting to realise she's been watching and worrying on the sidelines.

I don't want to add to her worries, so I try to reassure her. 'Chris and I are both busy people, but one of us will call the other at some point. Did I tell you he's a baker too?'

'Now, there's a coincidence,' she says. 'Is that why you swished up his profile?'

'Swiped right,' I correct her before remembering I didn't meet Chris on *LuvLocatr*. But Mum doesn't need to know that. I met him in what I've decided was a *LuvLocatr* adjacent way. It's almost the same thing.

'It was a coincidence,' I say. 'But it gave us plenty to talk about.'

'Where does he work?' she asks.

I'm about to tell her when I remember Mavis Sotherby. I don't want her hunting down Chris and reporting back to Mum. Apparently, Mavis does all her sleuthing work online, but there's no guarantee she won't get carried away one of these days and start gumshoeing in person. If she holds those silver surfer classes of hers in the village hall, she'll have access to the boxes of costumes the amateur dramatic society keeps behind the stage. If Chris tells me he's seen some woman dressed like one of Sweeney Todd's victims hanging around outside his bakery and muttering into a Dictaphone, I'll know what's going on.

'Somewhere in the Christchurch direction,' I say. 'I've forgotten the name of the bakery. Anyway, I have to run.'

Lily arrives at the Sugarloaf at the same time as me. She reaches for her key. 'How did last night go?'

'It was great, thanks.'

She nods and opens the door. 'That's good.'

In her place, Isabella would have given me an exasperated look and demanded all the details. Either Lily isn't as curious as Isabella or she has other things on her mind. She only has a few months before the baby arrives. It's such a huge thing in anyone's life that I'm surprised she can concentrate on the business at all.

I divide the first part of the morning between the kitchen and the shop. Business is brisk, and the cafe is soon full. Even Bernie's table is occupied. I hope Mrs Ogilvie doesn't turn up in the next half hour. She took huge offence the last time she arrived to find someone sitting at her table. I showed her to another one and tried to divert her attention, but she sat and stared at the customer fixedly until they turned bright red, gulped down their coffee and left. Mrs Ogilvie is not a woman to be trifled with.

Isabella arrives mid-morning, announcing she's been to see our suppliers and negotiated a reduction in costs.

'Now we're producing more on site, our order has quadrupled,' she announces, making a dive for the coffee machine. 'It doesn't seem right to keep paying the same prices. They argued, of course. They told me they've always supplied our bakery, and they barely make a profit as it is. I said I was sorry to hear that, and perhaps they would prefer to switch to customers who are happy to pay more. In the meantime, either they cut our costs or we'll go with McDonald and Sons, that new start-up in Southampton.'

'I haven't heard of them,' says Lily.

Isabella scoops coffee into the filter. 'That's because they don't exist.'

'What if our suppliers decide to search for them?' I ask.

'I'll say I got the name wrong. They won't bother. They know they're making a good profit from us. They were used to dealing with Mr Mason, who never questioned anything. It's about time they realised there are new kids on the block.'

'As long as they don't drop us entirely,' says Lily. 'Then we would be in trouble.'

Isabella takes a gulp of coffee. 'Don't worry so much. It's bad for the baby.'

'Since when do you know anything about babies?' says Lily.

'I know plenty!' says Isabella. 'I knew lots of things even before you were pregnant. For instance, the mother-to-be has to eat for two. That's the part I'm most looking forward to. Jack has filled me in with the rest, so I feel as though I'm an expert. If you go into labour while you're at work, you're in safe hands. Jack says you have to stare at pink crystals each time you have a contraction. I can't remember why. We don't have any of those in stock, but I expect our Bakewell tarts would do. And he says that when you're pushing, you should concentrate on something you really want. If it was me, I'd think of Abby's profiteroles. It's up to you, of course.'

Lily smiles. 'If you've been taking childbirth instructions from Jack, I'm not having you anywhere near me during the birth.'

'Spoilsport,' says Isabella. 'I've been knitting legwarmers like crazy because he says you must have one. My mum showed me how to cast on and knit in a circle. It's great fun. The only problem is that she's away this week, so I don't have anyone to tell me how to cast off.'

'I can show you how to do that,' I say. 'My mum taught me to knit when I was a child.'

'That would be great,' she says. 'I didn't want to wait for her to get home, so I kept going. It's about four feet long now. Lily will have to fold it over a few times before she can wear it, but it should keep her nice and warm. Jack didn't tell me why you only wanted one, Lily. Do you have to hop around the ward to make the baby come more quickly?'

'I'll explain it to you later,' I tell Isabella. 'But not in front of the customers. Mrs Ogilvie might walk in at any moment and be shocked. Now you're here, I'll make a start on the dough.'

'I'll help you,' she says. 'Lily will be fine in here.'

She follows me into the kitchen and picks up an apron. 'What would you like me to do?'

'You can wash your hands first,' I say. 'And put on a hair covering. I'll teach you how to make the basic dough.'

I show her how to measure the ingredients and switch on the machine. I love watching the ingredients puff and scatter as the mixers get to work, resisting being combined for as long as possible before giving in and embracing the inevitable.

'What's the deal with that leg-warmer thing?' she asks as we watch the dough spin and stretch and recombine into a creamy mass.

'It's all to do with the birds and the bees,' I say teasingly. 'I'm not sure you'll be able to handle it.'

'Oh, I know all about those!' she says. 'My mother believed in early biological education for her daughters. And don't forget I grew up on a farm. Is that all? I thought it was going to be something far more interesting.'

She watches the dough for a few more minutes. 'Speaking of the birds and the bees, how did last night go?'

I give a splutter of laughter. 'Your mind works in tortuous ways.'

'Not at all,' she says. 'You went on a date. It's the most obvious connection in the world. People don't join dating sites to find possible new members for their Mah Jong group.'

'It went very well, thank you,' I say primly, knowing this will drive her mad.

'If you don't give me the details right now, I'll march out to the bakery and ask Lily about that legwarmer at the top of my voice, *particularly* if Mrs Ogilvie is there.'

'Fine, I'll tell you!' I say. 'I don't want you to shock poor Bernie. We went to *The Wild Horse*.'

'I love it there,' she says. 'Did you have their Cointreau mousse?'

'I did. And Chris had the Crêpes Suzette.'

'And?' she says eagerly.

'That was all. We were too full for anything else.'

She fixes me with a steely gaze. 'Don't play games with me, Abby.'

I relent. 'I had a lovely time. I think he did too.'

'Did he kiss you? Are you seeing him again?' she demands.

'Yes, he did. And I don't know.'

'How can you not know?'

'Everyone seems to think I should wait for him to make the next move,' I say. 'At least, my mum does.'

'Nonsense!' she says. 'If you want to see someone, call them and suggest it. You aren't some fifties housewife.'

'I called to arrange the first date. It feels like his turn.'

She doesn't look convinced. 'I wouldn't wait.'

Lily puts her head around the door. 'Delivery for Abby.'

Isabella looks pleased. 'Is it flowers? I told you he liked you!'

'Not flowers,' says Lily.

'What then?' says Isabella. 'Chocolates, perfume, theatre tickets?'

'It may not be from Chris,' I say. 'It could be anything. An unpaid parking ticket, a free sample of soap, a summons for speeding.'

'I don't think it's any of those,' says Lily, handing me a small parcel.

'I'll open it later,' I say to annoy Isabella.

She snatches it out of my hand. 'You'll open it now, or I will!'

'It will serve you right if it's something boring,' I warn her. I pull back the paper and a card of buttons falls out.

Isabella picks it up and hands it to me. 'Why is someone sending you buttons?'

I read the note without letting her see it.

I'm all buttoned up tonight and tomorrow, but we could pick up the threads at the weekend if you're free.

'It's a private joke,' I tell Isabella.

'From Chris?' she says.

'Yes.'

She studies the buttons as though expecting them to contain some code.

'I give up,' she says at last. 'And you obviously aren't going to explain. All I want to know is whether it means he wants to see you again.'

I slip the card of buttons into my pocket. 'I think it probably does.'

Chapter Twenty

I call and arrange to meet Chris for lunch on Sunday. 'I'm paying,' I remind him.

'I know you are,' he says. 'It's the only reason I accepted.'

I thank him for the buttons. 'Are you planning on sending me the entire haberdashery department?'

'If it keeps you seeing me. The odd skein of wool seems a small price to pay for the pleasure of your company.'

'I'm not really a wool and fabric kind of woman,' I tell him. 'I do however collect gold bars and uncut diamonds. They sell them on the first floor of Bendine's, right next to the handbags.'

'Down one floor from the caviar and Cuban cigars?' he says. 'You aren't the only one with a list.'

We arrange to meet at twelve thirty and ring off. I'd like to talk to him for longer, but tonight is Mum's book club, and I want to make sure she goes. I'm hoping to persuade her to go out in the evenings more often, but it will take time. She tries to hide her anxiety from me, but I know her too well. She jumps at the smallest noise, and she's developed a habit of checking the house obsessively before she goes to bed. I try to do this for her and make a big deal of showing her the oven is off and the windows are closed. But I've heard her creep downstairs several times to check the back door is locked.

Apparently, this is normal when people have gone through something like she has. They're unable to control the big things in life, so they fixate on trying to control the smaller things. Still, it isn't healthy for it to continue long term, and I intend to keep an eye on her and get her some help if need be. In the meantime, she seems much better each time she goes out, so I encourage that.

Dad and I are planning to watch *Alien* tonight. I've made a big deal out of putting *It's a Wonderful Life* on the coffee table, where Mum is bound to see it. I've also brought home a box of doughnuts, at Isabella's insistence.

'They're past their sell by date,' she said, pushing the box into my hands as I was leaving work. 'I'd volunteer to do my duty, but it's my uncle's birthday tonight, and we're having a big family dinner. You and your dad should enjoy them.'

I didn't argue. Dad has always loved doughnuts. Mum doesn't buy them for him nowadays, as she insists on keeping him on the same healthy diet the hospital recommended when he first came home. But it's time she relaxed. I checked with the nurse last week, who agreed it was fine for Dad to enjoy his favourite foods. But I don't want to cause her any more stress, so I hide the doughnuts in my room until she's left, then fetch them down and show them to him.

His eyes light up as he stretches out his hand to take one. I watch him eat it, resisting the urge to fuss around him as Mum does, bringing him plates and napkins and wiping his fingers with a damp towel when he's finished.

Dad finishes his doughnut. I offer him the box again, but he shakes his head.

I pick up the remote. 'You'll regret that doughnut when you see what comes out of Kane's chest.'

He smiles but doesn't try to speak. I know he can manage several words now, but I don't like to push him. He should be allowed to take his own time. This is his recovery, not mine.

The film ends before Mum gets home, which gives me time to brush the crumbs off Dad's lap and fetch him a damp cloth from the kitchen. I hand it to him, trying not to watch him wipe his face. His coordination is shaky, and he misses his mouth several times, but I'm pleased to see him persevere. I don't have the heart to tell him he's missed a blob of jam on his cheek.

'Great job,' I say. 'You're getting better each day.'

He smiles again and nods. I don't want to ask him too many questions. He can answer if I give him enough time, but I don't know how he feels about being so slow and hesitant. He may not mind, or he may be embarrassed. I feel an overwhelming urge to connect with him, so I'll have to do the talking.

'I've met someone,' I say without giving myself time to think.

Why did I start with that? I could have talked about my job and my colleagues. I could have told him about our plans to cater for local events. Instead, I jumped right in and told him about Chris, like a teenager suffering from acute mentionitis about their latest crush.

'He's a pastry chef too,' I say. 'It's a bit of a coincidence. He works at The Slice Bakery in Parford. Anyway, he and I met recently, and we've started seeing each other.'

I study his face to see whether he's taking this in. I may be boring him, or he may be tired. It's past his usual bedtime. He focuses intently on my face as though he wants to take in what I'm saying.

'Mum thinks I met him on that dating app,' I say. 'That's not strictly true. I met a couple of people last week for coffee, but neither of the dates went well. I was on my way back to the car when I remembered Mum wanted some blue cotton, so I stopped in at Bendine's to pick it up. I was annoyed by the guys I'd met, so I wasn't paying attention to where I was going. Chris came around the corner, and we cannoned into each other. I dropped my bag. One of the cotton reels disappeared, and I couldn't find it, and Chris stepped on the other one!'

I don't know why I'm telling Dad this. It can't be of the slightest interest to him, but I'm unable to stop. It's the first proper conversation I've had with him since he came home from the hospital. I chat to him each day about trivial things and try to make positive comments about the weather and what I plan to cook for dinner. But it's the sort of conversation two strangers might have.

For the first time, I realise how much I miss my father. Mum is the chatty one, but I've always relied on Dad for advice and calm good sense. Since his stroke, that's all disappeared. I hadn't realised until now how much I've missed it. I wonder whether he does too.

I slip my hand into his, and he squeezes it. 'I've missed you, Dad. Would you like to hear the rest?'

He nods, and I go on. 'I had a complete meltdown when Chris stood on my cotton reel. It was ridiculous – a grown woman stamping her foot and shouting about a stupid reel of cotton. But it wasn't about that. I've been so angry about everything that's happened. I'm upset for you most of all, but I'm also upset for me and Mum. This whole thing feels so unfair, although people don't like you to say that. It makes them feel uncomfortable. They tell you things could have been worse, as though you don't know that already. I get so sick of people starting sentences with *At least.* "At least he got to the hospital on time. At least the doctors could give him the right treatment. At least he has your mum." Do they think I don't realise that?'

I stop abruptly. 'I'm sorry. Have I upset you?'

'No!' He says it with such vehemence that I jump. I've only heard him speak in a whisper since I came home.

He lifts his hand and strokes my hair. 'I hate it too.'

The words are slurred, but the meaning is clear. I reach for a tissue and wipe my eyes. 'I'm sure you do. I'm so sorry, Dad. I wish I could make it better for you.'

He takes a deep breath and looks at me directly. 'You do.'

I fight back the tears. I've done enough crying this week. I can hardly believe Dad and I are communicating. I don't care if it's in two-word sentences or that he can barely form the words. For the first time since all this happened, I dare to believe my father is in there somewhere. Not some stranger I'll have to come to know again, but my dad. The man who taught me to ride a bike and swim underwater.

'I'm so glad,' I say. 'With any luck, I'll be here for at least a year. If you need me for longer, I'll make Chris give me a job in his bakery.'

Mum's key turns in the back door before he can answer. She appears a moment later, flushed and cheerful.

'I've had a marvellous time! We barely talked about the book. Irene and Gordon Jarvis came home from their holiday in Spain yesterday. They filled the boot of their car with Chianti. They seemed eager for us to try it, so we did.'

'I knew that book club was an excuse for you all to get plastered every week,' I say. 'I hope you didn't drive home.'

'Gordon brought me,' she says. 'My car insurance covers anyone, so he drove me home and walked back.'

She catches sight of Dad and frowns. 'What's that on your face? It looks like jam.'

'That was my fault,' I say. 'I was eating a doughnut, and I leaned over to pick up the remote control. I must have dripped some jam onto Dad. Sorry about that.'

Dad shakes his head. 'Jam doughnut.'

'That's what I told Mum,' I say.

He shakes his head again. '*My* jam doughnut!'

I shrug and grin at him. 'I did my best. You're on your own now.'

Mum looks from Dad to me, then back at Dad, her face masklike. 'You've been eating jam doughnuts?'

He nods.

'And you told me about it?'

He nods again.

She flings her arms around him and bursts into tears. 'Oh, Geoffrey! That's the most wonderful thing I've ever heard!'

Chapter Twenty-One

Chris and I have lunch on Sunday. We exchanged so many details of our work histories and childhood memories over dinner on Wednesday that I wonder whether we'll have run out of things to talk about. Thankfully, this doesn't seem the case. The more I talk to him, the more I want to tell him about my life and hear more about his. I find myself telling him things I haven't shared with anyone except my family.

By the end of lunch, he knows more about me than I told Paul in the two years we were together. That was partly my choice. I wasn't aware at the time that I was giving Paul edited highlights of myself, but I see now that was the case. I sensed he wanted a certain version of me, and I presented it, for all the good it did me.

I tried to hold on to him by keeping back the parts of myself he had no interest in. It shouldn't be a surprise that didn't work. The bigger question is why I thought it was acceptable to edit myself in that way for anyone. It will never happen again.

I try to explain this to Chris, who seems to understand.

'We all do that to some extent,' he says. 'Especially when we first meet people. It's natural we should want them to see our best side. But we relax as time goes on, and we learn to trust the other person with the truth about ourselves. If they're worth that trust, of course.'

'That's just it,' I say. 'I never learned to trust Paul with the person I really was. I never gave him the chance to get to know the real me, at least not all of it.'

It's only been a few months since Paul told me he was moving in with Janine, but I already find it difficult to remember much about our time together. The whole thing feels shadowy. I resolve never again to lose a part of myself in someone else. If a relationship doesn't work when someone finds out who I am, it isn't the right relationship for me. Maybe I'll never find someone with whom I have that connection, but that's ok. Better to be alone than badly accompanied.

Or maybe I've already found the person with whom I can connect. I suppress this thought. I've had three dates with this man – two if I don't count the tearful coffee the night we met. It's far too early to invest much of myself in whatever this is. For all I know, Chris is only here to collect his free lunch. Once we're financially even, he may disappear, never to be seen again.

Paul kept a strict tally of who bought what when we went out. I didn't mind too much. I wasn't in the relationship for what I could get out of it. Looking back, I can see his lack of generosity was a mark of who he was as a person. I can't remember a single time he went out of his way to see me if it wasn't convenient or dropped in unexpectedly when I was ill.

Even when Dad had his stroke, and I called Paul in floods of tears, he asked whether I needed to go home straight away. He said it might be better to wait and see what the prognosis was in case it was only an ischaemic attack. I think I knew then, but my heart wasn't ready to face two losses, so I let it go. Chris wouldn't do that. I barely know him, but I'm sure of that. It doesn't mean I want to rush into anything with him, but it's a good start.

'What are you thinking about?' he asks. 'You've been staring out of the window for the past few minutes. Are you trying to work out where you parked so you can make a run for it and leave me with the bill?'

I return to the present with a bump. 'I was thinking about my dad and how awful it was when he had his stroke. I'm sorry.'

'Don't be,' he says. 'It takes you by surprise at the most inopportune times, doesn't it? I found myself thinking about my mum when I was supposed to be concentrating on the properties of American versus British wheat. I learned to go with it. If other people didn't like it, that was their problem. How's he doing now?'

I smile as I remember our movie night together and my realisation that Dad was still there.

'He's doing well, thanks. The doctors are pleased with his progress, and he's talking more. His therapist thinks he's chosen not to say much so far. She says it's quite common for people not to want others to see how difficult they find things, so they don't attempt them at all.'

'I can imagine doing that,' he says. 'We take so much for granted in life. All the little things like having a conversation with someone, being able to walk or cook dinner. It's devastating when that's taken away. We don't know who we are any longer. We have to build ourselves up piece by piece, never sure we'll be the same person when we've finished.'

'That's exactly it,' I say. 'Dad was such an active and decisive man. It must have felt awful to lose the ability to make his own choices. Mum would have insisted on speaking until we understood her. It's how she communicates. She always has. But Dad did the complete opposite. He withdrew into himself and kept his thoughts to himself. That's why it was so wonderful this week when he started to speak.'

I wipe my eyes. 'I'm sorry. It feels as though all you ever see me do is cry.'

He takes my hand. 'Don't be ridiculous. You've had a lot to cry about. I'm surprised you don't do it more often.'

'I hate it,' I confess, scrubbing at my eyes with a napkin. 'When something like this happens, everyone tells you that you have to be strong for the other person. I've lost count of the times I've heard people tell Mum she has to be Dad's rock. She's very patient, but in her place, I'd want to pick up that rock and hurl it at them.'

He laughs. 'It's a good thing you stuck to hurling coffee the other night. This is where that came from, isn't it?'

'I suppose so. It was terrifying being unable to control myself. It's why I took myself off the app. I'm not ready for it, and those poor unsuspecting seekers of relationships don't deserve it.'

'That's definite, is it? You aren't planning on giving it another go?'

I shake my head. 'I'm done with it. It's not for me.'

'I'm glad.' He looks at me with an expression that makes my heart beat faster.

'Why is that?' I say, although it's obvious what he means.

'There are far better things you could buy with the monthly fee,' he says. 'It seems a complete waste of money when you consider we're in a cost-of-living crisis.'

He laughs at my crestfallen expression. 'Abby, I'm joking. You know why I'm glad you've quit *LuvLocatr*. I really like you, and I'd love to spend more time with you and get to know you better. Also, I can't compete with all those successful guys you've been meeting on there.'

I smile back at him. 'I'd like that too. Speaking of wasting money, you have to stop buying up half the contents of the haberdashery department of Burdines.'

'It's a deal,' he says. 'If you promise to go out with me again, I'll promise not to send you those embroidery silks I saw when I was buying the buttons.'

'Embroidery silks?' I say. 'It isn't the eighteenth century. What did you expect me to do with those?'

'I was leaving it up to you,' he says. 'Maybe one of those cross-stitch things that says *Home is where the heart is*.'

'I'd have been more likely to cross-stitch you a sampler saying *Never contact me again*.'

'It sounds as though I don't know you as well as I thought,' he says. 'Perhaps we can remedy that on Wednesday over dinner? I'm sure we'll both be hungry by then.'

He lets go of my hand and picks up the menu. 'Speaking of which, would you like to try the coffee mint crème brûlée, or shall we stick with the more traditional cheesecake?'

Chapter Twenty-Two

Isabella comes into the kitchen a few weeks later, looking excited. 'Has Lily told you the news?'

I look up from the dough I'm kneading. 'I don't think so. Unless you mean the fact she has a midwife appointment this afternoon.'

'How is that news?' says Isabella. 'She has a midwife appointment every week. I'm talking about the Mix-up!'

'What mix up?' I say.

'*The* Mix-up!' she says. 'I'm glad she didn't mention it. I wanted to tell you all about it and start making plans. Lily is always so matter of fact. She isn't half as excited about it as I am.'

I pull off my hair net and follow her through to the shop. 'I still don't know what you're talking about.'

'Coffee?' she says. 'And grab yourself a cake or two. This may take a while.'

'It's your money you're wasting,' I say, selecting a cherry slice and sitting at Mrs Ogilvie's table. I'll move if she and Bernie arrive. I'm not in the mood for one of her gimlet stares.

Isabella carries the mugs of coffee over to the table and sits down. 'The Mix-up is happening again!'

'You still haven't told me what's got mixed up,' I say. 'Is it anything I can help with?'

'I hope so,' she says. 'We can't do it without you. Isn't it exciting? It all stopped during Covid, and we didn't think they'd restart it. But they have. We heard this morning.'

I sip my coffee while I wait for her to get to the point. I've taken a leaf out of Lily's book, and I now wait patiently until she's ready to tell me what new bee she has in her bonnet.

'You don't seem excited,' she says.

'I'm sure I will be when I know what I'm supposed to be excited about. So far, all I know is that something is muddled up, and you want me to help you sort it out.'

She waves her eclair at me. 'Nothing is muddled up. I'm talking about the *Mix-up*!'

'And yet I'm none the wiser.'

'The Mix-up!' she says again. 'You must have heard of it. It's been going for at least fifteen years. The New Forest Mix-up.'

'I'm afraid I haven't. Is it a big deal?'

'It's a huge deal!' she says. 'It's run by the tourist board to promote the area. The winning bakery holds the title for a year, and they get to rub all the neighbouring bakeries' noses in their failures.'

'That sounds fun,' I say. 'Is there a cash prize, or is a slice of lightly toasted schadenfreude the only reward?'

'Isn't that enough?' she says. 'Imagine being able to go into any bakery in the area wearing your prize winning sweatshirt that says *Take a hike, losers!*'

'Is that what they give the winner?'

'Probably not,' she admits. 'But it should be easy enough to get some printed. What do you say, Abby? Are you prepared to put your entire life on hold and place every waking minute at my disposal for the next two months?'

'Absolutely not,' I say.

She gives me a reproving look. 'This isn't the attitude I like to see in my staff members. What about the honour of the bakery?'

'I wasn't aware we had any. No one watching you fighting Lily for the last macaron last week would think of us as a dignified establishment.'

'That wasn't my finest hour,' she agrees. 'In my defence, I'd missed lunch.'

I take a bite of my slice. 'Tell me some more about this mix-up thing. What does it involve, apart from the honour of the bakery?'

'It's a multi-round competition,' she says. 'The entries are scored on technique and originality. You have to get through the qualifying round first. After that, there are a couple more rounds, and the three finalists are the bakeries with the highest overall total. The grand final is held in one of the secondary schools because they have enough ovens. It's a local tradition. Everyone comes to cheer on their team. The winner gets the rosette and a cup and bragging rights for the whole of the following year.'

'It sounds ok,' I say. 'I take it I'll have to do the actual baking?'

'Yes, but only because none of the rest of us can cook, which is a bit of an impediment for producing world-class baked goods. You're an amazing chef, Abby. I've seen some of the things you've produced. You're wasted on making cookies and muffins and pastries.'

'You're welcome to offer me a raise in acknowledgment of my superior cooking skills.'

'We're moving away from the point,' she says. 'It would be a feather in your cap if you won this for us. And wouldn't it be fun to beat Chris?'

'I hadn't thought of Chris,' I say. 'Does his bakery usually enter the competition?'

'Enter it? They won it three times in a row about seven years back. It's time someone showed them what's what.'

'Chris wasn't working there seven years ago,' I say. 'He was in France.'

'All the more reason to beat them this year, before he gets any ideas about his bakery being better than ours. Seriously, Abby, this would put us on the map. We've sunk a lot of money into buying the place and refurbishing it. Something like this could boost sales.'

She's right. It would be great publicity for the Sugarloaf. Not the running around wearing an offensive sweatshirt part. I'll have to talk her out of that as soon as possible. But winning any kind of award would be a sign this business is here to stay.

'I'm in,' I say. 'Are you sure it won't be a problem if Chris enters too?'

'Not at all,' she says. 'It's a great opportunity to sabotage our most dangerous opponent.'

'I would never do that!' I protest.

'Of course, you wouldn't. But it couldn't hurt for you to find out the code for his bakery's burglar alarm and who their supplier is,' she says with an innocent smile.

'I refuse to be involved in anything shady,' I say. 'There's no reason we can't win this thing if we put our minds to it. Besides, we don't even know The Slice is entering the competition.'

'I'm sure they will be,' she says.

'I'll ask Chris when I see him this evening.'

'Didn't you see him last night?' she says.

'So what? Is there some rule forbidding employees from going out on two weeknights running?'

'Not a written one,' she says. 'But I'll consider putting it into the staff manual if I ever get around to writing one. Do you see him most evenings? It must be serious.'

'I see him a few times a week,' I say. 'And we usually spend Sundays together. It's his day off too, which is lucky.'

I don't add that Chris went to considerable trouble to persuade his boss to change his day off. It's none of Isabella's business.

'Has he met your parents yet?' she asks.

'He has, but purely by accident. He dropped me home last week, and I left my handbag in his car. He couldn't text me to let me know because my phone was in my bag. He didn't want to leave it on the doorstep in case it was stolen. So, he brought it around the back and peered into the kitchen window to see whether I was there. Unfortunately, Mum was in there making a cup of tea. She came rushing through to tell me to call the police and lock all the doors because there was an intruder in the back garden *casing the joint.*'

Isabella giggles. 'Casing the joint? Does she think you're in some old gangster movie?'

'That would explain a lot,' I say. 'I went into the kitchen to see what was going on, and there was Chris standing by the back door, looking sheepish and holding my bag. I had no choice but to tell Mum who he was.'

'Fantastic!' she says. 'How did she take the news her only daughter was dating a burglar?'

'She was delighted. At least, she was when she calmed down. She insisted he come in for a cup of tea, and she made me take him to meet Dad.'

Isabella stops laughing. 'How did that go?'

'It was fine. Chris sat down and had a quick chat with Dad. He introduced himself and talked a bit about what he did and where he lived. He complimented the garden, which was a masterstroke. Dad loves his garden. I doubt Chris had time to see much of it while he was hiding in the shrubbery, but he mentioned a couple of the plants, and Dad nodded.'

'How about your mum?' says Isabella. 'What did she think of him?'

'She thought he was wonderful. She told me he seemed *A very nice young man.* I don't think she ever called Paul *A very nice young man.*'

'From the little you've told me about him, I don't think I would either,' she says. 'So, it's serious with you and Chris?'

I'm annoyed to feel myself blushing. 'I'm not putting any meaningless labels on it. But yes, it's going pretty well. He's lovely.'

Isabella clasps her hands and simpers. 'It sounds as though he's a real dreamboat.'

'I have pastries to make,' I say. 'Let me have the rules as soon as you have them.'

'A stud muffin!' she calls after my retreating back. 'A swell fella! A really neat young guy!'

I close the kitchen door and pick up my hairnet. I don't care how much Isabella teases me. I'm happier than I've been for a long while.

I switch on the mixer and tip in a generous scoop of raisins. I'll just have time to get these ready for their overnight rise before the shop closes. I want to get home as quickly as possible to make sure Mum doesn't start cooking dinner.

I feel guilty about leaving her so often, although she doesn't seem to mind. The least I can do is prepare dinner before I go.

I'm meeting Chris at the Red Lion for a drink tonight. It will be a good opportunity to talk about the Mix-up. There shouldn't be any problem with us competing against each other as long as we set some clear guidelines first and make sure we stick to them.

Chapter Twenty-Three

Chris arrives a few minutes after I do. He kisses me and collapses into a seat. 'I'm sorry I'm late. We had a crisis at work. We're catering a wedding on Saturday, and the oven packed up. We have a maintenance guy on standby, but he chose today to break his ankle and end up in the emergency room.

I wonder whether the Sugarloaf has people on standby to deal with this sort of crisis. I suspect not.

'What did you do?' I ask.

'We called my boss's cousin. He works in a bakery in Mickton. They let us use their oven. I don't know what we're going to do tomorrow if this guy can't hop over and fix it.'

'Can't you call a regular electrician?'

'We may have to if Glen isn't available. Rick won't like it. He's a pretty good boss overall, but he hates spending a penny more than he has to. It's why he's such a successful businessman.'

What would Chris say if I took this opportunity to ask him casually whether this Glen also services their burglar alarm? And if so, does Chris know what his birthdate is? I'm always surprised by how many people use basic personal information to set their codes.

'Have you heard about the competition?' I ask.

'We heard about it this morning. Rick is all fired up. He won it three times in a row a while back, and he never lets us hear the last of it.'

'You're entering, then?'

'Of course. Is the Sugarloaf having a go too?'

'Not only are we "having a go",' I say, 'but we're also expecting to win. Isabella says she'll fire me if we don't.'

'That's pretty much what Rick told me,' he says. 'It looks like we may both be out of a job by June. Maybe we should start up a business together.'

'It's not worth you even entering,' I say. 'Your boss sounds competitive, and I'd hate for you to disappoint him.'

He looks amused. 'I applaud your confidence. Have you done anything like this before?'

'I've watched Bake Off,' I say. 'I expect it's the same sort of thing.'

'Kind of,' he says. 'We won't have the same pressure they have, with the nation watching every move we make and television cameras everywhere. The first few rounds are held in various locations, and they're pretty low key. But the final is always a big deal. I remember going to one when I was training. It was terribly dramatic. One woman burst into tears, and the favourite set a stack of doilies alight while he was caramelising his cake. The sprinklers went off, and half the entries were ruined.'

'Thanks for the tip,' I say. 'I'll bring an umbrella.'

'That's a good idea if you get to the final,' he says. 'But there's some pretty stiff competition. About twenty bakeries enter, and some of them go all out to win.'

We order more drinks and take them out to the garden. It's a beautiful spring evening, and the early roses are out. We sit at a table and watch the bats emerge from a nearby spinney and try a few experimental wheeling turns before setting off to hunt for their evening meal.

'It's lovely here,' I say. 'I'm so glad to be home.'

'You still think of it as home?' he says.

'I'm as surprised as anyone. I've been away for ten years, but I grew up here, and my parents are still living in the same house. There was barely any adjustment at all.'

'Do you expect to live with them for long?' he asks.

'I'm not sure. This job is only for a year, so it doesn't seem worth looking for somewhere else until I know what I'll be doing next. Also, it's a lot easier to help Mum and Dad when I'm on the spot. I could never afford to rent around here, so I'd have to look for a room in town.'

He nods. 'I get that. Maybe you'll find another job in the area when this one finishes.'

'Maybe,' I say. 'I'm trying not to think about it. It isn't something I can control, so there's no point worrying about it.'

'I really hope you stay,' he says, his eyes warm.

I don't answer. This is a conversation people have when they've been together for years, not months. Or five weeks and three days. But who's counting?

'I'm not suggesting we move in together or anything like that,' he says when I don't speak. 'But I think this could turn into something, and I'd like to see where it goes. If that means making compromises, count me in.'

I feel a wave of warmth wash over me. I'm not counting any chickens either, but this relationship is going pretty well.

I lean over to kiss him. 'I feel the same way.'

'Now we've got that out of the way, do you think we could get something to eat?' he says. 'I was so busy trying to get hold of Glen today that I forgot to have lunch.'

'I'll fetch a menu,' I say. 'If I leave my bag out here, will it be safe, or will you rifle through it to discover my strategy?'

'I make no promises,' he says. 'Have you committed your ideas to paper? Rookie mistake.'

'I've jotted down a few ideas in my notebook, but you won't be able to read my handwriting.'

'In which case, I promise not to look,' he says.

We spend the rest of the evening chatting about the competition. The qualifying round is open to interpretation. We have to showcase our skills, whatever that means. The judges haven't specified anything in particular. I ask Chris what he's planning to do.

He shrugs. 'Whatever Rick tells me to do.'

'But you're the baker,' I say. 'You get to decide.'

'I'm not that bothered,' he says. 'Rick is desperate to win, so I'll leave it to him. That way, he can't blame me if we get knocked out.'

'I can't imagine letting my employers dictate to me like that,' I say. 'To be fair, I don't think they'd try. Isabella will have a thousand ideas, and Lily and I will have to talk her down, but she'll listen to us in the end. From what the pair of them have said, they see it as a team effort. I like that. My last employer never understood the word *team*. To him, it meant paying his staff as little as possible, calling them in at the last moment, yelling at them if they weren't available, and blaming them for everything that went wrong.'

'What are you thinking of doing for this round?' he asks.

I pull out my notebook and leaf through it. I always carry it with me. It's useful for jotting down recipe ideas and making notes about anything work related. I could use my phone, but Dad gave me the notebook before he had his stroke, and it makes me feel connected to him.

'I wondered about going with a UK theme,' I say. 'I thought we could make something from England, Scotland, Wales, and Northern Ireland. With any luck, not all the judges will be local.'

'Very patriotic,' he comments.

'I thought it might be fun. How about you?'

'I don't think Rick will demand I make Bara Brith or Cranachan, but who knows?'

Chris doesn't appear to be taking this competition as seriously as I am, which is fine. It means one fewer competitor for the Sugarloaf. I don't care whether he regards the whole thing as a bit of a joke, as long as he understands I don't.

If we win, it might convince Lily and Isabella to offer me a permanent job. It would be a great relief to be able to stay in this area. The nurse told us the other day that Dad was doing well, but we should prepare ourselves for a slow recovery. I'm in it for the long haul. As long as Dad gets back to his old self, I don't care how much time it takes.

The other reason I want to be in the area is Chris. I haven't said this to him, and I don't intend to. It would be ridiculous to make any plans based on a month-long relationship. I've learned my lesson from my time with Paul. Never make someone a priority who treats you as an option. It took me far too long to realise that was what I was doing. If Paul hadn't taken matters out of my hands by meeting and moving in with someone else at record speed, I'd still be trying to make our relationship work.

I won't make that mistake again. Whatever happens with Chris, I'm making my own plans and shaping the course of my own life. And it's unlikely there will be a long-term place for me in the bakery. Lily seems determined to return after her maternity leave, and she can manage the basic production with the help of a part time assistant. The bakery can't support three full-time staff, and the business belongs to her and Isabella.

Even if we win the competition, it's unlikely to have any long-term effect on my prospects. Unlikely, but not impossible, so I plan to do my absolute best, just in case. Besides, I like my new employers. They've been nothing but kind to me, and this job has made a huge difference to my entire family. Isabella is right to say that winning the Mix-up would put The Sugarloaf Bakery on the map, and I'm determined to do everything I can to make that happen.

Chapter Twenty-Four

It's all very well talking about winning this competition. We haven't even got through the qualifying round. The judges want a representative sample of our work, and I have no idea what they're looking for.

'We have to blow everyone away,' says Isabella. 'We don't want to go into the first round behind on points. It would be so demoralising.'

'Is there anything you'd like me to include?' I say.

Her eyes light up. 'Lots of things. Shall I give you a list of all my favourites?'

'You'll have to narrow it down,' I say.

She sighs. 'I was afraid you might say that.'

'I was thinking about UK recipes,' I say. 'We could do Eccles Cakes, Scottish shortbread, Welsh cakes, Barmbrack …'

'Great idea!' she says. 'How about scones too? Everyone loves a cream tea. The judges are visiting each bakery for this first round. We could serve the cakes with Earl Grey and English Breakfast tea to complete the theme. We could help things along with a nice slosh of whisky.'

'Sounds good,' I say. 'We'll need some nice china, and we'll have to close the cafe while the judges are here. We don't want them sampling our products with Bernie jumping up trying to get a bite and Mrs Ogilvie giving them the evil eye if they don't share nicely with him.'

She shudders. 'Can you imagine? I'll take care of that. They're coming on Monday morning, so that only gives us a few days to prepare. I'll arrange the practical details if you can do the baking.'

Lily arrives half an hour later, and we fill her in. She likes the idea of having a theme and promises to let everyone know the bakery won't be open to the public until lunchtime on Monday.

'We'll lose some custom,' she says regretfully, 'but people will understand. Mr Mason says his customers always turned up to support him back in the day.'

'Did he ever win?' I ask.

'I don't think he ever came close. So, we can do this for him too.'

'I'll do my best,' I say. 'Alice will need to come in on Monday to cover the shop.'

'I'll ask whether she's free,' says Lily. 'I can work Monday if need be.'

'Me too,' says Isabella. 'My uncle's accounts can wait for another day. This is far more important.'

I make up a few test batches. True to her promise, Isabella is an enthusiastic participant.

'This shortbread is the best I've ever tasted!' she proclaims. 'What's the secret ingredient?'

'Goose fat,' I say, and she chokes.

'It isn't?'

'As a matter of fact, it isn't. I don't have a secret ingredient aside from using good quality products and following the recipe.'

She gives me a relieved smile. 'I'm pretty adventurous when it comes to food, but that would have been a step too far even for me. As for following the recipe, that's the part I don't enjoy. It's so boring. I like to improvise as I go along.'

'Improvisation is fine once you've mastered the basics,' I say, removing the plate from her reach before she can eat another one. 'I need you to save room for the others.'

I hand her a scone. 'What do you think of these? Too crumbly?'

She takes a bite. 'Fabulous! Not too crumbly at all. I hate it when scones are too soft. You need some contrast with the cream and jam. Speaking of which, where do you stand on the whole question of which goes on the scone first?'

'I'm leaving it up to the judges,' I say. 'We'll give them each a bowl of cream and an assortment of jams and let them decide. I assume you have that side of things sorted?'

She swallows her last mouthful. 'I have. My mother is allowing me to borrow her afternoon tea set. It's Spode, and it's irreplaceable. She didn't want to lend it at first, but when she realised how important this competition was to me, she gave in. I wouldn't be surprised if she sent it over with an armed guard. She's also lending us some cut glass bowls. She says we may as well do the thing in style.'

'Great,' I say. 'I think that's everything covered. Who's making the tea?'

'Lily's mum,' she says. 'You haven't met her yet. She's so excited about the whole thing that Lily wanted to give her a role. She's in charge of making the tea and checking the judges have everything they need.'

Despite Isabella's confidence, I spend the next few days worrying about the competition. What if our oven breaks down at the last moment? I mention this to Lily on Saturday, who tells me her mother has promised we can use her oven if the worst comes to the worst.

'She's had it serviced especially,' she says. 'Mum never leaves anything to chance.'

'It sounds as though she's taking this competition seriously,' I say.

'We all are,' she says. 'It would be wonderful to win something like this. The publicity could make all the difference to the success of the Sugarloaf.'

I try not to think about this too much. I have to concentrate on getting through this qualifying round. It would be beyond humiliating if we were eliminated based on our core products. Especially if Chris's bakery gets through. I've promised myself not to see this as any kind of competition between us, but it's difficult.

Mum gets up early on Monday morning to make me breakfast.

'You're going to be fine,' she reassures me. 'Dad loved those Eccles cakes you brought home the other day. He insisted on eating two. I reminded him what the nurse said about a healthy diet, but he rolled his eyes at me.'

'I'm sorry,' I say, trying to hide a smile.

'I'm not!' she says. 'It's lovely to see the old Dad back again. I know I fussed over him too much at first, but I'm getting better. And he's right. Your baking is amazing.'

I say goodbye to Dad, who gives me a thumbs-up gesture.

I bend down to kiss him. 'I'll see you this evening. Would you like me to bring some more of those cakes home?'

He grins and nods. I check my reflection in the hall mirror and slip out of the front door. It doesn't matter what I look like because I'll be in the kitchen for most of the morning. But I don't want to let the Sugarloaf down.

Lily and Isabella are already there when I arrive, looking very smart. Isabella is wearing a crisp white shirt and black knee-length skirt, and she's slicked back her unruly blonde curls into a professional looking bun. Lily is wearing a black maternity dress with a white collar. There are two people here I don't recognise, although it's easy enough to guess the man is Jack. He looks exactly as Isabella has described him, friendly and rumpled.

'You must be Abby,' he says, holding out his hand to me.

'And you're Jack? I've heard a lot about you.'

The woman standing on the other side of Lily beams at me. 'And all of it good, I'm sure. Hello, my dear. I'm Angela Carson. It's so lovely to meet you. Lily tells me you're a wonderful cook.'

I give her an embarrassed smile. 'I don't know about that. It's been great working here. Lily and Isabella have made me feel right at home.'

'Of course, they have,' she says. 'Isn't this exciting? I was so pleased when Lily told me they were running this competition again. We've missed it over the past few years.'

'Do you need any help in the kitchen?' asks Jack. 'Apparently, I'm not smart enough to be working front of house. And to think I wore my best jeans for the occasion!'

'Can you cook?' I ask.

'I'm an excellent cook. Scrambled eggs, beans on toast, you name it.'

'Which would be wonderful if we were entering a Great British Breakfast competition,' says Isabella. 'But you won't be much use to us today unless you have an in with one of the judges.'

'I'm sure he'll charm them all,' says Mrs Carson. 'Everyone loves Jack, don't they, dear?'

Isabella makes such a comical face I almost laugh.

'I have everything covered,' I say. 'I'll call if I need anything.'

Isabella follows me to the kitchen. 'Are you ok, Abby? You look pale. You aren't coming down with something, are you?'

'I don't think so. I'm just a bit nervous.'

She looked surprised. 'Why would you be nervous? We have this one in the bag.'

'How can you be so sure? We don't know how many people have entered the competition or what they'll be serving. For all we know, everyone else is making intricate tempered chocolate creations in sugar cages. I wish I'd gone for something a little more adventurous now.'

'Take a breath,' she says. 'We've gone for exactly the right thing. The judges will think so too. I have complete faith in you.'

She gives me a reassuring smile and goes back to the shop, where I hear everyone talking and laughing. I wish I had her confidence. I'm convinced we're going to crash out in the first round, and it will be all my fault. Why didn't I at least make a few millefeuille or croquembouche?

It's too late for that now. All I can do is make sure everything is of the best quality possible. I spend the next two hours mixing and baking and trying not to think about what Chris is doing. There have been so many entries this year that the judges are spreading this first round over three days. They won't be seeing Chris until Wednesday. He and I have arranged to meet on Thursday for dinner, so I'll hear all about it then.

The shop bell jangles at eleven o'clock. Isabella comes into the kitchen, looking excited.

'They're here!' she whispers, although no one can hear us from the shop.

'How many of them are there?' I whisper back.

'Six. I wasn't expecting so many. I thought they'd send a couple to each bakery. I hope we have enough for them all.'

I wave to the trays of cakes. 'Unless they have appetites like you, we should have plenty. They won't want much if they're visiting other places today.'

Jack comes in carrying two afternoon tea plates. They're exquisite. The China is so delicate it's almost translucent. Tiny sprigs of roses and forget-me-nots twine around the edge of the plates, and the silver handles gleam.

'Lily's pushed two tables together,' he says. 'Thank goodness we have two of these cake stands. These cakes look amazing, Abby. We're an absolute shoo-in to go through to the next round.'

I want to tell him not to jinx the whole thing, but he'll only laugh at me.

'Can you arrange three of everything on these plates?' I say. 'I'll put the scones onto separate plates with the bowls of cream and jam.'

He and Isabella head back to the cafe with the cakes. Jack looks back as he reaches the door. 'I hope Lily's remembered to put those dog biscuits out of sight. I don't want the judges to decide they look interesting and take a bite.'

He grins at my horrified face. 'I'm trying to lighten the mood. You've done a wonderful job. Come and enjoy your triumph.'

I'd prefer to stay in the kitchen, but it would be churlish not to join everyone now I've been invited. I pull off my hairnet and smooth down my hair.

I walk into the shop and stand awkwardly by the counter. Isabella sees me and drags me forward. 'Here she is, the creator of this wonderful feast! Feel free to ask her any questions.'

The judges look up and smile but are too busy eating to say much. I hope that's a good sign.

One man reaches for an Eccles cake. 'I haven't had one of these for a while. My grandfather comes from Yorkshire, and he loved them.'

Isabella gives me a triumphant smile, but I'm not so sure. What if these don't measure up to his childhood memories?

He takes a huge bite, then wipes flakes of pastry from his moustache. 'Perfect! That takes me back.'

I realise I've been holding my breath and let it out in a gasp. One judge at least is on our side.

I look at the others, who are eating and exclaiming and making notes. One woman is chatting with Mrs Carson. They seem to be exchanging recipes, which may or may not be a good sign. I hope she isn't telling Mrs Carson how proper shortbread ought to be made.

The judges stay for a surprisingly long time. When at last they stand to go, the cake stands are empty. Hopefully, they'll write their appraisals while their brains are still fuddled with sugar.

I glance out of the window and almost jump. Mrs Ogilvie is standing outside, looking annoyed. She catches my eye and taps her watch. It's already five past twelve, and Lily told our customers we were opening at noon. Trust Mrs Ogilvie to take her so literally.

I make an unobtrusive motion with my hand, trying to indicate she should come back later. She seems to interpret this as a sign of hostility and glares back at me.

Isabella catches sight of her. 'Please excuse me for one moment.'

She snatches a dog biscuit from the bowl next to the till and slips outside, where I see her talking to Mrs Ogilvie before bending down and offering Bernie the biscuit.

'My goodness!' says one of the judges. 'We only expected to be here for half an hour. We've been so well looked after that we lost track of the time. Thank you for a wonderful morning. You're our first stop, so you've set the bar high.'

Lily looks pleased. 'That's nice to hear. When do we hear the results of the first round?'

'Not for a week or so, I'm afraid,' says the woman. 'After we've visited every bakery, we'll get together and discuss the results.'

The man with the grandfather from Yorkshire is the last to leave.

'That was a trip down memory lane,' he says as he passes me. He lowers his voice so the other judges don't hear. 'You've done extremely well.'

Chapter Twenty-Five

Isabella is jubilant when she hears what the judge said. I caution her not to get her hopes up, but she ignores me.

'That was Gavin, the head judge. Why would he have said that if he didn't mean it? It's obvious they were impressed. We need to plan for the next round. What is it?'

'It's the signature dish,' says Jack, who has stayed to clear up the plates and help Mrs Carson wash up.

'That's right,' she says. 'We don't have one, so we have to start thinking about it right away. Most of the other bakeries will have cakes they've been selling for a while because they're so popular. We need to come up with something spectacular. Maybe it should have a Yorkshire based theme.'

'I don't follow you, dear,' says Mrs Carson.

'Gavin said his grandfather came from Yorkshire,' explains Isabella. 'We could capitalise on that.'

'I don't think a Yorkshire theme is a good idea,' I say. 'We're a bakery in the New Forest, and this is a local competition to promote the area.'

She doesn't look convinced. 'I think we should bear it in mind. Yorkshire puddings with a Wensleydale filling might do it.'

'It isn't a savoury round,' says Jack.

She waves her hands. 'Abby can add a maple syrup glaze or something.'

'No, Abby can't,' I say. 'What's distinctive about the Sugarloaf? What do we make that no one else does?'

'Dog biscuits,' says Isabella. 'Do you think the judges would like those?'

'No!' Jack and I say together.

'What do you suggest, Abby?' she asks.

'We don't make anything unique,' I say, 'so we'll have to create something that represents the bakery.'

'Like what?' she says.

'I don't know yet. That's up to you and Lily. What makes this bakery different from the others in the area, apart from the fact its staff members eat most of the product?'

'I have no idea,' she says. 'We've added the cafe, but lots of bakeries have cafes.'

'That isn't enough,' I agree. 'We need something more. Something we could sell to the judges as the spirit of the Sugarloaf.'

Mrs Carson has been wiping down the tables. 'Have you asked your customers why they come here?'

'I've always assumed it's because we're local,' says Isabella.

'It's more than that,' says Mrs Carson. 'Plenty of people get all their food from the supermarkets, including their bread and cakes. And they can make themselves coffee at home for half the price. The gift store has closed, and the butcher's before that, but you have loyal customers who come back week after week. Ask them why.'

'It's an idea,' says Jack. 'You could give them a short questionnaire and put their name in a hat if they fill it out. You could offer the winner a free coffee and cake.'

He turns to Mrs Ogilvie, who's sipping her coffee and obviously eavesdropping. 'Would you be willing to fill in a questionnaire for us if it meant the chance to win a free coffee and cake?'

'Or a week's supply of dog biscuits,' says Isabella.

Mrs Ogilvie frowns. 'Can't you ask what you want to know with none of this ridiculous questionnaire business?'

'I suppose so,' says Isabella. 'What would you say is your favourite thing about this bakery?'

'Nothing,' says Mrs Ogilvie.

'Then why do you come here?' asks Jack.

'Because Bernie enjoys coming here,' she says. 'I would have thought that was obvious.'

Jack looks as though he's about to laugh, so I cut in before Mrs Ogilvie can take offence.

'That's an excellent reason. Do you have any idea why Bernie likes it so much?'

'Why don't you ask him?' asks Jack.

'Jack, could you help me move something in the kitchen?' says Isabella, giving him a quelling frown.

He follows her out of the shop, leaving me to placate Mrs Ogilvie.

'Bernie looks as though he's almost clever enough to speak,' I say. 'I'm sure he knows why he enjoys his visits here.'

'Of course, he does,' says Mrs Ogilvie. 'He's cleverer than most people I know.'

I take a chance and sit down opposite her. She doesn't give me her usual outraged stare, so I assume she doesn't mind.

'Why do you think he's fond of this place?' I say. 'Is it the staff?'

'Not that young man,' she says at once. 'He teases Bernie terribly. Bernie doesn't enjoy that. He has a great sense of dignity.'

I look down at Bernie, lolling on the floor and watching the customers with interested eyes. As I watch, he rolls over and stands up. He lifts his back leg to scratch behind his ear, misses his target, loses his balance and falls over. He grins up at me as though he's done something clever.

'I'm sure he has,' I say, pretending not to notice. 'No one enjoys being teased, although I happen to know Jack likes Bernie very much. I saw him sneak Bernie a broken dog biscuit when you came in.'

She looks surprised. 'Is that so? Well, I was never one to judge people too hastily. Live and let live is my motto.'

I can think of several mottos she appears to live by, and none of them connected with tolerance and goodwill towards the entire world. But I don't want to antagonise her.

'What about the rest of the staff?' I say. 'I know how much they all look forward to seeing him.'

Her face relaxes. 'I'm not surprised. That Lily is a sweet girl. I had my reservations about her at first, especially when she took up with that young man. But I've changed my mind about her and her friend since they bought the bakery from that old fossil and begged me to bring Bernie in here whenever I like.'

I remember Isabella telling me about the long running feud between Mrs Ogilvie and Mr Mason. It seems unkind to call him a fossil. He appears to be a bit of a worrier, but pleasant. He obviously thinks the world of Lily and, according to Isabella, her mother. Having met Mrs Carson, I'm not surprised. She has an infectious air of positivity, and I can't imagine her allowing anything to get her down for long.

'Why do you think Bernie enjoys himself so much here?' I persist.

She looks down at Bernie, who has noticed the reflection of a miniature dog in the chrome table leg and is trying to attract its attention.

'He likes the company,' she surprises me. 'He and I do very well together, but it's been terribly quiet at home since my husband died. Bernie is a sociable dog, and I don't want him feeling lonely. I bring him here so he can meet new people and enjoy different surroundings for a while. He always seems much brighter in himself after a visit here.'

'I understand how he feels,' I say. 'I'm sure he loves being with you, but we all need a change of scene sometimes. I used to work in Reading, and I was often lonely. Then I moved to Honeywell and started work at the bakery, and I don't have time to be lonely.'

She gives me a thoughtful look. 'You aren't married?'

'Not even close. I was with someone for a couple of years, but we broke up. It was a good thing because I needed to move back home for a while.'

'Change is always difficult,' she says in a surprisingly kind voice.

'When did your husband die?' I ask.

'Five years ago. Bernie still misses him.'

'I'm sure he does,' I say. 'I'm glad you're finding things for him to do to take his mind off it. From what I've heard, he's fond of our products. Does he enjoy the dog biscuits we make for him?'

'Most of them,' she says. 'They aren't always to his taste, but he appreciates people taking the trouble to think of him and find something he likes.'

She clips Bernie's lead to his collar. 'We must be going. We have to stop at the post office on our way home. Mrs Jayson doesn't like it if we go past without stopping in for her to say hello to him. She can be an awful chatterbox, but she loves Bernie, so I put up with it.'

I watch her leave the shop and set off for the post office with Bernie frisking around her heels. People can be surprising. Just when you think you have them pigeonholed, they show you an entirely new side of their lives.

Isabella has been standing behind the counter, watching us.

'I'm surprised she allowed you to sit down with her,' she says. 'The last time I tried that, she told me I'd never make a success of my business unless I occasionally did some work.'

I laugh. 'She's very perceptive. I'm glad she let me talk to her. There's no need for that questionnaire after all, so you can give her a free coffee the next time she comes in. She was very helpful, even if she didn't realise it. I know exactly what we should do for the next round!'

Chapter Twenty-Six

Mum and Dad are in the garden when I arrive home after work.

'We thought we'd have dinner outside,' says Mum. 'It's such a lovely spring evening. We've been enjoying the sunshine.'

It's encouraging to hear her use the word *We* with such confidence. She's spent the last few months talking about *Me and your dad.* I can understand why. After thirty-five years of operating as a unit, she's been forced to face the fact they're currently on different paths. It's no wonder she's been referring to them as separate entities, with one of them taking care of the other. It must be a complicated emotional situation for anyone to navigate. She's done it with grace and courage, but it's taken its toll. I'm pleased she sees them moving towards becoming a partnership again, even if it's not the one she's accustomed to.

'Are you seeing Chris tonight?' she asks.

'He's having dinner with his brother and their family. He invited me, but it feels too soon.'

'I don't see why,' she says. 'He's met us several times.'

'Only because I can never remember where I've left my things. If I hadn't left my bag in his car, none of you would have met for quite a while.'

'I don't understand that,' she says. 'When Dad and I got together, I couldn't wait for him to meet my parents.'

'Times have changed,' I say. 'You probably expected them to pay for your wedding too.'

Her face lights up. 'You aren't saying …?'

'No, I'm not! Chris and I have been seeing each other for about two minutes. Please don't start getting ideas.'

'Of course not,' she says. 'Your life is your own business, Abby. You know that. Dad and I would never dream of interfering. All I'm saying is that we both like Chris very much.'

'As long as you keep it to that.' I smile at her disappointed face. 'Chris likes you too. He said he and Dad had a good chat about football. Maybe they can watch a match together one of these days.'

I look at Dad, who gives me a thumbs up. I remember the Mix-up and the thoughts I've had about it.

'We're expecting to get through to the next round,' I say. 'We have to think about a signature dish. I've suggested we use the theme of inclusion.'

Mum looks doubtful. 'Do you mean you want to bake something gluten-free or vegan?'

'I mean we should include the entire village,' I say. 'Perhaps community would be a better word. The Sugarloaf Bakery doesn't yet have a signature dish because it's only just reopened, and Lily and Isabella haven't put their stamp on the place. It's time we came up with one. My idea is that we ask our customers to submit their favourite recipes and choose a representative selection. We can box them up and sell them as a local product. What do you think?'

'What a marvellous idea!' she says. 'You're so creative, Abby.'

'It was Mrs Ogilvie who gave me the idea. I was chatting with her this afternoon, and she was telling me why her dog enjoys coming into the Sugarloaf. It didn't take a genius to work out she was talking about herself, even if she wasn't prepared to admit it. It made me realise places like the Sugarloaf can be a lifeline. We should lean into that. People like to feel they belong somewhere. They want to know they're important, and others would notice if they weren't there. That's a lot to include in one box of pastries, but I'd like to try.'

'I'll have a look through my recipes this evening,' she promises. 'Geoffrey can help me. If there's one thing I can say about your father, he loves any homemade baking.'

She's as good as her word. She brings out her recipe file after dinner and chatters away as we leaf through it.

'I made this parkin the year you had chicken pox, Abby, and we had to have a bonfire at home instead of going to the village fireworks. It was a huge hit, and I had to make it every year after that. Everyone said bonfire night wouldn't be the same without it. And here's my recipe for garibaldi biscuits. Your dad has always loved those.'

We finish reading the recipes. It takes a while because there's a story behind each of them. It's lovely to see Mum so animated. She lights up as she recounts stories and memories, appealing to Dad at intervals to confirm her recollections. He seems happy to join in. It's the most relaxing evening we've had for weeks.

We finally settle on her recipe for ginger snaps. I take a picture on my phone and say goodnight. I've promised to be in early tomorrow to start a new batch of sourdough. It's Lily's favourite, and she asks for it every week. I don't know what nutrients the baby is lacking to make it demand sourdough each day, but I'm sure it knows what it's doing.

I spend the next day between the kitchen and the shop. Alice is now working four mornings a week, which takes some of the pressure off me. She's eager to help as much as possible in the kitchen, and I teach her how to make the basic doughs and cookie mixes. She's interested in the competition and makes several suggestions for the upcoming rounds.

'That's assuming we get through this one,' I say. 'Let's not get ahead of ourselves.'

I meet Chris for dinner after work. I'm feeling tired and would happily have settled for a takeaway in my pyjamas, but Mum would be shocked to think of Chris seeing me in my Paddington onesie. I don't like to tell her he's seen me in a lot less than that. She's aware I often spend the night at his, but she probably thinks we sit at opposite ends of the sofa all evening, not even taking off our coats, discussing the latest prices of wheat and barley futures.

I arrive before Chris and order myself a glass of wine, smiling to think of my angst over the etiquette of ordering myself a coffee a couple of months ago. That alone should have alerted me to the fact that dating apps weren't a good idea for me. Being with Chris is so easy and uncomplicated that it feels as though I've known him forever. He wouldn't care if I ordered a drink before he arrived. I doubt he would care if I ordered an entire meal if I was hungry and couldn't wait. It's the sort of relationship I didn't imagine existed until now, one in which we can each be exactly who we are while enjoying spending time together.

He arrives at the same time as my wine. 'How far behind am I?'

'Not far. This is only my seventh. You can easily catch up.' I grin at the server's surprised look.

We chat about our day and order our food. I wasn't hungry when I left home, even though I've been too busy all day to eat much. But the wine sharpens my appetite, and I enjoy my meal.

It isn't until we've finished our curry and are debating whether to split a dessert that Chris mentions the Mix-up.

'The scores will be published on Monday,' he says.

'So Isabella said. She's been like a cat on hot bricks all week. She'll be devastated if we don't get a good score.'

'What did you bake for your entry?' he asks.

'We went with the idea I first came up with. Around the UK in ten easy bites. How about you?'

'We did an all-fruit extravaganza,' he says. 'Rick is taking the local theme terribly seriously. He looked up all the varieties of heritage fruits grown in the area, and we made a range of tarts and muffins.'

'I'm impressed,' I say. 'I didn't think you cared enough to come up with something so original.'

'I don't,' he says. 'I told you Rick is making a huge deal about it. He hasn't directly threatened to fire me if I don't win a rosette, but he's been muttering about the guy who used to work for him. Rick's heard on the grapevine that he's left his London restaurant and is looking for work in this area.'

'His fancy heritage grapevine?' I say. 'Rick sounds a nightmare. I wonder whether he knows my old boss.'

'He's ok,' says Chris. 'Maybe a little intense at times. The Slice won the trophy three times in a row. He feels we have a reputation to maintain.'

'I can understand that,' I say. 'But Isabella feels we need to make a name for ourselves. She won't give up without a fight.'

'As long as you and I don't end up fighting, I don't care.'

'I agree,' I say. 'How are you doing with your signature round? Does The Slice have a signature dish?'

'We're well known for our meat pies,' he says. 'But savoury dishes have been excluded. We'll probably go with a variety of slices because of our name.'

'That doesn't sound too original,' I say. 'I wouldn't present the judges with a loaf of sugar simply because of our name.'

'Wait until you've tasted them before you judge,' he says. 'What are you planning to do?'

I tell him about my conversation with Mrs Ogilvie. He looks impressed. 'You're a dark horse, aren't you? Beautiful, a fantastic baker, and creative.'

'Don't forget my deadly aim with caffeinated liquids,' I remind him, embarrassed. It's been a while since anyone has called me beautiful. Paul occasionally called me gorgeous, but only when he wanted something.

'As if I could,' he says. 'I live in daily fear of offending you.'

'Not really?' I say, and he laughs.

'Not really. I'm happy to accept the coffee incident was a one-off due to the stress of meeting not one but two complete losers during the same two-hour period. Anyone could be forgiven for doing what you did.'

'Speaking of losers,' I say, 'would you like me to buy you a commiseration drink? It's never too early to get used to the idea of being beaten by a small but plucky new business.'

He doesn't rise to the bait. 'I never say no to a drink, commiseration or otherwise. We have plenty of time for one more before taking a taxi back to mine.'

'You should start practising your gracious loser face,' I agree. 'You never know how soon you may need it.'

Chapter Twenty-Seven

Isabella throws herself into our village project with enthusiasm. She arrives at work the next day carrying a folder.

'We need to name this *Operation Sweet Victory*,' she says. 'And keep it under lock and key at all times.'

'It isn't some top-secret spy mission,' I say. 'We're collecting a few recipes, that's all.'

'That isn't all,' she says. 'Not by a long shot. We have a good chance of getting through to the finals, thanks to you, Abby. We don't want our competitors pinching our ideas.'

'Are we planning to make our contributors sign an NDA?' I ask, amused.

'That's an idea!' she says. 'Who do I know who could give us free legal advice? I wonder whether there are any lawyers on the dating app. I'll have a quick look.'

'On the app?' I say. 'How does that help us?'

She gives an impatient shrug. 'You can be so slow. It's obvious. I'll look through the profiles and swipe right on all the lawyers. I'll meet them for a date, then casually turn the conversation to the subject of hypothetical non-disclosure agreements and how one might go about drafting one. If the date goes well, I could ask them to write one out on a napkin to show me.'

'I can see several problems with your brilliant idea,' I say. 'First, how do you know they'll match with you? You can swipe right all you want, but it won't help unless they do the same.'

She gives me whatever is the opposite of a modest smile. 'I'm not worried about that. I've never not had a match when I've swiped on someone.'

I'm about to make a sarcastic comment, but what's the point? If I looked like Isabella, I'd expect everyone to swipe right too.

'Fine,' I say. 'Let's assume you're right, and the entire male population of Hampshire is lining up to buy you coffee over the next few days. How will you persuade them your sudden interest in the minutiae of non-disclosure agreements is purely hypothetical, and you're far more interested in their favourite rock band?'

'It shouldn't be too difficult,' she says. 'Most men expect you to be interested in whatever interests them. I'll simper a little and say how confusing I find intricate legal documents, and however do they remember what all those technical terms mean? They'll be falling over themselves to explain it all to me with diagrams. If I play my cards right, I may come out of it with a free will or even the deeds to a new property.'

Lily has arrived while we've been talking. She hangs up her coat. 'Why do you need a will?'

'Because she's so annoying that we never know when one of our customers will take it into their head to dispose of her,' I say. 'We're discussing how we can keep our ideas for the next round a secret from our competitors. My solution is far simpler.'

'We hire undercover agents to watch the bakery?' says Isabella, brightening.

'No, I suggest we ask our customers to keep it quiet.'

She gives me a disgusted look. 'I thought when I hired you that you were going to be fun. You're a sad disappointment.'

'Abby's right,' says Lily. 'We'll get our customers on board with the idea of being a team. Everyone likes to win. Look at football supporters. Half of them don't know a hockey pitch from a soccer pitch and couldn't explain the offside rule to you if they tried. But they like being part of a group. Our customers will be the same.'

'What if they use other bakeries too?' says Isabella. 'They'll have split loyalties. It's a potential minefield. I think we should consider my idea again.'

'We'll only ask for recipes from people we already know,' says Lily. 'My mum knows everyone for miles around. She'd sniff out a saboteur within five minutes.'

The door opens, and Mrs Ogilvie walks in.

'Good morning, Mrs Ogilvie,' says Lily. 'Do you mind if we ask you a question?'

'You've already asked me why Bernie enjoys coming here,' says Mrs Ogilvie.

'It's a different question,' says Isabella. 'But before we get to that, I'm pleased to inform you that you were last week's winner of a free cup of coffee and cake of your choice. I'll make your drink while you decide which cake you'd like.'

To my surprise, Mrs Ogilvie agrees to submit a recipe for the competition.

'Goodness knows what she'll come up with,' Isabella warns me. 'You may come to regret asking her.'

'That's the whole point,' I say. 'We want to include everyone. The theme of the Sugarloaf is bringing the community together. That means everyone, even the ones who are a little prickly at times.'

'Prickly?' she says. 'I've seen fields of thistles with fewer spikes. I still think you may have bitten off more than you can chew.'

'You're confusing me with Bernie,' I say. 'Let's see what she brings us.'

I'm delighted to be proved right. Mrs Ogilvie turns up the following day with a piece of paper covered in spidery writing. She hands it to me and waits. I can just about make out the title – Lemon cream sandwich biscuits.

'Is this a family recipe?' I ask her.

'It's a Honeywell recipe,' she says. 'The vicar's wife used to make these biscuits every year for our Sunday School outing.'

Mr Mason is sitting at a nearby table. He looks up when she says this. 'The Sunday School outing to Cardigan Cove?'

'That's right,' she says. 'How do you know about that?'

His mournful face looks almost animated. 'I went on that trip twice. The Reverend Jarvis left the village soon afterwards to take up a posting in Gibraltar. The next vicar was unmarried, so the trips stopped. But I remember those biscuits.'

'How interesting,' I say. 'So, you both went on the same outing without realising. What year was that?'

Mrs Ogilvie looks at me as though I've offered Bernie strychnine, and I realise I've said the wrong thing.

Mr Mason is quicker. 'It was a while ago. I don't remember the exact date. I didn't think anyone else remembered those outings.'

He gestures to Mrs Ogilvie's table. 'I wonder whether …?'

She gives a gracious inclination of her head, and he moves his teapot to her table and sits down. Bernie greets him with a welcoming bark, and Mr Mason nods to him.

'Good, er, doggie.'

I leave them having an animated discussion of times gone past and the apparent delights of sardine sandwiches and brawn. It sounds revolting to me, but they seem to have fond memories of it all.

'You put your foot in it there,' Isabella murmurs to me. 'She must be ten years older than him. They won't have attended Sunday school at the same time.'

'I realised that when I saw her face,' I murmur back. 'But it was too late by then. Thank goodness for Mr Mason.'

I look at the pair of them, deep in conversation about people I've never heard of, despite having grown up in the village.

'Maybe this is the start of a beautiful May December romance,' I say.

Isabella gives a choke of laughter. 'More like Halloween to Christmas.'

'Don't be so ageist,' I chide her. 'Why shouldn't people later in life find happiness?'

'You're quite right,' she says. 'But Mr Mason is married. And he doesn't approve of Bernie.'

'That's a shame,' I say. 'I was already planning a Sugarloaf wedding. We could have a wreath made of doughnuts, and Bernie could be the ring bearer.'

'He'd be more likely to eat it,' she says.

She raises her voice. 'Excuse me, Mr Mason. We were wondering whether you'd like to submit a cookie recipe for the next round of the competition. We have to bake them ourselves, but we're collecting recipes from our customers to make it a village affair.'

'That's a good idea,' he says. 'I'll ask my wife whether she has any appropriate recipes.'

I lay a hand on Isabella's arm before she can speak. 'Thank you so much, Mr Mason. We look forward to it.'

He and Mrs Ogilvie resume their conversation.

'What?' says Isabella.

'You were about to ask why cookie recipes are women's work,' I say.

'Perhaps,' she says. 'I was even more curious why a man who ran a bakery for decades couldn't come up with his own.'

'He didn't bake his own products for the last few years,' says Lily. 'I hope he gives us something we can use. It would be good for us to be able to point to the continuity. And it would mean a lot to him. He didn't like letting the bakery go. He told me he could never have brought himself to sell it if it hadn't been me who'd made the offer. It didn't hurt that my parents underwrote part of the loan. He's always had a soft spot for my mother.'

I show them the paper Mrs Ogilvie gave me. 'I could only just read the title. We'll have to get a handwriting expert in to decipher the actual recipe.'

'My mum will be able to read it,' says Lily. 'It looks like my grandmother's handwriting. They must have taught it like that at school.'

'It looks as though Bernie stuck his paw in a pot of ink and did the polka all over the paper,' grumbles Isabella. 'Someone ought to have invented laptops much earlier. It would have saved us all a lot of trouble.'

Chapter Twenty-Eight

As Lily predicted, Mrs Carson has no trouble reading the recipe for Mrs Ogilvie's biscuits.

'I haven't had one of those for years,' she says. 'They're delicious.'

She's already given us the recipe for jumbles her mother-in-law gave her when she was first married.

'It works like a charm when people are tired and hungry,' she says. 'Many's the argument between Lily and Ben I've been able to stop by baking them a batch of these.'

'Ben always ate most of them,' says Lily.

'Don't you start all that again,' says Mrs Carson. 'You only have to say the word and I'll bake some for you and Jack. I'd cook for you more often, but I never know what you'll fancy these days. It changes all the time. Last month, it was calzone. But Jack says when he brought some home last week, you told him the smell made you feel sick. The poor man had to eat it all himself.'

'He's fine,' says Lily. 'He's always giving you sob stories about how badly he's treated because he knows you fall for them and cook him all his favourite foods to make up for it.'

'I enjoy it,' says her mother. 'He's such a lovely young man. We're so pleased to have him in the family.'

'What about Stephen?' says Isabella, and Lily laughs.

'Who's Stephen,' I ask.

'It's a long story,' says Isabella. 'I'll tell you some other time. Let's just say that Lily and I always refer to him as *The one that got away.*'

Mr Mason turns up a couple of days later carrying a notebook. 'My wife would have brought these in herself, but she's gone away for a few days to see her sister. She says you're welcome to use any of the recipes you like, but she recommends the treacle snaps.'

By Saturday, we have seventeen cookie recipes. I've baked a batch of all the likely-looking ones, and we've handed out samples to the customers and asked for feedback.

We settle on six recipes, and I make a second batch of each of them to check they're foolproof. Lily orders boxes with the name of our bakery and a picture of the village green with the church in the background.

I feel much calmer than I did before the qualifying round, when I wasn't sure what to expect. Lily keeps telling me to have fun and enjoy it, but Isabella insists we have to take the competition seriously as it could mean the difference between the bakery's success or failure in the event of another economic downturn.

Chris comes over for dinner the night before the next round. I've been unable to prevent Mum from inviting him to dinner several times since she met him. She takes me aside before he arrives this evening and murmurs discreetly that he would be welcome to stay over any time.

'It's only a five-minute drive to his flat,' I say, wilfully misunderstanding her.

Her face turns pink. 'I know that. But he may not want to go home every night. He may prefer the … company.'

'He does,' I say. 'He loves chatting with Dad about football. And he was most interested in what you had to tell him about geranium cuttings the last time he was here.'

I smile at her and walk out before she can come up with any more delicate euphemisms.

Chris arrives carrying an enormous bunch of chrysanthemums, which he hands to Mum. 'Abby said you like these. She also told me it was your birthday last week. I was sorry to miss it. I hope you had a good day.'

Mum looks flustered. 'I would have asked you to come to dinner with us, but Geoffrey had an appointment at the hospital that afternoon, and we went straight from there.'

'I wouldn't dream of crashing your family party,' he says. 'But I would have baked you something. Maybe not a cake. I'm sure Abby had that all under control.'

'She made me a Black Forest Gateau,' says Mum. 'I was so touched she remembered it's my favourite. We all had a slice when we got home. I haven't slept so well in years.'

Chris looks amused. 'Abby went to town on the Kirsch?'

'It's Mum's favourite part,' I say. 'She doesn't like to drink liqueurs. My grandmother always told her it was unladylike for a woman to be seen drinking them in public. But it's apparently fine to eat several slices of Black Forest Gateau or have three helpings of brandy butter at Christmas.'

'I'm with your mum,' he says. 'I've yet to come across a cake that couldn't be improved with a generous helping of spirits.'

I raise an eyebrow. 'I'll make a note to avoid your Victoria sponge.'

'My mum made me a Rum Baba for my fourth birthday,' he says. 'It was one of my dad's favourite cakes, and she completely forgot it had alcohol in it. Apparently, I ate a large slice, then fell asleep in the blancmange.'

'Oh, dear,' says Mum, distressed. 'I hope you were alright.'

'Not even a headache the following morning,' he says cheerfully. 'Mum felt terrible about it. I was more disappointed it wasn't a pirate ship cake.'

'Why a pirate ship?' I ask. 'Did you dream of becoming Jack Sparrow when you grew up?'

'I was desperate for a pet parrot,' he says. 'Mum and Dad vetoed that pretty sharply, so I decided I wanted a pirate cake to make up for it. But I forgot to tell her, so she made the Rum Baba instead.'

Mum still looks worried. 'Did you get a pirate ship cake the next year?'

'I wanted one, but we were on holiday for my fifth birthday,' he says. 'Mum had a look in the shops, but the closest she could come up with was some sort of caterpillar. I was going to ask for one again on my sixth birthday, but my sisters persuaded me that only babies liked pirates, and they talked Mum into making me a unicorn cake instead. They both loved unicorns.'

'You had a deprived childhood,' I tell him. 'Still, your memoirs will make interesting reading.'

'What a shame,' says Mum. 'Still, what's done is done, and you make wonderful cakes of your own now. I'm sure you'll both do very well in this next round. Abby tells me she received nine out of ten for presentation and ten out of ten for creativity in the qualifying round. Her father and I were so proud of her.'

'Chris did pretty well too,' I say. 'He got nine out of ten for both categories.'

Mum claps her hands. 'That's marvellous, Chris! I'm so proud of you.'

'You aren't meant to side with the opposition,' I say. 'You're supposed to be suggesting ways to sabotage him.'

She looks shocked. 'I wouldn't want to do that. I'm hoping you both get through to the final.'

I catch Chris's eye and see he's grinning.

'That's true. It would be more satisfying to beat him in the final,' I say.

'My girlfriend, ladies and gentlemen!' says Chris, dropping a kiss on top of my head.

'I don't know where she gets her competitive streak from,' Mum tells Chris. 'Certainly not from me.'

He shakes his head. 'It's a mystery, Sue. But it's a burden I have to bear.'

'You'll be fine,' she says. 'If you work half as hard as Abby, you can't fail to get into the final. I see her scribbling in that notebook of hers every evening. I'm sure she has lots of lovely ideas.'

Chris and I make dinner and watch the news with Mum and Dad. Mum is so pleased Dad is taking an interest in current affairs again that she doesn't object when he tries to throw a cushion at the screen each time his least favourite cabinet minister appears.

Chris leaves at ten o'clock. 'It's the big day tomorrow, and I'd better get ready. Is it ok to wish you luck?'

He sees my face. 'I know what you're going to say. You don't need luck.'

'You think you know me so well,' I say. 'But it's true. We're going to blow the judges away tomorrow and leave all our competitors in the dust.'

'I'll look forward to it,' he says. 'Our slices are also amazing, so don't get too cocky.'

'How about dinner on Wednesday evening?' I say. 'I'll have something to celebrate.'

'What a coincidence,' he says. 'So will I.'

He kisses me goodbye, and I watch him drive away before closing the front door.

Mum appears in the hall. 'Has Chris left? Dad asked me to make him a cup of tea, but I wanted to give you your privacy.'

'If you carry on like this, I'll forbid Chris from coming to the house at all,' I say. 'That will give us all the privacy you like.'

'Don't do that,' she says. 'I look forward to his visits. He's a lovely young man, and he's so good with your father. People are very kind. They drop by and chat to him, and I know he's pleased to see them. But some of them treat him as though he's a toddler. I'm sure they don't mean to, but they talk slowly and simply about the weather and the state of the roads. I have no idea why they suppose your father has the faintest interest in any of it. He never did before the stroke, so why should he now?'

'I've noticed that,' I say. 'Mrs Olsen dropped a cake around last week. It was kind of her, but she insisted on talking about the primary school fête for half an hour. I had to ask her to leave in the end. I said the nurse was coming. It wasn't true, but Dad gave me such a desperate look. Chris isn't like that at all. He talks to Dad about the things he's interested in, and he doesn't jump in with the correct word if Dad's struggling. Dad is far chattier with him than almost anyone else.'

'I've noticed that too,' she says. 'So, please don't stop inviting him around. I know it's early days, but I have the feeling you've found a good one.'

I give her a hug. 'It *is* early days, so don't get carried away. But I think you may be right.'

Chapter Twenty-Nine

Isabella and I drive over to the Swinford church hall together the following morning. Lily is coming later with Jack. We stack the boxes of cakes on the back seat, and Isabella drives at a ludicrously slow speed, taking corners with care.

We find our allocated table and set out our cookies. Gavin, the man who enjoyed our Eccles cakes, is the first judge to arrive.

'I've been looking forward to this,' he says. 'I can't wait to see what you have up your sleeve this time.'

'I think you'll be pleasantly surprised,' says Isabella.

'I'm sure I will be,' he says. 'The standard of competition has been high this year. Perhaps people are eager to make up for lost time. Oddly enough, someone had the same idea as you in the qualifying round and presented a range of British products. No Eccles cakes, more's the pity, but they made scones and Bakewell tarts.'

'That's strange,' says Isabella.

'I don't think so,' he says. 'It was an open round. There's nothing so likely as two bakeries coming up with a similar idea.'

'Which bakery was it?' she asks.

'I forget its name. The one at Monkford,' he says.

'The Baker Boys?' she says, frowning.

'I think that was the name.'

'I doubt anyone will have come up with the same idea as us this time,' I say.

The other competitors have arrived and are setting up their tables. I try not to stare at them, but Isabella has no such qualms. She walks up and down, inspecting the entries. She reaches the table furthest from ours, and her face freezes. She beckons to me to join her, and I hurry over.

'What is it?' I ask.

She glares at the man standing behind the table. He's a thickset man of about thirty with wiry brown hair. He looks oddly familiar, but I can't place him.

'What do you think you're doing?' she demands.

He gives her an aggressive stare in return. 'Oh, hello. I didn't know your bakery had entered the competition. That's brave of you.'

She ignores the obvious jibe. 'What are you doing? Is that a box of cookies?'

'Full marks for effort,' he says mockingly.

I look at the boxes in front of him. They're almost identical to ours. The only difference is that they've used a picture of their own village.

Isabella reaches over to open a box, but he stops her.

'Judges only,' he says in a sneering tone.

We're interrupted by Gavin, who has sensed trouble and come over to discover what's going on.

'Is there a problem?' he asks.

'Yes, there is!' says Isabella, just as the man says, 'Not at all, Gavin.'

'I'm pleased to hear it,' says Gavin. 'The judging is about to start, so we need all the contestants back in their places.'

I follow Isabella to where Lily and Jack are waiting.

'What was that about?' I ask.

She's about to answer when Gavin claps his hands for silence.

'Ladies and Gentlemen – welcome to the second round of the New Forest Annual Mix-up. I'm delighted to see so many of you here to offer support and encouragement to your local bakers. There are twelve competitors in this round. These are the bakeries who successfully made it through the qualifying round. We have invited each bakery to give us an example of what they consider to be their signature dish. I'm sure we're all excited to see what our competitors have come up with. So, without further ado, may I invite the team from Crusty Delights to show us what they've made?'

We all crane our necks to see what the team at the furthest table has produced. It's difficult to see clearly from this distance, but judging from the expression on the audience's faces, it's pretty impressive.

The judges gather around the table, tasting and conferring and scribbling notes. Gavin steps back and addresses us all again.

'What an excellent start to this part of the competition. In case you couldn't see, the team has entered a passion fruit meringue tart they tell me is such a firm favourite with their customers that they have a standing order of passion fruit from their suppliers. I shall certainly make a detour to Little Haywood next time I'm in the area.'

The judges move on to the second table, where they taste a triple-layer carrot cake sandwiched with a cream cheese and citrus filling. My heart sinks. I thought I'd been so ingenious with our idea for a signature dish. Now I'm not so sure.

The judges seem wowed by the first two entries. They may be less impressed with a few cookies.

Gavin and his team work their way around the room until they reach the table where Isabella was arguing with the man.

'And what do we have here?' asks the youngest judge, a woman with red hair and trendy purple glasses.

The man gives her an oily smile. 'Nice to see you again, Angela. After much thought and consideration, we decided the heart of any bakery is its customers. Therefore, we felt we could do no better than find out from them what makes them keep coming back to our establishment so we can give them more of the same.'

Isabella gives an audible gasp and almost stamps her foot. One of the judges gives her a disapproving look. I nudge Isabella and whisper. 'Isn't that exactly what we've done?'

'Yes, it is!' she hisses back. 'How did that treacherous snake, Dave Collins, find out what we were doing?'

'You know him?' I say.

She frowns. 'I wouldn't say I know him. I met him through the dating app.'

'You dated him?' I say, surprised.

She shrugs. 'One date only. Let's say his profile was less than honest.'

She pulls out her phone and opens the app. She scrolls swiftly down and points to a picture. I stifle a burst of laughter, and the same judge gives me a reproving look.

'I'd have swiped right on that,' I whisper, and Isabella nods.

I'm not sure where this guy had his photo taken, but the photographer must have had a magic lens. I look over at him, taking in his toilet brush hair and blotchy skin. I look back at Isabella's phone, where a face looks out at me that could easily be mistaken for Brad Pitt's younger brother.

'How did the date go?' I ask, trying to keep a straight face.

'It was shorter than he expected,' she murmurs back. 'We met for coffee, but before our order had even arrived, I had an urgent call telling me I was needed elsewhere.'

I grin. 'Lily?'

'She was my escape call,' she admits. 'Unfortunately, in the shock of meeting Dave in person, I forgot to wait for the actual call.'

'What did you do?'

'I gasped and said, "Oh dear! I was worried this would happen. It's my uncle calling me back home for a farming emergency. His prize cow must have gone into labour."'

'It wasn't the best excuse in the world,' I say. 'But you live next to a farm. It was a plausible scenario.'

She sighs. 'That's what I thought. Unfortunately, I'd forgotten to take my phone out of my pocket. When Dave pointed this out, I told him I'd set it to silent, and it had vibrated. He asked how I knew what the text said without looking. I was so flustered that I pulled out my phone, and we could both see there were no messages on it.'

'I imagine he was a bit annoyed,' I say.

'He was furious. He demanded an explanation, so I told him I'd made a mistake. My uncle doesn't send texts to that phone. He sends them directly to my burner phone. When he asked me to show him my burner phone, I said it wouldn't be appropriate on a first date because I'd hidden it in my underwear. For some reason, he didn't appear to believe me. Anyway, that was the end of our date. He didn't seem too pleased.'

'That explains his attitude to you,' I say. 'But how did he come up with the same idea as us today?'

She stops smiling. 'I don't know, but I intend to find out.'

The judges have moved on while we've been conferring. I wish I'd paid more attention to what Dave's bakery made. If this is a genuine coincidence, they won't have baked the exact same cookies as us.'

'And now for our final contestants,' says Gavin. 'The team from the recently reopened Sugarloaf Bakery in Honeywell.'

There's a smattering of applause, and I notice Lily's parents have arrived with Mr Mason.

We pick up our boxes of cookies and hand one to each judge. We explain the idea behind the concept, and the judges taste each cookie while Isabella and I watch anxiously.

'Another outstanding entry,' says Gavin. 'However, I'm a little surprised that two bakeries should have had the same idea.'

'So am I,' says Isabella grimly. 'And I'm determined to get to the bottom of it.'

'Do you mean to say you didn't exchange ideas with each other?' says Gavin.

She gives a derisive laugh. 'I wouldn't exchange the time of day with Dave Collins.'

Dave walks over to our table. 'That's not very nice of you. Isabella and I recently went on a date, Gavin. I'm afraid I wasn't feeling it, so it was only the one date. It seems to have hurt her feelings a little, which may be why she's behaving in such a hostile fashion today.'

I see Jack make a dart towards Isabella and grab her arm as it starts on its upward swing.

Gavin looks uncomfortable. 'Contestants' private lives aren't relevant to this competition. Perhaps we could put personal considerations on one side for now and discover why you both seem to have made the same thing.'

Isabella opens her mouth to speak, but Dave is quicker.

'I quite agree,' he says. 'But I thought you may have noticed that little unpleasantness before the competition, and I wanted to put it into context. For the record, I don't think The Sugarloaf Bakery cheated. Possibly, we weren't as discreet about our ideas as we might have been, and you know how word gets about. However, I'm happy to overlook it this time and allow each contestant to receive marks based on their own entry.'

Isabella breaks free of Jack and makes a lunge at him. Gavin looks shocked. Dave tries and fails to look pained. I see a smirk edging the corners of his mouth.

'That concludes this round,' interrupts the woman called Angela. 'The results will be posted on our website by tomorrow evening.'

The judges file out. Gavin is the last to leave. He stops at our table and points towards the open door. 'There's a dog sitting outside wearing a large rosette and a pink sweater. Do you see him too?'

I give a choke of laughter as I see Bernie sitting in the vestibule trying to chew through the ribbon holding his rosette in place. He's wearing an extraordinary pink jumper with lace edging.

I assure Gavin that I see him too.

He looks relieved. 'That's good. I've had a couple of funny turns this week. The doctor says it's nothing to be concerned about as long as I take my blood pressure tablets. But I wouldn't like to think I was seeing pink elephants or anything like that.'

He says goodbye and follows the rest of the judges. I walk over to the door, and Bernie prances inside, followed by Mrs Ogilvie. Bernie makes a beeline for our table and looks hopefully up at the boxes of biscuits.

'What are you wearing?' I ask, bending down to pat him.

He gives me an exasperated look. He would obviously prefer me to concentrate on more important things. He shakes himself, and the rosette drops off. I pick it up and inspect it. It says, *Good luck on your special day.*

'The post office didn't have a wide selection,' says Mrs Ogilvie.

'It's perfect,' I assure her. 'What a lovely gesture.'

She looks pleased. 'He's wearing his special jumper too.'

'It's very … interesting,' says Isabella.

Mrs Ogilvie detects the note of sarcasm in her voice and bristles. 'My sister made it for me a while ago. She sent it all the way from Australia.'

'Does she know Bernie is a boy?' asks Isabella with only the smallest quiver of laughter in her voice.

Mrs Ogilvie draws herself up to her full height, which is still somewhere under five feet. 'She made it for Maisie, who was the dog I had before Bernie. Anyway, I thought your generation didn't approve of pink clothes for girls and blue clothes for boys.'

'Quite right,' I say. 'Good for you and Bernie. Why should he be forced to conform to outdated and stereotypical notions of gender?'

Mrs Ogilvie looks somewhat mollified. 'He always enjoys wearing that sweater, and it seemed appropriate to make a bit of an effort today.'

Bernie lifts a hind leg and scratches behind his ear, then appears to notice the sweater. He snaps at the lace.

I hand him a piece of lemon shortbread. 'There you go, Bernie, on the house. It's your prize for being the best dressed dog in the village.'

He lies down and gnaws at it.

'I'm glad someone appreciates our entry,' says Isabella gloomily.

'Don't be like that,' says Mrs Carson. 'You all did a wonderful job. It's a pity the other bakery had the same idea, but these things happen.'

'I'm not so sure,' says Isabella. 'Fool me once, shame on you. Fool me twice, and I'll unleash the forces of hell on you.'

'Is that how it goes?' asks Mrs Carson. 'I'm sure that's not what we said in my day.'

Lily laughs. 'You're so nice that you probably said fool me twice and I'll give you the benefit of the doubt and offer to make you a cup of tea.'

'I'm not making a cup of tea for that man,' says Isabella. 'Not unless I can find something extremely nasty to put in it. What I'm going to do is find out how that snake heard about our ideas. When I do, I'm going to make him sorry he was ever born.'

Chapter Thirty

The judges post the results just as the bakery is closing the following afternoon. Isabella has been checking the website all day in between serving customers and muttering darkly about Dave Collins and what she'd like to do to him. I've remembered where I saw him before. I arrived early to meet Chris at the Red Lion last week and saw the pair of them chatting at the bar. Dave left when I arrived, and I forgot to ask Chris who he was.

'They've posted them!' shouts Isabella, and we all drop what we're doing and rush over to her.

There's a long silence as we peer at the screen. Lily is the first to break it. 'It could have been worse.'

'I don't see how,' says Isabella.

I look at the scores, my stomach plummeting with disappointment. We worked so hard on this round.

'We got full marks for execution and presentation,' says Lily. 'That's down to you, Abby. Well done.'

'But we were marked way down on originality,' I say. 'And that's down to me too.'

'No, it isn't!' says Isabella. 'It was a brilliant idea. Everyone thinks so. It wasn't your fault Dave Collins found out about it and copied it. The only comfort is that his bakery got marked down for originality too. And they didn't do as well as we did in the other category. I'd love to see his face right now.'

'Open his profile and look at it as much as you like,' I say.

She snorts. 'If I want to see young Brandon Pitt, I'll watch his movies.'

'Who?' says Lily, puzzled.

'A figment of Isabella's imagination,' I tell her. 'She's decided that Brad Pitt has a younger and more successful brother.'

'Meanwhile, back on planet earth,' says Lily, 'have we decided what we're doing for the next round? I saw they posted it on the website last night. It's rather vague, isn't it? *Everything Chocolate.* I wish they'd been a little more specific.'

'I think it's great,' says Isabella. 'It gives us plenty of scope for a show stealing entry. We can pull out all the stops.'

'We have to hold something back,' I say. 'Otherwise, we'll run out of ideas by the final.'

'I never run out of ideas,' she says. 'I've already had several. What do you think about a chocolate river running through a marzipan model of the bakery?'

'With Bernie playing the part of Augustus Gloop?' I suggest.

She sighs. 'I knew I'd heard of that somewhere. Fine, what about a chocolate mountain?'

'With what theme?' I say.

She looks puzzled. 'That *is* the theme.'

'I'm not following you.'

She gives an impatient sigh. 'The mountain is made of chocolate. It's a *chocolate* mountain.'

Lily interrupts as Isabella's eyes glaze over with a look of misty reverence.

'She's deluded, Abby. As far as Isabella is concerned, a mountain of chocolate is an art form in itself. She sees no need for a further theme.'

'I'll add it to my list,' I promise. 'I couldn't find my notebook this morning. I left home in a bit of a rush. I'll scribble your idea onto a napkin and write it in the book once I get home.'

'Have you come up with some ideas?' asks Lily.

I try to remember them all. 'I wondered about a Black Forest gateau or a Devil's Food cake. I texted Isabella last night to say I thought it might be fun to do a tasting plate.'

'That's a great idea,' she says. 'What do you think, Isabella?'

'I like the suggestion,' says Isabella. 'But could we make one of the cakes in the shape of a mountain? The Matterhorn, perhaps, or Everest.'

Lily smiles. 'We can talk about that later. In the meantime, those cookies won't arrange themselves into tasteful displays.'

'I don't see the point,' grumbles Isabella. 'The customers come in and buy them, which means I have to rearrange them. Why can't they look without buying? It would save me an awful lot of work. Do you remember those macaron displays you used to make when things were quiet in the shop? Why did you stop doing that?'

'I grew up,' says Lily. She catches herself. 'I'm sorry. I didn't mean to sound so tetchy. I didn't sleep well last night.'

'Was Jack kicking you?' asks Isabella.

'Of course not!' says Lily.

'My mistake,' says Isabella. 'You often talk about being kicked all night. I've always assumed you meant Jack. He seems like someone who'd be a restless sleeper.'

I intervene before Lily can answer. Her sense of humour is clearly at a low ebb today, and Isabella is in one of her most teasing moods.

'Have we agreed on a tasting plate as a working hypothesis?' I say. 'If so, I'll start making some sample batches and see what we all think.'

Thankfully, the delivery van pulls up outside, which distracts Isabella.

'I'll check the order,' she says. 'They promised to bring some of those coconut macaroons this week. I'm not signing for it if they haven't.' She grabs the printout and makes a dart for the door.

I make a batch of Danish pastries and put them in the oven. While I wait for them to bake, I pull out my phone and text Chris.

Congratulations on your score. I'm really pleased for you.

He answers almost at once. *You, too. We should celebrate.*

I'm not sure how to reply. He's seen the scores. He knows how badly we did.

I don't feel like celebrating, I type. *But you go ahead.*

I expect him to text me back, but he doesn't. Instead, my phone rings. I'm tempted to switch it off without answering, but I have to speak to him sometime.

'Abby?' he says. 'Are you ok?'

'I'm fine,' I say a little tightly. 'You've seen everyone's scores. Don't pretend I did well.'

He sounds surprised. 'I thought you did brilliantly. The Sugarloaf was the only bakery to get top marks for execution and presentation.'

'So what? They marked us right down on originality, which means we're going into the next round with one of the lowest overall scores.'

'That wasn't fair,' he says. 'Your idea was great. It was a pity Dave thought of the same thing.'

'It wasn't a pity,' I say. 'It was deliberate.'

He sounds amused. 'How so?'

'Think about it. He did the exact same thing we did – twice!'

'The first one is a bit of a stretch,' he says. 'Anyone could have come up with that UK theme. I'm not saying it was a bad idea, but it wasn't so original that two separate bakeries couldn't have thought of it.'

I bite back a sharp reply. Technically, he's right, but I was pleased with the idea when I came up with it.

'How about this last round?' I say. 'Our entry was even more original, yet Dave came up with the same thing again. That's pretty much a statistical impossibility.'

'Maths isn't my strong suit,' he says. 'I'll have to take your word for it. But even if you're right, so what? It's a stupid competition. Most people will never have heard about it, let alone care who wins.'

A thousand replies spring to my lips, all of them snappy. But Chris has had enough of me biting his head off for a while.

'You may be right,' I say, 'but that isn't how it feels to me. This competition is extremely important to me, and it isn't fair someone has sabotaged us like this.'

He still sounds amused, which annoys me. 'I'm sorry about that, but it's done now. Would you like to meet for a drink tonight and talk about it some more?'

If his tone wasn't so amused, I might have agreed. There's nothing I'd enjoy more than a nice relaxing evening with Chris. Mum and Dad are going to be so disappointed. They'll do their best to hide it, but I'll know what they're thinking. It will be a gloomy evening, and I'd love to escape it. But if I meet Chris, there's a strong possibility I'll lose my temper at some point, which won't help anything.

'I'm busy tonight,' I say.

'That's a shame. Anything that can be rearranged?'

'No!' I say. 'I've told you I'm busy. You'll have to celebrate on your own. Congratulations again.'

I don't care if he thinks I'm a sore loser. I can't sit drinking champagne with him tonight.

'Thanks,' he says. 'You, too.'

I take a deep breath. 'There's another thing I wanted to mention. It might be best from now on if you and I don't talk about the competition with each other.'

There's a long pause before he answers. 'You don't want to discuss it at all?'

'That's right. We should have made that rule right from the start. That was my fault, but it didn't occur to me.'

There's an even longer silence. When he speaks, his tone is cold. 'Let me get this straight. Are you accusing me of having leaked your ideas to Dave Collins?'

'No! At least, not deliberately.'

'I see. And this is based on what?'

I don't know why he's annoyed. It's the obvious conclusion to draw.

'I saw you with him in the pub last week,' I say. 'You were talking to him before I arrived.'

'And that was enough for you to decide I'd told him all about your plans for the competition and suggested he copy them?'

'Not the second part,' I say without thinking.

'Thanks,' he says. 'It's good to know you only suspect me of betraying your confidence.'

'I didn't mean it like that. But who else would it have been? You're the only person I've talked to about my ideas except for my family.'

'How about Isabella?' he says. 'She's always struck me as a chatterbox.'

'Don't be ridiculous,' I say. 'She would never do that. Besides, she hates Dave Collins. He's the last person she would talk to about anything.'

'So, it must have been me,' he says.

I'm starting to feel annoyed. I haven't accused him of deliberately sabotaging us. He probably didn't realise how important secrecy was to me.

'Chris, I don't want to argue with you,' I say as calmly as I can. 'I'm not accusing you of anything. Maybe you mentioned something to Dave when you saw him at the pub, and maybe you didn't. The damage is done now, but I don't want it happening again. If I don't talk about my plans with anyone, Dave can't steal our ideas, and we won't get marked down for lack of originality. And you and I won't keep fighting.'

'Sure,' he says. 'I'm sorry for taking up so much of your time. You must have plenty of things to do.'

The hurt in his tone is evident, and I feel a wash of guilt.

'Chris …' I begin.

'Have a great evening,' he says. 'Give me a call when you're free.'

And he rings off before I can answer.

Chapter Thirty-One

I get everyone on board with my idea of a tasting plate for the next round. We settle on Sachertorte, chocolate orange brownies, chocolate raspberry cheesecake with dark chocolate ganache, salted caramel chocolate tart, white chocolate lavender muffins, devil's food cake, and my favourite, Italian Torta Caprese.

I still can't find the notebook in which I jotted down my initial ideas. Mum has helped me search for it everywhere. She's even asked the nurses who come in, but there's no sign of it. I'm sure I had a few other ideas for what Isabella is now calling my Chocolate Paradiso, but we have plenty without them.

Alice's enthusiasm surprises me. She's only supposed to work four mornings a week, but she insists on coming in at other times to help with the planning and test the batches. She tells me she would love to train as a baker after her year off, but her parents want her to do a nursing degree. She's hoping to get enough experience at the Sugarloaf to persuade them she's serious about a future career in the catering industry.

I walk her through what I'm doing, step by step, and allow her to make one of the test batches herself. I offer to let her help me with the actual competition entry, but she refuses in horror.

'I'd be terrified of messing it up for you. My boyfriend says I lose my head at the slightest thing.'

'He doesn't sound supportive,' I say. 'Does he often put you down like that?'

'He's right,' she says. 'I get stressed about everything. I need to work on that.'

'You do if you're planning a career in hospitality,' I admit. 'Not every employer is as easy going as Isabella and Lily. What does your boyfriend do?'

'He's a mechanic,' she says. 'He's a bit older than me, so he's been working at a garage in Twyston for about ten years. He wants to own his own garage one day. His brother has his own business, and he says it's great being your own boss.'

It doesn't sound the best relationship to me, but there's no more point in me telling her this than it would have been for anyone to warn me Paul wasn't the greatest boyfriend ever. I hope Alice finds a way to follow her dream and do whatever makes her happy. She's still young enough to change boyfriends every five minutes. Hopefully, she'll move on and find someone better soon.

I resolve to give her as much encouragement as possible to attend the open days for the courses she's interested in. I can also invite her to spend time with me in the kitchen when she isn't needed in the shop, although that won't be for long. Lily is more than seven months pregnant, and she isn't sure how much longer she'll be coming into work. She wants to stay for the duration of the competition, if at all possible. She and Isabella constantly talk about how good it will be for the bakery if we get to the finals, and I'm determined to make that happen, even if I can't guarantee a win.

I haven't seen Chris since our phone conversation. We've exchanged a couple of polite texts but haven't found a mutually agreeable time to meet in person. I suspect neither of us has tried too hard. I'll see him on Saturday at the competition. Hopefully, I'll get the chance to talk to him afterwards and iron things out. In the meantime, I'm too busy to think about it much.

The morning of the third round is chaotic, and I wonder several times why I pushed to do something so complicated. We'd have been better off with something simple yet elegantly crafted. But it's too late for regrets, so I rush around putting the finishing touches on all the cakes and snapping at Alice and Isabella for getting under my feet. I feel guilty when I see Alice's crestfallen face, but this is nothing. She may be sensitive, but she'll have to overcome that before she's faced with a boss who makes Matt look like a guidance counsellor.

I pipe the last swirl of icing onto the Sachertorte with ten minutes to go and breathe a sigh of relief. Alice helps me to box up the cakes and carry them out to Isabella's car.

'I'm sorry I was short with you,' I say. 'I didn't sort out my timings properly. I'll walk you through it all later if you like and tell you where I went wrong.'

We arrive at Baywood church hall and set out our table. Chris is on the opposite side of the hall, and I'm relieved to see him give me a thumbs up when I arrive. I smile back, wondering why I've been so reluctant to meet him this week. He isn't the sort to bear a grudge for long, and he's had time to appreciate the reasonableness of my argument.

The judges arrive, and Gavin sniffs the air appreciatively. 'This is my favourite round so far. I'm extremely partial to a bit of chocolate.'

'Does anything stand out?' enquires Isabella with an innocent air, but he smiles and shakes his head.

This time, it's the Sugarloaf's turn to present first.

'We've decided to give you a tasting plate,' I tell the judges. 'It seemed an appropriate way to showcase several products at once. We've printed out menu cards with further information.'

The judges look impressed as they taste the cakes and thank us. They move onto Pies'n'Things, who have made an impressive layer cake using several kinds of chocolate. It's leaning to one side, and the ganache is a little too liquid, but the judges seem to like it.

I try to see what Chris has done, but his table is too far away. I'm sure he'll tell me about it afterwards. He and I don't have to talk about the upcoming rounds, but there's no reason we can't discuss the previous ones.

The judges reach Dave's table.

'And what delights will you be giving us today?' asks Gavin.

I peer around the crowd to see Dave looking smug, as usual.

'Well, Gavin,' he begins. 'After much thought, we've decided to tempt you with a tasting plate. After all, one piece of chocolate is never enough!'

With a familiar feeling of disbelief, I watch him hold out a plate to the judges.

'We have a variety of chocolate delights,' he says. 'A chocolate orange mousse, a beautiful Devil's Food cake, a caramel chocolate tart, a chocolate raspberry cheesecake, and white chocolate lavender muffins. And last, but not least, no chocolate round would be complete without a classic Sachertorte.'

Gavin doesn't speak for a moment. At last, he turns to the audience.

'Ladies and Gentlemen, it appears we have a small technical hitch. If you will excuse us for five minutes, we will resume the competition as soon as possible. In the meantime, I would appreciate it if the contestants from The Sugarloaf Bakery and The Baker Boys would join the judges in the foyer.'

Dazed, I follow Isabella and Lily to the door. Dave reaches it before us and politely holds it open, the trademark smirk still on his face. Isabella glares at him as she passes, and he chuckles.

Gavin turns to us, looking annoyed. 'Would one of you please explain what's going on?'

'Going on?' says Dave.

'Don't give me that!' says Gavin. 'The rules are quite clear that this competition is based on technical skill and originality of ideas. You both have a high degree of skill, but I can't say the same for your originality. We didn't think much of it when you produced a similar entry for the first round, but when you made the identical thing in the last round, we weren't impressed. As you will have noticed, we were forced to subtract marks from both of you for lack of originality. We thought that might be enough to bring you to your senses and prevent further collaboration. Obviously, we were wrong. We agreed that if it happened again, we would have no choice but to eliminate the offending bakeries from the competition.'

'You can't do that!' Isabella explodes. 'It's against the law.'

Dave raises an eyebrow. 'And what law would that be? The Cake Decorating Act of 1745? The Pastry Preservation bylaws? The Baking Equipment Noise Abatement amendment?'

Isabella gives him a murderous look. 'The law of natural justice.'

Gavin interrupts. 'We don't want to keep everyone waiting. Could one of you please tell me what's going on? Are you in cahoots?'

'We're in nothing of the sort!' shouts Isabella. 'You couldn't pay me to be in cahoots with someone like that. You could barely pay me to be in the same room as him.'

'I told you we had some … history,' Dave murmurs to Gavin, who nods.

I intervene before Isabella combusts entirely. 'I'm afraid you're right, Gavin. There has been some cheating involved in this competition. But The Sugarloaf Bakery is the innocent party. I don't know how The Baker Boys have found out our plans nor why they've chosen to bake the exact same things as us. They must have realised they would lose points for originality. But they've managed it somehow. It's horribly unfair to suggest disqualifying us when we haven't done anything wrong.'

'Abby's right,' says Dave. 'There has been cheating involved. But I can assure you it isn't on our part. Somehow or other, The Sugarloaf Bakery has discovered our plans and copied them. You're probably aware the new owners are completely inexperienced. Neither of them has any baking qualifications. And no one knows where their new baker comes from. For all we know, she has no experience either.'

'Don't be ridiculous!' I snap. 'I'm fully trained, and I've been working in this business for more than seven years.'

'Who was your last employer?' he counters.

How can he possibly know where I worked before I came to Honeywell? My heart sinks as I realise Chris must have told him. He wouldn't have seen it as important. If Dave asked him casually what he knew about me, Chris could easily have mentioned the North Street Bakery. If it comes to a showdown and Gavin demands references from my previous employer to show I really am a baker, I'm in trouble.

I check myself. The competition doesn't state that entrants must have been working in a reputable bakery for a certain number of years before they're eligible to enter.

'It's irrelevant how long I've been at the Sugarloaf,' I tell Gavin. 'Dave is trying to distract you from the fact he's been cheating.'

Gavin looks from me to Dave, then at Lily, who's looking distressed.

'Without tangible proof that only one of you has cheated, we are left with no option but to disqualify you both,' he says.

I expect Dave to argue further, but he doesn't. He gives a patient smile. 'The whole thing is most unfortunate, but I understand. I'm sorry you've been put in this position.'

Gavin looks gratified. 'I appreciate you taking it like that.'

He glances at Isabella, who's scarlet in the face. It's obvious who he believes, and I almost don't blame him. Faced with two contestants, one of whom is polite and measured, and the other of whom is red-faced and uttering threats, Gavin is hardly going to take our side.

I can't believe it's come to this. I desperately wanted to win this competition, or at least reach the final. We've worked so hard, and our entries have been better than most of the other bakeries. It feels so unfair to be treated like this. It's yet one more unfairness on top of the thousand unfairnesses since last December.

I turn away, fighting back the tears. I should have taken Chris's approach to the competition and told myself it didn't matter. He's right that it's a stupid local baking thing to promote the local area. The tourist board doesn't care about our cakes. They only want to raise the profile of the area and bring in more tourist money.

'I'm going back inside,' I mutter to Isabella. 'I want to be there to cheer Chris on.'

'Wait!' she says in a ringing tone that makes everyone jump.

What does she plan to do – attempt a last-ditch impassioned speech in the vein of *Mr Smith goes to Washington*? I hope not. I'd be delighted to hear one of Isabella's rants at any other time, but not today. I just want to support Chris, then go home and break the news to Mum and Dad as best I can.

'People are waiting,' says Gavin. 'We can't waste any more of their time.'

Isabella is scrolling frantically through her phone. 'I thought so!'

She holds out her phone to Gavin, who peers at it as though she's offering him a live lizard to admire.

'You announced the theme for this round a few hours after we'd finished the last one,' she says, waving the phone at him.

'I fail to see …' he begins, but she interrupts.

'You put the theme up on the website at five o'clock precisely. I remember it because I was checking our stock of doughnuts before we closed. Abby had left early because her mum had an appointment, so I texted her to let her know the theme. She texted back almost at once to say she'd had some good ideas.'

'That proves nothing,' interrupts Dave, but I'm pleased to see he looks a little rattled.

Isabella points to her phone. 'This text is time stamped five minutes after the theme was posted.'

She reads my text out loud. '*Why not do a tasting plate so we can show off a range of cakes? We could make Sachertorte, white chocolate lavender muffins, chocolate orange brownies, Torta Caprese. That's just off the top of my head. I'll make a proper list and bring it in tomorrow.'*

Gavin looks impressed. 'That seems conclusive.'

'No, it doesn't!' blusters Dave. 'They're all pretty standard chocolate dishes. All Abby had to do was to Google them. I'd be willing to bet Sachertorte was the first hit.'

'I'll take your word for it,' I say. 'As an experienced chef, I don't resort to basic internet searches for my ideas, but each to his own. Are you telling us white chocolate and lavender muffins would also be on the first page of the search results?'

He doesn't say anything. Gavin glances at the other judges, who nod.

'It would appear we have done you an injustice,' he says to me. 'If the team from The Sugarloaf Bakery would like to go back inside, we can resume the competition.'

He looks at Dave. 'You will hardly be surprised to hear your bakery has been eliminated.'

Dave shrugs. 'Whatever. I'm not losing sleep over some local competition with delusions of grandeur. I have better things to do with my time.'

He nods to his assistant, who follows him outside.

Isabella sticks her head out of the door and calls after them. 'Next year, you might like to try something more within your skill set. A vanilla sponge, perhaps, or chocolate chip cookies.'

She grins at their retreating backs. 'Fancy having so few ideas you have to copy from an inexperienced start-up.'

'You can gloat later,' I tell her. 'Everyone's gone back inside.'

We slip into the hall and watch the judges taste the final entries. I make my way through the crowd to stand near Chris's table. He's made a chocolate cake decorated with handmade white chocolate truffles. It looks beautiful. When the judges taste it, they clearly agree. They scribble in their notebooks, then turn to face the audience.

'Thank you for giving up your Saturday afternoon to support our contestants,' says Angela. 'The results will be posted on our website tomorrow, and the three contestants with the highest scores will go through to the final.'

The crowd disperses, and I walk over to Chris. 'That looks amazing.'

'Thanks,' he says. 'What was going on with you and Dave? We weren't sure whether you were coming back.'

'We nearly didn't,' I say. 'The Baker Boys made the same thing as we did again, and the judges almost eliminated us both.'

'Are you serious?' he says. 'They were going to throw you out of the competition for that?'

'Perfectly serious,' I assure him. 'Gavin has a point. This competition is partly about originality. How can they score the entries if everyone makes the same thing?'

'Does that mean you're out?' he says.

'Not this time. Thankfully, Isabella could prove we'd had the idea first, so Dave got kicked out instead.'

Chris gives me a serious look. 'You don't still suspect me of sabotage?'

'Of course not. You and I haven't talked about the competition since the last round.'

I remember our phone call. 'I'm sorry about what I said. Obviously, it couldn't have been you who leaked our plans or Dave wouldn't have known what we were planning for this round.'

He squeezes my hand. 'I'm glad we're ok.'

'More than ok,' I say happily. 'Isabella is busy lobbying Gavin to restore our lost points from the previous round. I expect she'll be successful. She's very persuasive when she wants to be. You and I should both do well this round. All's well that ends well.'

'I'm glad it worked out,' he says. 'What are you doing tonight? We were supposed to be drinking that bottle of champagne after the last round. It's still in my fridge.'

'It wouldn't still be in mine,' I say. 'You're a man of great restraint.'

He puts his arms around me and kisses me. 'Not for long. See you at seven?'

Chapter Thirty-Two

'We have to sort this out,' says Isabella on Monday morning. 'We were almost disqualified on Saturday. I'm not allowing that to happen in the final.'

'If we get to the final,' I say. 'We haven't seen the scores from the last round yet. And there's no guarantee we'll have our lost points restored from the previous one. If we don't, we have no chance at all of making it into the final.'

'Don't be such a pessimist,' she says. 'Of course, they'll give us back our points. They know how badly they wronged us. And our chocolate tasting plate was so amazing that we're bound to get top marks.'

There's no point arguing with her when she's in this mood.

'I didn't talk about our ideas to anyone,' I say.

'I believe you,' she says. 'But Dave go the information somehow. We need to find out how in case someone else decides to play the same trick in the final.'

'You don't suppose someone has bugged the bakery?' says Lily.

'I wondered about that,' says Isabella. 'But it's ridiculous. Where would they even put the listening devices?'

'Under the tables?' suggests Lily.

'In the flower arrangements?' I add.

Isabella jumps to her feet. 'Abby, you check the tables. Lily and I will do the flowers.'

I do as she says, feeling rather self-conscious. I hope no one comes in. What would they think if they saw three staff members crawling around the floor and pulling apart the centrepieces?

I sit back on my heels five minutes later. 'I've found nothing under the tables except for a few pieces of chewing gum. I've checked under the chairs too.'

'And the flowers have a clean bill of health,' adds Isabella. 'Except that I've snapped most of the stalks pulling them out of the oasis. We'll have to raid your mother's garden again tomorrow, Lily.'

Lily runs her hand under the counter and checks behind the till. 'Nothing here. I didn't think there would be. It's a little far-fetched to think someone is treating this competition like a Cold War operation.'

'Not so fast,' says Isabella. 'I'm only just getting started. There may not be hidden microphones in the bakery now, but that doesn't mean there were never any here.'

'Microphones don't have legs,' objects Lily. 'They're either there, or they're not.'

'That isn't true,' says Isabella.

'Are you talking about tiny high-tech robots?' I say. 'Because if so, I'm with Lily. It's too far-fetched for words.'

'I wasn't thinking of that,' she says. 'Although it's a great idea, so let's not rule it out. What I meant was that the microphones could literally have legs. They could be coming in with our customers.'

'How?' says Lily.

'In their pockets or pinned to their lapels,' says Isabella. 'I don't know how secret microphones work. Maybe someone has been wearing a wire.'

She wrinkles her brow in concentration. 'We're assuming it's someone with two legs. What if we're wrong?'

'You're assuming!' says Lily. 'Abby and I are simply waiting for you to finish.'

'I'm serious,' says Isabella. 'Who comes into this bakery several times a week and has four legs?'

'The Smith twins?' I suggest.

She ignores me. 'Bernie! It's perfect. He's always in here, and no one takes any notice of him. He lies under that table all morning, and none of us is careful what we say around him.'

'Does he take shorthand notes?' asks Lily with a giggle.

'I'm talking about his collar,' says Isabella impatiently. 'It would be the easiest thing in the world to clip a microphone onto it and record everything we say.'

I regard her with fascination. 'Are you saying Mrs Ogilvie is in on this? What would be her motivation?'

She shrugs. 'How should I know? She had a grudge against the Sugarloaf when Mr Mason wouldn't allow her to bring her dog inside.'

'But that's all over,' says Lily. 'She's quite happy now that dogs are allowed in. And she was pleased when we started baking biscuits for Bernie.'

'True,' says Isabella. 'But that could be a ruse. She could be playing the long game.'

Lily picks up the plates and mugs. 'You are a ridiculous woman. I refuse to believe Mrs Ogilvie has bided her time for three years and now has Bernie bugged on the off chance we might talk about our plans during the few hours a week in which she's here.'

She stalks off to the kitchen, leaving Isabella and me staring at each other.

'It isn't all that far-fetched,' she says.

'Yes, it is,' I say. 'Whatever's going on, it isn't that.'

'It would make a great thriller.'

'You should write it up and send it to Hollywood,' I tell her. 'In the meantime, I'm going to help Lily with the washing up.'

Chris comes over after work. He's promised to help me cook dinner to give Mum an evening off. He alternates his time between the kitchen and the garden, where Dad is enjoying the sunshine.

He opens the wine he's brought and pours us both a glass. 'How was your day?'

'Mixed,' I admit. 'Isabella made us spend the morning searching for bugs.'

'What sort of bugs?' he asks. 'Cockroaches?'

'Of course not! We had the health inspector in only last week, and we passed with flying colours. We wouldn't have done that if they'd found any cockroaches lurking.'

'Why is Isabella so worried?' he asks. 'I thought it was Dave who was sabotaging you. He's been kicked out now, so you're fine.'

'Maybe,' I say. 'But she's worried about how he found out. It was easy when we thought you'd told him. But you didn't know what we were doing in the last round, and he still found out somehow. If he could do that, so could someone else.'

He doesn't look impressed. 'Aren't you taking this a little too seriously?'

'I don't think you're taking it seriously enough,' I say. 'Someone is trying to sabotage this competition. Isabella is determined to get to the bottom of it.'

'Fine,' he says impatiently. 'In the meantime, can we enjoy a nice dinner without talking about the competition and who's sabotaging whom?'

'You aren't being very supportive,' I say.

'That's not fair. I understand you're taking this whole thing much more seriously than I am. What I don't understand is why. It seems to me you're being stupidly competitive about the whole thing and ruining what could be a bit of fun.'

I force myself to speak lightly. 'We're never going to agree about this. Let's forget it.'

'That works for me.'

He drops a light kiss on the top of my head and takes the bowl of salad out to the garden. I watch him go with a feeling of dissatisfaction. Agreeing to disagree is one thing. That comes under the heading of compromise, and everyone knows that's what good relationships are built on.

This feels different, as though he's belittling me and treating me like a child. Maybe that's how he sees me. It's an unsettling thought, but possibly true. Even the way we met points in that direction. I was throwing a mega tantrum, and he rescued me and bought me a drink to calm me down and prevent me from causing a further scene. He went on to send me joke gifts, referencing our initial meeting. If he saw me as an adult, he would have sent me flowers or chocolates, not buttons and knitting needles.

I follow him out to the garden, my mood darkening. I can tell myself not to be ridiculous, but the fact remains that Chris has always treated me like a child, and he still is. A small voice whispers I'm being unfair, but I tell it to shut up. My feelings are valid, and it's up to me to make sure they're heard. Paul never seemed to hear me or see me as an individual. He saw me as a pleasant addition to his life rather than someone with a separate identity. I'm determined not to let that happen again.

I don't talk much during dinner. I'm too preoccupied with my thoughts.

Mum glances at me a couple of times but doesn't comment until we're drinking our coffee. 'You don't seem yourself this evening, Abby. Are you tired?'

What does she mean I don't seem myself? Who else would I be? What she means is that I'm not acting in a way that makes her and everyone else comfortable, and she'd like me to revert to being that person. That's too bad. I'm not changing myself because someone else wants me to.

'I'm not tired,' I say. 'I'm a bit fed up, that's all.'

She glances at Chris, who doesn't speak.

'I'm sorry to hear that,' she says. 'But we're all here now, so can you try to put that aside for tonight and enjoy the evening? You and Chris have made us a lovely meal. Isn't it lovely, Geoffrey?'

'Delicious,' says Dad. He looks from me to Chris but doesn't say anything more.

'Are you up for watching the game this weekend, Geoffrey?' asks Chris.

Dad looks pleased. 'I'm looking forward to it.'

'Would you like to join us?' Chris asks me. 'I know football isn't your thing, but you might enjoy it. It's the final, and it's always a great atmosphere. I'm bringing pretzels. Your dad and I like to throw them at the screen when the ref gets it wrong.'

'You're right,' I say. 'Football isn't my thing. Why do you all want me to be someone I'm not?'

Mum gives me a warning look, which I ignore.

'I can decide for myself what I like and don't like,' I say. 'And what is and isn't important to me.'

'Of course, you can,' says Mum. 'No one thinks differently.'

I see her anxious face and relent. 'Just so we're clear.'

She perks up. 'I haven't told you my news yet.'

She leans forward and lowers her voice. I'm not sure who she thinks will overhear us. Mrs Robinson next door comes out to water her plants in the evening, but she's hard of hearing at the best of times. I don't imagine she's lurking in the shrubbery waiting to hear the latest piece of gossip that's come Mum's way.

'I had coffee with Mavis Sotherby this morning,' says Mum in a confidential tone. 'She's found out something rather disturbing.'

I shoot a quick glance at Chris. Surely, she hasn't been investigating him. The time to do that would have been when I first started seeing him. Mum wouldn't dream of having him checked out now she knows and likes him.

Mum lowers her voice even further. 'Mavis was in the Red Lion last night when someone approached her and asked whether she'd be interested in having a small flutter.'

'Like a butterfly?' I ask, confused.

'A bet!' she says. 'A wager.'

'What did they want her to bet on? Not a horse?'

She lowers her voice even further. 'You!'

'Me?' I say, startled. 'What about me?'

'Your competition!' she says and sits back to watch the effect of her words on us both.

'What?' Chris and I say simultaneously.

She looks pleased. 'I was shocked too. But it seems to be true. Apparently, half the village is in on it.'

'Betting on the winner?' asks Chris.

'That's right,' she says. 'From what Mavis says, you seem to be a hot favourite, Chris.'

He grins. 'How flattering. What about Abby?'

Mum's face falls. 'The person offered Mavis very long odds on Abby.'

'What a cheek!' I say.

Chris looks amused. 'Did Mavis take the bet?'

'She wasn't too forthcoming about that,' says Mum. 'I suspect she may have put a few pounds on.'

She sees my face. 'Don't look like that, Abby! We're in a cost-of-living crisis. No one's pension goes as far as it used to. She may have thought it too good an opportunity to pass up.'

'Why didn't they shorten the odds on me when they saw how well our bakery was doing?' I say.

'The question is, why are they allowing a book to be run in the first place?' says Mum. 'It's disgraceful. I've half a mind to tell the landlord of the Red Lion what's going on under his roof.'

'Unless it's the landlord who's running it,' I suggest.

'Does it matter?' says Chris. 'It's just a bit of fun.'

'That's easy for you to say,' I mutter. 'No one's betting against you.'

'What are the odds on Abby winning?' he asks Mum.

'Twenty to one, I think she said.'

He laughs. 'Maybe I should take a punt.'

Mum looked shocked. 'You'd bet against Abby?'

He gives her a reassuring grin. 'I'd bet on Abby, not against her. If she wins, I'd get an excellent payout. She and I could go away for the weekend together.'

I give him an icy look. 'No, thanks. What I want to know is why the bookmaker is so sure the Sugarloaf will lose?'

'They probably set the odds at the start of the competition,' says Chris. 'Don't forget you were a dark horse. You'd only just arrived in the village, and no one knew the first thing about you. They were hardly going to make you the favourite.'

'Maybe,' I say. 'But it seems strange they're still encouraging people to bet on me with those odds. You'd think they would do everything they could to steer them away from it. If I win, this bookmaker stands to lose a lot of money.'

'I asked Mavis to put ten pounds on you to win,' says Dad.

'Thank you,' I say, touched. 'I'll try not to let you down.'

'I didn't want him to, but he insisted,' says Mum.

'You don't think I have any chance?' I say.

She looks shocked. 'Of course, I do! But I don't like the idea of people placing wagers on my daughter. It isn't nice.'

'Are you going to bet on yourself, Abby?' says Chris. 'You could make a bundle if you won.'

'I'll pass, thanks,' I say. 'Dave probably put a large bet on himself, so he'll have lost money now he's been disqualified. From what Mum said, Chris is still the favourite, but why am I still seen as an also ran? I have as much chance of winning as he does.'

'I doubt anyone has thought much about it,' says Chris. 'It's just a few people having some fun by putting a fiver each way on the outcome.'

'Mavis says you have to bet on the two most likely candidates to win rosettes,' says Mum. 'She says you get even better odds if you pick the actual winner and runner up.'

'It sounds as though everyone is betting on Chris,' I say.

Mum jumps to her feet. 'Coffee, anyone? I'll make it.'

She's clearly eager to change the subject, so I stop talking about the betting. I can't help feeling annoyed that no one feels confident enough to shorten the odds against me. But it will make it all the more satisfying if I win. I'll mention it to Isabella when I next see her. Perhaps she'll suggest a betting syndicate to break the bank. We may persuade the poker club to join in.

We drink our coffee and chat about Dad's aqua therapy and the person who's coming around next week to assess him for an adapted car. He must be looking forward to the prospect of regaining some independence. It will take a while before he's back behind the wheel, but it gives him something to work towards. I've been frustrated by how slow the entire process has been and how few guarantees there are about his future recovery. He must be ten times more frustrated.

Chris helps me load the dishwasher. Neither of us says much while we work. I'm still annoyed by our earlier conversation, and he seems to take his cue from me.

'Are you coming back to mine tonight?' he asks.

'I have a seven o'clock start tomorrow,' I say. 'I need an early night.'

'Suit yourself,' he says. 'I think I'll make a move. I have an early start too.'

His tone is neutral, but his face is graver than usual.

'Chris,' I begin.

'It's fine,' he says. 'We all need our space. Let me know when you'd like to see me again.'

He kisses my cheek and goes out to the garden to say goodbye to Mum and Dad.

I want to run after him and tell him I didn't mean to be so grumpy, and I'd like to spend the night with him, but something stops me. Maybe Mum's right that I'm tired. I've been working hard over the past few weeks, then lying awake each night worrying about Dad and the competition and how safe my job is.

If I go home with Chris tonight, we'll end up arguing again, which is the last thing I want. I decide to leave it for now and call him in a couple of days after we've both calmed down.

Chapter Thirty-Three

'They've just posted the results!' Isabella says jubilantly the following morning. 'They've reinstated all our lost points, which means we're through to the final.'

I throw my arms around her. 'I can't believe it! Did we do well in the chocolate round?'

'We got nearly full marks,' she says. 'And there's an Asterix next to The Baker Boys. I hope Dave chokes on it.'

'How about Chris?' I ask.

'I don't want him to choke,' she says. 'Oh, you mean is he through to the final too? Yes, he is. He has three more points than us in total, but who's counting?'

I am, but I don't say so. Chris's entries have been amazing. He deserves his place in the final. Hopefully, it won't mean even more tension between us until the competition is over. But there's nothing I can do about that. Only two more weeks to go, then everything will go back to normal.

'Who's the third finalist?' I ask.

'Someone called Olivia Forde,' she says. 'I don't know much about her. She works in The Cookie Corner Bakery somewhere near Lyndhurst. She was the one who made that carrot cake with the citrus filling for the signature round.'

'I remember that,' I say. 'It was beautifully presented.'

'So was ours,' says Isabella. 'We're going to win this thing!'

'Don't get ahead of yourself,' Lily warns her.

'I'm not,' says Isabella. 'I'm quietly and appropriately confident.'

'What about the spies?' I ask. 'You were pretty upset about them last night.'

'I've decided to ignore them,' she says. 'Even if we're right, and I'm pretty sure we are, there's nothing we can do about it.'

'No surveillance equipment?' says Lily. 'No sneaking around outside our rival bakeries wearing false moustaches and fedoras?'

Isabella gives her a lofty smile. 'You wouldn't be any help. You're already the size of a house. We'd never be able to disguise you.'

'Hey!' says Lily.

'You look amazing,' I reassure her. 'Your skin is glowing, and your hair looks great.'

'I agree,' says Isabella. 'But you have to admit she wouldn't blend in too well during a heist.'

'What's the plan?' I ask. 'Do we prepare for the final as though no one has any idea what we're planning to do?'

'What choice do we have?' says Lily. 'Let's concentrate on getting through it without any mishaps. It's wonderful just to be through to the final, even if we don't win it.'

'No, it isn't!' says Isabella. 'I want to go all the way. Don't be so defeatist.'

I almost ask whether winning the competition would mean the bakery expanding their staff. I decide against it. It wouldn't be tactful with Lily here. She might think I was angling to take her job.

'What's the theme for the final?' I ask.

'*I love the New Forest,*' says Isabella.

'So do I,' says Lily.

'That's the theme!' says Isabella. 'The competition is being run by the tourist board, so it shouldn't be a surprise.'

'*I love the New Forest?*' I say. 'It's even vaguer than *Everything Chocolate.* What do you think we should do?'

'I'm not sure,' says Isabella. 'What do you think, Alice?'

Alice looks up from cleaning the coffee machine. When she first started working here, Isabella told her she wanted to be able to see her face in the steam nozzle at all times because it was a lot easier than searching for a mirror. Alice has taken her literally and spends several minutes a day polishing the chrome nozzle to within an inch of its life. I feel guilty each time I use the machine, knowing she's hovering behind me with her cloth.

'I have no idea,' says Alice. 'But I'd really like to help. I told my mum about the last round, and she was really proud. If I help with this one too, she may change her mind about me taking a catering course.'

I spend the next two days racking my brains to come up with a show-stopping idea involving forests, but without much success. Except for a short congratulatory text, I haven't heard from Chris, which isn't a surprise. He said he would wait for me to call when I was ready. I'm ashamed of the way I behaved at dinner last week. I don't agree the competition is unimportant, but there was no need for me to ruin a perfectly good evening over something so small.

I swallow my pride and call him after work on Friday. He sounds pleased to hear from me, which is a relief. He invites me over for dinner the following evening, and I accept, resolving not to allow myself to get worked up again.

He seems pleased to see me when I arrive, and I'm certainly pleased to see him. I've spent the past week wondering whether I've ruined the best relationship I've had in years. The best one I've ever had, if I'm honest.

We eat the spaghetti he's made and watch a movie. I'm not sure whether he expects me to stay over. It would have felt presumptuous to arrive with an overnight bag, but I have one in the car, should the need arise.

'That was a great movie,' I say when it finishes. 'Why haven't I seen it before?'

'*Die Hard* is a classic,' he says. 'I can't believe your dad didn't watch it with you when you were growing up.'

'Mum always chose the movies,' I say. 'She loves all the old black-and-whites. Dad went along with it.'

'Not all the time, surely. What happened to compromise?'

There's a slight edge to his tone that takes me by surprise.

'I'm sure they compromised,' I say. 'In fact, I know they did. Mum isn't keen on Scotland in summer because she hates the midges, but we took the caravan up there for holidays because Dad loves it. I'm sure he would have said something if he didn't like her choice of films.'

'Maybe,' he says. 'He and I are watching the football on Saturday, which won't be in black and white.'

'I'll bring you both snacks,' I say. 'And I'll refrain from commenting on the score and the colour of the away team's football strip.'

He laughs. 'This isn't your first match!'

'Not remotely. Dad used to make me watch them when I was small. Mum always refused, and he said it was no fun watching alone. He bribed me with jelly snakes and family packs of crisps.'

'I hope he bribes me with those too,' he says. 'Are you staying over tonight or do you have to get back?'

'I'm not sure. I didn't know what you wanted to do.'

He grins. 'I always want you to stay over. You know that. But I didn't want to push it after things have been so uncomfortable between us.'

'That's all over now,' I say. 'I'm sorry I was on edge the other night. I was tired, but I shouldn't have taken it out on you. My bag's in the car.'

His eyes are alight with laughter. 'Hedging your bets? Give me your key and I'll fetch it in.'

I take our glasses to the kitchen and wash them up while I wait for him. He returns a couple of minutes later, carrying my bag. 'What do you have in here? It weighs a ton. Are you moving in permanently?'

'I'm afraid not. Would one night do?'

'That sounds like an excellent compromise,' he says.

He lifts the bag onto the nearest chair. As he does, something falls out of his pocket.

I stare at it in horror. 'Is that my notebook?'

'Oh, yes. I meant to give it back to you earlier.'

'Where did you find it?' I say, my voice sharp with suspicion.

He looks surprised. 'At your house the other night. It had fallen onto the floor and been kicked under that mat in the hall. I saw the corner poking out and picked it up. I put it in my pocket while I carried the tray out to the garden. I must have forgotten about it.'

I try to keep my voice steady. 'Are you sure it was the other night?'

'Of course, I'm sure. Why do you ask?'

'Have you looked inside it?'

He picks up the notebook and hands it to me. 'I told you. I picked it up and put it in my pocket to give to you. I'd forgotten about it until now. Why, what is it?'

'Nothing!' I say snatching it from him and zipping it inside my bag.

He isn't deceived. 'It's clearly something important. I'm sorry I didn't give it back to you earlier. Is it your secret childhood diary? I missed a chance there, didn't I?'

'It isn't a diary,' I say, observing him carefully.

'How disappointing,' he says. 'Would you like to use the bathroom first?'

I can't believe this. How can he act as though nothing has happened? He didn't pick up that notebook the other night. I'm sure he didn't. This notebook has been missing for a few weeks. So, that's how Dave found out what we were doing in the last round. I didn't need to tell Chris any of the details. He already knew them.

'I can't believe you've done this!' I burst out, unable to contain myself any longer. 'I didn't want to think it was you who was stealing all our ideas, but who else could it be?'

'That's ridiculous,' he says.

'Even now, when you're caught red-handed, you don't have the decency to apologise.'

'Red-handed?' he says. 'Don't be so dramatic. I found your notebook and put it in my pocket, and now I've returned it to you. End of story.'

'You're right!' I fling at him. 'It *is* the end of our story. I trusted you, Chris! You seemed like such a nice guy.'

He no longer looks annoyed, more amused. 'I *am* a nice guy.'

'Don't give me that! A nice guy wouldn't steal his girlfriend's ideas. You pretended this competition wasn't important to you, yet clearly it is. You're prepared to go to any lengths to win.'

He throws up his hands. 'I didn't even want to enter. My boss insisted, so I went along with it. I didn't care whether we got into the final or were kicked out in the first round. I wouldn't go to any lengths to win. I wouldn't bother to go to the end of the street to win. Why do you have such a bee in your bonnet about it?'

I glare at him. 'I've told you why a hundred times, but you haven't listened. I'm not telling you again. You don't deserve it.'

He shrugs. 'Fine, let's leave it at that.'

I snatch my car keys from his hand. 'That's probably best.'

He looks confused. 'You're leaving?'

'Of course, I am. You just told me to leave it at that.'

He lays a hand on my arm, but I shake it off.

'You're getting this all out of proportion,' he says. 'Leave if you want to, but there's no need. Surely, you trust me?'

I don't answer, and his face goes blank. 'Really?'

I look at my feet. He doesn't speak for almost a minute. When he does, his voice is low. 'Abby, I thought you and I were serious, but I can't be in a relationship with someone who doesn't trust me. Anything else, we can work through, but not that. Now's the time to let me know. Do you trust me or not?'

My heart is pounding, and I'm on the verge of tears. More than anything, I want to fling myself into his arms and tell him I trust him. But something stops me.

I raise my eyes reluctantly to his face. 'I want to. I really do.'

He shakes his head in disbelief. 'I'm sorry to hear that, but it's better to find out now before things go any further.'

He bends down and kisses my cheek. 'All the best, Abby. I hope things work out for you.'

I want to stay and talk about this, but he's right. No relationship is possible without trust. If he'd asked me yesterday whether I trusted him, there would have been no question about it. I still want to believe there's some alternative explanation, but there isn't. All I can do is try to leave with the shreds of my dignity intact.

'You too,' I whisper. 'Good luck with the competition.'

I turn and leave before I start crying. I walk to my car, aware he's watching me. I half expect him to follow me and beg me to reconsider, but he doesn't. I switch on the car and drive down the road. As soon as I'm out of sight, I pull into the kerb and burst into uncontrollable tears.

Chapter Thirty-Four

I almost don't go home. I have wild thoughts of checking into a hotel or sleeping in the car. I change my mind when I remember the nearest hotel is about ten miles away, and there's no guarantee they'll have any vacancies. Also, I can't afford it.

Sleeping in the car feels even less attractive. I tried it once as a student and woke the following morning freezing cold and with a crick in my neck. I consider spending the night in the bakery. I have a key, and Isabella and Lily probably wouldn't mind when they heard what had happened. There isn't anywhere obvious to sleep there, but I doubt I'll get much rest tonight anyway. All I need is somewhere warm and safe, and I'm sure I could curl up in the corner of the office.

I'm about to drive over there when I remember I've left my key on my dressing table. I'll have to go home and get it. If I do that, I may as well sleep in my own bed. Hopefully, Mum and Dad will be asleep. I can sneak in quietly and leave again before they're awake.

I'd reckoned without Mum's burglar fixation. I park a few houses away and carry my bag as quietly as possible up the garden path before letting myself in at the back door. Mum has been talking about getting a security bolt, but she hasn't got around to calling anyone yet.

I tiptoe down the hall without putting on the light and start up the stairs, careful to avoid the creaky one. I've almost reached the landing and am congratulating myself on not having disturbed anyone when a dark figure looms up in front of me. I jump and let out a strangled squawk.

'Don't move!' a voice growls. 'I have you covered!'

For one terrible moment, I wonder whether I'm in the wrong house, but then I remember my key worked in the back door. It's hardly likely all the houses on our street would have the exact same lock fitted unless our local locksmith was a professional burglar. It would make a great detective story plot, but I reluctantly reject it. I've known Mr Dawkins since I was a child.

'Drop your weapons!' says the same gruff voice.

'I don't have any weapons!' I say indignantly before realising the voice is Mum's.

'It's me!' I say, switching on the landing light.

Mum blinks at me. 'Abby? What are you doing here? I thought you were a burglar.'

'Obviously. What's with the voice? Do you have a sore throat? You sounded fine earlier this evening.'

She looks pleased. 'Did you think I was a man?'

'Er …'

'I've been practising for weeks,' she says. 'Mavis Sotherby suggested it.'

'The internet sleuth?'

'That's right. She learned it on her self-defence course. If the burglar thinks there's a man in the house, they're far more likely to run away, especially if they think you're armed.'

'Are you armed?' I say, startled.

'Well, no,' she admits. 'I tried using Dad's old cricket bat, but it was too heavy to swing properly. Also, it smells of linseed oil, which is a bit of a giveaway even in the dark.'

My heart rate is slowly returning to normal. 'What are you using instead?'

'Nothing,' she admits. 'But I keep my hand in my dressing gown pocket in case they switch the light on. That way, they'll think I have a gun.'

'Another of Mavis' tips and tricks?' I ask, fascinated.

'That was my own idea,' she says. 'Mavis suggested the man's voice. She uses a Scottish accent, but I've never been able to roll my Rs.'

I'm even more fascinated. 'Why a Scottish accent?'

'She says it's the most menacing of all the accents,' says Mum blithely.

'Are you sure? I love Scottish accents.'

'Oh, yes! Think of *Braveheart.* I'd have been terrified to see all those warriors racing down the hill towards me. I'm sure a burglar would feel the same.'

Does she paint herself blue each night in case there are burglars queueing outside our house to steal the silver-plated gymkhana cup she won when she was twelve? Probably not or she would have treated me to the full glory of her woad face paint.

'You can put your gun away,' I tell her. 'I'm not a burglar, and I'm going to bed.'

'What are you doing here?' she says. 'Aren't you supposed to be at Chris's flat tonight? Did you pop home for something?'

I don't want to ask exactly what she thinks I've popped home for. The answer might embarrass us both.

'I decided not to stay,' I say. 'I have an early start tomorrow, and I never sleep well at his flat.'

I don't elaborate. She's welcome to think it's because I curl up decorously on his too small sofa all night.

Mum looks worried. 'Is everything alright?'

'It's fine,' I say curtly. 'I'll see you tomorrow.'

I make a dive for my bedroom before she can say anything more. She'll have to know that Chris and I have split up at some point, but not now. I can't bear a post mortem of our relationship with her dissecting every single word and action. She means well, but it would be too painful while I'm feeling so raw. She'll have to discuss it with Mavis Sotherby instead. From what I've heard of the woman, she'll have plenty of suggestions to make. I wouldn't put it past her to have a hitman on speed dial.

Despite all my resolutions, I arrive at work fifteen minutes late the following morning. I didn't fall asleep until the early hours, and I slept through my alarm. If Mum hadn't come in and shaken me awake, I'd still be in bed now.

'I'm so sorry,' I apologise as I race in.

'Don't worry about it,' says Isabella. 'I've only been here for two minutes myself, and we don't have any customers.'

'They probably arrived and left again,' I say. 'You know what a stickler Mrs Ogilvie is about opening on time.'

'I don't think so,' she says. 'I'd have seen her and Bernie stalking back up the street in high dudgeon. Are you ok? Your eyes are a bit red. Did you have a heavy night?'

She grins, and I try to smile back. Better that she should think Chris and I were out drinking half the night than guess what really happened.

She peers at me more closely. 'What's wrong?'

I pick up my apron. 'Like you say, I had a heavy night.'

'No, you didn't. I recognise a hangover when I see one, and this isn't one. Is your dad alright?'

I don't trust myself to speak, so I just nod.

She takes my arm and leads me into the office. 'You don't have to tell me what's happened, but it's obvious something has. Sit down, and I'll bring you a coffee and something to eat.'

'I'm not hungry,' I mutter.

'Well, I am. I'll be back in a moment.'

She disappears, leaving me to summon up the last vestiges of my self-control. If I tell her what's happened, she'll be horribly sympathetic, and I'll burst into tears. It's unprofessional enough arriving late for work without howling all over my employer.

She returns carrying two mugs and half a giant carrot cake.

'I didn't know if it was a one slice or two emergency,' she explains, cutting us both a large slice. 'I brought extra in case.'

I take a sip of the coffee. 'Thanks for this. I didn't have time for a drink this morning. I couldn't believe it when Mum shook me awake at eight thirty.'

'I wish mine would,' she says, taking a huge bite of carrot cake. 'But she says if I'm old enough to run a business, I'm old enough to get myself out of bed on time. I'm not sure what gave her that idea.'

'My mum's the opposite,' I say. 'She still thinks I'm a three-year-old, completely unable to manage my own life.'

'Even though you have good qualifications, a job, and a boyfriend?' she says, looking amused.

'I only have two of those,' I say, not meeting her eyes.

There's a pause while she studies me.

'I know you have the qualifications,' she says at last. 'I've seen your resume, and it's most impressive, although I suppose you could have been lying. That guy Matt wasn't as enthusiastic about you as he might have been. Assuming you weren't, I know you have a job because you turn up at the bakery every day, and Lily hasn't told me she's fired you. Which only leaves …'

I nod. 'We broke up last night.'

She doesn't answer immediately but reaches over and cuts my slice of cake into small pieces with my fork. It's exactly what Mum used to do when I was young and refusing to eat my food. Does Isabella think I'm a child too? Maybe I should stamp my foot and tip my plate on the floor. That would have the added effect of making me unemployed, which would only leave my qualifications as any sort of proof I'm an adult.

Without meaning to, I stab my fork into a chunk of cake and put it into my mouth. Isabella watches me with a pleased expression. She waits until I've finished the entire slice before speaking again. 'What happened, Abby?'

My eyes fill with tears. 'He stole my notebook.'

'He what?'

'The notebook I told you about. The one I was using to write down all the ideas I had about the competition. It disappeared a while ago, and I couldn't find it. When I was over at Chris's flat last night, it fell out of his pocket.'

She lets out a long, low whistle. 'That's pretty damning.'

'I know. First of all, I saw him talking to Dave in the pub, and Dave knew exactly what we were doing. Then he swiped my notebook.'

She frowns. 'The thing I don't understand is why Chris didn't use the ideas himself. Why did he give them to the other bakery?'

'Because that way he could eliminate two competitors,' I say. 'Dave and I would both lose points for originality, and Chris would be more likely to go through.'

She considers this. 'That makes sense. But he told me this competition wasn't important to him. He didn't want to enter it, but his boss insisted. Do you think that was a lie too?'

'He was probably telling the truth about that,' I say. 'But that was before the betting syndicate.'

She gives me a startled look. 'Betting syndicate?'

'That's right. Apparently, someone at the Red Lion started a book on this competition. People have been betting fairly heavily on it. If they've been betting on Chris's bakery, it makes perfect sense. His boss may be putting a lot of pressure on him not to lose the competition.'

She shakes her head in disbelief. 'It's a local bakery competition, not the Grand National. Why are people putting so much money on it?'

She thinks about this some more. 'And why has no one offered me the chance to take part? I could have bet on the Sugarloaf.'

She catches my eye and clears her throat. 'Sorry, I got distracted. So, you think Chris was trying to nobble both us and Dave to give himself a clear run at the title?'

I shake my head helplessly. 'I don't want to, but what else can I think? Someone told Dave what we were doing, and it certainly wasn't me. For all I know, he and Chris are in league together. Dave may not have cared about losing the competition as long as we were kicked out too. He probably gets his payment either way.'

'He's slimy enough,' she agrees. 'And he seems to think he has a grudge against me. I have no idea why. It can't be the first time someone's told him a few home truths while he's been on that app.'

I finish my coffee. 'Thanks for listening. I'd better get on with some work. We're lucky no customers have been in during the past half hour.'

She gathers up the plates. 'I turned the sign to Closed before I made the coffee.'

'Don't tell Lily,' I say. 'She hates you doing that.'

'What the eye doesn't see,' she says cheerfully.

She cocks her head on one side and listens. 'Perfect timing. I recognise that yapping noise. I'd better go and open the door before Mrs Ogilvie has an apoplexy.'

Chapter Thirty-Five

I get through the rest of the day as best I can, trying not to think about Chris. I want to call him and ask what he was thinking, but what's the point? We said all we needed to say last night. If I call him now, it's only because I don't want to accept what's happened, which won't help either of us in the long term. Even if he admits what he's done and apologises, I won't be able to trust him again. And he'll know I don't fully trust him, which is the death knell for any relationship.

I rack my brains for any alternative explanation for his behaviour, but I come up short each time. He may not take this competition as seriously as I do, but he takes it seriously enough to help his employer cheat, which is inexcusable.

I try not to look at my phone while I'm at work, but I can't help glancing at it now and then in case he's messaged me. I also jump each time I hear the shop door open. I don't really expect Chris to have sent me another of his weird and wonderful bouquets, but I can't help feeling disappointed when nothing arrives. He can't be too bothered about our breakup if he hasn't made the slightest effort to contact me and offer some sort of explanation.

I work for an extra fifteen minutes after we close, despite Isabella's protestations.

'You look exhausted,' she says. 'Go home and get some sleep.'

'I'm almost finished,' I say. 'I was late this morning, so it's only fair that I stay a bit longer.'

She rolls her eyes but leaves me to it. I lock up the bakery at five fifteen and set off home. I'm half expecting Chris to step out of a shop doorway and greet me, but he doesn't. So, that seems to be that. There's no point in me contacting him again, and he's unlikely to contact me. I suppose I'll see him in the final, which may be awkward. I decide to worry about that nearer the time.

Mum is waiting for me in the kitchen when I arrive home. 'I've made you a cup of tea. I've been worried about you all day.'

I take the cup she hands me and sit down at the kitchen table. 'There's no need to be worried about me. I'm fine.'

She doesn't look convinced. 'First of all, you came home last night when you were supposed to be with Chris. And this morning you overslept, which isn't like you. Is something going on, Abby?'

'Like what?' I parry.

'I don't know. But you're my daughter, and I'm perfectly aware when things aren't right. You don't have to tell me about it if you don't want to, but don't treat me like a fool.'

I lay down my cup. 'I suppose you'll have to know sometime. Chris and I broke up last night.'

Her face falls. 'Oh, sweetheart!'

She tries to put her arms around me, but I lean away. 'I'm absolutely fine. At least, I will be if you don't fuss around me.'

She looks a little hurt. 'I'm not fussing. I'm just trying to offer you some comfort.'

'I know you are, but it isn't necessary. You have enough on your plate with Dad without worrying about me too.'

'I have enough energy for more than one thing,' she says.

'I know you do,' I say more gently. 'I promise I'll tell you if I need anything.'

She nods and changes the subject. 'Dad had his physiotherapy today. He walked right down to the end of the garden.'

'That's fantastic! You must be so pleased.'

'We both are,' she says. 'It finally feels as though things are getting back to normal. He'll be able to go to a football match when the next season starts.'

I don't speak, and she flushes. 'I'm sorry, Abby. I forgot.'

I put my cup into the sink. 'Don't worry about it. Dad has plenty of friends who'll be only too pleased to go to football matches with him. He's only known Chris for a few months. He'll barely miss him.'

'That's not quite true,' she says quietly. 'Still, it's none of my business.'

I wonder whether to tell her what Chris has done. It might help her let go of her image of him as a saint. I decide against it. There's no point. We'll only end up picking over the past few weeks, with Mum suggesting increasingly wild explanations for Chris's behaviour, and me growing more irritated by the second.

We maintain a cheerful flow of chatter over dinner. Hopefully, Dad won't guess anything is wrong. I'm not quite ready to tell him yet. I wouldn't have told Mum if she hadn't been so nosy. Still, I can't put it off forever. Dad is as sharp as he ever was, and he'll quickly realise Chris isn't coming to the house anymore.

Mum suggests we all watch an episode of *Morse* after dinner, but I decline.

'Maybe another time. I'm really tired tonight. Do you mind if I have a bath and go to bed?'

I don't wait for her to reply but say good night and make my escape.

I make sure I'm at work on time the following morning. Isabella arrives late, but that's her prerogative. It would feel wrong if she didn't rock up at least ten minutes late most mornings. We don't talk about Chris. I spend the first two hours making a birthday cake for a local child while she looks after the shop and makes yet another unavailing attempt to persuade the poker group to cut her in.

She comes into the kitchen before lunch looking worried.

'What's wrong?' I say. 'Did you lose your shirt and have to pay for a round of Battenberg?'

She doesn't smile. 'Jack called. Lily's been admitted to the hospital.'

'She's in labour?' I say, surprised. 'I thought she had four more weeks to go.'

'She isn't in labour. She saw the midwife this morning, and her blood pressure has shot up. They've admitted her to the maternity ward so they can observe her.'

'That doesn't sound good,' I say. 'Is she going to be ok?'

She still looks worried. 'Jack says it's a precaution, but it must be horribly stressful for them both. He's going to call and let me know whether I can visit her tonight.'

I don't offer to go with her. She and Lily have been friends for years, whereas I'm a relative newcomer.

'Let me know if I can make anything for her,' I say. 'Lily likes those mini fruit crumbles, doesn't she?'

'I'll find out,' she promises. 'The hospital may have her on a strict diet.'

'What sort of a strict diet? I thought she was supposed to be eating for two.'

'I don't know much about these things,' she says. 'They may insist the baby eats lots of fruit or vegetables. Perhaps I should take her some of that carrot cake just in case.'

Alice looks up from the mixer. 'I hope everything is ok. Can you tell Lily I'll work extra hours if need be?'

'I will,' promises Isabella.

'Are you and Chris going to visit her?' Alice asks me.

Isabella gives me a quick look but doesn't say anything.

I take a deep breath. 'I'd love to visit Lily if it's convenient, but Chris won't be coming with me. You may as well know that he and I broke up a couple of days ago.'

'I thought you two were really good together,' says Alice.

Isabella saves me the trouble of answering. 'We all did. But he turned out to be a snake in the grass.'

Alice looks puzzled, so I explain. 'What Isabella means is that Chris has been sabotaging us throughout the competition. Apparently, someone's been running a book on it. Laying bets,' I add as she looks uncomprehending.

'What does that have to do with Chris?' she asks. 'Has he been organising the betting?'

'I don't think so,' I say. 'But he's been trying to rig the votes. He told his friend what we were doing for the first couple of rounds. When I stopped talking to him about our ideas, he stole my notebook and found out what we were doing that way.'

I turn away to lift the empty flour container off the shelf so I can replace it with a full one. There's an odd snorting noise behind me, and I turn to see Alice staring at me with a stricken look.

'Which friend did he tell?' she whispers.

'Dave Collins,' says Isabella. 'He has a bit of a grudge against me because we went on a date that didn't turn out too well. I didn't go as far as pouring a cup of coffee all over him, but we can't all be as enterprising as Abby.'

Alice sinks into a chair and, to my astonishment, buries her face in her arms and bursts into tears. Isabella and I look at each other uncomprehendingly.

I lay an awkward hand on Alice's shoulder. 'What's wrong?'

She sobs even louder. I give Isabella an agonised look. She sits down next to Alice and grasps her shoulder.

'Stop crying, Alice!' she commands.

When there's no response, she gives Alice a slight shake. 'Stop it, right now! Whatever it is, it won't help to behave like an overactive watering can. Take a deep breath and tell us what's going on.'

Alice takes the packet of tissues I hand her and blows her nose. 'I'm so sorry!'

'Don't be,' I say. 'Tell us what's wrong. Maybe we can help you.'

Alice's eyes flood with tears again. 'I don't mean I'm sorry about crying. I mean I'm sorry about what I've done.'

Isabella and I exchange glances. 'What have you done?' I say.

Alice gives a tragic wail. 'I've ruined everything!'

'I doubt it,' says Isabella. 'But I remember being terribly dramatic at your age, so I'll make allowances. It's a good thing I grew out of it and became the staid, unflappable woman you all know and love.'

Alice doesn't crack a smile. 'You don't understand! This is all my fault.'

Isabella gives an exasperated sigh. 'We seem to be going around in circles here. What's all your fault?'

'The competition!' says Alice. 'It wasn't Chris who told Dave what you were doing. It was me!'

I'm almost too astonished to speak. 'You leaked our plans to Dave Collins?'

She shakes her head. 'Not directly, but I told his brother.'

'I'm completely lost,' complains Isabella. 'How do you know his brother?'

A light bulb goes off in my head. 'Is he the guy you've been seeing?'

Alice gives a miserable nod. 'But I promise I didn't know he was Dave's brother. All Rick said was that his brother owns a business. He didn't say what kind of business. When I asked, he was a bit vague about it. I didn't like to ask any more in case it was something not quite legal. But I called him last night, and his flatmate answered and said Rick had gone to pick something up from his brother's bakery. I asked which bakery, and he said The Baker Boys.'

Isabella darts a quick look at me. 'That's Dave's bakery.'

'Did you tell your boyfriend what we were planning for the first couple of rounds?' I ask Alice.

She gives a frightened nod. 'He seemed so interested. He was always asking questions about the competition. I thought it was because he knew it was what I wanted to do, and he was being supportive.'

'What about the notebook?' asks Isabella.

'I don't know anything about a notebook,' says Alice.

I think hard. 'I thought Chris must have read the notebook because I'd stopped talking to him about what we were doing. Did you tell your boyfriend what we were baking for the chocolate round?'

Alice wipes her eyes. 'Yes. He thought it was an amazing idea. He was really impressed you were letting me help, and he asked me all about it.'

I feel as though I've swallowed an entire bucket of ice cubes. I've spent several weeks vaguely suspecting Chris and hating myself for it, followed by outright accusing him of some pretty horrible behaviour. No wonder he didn't want to see me anymore. Right at this moment, I'm not too keen on myself either.

I look up and catch Isabella's eye. I can see she's thinking exactly the same thing.

'You need to talk to him,' she says.

'What if he doesn't want to talk to me?' I say.

'That's a risk you'll have to take. Whatever you do, it's going to involve some serious grovelling.'

I'm quite prepared to grovel, but I have a horrible feeling it won't be enough. If Chris had accused me of the sort of behaviour I've accused him of, I'd never want to see him again. All I can hope is that he's a better person than I am.

Chapter Thirty-Six

I retrieve my bunch of carnations from the back seat of the car and carry them into the hospital. A woman at reception directs me to the maternity ward, where I find Lily lying at the far end of the room, her eyes closed. She looks pale and exhausted. Maybe I shouldn't have come to visit.

The nurse on duty notices my hesitation. 'She isn't asleep. I was talking to her a minute ago. I'm sure she'd love to have a chat with you. What beautiful flowers. I'll find something to put them in.'

She disappears towards the nursing station, and I walk over to Lily's bed. I lay the flowers on her bedside table, and she opens her eyes.

'Abby! How lovely to see you! Are those for me?'

'They are. Isabella told me on no account to bring lilies.'

She chuckles. 'She's quite right. Everyone does that, and I don't even like them. These carnations are beautiful.'

'I won't stay long,' I say. 'You look tired.'

She smiles. 'People keep telling me that. The doctor says I'm anaemic, and he's put me on an iron supplement before the baby is born. To hear everyone talk, you'd think I looked like a vampire.'

'Not quite that bad,' I say. 'But I don't want to tire you out. You must have lots of visitors.'

'Mum comes in every afternoon,' she says. 'And Jack spends as much time here as he can. You've just missed him. He's gone home to fetch some clean clothes. Isabella said she'd pop in tonight with some cake. She's convinced no one can survive a week on hospital food without supplements. I told her about my iron tablets, but she said she meant the other kind of supplement. I'm looking forward to seeing what she brings. She brought a bag of doughnuts last Tuesday, but she ate most of them while she was here.'

'I made a double batch of brownies yesterday,' I say. 'I expect there will be a few left over. I told Isabella we only needed one batch, but she insisted.'

Lily's face lights up. 'I love your brownies. The ones you baked for the chocolate round were amazing. Speaking of which, I hear you and Chris have made it to the final. You must be so excited!'

'Not as much as you'd think,' I say.

'Why is that? I thought you'd be over the moon. I know Isabella is.'

'It's got complicated.'

I tell her what happened between me and Chris and about Alice's confession. I don't mean to give her all the details, but it's a relief to talk to someone.

'It's a complete mess,' I finish, choking back a sob.

She leans over and hugs me. 'You poor thing. I'm so sorry. What are you going to do now? Have you told Chris about Alice?'

'I haven't spoken to him since that awful night at his flat,' I say. 'He made it clear we were over, and I don't blame him. If someone told me they didn't trust me, I'd dump them too. It's the most important part of any relationship. Chris never gave me any reason not to trust him, but I found one anyway. I don't know how I'm going to apologise.'

She considers this. 'I think it's more complicated than that. It wasn't entirely about trust, was it?'

'Probably not. I felt betrayed when he didn't understand why the competition was so important to me. I tried to explain it to him, but he never seemed to get it.'

'Why was it so important to you?' she asks.

'Isn't it obvious?'

'Not to me,' she says.

'Because of this job!' I say. 'I was desperate to get a job back home, and this one came up at the perfect time. I couldn't believe it when Isabella offered it to me. It meant I could be back with my parents. It's been awful, with Dad ill and Mum trying not to collapse under the strain. You and Isabella were so excited when the competition was announced. It meant so much to you both, which was understandable. Isabella has told me a hundred times how keen she is to win and how much good it would do the business. I thought if I helped you win the competition, you'd be more likely to keep me on at the Sugarloaf. Dad isn't fully recovered, and Mum will need me around for a while longer. I can't guarantee I'll find another job in this area.'

'That makes sense,' she says. 'Perhaps Chris should have tried harder to understand.'

I'm about to answer when there's a commotion at the other end of the ward. I turn to see Isabella in the doorway, throwing up her hands in despair.

'Stupid grapes!' she exclaims in annoyance. 'They've gone everywhere.'

She starts crawling around the floor, picking up grapes and putting them back into a paper bag.

Lily bursts out laughing. 'I hope she doesn't expect me to eat them after this.'

'They won't be for you,' I say. 'She'll have brought them to keep herself going while she visits you. I'd better help her.'

Isabella looks pleased when she sees me. 'Abby! I wasn't expecting to see you. I keep kneeling on these grapes. Can you grab a cloth before that nurse comes back? I always seem to annoy her when I visit. I don't know why.'

I pick up a box of tissues and crawl around behind her, cleaning up as I go. Isabella straightens up at last. 'I'm sure this bag was heavier when I brought it. Some of them must have rolled under the beds.'

She beams at Lily. 'Sorry about that. You have plenty of fruit anyway. I only brought them because your mum stopped by this afternoon and told me you needed to eat a healthy diet before the baby arrives. She appeared to be making a particular point, but I'm not sure what it was.'

She dives into her handbag and produces a box of brownies. 'Abby made these, so I'm sure they're healthy. Aren't they, Abby?'

'Naturally!' I say. 'I put plenty of walnuts in them.'

'There you go,' says Isabella, offering the bag to Lily. 'Walnuts are full of omega whatevers. And Abby uses chunks of dark chocolate, which is supposed to be good for you. It's almost like eating fruit.'

Lily takes a bite. 'I've missed your baking, Abby. Even Jack has taken my mother seriously. He brought me some wholegrain crackers last night and was most upset when I said they tasted like cardboard.'

'I'll make you an enormous batch of anything you like as soon as you've had the baby,' I promise.

'It will give me something to look forward to during labour,' she says.

'Can you bake an enormous batch for me while you're at it?' says Isabella. 'I'm sure labour will be an anxious time for me too.'

'When you've finished talking nonsense,' says Lily. 'Abby and I want to consult with you.'

'We do?' I say.

'Of course, we do. It may be difficult to get Isabella's attention, but when you do, she has some wonderful ideas.'

She tells Isabella everything I've told her about Chris and the notebook and the competition.

'I had no idea you thought the competition would affect your job,' Isabella says when Lily has finished.

'You talking about it non-stop may have had something to do with it,' says Lily.

Isabella looks contrite. 'I'm sorry about that, Abby. We should clear that one up before we go any further. Lily and I have been planning to offer you a full-time contract, regardless of when she comes back to work. The bakery's been doing extremely well over the past few months, and a lot of that is down to you.'

I give a gasp of relief. 'Do you mean that?'

'We do,' says Lily. 'We want to keep you as long as we can.'

'Chris is a little more difficult,' says Isabella. 'I can see why he was hurt. But not to worry, we'll come up with something.'

'Do you care about the competition?' she asks Lily.

Lily shakes her head. 'Right now, all I care about is keeping this baby safe and getting through labour.'

Isabella looks pleased. 'That makes the whole thing a lot simpler. We're through to the final, which is more than I expected. It would have been nice to win, but there's always next year.'

'I'll still try to win,' I say. 'Especially now you've been so kind about my job.'

She waves a hand. 'Don't worry about that. I love plotting and scheming.'

'She does,' says Lily. 'Don't argue with her, Abby. It's a waste of energy.'

Isabella breaks the last brownie into three pieces and hands them around. 'What we need is a showstopper, a big gesture like they do in movies. Chris isn't flying anywhere in the next week or two, is he?'

'Not that I know of,' I say.

'That's a shame. It rules out the frantic dash through the airport before he boards his flight. How about a soccer game?'

'He used to watch them with Dad,' I say, not taking her meaning.

'I don't mean that. Does he have a season-ticket or anything?'

'I'm afraid not.'

She looks disappointed. 'So, we can't put a huge apology on the score board.'

'I wouldn't even if I could,' I say. 'It isn't my style.'

'Killjoy!' she complains. 'Work with me here.'

'I have an idea,' says Lily. She lowers her voice, although there's no one in the adjacent bed. Isabella and I lean in closer to catch her words.

'Tell me what you think about this,' she says.

Chapter Thirty-Seven

I arrive at Mayfield High School on Saturday with my heart pounding. I haven't seen Chris since we broke up, and I haven't found the courage to call him. He meant what he said when he told me we had no future if I didn't trust him. He was right. No relationship can survive without trust. He was also right when he said I'd got this competition out of proportion. What I don't know is whether I'll be able to convince him that's no longer the case.

I follow the signs to the domestic science department. I'm the first to arrive. The first three kitchens have been set up for us. I dump my bags in the nearest one and unpack my ingredients.

I hear footsteps and force myself to turn around. It isn't Chris. It's Olivia, the third finalist. She's carrying four large bags and looking nervous.

'Can I use the kitchen next to yours?' she asks.

'Go ahead,' I say, pleased to think I won't have Chris working beside me.

He arrives five minutes later. 'Hi, everyone.'

His eyes meet mine, but I can't read their expression. 'Hello, Abby. How are you?'

'I'm fine, thanks,' I say. 'You?'

'I'm doing fine.'

He doesn't add anything else as he unpacks his ingredients in the remaining kitchen. I try not to watch him. I hoped he might display some sort of emotion when he saw me, even if it was anger. This calm indifference is worse than anything.

But it's too late to think about that now. All I can do is bake the most perfect cake possible and hope for the best.

Isabella rushes in a few minutes later, pink-faced and breathless. 'It took me ages to park. The school car park is packed, so I had to leave the car several streets away and run.'

She notices Chris and raises a questioning eyebrow.

I shake my head, and her face falls. Chris sees her and lifts a hand in greeting but doesn't speak.

'Did you bring the cake tins?' I ask, and she nods.

'Mrs Carson insisted on sending two sets, just in case.'

'What does she think I'm going to do to them?' I say.

'That's what I asked her, but she said better safe than sorry, and you'll be glad of them if anything happens.'

Chris glances up and catches my eye. Is that a look of amusement? I don't have time to decide before he looks away again.

We check the ingredients on my list. Isabella tries to taste the dark chocolate, but I swat her hand away.

'You only need one hundred grams!' she says, aggrieved.

The doors open at two o'clock, and everyone files in. I can't remember the last time I felt this nervous. It would be much easier if this wasn't a public round. It's nice that people have turned up to support the contestants, but it makes it far more stressful. I can hardly imagine what it feels like when the contestants have TV cameras on them too.

Mrs Carson squeezes my shoulder as she passes me. 'Good luck, dear. I know everything is going to go wonderfully.'

She walks over to stand with a man I assume is Lily's father. He gives me an encouraging smile and thumbs up. I haven't seen Jack yet, but I notice Mr Mason talking to Mrs Ogilvie. I'm glad they seem to have put their differences behind them.

The judges arrive and welcome everyone. Gavin makes a short speech about the importance of this competition to the New Forest community and says how delighted he is to see so many people here.

'You can wander around and watch the contestants as they work,' he says. 'Please don't talk to them or disturb them in any way. They only have two hours, and they need to concentrate.'

He looks at his watch. 'Are you all ready? No last questions? Then, off you go.'

He drops his arm as though starting a Grand Prix race, and there's an excited murmur around the room.

I weigh my ingredients into the mixer and switch it on. I needn't have worried about catching Chris's eye. We're all far too focused on what we're doing. I grease the cake tins and pour in the batter, hoping these ovens have accurate thermostats.

I set the oven timer and mix the first lot of icing. There's an excited yapping noise, and I look down to see Bernie straining at his leash. I don't know whether he wants to say hello or taste what I'm making. I jerk my head towards Isabella, who reacts quickly.

'Hello, Bernie,' she says. 'I thought you might be here today. Let's see what I've got in my bag for you.'

She leads Mrs Ogilvie away from the kitchen. A moment later, I hear a loud crunching noise. It hadn't occurred to me that Bernie would be here today, but I shouldn't be surprised. Mrs Ogilvie takes him everywhere she goes.

I mix up several more batches of icing while I wait for the cakes to cook. Half an hour later, the timer beeps, and I reach for a pair of oven gloves. I breathe a sigh of relief as I open the oven door. The cakes are perfect. They've risen just the right amount. Judging by the smell that wafts out, they're perfectly cooked.

I turn them out onto a cooling tray and step back. There's a murmur of appreciation from the people standing nearby.

'Doesn't that look marvellous, Martin?' says Mrs Carson. 'Abby is such a wonderful baker. Lily and Isabella are so pleased they found her.'

I concentrate on assembling the cake and finishing the more intricate aspects of my decorations, ignoring the comments and speculations of the onlookers. I step back with only five minutes left. There's nothing more I can do.

Isabella gives the cake an approving glance. 'I wish I could cook half as well as you, Abby.'

'I'm surprised you haven't learned,' I say. 'Baking seems to be a particular passion of yours.'

'That's true,' she agrees. 'But I prefer other people to do the actual work.'

'If you could refrain from sampling it until the judges have finished, I'd be grateful.'

'I'll do my best,' she promises. 'But it's been a long time since lunch, so there are no guarantees.'

Gavin claps his hands together, and there's a low murmur of excitement from the crowd.

'Will the contestants please stop what they're doing and step out of their kitchens?' he says. 'And will the audience please take their seats ready for the judging?'

He gestures to the three of us to join him, and we line up in front of the judge's table.

'We're all so excited to see your wonderful creations,' he says. 'But we like to talk to our contestants first. I'll start by asking each of you what everyone is dying to know – what have you made for us today?'

He hands the microphone to Olivia, who looks even more nervous than when she arrived.

She clears her throat. 'I've used a recipe for a spice and honey cake that William the Conqueror may have eaten around the time he established the New Forest. I've filled each layer with berries and nuts and organic cream, all locally sourced. I've decorated the cake with crystallised gorse petals.'

'Very nice indeed,' says Gavin. 'How about you, Chris?'

'I've made a raspberry and pineapple cake with a fondant topping,' says Chris.

'What was the inspiration for that?' asks Gavin.

'It just felt right,' says Chris.

He hands me the microphone without looking at me.

'And last, but not least,' says Gavin. 'Abby, can you tell us what you've chosen to bake this afternoon?'

'I've made a triple chocolate cake,' I say. 'It's a milk chocolate cake with white chocolate filling and a dark chocolate topping. It was inspired by … a friend.'

'Wonderful,' says Gavin. 'And now the moment you've all been waiting for, ladies and gentlemen. Olivia, would you present your cake to the judges?'

Olivia returns to her kitchen and emerges carrying a silver serving plate. I barely even look at it. My heart is thumping fast, and my legs feel wobbly.

The judges cluster around the cake, talking and exclaiming. Olivia slices it and hands the plates around. I look over at Mum and Dad. Mum looks tense, but Dad gives me a wicked grin. My heart slows to its normal pace. No matter what happens this afternoon, I have a lot to be thankful for.

'Thank you so much, Olivia,' says Angela.

The judges finish writing on their cards, and Gavin nods to me.

'Abby, may we see what you've made?'

The walk back to my kitchen seems to take hours. I'm painfully conscious of everyone's eyes on my back. I wish I'd made something different. What was I thinking? I'm about to make an absolute idiot of myself and become the laughing stock of the village. I dread seeing the look on Mum and Dad's face when they see what I've done. They were so excited at the thought of me winning the competition.

However, short of making a dash for it and hoping not to get lost in the maze of corridors on the way out, there's nothing for it. I'll have to go through with it. I pick up my cake and carry it out to the waiting judges.

I lay my cake on the table and step back, not meeting anyone's eyes. There's a ripple of laughter from the people in the front row as they crane forward to take in the details. I glance at Dave, who looks as though all his Christmases have come early. He has the look of a man who's about to win a large sum of money. It can't be helped, but I hope he invests it in something that goes bust within weeks.

Gavin is the first to speak. 'What an … interesting presentation. Can you tell us a little about your inspiration, Abby, particularly how it relates to the theme of *I love the New Forest*?'

I take a deep breath. 'I was inspired to bake this cake by hearing about someone's lifelong dream.'

I feel rather than see Chris make a movement behind me. I don't turn to look at him.

'When I entered this competition,' I go on, 'it felt more important than anything in the world.'

Gavin casts another fascinated look at my cake. 'I don't quite see …'

'I was obsessed with winning,' I say. 'It was all I could think of. I thought my job depended on it, and keeping my job was desperately important to me. I had family reasons for wanting to stay in the New Forest area. And later on, I had another reason.'

I don't dare look at Chris. He may not understand what I mean, or he may not care. The worst thing I could see on his face would be sympathy. I could cope with anything except that.

I clear my throat. 'To cut a long story short, I realised I had my priorities all wrong. Competitions are fine. They're fun if you take them in the right spirit, and I've enjoyed this one. But winning isn't everything, not by far. I've learned over the past few weeks that there are things that matter even more, such as family and friends and –'

'That's most commendable,' interrupts Gavin. 'And I'm sure we all join with you in these laudable sentiments. But I'm still not clear how *I love the New Forest* relates to –'

He leans over to study my cake more carefully. 'A pirate ship!'

Angela looks amused. 'Not just any pirate ship, Gavin. This one is pretty spectacular. The chocolate treasure chest filled with gold coins is a work of art in itself. And is that a parrot hiding in the rigging?'

'That's right,' I say. 'I'm afraid I can't explain any more about why I made this cake today. I'm aware it doesn't fall under the mantle of how wonderful the New Forest is, at least not in the way you envisaged. But this cake is meaningful to me, and this is how I interpreted the brief.'

'And what would you say was the meaning?' says Angela, still looking amused.

'That people are more important than rosettes,' I say. 'We all have hopes and dreams. They aren't always possible to achieve. But sometimes they are. When that's the case, we should do our best to make them come true for the people we love. And if that means losing a stupid competition, so be it.'

I catch myself. 'Not that this is a stupid competition …'

She smiles. 'I think we all know what you mean. Thank you for your entry and your explanation. I'm sure we'd all like to hear a little more of the story behind it, but perhaps it's not yours to tell.'

'I'm afraid it isn't,' I say. 'We can only tell our own story, and this one is mine. I wanted to show that I've learned what's important in my life. If I had my time over again, I'd behave differently. Also, I'm afraid you won't be able to taste it. It's a pity because it's an excellent cake. But that's the way it is.'

'You realise if you won't let us taste it, you won't receive a score?' says Gavin.

'I know. But this isn't my cake. It belongs to someone else, and it's up to them what happens with it.'

I half expect Chris to say something, but he doesn't. Isabella gives me a sympathetic smile, and I look away. I don't want to burst into tears before the entire room.

Gavin nods. 'If that's the case, there's nothing to do but proceed to our final entrant. Chris, would you like to show us what you've prepared?'

'Certainly,' says Chris.

I watch him walk to his kitchen with a sinking heart. Did he understand what I was trying to say? I didn't want to be more explicit and embarrass him in front of everyone, but he must remember his birthday and the cake he longed for. Was that story less meaningful to him than I thought? In which case, I've thrown away the competition for nothing and made a gigantic fool of myself into the bargain.

Chris walks over to the judges and lays his cake on the table. I don't dare to look. No one speaks for a moment. Is this the most amazing cake they've ever seen, and none of them can find words? I hope he hasn't stuffed it up. I want him to win.

'This is the oddest Mix-up final I've ever been involved with,' says Gavin at last.

I take a deep breath and open my eyes. Chris has baked a large, square cake, covered with smooth pink fondant. A pair of chocolate knitting needles sits on one edge, balanced on what looks like a ball of rainbow coloured wool. On closer inspection, I see he's iced each intricate strand separately.

I follow the end of the wool to where it's formed itself into curly letters.

I'm sorry things came unravelled. Can we make some repairs?

I stare at it, unable to speak. Chris turns to face me.

'I'm so sorry, Abby. I didn't realise how important this competition was to you. Your father explained it to me, but not until after we'd broken up, by which time it was too late.'

I give my parents a startled glance. Mum still looks bewildered, but Dad just shrugs and smiles.

'We had a long talk when I dropped by to watch the football final with him,' says Chris. 'He's a wise man, your dad. I'd say it won't be long before he and your mum are back on track to achieve their dreams.'

I didn't expect Chris to continue to visit Dad after we broke up. But it shouldn't surprise me. It's who he is. It's who he's always been.

'I didn't know how to tell you how sorry I was for what happened,' he goes on. 'I knew what you'd been going through, and I should have understood how important this competition was.'

I take a step towards him, hardly able to believe what he's saying. 'Does that mean you'll give me another chance?'

'If you'll still have me,' he says, pulling me into his arms and kissing me. We stand locked together for what seems like hours until the noise of the crowd applauding brings me back to reality. I pull away and look around. Dad has his arm around Mum, who's crying. Isabella has jumped to her feet and is waving her arms, making loud whooping noises.

'I made that cake for you,' I tell Chris. 'It's a …'

'I know,' he says. 'It's perfect. I can't believe you threw the competition when you were so close to winning.'

'There will be plenty of other years,' I say. 'This is a one-shot deal. Don't get used to it.'

Gavin waves his arms for silence, and the applause dies down.

'This is all most irregular,' he says. 'Are we allowed to taste this cake, or is it also out of bounds?'

'Of course, you can taste it,' I say.

'You can taste my pirate ship too,' says Chris. 'Just don't touch the parrot or the treasure chest.'

Gavin shakes his head in confusion and picks up a knife. The crowd falls silent as the judges huddle together and confer. I stand close to Chris, my hand tucked in his. I no longer care what score they give me. I've already won the only thing I care about.

The judges step back and Gavin consults his notes before clearing his throat. 'Ladies and gentlemen, this has been one of the most unusual competitions I've ever attended. Then again, nothing about these past few years has been usual, so perhaps this year's Mix-up reflects that. In the spirit of which –'

He's interrupted by a crashing sound as the door bursts open. There's a ripple of excitement among the crowd as everyone turns to see what's happening.

To my astonishment, I see Jack, red-faced and out of breath, with his hair standing on end.

'It's Lily!' he gasps. 'She's had the baby!'

Chapter Thirty-Eight

There's a stunned silence before Mrs Carson leaps to her feet with a scream. 'Is she alright?'

Jack beams at her. 'She's fine. I'm sorry to have broken the news so abruptly. I should have told you privately that you're the proud grandmother of a beautiful baby girl. But the cat's out of the bag now.'

Mrs Carson gives another shriek. 'Did you hear that, Martin? We have a granddaughter!'

She rushes over to Jack and flings her arms around him. 'Congratulations! I'm so happy for you both.'

She dissolves into tears, and he pats her on her shoulder. 'Everything's fine. It all happened in a rush. One minute, Lily was saying if I brought her any more unflavoured popcorn, she'd be consulting a divorce lawyer. The next thing we knew, her waters had broken.'

Isabella rushes over to hug Jack. 'I was sure you'd annoy the baby into being born if we gave you half a chance! Who does she look most like, me or Lily?'

He laughs. 'Right now, it's hard to tell. She's like a tiny, crumpled flower petal, all soft and pink.'

She frowns. 'I've spent almost as long with her as her mother has. She might at least have acknowledged her aunt Isabella. When can I meet her?'

'When her grandparents have seen her,' he says. 'Lily's eager to see them as soon as possible. She wants to introduce them to baby Daisy.'

Mrs Carson dabs at her eyes with a tissue. 'Daisy? What a beautiful name. We'll come whenever you like.'

'Is the competition over yet?' asks Jack. 'That's why I'm here. I came home to collect a few things for Lily, and she insisted I drop in and hear the result.'

'I can call you,' says Mrs Carson. 'You'll want to get back to Lily.'

'She's in no rush,' says Jack. 'She and Daisy are in their own little bubble. I barely got a look in. At one point, Lily waved in my direction and said, "That man's your father." But that was the extent of my involvement.'

Mrs Carson turns to the judges. 'Can we move things along, please? I have a granddaughter to meet.'

Everyone sits down again, and the room falls quiet.

'As I was saying,' says Gavin, 'this has been a rather unusual competition. But the judges are in complete agreement that this year's Mix-up prize should go to Olivia Forde from The Cookie Corner.'

There's a storm of applause, in which Chris and I join. Dave looks as though he's bitten on a lemon. Obviously, he'd bet on Chris to win.

Gavin waves for silence. 'The judges were unable to award two of our competitors points for sticking to the theme and were most reluctantly about to disqualify them both. However, judging from the reaction of the crowd, they seem to feel that Love *In* the New Forest is a legitimate interpretation of the brief. We have therefore decided to call it a tie. The Sugarloaf Bakery and The Slice Bakery will share second place.'

Chris slips an arm around me, and I rest my head on his shoulder.

'That works for me,' I say happily.

'Me too,' he says.

I look at Dave, who's glaring at the judges. He turns to gesticulate at a man in the next row. I recognise him as the barman at the Red Lion. The man grins and shakes his head, and Dave looks like a pricked balloon.

Angela steps forward. 'As you will be aware, the audience has the opportunity to taste the cakes once the judging is final.'

'I'll make you another,' I whisper to Chris.

'I want one each year for my birthday,' he whispers back.

Everyone clusters around the judges' table, tasting the cakes, chattering and laughing. Chris takes my hand and leads me over to where Mum and Dad are sitting.

'Good lad,' says Dad.

'Thanks for interfering,' I say, and he smiles.

'Well, isn't this lovely?' says Mum. 'I knew you two would get back together eventually.'

'I didn't,' I say.

She pats my arm. 'That's because you never listen to anything your mother tells you.'

I push my way through the crowd and return with two plates of cake, which I hand to my parents.

'These all look lovely,' says Mum. 'Although I'm not sure what possessed Abby to bake a pirate cake.'

'It's a mystery,' says Chris. 'But I've learned never to ask your daughter questions. It's easier to let her go her own way.'

'I'd have thought a nice Black Forest Gateau might have been more appropriate,' says Mum. 'Still, it tastes delicious.'

She inspects her plate more closely. 'Is this a fondant thimble, Chris?'

'I've learned never to ask Chris questions,' I say. 'It's easier to let him go his own way.'

Isabella and Jack come over to join us.

'I wanted to congratulate you before I left,' says Jack. 'Lily will be delighted.'

I hug him. 'This is a just cake competition. You've won the real prize. Congratulations! It's wonderful news.'

I'm amused to see him turn pink. He's obviously bursting with pride and trying not to show it.

'I'm sorry there's no cake left to send Lily,' says Isabella. 'I tried to bag an extra slice for her, but it had all been eaten. I'll bring her something from the bakery.'

'She's in a world of her own,' says Jack. 'She wouldn't notice if you brought her a plate of digestive biscuits.'

'Congratulations!' says Isabella when he's gone.

'Me or Chris?' I say.

'Both,' she says. 'And not just on the prize. I'm glad the pair of you have seen sense.'

'You didn't mind the Sugarloaf coming second?' I say.

She laughs. 'All I care about is that Dave didn't win his stupid bet. Alice asked his brother about it right before she dumped him. Apparently, Dave bet heavily on Chris and Olivia to win the rosettes, with a side bet on Chris coming first. When he realised how good you were, Abby, he decided to sabotage you. He didn't care about being eliminated himself, as long as you lost points and didn't make it to the final. I saw him arguing with Matthew Lawson just now that Chris coming joint second still counted, but he didn't seem too hopeful of changing his mind. Serves him right.'

'Your disastrous date probably gave Dave another incentive to get us out of the competition,' I say.

'True,' she says. She turns to Chris. 'Do you mind sharing second place?'

'I came here this afternoon with one aim,' he says. 'And it wasn't winning first prize. Besides, Olivia's cake was spectacular. That medieval recipe was incredibly creative. She deserved to win.'

'I agree,' I say.

The room is clearing, and the judges are packing up to leave. Now the cakes have been eaten, people are drifting away.

Mr Mason joins us. 'Congratulations on your achievement. The Sugarloaf Bakery has never reached the final before.'

'We all benefited from your advice and expertise,' says Isabella, and he looks pleased.

A sharp yap makes me jump. Bernie has slipped his leash and run over to greet us.

I bend down to pat him. 'Hello, Bernie! I was surprised when I saw you here today.'

Mrs Ogilvie trots over to us, waving Bernie's lead. 'Naughty boy! I told you to stay with Mummy.'

Bernie looks unrepentant as he allows her to clip his lead onto his collar.

'Did Bernie taste any of the cakes?' asks Isabella.

Mrs Ogilvie looks defiant. 'As a matter of fact, he did. Not the chocolate cake, of course. But the judge gave me a rather large helping of the other two, and I couldn't finish it all.'

'And which cake did he vote for?' asks Mum, stooping down and ruffling Bernie's head.

'Abby's, of course,' says Mrs Ogilvie. 'It was by far the best entry.'

'Bernie is a dog of great taste and discernment,' says Isabella. 'He should become the Sugarloaf's mascot. What do you think, Mrs Ogilvie? With him at the helm, we can't fail to win the competition next year.'

Mrs Ogilvie beams. I'm surprised her face can make that shape.

'Bernie would like that very much,' she says. 'It isn't the same as being in the films, but he would be around far fewer undesirable people.'

'That's a matter of debate,' Chris murmurs in my ear.

The judges come over to congratulate us.

'Your cakes were a little unorthodox,' says Gavin. 'But I have to admit they tasted delicious. You might both consider something more visually traditional next time.'

'Perhaps next year, Abby and Chris could bake a joint entry,' says Mum coyly.

'Not a hope,' says Isabella. 'The Sugarloaf Bakery will bake the winning entry next year and take all the credit for it.'

Chris and I pack up our bags, and head for the door. Mum invited us for dinner, but she didn't seem surprised when we refused.

I stop in the doorway and look back at the people milling around, talking and laughing.

'It's been quite an afternoon,' I tell Chris. 'First the final, and now Jack and Lily's new baby.'

'And you and I are back together,' he says, bending his head to kiss me.

I slip my arms around his neck and kiss him back. He smells like vanilla and nutmeg, and his lips taste of the dark chocolate I used for the treasure chest.

'I'm going to "whisk" you away for a celebratory dinner,' he says.

'Are you making a baking pun on top of those awful knitting ones?' I ask. 'If so, I may have to reconsider my decision.'

'That's a shame,' he says. 'I've been planning these baking puns for a while. "Of all the women I've ever known, you take the biscuit. You never crumble under pressure. I doughnut know what I'd do without you." I'm working on a few more that involve being half-baked or crusty.'

'I'm sure you are,' I say. 'But I'd appreciate you keeping them to yourself.'

He grins. 'Fine. The important thing is that I've got you back. That's good enough for me.'

The expression in his eyes as he looks into mine makes my heart beat faster.

'Do you think we'll make it work this time?' he says. 'I couldn't cope with losing you again.'

Maybe there's something in these baking puns, after all.

'Of course, we will,' I say, reaching up to kiss him again. 'A piece of cake!'

A Sweet Romantic Comedy

A Sugarloaf Surprise

ROSEMARY WHITTAKER

Chapter One

The car makes one final choking noise and sputters to a halt. I pull in to the side of the road before it gives up entirely. I look around, wondering where I am. Somewhere on the edge of the New Forest, I believe. I noticed a sign a few miles back saying *Beware – wild ponies*. I'm not sure whether I'm supposed to beware of them, or they of me. The picture didn't make it clear.

The sign would have been correct to warn the ponies to beware of this car. I find it terrifying, and I'm sitting inside it. But not for long. I remember my driving instructor warning me never to stay in a broken-down car.

I climb out and scramble up the grassy bank to peer over the hedge. There are several fields of bright yellow flowers, but no people. There ought to be a farmer pacing his meadows and counting the flower heads, or whatever it is they do. Failing that, a shepherd. I look around for some sheep. But either they're hiding in the yellow flowers, or they've gone for a walk.

I sit on the bank and think hard. I have no clue where I am. I took a shortcut a while back because my phone suggested traffic was building up on the main road, and I thought it must know best. But it immediately followed up on its helpful suggestion by shutting down due to low battery. I switch it on again to check the map. The screen obligingly flashes into life, but there are no bars. I try to call the rental car company, but there's no connection.

It's a beautiful day. The sun is shining, and the birds are chirping. The yellow flowers are swaying gently in the breeze. I take a deep breath and try to enjoy the moment. Maybe this breakdown is a sign I should slow down and appreciate the simple things in life.

I heave a sigh and lean back against the hedge. This is just my luck – stuck in the wilds of the countryside with no phone signal and a broken-down car. What am I supposed to do now? I could try walking, but I have no idea in which direction. I could be wandering around for hours. What if I stumble upon the wild ponies? I don't feel prepared to face them on my own.

I switch off my phone again. I need to preserve whatever battery is left. Goodness knows when I'll reach civilisation again. This phone could be all that lies between me and complete disaster. I could sit here and wait for another car to come by, but I suspect I'd be here for a long time. I don't remember passing any other vehicles during the past ten minutes. Not even a tractor. Failing that, I'll have to start walking and hope I choose the right direction. If not, I may walk for miles before finding myself lost in a marsh or up to my neck in quicksand.

I remember I still have a half-eaten bar of chocolate in the dash pocket of the car. It's a cheering thought. With sensible rationing, it should help me survive for a couple more hours. And it's bound to rain soon. It always rains in the countryside. That's probably why they choose to grow crops there, rather than in cities. I won't have to worry about dying of thirst before I'm rescued.

It's the end of May, and the weather has been delightfully warm all week. On the other hand, the nights are still chilly. That decides it. I'm taking a chance and setting out in search of civilisation.

I scramble down the bank and extract my handbag from the car. I pull on my jacket and shove my phone into my pocket in case I can figure out a way to charge it from a nearby telegraph pole. I look up and down the narrow lane and decide the direction in which I was driving looks more promising than the one from which I came. I set off purposefully, but I haven't taken more than fifteen steps when I hear an engine, although I can't see any sign of a car. It may be on a parallel road to me, which would be frustrating. The sound grows louder, and a red sports car comes into view.

I'm so relieved that I almost forget to flag it down. Luckily, it's already slowing as it approaches. The driver must be wondering who's dumped a vehicle in the middle of nowhere and wandered off. Maybe he's planning to return with a truck and steal it. Horrified by the thought of having to explain myself to the rental company and possibly being charged a huge deposit, I turn and retrace my steps.

The driver has climbed out and is inspecting my car. He gives me a cheerful grin when he sees me. 'Hello, there! Having a bit of car trouble?'

'It's a rental,' I say. 'I have no idea what's wrong with it. It started making funny noises about an hour ago, and they got worse.'

'What sort of funny noises?' he says, looking amused.

'Just funny noises. Like sausages sizzling, or a popcorn machine, or a soda can after it's been shaken up.'

'And what did you do when you heard it?'

'I turned the radio up.'

I'm annoyed to hear him laugh. 'Of course, you did.'

'What else was I supposed to do? I'm not a mechanic.'

'Maybe find a mechanic?' he suggests. 'Or call the roadside services?'

'They aren't included in my rental package. The man told me this car was serviced only last week, and I didn't want to pay extra for something I wouldn't need. Besides, I was in a hurry. I wanted to get to my bed and breakfast before dark.'

'And now you won't get there at all.'

'Can't you fix it?' I say.

'I'm not a mechanic. I'm a photographer. There isn't a lot of overlap.'

I give a despairing sigh. 'Didn't they teach you how to maintain your camera at photography school? It's probably not much different.'

'I'm afraid not,' he says. 'It's a pity a chef didn't come along instead.'

'A chef?'

'As soon as you told them it sounded like sausages frying, they'd have it diagnosed in an instant. Sausages frying – transmission failure. Popcorn machine – overheating. Soda explosion – leaking brake fluid.'

Despite my annoyance, I find myself laughing. 'Thanks for trying to help, anyway. Could you possibly give me a lift into the next town? Even if there aren't any chefs on duty, I may be able to locate a mechanic.'

'I can do you one better than that,' he says. 'We're about five miles away from Honeywell. I'm staying in the village. You can call the rental company and ask what you should do.'

'I expect they'll say it's my fault,' I say gloomily. 'They weren't terribly helpful to begin with. And look what they've given me. They said it was a nice little runaround.'

He gives my car a disparaging glance. 'I wouldn't have thought it could do much more than stagger around.'

'Exactly! And now it's not even doing that.'

'Which is why they'll have to pay to fix it,' he says. 'If you're lucky, you may even get a night's accommodation out of them. Where were you trying to get to?'

'Dorchester.'

'That's about thirty-five miles from here,' he says. 'Where are you coming from?'

'Why?'

'I don't understand how you ended up here,' he says. 'We're nowhere near a main road.'

'I took a shortcut.'

'Who told you it was a shortcut?' he says, a glint of amusement in his eyes.

'It looked as though it *ought* to be a shortcut. The traffic was moving slowly, and my phone said it was getting worse. I thought I could bypass it and rejoin the main road later. But the road started winding away in a completely different direction. I tried to check the map, but my phone battery was almost dead. When I managed to switch it on again, I realised there was no connection.'

'It's a bit of a dead spot around here,' he agrees. 'It picks up again as you get closer to Honeywell. We have excellent connection there.'

'Congratulations! But that's not much help to me.'

'True, but I can give you a ride there. You can't sit here all day. You're lucky I came along when I did. You could have been here for hours.'

He opens his car door. 'That heap of junk will be fine here for an hour or two until they send someone out.'

I take a step towards his car, then stop. This may not be the best idea. I'm alone in a deserted area without a phone connection, and I have no idea who this man is.

He notices my hesitation. 'I'm Will Matthews. I'm a photographer, down from London for the summer. I have a few commissions in this area. One of them is to photograph places of interest for a book on local history, including Honeywell. That's where I'm currently staying. If I could get any connection, I'd show you my firm's website. It has my photograph on it somewhere. As it is, you'll have to take my word for it.'

I study his face carefully. He looks all right, but that doesn't mean anything.

'If you'd rather stay here and wait for a mechanic, that's fine,' he says. 'I don't know when they'll send one, but it may not be for a while. I have a bag of apples in my car I can leave for you. I also have three dozen eggs I bought from a farm shop a few miles back.'

'What do you expect me to do with eggs?' I say.

'That's up to you. If you happen to have any brandy in the car, you could make an eggnog.'

'If I had any brandy in the car, I'd have drunk it by now,' I say. 'It's been a rough week, and this breakdown has just about put the lid on it.'

'If I hadn't come along when I did, you'd have been forced to spend the night here,' he says. 'You'd have needed the brandy to stay warm. What would you have done if you'd drunk it all?'

'I have half a bar of chocolate,' I say. 'I was trying to work out how long that would last.'

'It's better than nothing,' he says. 'But not as good as my apples and eggs.'

'Raw eggs,' I remind him.

'True, but you may have seen them differently if you'd been stranded here all night. You'd be thinking longingly of steak tartare long before dawn.'

'I doubt it,' I say. 'Anyway, I wasn't planning on spending the night here. I was setting out to look for help when you arrived.'

'I saw that. There was a touch of the Captain Oates in the way you were striding along. "Now, there's a woman who may be gone some time!" I said to myself.'

'Was I at least going in the right direction?' I ask.

'It depends on what for. If you take a keen interest in automatic crop sprinklers or the latest fashions in scarecrows, you'd have had a wonderful afternoon. If you were dead set on finding a mechanic, not so much. We're only a few miles from Honeywell as the crow flies, but it's in that direction.' He points towards a clump of elms.

'Have you decided what you want to do?' he adds. 'Shall I go on ahead to warn the villagers that hostile townies are lurking nearby, or would you like a ride in so you can tell them yourself?'

I decide to take the risk. I don't want to sit here all afternoon.

'I'll come with you,' I say. 'Are you sure you know where we are?'

'I am. I can tell the rental agency exactly where to find your car.'

'If you insist on calling it that,' I say. 'I assume there's somewhere I can eat at this Honeywell place?'

'There's a very nice bakery. You won't need to bring your emergency chocolate ration with you. Leave it in the car for the next time you break down.'

'And your eggs are safe for now,' I say, settling myself into the front seat of his car. 'Why do you need so many? Are you making a giant omelette?'

'It's the school sports day tomorrow. I promised the head teacher I'd supply the eggs for the egg and spoon race.'

'It's lucky I didn't eat them,' I say. 'They'd have had to use something else for the race.'

'Like ping-pong balls?' he suggests, turning his car to face the opposite direction.

'Not ping-pong balls! They'd fall off the spoons if there was the slightest breeze. You'd need to use something much heavier. But not heavy enough to cause damage if it flew off and hit the other competitors.'

'You've obviously given this some thought,' he says. 'Are you an engineer or an assault course designer?'

'Not even close. I'm a veterinary nurse.'

'I take it from the fact you're lost that you aren't a local?' he says, turning onto a larger road, signposted Honeywell in one direction, and Ringwood in the other.

'I've never been in this part of the world before,' I say.

'Are you on holiday?'

I don't answer for a moment.

'It's none of my business,' he adds. 'I'm just naturally nosy.'

I don't know why I hesitated. I'll never see this man again. I should have agreed I was on holiday and left it at that.

'It's a sort of holiday,' I say. 'I wanted to be away from my flat for a few days, while …'

'It's always good to take a break,' he says.

He turns the subject and points out various landmarks – a disused mill, and a pick your own strawberry farm. I'm grateful for his understanding.

He turns off the main road and weaves his way along several smaller lanes.

'There's Honeywell church,' he says, indicating a grey stone building on our right. 'The primary school is right next to it.'

We come to a crossroads, and he points to the sign. 'This is Honeywell high street. The Red Lion is over there, if you still want that brandy. Otherwise, you can get something to eat at The Sugarloaf Bakery. They'll do you an excellent cream tea. They also sell sandwiches and pies if you're after something more substantial.'

'What about the rental company?' I ask.

'Call them now,' he says, handing me his phone. 'My phone has plenty of charge.'

I dial the number and speak to a woman who tells me her boss has gone to lunch, but she'll get him to call me as soon as he gets back.

'Let's hope it isn't a three hour lunch,' I tell Will. 'I need them to sort something out for me as quickly as possible.'

'I'm sure it won't be,' he says. 'In the meantime, are you going to the pub or the bakery?'

'Which do you recommend?'

'The bakery,' he says without hesitation. 'I go there almost every day. They'll sort you out with a phone charger if you ask.'

'The bakery, it is.'

'Good call,' he says. 'You won't regret it.'

'It's awfully kind of you to go to all this trouble,' I say. 'You didn't have to.'

He grins. 'I couldn't leave you wandering around in the depths of the New Forest countryside, getting yourself more and more lost and falling into peat bogs.'

'But you were heading in the other direction. I've made you late for wherever you were going.'

'Not really,' he says. 'I was supposed to be photographing Wyndham Keep this afternoon. But I can do that anytime.'

He pulls up outside the bakery. 'Here we are. You must be ready for something to eat after all the excitement.'

'I could do something with a sausage roll or a sandwich,' I say. 'And those cream teas sound tempting.'

'You won't regret it,' he says. 'I may even join you there later. By the way, what's your name? I can't keep on calling you Jane Doe.'

'Olivia Sullivan,' I say.

I close the car door, and he rolls down the window. 'I've always liked that name. My aunt had a cat called Olivia.'

He gives me a friendly wave and drives away.

Chapter Two

I push open the bakery door and step inside. There's a counter in front of me, filled with brightly coloured cakes. I suddenly realise how hungry I am. It's been a long time since breakfast. I was planning to eat lunch in Dorchester, and it doesn't look as though I'll arrive there before dinner. But I could still be wandering around the countryside, getting progressively more lost. There are worse places to find yourself at lunchtime than a bakery.

A woman appears and greets me with a cheerful smile. 'Hi, I'm Isabella. How can I help you?'

'I'm not sure,' I say. 'There's so much to choose from.'

'That's our motto here at the Sugarloaf,' she says. '*Never knowingly underwhelmed.*'

'Is it really?'

She laughs. 'No, but it ought to be. Would you like some recommendations?'

'I was hoping to get some lunch.'

She looks at the clock hanging over the counter. 'It's half past three. Please tell me you mean second lunch?'

'I don't. My car broke down somewhere around here, and a helpful passer-by gave me a lift to Honeywell. He said this bakery would be a good place to eat.'

'He was almost right,' she says. 'It's the absolute best place to eat. There's the Red Lion too, but they don't have much in the way of lunchtime desserts, which I always think are the most important part of a meal.'

She shows me to a table and hands me a menu. 'We can offer you a variety of sandwiches and pies.'

'The man who gave me a ride mentioned something about cream teas,' I say, scanning the menu.

She looks pleased. 'We do the best cream teas for miles around.'

This woman doesn't seem overly troubled about modesty. She sees my expression and bursts out laughing. 'Someone has to say it, and it may as well be me. We make amazing cream teas. Our pastry chef has a secret recipe for scones that she refuses to share with me. It doesn't make any difference because I can't cook. Whatever she puts in them, they're delicious. We came second in the New Forest Mix-up last year, and I'm convinced it was partly because of our scones.'

'Do you have any chicken and leek pies left?' I ask.

'I had one earlier,' she says. 'But there were still a couple left. I don't think anyone has bought them.'

She disappears behind the counter and emerges with a pie. She puts it onto a plate and adds a few sprigs of salad.

I take a bite and sigh in contentment. 'This is delicious. Do you bake on the premises?'

'We do,' she says. 'We decided we wanted to make all our own pies and cakes when we bought the place.'

I remember my phone. 'The man I met said you might lend me a charger. My phone is flat, and I need to make some calls. I should have checked it before I set off this morning.'

She looks at the phone I hold out to her. 'No problem. That's the same one I have. I'll plug it in for you. You should be at least half full by the time you leave. I mean, your phone will. You'll be completely full.'

A woman comes out of the room behind the shop. 'Do we have any dried raspberries?'

Isabella nods. 'They're in the storeroom. I didn't get around to unpacking that last order. Were your ears burning just now? Our customer was saying how good your pies are.'

'This is Abby, our pastry chef,' she tells me.

'Hi,' I say to Abby. 'I'm Olivia.'

'I run the bakery with my partner, Lily,' says Isabella. 'She isn't here today because her baby has typhoid.'

'Typhoid?' I say, startled.

'A cold,' corrects Abby with a grin.

'Possibly,' concedes Isabella. 'I'm no baby expert. All I know is that I had to cover for Lily today because Daisy is seeing an infectious disease consultant from the rare tropical diseases department at the local hospital.'

'She means the health visitor,' says Abby. 'Nice to meet you, Olivia. I'd better get back to my cookies. Isabella eats most of them if she's left alone in the shop for too long, so we're always running out.'

'She and Lily are always making comments like that,' says Isabella. 'I can't think why. I taste the occasional product, but that's all. It's all part of being a conscientious bakery owner. Have you finished your pie? Would you like another?'

'I'm fine, thanks. It was the best pie I've eaten in a long time.'

She looks pleased. 'You must come in again and try one of our other flavours.'

'I won't have time,' I say regretfully. 'As soon as my car is fixed, I need to drive Dorchester. I've booked a room there tonight.'

'I'll fetch your cream tea,' she says. 'Do you have any preference for jams, or shall I bring you an assortment?'

'I'm not sure I can manage anything more after that pie,' I say.

'Of course you can! Our cream teas don't take up any room at all. I often eat one before I go home, and I'm still ravenous by dinner time.'

'You don't look as though you've ever eaten a cream tea in your life,' I say.

She laughs. 'Appearances are deceptive. I've eaten plenty of them. I tell you what. If you can't finish it, I won't charge you for it. You can't say fairer than that.'

She disappears into the kitchen and returns a minute later carrying a tray with a plate of scones, several small bowls of jam and cream, and a pot of tea.

'I've brought all the jams we have,' she says, setting down the tray and unloading it. 'My favourite is the gooseberry. Lily's mum makes it. She grows a lot of soft fruit, and she always makes too much jam, so we buy it from her and use it in the shop.'

I split open a scone and spread some of the jam on it. I sandwich it with a generous dollop of thick cream and take a bite. Isabella watches me anxiously.

'It's wonderful,' I say, swallowing my mouthful. 'I may finish it after all.'

'I knew you would!' she says. 'Everyone says they don't have room, but they never leave anything on their plates.'

She looks at her watch. 'It's only an hour before we close. I think I'll liberate a couple of scones. That gooseberry jam is making me hungry.'

'Why don't you join me?' I suggest. 'You don't seem busy in here, and I'd enjoy the company.'

She looks delighted. 'You're the best kind of customer. My two favourite hobbies are talking and eating. It's wonderful when I can combine the two.'

She disappears into the kitchen again, and I pour myself a cup of tea.

The shop door opens, and Will comes in. He looks pleased when he sees me. 'You're still here.'

I point to my plate. 'I may be here some time.'

'That's good. I was worried about you when we met. You looked so forlorn.'

'I was hungry,' I say. 'I hadn't had lunch, and I wasn't sure whether I dared eat that chocolate bar. I feel much better now. Thanks for rescuing me.'

'It was my pleasure,' he says. 'I came to tell you that the rental people called me. They must have thought you used your own phone to call them earlier. They've sent the local mechanic out to see your car. He's put the car on his truck and brought it back to Honeywell to have a look at it. What do you want to do next – wait for it to be fixed or ask the company for another one?'

I spoon raspberry jam onto my second scone. 'What I want is to sue the rental place for millions before pushing the car into the nearest river.'

'You can't do that,' he says. 'The council has extremely strict laws about fly-tipping.'

'I said push,' I remind him. 'I don't have to tip it in if the mayor will make a fuss.'

'Honeywell doesn't have a mayor,' he says. 'But the council would definitely object to finding a car in the river. We'll have to come up with another plan.'

'Another plan for what?' says Isabella, appearing with the scones. 'Hi, Will. Sorry I wasn't here when you arrived.'

He looks at her plate. 'You were probably otherwise occupied. Were you busy haranguing Abby about not making enough scones for your daily tea break?'

'I never harangue,' she says. 'I may have mentioned our stocks of eclairs are running low, but that's just business.'

She sits down at my table. 'Is this man bothering you, Olivia?'

I catch Will's eye and laugh. 'Yes. He's raising all sorts of objections about where I want to leave my car.'

'Olivia's a visitor,' she tells him through a huge mouthful of scone. 'She can park her car pretty much where she likes.'

'She wants to park it in the river,' says Will.

Isabella picks up another scone. 'I'm sure she has her reasons.'

'Will's the man who rescued me,' I tell her.

'Are you sure? I thought you said the man who brought you here was charming.'

I flush. 'I don't think I said charming. I expect I said helpful.'

'Probably,' she agrees. 'Will isn't charming. He's quite grumpy, really.'

He rolls his eyes. 'I told you I didn't have time to photograph all your cakes this week, that's all.'

'Are you putting the pictures on your website?' I ask Isabella. 'That's a good idea.'

'If that were the case, I might have made time,' says Will. 'But Isabella wanted the pictures for personal use.'

'What sort of personal use?' I say, puzzled.

His lips twitch. 'You know how people photograph their shoe collections or their antique bells? Isabella has decided she wants a photo shoot of all her favourite cakes. Something to look at during the long winter evenings.'

'It's an excellent idea,' says Isabella. 'Far more interesting than that stupid coffee table book you're working on.'

'That coffee table book will pay my bills,' he says. 'I suspect your collection of cakes won't.'

He turns to me. 'To make matters worse, Isabella wanted to pay me in kind.'

'You should consider it,' I say. 'Have you tasted her chicken and leek pies?'

'Well, no, but …'

Isabella gives him a triumphant smile. 'There you go. You're deciding without knowing all the facts. I told you he was judgemental, Olivia.'

'You said grumpy,' he reminds her.

'And pedantic,' she says.

The shop door opens again before he can answer. Isabella lays down her scone. 'I'll be right back.'

She walks over to the counter and starts talking to the customer.

'She's incorrigible,' says Will. 'But she's great fun. And when it comes to food, she leaves strong men collapsed in her wake.'

'She's really nice,' I say, wondering whether he and Isabella are seeing each other. It would explain their easy camaraderie.

He's a lucky man, if so. She's stunning. Add to that her sunny, friendly nature and infectious laugh, and I'd be surprised if half the male population of Honeywell weren't beating down the door of the bakery.

I shoot a surreptitious look at Will. I'm forced to admit Isabella wouldn't be doing too badly if she dated him. He's tall and strongly built, with dark, wavy hair and deep brown, amused eyes. Well, good luck to the pair of them. It's nice to know some relationships work out.

'Have you decided what you'd like to do tonight?' he asks, bringing me back to reality. 'Did you say you had a room booked in Dorchester?'

'That's right, but I don't know how I'm going to get there. Is there a bus or a train I could catch?'

'Possibly, but it's getting late. And you'd have to come all the way back here to collect your car, assuming you still want it. You might be better off cancelling your booking and staying here for a couple of nights.'

I look around me. 'Here?'

He laughs. 'I don't mean the bakery. That's Isabella's dream, not yours. But we could easily find you a place to stay for the night. There's plenty of accommodation in Honeywell. The holiday rush hasn't yet started.'

Isabella reappears. 'If I have to tell Mrs Glennister one more time that we don't sell soap powder! What are you two talking about?'

'Where Olivia is going to stay tonight,' says Will. 'I've suggested she finds somewhere around here until her car is ready.'

'That's a good idea,' she says. 'She can stay with me.'

'Great!' says Will.

'No, I can't!' I exclaim.

Isabella sits down and resumes her cream tea. 'Why not? We have a spare bedroom. You wouldn't be any trouble.'

When she says we, does she mean her and Will? I don't want to be a third wheel.

'My mum's away this week,' she says. 'So, the standard of cooking won't be up to much. I'm more of a baked goods girl myself. But we could order a takeaway.'

'That's ridiculous,' I say. 'I couldn't possibly land myself on you.'

'Why not? You have to sleep somewhere.'

'Don't bully the poor girl,' says Will. 'She probably doesn't want to spend any more time with you than she must, but she's too polite to say so.'

'That's not it at all!' I say.

'Of course, it isn't,' says Isabella. 'Why wouldn't she want to stay with me? Isn't that what you're doing here in the first place, Olivia? Having an adventure?'

'Not really. I was –' I break off, not sure how to describe to her what I'm doing. I'm not even sure how to describe it to myself.

'It's none of our business,' interrupts Will. 'Don't let Isabella bully you into doing anything you don't want to. We can find you somewhere else to stay.'

'I'm not bullying her!' she says indignantly. 'Am I, Olivia?'

Her expression is so much like an excited puppy that I laugh. 'Of course not. It's extremely kind of you. But I'm a complete stranger. I can't impose on you like that.'

'We won't be complete strangers after you've spent the night with my family and seen my sister's collection of gargoyle mugs,' she says. 'They may give you nightmares, but that can't be helped. Is that all?'

'Well, yes.'

She swallows her last mouthful of scone. 'Great! Your phone should be charged by now. You can call the place where you were supposed to be staying tonight and let them know you've had a better offer!'

Chapter Three

It feels strange to be setting off to a complete stranger's house for the night. But it's been a strange day, so I decide to go with it. To be honest, it's been a strange few weeks.

'My car's just over there,' says Isabella. 'I always try to park near the shop, but the customers usually beat me to it. I probably ought to get here before they do.'

'You must be running a popular business if the customers are queuing outside even before you open.'

She grins. 'It's the other way around. I mean, they're waiting for me to arrive and open the shop. I'm not the greatest timekeeper.'

'If that cream tea is a sample of your usual products, they probably don't mind.'

She looks pleased. 'Abby's a great baker, isn't she? She's been with us for just over a year. She came to cover Lily's maternity leave, but she stayed on. I can't imagine how we'd cope without her.'

'Lily is your partner?' I say.

'That's right. We bought the bakery together a few years ago. It's been in the village for ever, but business wasn't good. We wouldn't have been able to afford the bakery if it had been, even with both our families underwriting the loan. We expanded into the shop next door when they closed down, so now we have the cafe too. It was touch and go there for a while. We were drowning in debt, and there was no guarantee we'd be able to make a go of it. But we managed somehow. Business picked up, and now we're doing fine.'

'That's good,' I say. 'A lot of businesses seem to be struggling at the moment.'

'It helps that we're the only bakery for miles around,' she says. 'Honeywell isn't large, but most of the other villages near here are even smaller. So far, none of them has decided to open a bakery. I hope they never do. As it is, people who used to go into Christchurch or Ringwood are coming to us.

'I'm not familiar with the area,' I say. 'I grew up in Bath.'

'What do you do for a living?' she asks. 'Are you a mosaic tiler?'

'Why would you think I was a tiler?'

'My parents used to take me to Bath for the weekend when I was younger,' she says. 'I remember visiting the Roman baths and seeing lots of mosaics.'

'Made by the Romans,' I say.

'Originally,' she agrees. 'But they must have been redone plenty of times since then.'

I dart a look at her and see she's laughing.

'What else did you do in Bath?' I say.

'Oh, the usual. We visited the Abbey, took Jane Austen tours, and had tea at the Sally Lunn tea shop.'

She brightens. 'There's the most incredible fudge kitchen down one of the side streets. My parents always took me there if I didn't make a fuss about yet another tour of the Abbey. Do you know it?'

'I think I know the one you mean. They hand out free samples so you can choose a flavour.'

'That's the one!' she says. 'I used to go in wearing my hair in different styles to see how many samples I could get in one afternoon.'

'Did it work?'

'Amazingly, it didn't. My father had to buy several pounds of fudge to placate them. It was a win-win situation for me.'

'You appear to have a very sweet tooth,' I say, remembering the cream tea.

'I have several very sweet teeth,' she says placidly. 'And a fast metabolism.'

'Lucky you. I wish the fairies who attended my christening had been as thoughtful.'

'You have a great figure,' she says. 'And those fairies gave you that amazing red hair. I always wanted red hair. Proper red, the sort that looks as though your head has caught fire when you're watching a sunset.

'And I always wanted blonde hair like yours,' I say. 'I spent most of my childhood being teased about my hair. However, short of spending an absolute fortune on hair dye, we're stuck with what nature gave us. We'll just have to make the best of it.'

'Until they perfect the art of head transplants,' she agrees. 'Here we are!'

She swings the car up a gravel driveway and pulls up outside an old stone house, hidden from the road by a row of poplars.

'The Lodge,' I read, peering at the sign over the front door.

'That's us.'

She jumps out of the car and picks up my bag. 'I live here with my parents and younger sister. My uncle and his family live up there in the main house.'

She gestures towards a massive building a quarter of a mile away up the hill.

'That looks like Downton Abbey!' I say, awed. 'Does your uncle have butlers and housemaids and chauffeurs and tweenies?'

'I've never noticed any while I've been visiting,' she says. 'But there's a large cellar and several attics, so who knows?'

'Your house looks lovely too,' I say. 'I wouldn't really want to live in a mansion. I like cosy houses.'

'They only live in one wing,' she says. 'They rent the rest of it out for conferences and as holiday lets.'

'Does it have a ghost?'

'Several,' she says, and I can't tell whether she's joking.

She opens the front door and ushers me inside. 'Welcome! I'll see whether anyone's home.'

She drops my bag in the hall and disappears. She returns a minute later. 'No one seems to be around.'

I feel a momentary qualm at the thought of being alone in the house with a complete stranger. For all I know, the house may not even belong to her. She may have broken in, disposed of the occupants, stolen their keys, and set up house here.

The front door opens, and I spin around, half expecting to see a police officer. But it's a young woman. She's several years younger than Isabella, but it doesn't take a genius to realise this must be her sister. They're incredibly similar, right down to the blonde curls and vivid blue eyes.

'Hi, Issy,' she says casually. 'Is dinner ready?'

'Not unless you've made it,' says Isabella. 'Georgia, this is my friend Olivia. Olivia, this is my sister, Georgia.'

Georgia lifts a hand in greeting. 'Hi, nice to meet you.'

She turns back to Isabella. 'I'm going out in half an hour. Is there anything to eat?'

'The kitchen's that way,' says Isabella, pointing.

Georgia sighs and disappears. We hear the crashing of pots and pans, followed by a muffled exclamation.

She reappears a few minutes later. 'I ate that pie in the fridge. I hope you weren't saving it for anything. I couldn't find anything else, and I was starving.'

'Where are you going?' says Isabella.

'Matthew's taking me for dinner at the Wild Horse. I'd better get a move on. The table's booked for seven.'

'Did you miss lunch?' I say sympathetically.

Georgia gives me an odd look. 'No.' She disappears upstairs.

Isabella doesn't appear to find anything unusual in this exchange. 'I'll show you to your room. Then we can think about dinner. I was going to have that pie, but Georgia has beaten me to it. I don't think there's much else in the house. I meant to go to the supermarket at lunchtime, but our supplier was late, and Abby couldn't wait in for them.'

'We could order a takeaway,' I say. 'I'm paying.'

'I was going to suggest we went to the Red Lion,' she says. 'That way, you can meet some of the locals and get to know them.'

'That would be nice. But I'm just passing through. I'll never see any of them again.'

'Maybe,' she says. 'I need a shower. Shall we leave in about half an hour?'

She shows me to the guest bedroom. I sit on the bed and stare out of the window, thinking about the strange turn my day has taken.

I set off this morning in a functioning car, heading for Dorchester, determined not to think about the past few days. I've ended the day with no car at all, sitting in a strange bedroom, in the house of a complete stranger. And now I'm about to go to the pub to meet the local inhabitants of a village of which I'd never heard until today.

I take a deep breath, trying to clear my mind. I can't allow myself to think about everything that's led me to this point. I came here to escape, to find some peace and quiet. The last thing I need is to get caught up in someone else's drama.

A knock on the door brings me back to reality. Isabella pokes her head around. 'Do you have everything you need?'

'I have, thanks. It's a lovely room. You must let me pay for it.'

'You can buy me a drink and call it even,' she says. 'Are you ready?'

I pick up my bag. 'As I'll ever be. I'm not particularly hungry, but I'm happy to watch you eat.'

'Wait until you've smelled Shelley's game pie,' she says. 'I guarantee you'll be ravenous.'

Chapter Four

The Red Lion is full when we arrive. No one seems to notice I'm here, which suits me fine. I'm only passing through, and I have no desire to learn the names of people I'll never see again. All I want is a quiet dinner and a chance to relax before diving into the comfortable bed in Isabella's spare room.

'I'll get us a couple of menus,' she says. 'You find us a table. There's one over there by the window. Or would you rather eat outside? They have a lovely garden.'

'Good idea,' I say. 'It will be quieter.'

'Don't count on it. Half the dog population of Honeywell is out there at the first hint of a warm evening. Do you mind dogs?'

'I love them. I'll see you out there.'

Isabella's prediction is slightly exaggerated. Most of the outside tables are occupied, but I only count three dogs – an elderly golden retriever who's trying and failing to catch a butterfly, a Jack Russell eating chips off the grass, and a chihuahua scrambling up its owner's leg.

I sit at the last empty table and look around me. The garden is enormous. The part nearest to the building is fenced in, but there's a gate in the fence, beyond which half an acre of rough grass leads down to what I assume is a small river. I can't see the water, but something about the row of willow trees suggests they're growing there for a reason.

Isabella appears and dumps the menus onto the table. 'I don't really need one. I already know what I'm having.'

'The game pie?' I say.

'I wasn't joking when I said it's the best I've ever tasted. Why don't you try it?'

'I had pie for lunch,' I remind her. 'One of the nicest I've ever eaten.'

'But that was lunch,' she says. 'It's half a lifetime ago. Why can't you have pie for dinner too? Is there some new law I haven't heard about?'

'Not exactly a law. But I've heard the Royal family ostracises anyone who dares to consume pastry more than once a day.'

'I don't dare ask what they have to say about cake,' she says.

'Never more than once a week.' I laugh at her horrified expression.

'I considered marrying Prince William when I was younger,' she says. 'I realise now I had a lucky escape.'

She picks up the menus and heads back towards the pub.

'You forgot my card!' I call after her. 'I'm paying for this.'

She waves her hand. 'You can get the next one.'

She disappears before I can protest. I'll have to make a bank transfer or something. There won't be any 'next one'. With any luck, my car will be fixed by tomorrow morning, and I'll be able to resume my journey.

The whole point of my trip is to keep moving and avoid having to think about what's happened, or what my future might hold. Stopping in Honeywell wasn't part of the plan. That isn't too important. I'd have had to stop somewhere tonight, and this seems as good a place as any. But I have no intention of making a prolonged visit. I plan to be away from London for at least a week and to stay in a different place each night. Constant change is the best remedy I know for keeping the mind off difficult subjects. But I'm here for tonight. I may as well make the best of it and treat it as an adventure.

Isabella reappears. 'That was a close call. Matt told me there were only two servings of game pie left. I don't know what we'd have done otherwise.'

'Ordered something else?' I suggest.

She gives me a horrified look. 'I'll let that pass because you're a newcomer. You won't speak so lightly about such things once you've been here for a while.'

'I'm sure I wouldn't. But I'm not a newcomer. I'm a sojourner.'

'A what?'

'A traveller,' I elaborate. 'An out-of-towner, a passer through.'

'I know what it means,' she says. 'I may not be royalty, but I have an excellent vocabulary. However, I'm not sure it applies to you.'

'I'm pretty sure it does. I may have taken a slight detour, but it's only for one night. I'll be on my way tomorrow.'

'But why?' she says. 'Don't you like Honeywell?'

'What I've seen of it looks lovely.'

'It *is* lovely,' she says. 'I often feel sorry for all the people in the world who don't get to live here.'

'That's an awful lot of people to feel sorry for. What's the population of Honeywell?'

'About two thousand,' she says.

'Which makes nearly eight billion people who don't live in Honeywell.'

'Minus two thousand,' she reminds me. 'It *is* an awful lot of people to feel sorry for. Is it any wonder I feel exhausted at the end of each day?'

'I've been living in London for the past eight years,' I say.

'Poor you.'

'I don't see why,' I say. 'I quite like it.'

She gives me a keen look. 'Why do I think that isn't quite true?'

'Because you seem to be some sort of paid brand ambassador for Honeywell?'

'They don't pay me,' she says. 'But wouldn't it be great if they did? I could lie in bed all morning. I *hate* getting up early. After a light lunch, I'd wander around the village for an hour, telling everyone I met what an incredible place Honeywell is. After which, I'd collect my cheque and use it to pay for a cream tea.'

'I thought you owned the Sugarloaf,' I say. 'You don't have to pay for what you eat.'

'But I wouldn't own it if I took on this new job. I couldn't do both jobs justice. I'd have to sell my share of the bakery. Either Lily would buy me out, or I'd have to sell it to some awful London type, who would treat it as a weekend bakery.'

She catches my eye. 'Someone like you, in fact! The locals are always complaining about the horrible Londoners who buy second homes in the village and drive up house prices until no one can afford them.'

'They sound awful,' I say. 'I'd better not to spend any more time here. If anyone hears I come from London, they'll be after me with pitchforks.'

'That depends,' she says. 'Do you own a mansion in Mayfair?'

'Not even a house on Park Lane,' I say. 'We've … I've been renting a flat in Putney.'

Our food arrives before she can comment. Her eyes light up when she sees our plates. 'Take a bite of that and tell me you aren't hungry.'

I dig into the pie, which emits a cloud of fragrant steam. I'm suddenly ravenous. Maybe it's something in the air of this place. Isabella seems to be perpetually hungry.

I take a bite. 'You're right. This is the most delicious pie I've ever tasted. Including the one you gave me this afternoon!'

'I told you so,' she says, pleased. 'I'm not even insulted by the comparison.'

'That's good because, compared to this one, your pie is barely a prototype pie.'

'Hey!' she says.

'It's true,' I say through another mouthful. 'If all the pies in the world were arranged next to each other, yours wouldn't even be on the same continent as this one. The only use people would have for your pies would be as doorstops or weapons in some pie-related combat.'

'Hey!' she says again. 'I made that pie. I helped to make it, at any rate.'

'You told me Abby made it,' I say.

'Technically, that's true. But I was in the kitchen while she was making it. At least, I was for part of the time.'

'That's very impressive,' I say, selecting a chip and dipping it into the gravy. 'It sounds as though you're some sort of patron saint of baked goods.'

'That's an excellent way of putting it,' she says. 'It isn't often I meet someone who gets me like you do.'

'All the more reason for you to stay on as manager of the bakery. Think what a loss it would be to the village if you took up this tourism job.'

She finishes her pie. 'You really do get me! Anyway, I can't consider other employment at the moment. I'm not sure when Lily will be back, so Abby and I will have our hands full for the foreseeable future. I can't leave her in the lurch.'

'I'm sorry to hear Lily's child is ill,' I say. 'How old is she?'

'Almost a year. Her birthday is on June 4th. I'm her godmother, so it's my job to keep tabs on all that sort of information.'

'Don't her parents do that?' I say.

'I have no idea. Lily may have it scribbled down somewhere, but I wouldn't trust Jack to remember anything more important than dinner time. It doesn't matter. That's what I'm here for.'

'What kind of godmother are you?' I say. 'Are you like the ones who turned up at Sleeping Beauty's christening and gave her those gifts of grace and beauty and whatever? Or are you more like the one who sulked because she wasn't invited and came up with all that ridiculous nonsense about a spindle?'

'I'm not like any of them,' she says. 'It would have been a complete waste to give Daisy gifts like beauty and brains. She's the prettiest baby I've ever seen. She's super intelligent too. She knows her godmother already. She calls me Whizzy.'

'It suits you,' I say. 'You don't seem to sit down much.'

'Except for meals,' she agrees. 'She also knows I'm the person who always has cake in their bag. She makes a beeline for it as soon as I walk in the door. She can crawl even faster than I can.'

'Somehow, it doesn't surprise me that you always have cake somewhere about your person,' I say.

She doesn't look insulted. 'Be prepared for anything, my mother always said. She was talking about men, but it applies to cake too.'

She stretches out a hand. 'Are you going to finish those chips? Do you mind if I do?'

I push my plate towards her. 'Go ahead. But save room for dessert.'

She eats the last few chips and wipes her fingers. 'Always. Shall I get us some dessert menus?'

'I was joking. After that pie, I'm not sure I ever want to eat again.'

She stands and brushes pastry crumbs onto the grass. 'You won't say that when you've tasted their crème brûlée. It's amazing.'

'I'm sure it is,' I say. 'You were right about the pie.'

'And I'm right about this,' she says. Without giving me the chance to protest, she disappears inside the pub.

I lean back and let the evening sun soak into me. This is one of the most peaceful places I've ever visited. It isn't only the lack of traffic and hordes of commuters rushing home about this time. It's the village itself. There's something special about it. I can't quite put my finger on what it is. But I'm starting to think Isabella is right to feel sorry for all the people who don't live here.

Chapter Five

Isabella returns a few minutes later carrying two glasses. 'I forgot to mention this pub sells the best local cider I've ever tasted.'

'Is there anything this pub doesn't sell the best of?' I ask, laughing. 'First, there was the game pie, and now the cider.'

'You haven't tasted it yet,' she says, handing me a glass. 'And you haven't tasted their creme brûlée either. I was right about the game pie, wasn't I?'

I take the glass she hands me. 'You were. It was amazing.'

'There you are, then. You have to learn to trust me. Once you've been here for a while, you'll realise I'm an infallible source of information concerning anything edible or drinkable.'

I take a sip of the cider. I don't want to add to Isabella's inflated sense of self-importance, but it's beyond delicious. It's like distilled sunlight. It's as though someone has concentrated the flavour of a hundred different varieties of apples into one glass of sparkling amber liquid.

Isabella is watching me, a gleam in her eye. 'I'm right, aren't I?'

I fling caution to the winds and risk the truth. If her ego explodes, that's nothing to do with me. 'I think I've died and gone to heaven.'

'That's exactly how I felt when I first tasted it!' she says. 'My boyfriend Stephen brought me here, and he said I ought to try it. It was our second date, and I wasn't sure whether to agree to a third one. But this tipped the balance!'

'Does Stephen live locally?' I say, and she laughs.

'He's not my boyfriend now. That was ages ago. About three years, in fact.'

I try to read her expression to see whether this is a painful memory for her. It doesn't appear to be.

'I'm sorry,' I say. There doesn't seem anything else to be said.

'Why?' she says. 'That's all in the past now.'

I take another sip of the cider, wondering whether they sell it in bottles. If they do, I intend to load up the boot of the rental car with as much as it will hold.

'Three years isn't that long,' I say. 'Not after a painful breakup.'

'But this wasn't a painful breakup,' she says. 'We were only together for a few months, and we were completely wrong for each other. It turned out it was Lily he wanted all along, not me.'

'Your partner wanted to be with Lily?'

I don't want to pry, but this sounds as though it could be an interesting story. I can't imagine continuing to work with someone after they'd gone off with my boyfriend.

'That's right,' she says. 'It's how she and I met.'

'Don't tell me. You were busy screaming at her to keep her claws out of your man, and it somehow morphed into a decision to buy a bakery together?'

She finishes her cider. 'Not even close! Stephen and Lily used to date, then he broke up with her. He met me the following year, and we got together, but he decided it had been a mistake to let her go.'

'So, she's with him now?'

She waves an airy hand. 'Oh, no. She's with Jack now, and they have baby Daisy.'

I decide not to pursue this any further. Isabella isn't the most coherent storyteller. A server comes out of the pub, carrying two plates.

Isabella waves. 'Over here, Dave!'

He puts the plates in front of us. Isabella looks delighted. 'Extra-large ramekins, I see.'

'Matt told me who'd ordered them,' he says.

She doesn't look abashed. 'Olivia, this is Dave. He's in charge of …'

'Portion control?' I suggest, and he grins.

Isabella ignores me. 'Dave, this is my new friend Olivia. She's moving to Honeywell, so we need to make her welcome.'

Dave shakes my hand. 'Nice to meet you, Olivia. And welcome to the village.'

'Nice to meet you too,' I say. 'But I'm not moving here. I'm just passing through.'

He gives Isabella a confused look. She picks up her spoon. 'Don't worry about Olivia. She's a little behind the curve, but she'll catch up. See you later, Dave.'

'Try this crème brûlée,' she tells me. 'I'm about to go three for three.'

I don't move. 'Why did you tell him I was moving to the village?'

'Daisy's cold has turned into bronchitis,' she says. 'Lily's had to take her to the hospital. She won't be back in the bakery for a week or two. We'll need an extra pair of hands at the Sugarloaf.'

'But what does that have to do with me?'

She looks exasperated. 'Isn't it obvious?'

'Not to me.'

'Eat your pudding!' she says, sounding like my mother when I was a child and refusing to try a new vegetable. 'It can't be a coincidence that you arrived in the village on the very day we heard Lily would be out for a while.'

'Of course, it can. Coincidences happen all the time.'

'Not this one,' she says stubbornly. 'I knew as soon as I saw you that you were going to be around for a while.'

'I'm sorry to disappoint you, but in this case, your intuition has failed you. I'm carrying on to Dorchester tomorrow. I may come back through Honeywell on my way home. If this crème brûlée is as delicious as it looks, I'll make a point of it. But that's all. You can get a temporary staff member from an agency. You must have had to use one before.'

'I could find hundreds of people,' she says. 'But that isn't the point. I've found you.'

'Technically speaking, I found you,' I say. 'Even more technically speaking, Will found me and brought me here. And he didn't mention there were any conditions attached. He didn't say, "I'll rescue you, but only if you guarantee to spend at least a week in Honeywell." I'd have refused to come with him if he had.'

'You'd still be sitting there,' she says. 'There isn't much traffic along that lane.'

'I wouldn't still be sitting there. I'd have been bound to have been rescued by now. Some handsome farmer would have come along and seen my plight.'

'That would be Mr Marshall,' she says. 'He's in his seventies, and I wouldn't call him handsome. Not unless you have a thing for bloodshot eyes and a threatening manner. Maybe you do. People have different tastes. Far be it from me to judge.'

'It wouldn't have been Mr Marshall,' I say. 'It would have been his handsome young assistant. I'd have helped him to deliver a calf. He'd have been so grateful that he'd have given me a lift to Dorchester.'

'It's mostly sheep in these parts,' she says. 'And they aren't much use to stray travellers. If you have visions of them being trained to rescue passers-by with little kegs of brandy tied around their necks, you can forget it. Sheep are practically untrainable. I ought to know. My uncle has an enormous flock of them, and he ropes me in to help at lambing time. Delivering a lamb in the middle of a field on a freezing February night isn't actually as much fun as you might imagine.'

'But this is May,' I say. 'I wouldn't mind helping to deliver a calf. I've done it before.'

She looks interested. 'Have you, indeed? Was that in pursuit of another handsome young assistant farmer?'

'Not exactly. I'm a veterinary nurse. I was attached to a rural practice during part of my training. I helped out occasionally on the farms.'

'I'm impressed,' she says. 'Is that what you do in London?'

'It's what I've been doing for the past few years.' I haven't decided how much detail to give her about my life. Not too much. I'm only passing through.

'Does that mean you're no longer doing it?' she says.

'You don't have to tell me if you don't want to,' she adds, noticing my expression. 'Lily is always telling me not to be so nosy. I just wondered, that's all.'

I almost take the lifeline she's handed me and change the subject. I'm not sure why I don't. Maybe it's the cider, or maybe it's the strange day I've had. I feel a sudden urge to confide in someone. And who better than a complete stranger, a person I'm never going to see again?

'I resigned last week,' I say.

'Do you have another job to go to?'

'Not yet. I was going to look for work after this trip.'

Her eyes gleam. 'So, you aren't currently employed, and you don't have a new job lined up?'

'There's a vast difference between a veterinary nurse and a baker,' I say.

'A bakery assistant,' she corrects me. 'Abby does the actual baking. We're looking for someone to help in the shop and the cafe. You could do that on your head.'

'That would be a little unorthodox.'

'Then you can do it the right way up. Come on, Olivia. What's stopping you?'

'I have to get back to London,' I say.

'Why is that?'

'Because my life is there. Because you can't up sticks and move whenever the fancy takes you. It isn't what adults do.'

'Plenty of adults do that,' she says. 'My mother was born in Scotland. When she met my father, she upped sticks without a second thought and moved to Little Compton.'

I allow a hint of exasperation to creep into my voice. 'That's different. She had a good reason.'

'And you don't?'

'No, I don't.'

She finishes her pie. 'Working at the Sugarloaf Bakery is a good reason in itself. You're new to the area. You'll learn. But you haven't mentioned any other reason you shouldn't stay here for a while. Are you married?'

'I'm not married, but I've been living with someone for the past five years.'

She arches an eyebrow. 'Again, the use of the past tense. Do I infer you're no longer living with him, or her?'

'I left Charlie a week ago.'

'It's always nice to be the one who does the leaving,' she comments.

'It's nicer to be in the position where you don't want to leave.'

'True,' she says. 'Would you like to talk about it?'

'Not really. But it's the reason I'm taking this trip. I wanted to give him time to cool down in case he was angry.'

'Is he likely to be angry?'

'Who knows? Probably. He's not too keen on other people making decisions.'

'What about your accommodation?' she says. 'Do you have somewhere to go back to?'

'It was Charlie's flat. He bought it before we met, so it's entirely in his name.'

'Better and better,' she says. 'You don't have anywhere to live, you don't have a job, and you're already in the area. What's to stop you adding some extra time to your trip to help out an old friend?'

'You aren't an old friend,' I say without thinking. 'I'm sorry, Isabella. That came out wrong.'

She tries to look affronted but spoils the effect by grinning. 'You can be very harsh at times. Despite that, the job offer is still open.'

I look past her at the meadow leading down to the river. She's being ridiculous. This place is lovely, but it's the sort of place you come to for a holiday, not to stay permanently. It's different if you were born here, as she was.

'I can't,' I say. 'And I'm too tired to argue about it anymore. It's been a long day, and I really need some sleep. Can we get the bill and go?'

'I've already paid for the meal,' she says. 'I'd have done so even if I didn't know you'd be staying here. But I won't bother you anymore.'

She looks at my plate. 'You haven't even tried your crème brûlée. That's a serious mistake. Taste it, at least. If you don't like it, I'll finish it for you.'

'Fine.' I plunge my spoon into the brûlée and lift it to my mouth.

She stops me before I can taste it. 'I said I wouldn't try to persuade you any longer, and I won't. But just remember I was right about the game pie, and I was right about the cider. Two seconds from now, you're going to realise I was right about this too. We don't have to talk right now about you working at the Sugarloaf. But I'm telling you it's a great idea for both of us. Think about it. Remind yourself this strange woman has been right about three things within the space of an hour, so the odds of her being right about a fourth thing are pretty good.'

'Strange woman is right,' I say.

'And you'll think about the other thing?'

'I'll think about it. That's the best I can offer. But don't get your hopes up. It's a ridiculous idea, and I can't see myself changing my mind.'

'That's a deal,' she says. 'Now, get a move on with your dessert. The pub will be closing soon, and I forgot to bring a doggy bag.'

Chapter Six

I sleep surprisingly well. I don't usually enjoy staying in strange places, but no sooner does my head hit the pillow than I'm fast asleep. I don't stir until there's a light tap at the door, and Isabella peeps around it.

'I hate to disturb you, but I'm leaving for work in twenty minutes. I didn't want you to wake up and find yourself all alone in a strange house.'

Does she know I almost cut and ran when I arrived here yesterday? She'd probably find it amusing. She seems to find most things amusing.

'I'm sorry I slept so late,' I say with a yawn.

'It's the country air,' she says. 'It has that effect on me too. I can never get up in the mornings.'

'Aren't you used to the air by now?' I ask, swinging my legs out of bed.

'You'd think! But it doesn't seem to have worn off yet. What would you like for breakfast?'

'Don't worry about that. I rarely eat it.'

Her eyes widen in horror. 'How can you rarely eat breakfast? It's the most important meal of the day!'

'Says who?'

'Everyone! My mother, for one. She told me never to trust a man who doesn't eat breakfast.'

'Is that her criterion for selecting a man?' I say.

'Oh, no! She has a very long list. She made me learn it by heart before she let me date anyone. I'll tell you about it some other time.'

'I'm sure I'll find it very useful,' I say. 'In the meantime, would you mind if I took a quick shower? I was too tired when we got home last night. After that, I'll get out of your hair.'

'Aren't you coming to the bakery with me this morning?'

'A ride into the village would be very welcome,' I say. 'Maybe you can point me in the direction of the garage. Hopefully, the mechanic will have my car ready to go.'

'The mechanic rang about half an hour ago,' she says. 'He says the big end has gone in the engine, and he'll have to order another one, which could take days. He told me to ask whether you'd like him to do that or tell the rental company to send over a truck and tow it?'

I sigh in frustration. 'They promised me it was in great repair and had recently been serviced.'

'Maybe you're a terrible driver,' she says.

'I'm not. I don't drive too often in London, but I passed my test over ten years ago, and I've never had so much as a speeding ticket.'

'Would you like some of mine?' she says. 'My father says if I get any more, he'll remove me from his insurance.'

'Why are you on your father's insurance?'

'It has something to do with the farm,' she says vaguely. 'I do the books for them. As I told you yesterday, I also deliver the odd lamb. Apparently, that makes it ok for my car to be registered as a business vehicle.'

'I'll pass on your very kind offer of sharing your tickets with me. I only have last month's pay cheque to see me through until I find another job. I can't afford to waste any of it. I shouldn't have taken this trip, but …'

'Of course, you should.' She gives me an encouraging smile. 'And don't forget you've already found another job. It's ready and waiting for you. You only have to say the word.'

I feel my resistance beginning to crumble. 'This is ridiculous. You only met me yesterday. I could be anyone at all. I could be a murderer on the run from justice.'

She looks interested. 'Are you?'

'Not to date, but I like to keep my options open.'

'That's wise,' she says. 'I'm pretty sure murderers are one of the things on my mother's list. In the meantime, while you're waiting to decide whether or not you are, why not come and work with me?'

'I don't have anywhere to stay.'

'You can stay with me until you find somewhere better. This village is absolutely crawling with places to stay. You can't go ten yards down the street without tripping over a bed-and-breakfast or an Airbnb.'

'I haven't brought enough for a long stay,' I protest.

'Did you leave everything at that man's flat?'

'I packed up my clothes and a few belongings. I didn't dare take anything we bought together. Charlie would have gone mad if he'd come home to find things missing. He'd probably have called the police.'

'Didn't you discuss how you were going to divide everything up?' she says.

'We didn't discuss anything. I didn't tell him I was leaving.'

She looks amused. 'It didn't occur to you to mention it in passing?'

'It wasn't like that. It's difficult to explain. Either he'd have been angry, or he'd have talked me out of it.'

'It sounds as though you did the right thing,' she says. 'Did you leave a note?'

'I did. It felt too impersonal to break up by text.'

'Please tell me you pinned it to his pillow,' she begs. 'That's what everyone does in movies. Or they leave an envelope on the dressing table. I've always wanted to do that, but my handwriting is atrocious.'

'Why does that matter?' I say.

'Oh, you know! The heroine writes the man's name on the outside of the envelope in a beautiful flowing script. If I tried that, the man wouldn't know who it was for. He'd find an envelope on his pillow, and he'd have no idea it was intended for him. It would be terribly anticlimactic.'

'I'm pretty sure Charlie would have known the note was for him,' I say, laughing.

'What did it say?'

'Just that things weren't working out, and I'd decided to leave.'

'Short, sweet, and to the point,' she says. 'I approve. After all, what is there to say when you break up with someone? You're telling them you don't want to be with them anymore. There's no real way to sugar coat that. Unless you go down the route of saying it's not you, it's me. And I don't expect it was you.'

'I should have left years ago,' I say. 'I don't know why I didn't. Anyway, all I have with me now is a suitcase of clothes and a few pairs of shoes.'

'What else do you need?' she says. 'I know you brought a toothbrush because I offered to find you one last night and you refused.'

'Maybe I only brush my teeth once a week,' I say.

'No, you don't. You wouldn't have such nice teeth if that was the case. And I wouldn't have offered you the job. I'm extremely hot on dental hygiene for my employees. It's one of the first questions I ask at interview.'

'Really?'

'Not really,' she says. 'I'm also sure you packed deodorant and shampoo. Your hair is clean and shiny, and you smell fine.'

'Is there anything else about my personal appearance you'd like to comment on?' I say. 'Don't be shy. It appears to be *Say what you think* day.'

She looks remorseful. 'I'm sorry, Olivia. I'm afraid that every day is *Say what you think day* for me. I didn't mean to be rude.'

'You weren't,' I assure her. 'On the contrary, you've told me my hair isn't greasy, my teeth don't have bits between them, and I don't smell. That's all very complimentary. I'll be sure to include it in my resume when I apply for my next job.'

'The job after this one,' she corrects me. 'You can look around for vacancies while you're working at the Sugarloaf. I'll even let you leave early for interviews. You can't say fairer than that.'

She looks like an eager terrier waiting for me to tell her where I've hidden its bone.

'I still think it's a ridiculous idea,' I say.

She claps her hands together. 'So, you'll do it?'

I cast around for reasons to say no – unarguable, incontrovertible reasons to which even Isabella must give way. But I can't come up with any. When I left London two days ago, all I could think about was getting away and leaving the past behind me. I didn't want to face dealing with the fallout with Charlie. All I knew was that I wanted a break. I *needed* a break.

So, I jumped on a train and set off. Somehow, without quite knowing how, I ended up here and met Isabella, and she offered me a job. Only a temporary job, but that's fine. I don't want to work in a bakery for the rest of my life. I need to decide what to do next.

But I'm exhausted. Leaving Charlie has taken every ounce of energy I possess, and I'm drained. The idea of returning to London and finding a job and accommodation makes me want to lie down and go to sleep. It will have to be done, but I can't bear to think about it. And the opportunity not to think about it for a while is being handed to me on a plate.

Isabella is offering me the prospect of a few weeks' respite, the chance to consider what I want from my future without having to deal with anyone else's opinions. Why am I resisting it? It's time I made my own decisions and my own mistakes.

The worst that can happen is that Lily comes back to work, and she and Isabella tell me they don't need me anymore. In which case, I can return to London and resume my life there.

I'm not sure what's the best that can happen. It's been so long since I've thought about my future with any optimism. But that won't always be the case. When I left Charlie, it was because I knew it was time to make a change. If I didn't do it now, I knew I never would. This isn't the change I expected to make, but who cares? It's a change, and everyone says a change is as good as a rest. I'm sure that's somewhere on Isabella's mother's list of life lessons.

Isabella is looking at me with a hopeful expression.

Why not?' I say. 'You seem to need some help, and I don't appear to have anything to do for the next few weeks. It's Kismet!'

'You may mock,' she says, 'but I believe in Kismet.'

'You realise it isn't a fancy French pastry?'

'I'm aware,' she says. 'Seriously, Olivia, this is great. I hate taking on temps. It takes longer to explain stuff to them than to do it myself.'

'You have no idea how slow I am to pick things up,' I warn her.

'You'll be fine. You have all the qualifications. You laugh at my jokes, you like my pies, and you brush your teeth. We're going to get along well. Get dressed as quickly as you can, and we'll go to the bakery and get you fitted for a Sugarloaf overall.'

Chapter Seven

Isabella's induction course is short and concise. It doesn't take me long to pick up the essentials. I've used one of these tills before, which she's delighted about.

'I hate having to teach people how to use it,' she says. 'I'm fine with the basics, but I always forget what I'm supposed to do for a refund.'

'Do you have to issue many refunds?'

'The occasional one. You wouldn't believe how fussy some customers can be. The crust is too brown, or too pale, or they told Albert to ask for thin slices, and the ones he brought home don't fit in the toaster, even if you push them hard. I used to argue, but I gave up. It's easier to smile and give them a refund.'

She shows me how to use the coffee machine, which is rather more complicated. She promises to give me a longer lesson this evening. In the meantime, we both agree it would be better not to unleash me onto unsuspecting customers.

'You'll be fine after some more training,' she says. 'I confidently expect you to win employee of the month before you've been with us for a year.'

'I need to win it long before that,' I say. 'I'm here until Lily returns, and then I must move on. I have my entire life to sort out.'

'Of course, you do,' she says reassuringly. 'Daisy won't be in the hospital for long. At least, I hope she won't. I'm going to visit her tonight.'

'In your capacity as godmother?'

'Absolutely!' she says. 'It's one of a godmother's first duties to sneak chocolate buttons into her goddaughter's hospital room.'

'Won't Lily mind?'

'Not if I take her a packet too.'

I give a snort of laughter. 'That's not what I meant.'

The door opens, and Isabella nudges me. 'Your first customer. Remember what I told you – shoulders back, chin up, look them in the eye, and make sure you know how thick they like their slices *before* you switch on the machine.'

I'm about to greet the customer with the mantra Isabella has taught me: 'Welcome to the Sugarloaf bakery. How may I help you?' when I realise it's Will.

'Oh, hi!' I say.

Isabella clears her throat loudly.

'Welcome to the Sugarloaf bakery. How may I help you?' I add.

Will's eyes open in surprise. 'She has you working here?'

I give him a dejected smile. 'I'm afraid so. When she found I couldn't pay for my night's accommodation, she insisted I work it out in indentured labour.'

He grins. 'Seriously, what's going on?'

'I'm thinking of retiring soon,' says Isabella. 'I'm anxious to leave my half of the bakery to someone worthy of the honour. I've tried out several candidates, but terrible things have happened to them. One of them fell into the dough mixer, another ate too many eclairs and exploded, the third one –'

'I get the picture!' he interrupts. 'I suppose Olivia found the final golden ticket in her strawberry tart?'

She looks delighted. 'I love it when people get my literary references.'

'It was very obscure,' he says. 'Luckily for you, I'm extremely well read.'

He turns to me. 'You're my last hope for a sensible explanation. Why are you standing behind the counter, wearing a Sugarloaf overall?'

'I'm sorry about my co-worker,' I say. 'It was a perfectly reasonable question, and I don't know why she was being so evasive. The real answer is that I'm taking part in Secret Millionaire.'

He rolls his eyes. 'Is there any point in me asking for a coffee, or will I get gravy instead?'

'You'll have to ask Isabella,' I say. 'Apparently, I'm not fit to be let loose on the population of Honeywell without extensive further training.'

'I'll bring it over,' says Isabella. 'I'll throw in a cookie for free as an apology.'

'That's very kind of you,' says Will. 'I accept.'

She opens the sliding door behind the counter and picks up a cookie. 'Don't get too excited. They're out of date. I was about to throw them away.'

'By which you mean put them in your bag to take home?' he says.

She hands him the plate. 'Whatever! You say potato …'

'The mechanic says he can't fix my car today,' I tell Will.

He looks surprised. 'Are you sure? He'd just given it a test drive when I walked past the garage a minute ago.'

'Quite sure,' I say. 'That must have been a different car. He called Isabella this morning and told her he needed to order in a part, which could take a while.'

'It wasn't a different car,' he says. 'It was the one you were driving yesterday. The same number plate and everything.'

I glance over at Isabella, who's turned pink. 'Are you sure you got the message right?

She shrugs. 'Who can say? He said something about cars and parts and fixing problems. I'm not technical. I never pretended to be.'

'Did you tell me he couldn't fix my car so I'd agree to stay longer?' I ask sternly.

She gives me an inscrutable look. 'Or did he make his message confusing because the universe wanted you to remain in Honeywell?'

'I'm betting on the first one,' says Will. 'What do you think, Olivia?'

I ought to be angry, but somehow, I'm not. If anything, I'm grateful to Isabella for buying me enough time to make this decision.

'I'm inclined to go with the second one,' I say.

He smiles. 'So, she's persuaded you to stay with us for a while?'

'Just for a week or two,' says Isabella. 'While Daisy isn't well.'

'That's great,' he says. 'It will be nice having you around. And there are worse places than Honeywell to take an unscheduled hiatus.'

I like that description. I'm not taking an enforced time-out. I'm enjoying an unscheduled hiatus.

'It's time for your break, Olivia,' says Isabella. 'Why don't you sit and chat with Will while I get you a coffee?'

'It's only ten o'clock. Have I been working for long enough to take a break?'

'Of course, you have!' she says. 'I don't want you resigning on your first day due to overwork. I'll make you a latte. I've been trying to do those pictures on the foam. I'm getting much better at them. What would you like?'

'What can you do?'

She considers. 'I can do footballs, netballs, and ping-pong balls. The other day, I managed a very nice balloon.'

'I'm not terribly sporty,' I say. 'Unless you count ice-skating. I love that.'

She frowns. 'I can't do an ice skate, if that's what you're after. I'll tell you what. I'll do you an ice hockey puck.'

'I'm sensing a common theme here,' says Will. 'Are we to understand you've mastered the art of making circles on the foam?'

'That's right,' she says. 'I'm hoping to expand my repertoire to squares soon, but I don't want to run before I can walk.'

She brings me my latte, and Will and I dutifully admire my ice hockey puck. I wouldn't have guessed what it was if Isabella hadn't told me. But it doesn't matter. The latte is excellent.

'You didn't have breakfast!' she exclaims suddenly. 'I'd completely forgotten that in all the hurly-burly of giving you my intensive training course. You must be passing out, Olivia. What can I get you? Will, stand ready to catch her if she faints.'

'He's done enough rescuing of damsels in distress for one week,' I say. 'I'm fine. I rarely eat until lunchtime.'

She shudders. 'Is that a London custom? No wonder I've never wanted to live there. It sounds horrific.'

She makes a dive for the counter and emerges with a cookie on a plate, which she hands to me. I break it in half and hand her a piece. 'I appreciate the thought. I'm not really hungry, but this looks good. Why don't we split it?'

'Isabella doesn't usually share her cakes,' says Will. 'You're a beneficial influence on her already.'

'I'm not sharing,' she says with her mouth full. 'Olivia is. It's a very different thing.'

'Shall I let the mechanic know you're staying in the village and no longer want the car?' he asks me. 'He can arrange for it to be picked up, and you can call and sort out a refund.'

'Thank you. Is everyone in the countryside so helpful and community spirited?'

'He isn't from the countryside,' says Isabella. 'He comes from London, like you.'

'Which part?' Will asks me.

'You can talk about all that later,' says Isabella. 'In the meantime, Olivia's break is over. Can I get you anything else, Will?'

He shakes his head. 'I should get going. I'm driving to Mitcham this morning to take some pictures of the church. The light should be just right. I'll see you both later.'

He gives us a friendly wave and disappears.

'I'm sorry about that,' says Isabella. 'I shouldn't have mentioned you came from London. It isn't anyone else's business.'

'I'd prefer not to talk about my life there,' I say.

'I know,' she says contritely. 'But I'd already mentioned it before I realised. That's why I said your break was over. It isn't really. You have ten more minutes.'

'I don't need ten more minutes,' I protest. 'It's your turn for a break. I can watch the till.'

'If you're sure,' she says. 'I wouldn't mind a coffee. I only had a small one before we left this morning.'

She switches on the coffee machine again. 'Your hockey puck came out so well that I'm going to be daring and attempt a rugby ball.'

Chapter Eight

Isabella hands me a piece of paper the following afternoon.

'I dropped in at the estate agents on my way back from lunch,' she says. 'They have two properties they're trying to rent out at the moment. The only problem is that you'd have to sign a six-month lease.'

'I'm not doing that,' I say. 'Lily may be back at work next week, and where would that leave me?'

'Living in Honeywell,' she says. 'I don't need to remind you it's the best place in the world to live.'

'So you keep saying. But living here with a job is one thing. Living here without one is quite another. It isn't the cheapest of areas.'

'You can stay with me for as long as you like,' she says. 'I don't know when my mum's coming home, and Georgia is almost never there. I'd enjoy the company.'

'Your dad is there,' I remind her. 'At least, you've told me he is. I haven't seen any evidence of it so far. For all I know, he's a figment of your overactive imagination.'

'He is not!' she says indignantly. 'He came in late last night and left early this morning. It's always a busy period on the farm at this time of year. They're muck-spreading this week.'

'Lovely for them,' I say. 'Don't you want to join in?'

'I used to when I worked for them full time. It was more fun than being stuck in the office doing the accounts. But I've stopped doing that sort of thing since we bought the bakery. The customers don't appreciate being served by someone smelling of manure.'

'Even accepting your father exists,' I say, turning the conversation back to the original subject, 'he won't want some complete stranger camping out in his house for weeks. I need to find myself something a little more permanent.'

'There's always Tom and Diane's place,' she says.

'Who are they?'

'They keep a bed-and-breakfast up by the crossroads. It's usually full in the school holidays, but not so much during term time. I expect they'd give you a reasonable rate if you booked a room for a few weeks. And you don't eat breakfast, which means it would be even cheaper! You'd like it there. It's a little run down, but the garden is lovely.'

I resolve to see for myself how run down this place is before committing myself to anything permanent. Isabella seems the sort who would be up for any adventure. But I want to make sure I won't be expected to sleep on bales of straw or use a hand pump to wash each morning.

Still, if it's clean, and I can afford it, it would be nice to find a place of my own. Isabella is lovely, and the bed she's given me is the most comfortable I've ever slept on. But it feels increasingly surreal to be staying with a complete stranger in a place I never intended to visit. I've decided to go with the flow and enjoy my time here, but I'd prefer to do it on my own terms.

The shop bell rings, making me jump. I haven't yet got used to the sharp, jangling noise that warns us of a customer. Maybe when I've been here for a while I'll relax and take the whole thing more in my stride. I look up to see Will standing there.

'Hey, how's it going?' I say.

'Aren't you supposed to say, "Welcome to the Sugarloaf? How may I help you?"'

'Only when Isabella is around. Did you want to see her? She's in the kitchen. I can fetch her.'

'I wanted to see you,' he says. 'How's your hunt for accommodation going?'

'It isn't, but I need to sort out something soon. I can't keep living with Isabella's family forever. Even if they don't know I'm there.'

He raises an eyebrow. 'They don't know you're there? Does she sneak you in through the back door when everyone is at dinner and force you to use the servants' staircase?'

'There's a servants' staircase?' I say.

'There's bound to be. Doesn't she live in the Manor House in Little Compton?'

'Her family lives in the Lodge. Her uncle lives in the Manor House.'

'How disappointing,' he says. 'I was hoping for the grand tour. I thought there might be some historical features I could photograph inside the house. Perhaps there are some in the garden.'

'I don't know. I haven't been up there yet. But there's a sundial in Isabella's garden which is missing the metal bit.'

'Isn't that the most important part?' he says.

'That's what I thought, but Isabella says not. She says it's the perfect height for her morning coffee.'

'Less of a sundial and more of a table?' he says.

'I suppose so. She puts her phone on it, set with an alarm to tell her when it's time to leave for work. Do you think that counts as a time-keeping device?'

'Definitely,' he says. 'But I'm not sure I could persuade my editors to give it a double page spread.'

'That's a shame. There's also a gnome with a broken fishing rod, if that's any help?'

He laughs. 'I appreciate the suggestion, but the editors are distressingly narrowminded. They commissioned this book as a record of the historical features of the New Forest. It would take a better man than me to persuade them that modernised sundials and vegan gnomes would make a suitable alternative.'

'You don't know the gnome is vegan,' I say. 'All you know is that he doesn't eat fish. At least, not fish he catches himself. But that's true of most of us. I love fish and chips, but I prefer someone else to do the work.'

'I'll have to take you to the Red Lion one Friday,' he says. 'They make the best fish and chips I've ever tasted.'

'Not you too! Do you and Isabella have shares in the Red Lion? She's always saying they serve the best food for miles around.'

'I expect she took you there for game pie,' he says. 'She seems to eat her body weight in that when she can get it.'

'Not just the game pie. I had to try their crème brûlée too. And their homebrewed cider.'

Isabella appears, her arms full of loaves. 'Is Olivia giving you what you want?'

'Am I what?' I say.

She waves a hand towards the cakes, almost dropping a loaf as she does so. 'Have you found whatever he came in for?'

'I don't know what he came in for,' I say.

'I'd like a couple of Abby's jam doughnuts,' says Will. 'But I really came to find out whether Olivia has found herself somewhere to stay.'

'She's going to check out Diane and Tom's place,' says Isabella.

'Why would she do that?' he says.

'Because I need a place to stay,' I tell him. 'I thought we'd established that.'

'I don't think you'd be very comfortable there. The guestrooms are in the attic, and the roof has been leaking ever since that hailstorm last month.'

Isabella looks dubious. 'It may not be too bad.'

'My parents stayed there last week,' he says. 'I'd have had them at my place, but I'm only renting the one room. Mum said there were three buckets in their bedroom, and she and Dad had to keep moving them because the leaks couldn't decide where they wanted to settle.'

'Maybe they've fixed it by now,' I say.

'No, they haven't,' he says. 'The insurance company told them there were so many broken tiles on the roof before the storm, it was an accident waiting to happen. So, they're refusing to pay up. Tom was in the Red Lion last night. He says Diane is incandescent. She wants to sell up and move to Southampton. Anyway, you can't stay there, Olivia.'

'She has to stay somewhere,' says Isabella. 'She'd be very welcome at our house, but she doesn't like the idea. And she doesn't want to sign a six-month lease.'

'That's understandable,' says Will. 'That's what I stopped in to tell you. I asked my landlady if she had any ideas, and she said her friend Eleanor across the road is looking for a lodger. Her old one left last week, and she can't afford the mortgage unless she lets out her spare room. What do you say, Olivia? Would you like to take a look?'

'I'd love to,' I say. 'I assume Eleanor's house has a roof?'

'I have a good view from my bedroom window,' he says. 'It appears to have a roof. Otherwise, the chimney pot would have fallen down into the garden.'

'Appearances can be deceptive,' says Isabella darkly. 'So, your accommodation has a roof. Big deal! For all you know, this Eleanor woman has knocked down all the internal walls and put up a giant bouncy castle.'

'In which case, I'll give Olivia my room and move in with Eleanor,' says Will. 'I love bouncy castles!'

'Or she might be a hoarder,' she goes on without listening. 'Olivia won't be able to move without tripping over collections of novelty teapots or antique toasters.'

'Even more reason for me to move in,' he says. 'I love antique toast.'

'Or she might host open mic nights and force Olivia to do comedy routines.'

'I'd come and listen to that,' he says.

'Or keep chickens indoors,' she finishes. 'Olivia won't be able to sleep because of the rooster crowing.'

'But think of having fresh eggs for breakfast every morning,' he urges. 'Seriously, Isabella, why don't you want her to move in with Eleanor?'

'Because it would be a lot more fun if she stayed with me,' she says.

I give her an impulsive hug. 'I love staying with you, but I'd prefer to be independent. If this Eleanor isn't as awful as you think, maybe you could come and sleep over one night.'

'Fine,' she says. 'But only if it's open mic night, and you let one of the chickens sleep in my room.'

I put a couple of doughnuts into a bag and hand it to Will. 'I'm afraid all the strawberry ones have gone. But the raspberry ones are very good.'

'What a coincidence,' he says. 'I believe strawberry is Isabella's favourite flavour.'

She ignores him. 'Can you tell this Eleanor woman we'll be over after work to look at the room?'

'You're coming too?' I say.

'Of course. I want to check out the sound system.'

'I'll find out when she's free,' promises Will. 'I'll give you a call later.'

Chapter Nine

He holds the door open for an elderly man before disappearing out of the shop and striding away down the high street.

'Hello, Mr Mason,' says Isabella. 'How are you today?'

The man gives her a perplexed look. 'Oh, I'm … that is to say …'

'That's good,' she says. 'Mr Mason, I'd like you to meet our newest member of staff, Olivia Sullivan. Olivia, this is Mr Mason. He used to run the Sugarloaf bakery. Lily and I bought it from him when he retired.'

He peers at me over his half-moon spectacles. 'It's very nice to meet you, my dear. I didn't realise Lily and Isabella were taking on any more staff.'

'We aren't really,' she says. 'Lily is out because Daisy isn't well. Olivia has kindly agreed to fill in for as long as she's needed.'

'How nice,' he says. 'I hope Daisy will recover soon. She was named after my wife, you know,' he tells me in a pleased tone.

'That's lovely,' I say. 'It's a beautiful name.'

'What can I get you today, Mr Mason?' Isabella prompts him.

He looks puzzled. 'Get me?'

'From the bakery,' she says. 'Or are you here for a cup of coffee?'

'I'm afraid I don't have time,' he says, looking at his watch. 'I only popped in for a … now, what did I pop in for?'

We regard him with fascinated attention as he frowns and stares into the distance, his lips moving slightly.

'A cob loaf!' he exclaims at last. 'Daisy told me we were almost at the end of ours and asked me to collect one on my way home.'

He catches my eye. 'Daisy my wife, I mean. Not little Daisy, her namesake.'

I keep my face straight. 'I assumed that was who you meant. Although I haven't met little Daisy yet. For all I know, she may be very advanced and write her own shopping lists.'

He frowns. 'I don't think so, my dear. She's only a few months old.'

'She's almost a year old,' says Isabella. 'If you remember, she was born during the final of the New Forest Mix-up.'

'My goodness!' he says. 'Has it been that long?'

'I'm afraid so,' she says. 'They aren't running the competition this year. They said it's because of a lack of funding. But Lily and I are sure that, having seen our entry last year, all the candidates have backed out. We put them all to shame, Olivia. It was a travesty we didn't win. Abby made the most amazing pirate ship.'

'What was the theme?' I ask.

'*I love the New Forest.*'

'Are there many pirate ships in the New Forest?'

'That's what I asked Abby,' says Mr Mason. 'I don't remember what she told me, but I'm sure she knew what she was doing.'

Isabella laughs. 'She did. It's a long story, Olivia. Remind me to tell you sometime. Anyway, we've scared off all our competitors. Hopefully, they'll run it again next year, once people have forgotten how good we were.'

Mr Mason picks up his loaf. 'I must be going. I told Daisy I'd be back before lunch.'

He glances at me again. 'My Daisy, I mean. Not –'

'I understand,' I assure him. 'Enjoy your bread.'

He potters out, and I turn to Isabella. 'Did he really run the bakery before you?'

'He did. Why do you ask?'

'No reason. He seemed a little confused about where he was. I half expected him to ask you for some batteries or a bunch of asparagus.'

'He's always like that,' she says. 'He was exactly the same when Lily started working for him. He'd got rather stuck in his ways, and it was hard to convince him to change anything. I don't think he'd have retired at all if we hadn't offered to buy the bakery. I'm glad he did. He seems very content nowadays. He comes in and tells us everything we're doing wrong. We smile and thank him for his advice and carry on as we were, and everyone's happy.'

'Is baby Daisy really named after his wife?' I say.

She smiles. 'He likes to think so. I suspect it has more to do with daisies being Lily's favourite flowers.'

She looks at her watch. 'How do you feel about holding the fort while I run out for half an hour? Abby's in the kitchen if you get into difficulties.'

'Are you sure I'm ready?' I say.

'Why not? You know where everything is, and you can handle the till. After last night's intensive training session, you're able to make lattes and cappuccinos. You're a lot more ready than I was on my first day here. I dropped one of those giant bags of flour when I was carrying it in from the delivery van. The bag exploded, and the flour went everywhere. It was like a blizzard in here. We were brushing off the customers for hours. We had to give them all free cake to calm them down. And the day we opened the café, I overfilled the milk jug and left the steam nozzle in for too long. It foamed up and went all over the floor. A customer trod on it and skidded halfway across the cafe. I think we gave away that entire day's profits in free cake.'

'I'm feeling more confident already,' I say. 'As long as no one asks me to foam their milk or carry their flour, I should be fine.'

She grins. 'That's the Sugarloaf spirit! I'll be back as quickly as I can.'

She disappears, and I nervously take my place behind the counter. I don't know why. There isn't much that could go wrong. If by some chance I spectacularly mess everything up and lose all the stock or offend a customer, this isn't a career on which I've been staking my entire future. I can apologise and move on, and Isabella can ring the temp agency and ask them for someone more competent.

Anyway, Abby is here. She's making pastries this afternoon, but I'm sure she'd abandon them to their fate and rush into the shop if I screamed loudly enough. I brace myself for an onslaught of customers, but it doesn't come. The bell remains obstinately silent. There are very few people on the high street at this hour. The morning rush has subsided, and the people on their way home from work haven't yet appeared.

I'm startled out of my musings by a commotion at the far end of the street. An elderly woman has crossed the road with her dog, who is now lying on the grass verge. She's dropped her bags of shopping and is kneeling next to him. I look up and down the high street, but no one seems to be around.

'Abby!' I shout. 'Can you look after the shop for a minute?'

Without waiting for her to answer, I dart out of the door and run down the street.

'What happened?' I gasp as I reach the woman. 'Did he get hit by a car?'

She frowns up at me. 'Of course, he didn't get hit by a car! He has excellent road sense. My vet says he's rarely seen a dog with such intelligence.'

I kneel next to her. 'That's a relief. What's happened to him? Does he suffer from fits?'

She gives me an outraged glare. 'My dog has never had a fit in his life!'

'That's good to hear. So, what's wrong with him?'

As if hearing my voice for the first time, the dog rolls over and looks up at me.

'Hello, old fellow,' I say in a soothing voice. 'What's going on?'

As if in reply, he holds up his front paw. I grasp it lightly and inspect it. I gently run my thumb over his pads, and he winces. I look at it more closely. 'What's making you so sore? Oh, I see! Let's get that out.'

I reach into my pocket for a pair of tweezers, but the woman stops me. 'What do you think you're doing?'

'He has a thorn in his paw. I'm taking it out for him.'

'No, you aren't! I'm not having a complete stranger poking around my dog's paw. How do you know he has a thorn?'

I point with the tweezers. 'Because I can see it right here.'

Without waiting for her to answer, I catch the end of the thorn and pull it out. 'There you are, old man. You're good to go.'

The dog rolls over and jumps to his feet. He capers in circles around his owner, while she tries to prevent him from tangling his lead around her legs and pulling her over.

I put a hand on his collar. 'Easy there. I'm glad you're feeling better, but you need to calm down.'

I keep a firm grip on him, hand the end of the lead to the woman, and watch while she untangles herself. She looks up at me with an expression of annoyance and relief.

'Thank you,' she says gruffly.

'No problem.' I ruffle the dog's head. 'You need to look where you're walking.'

He gives me an imbecilic grin and licks my hand.

I suddenly remember where I am and what I'm supposed to be doing. 'I must go! I've left the shop unattended.'

I dash back up the street and into the bakery, where I find Abby standing behind the counter.

'Are you ok?' she says. 'I heard you yell, but you'd disappeared by the time I arrived.'

'I'm fine. I had to rescue a dog. I'd better wash this mud off my hands.'

I return a minute later to find the elderly woman and her dog have followed me into the bakery. The woman is frowning more heavily than ever, and I wonder whether she's come in to complain about me. She didn't seem too happy when I produced my tweezers. But I couldn't leave her dog to limp around with a thorn in his paw. If she wants to complain, she can go ahead.

'There she is!' says the woman, pointing to me.

'Look!' I say with a trace of impatience. 'What did you expect me to do? Your dog was in pain or he wouldn't have been lying down like that.'

'Olivia,' interrupts Abby. 'This is Mrs Ogilvie, one of our regular customers. Mrs Ogilvie, this is Olivia. And this is Bernie. But I don't need to introduce you to him. I gather you've already met.'

'That's right,' I say. 'I saw him lying by the side of the road and went to see what was wrong. Luckily, he only had a thorn in his paw.'

Abby laughs. 'Did he do his full collapse in agony routine?'

She gives Bernie a stern look. 'I've never seen such a drama king in all my life.'

He grins up at her hopefully, and she rolls her eyes. 'Just a small one.'

She reaches into the box next to the counter and hands him a biscuit.

'Should he be having that?' I say.

'We make them for the local dogs, using a recipe the vet suggested. We bake a variety of flavours.'

She doesn't appear to be joking, so I decide to leave it.

'May I buy you a cup of coffee?' says Mrs Ogilvie.

For a moment, I think she's talking to Bernie, and I open my mouth to protest. Dog biscuits are one thing. Coffee is quite another. Then I realise she's addressing me.

'That's very kind of you,' I say. 'But there's really no need. And it isn't my break time.'

'It is,' says Abby. 'I've finished the pastries. I was coming through to tell you to have some lunch. I'll make your drinks.'

Mrs Ogilvie sits at the table by the door. Bernie obviously knows the bakery well because he's already lying under the table, chewing his biscuit.

I sit down at Mrs Ogilvie's table, and Bernie gives my ankle a welcoming lick.

'He seems quite happy now,' I say.

'Yes, he does,' says Mrs Ogilvie. 'It occurs to me I forgot to thank you.'

She says it rather stiffly, but with obvious sincerity. I'm pleased she's dropped her hostile attitude.

'You're very welcome,' I say. 'I've taken a lot of thorns out of dogs' paws over the years.'

'Do you have a dog of your own?' she says.

'I've been living in London for the past few years,' I say. 'Our tenants' association doesn't allow pets. I'd love a dog of my own, especially one like Bernie. I'm fond of cavoodles. They're a lovely breed.'

She unbends further. 'I've always kept cavoodles. They're very intelligent. And they make excellent watchdogs.'

I look at Bernie, who's dropped his biscuit and doesn't seem to have realised it's stuck behind his ear. He's staring around the shop as though suspecting one of the customers of having abstracted it when he wasn't looking.

'They are wonderful,' I agree.

Clearly, this dog is the light of her life, and she won't take kindly to any criticism of him. Besides, she's right. Bernie may not be receiving his invitation from Mensa any time soon, but he obviously has a lovely temperament. I've been around enough dogs to tell at a glance which of them are highly strung and need extra care. Bernie appears to have been passed over when they were handing out high strings.

I remove the biscuit from behind his ear and hand it to him. He snatches it from me with evident delight, then drops it on the floor and rolls over on it. He looks at me with the patient air of a dog accustomed to being handed treats that promptly grow legs and has become resigned to it.

'You'll figure it out,' I tell him.

Mrs Ogilvie takes a sip of her tea and gives an approving nod. 'They make a very nice cup of tea here. I never drink coffee in the afternoon. Some people do, but I don't understand why.'

I take a sip of my latte. 'I'm sure tea is much better for you, but I still prefer coffee.'

'How do you know so much about dogs?' she says.

'I'm a veterinary nurse.'

She looks surprised. 'What are you doing working here?'

'That's an excellent question. I'm not quite sure. My car broke down a few miles from here, and the man who rescued me brought me to Honeywell. I only meant to stay the night, but Isabella talked me into staying for a few weeks.'

Abby looks up from the coffee machine. 'Lily's little girl isn't well, Mrs Ogilvie. Lily has taken some time off to look after her.'

'I'm sorry to hear that,' says Mrs Ogilvie. 'I hope it isn't too serious.'

'I talked to Lily last night,' says Abby. 'She expects to bring Daisy home in a few days. But she won't want to return to work until Daisy is recovered. Olivia is kindly helping us out until then.'

'I should get back to work soon,' I say. 'It would be a good idea to rub some antiseptic ointment into Bernie's paw when you get home, Mrs Ogilvie. Keep an eye on it for a day or two. Puncture wounds can become infected. But this one was superficial. I'm sure Bernie will let you know if it gets worse.'

Abby winks at me. 'He'll let the whole village know. You saw him in action today.'

Mrs Ogilvie ignores her. 'We must be getting on. We have to call in at the post office before it closes, and you know what a chatterbox Mrs Jayson can be.'

She clips Bernie's lead to his collar, and he jumps up and sprints towards the door.

'Haven't you forgotten something?' I ask him, pointing to the place where he was lying.

He skips back, grabs the last piece of biscuit, and disposes of it in two noisy crunches. Clearly, he doesn't want to risk it growing legs again and trotting off to hide in a dark corner.

Mrs Ogilvie gives me a gracious inclination of the head as she leaves.

'You've made a hit, Olivia!' says Abby as the door closes behind her.

'How so?'

'I've never seen her offer to buy someone a coffee before. She must like you.'

'I think she likes her dog. She looked terribly upset when he was lying there. That's why I thought something more serious had happened to him.'

'That's why Bernie does it,' she says. 'If you knew the number of biscuits he'd conned her out of with his dying swan act …'

'She said he was very intelligent,' I agree. 'She could easily have removed the thorn herself. I'll show her how the next time I see her.'

'She comes into the bakery several times a week,' she says. 'You're bound to see her again soon. Wait until Isabella hears about this! Seriously, Olivia, you have no idea what a hit you must have made. Isabella told me Mrs Ogilvie refused to learn her name for more than a year. Even now, she occasionally refers to her as Imogen.'

I laugh. 'I'll have to remember that one.'

'It's as if you'd saved the life of the son of a Mafia boss,' she pursues. 'You'll probably find the villagers doff their caps as you pass by. The word will go round that anyone who lays a finger on you will be answerable to Mrs Ogilvie. Your money will no longer be good in any of the shops on the high street.'

'Which would suit me fine,' I say. 'I have about twenty-five pounds to last me until payday, and I'm looking at a room this evening. If I take it, the landlady will want a deposit.'

'Don't worry about that,' she says. 'Mrs Ogilvie will beg you to stay with her for free and offer to make you an allowance.'

'Sounds good,' I say. 'In the meantime, Isabella's car has pulled up outside. It seems to me this is the perfect time to strike while the iron is hot and demand a raise.'

Chapter Ten

Will calls me just before closing time and tells me Eleanor will be home this evening and is happy for me to drop around whenever I like.

'Unless you've seen the room by then and decided you want it,' I say.

He laughs. 'I'll admit I was temporarily seduced by visions of antique teapots and free-range chickens. But I'm happy where I am, thanks. The room's all yours if you want it.'

Isabella pulls a face when she hears this. 'I still think you ought to change your mind and stay with me. But I'll come along with you this evening. I'm sure I can find a few flaws and point them out to you.'

We drive back to Honeywell after dinner. A middle-aged woman opens the door to us.

'Is one of you Olivia?' she says. 'Will said you might drop around this evening.'

'That would be me,' says Isabella. 'I have to warn you I'm very picky, and I drive a hard bargain. I've turned down hundreds of rooms already.'

The woman looks at her more closely. 'You're Isabella Campbell, aren't you? Don't you work at the Sugarloaf bakery with Angela Carson's daughter?'

'Run!' Isabella hisses in my ear. 'She's onto us.'

I give her a quelling look. 'I'm Olivia, and you must be Eleanor. Please ignore my friend. She's had a difficult day.'

I turn to Isabella. 'Would you like to wait in the car?'

'No, I promise I'll behave.' She grins at the woman. 'Sorry about that. I've been trying to persuade Olivia to stay with me, but she insists on looking for her own place. I'm doing my best to put her off.'

Eleanor doesn't look put out. 'Are you both coming in?'

Isabella gives her a contrite look. 'I'll take my shoes off.'

'No need,' says Eleanor. 'It's all hard floors downstairs.'

'Even more reason to take them off,' says Isabella. 'I can slide around in my socks. On second thoughts, perhaps it would be better if I went across the road to visit Will. Come and find me when you're ready, Olivia.'

'Great idea,' I say, relieved.

'Olivia is an ideal tenant,' she tells Eleanor. 'She's tidy and quiet, and she doesn't hog the bathroom for hours.'

'I'm sorry about Isabella,' I apologise as Eleanor leads me into the house.

'No problem,' she says. 'I like people with a sense of humour.'

Is she saying I don't have a sense of humour? Should I do a dance or tell her a knock-knock joke to prove what a riot I am?

'She's very nice,' is all I can think of to say.

Eleanor opens the nearest door. 'This is the living room. It faces west, so it's lovely in the evening. The dining room is through those double doors. There are French windows leading out to the garden.'

I look around appreciatively. The living room walls are painted a pale lilac, which sets off the honey-coloured wood of the floor. There are two comfortable looking sofas, a coffee table covered in newspapers, and several bookcases filled to overflowing with books.

This is my kind of room. Charlie is obsessed with neatness and would hate everything about it, which only makes me like it the more. He'd be horrified by the newspapers thrown down at odd angles, and the non-matching sofas.

There's a vase of flowers on the mantlepiece, the delicate scent of carnations mixing with the crisp bouquet of freshly cut roses. The afternoon sunlight dances in waves across the room, creating a ripple effect on the floor. I take a deep breath and feel my entire body relax for what seems the first time in weeks.

Eleanor leads me down the hallway. 'That's the kitchen. There are three bedrooms upstairs. The smallest one is barely a bedroom, and I use it as a study. I have the largest bedroom with the ensuite. My lodgers have the middle room and use the main bathroom.'

The bedroom she shows me is lovely. I'm thankful to see it's at the back of the house, facing out over the garden. I'm not sure which way Will's bedroom faces, but it would have been embarrassing if both our bedrooms were at the front. I'd have had to keep my curtains closed at all times.

Eleanor's voice breaks into my musings. 'What do you think?'

'It's perfect!' I say with enthusiasm. 'When can I move in?'

'Don't you want to know how much I'm charging?' she says, looking amused.

'Will mentioned that when he called. The only problem will be finding a deposit. The rent is no problem, but it may take me a while to sort out my finances.'

I feel my face flame. 'They're … tangled up with someone else's at the moment. It could take a while to untangle them.'

'It's difficult when that happens, isn't it?' she says. 'I'm happy to waive a deposit, especially as Will tells me this is a temporary thing for you. How long are you staying in the area?'

'I have no idea. It could be a couple of weeks, or a couple of months.'

'No problem,' she says. 'If you pay each week in advance, that works for me.'

'Are there any house rules I ought to know about?'

'Lodgers must be in their rooms by nine o'clock each night,' she says. 'No gentlemen visitors at any time. Any other visitors by negotiation. But only once a week, and they must bring their own toilet paper and soap. I'm not running a hotel here.'

She sees my face and bursts out laughing. 'Olivia, I'm kidding! Just behave like a reasonable human being, and I'll be happy. I'll do my best to do the same. I've got on fine with all my lodgers so far. I don't imagine things will be any different with you.'

She smiles. 'That friend of yours won't be visiting, will she? I couldn't cope with that.'

'Isabella? Not if you don't want her to. But she's lovely when you get to know her. And she's been very kind to me.'

'I'm kidding,' she says. 'Ask anyone you like. This is your home too for as long as you live here.'

I laugh. 'Sorry, my sense of humour needs some work. I've been living with someone who had lots of rules, but he wasn't joking.'

She pulls a face. 'That's not good.'

'No, but it's my fault. I should have left a lot sooner.'

'Don't think like that,' she says. 'It can take a while to realise what people are like. Years, sometimes. I should have divorced my husband long before I did, but I got tangled up in the fallacy of sunk costs and kept telling myself I had more to lose than gain. It wasn't until I'd left him that I realised quite how bad things had got. And he didn't have any weird house rules.'

'That's exactly it!' I say. 'By the time I'd been with Charlie for several years, it felt as though there was too much history to throw away without a far better reason than I could come up with. Whenever I tried to discuss my concerns with him, he had a way of pushing them all back on me and making me think everything was in my head. I thought I was losing my mind.'

'I'm sorry,' she says. 'No one should have to live like that. Have you left him permanently?'

'I hope so. I told myself it was only for a week or so because that was the only way I could get up the courage to leave. This job came up at the perfect time for me, although I didn't realise it at first. I'm hoping it will give me some space to think things through and put some distance between me and everything that's happened. I'm still not sure whether I've made a mistake.'

She looks at my flushed face. 'I don't know you, and I don't know what's been happening in your life over the past few years. But I'm a great believer in instinct, gut feelings, intuition, whatever you want to call it. I suspect when you've had time to settle down and think, you'll realise you did the right thing.'

'I don't feel able to think clearly about anything at the moment.'

'So, don't!' she says. 'You've been given an unexpected opportunity to take some time for yourself, away from whatever's been going on. Take it! You have a job, which ought to keep you busy. If you're working with Isabella Campbell, I doubt your days will be too dull. You've found yourself somewhere to stay and, despite what she hinted just now, your landlady really isn't the boarding house supervisor from hell. Honeywell is a lovely village, and the New Forest is beautiful in the summer. I suggest you make the most of it and don't worry too much about the future.'

I follow her downstairs, and she hands me my coat.

'Can I move in tomorrow night?' I ask.

'Move in whenever you like,' she says. 'I'll give you my phone number, and you can call me directly instead of going through Will.'

'Good idea. I'm very grateful to him for mentioning this place. Do you know him well?'

'Not really,' she says. 'He hasn't been in the village for long. He seems like a nice guy.'

'He is. That's twice he's come to my rescue. First, he picked me up when my car broke down and brought me to Honeywell. And now he's found me somewhere to live.'

'Is that right?' she says with a smile. 'They say the third time's a charm.'

I don't know what she means by this, and she doesn't elaborate.

'See you tomorrow, Olivia,' she says and closes the door.

I look across at Will's house. There's a light on in the downstairs front room, but none upstairs, so he and Isabella probably aren't up in his room. Not that it's any of my business.

I set off down the garden path, wondering what I'll find when I arrive. If Will's house has wooden floors like Eleanor's, I'll probably discover him and Isabella skidding around the living room in their socks.

Chapter Eleven

Mrs Ogilvie turns up at the bakery a few days later with Bernie in tow. He races in and leaps up at me, trying to lick my face.

'Stop that at once, Bernie!' she says. She gives me an apologetic smile. 'He doesn't usually do that. I think he recognises you and is saying thank you.'

'No need,' I say, catching Bernie's paws and putting him back on the floor. 'Judging by the speed at which he charged in here, he hasn't suffered any ill effects.'

'None at all,' she says. 'I applied some of the ointment as you told me, and I kept a close eye on him, but he seemed fine. I would have taken him to the vet at once if he had been limping.'

'Good idea,' I say. 'Any advice I gave you was in a purely advisory capacity as a private citizen. I'm not qualified to diagnose or prescribe or anything like that. If in doubt, always call your vet.'

'Oh, I do!' she says. 'He loves Bernie, and he's always delighted to see him, even if it turns out there's nothing much wrong. And Bernie loves Dr Marsden, don't you, darling?'

Bernie grins up at her and wags his tail.

'Dr Marsden says Bernie is one of the most intelligent animals he's ever had to do with,' she tells me proudly.

I don't mention that vets say that about all their patients. I've seen one tell a young boy that his goldfish displayed remarkable skill and dexterity in dodging through the weeds and avoiding crashing into the toy castle in his tank.

But it would be unkind to remark on this. Mrs Ogilvie is obviously besotted with Bernie, and he seems very fond of her. He must be good company for her. I'm not sure what her personal circumstances are, except that Isabella mentioned she was a widow. Whatever their situation, most people benefit from having a pet.

'He looks very alert,' I say.

Bernie promptly collapses under the nearest table, rolls onto his back and starts to snore.

'I hope you've come in for a drink,' I say. 'Bernie doesn't look as though he intends to make this a brief visit.'

She pulls out her purse. 'I'd like a cup of tea please, and a slice of Battenberg.'

'Coming right up.'

She watches me carefully as I make her tea. I hope I'm doing it properly. It isn't as complicated as using the coffee machine, where I have to remember whether or not the customer wants caffeine, and whether they've requested extra-hot, extra-strong, or extra foam. And that's before we get onto the question of which milk they require. All I have to do with the tea is to pour in boiling water and make sure the cup isn't chipped.

Mrs Ogilvie takes a sip and nods. 'Very nice. The last girl who was here used to make it far too weak.'

'You mean Lily?'

She shakes her head. 'Lily makes a nice cup of tea. I'm talking about Alice. She wasn't here for long. She was a pleasant enough girl, but she could never learn to warm the pot, and she had no idea how many tea leaves she was supposed to use. Why don't you join me?'

I look at my watch. 'I'm due for a break in five minutes. As long as Isabella is here by then, I'd love to.'

For a wonder, Isabella arrives four and a half minutes later. She pulls off her coat and gives me a cheerful smile. 'You must be impressed by my punctuality. I had to run the last quarter of a mile. It's all your fault. You weren't there to wake me up this morning.'

'What about your alarm?' I say.

'I believe it rang once or twice,' she says. 'The second time it rang, I swiped at it, and it crashed onto the floor. I didn't hear a thing from it after that. I'll have to buy a new one.'

'Or you could use your phone,' I say.

'No, I couldn't. The last time I did that, I was so startled that I made a grab for it, knocked it halfway across the room, and smashed the screen. I'm not risking that again.'

'Maybe Georgia could wake you up?' I suggest.

'Fat chance! My sister wouldn't wake up if a bomb went off. When she was younger, I used to pour cold water on her, but even that didn't work. She used to mutter and grumble, then roll over and start snoring again. The only thing that's ever been known to wake her is the smell of frying bacon. One hint of that, and she's out of bed in a flash.'

'Couldn't you go downstairs and fry bacon each morning?' I suggest.

'What would be the point of that? I'd have to be awake to do it. Then I wouldn't need Georgia.'

'Someone ought to invent an alarm clock that pumps out smells instead of screeching in your ear,' I say. 'I'd love to wake to the scent of freshly baked bread each morning.'

'You spend your entire day smelling freshly baked bread,' she says. 'You should come up with something more original.'

'Popcorn,' I say after a moment's thought. 'I love the smell of buttered popcorn. It always reminds me of going to the movies with my parents when I was a child.'

'It certainly beats bread,' she says. 'I'm not sure what I'd programme my alarm to smell of. I'll have to give it some thought.'

'And wait until someone's invented it,' I say. 'Is it ok if I take my break now that you're here?'

'Of course.' She drops her bag behind the counter. 'Hello, Mrs Ogilvie. How are you today?'

Her eyes fall on Bernie. 'Is he asleep, or is he pretending to have hurt himself in the hope we'll ply him with one of Abby's biscuits?'

'Bernie would never do that,' says Mrs Ogilvie. 'He's an exceptionally brave dog. It worries me sometimes how little fuss he makes. He might not let me know if something was really wrong with him.'

Isabella's lips twitch. 'I don't think you need worry about that too much. I'm sure he'd let you know.'

'He's extremely intelligent,' I say, shooting her a warning glance.

I make myself a coffee and sit down at Mrs Ogilvie's table. Isabella looks surprised, but she doesn't comment.

We chat about Bernie for a few minutes, and I hear his entire life history. How he came to live with Mrs Ogilvie just before her previous cavoodle, Maisie, died. What a joy he's been to her, and how many tricks he's learned.

'I've never seen him do any tricks,' says Isabella. 'What can he do?'

'Bernie doesn't like to perform in public,' says Mrs Oglivie. 'He's an extremely shy dog.'

'Do you live in Honeywell?' I ask her.

She nods. 'Bernie and I live in one of the cottages down by the water meadow.'

'I'm renting a room in Cherry Street,' I say. 'Do you know it?'

'I know all the roads in Honeywell,' she says. 'I've lived here since I was five years old.'

'Goodness! So, you're the person I should come to if I want to learn anything about the village?'

'I can tell you all about its history,' she says. 'But I don't know as many people as I used to. Plenty of them have moved on since I arrived here, particularly the younger ones. There isn't much work in the area, and house prices have risen a lot.'

'Have you lived in your cottage for long?'

'Since Edward and I were married,' she says. 'That was almost sixty years ago.'

Her mouth tightens. 'He left me six years ago. He had a heart attack. One day he was there, and the next day he wasn't.'

'I'm so sorry,' I say with genuine sympathy. 'I can't imagine losing someone after spending so long together.'

'I had Bernie,' she says. 'Edward and I had only just got him. I don't know how I would have managed without him. He gave me a reason to get out of bed each morning. Gradually, it became a habit, and things got back to normal.'

'Not quite normal,' says Isabella gently, and Mrs Ogilvie shrugs.

'Perhaps not, but it happens to us all in the end. You're still young, so you won't understand that.'

'I haven't lost a husband, but both my parents died when I was eighteen,' I say. 'So, I understand a little of what you went through.'

To my surprise, she stretches out her hand and gives mine a squeeze. 'You poor thing. That's a terribly young age to lose your family.'

'It is,' says Isabella in a low voice. 'I'm so sorry, Olivia.'

I take a sip of my coffee before answering. 'It was pretty rough. They died in a car crash during my first year of university. But I got through it because I had to, much like Mrs Ogilvie says. Only I didn't have a beautiful cavoodle puppy to distract me. University halls don't allow pets.'

'You must get a dog as soon as you can,' says Mrs Ogilvie. 'I always pity people who don't have dogs.'

'Some people are allergic to them,' says Isabella. 'My sister Georgia knows at once when there's a dog or a cat in the vicinity. Her eyes stream, and her face breaks out in hives.'

'Cavoodles are hypoallergenic,' says Mrs Ogilvie primly.

'So is Georgia, but that doesn't stop me from having an adverse reaction to her now and then,' says Isabella. She grins at us and disappears into the kitchen.

'That young lady is entirely too fond of a joke,' says Mrs Ogilvie.

'She's great fun,' I say. 'I'm enjoying working here.'

Bernie stirs and sits up. He looks around him, blinking.

'He's hoping for a dog biscuit,' says Mrs Ogilvie. She hands me her credit card. 'I wonder whether you would mind fetching one for him.'

'I'd be delighted. Does he have a favourite flavour?'

'He enjoys them all,' she says. 'He's a very polite dog.'

'I can see that.' I choose the largest biscuit and hand it to Bernie, who falls on it in delight.

I sit down again. 'I have five minutes left of my break, and I intend to take all of it. It's taking me a while to get used to standing all day, and my legs don't appreciate it. I thought I had a busy job as a veterinary nurse, but I was moving around rather than standing behind a counter. I'm making the most of these few minutes. Why don't you tell me some more about the village?'

She considers. 'I'm not sure where to start. I moved here with my parents when I was five years old, nearly seventy-five years ago. We moved into the cottage the day before my birthday. I remember I was terribly excited to have a party in the garden. Before that, we lived in the flat over my father's shop in Christchurch.'

'What kind of a shop was that?'

'It isn't there now,' she says. 'He ran the ironmongers. We sold a bit of everything. I used to love to spend the morning in there with him when my mother had to go out. It was convenient for him to live over the shop. But it didn't pay, and it closed down when I was five. So, we moved to Honeywell, and my father became a farm labourer. That row of cottages was tied to the farm. They aren't now, but that's why they were originally built.'

'So, you celebrated your fifth birthday party in your new house?' I say.

She gives me an unexpectedly sweet smile. 'It was a wonderful day. I was always glad my birthday was in August because it was the middle of the school holidays. We invited the entire class, and almost all of them came. We played pass the parcel and musical chairs, and my mother made a beautiful chocolate blancmange in the shape of a rabbit. It was the best birthday I could have imagined.'

'You said your family moved to that house nearly seventy-five years ago,' I say. 'I don't want to be rude, but does that mean you'll soon be eighty?'

'I will,' she says. 'But I'm far too old to be making a fuss about birthdays. They're for children, not for old women.'

'Nonsense!' I say. 'Bernie is neither a child nor an elderly woman, but I'd be willing to bet you celebrate his birthday.'

Is that a pink flush on her cheeks? 'Just a small celebration to mark the occasion.'

'When is it?' I ask.

'As it happens, it's the same day as mine. At least, I think it is. We didn't get him until he was nearly a year old. The person who adopted him became ill, and Edward and I took him in. We asked the date of his birthday, but they couldn't remember exactly. All they knew was that they had taken him home when he was eight or nine weeks old, so he must have been born sometime in the middle of August. Edward said he and I should have a joint celebration. And so, we did. It was great fun. We made a maze for him to run around in the garden, and he had his favourite biscuits.'

Her face looks animated as she thinks back to Bernie's puppyhood. 'We had no idea Edward wouldn't be there for Bernie's second birthday. I bought Bernie a cake that year, but I didn't have the heart to do more.'

'But eighty is a pretty special birthday,' I say. 'Surely, you plan to celebrate?'

She shakes her head. 'It's a lot of nonsense. Bernie will have his cake, as usual. He would never forgive me if I forgot his birthday. But that's all.'

'Do you have any family in the area?'

'No family,' she says. 'And very few friends. I have a sister who lives in Australia, but I don't hear from her often.'

'What a shame,' I say. 'How old will Bernie be this year?'

'He'll be seven years old!' she says proudly. 'The vet says he has the energy of a dog half his age.'

'He has a great zest for life,' I agree. 'I expect he keeps you busy.'

Isabella comes back into the shop. 'I hate to disturb you, but I have to run out for a few minutes. The supplier has forgotten our dried fruit, and they aren't answering their phone. Abby was supposed to be making Eccles cakes today, and she's stomping around the kitchen in a blind fury.'

'I've never seen Abby stomp,' I say. 'Neither have I seen her furious.'

'Possibly not,' says Isabella. 'But I could swear someone in the kitchen was.'

She catches my eye and laughs. 'All right, it was me. I love Abby's Eccles cakes. Anyway, I have to pop over and threaten to sue our suppliers or withdraw our custom or something. Will you be all right on your own?'

'Of course.'

Mrs Ogilvie clips Bernie's lead to his collar. 'We must be going too. Thank you for a pleasant chat.'

'I've enjoyed it,' I say. 'I'm looking forward to hearing more about Honeywell. I've never been in this part of the world before, and it's wonderful to have a walking encyclopaedia to consult.'

She looks pleased. 'Bernie and I will pop in again tomorrow. He loves the walk up here.'

Bernie jumps up and licks my face before I can stop him.

'Naughty boy,' says Mrs Ogilvie in an indulgent tone.

She gives us both a gracious wave and follows Bernie out of the shop.

Chapter Twelve

Isabella calls round to see me the following evening.

'I thought I should come and check out your new place,' she says as soon as I answer the door.

'You saw it when I came to look at it.'

'Only from the outside,' she says. 'You made me leave before I'd seen the bouncy castle. Is it all you dreamed it would be? Is there a rota, or can you use it whenever you like?'

'I'm sure there would be, if we had one.'

'Don't you?' she says, disappointed. 'Not even a tiny one in the garden?'

'I've inspected every inch of the place, and I haven't been able to discover so much as an inflatable air bed in the garden shed.'

'You should have stayed with me,' she says. 'My uncle opens up his gardens one weekend each summer to everyone in the village. He gives all the children pony rides in the paddock behind the house.'

'That sounds rather strenuous for him,' I say.

She sighs. 'You don't know the first thing about country life, do you? We use an actual pony. It's a kind of small horse.'

'Thanks,' I say. 'My training didn't cover anything bigger than a hamster.'

'I thought that would be the case,' she says. 'Which is why I filled you in. Feel free to ask me anything you want about animals. We could have an animal of the week at the bakery and learn all about them. We'd start small and work up to the large ones, like elephants. I vote we begin with sheep. I know lots about those. More than I care to, if I'm honest.'

'You're too kind,' I say, ushering her inside. 'What were you saying about ponies?'

She slips off her shoes. 'I'd better not annoy your landlady any more than I already have. Oh, yes. My uncle's open day. They serve tea in the rose garden, and the children have pony rides. And he puts an enormous bouncy castle on the lawn. It's my favourite weekend of the year. They don't come to take it away until the following morning, so I get it all to myself for the night. I bet you're kicking yourself now, aren't you?'

I follow her into the living room. 'I'm devastated. But it would be bad manners to walk out on Eleanor before I've been here for a week, so I'll have to live with it. Besides, I'm not likely to be here in August. Lily will be back at work long before that, and I'll be on my way.'

'Where to?' she asks. 'You don't want to go back to London. Why not stay around here?'

'I'll think about it. Would you like a drink?'

She sinks into the sofa. 'I thought you'd never ask. I've had a long journey to get here, and I'm parched.'

'Did you walk over to Honeywell?'

'No, I drove. But you have an exceptionally long garden path. I wasn't sure I'd make it.'

Are you in Honeywell to see me, or did you drop in on your way to see Will?'

'To see Will?' she says. 'Am I supposed to be meeting him tonight?'

'I have no idea. I thought maybe you and he were …'

She gives a snort of laughter. 'I'm sorry. It's just the idea of me and Will.'

I'm surprised to hear her speak so decisively. He's an attractive guy, and the pair of them seem to get on well.

'I didn't mean to offend you,' I say. 'I just wondered whether …'

'Not even close,' she says. 'Will's great, and I really like him. But I haven't considered him as boyfriend material.'

I feel almost offended on Will's behalf. He isn't here to defend himself, so maybe I should.

'I don't see why,' I say. 'He's a good-looking guy, and he's thoughtful and kind, which you can't say about everyone.'

'He *is* good-looking,' she agrees. 'I wonder why I've never thought of it before. It's strange, when you come to think of it. But he still isn't my type.'

'What is your type?'

'It's hard to say. I've dated plenty of men you'd have said were nothing like each other. But they must have been my type, one way or another. I'm not sure what the connecting factor is. It isn't colouring or body type. I've dated blonds and brunettes. And there was one man who was completely bald but who made all the men around him look as though they were trying far too hard with their ridiculous heads of hair. I really liked him.'

'What happened?' I say.

'Oh, he had to go to Alaska or somewhere with his job, and I didn't fancy it.'

I have a vision of a Bear Grylls type striding across the Alaskan Tundra. 'What did he do for a living?'

'He was an actuary,' she says. 'Maybe it was Alabama or Africa. It was definitely somewhere that began with an A. Altrincham, perhaps?'

'And you still didn't fancy it?'

'I like to travel,' she says. 'But I like this place too. And Lily and I were in the middle of buying the bakery. The timing was wrong.'

'That's a shame. Maybe he'll move back here sometime, and you can reconnect.'

'I doubt it,' she says. 'He messaged me a few months later to say he'd met someone, and he was getting married.'

'I'm sorry.'

'Don't be. There are plenty more fish in the sea, even around Honeywell.'

'But not Will?' I don't know why I'm pursuing the subject. It's nothing to me what two complete strangers choose to do. I'm just intrigued.

'Not remotely,' she says. 'He's all yours.'

I jerk upright. 'What makes you say that? I told you I've just come out of a difficult relationship. I'm not thinking about another one for a long time, if ever.'

'My mistake,' she says. 'Are you going to give me the grand tour?'

I show her the rest of the house. She surveys my bedroom thoughtfully. 'It's rather bare, isn't it?'

'I told you I didn't bring much with me when I left. Most of the things in Charlie's flat were there when I arrived. And the things we bought together aren't mine.'

'They aren't his either,' she says.

'But he isn't the one who called it a day and left.'

She sits on the end of my bed and regards me thoughtfully. 'You're allowed to decide a relationship isn't working for you.'

'But you usually do the other person the courtesy of discussing it first.'

'Why didn't you?' she says.

I'd decided not to think about Charlie for a while, but the temptation to discuss him is too much. Isabella is a sympathetic listener, and I doubt she'll try to persuade me I've made a mistake.

'Don't talk about it if you'd rather not,' she says. 'It's your own business, no one else's.'

'I'm not sure where to begin. And I'm scared that if I start talking, I'll never be able to stop.'

'I know the feeling,' she says.

'That's different. You love the sound of your own voice.'

'True,' she agrees. 'But I'm also able to shut up for a while and listen to a friend. I won't comment if you don't want me to. Despite my undeserved reputation for chatter, I'm excellent at keeping secrets. I found out Lily was pregnant before Jack did, and I never said a word.'

'How did you find out?' I say. 'Godmotherly second sense?'

'It could also have something to do with the fact she turned a delicate shade of green one morning and rushed out of the shop. I remembered she'd gone off her favourite cookies, and I put two and two together.'

'Trust you to notice that,' I say.

'The point is that I didn't breathe a word to Jack when he came into the shop later that day.'

'There isn't much to tell,' I say. 'I've been living with Charlie for the past four years. We met at university and dated on and off for a while. I wasn't sure about moving in together, but he was adamant it made sense. He'd bought himself a flat, and he said it was ridiculous for me to keep paying rent on my studio flat when I could move in with him. He said we could put my rent into a savings account and use it to buy somewhere bigger when we started a family.'

'I can see that makes financial sense,' she says. 'But you weren't sure about it?'

'It was just cold feet. He was right to say we should give it a try. I moved in, and I've been living there ever since.'

'Saving your rent money?' she says.

'I believe so.'

'What do you mean? You must know whether you've been saving it.'

'I'm sure we have. Charlie is weird with money. He's always moving it around and changing accounts to get better interest rates. I couldn't keep up. It seemed easier to leave it to him. He's better at that sort of thing than I am.'

'But it's your money,' she says.

'I said that once, but he pointed out I would have been paying rent anyway, so it didn't make much difference to me.'

She doesn't look convinced. 'I wouldn't let anyone tell me what I could and couldn't do with my own money.'

'It wasn't like that. He liked to be in charge of the day-to-day logistics, and I wasn't too bothered. He must have been investing it well because he told me a few weeks ago we had enough for a deposit on a house. With the sale of his flat, he said we'd be able to afford a three bedroom outside London.'

'Is that what you wanted?' she says.

'I thought so. But now I'm not so sure.'

'Did you tell him that?'

I think back to the row Charlie and I had the evening he told me we could finally afford to move house. He was right to be confused and upset. I'd been happy to go along with all his plans until then. I don't know why I suddenly raised objections. He didn't speak to me for a couple of days, which is always the way he handles disagreements. He says it's better than constant arguments. But I hate it. I'd far rather discuss things rationally and come to some sort of compromise that works for us both.

'I told him I didn't feel ready,' I say. 'He was pretty upset, as you can imagine. First, he said I'd wasted six years of his life and treated him like a fool. Then he said I'd used him for cheap rent. But that wasn't true. I offered to pay half of his mortgage from the day I moved in, but he refused. He said he was easily able to afford it himself, and it made much more sense to put my money into high yield deposit accounts, so that's what we did. I paid him the same amount as I paid my old landlord.'

'But without being on the deeds,' she says. 'I don't think much of that.'

'Charlie said it didn't matter. He said when we bought a house, it would be a joint purchase because I'd be putting my money into it too. I can see his point. When I first moved into the flat, I hadn't put anything into it, so there was no reason for me to have a share in it.'

'Did you split the other bills?' she asks.

'I bought most of the food, and I paid the utility bills. Charlie never wanted the heating on, and I hate being cold, so it was only fair that I paid.'

'Let me guess,' she says. 'You cooked and cleaned too?'

'Only because he worked longer hours than me. It would have been unreasonable to expect him to come in from a long day at work and start cooking and cleaning when I'd only been at work from nine to five. Anyway, that's how we saw it.'

'It sounds idyllic.' She sees my expression and sighs. 'I'm sorry, Olivia. I won't say any more. If it worked for you, it worked for you. Why did you hesitate when he started talking about moving somewhere bigger?'

'I have no idea. Charlie told me I was panicking because I'm not good with change. He was great about the whole thing after he'd calmed down. He said he knew what I was like, so he should have broached the subject more carefully with me. He promised not to mention it again for a week to give me time to get used to the idea.'

'And did you?' she says.

'Almost. I persuaded myself I was being immature and panicking about nothing. Charlie was right to say this was something we'd discussed several times over the years. How was he to know I'd react like that?'

'You realise you're allowed to react in any way you like?' she says.

'Maybe. But I'd go to bed each night convinced this was what I wanted, and that everything was fine. Then I'd wake up each morning in a cold sweat, wanting to run away. None of it was Charlie's fault. It was my fault for being miserably indecisive.'

I look past her out of the window. The elm trees at the bottom of the garden are in full leaf, and a nuthatch is swooping in and out of a hole in the tallest one, its beak full of fluff. It seems to have no difficulty in making a home for itself and starting a family. I doubt it had to spend the winter months being persuaded by its mate that now was the perfect time to find a bigger hole and make it their forever nest. I don't know why I'm less decisive than a nuthatch.

'What happened next?' Isabella prompts me. 'Did you decide one way or the other? Given that you're sitting on a bed in Honeywell talking to me, I assume you must have done.'

'Not really. I got up one morning and went to work and gave in my notice. It felt as though I was on autopilot. I half hoped my boss would persuade me to stay. But she accepted my resignation at once and even offered to waive my notice period. I thought she must have someone else she wanted to bring in, but I don't think so. I heard her on the phone to the temp agency that afternoon, and I know how much she dislikes having to use temps. It's a lot of extra work for her.'

'That was nice of her,' says Isabella. 'Not many employers would be so understanding.'

'Especially when there was nothing to understand,' I say. 'As far as she was concerned, an employee who had been with her for several years had decided to move on. I almost asked her about it, but something stopped me. I was too relieved to want to rock the boat.'

'How did Charlie react to the news you'd quit your job?'

'I didn't tell him. I have no idea why. He would have been delighted. He was always telling me I should cut down my hours to give me more time to look after things at home. He said he was earning enough to support us both, and it would be good practise for when we had children.'

'When was this?' she says.

'Last week. I didn't go in to work the following morning. Instead, I waited until Charlie had left the flat, threw my clothes into a suitcase, and called a taxi. I took the first train to Southampton, picked up a rental car, and set off. The rest is history.'

She squeezes my hand. 'Good for you. Is this a temporary thing, or is it permanent?'

'I don't know. I had this overwhelming feeling I needed to escape. I wasn't sure from what. I haven't allowed myself to look more than a couple of days ahead.'

'That's wise,' she says. 'For what it's worth, I don't think you have a problem with change. Look how well you've settled into Honeywell.'

'But that's only temporary. It feels like an extended holiday. Buying a house and settling down is a different thing entirely.'

She jumps off the bed. 'Perhaps. But it isn't always a good idea to accept what other people tell us about ourselves. Are you hungry?'

'A little. Why?'

She pulls me to my feet. 'I've remembered the kitchen at the Red Lion stays open late on Thursdays. I haven't had a thing to eat since this afternoon. What do you say to walking down to the pub to see whether there's any of Shelley's game pie left?'

Chapter Thirteen

Isabella doesn't mention Charlie again, for which I'm grateful. There's nothing to say. I've left, even if I'm unable to articulate why. I'll have to talk to him at some point, but I'm not ready to do that yet. Maybe I won't have to. He may be so angry with me for what I've done that he won't want to see me or speak to me again.

It's a pleasant thought, but I doubt it. Charlie has always expected me to come around to his viewpoint and accept I was in the wrong. And I'm definitely in the wrong this time for leaving him without a word. I'd be devastated if someone did that to me. Nevertheless, I keep his number blocked and don't check any of my emails. I'll have to contact him sometime, but not now.

I'm having a great time in Honeywell. Not only is it a lovely village, but I'm enjoying working in the bakery. Isabella and Abby are friendly and uncomplicated, and I don't reach the end of each day feeling as though the weight of the world is on my shoulders and crushing the life out of me. It's been too long since I took a holiday. Charlie hates being away from home for more than a few days at a time, and I've never yet booked somewhere with which he hasn't found fault.

I don't know what he'd think of Honeywell, but I suspect he wouldn't be too impressed with it. Not that it matters, as there's very little chance of him arriving on my doorstep. I haven't told anyone where I am, and Honeywell is the last place he'd think to look.

There are no cinemas or theatres here, and the closest thing to fine dining is the Red Lion. The food there is excellent, but it doesn't have any Michelin stars, which is the yardstick by which Charlie measures any new place.

I finally meet Lily, the co-owner of the bakery, and Isabella's business partner. She comes into the bakery one afternoon while I'm serving there alone. It's Abby's afternoon off, and Isabella is in the office doing the accounts.

I greet her politely when she comes in. 'Good afternoon. How may I help you?'

'You must be Olivia,' she says.

'That's right.' I study her carefully, but I'm sure I haven't met her before.

'I'm Lily,' she says, holding out her hand. 'I expect Isabella's mentioned me.'

'She has!' I say. 'How's your little girl doing?'

'Much better, thanks,' she says. 'She's coming out of hospital tomorrow morning.'

'What a relief for you.'

She nods. 'It's been awful. It's the first time she's been properly ill. I feel as though I haven't slept in weeks. Daisy's dad is great, and my mum has been wonderful, but Daisy has wanted me with her all the time. I'm exhausted.'

I look at her more carefully and see she's telling the truth. She's pale, and she has dark circles under her eyes.

'Lots of the customers have been asking about her,' I say. 'Everyone seems to know her.'

'My mum often brings her in here. She looks after her three days a week, and they come in to choose something to take home for tea. It's Daisy's favourite place in the whole world. Have you met Bernie yet?'

'Several times,' I say. 'He's gorgeous, isn't he?'

'He's lovely. Daisy adores him. She runs over to give him a hug whenever she sees him. He's very gentle with her. He licks her face, but he doesn't jump up at her.'

'He doesn't afford me the same courtesy,' I say. 'He launches himself at me whenever he sees me and tries to knock me over.'

'I take it you've met his owner too?' she says.

'I have. She's rather sweet.'

Lily gives me an awestruck look. 'If there's one word I never expected to hear applied to Mrs Ogilvie, it's sweet.'

'She has a brusque manner,' I agree. 'But she's devoted to that dog. It's a rule with me that anyone who loves animals can't be all bad.'

'True,' she says. 'It took her a while to warm up to me, and I'm not convinced she's quite got there with Isabella. But I'm glad you've been getting on with her all right.'

'So far,' I say. 'Did you know it's her eightieth birthday in August?'

'How do you know?'

'She told me recently. We were talking about the history of the village, and she mentioned she moved into her cottage when she was five, almost seventy-five years ago.'

'Goodness!' she says. 'That's quite an achievement. How is she celebrating?'

'That's the thing. I don't think she is. She said she'd be getting a cake for Bernie, as usual, but nothing more. It seemed a little sad. In fact, I was wondering …'

Isabella appears behind us. 'Hi, Lily! I didn't hear you come in. How's my favourite goddaughter?'

'That depends,' says Lily. 'How many do you have?'

'Only the one at present,' says Isabella. 'Unless you have something to tell me?'

'Decidedly not!' says Lily. 'And can you be a godmother to more than one child in the same family?'

'Just watch me!' says Isabella. 'How's she doing?'

'Much better,' says Lily. 'The doctor says we can bring her home tomorrow, all being well.'

Isabella hugs her. 'That's wonderful! You must be so relieved.'

'And nervous,' says Lily. 'I've hated her being in hospital, but I've felt safe while she's there.'

Isabella gives her a reassuring smile. 'You'll be fine. Jack will take the pair of you straight back if anything changes. Or your mother will. If they're both too drunk, you only have to call me, and I'll be there in three minutes.'

'How about if you're drunk?' says Lily.

'I'm never drunk,' says Isabella. 'And I shall make it a point not to have more than one small glass of cider until I'm sure Daisy doesn't need me.'

'You had four the other night,' I say, and she frowns.

'I don't think you can be right. A responsible godmother is always available, always sober, and always prepared.'

'Like a girl guide?' I say.

'Exactly! I was a guide for almost six weeks.'

'What happened?' asked Lily. 'Didn't you like it?'

'I loved it,' says Isabella. 'But the leaders told my mother there were only two of them, and I required a whole leader all to myself. So, they had to respectfully decline the honour of my continued presence.'

'What did you do?' I ask, fascinated.

'Exactly what I was supposed to,' she says. 'I was almost halfway through my helpfulness badge, which was annoying. I only had a few more deeds of kindness to perform. After that, I wanted to try for my fishing badge.'

'I'd love to hear the leaders' side of it,' says Lily.

'So would I,' says Isabella. 'But my mother advised against it. I don't know why. She was probably worried they would realise their mistake and be upset. Anyway, that's all in the past now. Is Olivia looking after you?'

'I haven't had the chance,' I say. 'I was about to ask what Lily would like when you came through and distracted us with tales of your childhood exploits.'

'The exact word my guide leaders used,' says Isabella. 'How odd!'

'I'm a little disappointed to see you've lowered the standard of staff training,' says Lily. 'When I first started working here, I had to say, "Thank you for visiting us at The Sugarloaf Bakery. I hope your experience was everything you hoped for," whenever a customer left.'

'But you haven't left yet,' says Isabella. 'How do you know Olivia wouldn't have said it when you'd finished?'

'I stand corrected,' says Lily. 'I came in to collect Mum's wholemeal loaf before you sell out. She and Dad have gone to Southampton for the day, and she was worried she wouldn't be back before the bakery closed. I told her I'd drop it on her doorstep on my back to the hospital.'

'I've already put one aside for her,' says Isabella, handing her a wrapped loaf. 'And what can I get for you?'

'I'm fine, thanks,' says Lily. 'I had lunch at home.'

'Nonsense,' says Isabella. 'You have to keep your strength up at times like this. Don't forget you're eating for two.'

'I most certainly am not,' says Lily. 'The only person eating for two around here is you.'

I stifle a laugh, and Isabella gives me a wounded look. 'You aren't supposed to take her side.'

'I'd better get going,' says Lily. 'I told Jack I'd be back at the hospital ten minutes ago.'

Isabella drops a couple of brownies into a bag and hands it to her. 'Please give these to my goddaughter. Tell her that Whizzy sent them.'

'She can have one bite,' says Lily. 'Jack and I will eat the rest. Nice to meet you, Olivia. Thanks for standing in for me at such short notice.'

Isabella nudges me in the ribs. 'Olivia, our customer is leaving,' she says in an encouraging tone.

'What?' I say. 'Oh, yes! Thank you for visiting us at The Sugarloaf Bakery today. I hope … I'm sorry, I've forgotten the rest.'

Isabella tuts. 'So much for my intensive staff training. You see how it is. This younger generation won't be taught.'

'I'm twenty-nine,' I say.

'Then there's no hope for you. Please excuse her, Lily. I'm sure your experience today was everything you hoped for and more. I'll come over to see Daisy this evening if that's ok?'

'Are you sure?' says Lily. 'She'll be out tomorrow morning.'

'Quite sure,' says Isabella.

She watches Lily leave. 'There's a rather nice cafe in the hospital foyer that stays open until seven. They reduce their prices around six thirty. It would be a pity not to visit it one last time.'

'And you might pick up a nice doctor while you're at it,' I say. 'Your eyes will meet over the one remaining slice of reduced-price banana bread. You'll both reach out for it at the same time, and …'

'If he thinks I'm going on a date with him after that, he can think again!' she interrupts. 'So much for the healing profession.'

'Have fun, anyway,' I say. 'There was something I meant to mention to you before I left. I started talking about it with Lily, but you interrupted us. Did you know Mrs Ogilvie is about to turn eighty?'

'I had no idea,' she says. 'She does pretty well for her age, doesn't she? She's always out and about with Bernie.'

'She told me the other day she isn't celebrating it,' I say. 'I thought that was rather sad.'

'How can you not celebrate your eightieth birthday?' she exclaims.

'That's what I thought. But I barely know her. It isn't my place to say anything. You know her much better than I do. Maybe you can persuade her it would be a shame not to celebrate such a milestone birthday. She says she doesn't have any family around here, but she must know plenty of people if she's lived here all her life.'

'I never see her with anyone,' says Isabella. 'But she must have some old friends living here.'

'I was wondering whether we could throw a small party for her at the Sugarloaf?' I say. 'She seems to be a regular customer.'

'That's a great idea!' says Isabella. 'Do you mean a surprise party?'

'I don't know. Do you think Mrs Ogilvie is a surprise party sort of person?'

'Why not?' she says.

'Some people don't like surprises. I'm not too keen on them myself.'

'I'd love one,' she says. 'But I'm not Mrs Ogilvie. Could you talk to her and find out?'

'Ask her whether she'd like a surprise party? Wouldn't that give the game away?'

'We'll have to find out some other way,' she says. 'Who does she know who comes in here?'

'I have no idea. I've only met her a couple of times.'

'There's Mr Mason,' she says. 'The pair of them used to be sworn enemies, but they get on a lot better now. I could ask him what he thinks.'

'The man who owned the bakery? He seems a little indecisive. And forgetful. Do you think he'd be able to keep it a secret?'

'Maybe not,' says Isabella. 'But I'm glad you mentioned it. I'd hate to think of her celebrating her birthday all by herself. Besides, it's about time the Sugarloaf held a party. We had one when we re-opened, but that was ages ago. I'll mention it to Lily tonight. I can't imagine she'll have any objection. Assuming she's on board with the idea, you and I should start organising it at once.'

Chapter Fourteen

Will comes into the bakery the following morning.

'Hi, Olivia,' he says when he sees me. 'Just the person I was hoping to bump into.'

'The odds were pretty good,' I say. 'I'm here every day except Wednesday and Sunday. How can I help you?'

'I was wondering whether you'd like to come to Harfield with me tomorrow,' he says. 'Tomorrow being Sunday, one of the days I'm reliably informed Isabella won't have your nose to the grindstone.'

'What's at Harfield?' I say.

'There's an old water mill I've been wanting to photograph for the past week. Every time I start off in that direction, the sky clouds over. I was thinking about going first thing tomorrow and taking a picnic. The forecast is good. You haven't seen much of the area, so it would be a chance to remedy that.'

Isabella comes into the shop, carrying a ledger. 'Hi, Will. What are you doing here?'

He frowns as though in concentration. 'Now, what would I be doing in a bakery? Oh, yes, I remember. I've brought my dry-cleaning in. Olivia says it will be ready tomorrow.'

'Don't mess with me,' she says. 'I'm not in the mood. I'm off to see our accountant. I always have the most dreadful fear he'll discover I've been cooking the books and report me to the Inland Revenue.'

'Have you been cooking the books?' he asks with interest.

'Not to the best of my knowledge,' she says. 'But you never know. It's the sort of thing that might happen when I'm distracted. I'd be off to prison before I could say chocolate éclair.'

'Which would probably be the thing that distracted you in the first place,' I say.

'Very true. I'd better get going. It would look suspicious to be late. He'd be bound to think I had something to hide.'

'Will asked me whether I'd like to see Harfield water mill tomorrow,' I tell her. 'Will I be safe?'

She stops with her hand on the door. 'With Will? I'd say the chances are slightly better than even, but don't hold me to that.'

'At the mill, I mean. Is there likely to be a landslip that tips us both into the mill stream?'

'Hard to say,' she says. 'But you should go. My parents used to take me and Georgia there when we were younger. We fell into the stream once, but it wasn't because of a landslide.'

'And I wasn't there to take the blame,' says Will. 'What happened?'

'Georgia was being even more annoying than usual,' says Isabella. 'I forget why. Got to go!'

She rushes out and jumps into her car, and we watch her drive away.

'I hope you feel reassured by that,' says Will. 'You should be safe as long as you're not too annoying.'

'It sounds like fun,' I say. 'Did you say you wanted to take a picnic?'

'I did. But I'll sort that out.'

'No need. Isabella lets me have anything I want once it's past its sell by date. If you can put up with stale sandwiches and yesterday's brownies, we'll be fine.'

'If you're sure,' he says. 'I'll bring something to drink. I'd offer to pick you up, but you live opposite me. Shall we aim to leave around nine o'clock tomorrow morning?'

I remember what I discussed with Isabella last night. 'Do you have a moment?'

'I have nothing but moments,' he says. 'That's the beauty of being on assignment. There's no one to check up on you.'

'Until they ask for your portfolio,' I remind him.

'True, but they won't do that this week, so I'm fine. Is there something you want to discuss? If so, may I have a cappuccino? Have you mastered those yet?'
a

'If you don't mind the foam being somewhat uneven,' I say. 'And if you aren't expecting elaborate art.'

'Something simple like the Sydney Opera House will be fine,' he says. 'Can I buy you one too? You could gulp it down between customers.'

'I'm allowed as much coffee as I can drink,' I say. 'It's one of the many perks of this job.'

'What are the others?' he asks.

'I've already told you about the cakes. I can't remember the rest of them right now, but I know Isabella enumerated them at length on my first day here. I seem to recall one of them was her sparkling conversation and inexhaustible supply of trivia.'

'I hope she pays you well,' he says, sitting at the table next to the door. 'Before you say anything, I'm aware this is Mrs Ogilvie's table. I'll move the second I see her sailing down the high street.'

'It's more Bernie's table,' I say. 'Isabella gave me strict instructions that he's only allowed to sit at the table by the door. He isn't allowed to rampage all over the shop. He doesn't strike me as much of a rampager, anyway. He knows where the basket of dog biscuits is kept, and he likes to stay within striking distance.'

'He's a bright little fellow,' he agrees.

I hand him his cappuccino, and he peers at the surface. 'I thought I requested the Opera House.'

'I'm more of a fan of portraits,' I say. 'This is modelled on one of Picasso's more famous works.'

'Which one?'

'I have no idea. But if you squint hard, that blob looks like a nose.'

'It looks nothing like my nose,' he says. 'Or yours either. But the clump of chocolate powder next to it looks rather like an eyebrow, so I'll give you the benefit of the doubt.'

He takes a sip. 'It tastes fabulous, which is the main thing. I'd never have known you hadn't been doing this for years. You're wasted as a veterinary nurse.'

'I mix up an excellent solution of glucose and vitamins too,' I say.

'I'll try that next time I'm in,' he says. 'You said you had something you wanted to talk about?'

'It's about Mrs Ogilvie. I was chatting with her the other day, and she mentioned her eightieth birthday is coming up soon. At least, she was talking about how long she'd been living in her cottage, and I did the maths. She isn't planning to celebrate it, so I thought it would be nice to throw her a small party at the bakery. Isabella and Lily like the idea. But it was my suggestion, so I should do most of the work.'

'It's a great idea,' he says. 'I'll be happy to help out in any way I can.'

'I'm glad you said that. It makes it less awkward to ask you for a favour. I wondered whether you might be the official photographer.'

'You *are* pushing the boat out,' he says. 'How big will this party be? Do I need to run up to London to fetch my tux?'

'That's up to you. It won't be a fancy party, but it struck me we have a professional photographer right here in the village, so we should make use of him. Will you still be here in August?'

'I should be,' he says. 'I'm happy to take photographs for you. Let me know if there are any other ways I can help. I really should get going now. I promised my landlady I'd help her to put together a bookcase this afternoon. Apparently, her husband hasn't got around to it, and she's getting desperate. She may regret her impatience when she sees what kind of a job I do. Flat pack furniture is not my forte.'

'I'll remember that if I decide to put up an awning for this party,' I say. 'We don't want it crashing down on the customers' heads.'

'It would make a wonderful picture,' he says. 'I could sell it to the tabloids for millions and never have to work again.'

'But they'd sue the bakery, and Isabella wouldn't like that. Maybe we should stick to balloons.'

'We can discuss it properly tomorrow,' he says. 'See you at nine o'clock, Olivia.'

Chapter Fifteen

Will is waiting by his car when I arrive the following morning.

'It's a lovely day,' he says. 'I ought to get some good shots of the mill.'

'How far is it?' I ask, climbing into the car and dumping my bag of food onto the back seat.

'About forty-five minutes if the traffic isn't too bad. We'll head towards Lyndhurst, then turn off towards Harfield.'

He sets off in the direction of the high street.

'Do you want to stop and get a coffee for the road?' he asks as we approach the Sugarloaf.

'Absolutely not! This is my day off. If we go into the bakery, Isabella is bound to discover there's somewhere she needs to be, and I'll end up covering for her. Keep driving. If she comes out of the bakery, pretend not to see her, and put your foot on the accelerator.'

'I'm not sure I like this attitude,' he says. 'As a new employee, I'd have thought you'd be only too pleased to make a good impression.'

'A new and extremely temporary employee,' I say. 'That makes all the difference.'

'You can't be all that temporary,' he says. 'You've promised to organise a party in August.'

'I know, and I'm already regretting it. That's more than two months away.'

He glances over at me. 'Don't you like Honeywell?'

'I love it. But it isn't real. I keep expecting to wake up in my bed in London.'

'Which part of London?'

I wish I hadn't mentioned London. It's the last thing I want to talk about.

He notices my hesitation. 'I only asked because that's where I've been living for the past few years. I have a flat in Hammersmith.'

'I was in Putney,' I say reluctantly.

'Honeywell is a bit of a change from either of those,' he says. 'I've been having a great time down here. I'm spinning it out for as long as I can.'

'How long is your assignment?' I say, happy to move on to safer ground.

He shrugs. 'It's a bit of an open question. I've been working for a commercial photography company for the last few years as a semi-permanent freelancer.'

'That seems a bit of a contradiction in terms,' I say.

'I suppose it does. I'm not a permanent employee, and I don't want to be. But they give me enough contracts that I may as well be. They had someone lined up for this job, but it fell through. I happened to be free, so I agreed to take it on.'

'But it can't make financial sense for you to spend longer on it than you need to,' I say. 'All the freelancers I know are racing to line up their next contracts as quickly as possible.'

'That was me until recently,' he says. 'But I realised that wasn't how I wanted to live. The company have offered me a permanent position, and I'm considering it. But I'd already decided to take a few months off before this job came up, and this seemed an ideal opportunity.'

'Is there a deadline for publication?'

'September,' he says. 'It's coming out at Easter, and they want the photos well before then. It shouldn't be a problem.'

I want to ask him why he needs this time off, but I don't dare. He would probably tell me, but he'd be bound to ask questions in return, and I'm not ready for that.

He reaches into the glove compartment. 'I don't have the half bar of chocolate I hear is the basic requirement for any journey over three miles, but I have a tin of travel sweets if you'd like one.'

I take a sweet and hold out the tin to him. He doesn't take his eyes off the road. 'I'd like a red one, if there are any.'

'I just took the last one,' I say apologetically. 'I'm sorry. They're my favourite.'

'How about an orange one?' he says.

I relax, realising my shoulders have tensed up and my heart has started to race.

He glances at me. 'You aren't feeling carsick, are you?'

I shake my head. 'I don't get carsick. I'm fine, thanks.'

I drop the sweet into his outstretched palm and take a few deep breaths to steady myself. I must learn not to overreact in this sort of situation. So, I took the last red sweet without thinking. Big deal. But it takes me a couple of minutes before I feel completely calm.

I sense Will turning his head to look at me a couple of times, but he doesn't speak until we reach the turning.

'We head west along here for a few miles, then turn off towards Harfield,' he says. 'We can get a coffee there without running the risk of anyone asking you to stand in for them.'

'Didn't you bring a flask? You're supposed to be in charge of drinks.'

'My landlady didn't have one,' he says. 'I settled for a bottle of wine instead. It seemed a reasonable substitute. I even brought my penknife with the bottle opener attachment.'

'Red or white?'

He gives me a smug look. 'I wasn't sure which you preferred, so I went for rosé.'

'Still or sparkling?' I say, and he laughs.

'Is it a dealbreaker?'

'Not at all. I just wanted to worry you.'

'Would you have demanded I took you home if I'd brought the wrong one?' he says.

'Maybe.'

'I knew it! "Now, there's a woman who's difficult to please," I said to myself the first minute I saw you.'

'Is that what you really thought of me?'

'No. What I really thought was, "Now, there's a woman who has terrible taste in cars." Why do you ask?'

'No reason,' I say. 'It's just something someone used to say to me quite often.'

He shoots me a quick look. 'Someone important?'

'I thought so.'

'But you don't still think so?'

'Probably not.'

'Good,' he says. 'No one needs that sort of negativity in their life. Do I take the first or the second left on this road?'

I look at the GPS and guide him for the next few miles.

He pulls up at last outside a small row of shops. 'This is Harfield. At least, I hope it is. Shall we find ourselves some coffee before we set off for the mill?'

I look around. 'I don't see any mill.'

'That's because it's a couple of miles from here,' he says. 'But this is as far as the road goes.'

'There isn't even a track?'

He smiles. 'I should have said this is as far as I'm prepared to take the car. She doesn't like bumping and jolting along stony tracks.'

'Now, there's a car who's difficult to please,' I say, and he laughs.

We set off ten minutes later, clutching our cups of coffee and the picnic basket.

'When you say two miles, do you really mean five?' I ask.

'Not if the map is correct,' he says. 'Don't you like walking?'

'I love walking. I'm less keen on getting lost. Particularly after my recent experience.'

'I can understand that,' he says. 'But look how well it turned out. You were rescued almost at once, and you started a whole new life.'

'I don't know why everyone keeps saying that! I haven't started a whole new anything. All I'm doing is taking some time off while I decide what to do next. It isn't much different from what you're doing, and no one tells you that you've started a whole new life.'

'You may be right,' he says. 'But it feels different. I'm just taking a few months off from a job I love.'

'How do you know I don't love my job?' I say.

'I don't. Do you enjoy it?'

'I do, although I'm ready for a change. I've been working for a practice in Wimbledon for the past six years.'

'Are you going back after your break?'

'I don't think that's a good idea,' I say. 'Not because of the job itself, but there are other things …' I'm not sure how to finish the sentence. No matter how hard I try to avoid the subject of my past, it keeps sneaking up on me regardless.

'There must be a lot of that sort of work around Honeywell,' he says, not appearing to notice my confusion.

'I like small animal work,' I say. 'I haven't had much experience with rural practices. Just the odd cow and sheep during my training, but nothing since then.'

'London probably isn't overrun with people keeping sheep and cows in their high-rise flats,' he says.

'You'd be surprised what some people consider as pets. But you're right. Our practice mainly treated cats and dogs and rabbits and hamsters.'

'No snakes?' he says.

'A few. Don't tell me you're a secret snake lover and keep a pet boa constrictor in your Hammersmith flat? What have you done with it while you're down here?'

'I brought him with me,' he says. 'Haven't you noticed him wandering around the front garden each morning, enjoying the sunshine?'

'I must have missed that. I have extremely early starts at the bakery. Do you really keep a snake?'

'Absolutely not!' he says. 'I'm terrified of them.'

'Even little ones?'

'Particularly little ones. At least, with the big ones you know where they are. The small ones could be anywhere, and you'd never know.'

'You'd better watch your feet,' I say. 'There are adders in the New Forest. They're fairly rare, but we might spot one.'

'Not this year,' he says. 'They've been banned. I checked before I agreed to come down here.'

'Banned?'

'That's right. My manager assured me there would be no snakes in the area for the entire duration of my visit.'

I burst out laughing. 'If it makes you feel better to feel they've been banned this year, I'll go along with it. Is it just snakes you don't like? How do you feel about spiders?'

'They're even worse,' he says with a shudder. 'Snakes tend to live outside. Spiders have no such boundaries. There was one in the bath the other day, and I had to go downstairs in a towel and ask my landlady to remove it.'

'What was it doing in the bath?' I ask.

'I didn't look too closely. The back crawl, I think.'

'Next time you find a spider in the house, and the landlady isn't around, you can call me,' I say. 'I can be there in twenty seconds.'

'What if you don't answer your phone?' he says. 'Could I throw stones at your window?'

'My landlady is very nice, but I expect she'd draw the line at that.'

'Is your bedroom at the front of the house?' he says.

'It's at the back. Why do you ask?'

'Because mine's at the front. We could have set up a signalling system with candles. One flash for a house spider, two for a tarantula, three for a very small snake, and four for a python.'

'My landlady may think you're trying to proposition her.'

'The phone, it is,' he says. 'But please keep it on you at all times.'

'Is that the mill over there?' I point towards a clump of trees. I can just see the outline of a roof behind them.

'Let's have a look at the map.' He waves his phone around. 'There doesn't seem to be any connection.'

I watch him, amused. 'Why does everyone do that? Do they think there are stray telecommunication waves floating around, and all they need to do is catch one?'

'I don't know what else to do,' he says. 'Except for climbing up a very high tree. That seems to work in movies.'

'I'm happy to watch you try,' I say. 'Are we at least going in the right general direction?'

He switches off his phone. 'I thought we were. But this path keeps twisting and turning, and I'm losing track.'

'In which case, we should definitely head for that building over there. There may be someone we can ask.'

I strike off up the side path towards the clump of trees, and Will follows me.

'Can you hear something?' I say.

'What sort of something?'

I point towards the trees. 'I thought I heard voices.'

'Are you sure it isn't music?' he says.

'You may be right. Come on, there's bound to be someone who can tell us which way the mill is.'

We quicken our pace and head up the slope towards the trees. The bursts of noise and laughter grow louder as we approach.

'Do you think they're having a rave?' says Will.

'It would be a strange time to have one. Don't they usually take place in deserted warehouses in the middle of the night?'

He raises an eyebrow. 'You seem to know an awful lot about them. I'll defer to your superior knowledge.'

'That's the only thing I remember. I'd be willing to bet Isabella knows a lot more about them than I do. You should ask her if you want more information. She's probably the local organiser.'

'It wouldn't surprise me,' he says. 'The noise seems to be coming from the other side of the trees. Maybe they'll invite us to join them. I'm glad I brought that bottle of rosé now. It's like currency in those places. It should stop anyone from attacking us.'

A movement among the trees catches my eye. A moment later, a man appears. He's dressed in a full-length leather apron and is holding what looks like a large hammer.

I take an involuntary step backwards, and Will laughs. 'He's a blacksmith. He's probably working on one of the farms around here. He's bound to know where we are.'

The man sees us and waves. We walk towards him. I keep a wary eye on his hammer, but he doesn't seem as though he's about to swing it at us.

'Hi!' calls Will when we come within earshot. 'We were hoping you could tell us where we are.'

The man stops and considers. 'You are in the fair vale of Mitcham.'

'Where?' says Will. 'We're trying to find the old water mill. Is it somewhere around here?'

'There is a water mill yonder,' says the man, pointing. 'Master Twyford built it nearly two score years ago, and a great wonder it is.'

I glance at Will, who looks as puzzled as I feel.

'I'm not talking about a modern building,' he says. 'We're looking for the water mill. My GPS says it's in this general direction, but there's no signal, and we're lost.'

'GPS?' says the man.

'Satellite,' I explain. 'I should have brought the map from the car, but I thought we'd have enough connection if we got lost. Evidently not.'

'Your cart?' he says. 'Where is it?'

'Car,' says Will. 'We left it in the village.'

'Which was unwise,' says the man. 'There are thieves in that village. Nothing is safe.'

Will looks startled. 'Car thieves? Perhaps we'd better …'

'It's fine,' I say. 'I saw you lock it, and it has an alarm. I'm not walking all the way back there to check on your precious car.'

He doesn't look convinced, but I'm rapidly losing my patience. 'I mean it, Will. I want my lunch. Let's find this mill and have something to eat.'

'An excellent idea,' says the man. 'Make your way through yonder thicket, and you will find all the food you want.'

'Another village?' says Will.

'Exactly!' says the man.

He turns and strides off the way he came, beckoning to us to follow.

I hang back. 'I'm not going with him. He seems a little strange. Maybe we should head back to the village after all and check your car. Someone there is bound to have a map we can use.'

A look of comprehension flashes over Will's face, and he grins. 'I think we'll be fine. Come on! He's almost out of sight.'

He takes my hand and starts jogging along the path after the blacksmith. I almost pull away and turn back the way we came. But his hand feels oddly comforting. He's tall and strongly built. He can probably cope with most things. As long as the blacksmith doesn't start waving his hammer around. Will's penknife may not be a match for that, even with the bottle opener attachment.

We weave through the clump of trees and stop dead. Below us is a large field with hundreds of people in brightly coloured clothes milling around. Several men on horseback are playing what looks like a game of polo. Scores of tents are spread across the field, and the sound of music and laughter rises up to meet us.

A woman carrying a large bundle is climbing the hill towards us.

'Welcome, strangers!' she calls when she sees us. 'I did not think to see so strangely clad a couple on this fine June morning.'

'Sorry about that!' says Will. 'We didn't expect to be here today, or we'd have made more of an effort.'

'And speaking such a strange tongue,' she says. 'Are you from foreign parts?'

'If London counts,' he says.

'A foreign place, indeed! Still, if you are loyal servants of the crown, I bid you welcome.' She wanders over to talk to a nearby group of people.

I stare at the scene in front of me. 'Have we stumbled into Brigadoon?'

'Wouldn't that be something?' says Will. 'The real explanation is rather more prosaic. I remember seeing a flyer when I was in Lyndhurst last week. It's the annual medieval fair.'

'That's a relief! I thought for a moment the blacksmith was about to murder us both.'

'He may still plan to,' he says. 'But on the off chance he's forgotten about us and found himself another victim, shall we go and explore? It would be a shame not to take a look now we're here.'

'Fine,' I say. 'But just in case that blacksmith is still hanging around, you can go first.'

Chapter Sixteen

I follow him down the hill towards the field.

'I feel rather underdressed,' I say. 'Or overdressed. I'm not sure which.'

'You're fine,' he says. 'That summer dress isn't vastly different to what some of the women here are wearing.'

'Thank goodness I'm wearing a long dress. Can you imagine what they'd call me if my knees were showing?'

'I'm not worried about my knees,' he says. 'These jeans cover them. But I feel I'm lacking something regarding the rest of my outfit.'

He looks at a group of men standing by the entrance to a nearby tent. 'They knew how to do sleeves in those days. Those shirts make me feel distinctly underdressed.'

'There aren't too many T-shirts around,' I agree.

'Maybe I can buy myself something to wear.'

'Are you serious? We'll only be here for an hour or so.'

He looks around him. 'There seems plenty to see and do.'

'They won't throw you out because you've turned up in a Hugo Boss T-shirt.'

'Selfridges,' he corrects me. 'My mother gave me a voucher for my birthday last month. I thought I'd better spend it before I lost it, which is what I usually do with vouchers. If I'd known I was coming here, I'd have spent it on something more appropriate.'

'I don't think puffy sleeves and leather jerkins are in this year.'

'You're wrong,' he says. 'They were all over the catwalk in Milan. And those long, pointy shoes were everywhere. If I'd had the forethought to buy myself a pair, I wouldn't be sticking out like a sore thumb right now.'

'Despite the jeans?'

He gives me a reproving look. 'These aren't jeans. They're cotton hose.'

'I stand corrected. Shall we stand here all day arguing about fashion, or shall we see what's going on?'

'Give me a moment to stash this picnic basket behind a tree, and I'm all yours.'

We wander around the field, watching the performers walking on stilts and juggling. One man is playing a lute badly, but at least he's trying.

'I can't make out whether that's supposed to be Greensleeves or Ticket to Ride,' whispers Will.

'Shhh! He'll hear you. I know the Beatles are timeless, but they weren't around in medieval times.'

'True,' he says. 'I think he's actually playing That'll be the Day. He's obviously a Buddye Hollye fan.'

'I like it,' I say. 'And he looks as though he's having fun. He isn't bothered by what other people think, which is a good thing. I wish I could be more like that.'

'Are you bothered about what people think of you?' he asks.

'Yes.'

'You shouldn't be.'

I give a fake start. 'My goodness! Why hasn't anyone told me that before? This is life-changing information!'

He smiles. 'Fair enough. But it's a shame to waste our lives trying to be what we think other people want us to be, when we're fine as we are.'

'What if we aren't?'

He shoots me a quick look. 'Are you asking generally or specifically?'

'I don't know. A bit of both.'

'I'd give you the same answer either way,' he says. 'We're all of us fine, just the way we are.'

'What if we burgle houses or hack into nuclear facilities and steal the codes?'

'That's oddly specific,' he says. 'Do you make a habit of doing either of those things?'

'No, but it's a cliché to say everyone is fine just the way they are. It's patently obvious that's not true in a lot of cases.'

'You've got me there,' he says. 'But my point still stands. What do you think is so wrong with you?'

'I'm not talking about anything in particular,' I say. 'But you hardly know me. You've met me a couple of times in the bakery, and we've been for a walk and got lost. It isn't nearly enough to make a judgement about what kind of person I am.'

'Maybe not,' he says. 'But if you look at it the other way around, I don't know anything bad about you. Time for a different judgement when I discover you're a cat burglar who targets antique snuff boxes.'

'That also seems oddly specific,' I say. 'Is that what you get up to when you aren't in Honeywell?'

'Nothing so exciting,' he says. 'I work, I go home and I make dinner. I forget to water my plants, then realise they're plastic, so it doesn't matter. Occasionally, I play tennis. It may not be everyone's idea of fun, but it suits me, so I'm sticking with it. How about you? What do you like to do in your spare time?'

'I never seem to have any. I go to work. I come home and clean the flat.'

'That can't take long,' he says. 'It won't get too messy if you're out at work all day.'

'No, but my … flatmate was quite fussy about how it was done. He worked longer hours than I did, so it seemed only fair for me to take care of things at home.'

He pulls a face. 'I wouldn't house share with someone who told me what to do with my spare time. Especially when it's something as boring as housework. Why didn't you tell them where to go?'

I don't meet his eyes. 'It was more complicated than that. When I say housemate, I mean partner.'

'Ah,' he says. 'That makes a difference. But not a huge one. Is that what you're going back to when you leave Honeywell?'

'No. At least, I don't think so. I left him last week.'

'That sounds like an excellent decision to me,' he says.

'Maybe.' To my dismay, I feel my eyes filling with tears, and I turn away before he can see.

He squeezes my hand. 'There's no need to talk about it now. Look at us – we're as far away from real life as it's possible to be. We're living in Mediaeval England. It would be a pity not to make the most of it.'

I smile back at him. 'You're right. This is fun. I saw a stall selling what looks like pies. Shall we contribute to the local economy and try a couple?'

He reaches into his pocket. 'Always assuming they accept modern doubloons.'

'Aren't those Spanish?'

He opens his wallet. 'Who knows? It may be too much to expect them to take Ye American Expresse. But with any luck, they'll change some of these coins into shillings and sixpences for us. Don't let's stand around talking any longer. Let's go and negotiate with the peasants.'

Chapter Seventeen

We find a stall selling pies, and Will buys two.

'We could have stayed in Honeywell and eaten these,' I say.

The stallholder overhears us. 'I know not of this Honeywelle, but I doubt they could compete with our pies, which are known the length and breadth of the kingdom. We have sold them to noblemen and commoners, as far away as London Towne.'

'I must remember to take a look next time I'm in Starbucks,' says Will.

We sit on the grass a little way from the stall to eat our pies.

'Aren't you hungry?' asks Will. 'I thought you were eager to get to the mill so we could have our picnic.'

'I'm ravenous,' I say. 'But I'm waiting for you to try yours first.'

He gives the pie a dubious poke. 'What do you think is in it?'

'How should I know? But you're about to find out.'

'Funny,' he says, 'I had the exact same idea.'

'You won't win this argument,' I say, 'so you may as well give up now. This is the age of chivalry. I'm looking to you for gallantry and courteous behaviour and all the rest of it. That means being the first to try that pie and letting me know whether it's safe.'

'Fine!' He takes an enormous bite and chews.

'Well?' I say.

'Interesting,' he mumbles. 'Definitely a hint of some small mammal, but I can't place it. Rat, perhaps? And there's something slimy. I suppose it could be a frog? It's difficult to tell. The bones are a little crunchy, but the overall flavour isn't too bad.'

He sees my instinctive recoil and laughs. 'You deserved that for making me eat it first. It's very nice. I think it's lamb. And there's some sort of spice I can't place. It's quite pleasant.'

I pick up the pie and take a tentative bite. 'It's lovely!'

'I imagine they're here to make a profit,' he says. 'I expect they get some local bakery to deliver them, then add a few doubloons to the price.'

'Farthings,' I remind him.

'Inflation means we're way past farthings,' he says. 'Sovereigns, perhaps, or guineas. It's a good thing I brought some money with me.'

'I have about ten pounds in my purse,' I say. 'Enough to buy us a drink, at least. Unless you want to retrieve your bottle of wine?'

'Absolutely not,' he says. 'They didn't have supermarkets in mediaeval times.'

'You don't know that for sure. You're a photographer, not a student of mediaeval history. I bet they did have supermarkets. They'd have called them things like Ye Olde Cooperative or Sainsburyshire's. They'd have people standing at the ends of the aisles, handing out free samples of potions.'

'And the shopping baskets would be made of chain mail,' he says.

'And there would be express checkout lanes for knights and lords.'

'Don't be ridiculous!' he says. 'They would have sent their jesters and fools to do their menial work.'

'Not if they wanted to get exactly what they'd written on their list. Noblemen wouldn't allow for random substitutions. I wonder whether they had mediaeval loyalty cards.'

'Probably,' he says. 'They would periodically receive an illuminated piece of parchment, telling them that armour polish was on special that week. You were so quick to assume modern day society was superior. And all along, people in the Middle Ages were having a wonderful time.'

'If they spent all their time wandering around fields and eating pies and jousting, they must have had lots of fun,' I agree.

'Have you finished your pie?' he says. 'Would you like something else?'

'I wouldn't mind something to drink. I don't suppose there's any chance of finding a coffee around here?'

He pulls me to my feet. 'I doubt it. I seem to remember that coffee didn't arrive in the country until about the sixteenth century.'

'Even in the supermarkets?'

'We didn't learn about those in our history lessons, so I can't help you. I can see what looks like a beer tent over there.'

'Even better!' I say. 'I assume mediaeval beer is similar to ours? It doesn't have frogs' legs floating around in it, or anything equally horrible?'

'Only if you pay extra.'

'I'm not doing that. I don't want to run out of doubloons too quickly.'

'You aren't a pirate,' he says. 'How many times do I need to remind you?'

'Arrr!' I hop ahead of him towards the beer tent.

The man serving behind the makeshift bar greets us pleasantly. 'Good morrow, friends. How may I be of service to thee?'

'We're looking for beer,' I say, adding without thinking, 'Prithee.'

I catch Will's eye and laugh. 'You order, if you think you can do any better.'

'Not at all. You have it covered.'

The bartender smiles at me. 'For thee, my lady, I recommend small beer.'

'Why?' I say. 'Don't you know that women drink pints these days?'

'You misunderstand,' he says patiently. 'Small beer is that which is brewed to be less intoxicating, and so may be consumed in greater quantities without ill effect to man or woman.'

'Sounds good to me,' says Will. 'I'll have a gill of that. Or a flagon, or whatever you use to serve it.'

'How about a skip?' I say. 'Do you serve anything besides this small beer?'

'Assuredly,' says the man. 'We serve the finest ale in all the county.'

'I'll have a barrel of that,' I say. 'I think it's best that my friend here sticks to small beer. He doesn't have a strong head.'

'Ale sounds good too,' says Will. 'Maybe I'll try both.'

'We are also serving mead,' says the man. 'Brewed with the honey from Master Lovelock's bees. The finest bees in all of Hampshire, and singularly free from plagues and agues.'

'I'm delighted to hear it,' I say. 'I'd love to try some mead. I've read about it, but I've never tasted it.'

'You're in for a treat,' says Will. 'I had some last year at a Christmas fair, and it was Ambrosia.'

'In which case, you were honoured above the lot of mortals,' says the man.

'Sure,' says Will. 'Lucky me! Ok, that's two flagons of your finest mead, please. What is that? A farthing?'

'Alas,' says the man, 'the taxes on grain have been such this year that prices have risen beyond belief. The King is determined upon war with France, so the taxes continue to rise.'

I hand him a ten-pound note. 'How much will that buy?'

He hands us both a tankard of mead. 'As it happens, the amount you offer is almost correct. Be not alarmed, for a tithe of the merchants' profits goes to the local infirmary for the young.'

He points to a sign pinned to the flap of the tent, proclaiming in heraldic script, *This Mediaeval Fair supports Reardon Children's hospital.*

'That's great,' I say.

'Indeed it is, fair maid. Therefore, reach deep into the recesses of thy pockets and spend freely as you go about.'

'That's pretty much all the cash I have,' I say. 'Unless you take debit cards.'

'I myself do not,' he says. 'But I have heard tell of others present here today who dabble in the witchcraft of magical waves throughout the ether.'

We finish our mead, which is, as Will predicted, delicious. It tastes like the essence of sun-kissed meadows, with bees drifting lazily through the wildflowers.

I take a deep breath. 'If there's a definitive description of liquid gold somewhere, this would be it.'

I follow Will out of the tent, where we almost bump into a woman juggling flaming torches.

'Do you fancy a go?' says Will.

'Not after that mead. I'd burst into flames as soon as I breathed.'

'It was strong, wasn't it?' he says. 'But it beats my bottle of rosé hands down. Why is that man waving at me?'

'I think he wants to fight you.'

'What?' he says, startled.

'He's waving a stick at you. What else could that mean?'

'Maybe he thinks he's a wizard?' he suggests.

'Anything's possible. Why don't we ask him?'

The man waves again. 'A joust, young master, a joust! Cry not craven before thine fair companion.'

'I can't ride a horse,' says Will.

'Tis of no matter, sire,' says the man, taking his arm. 'For this is merely tilting at the quintain. A practice beloved of all young knights in training.'

'There you are,' I say with an encouraging smile. 'It's only tilting. Off you go! I'll stand here and applaud.'

'Why don't you do it if you're so keen?' asks Will.

'I'm a woman!' I say in a shocked tone. 'I'd be put on the ducking stool if I tried something like that.'

'Only sixpence a try,' says the man. 'The successful tilter wins a ribbon for his lady.'

'You can't buy too many ribbons for sixpence,' says Will.

'Five pounds in modern money, sire. But what is that against the chance to impress the fair maiden and win her heart with your skill and daring?'

Will sees my quick grin and sighs. 'If I must. Do you take debit cards?'

'No problem, mate,' says the man.

He hands Will a stick. 'At thine own pace. The target is yonder. Run fast and strike it true, then quicken thine pace so as to avoid the sandbag which pursues thee.'

Will looks alarmed. 'No one said anything about being hit with a sandbag.'

'Cry not craven!' I remind him. 'Besides, we've already donated to the hospital. I mean, the infirmary. I'm sure they'll be only too happy to patch you up.'

He gives me an ironic look but picks up a stick. With a doubtful glance at the target, he sets off towards it at a quick trot, waving his stick wildly. A man standing near the target, chatting with a woman on stilts, jumps out of the way.

Will hits the target right in the centre. He gives a jubilant shout, which is cut off a split second later as the sandbag swings around and hits him in the back of the head, sending him flying. He lies on the grass without moving, and I run towards him.

He rolls over, groans, and sits up. 'What happened?'

'You forgot about the quicken thine pace bit,' I say.

He rubs his head. 'Is that what he meant? He could have made it clearer.'

I help him to his feet. 'I don't see how. He was speaking the King's Englishe to you. It isn't his fault you weren't listening properly.'

He returns the stick to the man, who smiles. 'A valiant attempt. Wouldst thou perchance wish to essay the task once more? Tis only another sixpence.'

'There's no perchance about it,' says Will. 'I'm not tilting at another target as long as I live.'

The man shrugs. 'As you wish. 'Tis not the spirit the King would wish to see in his yeomanry, but no matter.'

I interrupt before Will can make an unpatriotic remark about King Richard, or whoever is supposed to be on the throne right now.

'He hit the target right in the middle,' I say. 'Doesn't that mean he wins a ribbon?'

'Naught but a broken head,' says the man. 'The rules are very clear.'

'Not even a little one?' I plead. 'You've already flouted about ten health and safety regulations in running this so-called game.'

He sighs. 'That one so young should descend to blackmail and extortion. I shall not yield to base threats. Yet, for the sake of thy bright eyes shall I let thee choose a riband for thy wrist.'

'That's more like it,' says Will. 'Which one would you like, Olivia?'

'The maiden art named after a future Lord Protector of England,' says the man. 'Thy patriotism shines like a light in a dark world.'

'I'm not sure you're supposed to know about Cromwell yet,' I say. 'You'd better not mention it again or you'll be accused of witchcraft. I'd like a yellow one, please.'

He hands me the ribbon, and I tie it around my wrist as we wander towards the next tent.

'Are you going to win me a whole rainbow of ribbons?' I ask Will.

'Not a chance. They'd probably make me eat a live frog to get the green one. You'll have to be happy with the one you have.'

A man sitting behind a stall runs out as we pass. 'Good morrow, fair strangers. I am Frances Whytleafe. I am able to take thy likeness in fewer than fifteen minutes of the clock.'

I look at the easel standing next to his stall. 'A cartoonist! Can I pay for him to draw you, Will?'

'Not a hope,' he says.

'Oh, go on. It would be fun.'

'How if I should make a likeness of you both together?' suggests the artist. 'It would be both a memento and an economy. I shall remove twenty-five percent from the final reckoning.'

'I hate having my picture taken,' I say.

'But you're happy enough for me to have mine done,' says Will. 'And it isn't a photograph. Cameras weren't invented in mediaeval times.'

'How do you know?' I grumble. 'Did they teach you that in your history of cameras class at photography school?'

'No, but we covered it in magical inventions of the future,' he says. 'Otherwise known as digital technology.'

'I still think you ought to have your picture done while I watch.'

'And I don't,' he says, grasping my wrist and leading me towards a chair.

'Wonderful!' says the man. 'I shall create a portrait of thee both to gladden thine hearts and remind thee for many years to come of this day.'

'As long as you make it quick,' I say.

'And what are thine interests and dispositions?' he enquires. 'Thy passions and daily pursuits?'

Will and I look at each other.

'He's a photographer, and I'm a veterinary nurse,' I say. 'But I'm working in a bakery at the moment.'

'And how dost thou utilise thy spare time?' he enquires.

'What *do* you do in your spare time?' I ask Will. 'Apart from driving that red car around the countryside rescuing people.'

'Indeed?' says the man. 'A knight errant, I perceive.'

'Otherwise known as a driver with a map,' says Will. 'Olivia's rental car had broken down, and I happened to drive past and see her. That's how we met.'

The artist nods. 'And how does the young maid employ her spare hours when not attending to her livestock?'

I open my mouth to answer, then shut it again. I don't want to tell him I have no hobbies or interests. Or rather, I don't want to tell him that in front of Will. How did that happen? I used to have hundreds of hobbies. Why did I stop doing them? I grew up, I suppose. Most adults don't have time for hobbies. At least, responsible, mature adults don't.

'No matter,' says the man when I don't answer. 'I have already seen into the depths of both thy souls and shall create a likeness accordingly.'

He directs Will to sit next to me, produces a pack of pastel crayons, and starts to sketch.

'Why did I let you talk me into this?' I mutter to Will, trying not to move my lips. I realise this is ridiculous. We aren't having our photo taken, where there's a risk of camera blur. The artist already knows what we look like, and the odds of the final image being in any way recognisable are slim. If he were a proper artist, he wouldn't be wasting his Saturday afternoon touting for business at a mediaeval fair.

'Because it's fun,' Will murmurs back. 'There's nothing wrong with having fun.'

'I'll take your word for it.'

The man draws for ten more minutes, humming a madrigal to himself as he sketches. At last, he lays down his crayon. 'Before I show thee the result, I shall require payment.'

I'll bet he does. I knew he'd be terrible. If he allows us to see the picture first, he knows we won't pay.

'Here you go,' says Will, tapping his card on the reader.

He looks at the paper the man hands him and laughs. 'And you said no one had ever taken a good picture of you, Olivia!'

I peer over his shoulder and burst out laughing. 'That's amazing!'

The man gives us a modest smile. 'You are too kind, my lady.'

'You must be a professional artist in real life,' I say.

'I work in a gallery in Bournemouth. I show my work there occasionally.'

'What brings you here today?' I say. 'You don't appear to have many customers.'

'Because I enjoy it,' he says. 'I come here every year. I love it.'

'You mean, like a hobby?'

'Exactly.' He switches back into character. 'I thank thee for thy custom. Shouldst thou encounter other young couples amidst the throng, who would be glad of this experience, please mention my name and direction unto them.'

'We aren't a couple …' I begin.

'We'd be delighted,' says Will.

Chapter Eighteen

It isn't until we see one of the stallholders taking down their tent that I realise how long we've been here. After having our portrait done, we went to the crafts tent and tried our hand – unsuccessfully – at pottery. Will's attempt was more recognisable as a vase than mine, but I couldn't advise him to give up the day job on the strength of it. After a brief stop to sample the spiced gingerbread, we watched a wedding reenactment which would have put many of today's bridezillas to shame. Somehow, the afternoon seems to have got away from us, and it's now early evening.

'Do you know what time it is?' I ask Will. 'I don't wear a watch, and my phone's out of power again.'

'We could find ourselves a sundial,' he says. 'If only you'd had the forethought to steal Isabella's while you were living with her.'

'It was broken. The only thing it was useful for was to tell her when it was time for her morning coffee.'

He pulls out his phone. 'It's six thirty! How did that happen?'

'Is there anything else you wish you'd done while you had the chance?' I ask. 'There's still time if we hurry. How about another tilt at the quintain? I'm sure your abject failure has been niggling at you all afternoon.'

He smiles. 'Not even a bit.'

'But I want a pink ribbon,' I complain.

'So, go to a craft shop. They'll sell you metres of the things. I've done everything I want to. It's been a wonderful afternoon.'

'Hasn't it?' I say. 'I'm sorry about the mill. You'll have to come all the way back another day, assuming you can work out where it is.'

'Shall we see whether our picnic bag has survived or been discovered by marauding peasants and auctioned off to the highest bidder?'

'Do peasants maraud?' I say, following him up the hill to where he left the bag.

'If they catch sight of day-old cakes and bottles of sparkling rosé, they do.'

He reaches the tree and looks behind it. 'Lucky for us, they didn't find it. Let's get out of here before anyone sees us and gives chase.'

'Do you think we'll find the village again, or are we doomed to wander in circles all night?' I say as we emerge from a thicket of trees.

'I'd give us pretty good odds,' says Will. 'Although it may take a while. Are these the same trees we walked through this morning – where we met the blacksmith?'

'They look the same. They have trunks and leaves.'

'It's a good start,' he says. 'But somehow, I don't think it's enough. What a pity we're city dwellers. I'm not sure I can tell an oak from a rowan.'

'The trees this morning were right on the top of a hill,' I say. 'These are halfway up the slope. I'm not even sure it's the same hill. Someone seems to have moved it.'

Will squints at the sky. 'The sun appears to be going down over there – although I wouldn't trust it not to change its mind at the last moment. If it continues in the same direction, that means we know which way is west.'

'Great!' I say with enthusiasm, adding more uncertainly, 'How does that help us? Is the village due west from here?'

He grins. 'You've put your finger on the problem. It's definitely west of somewhere, but I have no idea where. That's my bright suggestion down the drain. It's your turn. Can't you retrace our tracks from this morning? There's bound to be a trail of pastry crumbs.'

'Wouldn't the birds have eaten them by now?'

'I don't know,' he says. 'Do birds eat cake? I thought they lived on berries and worms.'

'London birds eat cake. I've seen them hanging around picnickers in the park, finishing their sandwiches and biscuits and anything else they can get their beaks on. I don't suppose country birds are any fussier.'

'There's nothing for it,' he says. 'One of us will have to pick a direction and see where it takes us. I'd prefer it to be you. If it goes wrong, I'd prefer to blame you than have you blame me.'

'Don't you have a sixth sense of where your car is?' I say. 'You seem very attached to it. Listen closely. It may be calling to you.'

He tips his head on one side. 'Either it's asleep, or it's got fed up waiting for us and headed home.'

'It's this way!' I say with false confidence, pointing to a narrow track.

'Are you sure?'

'Not in the least. But it's either that or going back to the fair.'

We follow the track for half a mile without any sign of the village.

'We'll give it five more minutes, then it's your turn to choose a direction,' I tell Will.

'Fine, but I don't think I'll need to. I have a good feeling.'

'Is the car calling to you?'

'You misunderstand the nature of my relationship with that car,' he says.

'You don't love it beyond sense or reason?'

'Oh, that! You may be right.'

'I've never considered keeping a car in London,' I say. 'The public transport is so good, and then there's the congestion tax.'

'I don't keep a car in London,' he says. 'This is a rental car. I thought you realised that.'

'A rental car? Like mine?'

'Not exactly like yours,' he says. 'My car goes.'

'Fair enough. But my car went fine until it didn't. How was I to know it was possessed of evil intent? The rental agent didn't issue me with a bell, book and candle and a handbook for performing an exorcism.'

'That's true,' he says. 'But the name of the company ought to have tipped you off. *Econowheels!* It doesn't exactly inspire you with confidence.'

'On the contrary,' I say. 'It exudes solid, reliable efficiency, combined with laudable thrift. Essential in these difficult economic times.'

'Personally, I like a car I can drive for more than thirty miles before it packs up.'

'Each to his own. So, your sports car doesn't belong to you? I had an image of you zooming down from London, forcing all the pedestrians to leap into hedges as you passed, while you yelled, 'Poop, poop!''

'I'm sorry to disappoint you,' he says. 'But I'm not Mr Toad.'

'It must be costing you quite a bit.'

'An allowable extravagance,' he says. 'I'm not taking a holiday this year. I was supposed to be going to Greece, but that didn't work out. I'm treating this assignment as my annual holiday, so I thought I'd splash out.'

'Honeywell is quite a change from Greece,' I say. 'What made you change your plans?'

He doesn't answer, and I glance at him to see his face has settled into a masklike expression.

'I'm sorry,' I apologise. 'It's none of my business.'

He shrugs. 'It's fine. I was going there with my girlfriend Melissa, but we broke up about six months ago. We'd already booked the holiday, so she went with her new boyfriend instead.'

'Ouch!' I say sympathetically. 'How long have they been together?'

'About seven months.'

It takes me a moment to digest this. 'Ouch!' I say again. 'I'm sorry I asked.'

'No, it's fine. At least they had the decency to refund my deposit, so I decided to use it for something fun.'

'That's a good idea. A red sports car may not be my idea of fun, but we're all different. I hope it's everything you ever dreamed of.'

'And more!' he says. 'It's a real babe magnet.'

'Is that right? I've seen you driving around the village, but I've never noticed anyone in the passenger seat. Do you make them lie down on the back seat and hide until you're out of view?'

'No, but that's a great idea. Anyway, how can you say you've never seen anyone in the passenger seat? I drove a beautiful woman through the village only this very morning.'

I make a gagging sound, and he laughs. 'I'm winding you up. And I don't actually refer to women as babes.'

'I should hope not.'

'We've established what I do for fun,' he says. 'I drive fast cars around the countryside to fulfil my childhood Wind in the Willows fantasies. How about you? What constitutes your idea of fun? It obviously isn't driving a functioning car, so what is it? What makes Olivia Sullivan tick?'

I try to answer lightly. 'You know what I do for fun. I look after animals, and I serve annoying customers in the bakery.'

'You've only been doing that for a week,' he points out. 'What did you do until now?'

'I've been busy with work.'

'You said you worked regular hours,' he reminds me.

'What are you, a high court judge?'

He looks surprised. 'I'm sorry. I didn't mean to upset you.'

'I know you didn't. I'm sorry if I over reacted. It's a touchy subject, and I'd rather not talk about it now.'

'No problem.'

We walk in silence for a few more minutes. Is he angry? Is he upset? I can't tell, and my entire body is tensing up in response. It's a familiar feeling and one I'd hoped not to have to feel again. This silence is worse than anything.

'Will,' I say hesitantly.

I'm surprised to see his answering smile. 'Yes?'

'I'm sorry I snapped at you. I was out of order.'

'You had a perfect right not to answer,' he says. 'What you do in your spare time is your own business. You don't have to tell me just because I asked. I have a pretty good idea what it is, anyway.'

'You do?'

'Yes. You teach monkeys to water ski.'

The knot in my stomach unclenches. He doesn't look angry, more amused.

'Close, but no cigar,' I say. 'I'm actually a part-time snake-charmer.'

I see his instinctive flinch and laugh. 'I've taken my preliminary certificate, and I'm almost ready for the advanced one.'

'No details, please!' he says in a faint voice.

'But you asked,' I say. 'And I rudely cut you off. Now I'm making it up to you with a full and frank description of my course. First, we learned how to hypnotise a tiny garden snake by singing it a special lullaby. After that, we moved on to garter snakes. We taught them how to retrieve small objects from our bags. Then it was onto the medium-sized snakes. They were far more difficult. But we eventually trained them to arrange themselves to spell different words.'

'I'm sure you were an apt student,' he says. 'But you should know I'll have nightmares tonight after this conversation.'

'I can't imagine why. Anyway, having passed my level one snake-handling exams with flying colours, I'm planning to tackle level two. It will take an enormous amount of work, but it will be worth it. You can come and watch the final exam if you like.'

He turns pale. 'How much would it cost to persuade you to give me the wrong date?'

'Why would I do that? You'll love it. First, our snakes have to navigate an intricate maze. After that, it's the dance off. They have five minutes to perform the rumba, the tango, and contemporary freestyle.'

'No jazz?' he enquires.

'It used to be on the curriculum, but the trainers felt it wasn't taxing enough. The snakes were simply phoning it in because they knew no one could tell the difference. It's just like playing it. All you have to do is produce a jumble of notes and claim it's improvisational jazz.'

'Shows what a lot you know about jazz music,' he says.

'I know it's cheating when it comes to snake dancing,' I say. 'Don't tell me you're a jazz aficionado?'

'I've been to the occasional concert,' he admits. 'Thankfully, I've never seen a snake there.'

'That's because they're at the bar, downing snake bites.'

He gives a shout of laughter. 'You win! I wouldn't –'

He breaks off and points. 'Would you believe it?'

'What?' I stop dead too. 'Is that …?'

'It must be,' he says. 'Isn't that always the way? As soon as you stop looking for something, it appears right in front of you.'

'That also happens when you bring a map,' I say, speeding up to keep pace with him.

He isn't listening. 'It's beautiful. What a magnificent setting!'

'Master Twyford knew what he was doing when he built it,' I agree.

'Master who?' says Will. 'Oh, him! He most certainly did.'

Chapter Nineteen

The path drops steeply in front of us, and we follow it down to where the mill stands by the stream, bathed in the early evening sunlight. It couldn't have found itself a more perfect setting, surrounded by trees and hidden from view until the very moment passers-by stumble across it. I wouldn't be surprised to hear it only appears on sunny evenings, or in the depths of winter when the moon is full and the owls set out on their nightly hunting sprees.

The mill seems to have stood there for so long that it's become a part of the scenery. It appears to have grown out of the surrounding landscape, rather than having been built. The wooden paddle is intact and looks as though it could move at any moment. But the stream flows past and around it without it appearing to notice. It's a mill in retirement, determined not to be sucked back into the workaday world.

'I'm so glad we found it,' I say, dropping my bag on the bank of the stream and sitting down. 'You'll know where to look for it when you come back.'

Will opens his bag and pulls out his camera. 'Come back?'

'I thought you wanted to get a picture of it in the sunshine.'

'I did, but this is even better. Look at that sky.' He gestures to where the setting sun has turned a lilac bank of cloud into flame.

'Don't the publishers tell you exactly what they want?'

He screws a lens onto the camera. 'Sometimes. But this brief was fairly generic.'

I pull out my phone. 'I want a picture too. It won't be as good as yours, but my phone camera isn't too bad.'

'I'll take one especially for you,' he says. 'It's the least I can do after dragging you all over the countryside today.'

'I've had a great time. I'd love you to take a photograph for me, but I'll take one of my own too. I want to remember today through my own eyes as well as yours.'

He takes a few steps backwards. 'I'll take a couple of preliminary shots to test the light. Do you mind if I use you for scale?'

'As long as I don't end up in the book. I've told you. I look awful in photographs. No one has ever taken a good picture of me. And don't tell me that's because you've never taken one of me. I've heard it all before.'

'I wouldn't dream of saying anything of the kind,' he says. 'I'm perfectly willing to accept that every image anyone has ever taken of you is hideous.'

I laugh. 'Except for the picture that man drew of us at the fair. I liked that.'

'So did I. From now on, you should stick to having your caricature drawn and avoid all cameras for fear of breaking them. In the meantime, I'll take a couple with you in them to assess the composition. You don't have to look at the camera. You can turn your back if you like. I need a figure. Anything would do – a deer, a fox, a badger. As there don't seem to be any of those around at the moment, I'll have to make do with you.'

I gaze out over the water, feeling self-conscious. It's one thing to accept I look horrible in photos, despite the photographer's best efforts. It's another to know Will is taking pictures of me, secretly expecting them to turn out wonderfully so he can demonstrate his superiority with a camera. He'll have a shock when he sees them later, but there's no use trying to persuade him. He'll have to find out for himself.

'That's great,' he says a couple of minutes later. 'I'd like to get some from the far side of the stream. I want to catch the way the evening sun strikes the grey stones. Are you coming?'

'I'll stay here and guard the picnic and the rest of your camera equipment,' I say. 'Take your time. I'm enjoying the break.'

He disappears around the bend in the stream. He reappears a minute later on the far bank and starts to photograph the mill from different angles. I watch him for a while. It's interesting to see this side of him, no longer light-hearted and full of jokes, but serious, absorbed, completely lost in what he's doing.

After a while, I stop looking at him and become lost in my own thoughts. I don't know why I've been feeling the need to rush back to London so quickly. There's nothing for me there. It's strange to think I've spent nearly a decade of my life in the city and left no lasting impression. I've made very few friends, built nothing, and had my confidence ground down by staying in a relationship I should have known a long time ago was wrong for me. I can't blame Charlie for everything. I saw very early that it was his way or nothing, and I should have got out then. I'm not sure why I didn't.

He was so supportive after my parents died, and I clung on to that. I had no wider family in the area, and I was grateful when Charlie took on the role of being my support, my guide, and my rock. I hardly noticed when that morphed into him becoming my mentor, the person who always knew better than me and was sure of the direction I should take. By the time I emerged from the emotional vacuum into which I'd been flung when my parents died, Charlie and I had settled into a pattern, and it was less exhausting to accept it than break out of it.

I'm not going back to him. I wasn't sure of that when I left London, but after a couple of weeks in Honeywell, things have become clear. Charlie may be right for someone, but that person isn't me. It's time for me to take responsibility for myself and pick up the reins of my life that I dropped when my world fell apart. I'll be turning thirty next year, and now seems as good a time as any to stop and take stock. I don't want to reach Mrs Ogilvie's age and realise I'm still contracting out my life and my decisions to someone else.

She's half a century ahead of me, which seems like forever. For all I know, she may wake up each day wondering where those fifty years went, and what happened to that thirty-year-old woman who looked forward to her life with such hope. I hope not. I hope she looks back and is happy with the choices she made. I hope I'll be able to do that too when I'm her age. But that won't happen if I continue to allow other people to tell me what to do.

I'm so grateful to Isabella for finding a way to stop me in my tracks and keep me in Honeywell for a while. I'll never know how she knew what I needed. But somehow, she did. In her usual impulsive way, she reacted without stopping to consider all the things that could go wrong. Of all the people in the world I could have met on the day my car broke down, I'm so lucky I met her. And Will too. He was the catalyst, and I'm grateful to him for that.

His voice breaks into my musings. 'I'm pretty much done here. Would you like to stay here for a while longer or try to find the car?'

'It's so beautiful here, so calm and peaceful,' I say. 'I feel as though I could stay all night. But perhaps we'd better try to get back to Harfield. Do you have any idea where it is?'

'I'm pretty sure it's over there,' he says, pointing. 'Do you see those roofs and the church spire? That looks like Harfield. It also makes sense when I think about the direction we were supposed to take to get to the mill this morning. When we started along the path behind the church, we should have taken the right-hand fork rather than the left. That would have brought us almost directly to the mill. We couldn't see it from the village because it's in this hollow. Instead, we took the left hand fork and ended up somewhere completely different.'

'I'm glad we took the wrong turning,' I say. 'Otherwise, we wouldn't have found the fair, and I've had a wonderful day. And it all worked out in the end.

We found the mill, and you got your pictures. With any luck, we may even locate the car again before dark.'

He zips his camera into its bag and slings it over his shoulder. 'I agree. It's been a lot of fun. Thanks for coming with me, Olivia. I hope you have enough energy to walk back to the village. I'd offer to fetch the car and attempt to drive across country to you, but I'm not convinced I'd ever find you again if I did.'

'We should stay together,' I say, following him across the grass to the stony track. 'There's no guarantee your car will be there, even if we do find Harfield. Remember what the blacksmith told us about the gangs of marauding thieves stealing carts from the surrounding villages?'

'If it isn't there, we'll have to take the mediaeval equivalent of an Uber, whatever that turns out to be.'

'It depends on your income,' I say. 'If you're wealthy, you send a carrier pigeon ahead, and your carriage will be waiting for you when you get to the village. If not, you have to use Dial a Donkey and hope for the best.'

'Both of those sound fun,' he says. 'But I can see the village street now, and my car seems to have successfully evaded the bands of thieves. Unless you're dead set on that donkey, how about I drive you home? Maybe we can stop for dinner somewhere on the way. It's a long time since we ate that pie.'

Chapter Twenty

Isabella greets me eagerly the following morning. 'How did it go?'

'It was great,' I say. 'We had the most amazing day.'

'I knew you would! I'm so glad you two have got together.'

'Got together?' I say. 'What are you talking about? I went to keep him company while he took some photographs, that's all.'

Her face falls. 'I thought you had an amazing day.'

I open the till and check we have enough change to start the day. 'We did. But people can have a wonderful time without it meaning anything more than that. Will and I are just friends. That's all we'll ever be.'

'I don't see why. He's a great guy.'

'He is,' I say. 'And he's single. As are you. Which makes you perfect for each other.'

She pours us both a cup of coffee. 'That's ridiculous. Plenty of people are single. It doesn't mean I have to get together with them just because I'm single too.'

'Exactly,' I say.

She laughs. 'Point taken. But I didn't think you'd be good together because you're both single, although that obviously makes it a lot easier. I thought it because you get along so well.'

'As do you,' I point out.

'But I've already told you I'm not interested in him.'

'And now I'm telling you that neither am I. Poor Will. How is he going to cope?'

The doorbell jangles, and I spin around to see who it is. It would be just my luck for Will to be standing there, having overheard my last comment. But it's a woman I haven't seen before.

'Hello, Mrs Carson,' says Isabella.

The woman beams at her. 'How are you today, my dear?'

'Very well, thanks,' says Isabella. 'How's Daisy?'

The name Carson rings a bell. This must be Lily's mother. She catches sight of me and beams again.

'You must be Olivia! It's lovely to meet you. Lily told me you're kindly helping out while she's away. Daisy is much better, thank you, Isabella. I'm about to pop over to see how she and Lily are doing after their first night at home. I thought I'd pick up a little something to take with me. What do you suggest?'

'As her godmother, I can tell you Daisy loves our brownies,' says Isabella. 'So does Lily. I'd better give you a boxful in case Jack is around too.'

'I think I'll take one of your apple turnovers,' says Mrs Carson. 'Daisy loves those. She gets the cream everywhere, but I always clean her up before Lily gets home, so she's none the wiser.'

'Daisy is lucky to have a godmother and grandmother who understand her so well,' says Isabella.

'And how are you settling into Honeywell?' Mrs Carson asks me. 'Please let me know if there's anything you need.'

'I'm not exactly settling in,' I say with a glance at Isabella. 'I'm only here temporarily. But thank you for the offer.'

'You're staying with Eleanor Marsh, aren't you?'

'That's right,' I say. 'How did you know?'

'Angela knows everyone in this village,' says Isabella. 'How long have you and Martin lived here?'

'Thirty-five years,' says Mrs Carson. 'I was expecting Ben when we moved in, and the sale was delayed several times. The lease on our rental house was running out, and I told Martin I half expected to give birth in a tent. But everything turned out for the best. We moved in a few weeks before he was born, and we've been there ever since.'

'I can't imagine living anywhere for that long,' I say. 'It sounds rather nice. I was talking to Mrs Ogilvie the other day, and she told me she'd been in the village for seventy-five years.'

'Is that right?' she says. 'How marvellous! I know her a little, but she keeps herself to herself. I was pleased when I heard she'd started coming to the bakery more regularly. It must be good for her to see different people and have a bit of a chat.'

'Olivia wants to throw her a party,' says Isabella. 'She's turning eighty in August, and she has nothing planned.'

'What a lovely idea!' says Mrs Carson. 'I'm sure Mrs Ogilvie will be delighted.'

'Isabella and I aren't quite so sure,' I say. 'What if she doesn't like surprises? What if she doesn't like parties?'

'Everyone likes parties,' she says. 'Where were you thinking of holding it?'

'At the bakery.'

She frowns. 'Isn't that rather small? You can only seat fifteen people.'

'I don't think that matters,' says Isabella. 'She may not know fifteen people.'

'Planning it is proving more difficult than I thought,' I tell Mrs Carson. 'It's supposed to be a surprise party, so I can hardly ask Mrs Ogilvie for a list of guests. But I don't know anyone in the village, so I'm not sure where to begin.'

'Leave that to me!' she says. 'I can find out who her friends are and invite them if you like.'

'That would be wonderful,' I say. 'If you're sure you don't mind.'

'Not in the least. I'd enjoy it. It will give me the chance to catch up with people I don't see regularly. I'll make a start this afternoon. What were you planning to do about food?'

Isabella waves towards the counter. 'We can manage sandwiches and sausage rolls and baked goods. Abby has offered to make a birthday cake for Mrs Ogilvie and Bernie. It seems they share a birthday, so we can make it a joint celebration.'

'As long as it isn't a pirate ship,' says Mrs Carson, and they both laugh.

'I must hear that story sometime,' I say. 'Everyone seems to know it but me.'

The doorbell jangles again, and Will walks in. Isabella gives me a meaningful look, which I ignore.

'Hi, Will.' I say. 'What can we get for you?'

'One of your chicken pies, please. I'm off to Overton today to photograph the inside of a Norman church. Hello, Mrs Carson. How are you?'

'I'm very well,' she says. 'It's lovely to see you again, Will.'

She lowers her voice and addresses me. 'Does he know about the *p a r t y*?'

'He does,' says Will, his eyes alight with laughter. 'He can also spell.'

She laughs. 'I'm sorry. I'm so used to being with my granddaughter. We have to spell out all sorts of things now she understands words like cake and ice cream and bath and bed.'

'It's a great idea,' I say. 'Abby and I have to do that when Isabella's around or she discovers the fresh batches of cakes before the customers can get near them.'

'The joke's on you,' says Isabella. 'I only pretend not to understand you.'

'I must be going,' says Mrs Carson. 'I'll let you know how I get on with the guest list.'

She gives us all a cheerful wave and trots out.

'Mrs Carson seems very nice,' I say.

'She is,' says Isabella. 'She's one of those people who can only see the good in others. The strange thing is, it seems to make everyone around her nicer. Even me!'

'If you weren't already perfect,' I say.

'That's true. But you know what I mean.'

'Very rarely,' I say. 'Just the chicken pie, Will?'

He looks at the counter. 'Perhaps I'll take one of your *c o o k i e s* as well.'

Isabella picks up an empty pallet. 'I've already told you that trick doesn't work with me. Anyway, I sold the last cupcake this morning, so you'll have to make do with a cookie instead!'

She gives him a satisfied smile and marches out to the kitchen.

Will watches her go. 'Do you think she's really illiterate?'

'She's running a business fairly successfully,' I say. 'I expect she'll be fine.'

I hand him the two paper bags. 'Are you sure I can't get you anything else?'

'I'm good for now, thanks.'

He pauses by the door. 'Am I officially allowed to know about the *p a r t y*?'

'The cat seems to be out of the bag now,' I say. 'And it wouldn't be a smart move to keep the official photographer in the dark about the arrangements.'

'That's what I wanted to talk to you about,' he says. 'I wasn't sure what to give Mrs Ogilvie for a birthday present.'

'You're taking the photographs. Isn't that her gift?'

'In doing that as a favour for you,' he says. 'For all I know, Mrs Ogilvie may be like you and hate having her picture taken.'

'I'm starting to wish I hadn't told you that. But I haven't thought about a present. I suppose we ought to get her something. I have no idea what.'

'I was thinking about it last night,' he says. 'And I remembered how much she loves that dog of hers. Do you think she'd like a professional portrait of him?'

'That's a wonderful idea!'

'I'm glad you like it,' he says. 'But I can't work out how to take the pictures without her knowing. The pair of them are always together.'

'That's true. It's one thing to grab your phone and take a quick picture of Bernie. It's another to pull out that huge camera of yours and start clicking away. She'd be bound to suspect something.'

'That's what I thought,' he says. 'It will take some thinking about. I'll need your help if you're up for it.'

'I'll help in any way I can,' I say. 'But I know nothing about photography.'

'Not to take the actual picture. But you could be useful in diverting her attention.'

Isabella returns carrying a fresh palette of loaves. 'Diverting whose attention? Not mine?'

'Not this time,' he says. 'Although I wish it were. I have a feeling it would be exceptionally easy.'

'I'd only have to dance around, waving a cake,' I say. 'You'd get as many pictures as you wanted in no time.'

'I'm sorry,' says Isabella. 'You lost me at waving a cake. What are we talking about?'

'What we're giving Mrs Ogilvie for her birthday,' I say. 'Will suggested a portrait of Bernie, but we can't think how to separate him from Mrs Ogilvie without her suspecting.'

'You could try that cake thing,' she says.

'And if that doesn't work?' says Will.

She bites her lip. 'I'm not sure. But I expect I'll come up with lots of good ideas if you give me a day or two.'

'Great,' he says. 'I'll leave it to you two to form a plan. I should get going.'

He hands me a large envelope. 'I've taken a picture of this for my records, but I thought you should have the original.'

'What is it?' asks Isabella when he's left.

'I have no idea.'

'Are you sure?' she says. 'It looks official. Did you and he get married while you were out yesterday?'

'I think I'd remember something like that.'

'Not necessarily,' she says. 'It's the kind of thing that could slip anyone's mind if they were busy. If it isn't a marriage certificate, what is it? Your letter from Hogwarts? An invitation from NASA to head up their next space mission?'

I undo the clasp and ease back the flap. A piece of paper slides out. It's the picture Will and I had done at the fair.

'Let me see!' urges Isabella. She turns over the paper and bursts out laughing. 'This is wonderful! Where did it come from?'

'It's a long story,' I say. 'Will and I ended up at a mediaeval fair yesterday afternoon. There was an artist there doing caricatures. He asked us how we met, and this is what he came up with.'

'We'll have to frame it,' she says. 'We'll put it up behind the counter so everyone can see.'

I remove it from her grasp. 'We'll do nothing of the kind.'

'But it's amazing.' She studies the picture more carefully. 'It's exactly like you. It's a good picture of Will too. Doesn't he look dashing on that white charger?'

'Are you changing your mind about him now you've seen him in a whole different light?'

'I wavered for a moment,' she says. 'But the maiden he's rescuing isn't me. It's you. Look at you, sitting on the grassy bank, making a daisy chain. "He loves me, he loves me not, he loves me …"'

'Whereas in real life, I was setting off to save myself,' I say.

'But look at him in his shiny suit of armour,' she says. 'He wants to rescue you.'

'Not everyone wants to be rescued,' I say rather tartly.

'But it's nice to have friends who look out for you. You can save him the next time, if you like. Anyway, it's a lovely picture.'

'I like my dress,' I say. 'It looks like a nightmare to wash, but it's beautiful.'

'It is,' she agrees. 'That embroidered bodice is gorgeous. I expect mediaeval peasants spent most of their money on dry-cleaning.'

'I'm not a peasant,' I say. 'If I were, a knight would never have stopped for me.'

'Will might,' she says.

'He'd be a rubbish knight if he did. He'd get drummed out of the guild.'

'It's a lovely picture,' she says. 'If you won't hang it in the bakery, frame it and hang it in your room. I told you it was looking rather bare. Now you have something personal to put on the wall. I'm willing to bet you'll have plenty more before you leave Honeywell.'

Chapter Twenty-One

Mrs Carson appears the following morning looking pleased with herself.

'I've been talking to Mavis, and she's helped me to make a long list of people to invite,' she announces as she bursts into the bakery.

'Hello, Mrs Carson,' I say. 'Who's Mavis?'

She looks surprised. 'I thought everyone knew Mavis Sotherby. You must have met her by now.'

'I don't think so. Most customers don't tell me their name. They just tell me what they want.'

'Oh, Mavis would have introduced herself,' she says. 'She'd want to find out everything about you. She has a mind like a computer hard drive!'

'Is that so?' I say, amused. 'I didn't realise you were interested in technology.'

'I go to her class each week,' she says. 'She teaches us all about files and folders and Office, and I don't know what. What that woman doesn't know about computers isn't worth knowing.'

'I wish she'd teach me how to install my new book-keeping program,' says Isabella, emerging from the office with her arms full of files. 'I've seen our accountant, and he insists we move to something more standardised. Apparently, this is the latest program, and it will practically do my books for me. I'm all for that, but it's no good if it won't install.'

'Would you like me to have a look at it for you?' says Mrs Carson. 'We learned all about installing programmes last week.'

Isabella looks alarmed. 'I'm fine, thanks. You have enough to do without worrying about our computing system.'

'If you're sure,' says Mrs Carson. 'But you only have to say the word, and I'll ask Mavis to pop in and sort you out. She'll have it up and running for you in minutes. She'll do the accounts too, if you ask her nicely.'

Isabella looks even more alarmed. 'I'm sure I'll be fine.'

'Mrs Carson says she's already sorted out the guest list for the party,' I tell her.

'Aren't you a marvel?' says Isabella. 'How did you manage that?'

'It was simple,' says Mrs Carson. 'I told Mavis all about it at last night at our class. She talked to the members and told them about the plan. It's surprising how many of them know Mrs Ogilvie, at least by sight. Mavis looked through the list of previous attendees and promised to call them too.'

'I hope Mrs Ogilvie isn't one of them,' I say.

'We're safe there,' says Isabella. 'Can you imagine her in a computing class? She'd insist on bringing Bernie, and he'd have all the wires tangled up before Mavis could blink.'

'Pets aren't allowed,' says Mrs Carson. 'Mavis is very strict on that point.'

'There you go,' says Isabella. 'So, all we have to worry about is one of the members mentioning the party to Mrs Ogilvie.'

'Mavis swore us all to secrecy,' says Mrs Carson. 'I'm sure no one would want to spoil the surprise.'

'With any luck, most of them will have forgotten all about it by next week,' says Isabella.

Mrs Carson gives her a reproving look. 'That's not very nice, dear. Several members of the class may be elderly, but there's nothing wrong with their memories. I think it's admirable they're getting out there and learning new technologies. Mr Pollard learned to put his digital photos into a zip file last night and attach them to an email to his daughter in Hong Kong. We all gave him a round of applause when we saw it had been delivered.'

'You're quite right,' says Isabella. 'I shouldn't be making jokes about the Silver Surfers. I'm the one who can't install this program. Maybe I should ask Mr Pollard to give me a hand.'

'The important thing is that we have some guests,' I say. 'I was beginning to think it would be just us and Mrs Ogilvie, which wouldn't have been the greatest surprise party.'

'Don't worry about that,' says Mrs Carson. 'Everyone thought it was a wonderful idea. There may be too many people to fit into the bakery, but Mavis and I have had some ideas about that.'

'We'll need rough numbers soon,' I say. 'I need to know how many we're catering for.'

'I'll let you know in good time,' promises Mrs Carson. 'I must go now. I promised Lily I'd watch little Daisy this morning while Lily gets her hair cut. It will do her good to get out on her own for a while. Maybe she'll pop in here for some lunch when she's done. Tell her there's no need to rush home. Daisy and I will be pressing flowers this afternoon.'

'Can I send something for your elevenses?' says Isabella. 'On the house, naturally.'

'I wouldn't dream of it,' says Mrs Carson, pulling out her purse. 'What would your accountant say if he found out you were giving away the stock for free? Now, what would Daisy like?'

She leaves a few minutes later, clutching a box filled with goodies.

'I wish my grandmother had been like that,' says Isabella. 'Mine always told me little girls should be seen and not heard. And not seen too much, either.'

'You must have been the ideal granddaughter for her,' I say. 'Tidy, polite, restrained, always happy with a piece of embroidery …'

'I wouldn't know one end of an embroidery needle from another,' she says. 'Although I was planning to do my needlewoman badge when I was a girl guide.'

'What were you going to sew?'

'A cushion or something? I'm not sure what people make nowadays. But my friend Suzanne was taking hers, and I didn't want to be left out. I wonder if they offer an accountancy badge? That should be doable with a little effort. I should check whether Honeywell still has a guide troupe. It may not be too late.'

'They won't know what's hit them,' I say. 'In the meantime, how about working towards your party planner's badge? I could do with some help. I haven't organised anything like this before.'

'You'll be fine,' she says. 'Angela is doing the guest list, Will is doing the photography, and Abby will end up doing most of the food. All you have to do is make a few banners, buy some balloons, and organise a few games.'

'Games? It's an eightieth birthday party!'

'So what?' she says. 'I'd want games at my eightieth party.'

'Like what? I can't imagine sending everyone off to play hide-and-seek around the bakery or organising a game of musical rocking chairs. And before you suggest a pie-eating competition, I'd have to buy in a ton of indigestion tablets. Besides, you'd almost definitely win, which wouldn't be fair.'

'Fine,' she says, 'But I'm having that for my eightieth. Not only pies. Sausage rolls and doughnuts too.'

'We still have to think how to get this picture of Bernie,' I say. 'Mrs Ogilvie is always with him. Do you have any good ideas?'

'For kidnapping her? I'm sure I can come up with some.'

'I was thinking of something less drastic,' I say.

'Then, no!'

'I expect Will can think of something,' I say. 'We only need Bernie for a couple of minutes.'

'Doesn't that depend on what you plan to do with him?' she says. 'What sort of picture does Will have in mind? Is he planning an action shot or does he prefer the stiff, royal type of portrait, with Bernie in a ruff, looking annoyed?'

'Who wouldn't look annoyed if they had to wear a ruff? I'm leaving it up to Will. He's the expert.'

'Does he do many portraits?' she asks.

'I don't know. I haven't asked him much about his job. But how different can it be from photographing a building or a person? Doesn't the camera do most of the work?'

'Don't ask me,' she says. 'All the pictures I take with my phone come out blurred.'

'That's because you never stand still long enough.'

'Bernie won't stand still for long either,' she points out. 'At least, not as long as the Eiffel Tower or the Empire State Building.'

'That's Will's problem,' I say. 'This was his idea. I'm only his helper.'

'He'll probably want you to dress up as something bizarre to distract Mrs Ogilvie,' she says.

'He'd better not. But if he does, you can help him. I suspect you'd enjoy dressing up as an elf or a plumber.'

'What a strange idea you have of me,' she says. 'Anyway, this party is your thing, so you're the one who has to organise it. Abby and I are just providing the food and the premises. We're far too busy for anything else.'

Chapter Twenty-Two

Lily comes into the bakery the following morning with her daughter. It's the first time I've met Daisy, and I'm amused to see she's a tiny replica of her mother – small and slight, with straight fair hair and dimples.

'This is my friend Olivia,' says Lily when she sees me. 'Olivia, I'd like you to meet my daughter.'

She says it with such obvious pride that I smile. I'd feel exactly the same way if I had a mini-me as cute as Daisy. She's wearing a blue pinafore dress with a white daisy print, and a matching Alice headband.

'It's lovely to meet you,' I say, coming around the counter and bending down to talk to her.

Daisy sticks her thumb in her mouth and looks up at me with huge blue eyes.

'Can you say hello to Olivia?' prompts Lily.

Daisy removes her thumb and stares up at me. 'No.'

'I'm sorry,' says Lily. 'She'll warm up to you when she knows you better. She isn't good with strangers.'

'That's fine,' I say. 'I like a woman with a mind of her own.'

'Would you like a babyccino?' I ask Daisy. Isabella has taught me how to make those, so I imagine Daisy has come across them before.

She removes her thumb again and beams at me. 'Yiss!'

'Yes, please,' Lily corrects her. 'You couldn't have offered her anything she'd like better, Olivia. Mum always buys her one when they come in. They sit at that table over there with their drinks and chat about everything that's going on. At least, Mum does. She's a great talker. And Daisy says, "Yiss," and "No," and occasionally, 'More!"'

'It sounds as though she's developed all the most important vocabulary,' I say. 'I hear she can also say, "Whizzy."'

Daisy's eyes light up. 'Whizzy?'

'She'll be back in a few minutes,' says Lily, carrying her over to the nearest table.

'She's adorable,' I say. 'I don't know much about young children. I'm more used to kittens and puppies. She seems pretty healthy now.'

'She's much better,' says Lily. 'She gets tired a little earlier than usual, but she's picking up fast. Children bounce back far more quickly than we do. I'm exhausted from spending a week on a camp bed in the hospital. The nurses came around every couple of hours to take Daisy's temperature. She slept through the whole thing, but I didn't.'

'I remember that from when I had my appendix taken out a few years ago,' I say. 'I used to roll over and groan and try to hide under the pillow, but the nurse wasn't having any of it. She shone the torch on my face until I allowed her to take my temperature and check my pulse. I'm not sure which of us was more relieved when the doctor said I could go home.'

'I know how pleased I was,' says Lily, taking the two mugs I hand her – one adult-sized mug, and one tiny mug with pink rosebuds that match the pink marshmallow I've balanced on the saucer.

She hands the smaller one to Daisy. 'Remember to sit up straight and hold your cup carefully, just like Grandma showed you.'

Daisy buries her face in the mug, emerging a second later with foam around her mouth and a dab of chocolate powder on her nose.

Lily picks up a napkin and wipes her face. 'Good try. We'll have you trained in no time.'

Daisy snatches Lily's spoon and bangs it on the table.

'Careful with that!' says Lily, taking it away from her.

Daisy is about to protest when the shop door opens and Isabella walks in.

'Whizzy!' shouts Daisy.

'Dizzy!' says Isabella, catching her up in her arms and swinging her into an enormous hug.

'I've asked you not to call her that,' says Lily, but without much hope.

'She's my goddaughter,' says Isabella. 'All godmothers have pet names for their godchildren.'

'But she's starting to call herself that too,' says Lily. 'One of the doctors at the hospital was quite alarmed when she said it last week. They made her sit down.'

Isabella laughs. 'I should teach her to say something useful like, "Low blood sugar!"'

She puts Daisy back in her chair and sits next to her. 'Are you hungry?'

'Yiss!' says Daisy joyfully.

'It's almost lunchtime,' says Lily. 'Grandma is making us toasted sandwiches. We only popped in to give Olivia this note.' She hands me an envelope.

'Is it from Will?' says Isabella, and I'm annoyed to feel myself flush.

'It's from Mum,' says Lily. 'Were you expecting something from Will?'

'Of course not,' I say.

She and Isabella exchange the briefest of glances as I tear open the envelope and scan the contents.

'That's kind of your mother,' I tell Lily. 'Can you tell her I'd be delighted?'

'Delighted about what?' says Isabella.

'Mum's invited Olivia and Will to tea on Wednesday,' says Lily, and she and Isabella exchange another quick look.

'Only because we're trying to photograph Bernie,' I say before Isabella can say anything.

'Mum's invited Mrs Ogilvie too,' explains Lily. 'She thought it would be an excellent opportunity for Will to be around Bernie without raising Mrs Ogilvie's suspicions.'

'I'm the decoy,' I say. 'My job is to distract Mrs Ogilvie so Will can get a picture of Bernie.'

'She could have asked me,' grumbles Isabella. 'I'm far more distracting than you are, even when I don't mean to be. I'd be bound to trip over something or break a cup or pour tea into someone's lap. It would give Will the perfect opportunity to take as many photos as he wanted.'

'We'll keep you in reserve for next time,' I promise. 'We don't want to bring out the big guns until we need them. Anyway, you're working on Wednesday. It's my day off.'

Isabella grins. 'I'm only teasing. You don't want me playing gooseberry.'

'Time we were going!' says Lily before I can answer. 'See you on Wednesday, Olivia. I'll tell Mum you'll be there.'

She lifts a protesting Daisy off her chair and straps her into her stroller. 'Say goodbye to Olivia and Whizzy, sweetheart.'

'Bye, Whizzy! Bye, Wovy!' shouts Daisy.

We watch them set off down the high street.

'I hope I didn't go too far,' says Isabella as they disappear around the corner.

'You always go too far,' I say. 'But I'm used to it.'

'Good. You turn such a lovely fiery red when I tease you about Will. It matches your hair.'

'Whereas you say the most outrageous things without turning the faintest pink.'

'Long years of practise,' she says. 'You'll get there if you persevere.'

She picks up the mugs. 'I see you've put my training to good use. Daisy loves her babyccinos.'

'I'm not sure she drank much. Most of it went on her face and over the table.'

'As I say, practise is the key,' she says. 'I'm preparing her for the day when she can drink the real thing. It's basic godmother stuff. Anyway, I must get back to the accounts. I've installed the program now, which is a step in the right direction. But the columns keep on jumping around. No wonder Mr Mason stuck to pencil and paper for all those years.'

I don't see Will until Wednesday afternoon. He texts me on Friday to ask whether I'd like to go to Whitfield Castle with him on Saturday, but I have to tell him I'm working. I feel a pang of regret that I have to refuse. I had such a good time with him last Sunday, and I'd love to do it again. But I have no intention of starting anything with him. In which case, it's better not to go out with him too regularly, fun though it might be.

It's nothing personal. I have no intention of starting anything with anyone for a long, long time, if ever. I haven't yet worked out why I stayed so long in a relationship that caused me to lose myself so entirely. Until I've done that, I'm in danger of repeating the whole thing with someone else. On the face of it, Will is nothing like Charlie. But the Charlie I met and fell in love with was nothing like the man he eventually turned out to be. And I didn't see the signs until it was almost too late. Better to stay away from men altogether than to sleepwalk into another disaster.

Anyway, I have no reason to think Will sees me as anything other than a friend. If my first instincts were right, he may be interested in Isabella. It appears she isn't interested in him, but he doesn't know that. And I refuse to be anyone's rebound if I ever reach the stage of considering a new relationship.

I sleep late on Wednesday morning. I no longer wake each morning at daybreak, trying and failing to doze off again. These days, I'm asleep almost as soon as my head hits the pillow, and I don't wake up until my alarm rings. Isabella is convinced it's the Honeywell air. She says she's lived in this area for her entire life and has always slept like a log, so that proves it.

I suspect she would sleep beautifully anywhere. I've never met someone as full of energy and life. She has the enviable quality of being comfortable in her own skin. She's happy with who she is, without being in the slightest conceited or self-satisfied. She enjoys life and all it throws at her, and she loves people.

I can't imagine her ending up with someone like Charlie. She would have pushed back at the first sign of his trying to control her, and he would have backed off. Whether he would have changed is another matter. Probably not. The more I see of people, the more I sense they're unlikely to change in anything but their outward behaviour. By the time they reach their thirties, most people's characters are fixed.

I'm aware that I follow this pattern too. I am who I am, and I have to find a way of coming to terms with that. I can't beat myself up forever for ending up in a relationship like the one I had with Charlie. But I should work out why I did what I did and try to change that pattern before it leads me into permanent disaster.

Chapter Twenty-Three

I arrive at Mrs Carson's house at three o'clock on Wednesday. I almost texted Will to ask whether he wanted to walk over there together but decided against it. I don't want to look as though I'm unable to do anything for myself. And I'd prefer not to give the slightest impression that I think this is a date. I don't know why I'm being so touchy about this. Will hasn't indicated he sees me as anything more than a friend, even though he's had several opportunities to do so.

That evening at the mill could, in retrospect, have been one of them. It was a romantic setting, with the sunset and the ancient building, steeped in the history of centuries past. It was so quiet and secluded that it felt as though we were hundreds of miles away from any other living thing, despite being only half an hour from civilisation. If someone were planning a romantic evening, which we weren't, they'd need to go a long way to beat it.

Instead of which, Will told me I was nothing more than a substitute for a badger or a fox, left me alone while he wandered around taking pictures, and didn't even open the bottle of wine he'd brought. That may have been because we'd already been drinking mead and he was driving. But the point is that he showed no sign of being affected by the romantic setting, which means I have nothing to worry about and no complications ahead of me.

Mr Carson answers the door. He's a jolly-looking man of about sixty with a salt and pepper beard and twinkling grey eyes.

'I'm Martin,' he says. 'And you must be Olivia. My wife's in the back garden. Would you like to use the side gate? It's quicker than going through the house.'

I follow him around the side of the house, where we find Mrs Carson sitting on the patio, chatting with Mrs Ogilvie.

She jumps up when she sees me. 'Olivia! How lovely. Thank you for coming.'

'It was kind of you to invite me,' I say. 'Good afternoon, Mrs Ogilvie.'

I look around the garden. 'Where's Bernie?'

It hadn't occurred to me he might not be here. I hope Mrs Ogilvie hasn't taken him to the vet or left him with the dog groomer for the afternoon. That would shatter all our plans.

Mrs Carson ghosts me a wink. 'He's somewhere at the bottom of the garden, playing with Will. I suggested they had some fun together while Mrs Ogilvie had a rest after her hot walk over here.'

'What a good idea,' I say. 'Shall I see how they're getting on?'

'Why not? Tell Will we're having tea around four o'clock, but I can delay it if he and Bernie are busy.'

I set off down the garden in search of Will. With any luck, he'll have taken several pictures by now, and we can select the best one later. I reach the end of the lawn and see a small shrubbery on one side, hidden from the house. As I expected, Will and Bernie are here. But Will isn't crouching down, snapping away in his best professional photographer manner. He's sitting on the grass, ruefully surveying his camera.

'What happened?' I say.

Bernie rushed over to me and leaps up to lick my face.

'Gently!' I say. 'It's nice to see you too, but I washed my face only this morning.'

Will looks up from his camera. 'I almost had it! He was sitting on that clump of grass, grinning at me. I crawled towards him and was about to take the shot when he noticed me and jumped up. He raced over to lick me, and I dropped the camera. I've broken the lens!'

I take an instinctive step back. 'I'm so sorry, Will. I really am.'

He looks surprised. 'It's fine. It isn't the first time. It's a hazard of the job. It's a little inconvenient because I've left my spare lens at home.'

'Is it insured?'

'All my camera equipment is insured,' he says. 'Are you ok, Olivia? You look quite pale.'

'Do I? I'm upset for you. You must be so annoyed.'

'With Bernie?'

'I suppose so, although it isn't his fault. But it's made things difficult for you. You have every right to be annoyed.'

He looks puzzled. 'I don't see why. It's not the end of the world. I've broken a lens. So what? I have other lenses. I'll fetch the other one later.'

He gets to his feet and snaps his fingers at Bernie, who's trying to dig up the nearest bush. 'Come on, mutt! Mrs Carson won't love you any more if she sees you doing that.'

I follow him back up the garden to where the two women are sitting, deep in conversation.

Will greets them cheerfully. 'Bernie's had a good run around. Now he's ready for a nap, aren't you, old man?'

Bernie promptly collapses at Mrs Ogilvie's feet and starts snoring.

'Isn't he a wonder?' says Mrs Carson. 'You'd almost think he understood what we were saying.'

'He does!' says Mrs Ogilvie. 'My vet says Bernie is the most intelligent animal he's ever come across.'

'That doesn't surprise me,' says Mrs Carson. 'He's a lovely dog. So well-behaved and docile.'

Will and I glance at each other and look hurriedly away. Mrs Ogilvie doesn't appear to notice.

'I'll pop the kettle on, shall I?' says Mrs Carson. 'I'm sure we're all ready for a cup of tea.'

I follow her into the house. 'Can I help you with anything? I brought a box of cakes from the bakery.'

'You didn't need to do that!' says Mrs Carson as though I've trekked across the Antarctic to bring her favourite walrus steaks instead of picking up a few cakes and cookies from my place of work.

'And Will brought us a bottle of wine!' she says. 'The pair of you are spoiling us. I popped it into the fridge to get cold. It's a lovely bottle of sparkling rosé. Just the thing for an afternoon in the garden. So thoughtful of him.'

I'm glad someone's getting use out of the wine. I smile as I remember the glasses of mead we drank. It was an unforgettable experience.

'You look pleased about something,' she says. 'Did Will get some pictures of Bernie?'

I come back down to earth. 'I'm afraid not. He was about to, but Bernie jumped up at him at the last minute, and he dropped his camera. I'm afraid he's broken his lens.'

'How annoying for him,' she says placidly. 'I hope he has another one.'

I'm taken aback by her response. First, Will didn't seem put out, and now Mrs Carson says it's merely annoying. I thought one of them would recognise the gravity of the situation. However, it's not my business if Honeywell inhabitants do things differently.

'Maybe he can pop home in a while and pick up another one,' she suggests.

'That's what he said.'

'Marvellous!' She hands me a plate of scones. 'Would you mind taking that out to the garden? I'll bring the tray of tea things.'

I find Will chatting with Mrs Ogilvie about gardening. I give him a meaningful look as I put the scones on the table.

'Didn't you say you needed to run home for a few minutes to fetch something you'd forgotten?'

He gives me a bland smile. 'I was telling Mrs Ogilvie I'd like to take some pictures of the flower beds, but I don't have the correct lens with me.'

'A macro lens!' Mrs Ogilvie informs me.

'Do you know about photography?' I say, surprised. I half expect her to tell me she used to do it as a child. But she would have been using a Brownie, and I doubt they had macro lenses.

'Will has been telling me all about the different lenses he uses,' she says. 'It's fascinating. My husband used to dabble in photography. He set up a dark room in his shed, and he developed his own pictures. I didn't like the smell, so I didn't help him. I used to send our holiday snaps to Boots, and they sent me back a packet of photographs by return post. Will doesn't even do that. He says it's all on his computer.'

She looks genuinely interested, and I wish I had something intelligent to add to the conversation. I haven't asked Will much about his work. This is partly because I've been avoiding reciprocal questions. But partly it's because I've been too wrapped up in myself and my own troubles to take much interest in what anyone else is doing. I don't even know what his next project is, or where. For all I know, he may be off on assignment to Cairo soon to photograph the pyramids.

Mrs Carson appears with the tea tray. 'Help yourself to scones! I baked them this morning. Did I hear someone mention computers? Were you talking about the Silver Surfers?'

'What's that?' says Mrs Ogilvie.

'Mavis Sotherby organises it,' says Mrs Carson. 'She teaches the older generation how to get the most out of their computers. It's a wonderful idea. I pop along whenever I can. I've learned all about attachments and files, and I don't know what else! Martin is most impressed. I showed him how to back up his digital photos yesterday, and he said the end times had come.'

'Would you like to attend the classes, Mrs Ogilvie?' asks Will.

'They aren't for people like me,' she says. 'I don't own a computer.'

'Of course, they're for people like you!' exclaims Mrs Carson. 'Everyone should know how to use one. They're an essential part of modern life.'

Mrs Ogilvie doesn't look convinced. 'Aren't they terribly expensive?'

'They can be,' says Will. 'But a basic second-hand laptop doesn't cost much.'

I hope he doesn't push this. I don't know how much money Mrs Ogilvie has. For all I know, she may spend all her spare income on Bernie instead of putting the heating on or eating properly.

'I don't have one either,' I say, taking another scone and spreading it thickly with jam.

'Really?' says Will.

'I had a PC in London. But it was in my flat, and I've moved out.'

He shoots me a quick look but doesn't comment.

'But you have a phone,' Mrs Ogilvie surprises me. 'I've seen you using it to look things up.'

'True. I'd be lost without my phone.'

'And sometimes you're lost with it,' says Will. 'The first time I met Olivia, her car had broken down. She couldn't get any phone connection, so she didn't know where she was.'

'How dreadful!' says Mrs Carson. 'So, that's how you ended up in Honeywell?'

'Pretty much,' I say. 'If Will hadn't been living here for the summer, he'd have given me a lift to somewhere else, and I'd never have met you all.'

'These things are meant to be,' she says. 'I've always thought that.'

'I almost didn't agree to stay,' I say. 'It seemed so ridiculous to arrive out of the blue and end up working here. If this were a Hollywood movie, I'd say it was too far-fetched for words.'

'If this were a Hollywood movie,' says Will, 'you'd have been a criminal running from justice. Or an innocent tourist who gradually became aware of spooky goings on in the village. At first, you'd have thought it was idyllic, but you'd have started to notice strange happenings. No one would be who they seemed. Everyone would have a secret to hide. By the end of the movie, you'd be running for your life through the forest, armed only with a torch with a failing battery. To make matters worse, you'd have absolutely no phone connection!'

'My goodness!' says Mrs Carson. 'You do have a vivid imagination, Will. I'm sure it would have been nothing like that. If Olivia were in a film, she'd be the beautiful heroine in search of adventure. She'd arrive in Honeywell and meet the love of her life. She wouldn't know he was the love of her life to start with. No one ever does. She'd meet three young men and have to choose between them.'

'I hate making choices,' I say. 'Couldn't someone do it for me?'

'Oh, no, my dear! That isn't how it works at all. We all have to choose our own path in life. Isn't that right, Will?'

'I'm sure it is,' he says.

'Who are these men I'm going to meet?' I say.

She gives me a slight smile. 'That isn't for me to say. That's for the scriptwriter.'

'They need to hurry,' I say. 'I'll be leaving Honeywell soon, and I haven't met many people at all.'

'There was the blacksmith,' Will reminds me.

'I'd forgotten him,' I say. 'But I don't somehow see him as the love of my life.'

'Mr Makepeace?' says Mrs Carson, bewildered. 'He's married with five young children.'

'I believe Will is thinking of a different blacksmith,' I say. 'And I can rule him out. That leaves two more men. There was the man in the beer tent. I don't remember much about him, but he served me some of the finest mead in all the land. I'll keep him on the list.'

'Which leaves only one more,' says Will. 'Think hard, Olivia. Didn't you notice anyone jousting or wrestling who filled your girlish heart with unnamed hopes and dreams?'

'The only man I remember was tilting at the quintain,' I say. 'He started off well, but he ended in an undignified heap on the grass.'

'But he won you a ribbon,' he reminds me.

'True.' I hold up my wrist to show him.

He looks pleased. 'You're still wearing it.'

I shrug. 'I couldn't find any scissors.'

Mrs Ogilvie lays down her cup. 'Are we still talking about computers?'

'I'm sorry,' I apologise. 'Will and I visited the mediaeval fair the other day. We were talking about that.'

'Were we?' says Mrs Carson. 'No wonder I'm confused. I was talking about romantic comedies. Did you have a lovely time?'

'We did,' I say. 'At least, I did. We didn't mean to go there. We were looking for Harfield Mill, but we took a wrong turning and ended up at the fair.'

'It sounds as though you took the right turning,' she says. 'I'm always telling Martin we should visit that fair. They're holding it again at Christmas. Perhaps we should go this year. I'm sure they have some lovely mulled wine.'

'What do you say, Olivia?' says Will. 'Shall we try it again at Christmas?'

'There's no point,' I say. 'It's the sort of place you only find when you aren't looking for it. If you try to make arrangements in advance, it disappears. Besides, neither of us will be here by then. I'm leaving as soon as Lily comes back to work, and you'll have taken all your pictures by the autumn. After that, you'll be off to who knows where?'

'That's such a shame,' says Mrs Carson. 'I was hoping you'd stay with us much longer, Olivia. We've only just got to know you.'

'It is a pity,' agrees Mrs Ogilvie. 'Honeywell seems to suit you.'

'It does?' I say.

She nods. 'You look far more relaxed than when you first arrived. Besides, I enjoy chatting with you when I come to the bakery. So does Bernie.'

I smile at Bernie, lying on his side with his legs twitching. He's chasing something in his sleep, but I'm not sure what. I wonder whether Isabella does this in her sleep too. Maybe she dreams of racing to the Red Lion before they run out of game pie.

'It's a beautiful place to live,' I say. 'You're all very lucky.'

'What's stopping you from staying longer?' says Mrs Carson.

'It isn't my home. You can't just rock up to a new place and decide not to leave.'

'Why not?' asks Will.

'Because life doesn't work like that. You know it doesn't.'

'Not usually,' he agrees. 'But there's no reason you shouldn't stay here if you want to.'

'You're so full of suggestions about what other people should do,' I say. 'Why don't you follow your own advice?'

I expect him to look annoyed, but he doesn't. 'My home is somewhere else.'

'So is mine!' I counter.

'Where's that?'

I start to speak, then stop. I was about to say London, but that's no longer true. I could move back there if I chose. But I wouldn't be going home. I'd be going there to start a whole new life.

Mrs Carson gives me an encouraging smile. 'Where do you call home, Olivia?'

I'm aware of Will's eyes on me as I answer. 'I don't call anywhere home at present.'

'Where does your family live?' asks Mrs Ogilvie.

I stare down at my lap. 'I don't have much family. As you know, my parents died when I was eighteen. I'm an only child, and so were they. My last remaining grandparent died when I was twenty-one.'

Mrs Carson looks horrified. 'You poor child! I had no idea. So, you've been living all by yourself for the past goodness knows how long?'

I feel my face turn red. 'Not exactly. I'd just started university when my parents died, and I spent the next four years there. First, I was in halls, and then I shared with friends for a couple of years. After I graduated, I got a job as a veterinary nurse. I lived in a share house for a few years, then I moved in with my boyfriend.'

She looks relieved. 'So, you do have someone?'

'Not really. He and I recently broke up. That's why I left London. I decided to take a trip for a week or two. I hadn't had a holiday for years. Charlie – my boyfriend – didn't like them, so we hardly ever went away.'

'That's a shame,' she says. 'I love Honeywell, but I love seeing new places too.'

'I was planning to explore the Purbecks,' I say. 'It seems a beautiful part of the world. Still, I can do that some other time.'

'Are you looking for a new job?' she asks. 'Or will you be going back to your job in London?'

'I gave in my notice before I left. And I don't want to go back to that area. There's too much chance of running into Charlie.'

'There are plenty of veterinary nurses around here,' says Mrs Ogilvie unexpectedly. 'There are two working at the practice Bernie and I attend.'

'I expect there are,' I say. 'But I'm not sure whether I want to keep doing that.'

'I thought you loved working with animals,' says Will.

'I do. But I really wanted to specialise in surgical nursing.'

'I didn't know that,' he says. 'What stopped you?'

I open my mouth to say that Charlie did, but I close it again. It's only half true. He was strongly against the idea, but he couldn't have prevented me if I'd been determined to do it.

'I was put off by the length of the course,' I say. 'I have a biology degree, which is a start. But I'd still need to undertake another couple of years' training, which is a huge commitment at my age.'

'Your age!' says Mrs Carson. 'You're still a baby.'

'I'll be thirty next year.'

'That's what I mean. You're far too young to be worried about things like that. If I can learn how to export files at my age, you can think about retraining for a different career.'

'It wouldn't even be a different career,' says Will. 'You're already working in that field.'

'I know!' I say impatiently. 'Do you think I haven't thought about all that?'

'What's stopping you?' he says more gently.

I swallow hard. 'Me! I'm stopping myself. I've spent four years living with a man who thought he knew what was best for me. Not just the small things like how to decorate the flat or which car to drive. The big things too. He spent all his time telling me I was less competent than he was, and I should allow him to make all the decisions about how I spent my money and my spare time. In the end, I came to believe he was right. I believed I was lucky to have him. He had such a clear sense of purpose for our lives, and I had none.'

'That's hardly surprising after what happened to you at eighteen,' says Will in a low voice.

'Maybe,' I say. 'But that's more than ten years ago. I ought to have got over it by now and found my way. About a year ago, I began to think I was ready to do that. But by then, it was too late. Charlie had our future all planned out for us, and it felt unfair for me to change everything on a whim. I persuaded myself I was being ridiculous and having an early midlife crisis.'

'What happened?' says Will, his eyes fixed intently on my face.

'I have absolutely no idea. I thought I'd got it all under control and was happy with the plans we were making. I really believed that was true. But I woke up one morning, and everything had changed. I can't say exactly how, but it had. You know how you go on holiday somewhere, and you're exhausted by the journey, so you fall into bed as soon as you arrive and go to sleep? When you wake the following morning, there's a minute when you don't know where you are. Everything's changed, and you don't recognise anything around you. It was a bit like that for me. It was as though I'd woken up in a strange place, not knowing where I was or how I'd got there. The only thing I recognised was me. And it wasn't the me of the past ten years. It was the me from when I was eighteen, before my parents died. It felt as though no time had passed since I was that girl – that the intervening years had been a dream. An extremely vivid one, but still a dream.'

I stop, unable to go on. Mrs Ogilvie breaks the silence. 'That was the real you. It was the other person who was a dream.'

I looked her in surprise, and she flushes. 'It was the same when Edward died. The person I was until then was entirely different to the person I am now. Sometimes, I look at myself, and I hardly recognise myself and what I've become. It's like you say – it's all a vivid dream. It's one of the reasons I love Bernie so much. He knew me before Edward died. He loved the person I was then, and he hasn't stopped loving me.'

As if he hears his name, Bernie twitches an ear and half opens his eye to look at her.

She smiles down at him. 'You're a silly old boy, but I don't know what I'd do without you.'

I surreptitiously wipe my eyes. I had no idea anyone would understand. I should have said something sooner. It might have helped us both. It's strange to think there's another person in the world feeling exactly the same as I do, and that I should have bumped into them like this.

Maybe it isn't so strange, after all. Maybe I'm less alone than I feel. I've resisted talking to anyone in Honeywell about my previous life. I didn't think they'd understand. Yet, here I am, blurting out my deepest secrets to a group of strangers. Not only are they listening with sympathy, but one of them is telling me they feel the same as I do.

I've spent the past ten years feeling horribly alone. Is it possible that all I needed to do was to reach out and tell someone how I felt? If I'd found the courage to do that, would everything have been different?

I'll never know the answer to that, but it doesn't matter. No one can change the past. All they can do is plan the future. I've delegated that responsibility to someone else for far too long. Not so much delegated as allowed him to snatch the reins of my life from my own hands. But that's finally over, and I'm free. The person I was before this all happened is still there somewhere, hoping I'll ask her what she wants. I resolve to do everything in my power not to let her down.

Chapter Twenty-Four

Will disappears after tea, saying he needs to pick up his lens so he can take some nice shots of Mrs Carson's herbaceous border. I offer to help Mrs Carson with the washing up, but she refuses.

'You and Mrs Ogilvie enjoy the sunshine and have a pleasant talk. Martin is somewhere in the house. He can dry the plates for me.'

'Don't you have a dishwasher?' I say. 'I must help you.'

She flaps her hands at me to sit down. 'I have a lovely dishwasher. But I enjoy doing things like this by hand. It's an opportunity to chat with Martin.'

She disappears into the house with the tray, leaving me with Mrs Ogilvie. I wonder whether I should bring up the subject of our earlier conversation, but I'm not sure how. For all I know, she may be embarrassed at having shared something so personal about herself. I know I am. But I also feel strangely light. I've been carrying around this huge, shameful secret for weeks. When I finally found the courage to unburden myself, I discovered it was neither huge nor shameful. I've made some poor decisions over the past few years, but so have millions of other people. They recognise them and find a way to fix them.

I met someone who wasn't right for me, and I stayed with him far too long and allowed him to dictate the terms of my life to me. I didn't realise that was what I was doing. Now that I do, it's up to me to change course. It's no big deal. Lots of people find a new path even in their sixties and seventies.

Mrs Carson is right. I'm young. I have plenty of time. I can stop lying awake at night, worrying myself sick about the terrible decisions I've made and all the doors I've closed to myself. That's the great thing about doors. They close, but they can also open. Even if they're locked, you can find the key if you look hard enough. If the worst comes to the worst, you can break them down.

I've almost forgotten where I am, and it's a shock when Mrs Ogilvie speaks. 'Do you think I could learn to use a computer?'

I take a moment to remember where I am. 'Definitely. Anyone can use one. They aren't half as complicated as you'd expect.'

'So everyone says, but I'm not sure I'd cope. It's difficult to learn new things at my age.'

'You aren't eighty yet!' I tease her. 'It wouldn't take you long. Do you have any special reason for wanting to learn?'

She hesitates. 'Angela has been talking to me about those email things.'

'You'd like to send an email? Good for you! I can help you with that if you don't want to go to those classes. Although they sound like fun. You might enjoy them.'

'Angela says they hold them in the evenings,' she says. 'I couldn't leave Bernie by himself. He wouldn't like it. And I don't suppose they'd allow him into the classes.'

'It would be terribly boring for him,' I say. 'He wouldn't know what was going on or why no one was paying any attention to him. But that isn't a problem. I'd love to come and babysit him. I mean doggy sit. Or I could take him for a walk. It would only be for an hour or two.'

'No one but me has ever looked after him,' she says doubtfully. 'Still, you aren't the same as everybody. You're trained.'

'That's right,' I say. 'I can't perform operations, but I can do most other things. And you can give me the vet's number, in case.'

'It's an idea,' she says.

'It's a great idea,' I urge. 'We should get you enrolled at once. The quicker you start, the sooner you'll be able to send an email. Do you have any one particular in mind?'

'My sister in Australia,' she says.

'How do you contact her at the moment? Do you call her?'

Her face closes. 'We haven't spoken for a while. If we need to pass on any information, we write a letter.'

Obviously, this is a touchy subject, and it's none of my business. But she's the one who brought it up, so I risk a further question. 'How long is it since you saw her?'

'About six years.'

'Have you never been over to visit her?'

'I can't,' she says. 'I have Bernie. My sister lived in Winchester until she left England, so we saw each other quite often. She moved to Australia just before Edward died. We were supposed to join her. We were all planning to buy a house together in Melbourne. Mabel went on ahead, while we got ready to sell the house here and pack up our things. Then Edward had his heart attack, and everything changed.'

'Of course, it did. Did you think about joining her later?'

She shakes her head. 'Edward and I had planned to take to take Bernie over there with us, but he wasn't well enough. Mabel and I had a bit of a falling out over it. She said I should have waited and got myself a dog in Australia. Then she said I should bring Bernie with me. Animals fly all over the world nowadays, and she was sure he would be fine. But the vet wasn't too happy about it. Bernie had respiratory problems when he was a puppy, and I didn't know how he would manage on an airplane. I couldn't take any unnecessary risks with him. He was all I had left. I'm sure Edward wouldn't have wanted me to risk Bernie's safety.'

'Does Bernie still have respiratory problems?' I say.

'No, he grew out of that, thank goodness. But by then it was too late. Even if I'd wanted to move over there, I don't think Mabel would have wanted me.'

'I'm sure that's not true. Your sister was disappointed. People say things they don't mean when they're upset.'

She purses her lips. 'I wrote to her a couple of years later and suggested she came back home to live with me. I have a second bedroom in the cottage. But she said she was happy where she was, and she wasn't the one who had changed the arrangements.'

I'm not sure what to say. It seems Mrs Ogilvie's sister is as stubborn as she is. I can imagine the situation, with neither of them being prepared to make the first move to apologise and climb down. It's a pity, at least for Mrs Ogilvie. I don't know what kind of social life her sister has in Melbourne, but it's obvious Mrs Ogilvie is lonely and isolated.

'It's lovely you want to learn how to send her an email,' I say at last. 'Do you know whether Mabel has a computer?'

'I expect she does,' says Mrs Ogilvie. 'She was always one to move with the times.'

'Is she your older or your younger sister?'

'I'm the eldest daughter,' she says, looking so forbidding I don't dare ask for any further details.

Mrs Carson appears at the French windows, and I wave to her. 'It looks as though Mavis Sotherby has one more recruit for the Silver Surfers.'

She looks delighted. 'How exciting! Who's that?'

'Mrs Ogilvie. Do you think there will be room for one extra?'

'Of course, there will. What a marvellous idea. I'm afraid she won't be able to bring Bernie.'

'Not a problem,' I say. 'I've persuaded Mrs Ogilvie to allow me the honour of taking care of him that evening. I can't wait.'

She looks relieved. 'How kind of you. I'll give Mavis a call this evening. The classes are on Friday from six o'clock until eight o'clock.'

I half expect Mrs Ogilvie to veto the entire plan, but she doesn't. Maybe she's so carried away by the whole thing that she'll go home this afternoon and book herself a last-minute ticket to Australia. I'll arrive to collect Bernie on Friday, only to find a for sale sign on the lawn and the front door swinging open.

Will appears around the side of the house, holding a small bag. 'I have the lens. I'll start by taking a few pictures of the flowers in the rockery to assess the light.'

He wanders around the garden, bending down and photographing individual blooms. He straightens up and beckons to me. 'Olivia, can you give me a hand?'

'What a wonderful idea!' says Mrs Carson. 'It's getting rather hot out here, Edith. Shall we sit in the house?'

Mrs Ogilvie gets to her feet, and Bernie wakes up. I click my fingers at him. 'Come and have a run around with me while Will photographs the flowers.'

Bernie races over and jumps up at Will, who takes a hasty step back. 'You can wash Olivia's face, not mine. At least, not when I'm holding this.'

Mrs Carson and Mrs Ogilvie disappear into the house.

'Where do you want him to pose?' I say.

'I don't know,' says Will. 'Could you play with him a bit while I try to get some natural shots?'

'Only if you promise not to take any pictures of me.'

'I'll do my best,' he says. 'I can crop you out later, anyway. Unlike you, I have access to one of those newfangled computer things.'

I give him a pitying look. 'I edit all my photos on my phone.'

'Aren't you the technophile?' he says. 'I should have come to you instead of taking a photography course.'

'Did you study photography for your degree?'

'Not a degree, as such, but I took a certification,' he says. 'I printed it out, and everything. Remind me to show you some time.'

'What sort of certification?' I ask, moving Bernie away from the geraniums, where he's busily engaged in checking for bones Mrs Carson may have buried there for a rainy day.

'It was an online course,' he says. 'The company was based somewhere in the Caymans, if I remember correctly. I can't go back and check because they went bust soon afterwards.'

'How long was the course?'

'Two days. But it was fairly intensive. We weren't allowed to miss any of the modules. We covered the whole subject pretty thoroughly. It was two thousand pounds well spent.'

'Really?' I ask incredulously.

'No, not really,' he says. 'Sorry, Olivia. I couldn't resist. You seem to have such a low opinion of what I do.'

'That isn't true! I don't know much about it.'

'That's easily remedied,' he says. 'What would you like me to tell you?'

'Where did you really train?'

'I did a fine arts degree at Goldsmiths. I planned to go into textile design, but I got involved in a black-and-white photography project during my second year, and I was hooked.'

'Is that what you like best? Black-and-white photography?'

'Not necessarily. I choose the most appropriate medium for whatever I'm doing. Bernie, for instance' – he nudges Bernie with his toe to stop him from beginning a second excavation in the begonia bed – 'will look better in colour. It will catch his lively personality. He doesn't strike me as a candidate for a moody, atmospheric shot.'

As if to prove us wrong, Bernie sits down in front of the flowers and gives me a soulful look. It's the look of a dog who is often misunderstood but who takes all the buffets and blows of life with saintlike patience.

'That's the one!' whispers Will, reaching for his camera. 'Don't distract him, Olivia. In fact, don't breathe for the next five minutes if you can manage it.'

He bends down until he's almost on a level with Bernie. For a wonder, Bernie doesn't move. His attention has been caught by a butterfly above his head. He watches it, entranced.

Will straightens up. 'That should do it. We couldn't have planned it more perfectly if we'd tried.'

He shows me the screen on his camera.

'That's incredible!' I say. 'Mrs Ogilvie will love this. I can't wait to see it printed out full size.'

Even seen in miniature, it's an impressive picture. Bernie is sitting in a patch of sunlight, surrounded by flowers. The sun catches the golden fur around his head, turning it to gold. The butterfly hovers tantalisingly near his face. Bernie is looking up at it as though he's Saint Francis of Assisi and has spent his entire life talking to all other living creatures and administering to the poor.

'How did you get the butterfly in focus as well as Bernie's face?' I ask. 'When I take pictures of two different things, one of them is always slightly out of focus.'

Will gives me a smug look. 'That's the beauty of a course like the one I took. On day two, they taught us about the twiddly bit you turn on the lens that does something or other with the focus. Like I say, it was two thousand pounds well spent.'

'Fine,' I say. 'Don't tell me. I wouldn't understand, anyway. Are you taking any more pictures?'

'Not unless Bernie does something exceptional like dancing on his hind legs while reciting The Wreck of the Hesperus. Or he gets another thorn in his paw.'

'How would that help?' I say.

'You could bend down and administer to him. It would make a wonderful picture. You in your nurse's uniform, tenderly caring for a helpless creature. I could show it at the Royal Exhibition. It would be bound to get us at least a highly commended.'

'I have a better idea,' I say. 'I'll jab a sharp stick into your hand and take pictures of Bernie removing it. That should win us more than a highly commended.'

He shakes his head as he zips his camera back into its bag. 'Sometimes, I don't think you take either my career or me seriously.'

'I don't. In fact –'

I break off as a squirrel appears from somewhere behind the flower bed. It streaks across the lawn at top speed. Bernie, all traces of his former angelic pose disappearing, pelts after it as fast as his legs will carry him.

Will makes a grab for his camera bag and fumbles with the zip, while I dart after Bernie, shouting at him to leave the poor squirrel alone. He takes no notice, and I speed up, still shouting.

I round the corner just as the squirrel makes a dash for the nearest tree and launches itself towards the trunk. Without thinking, I pull out my phone and point it at the tree. I click several times as Bernie makes an ineffectual leap for the lower branches. He lands on his back and rolls over. With a quick look around to make sure no one has noticed his humiliation, he trots into the house.

Will appears behind me. 'Why did I put my camera away? That would have made the most amazing sequence.'

I look down at my phone screen and smother a laugh.

'What?' says Will, and I wordlessly hold out my phone.

His eyes widen. 'That's not possible.'

I give a nonchalant shrug. 'It's nothing. They taught us how to take pictures on day one of the course on how to use a mobile phone. Step one – switch on your phone. Step two – point and shoot.'

He bursts out laughing. 'Touché! That's an amazing photo. Well done.'

I look at the picture again and have to agree. It may be an absolute fluke, but that doesn't detract from the beauty of the shot. It's a moment of sheer, unadulterated canine joy. Bernie, with the joyful light of determination in his eyes, is leaping towards the squirrel like an acrobat defying gravity. His fur is practically sparking with electricity.

The squirrel is a few feet above his head, looking back over its shoulder with what seems like a look of derision. It's a shot in a million – the sort of picture you could never in a hundred years expect to achieve unless you weren't trying to. A concatenation of chances no one could plan, but which come together in the most perfect way imaginable. Much like my time in Honeywell.

I beam up at Will, all thoughts of teasing him forgotten in the joy of the moment. 'I can't believe I did it!'

'You're amazing, Olivia. Has anyone ever told you that?'

And, without waiting for me to answer, he pulls me into his arms and kisses me.

Chapter Twenty-Five

For a second, I'm too surprised to react. I almost respond to the kiss. It feels the polite thing to do. But my brain kicks into gear before I can do anything to make this whole situation more confusing than it already is.

I step back, and he releases me at once. 'Olivia?' he says, his voice shaky.

I'm not sure what to do next. Romantic conventions would seem to dictate that I slap his face, but that seems extreme for one quick kiss. It must have been the surge of adrenaline after the mad dash across the lawn and subsequent successful photograph that made Will lose his head. I can understand that. I almost kissed Bernie myself when I saw the picture.

'My picture isn't that good!' I say, trying for a light tone.

He looks dazed. 'What picture?'

I wave my phone at him. 'This one!'

He hardly seems to hear me. 'I've wanted to do that for a long time.'

'Do what? You mean kiss me? That's ridiculous.'

'No, it isn't. When I saw you stomping off down the road that day, I knew it was the start of something special.'

'I didn't stomp,' I say defensively. 'I set off in a purposeful manner.'

'When you turned around and walked back towards me, I felt as though I'd won the lottery.'

This isn't the point. All he needs to do is to acknowledge he got carried away with the emotion of the past ten minutes and did something stupid. Then we can put it behind us.

'Never mind about all that,' I say. 'It has nothing to do with what just happened.'

'It has everything to do with it,' he says. 'I'm trying to tell you how I feel about you, but you aren't making it easy.'

'Because that isn't how you really feel. Don't make this something it isn't. You kissed me. It wasn't the best idea, but I can see why you did it. Can't we forget it and carry on as we are?'

'Is that what you want?' he asks in a low tone.

'We're both leaving this place soon, and we won't see each other again. Even if we … if you wanted something else, it couldn't happen. You're going back to London, and I'm not. It isn't a recipe for a happily ever after.'

He starts to speak, but I stop him. 'Besides, I'm not interested in another relationship. Not now. Possibly not ever. I'm not good at them.'

'That's nonsense!' he says. 'Everyone has a few relationship disasters. You learn from them and move on. The human race would have died out by now if everyone who had a break up stayed single for the rest of their lives.'

'That isn't my problem. I don't owe it to humanity to repopulate the earth. It's overcrowded, anyway.'

He smiles. 'I didn't put that too well, did I? Are you telling me you plan to stay single because of one bad relationship?'

'A disastrous one,' I correct him. 'And I don't know. I haven't given it much thought.'

He reaches for my hand. 'Do you think you could consider it now?'

I pull my hand away. 'Why should I? Why can't you listen to what I say and respect it? Why does every single person in my life think they know better than me what I want and what's good for me?'

'They don't,' he says. 'At least, I don't. I know you've been living with a complete loser, but please don't judge all of us by one man.'

'Not all men? How many times have I heard that?'

'That isn't what I meant!' he says. 'But I'm not Charlie. I'm nothing like him. Why refuse to give me a chance because he was a controlling jerk?'

It's possible that he's right. But how can I know? Charlie didn't start off by controlling my every movement. I wouldn't have stayed with him if he had. It all happened imperceptibly, without me noticing. By the time I did, I was trapped, and I couldn't tell what was real and what wasn't.

'Perhaps that wasn't fair,' I say. 'You may be nothing like Charlie. You don't seem to be. But I no longer trust my own judgement.'

'I could give you references,' he says with a half-smile. 'I'm sure I could find people to vouch for me.'

'You mean old girlfriends?'

He recoils. 'I do not! That would be weird. I meant professional references. A tutor from college, my bank manager, the local vicar, that sort of thing.'

'Do you know your local vicar?'

'I do. I took the pictures for his church's five-hundredth anniversary. He was delighted with them.'

I can't help smiling. 'I'm sure he was. But that doesn't mean he has the faintest idea who you are as a person.'

'He knows I'm punctual, and my prices are very reasonable.'

'Punctuality is important when you're dating,' I agree. 'But unless you charge people to date you, the other part isn't relevant.'

'I don't,' he says. 'To prove it to you, I'd like to buy you dinner tonight. And I promise to turn up on time.'

I almost agree, but something stops me long enough for common sense to kick in. 'It's very kind of you, but the answer is no.'

'No for tonight, or no forever?' he says.

'No forever. I'm sorry, Will. You seem like a nice guy, but so did Charlie.'

'Do you plan to judge everyone by how he behaved?'

'Perhaps, but that's my prerogative.'

He shrugs. 'True enough. What do you plan to do when you leave here? Where will you go?'

'I'm not sure. I'm finding it difficult to make any plans. Whenever I try, my brain spins off the subject and ends up somewhere different.'

'That's very natural,' he says. 'Maybe you should allow someone else to help.'

'Who?' I say, not catching his meaning.

'Me,' he says. 'I'm going back to London soon. You'd be welcome to stay with me until you're back on your feet. I have a two-bedroom flat, so you'd have a space of your own …'

'No!' I burst out before he can finish. 'You don't get it, do you? You're the same as everyone else. You think you know what I want and what I need. All you have to do is tell me what you have planned for my life, and I'll fall into line. I thought better of you, which shows I'm right to doubt my judgement.'

'I didn't mean it like that,' he says.

'No one ever does. There's no point in continuing this discussion. You and I are not happening, Will, and the sooner you accept that, the better. I have to go.'

I turn abruptly and follow Bernie into the house. I find him sitting on the sofa next to Mrs Ogilvie, who's looking at a photo album.

Mrs Carson jumps up when I come in. 'Have you and Will got what you want?'

'Not exactly,' I say in a low voice.

'What a shame,' she says. 'Perhaps the pair of you can try again another time?'

I ruffle Bernie's head, and he licks my hand. 'I'm afraid I have to go. I promised my landlady I'd be home in time to help her with something.'

I hope to goodness she doesn't ask me what. I can't imagine what tenants help their landladies with. Re-tiling the roof, perhaps, or sharpening the lawn mower blades?

'Is Will going with you?' she says.

'He's in the garden. He's still taking pictures of the flowers. I've said goodbye to him. I really must go now. Thank you so much for inviting me. Goodbye, Mrs Ogilvie. Bye, Bernie.'

I leave the room before she can answer. I walk down the drive, my head spinning with the events of the afternoon. What was Will thinking? He had no right to kiss me like that without asking. He must have assumed I felt the same as him, but he had no business doing so. He could have had the decency to ask first. And what was all that about me going to stay with him in London? Clearly, he's put some thought into these plans. I wonder how long he's been thinking about them and why he hasn't mentioned them to me.

I'm so tired of people planning my future without even the basic courtesy of consulting me. Isabella was the first. She decided when she met me that I ought to live in Honeywell, and she tricked me into it. Now Will thinks I ought to go back to London and the life he's planned out for me. And he hasn't even tried to trick me into it. He assumes I'll be fine with it, which is worse.

Is this my fault? Do I give out vibes of complete incompetence? In which case, was Charlie justified in taking over my life once it became clear I would never do so myself? He may have waited for years, hoping I'd step up and take responsibility for myself and only picked up the reins when he saw I wouldn't.

It's a depressing thought, but I hope it isn't true. I coped fine until I met him. I got a good degree and had great plans for the future until he persuaded me I was being selfish in refusing to think what was best for us as a couple.

I pick up the pace as I walk home. The faster I walk, the more difficult it is to think about my life and what a mess it is. I'm almost running by the time I reach Cherry Street. I slow to a jog and wait until my breathing has returned to normal before walking sedately up the garden path. I don't want Eleanor to catch sight of me and ask questions.

The way my afternoon has been going, she'll probably tell me she's been giving my future a lot of thought, and she's decided the best thing for me is to stay in Honeywell and join her in a property investment business.

Chapter Twenty-Six

'How did it go?' says Isabella the moment I walk into the bakery the following morning.

'How did what go? Oh, you mean the thing with Bernie? We got some photos of him.' I hang my bag on the hook and reach for my overall.

'That's good,' she says. 'But I meant how was the afternoon overall? Did you and Will have a nice time?'

'I wish everyone would stop going on and on about Will!' I snap.

She looks surprised. 'I wasn't going on about him. I was asking how your afternoon went.'

'Well, don't!'

She doesn't say anything more, which surprises me. She's usually such a chatterbox.

I switch on the coffee machine and stare out of the window while it warms up. Why did Will have to spoil things like this? First by kissing me, although I did my best to give him a way to back down from that. Then by pursuing the subject and telling me what I ought to be doing with my life. Why couldn't he have followed my lead and made a joke of the whole thing?

'Abby's been making custard slices,' says Isabella.

'And?' I say.

'I thought you might like one.'

'I'm not hungry. I'll make myself a cup of coffee, then check the orders.'

'I've already done that,' she says. 'I checked them while you were staring into space, muttering about men.'

I blink. 'I did no such thing. I haven't said a word since I got here.'

'You said it with your eyes. If ever a woman had a face that was easy to read, it's you, Olivia. What has he done?'

'What has who done?' I counter, but it's no good. She's like Bernie with a bone.

'Will, of course. You left here all excited about having tea with him. Now you're like a bear with a sore head. I doubt Mrs Carson said anything to upset you. That woman's a living saint. And for some inexplicable reason, you seem to get on well with Mrs Ogilvie. Which only leaves one person.'

I drop into the nearest chair and sigh. 'If I said I'd prefer you to leave it for now, would you take the slightest bit of notice?'

She steams the milk. 'That's hard to say. Possibly, if you were very stern with me. But I know you'd like to talk about it, and there's no one else here at the moment, so why don't you?'

'Perhaps because I'm sick and tired of people telling me what to do. It seems everyone around here knows what I want, and how I feel. Is that a Honeywell thing, or are you all bored?'

The smile disappears from her face. 'Is that how you really see us?'

I want to back down, but I'm not sure how. 'You must admit you've taken control of my life and told me what to do.'

She hands me a mug. 'I don't think so. I gave you a way out when it seemed as though you needed one. That's all. It was your choice to take it. You could have said, "No, thank you," and kept on driving.'

'And you wouldn't have been disappointed and tried to change my mind? Come on, Isabella. You did everything you could to trick me into staying here. First, you told me the mechanic couldn't fix my car. Then you talked me into working here.'

'I wanted you to stay,' she says, sitting down opposite me. 'Is that a crime? You looked as though you needed time out, and I needed some help. Why not do something that was in both our best interests?'

'Maybe. But I'm still here weeks later.'

'You're free to leave at any time,' she says. 'Why haven't you?'

'I don't know. Maybe I should.'

She takes a sip of her drink. 'What happened yesterday?'

'Nothing! At least, nothing much. We were having such a lovely afternoon together. Then Will went and spoiled it all by kissing me.'

I half expect her to give one of her trademark whoops and throw her arms around me. She doesn't.

'Did you mind?' she says.

'Of course, I minded! I told him not to do it again.'

'I thought you liked him,' she says mildly.

'I do like him. I imagine most people do. What does that have to do with it?'

She bites into a gooseberry slice. 'You must have known how he felt about you.'

'I didn't. I still don't. He got carried away when we took a great shot of Bernie yesterday, that's all. It doesn't mean anything more than that.'

'If you say so.'

I eye her resentfully. 'Why don't you believe me? I only met Will a few weeks ago. And you both know I've just got out of a bad relationship.'

'True,' she says. 'But there's no reason why you shouldn't meet someone else and move on. Most people do.'

'Not me. I'm not good at relationships.'

She snorts. 'Don't give me that! You must have had other relationships before this Charlie. What happened with those?'

'I dated a few people during university,' I say, 'but I wasn't ready for anything serious. Charlie was the first man I stayed with for long enough to move in with and think about spending the rest of my life with. And look how that turned out.'

She props her chin on her hands. 'He sounds awful. I can see how he might have ground you down. But that's all over now. You have to move on with your life.'

'I don't want to move on with my life,' I say. 'At least, not until I've worked out why I made such a poor decision.'

'What's the answer?' she says.

'I'm terrible at relationships?' I hazard.

'No one is terrible at relationships,' she says. 'There's nothing to them. Be yourself and find someone who likes who you are.'

'That's nonsense. It's far more complicated than that.'

She picks up a white chocolate cookie and bites into it. 'Only if you make it complicated.'

'That's not true,' I say. 'You can like someone a lot but discover you're completely incompatible.'

'Is that what happened with Charlie?'

'I'm not sure. All I know is that I couldn't stay there another minute.'

'Were you in love with him?' she says.

'I don't know.'

'Which means no. If you're in love with someone, you know about it.'

'I thought I was at first,' I say. 'But things started to go wrong after we moved in together. That was my fault, not Charlie's. I'm not terribly tidy, and I wasn't good at prioritising our relationship in the way I should have done.'

'That's rubbish,' she says. 'Who cares how tidy you are? Anyway, I've seen your room at Eleanor's house, and it's fine. And what does that mean – prioritising your relationship?'

'I kept thinking of myself as single,' I explain. 'I can see why that hurt Charlie. Whenever an opportunity to do something came up, I only thought about whether I wanted to do it, not whether we wanted to do it.'

She looks bemused. 'What's wrong with that? You don't become one half of yourself just because you're in a relationship.'

'But you ought to think about the other person and be prepared to compromise.'

'From what you've told me, you did an awful lot of compromising,' she says. 'Did he do any at all?'

'He was always thinking of me and what was best for me. All his plans were for us as a couple.'

'Did those plans include things you wanted too?'

'That's the problem,' I say. 'I've never been good at thinking about the future. But one of us had to.'

'Why do you think that is? I mean, why haven't you thought about your future?'

'I'm too unfocussed,' I say. 'I've never known what I wanted, and I don't make proper plans.'

'Neither do I,' she says. 'I like to live for the day. So, you allowed other people to make plans for you?'

'Only because I didn't know what I wanted. I couldn't even decide what to study at university.'

She looks amused. 'You stuck a pin in a list of subjects?'

'Not exactly. But my tutors all agreed I was better at science than any other subject. It made sense.'

'And what happened after you graduated?' she says. 'Did your lecturers tell you which jobs to apply for?'

'No, I decided that for myself. Charlie was happy enough with my choice. He's a high earner, so he wasn't too bothered by what I did.'

'That's big of him,' she comments.

'You're taking everything I say the wrong way!'

She considers me carefully. 'Do you know what I think?'

'I don't, but I imagine you're about to tell me.'

'I think you've spent so long being told what to do by other people that you've never got to know yourself. The first day I met you, you seemed almost relieved when I told you what to order because you didn't have to decide for yourself.'

'Or because I genuinely didn't care,' I say. 'Not everyone sees food in the same way you do.'

'I know!' she says. 'I can never understand it. But it wasn't a one off. I've noticed since then that you have great trouble in deciding about the smallest thing. I don't think you were born an indecisive person. I think you became one because the people around you thought they knew what was best for you. Maybe it came from good motives. Maybe they thought they were protecting you. But here you are, with no idea of what you want from life because you've never been allowed to think what that might be.'

Her expression softens. 'I'm sorry, Olivia. I know I'm interfering, just like everyone else in your life. But I hate to see you thinking of yourself as someone who has to do what others want her to do because she's never learned what she herself wants.'

'I get that,' I say. 'But that's all the more reason not to jump into a new relationship.'

'I suppose so,' she admits. 'But I'd hate for you to let something good slip through your fingers because you think you're terrible at relationships.'

I pick up my hairnet. 'I'll bear that in mind. I've promised to give Abby a hand planning the party food, so I'd better go.'

'And those books won't cook themselves,' she says. 'Off you go. But think about it, ok?'

'I will,' I promise, although I'm not entirely sure what I'm supposed to be thinking about. In the meantime, I have a party to plan, and I'm determined to make sure it's perfect in every way. Philosophical reflections will have to wait.

Chapter Twenty-Seven

I don't expect Will to come into the bakery again for a few days, if ever. He must be upset things didn't go the way he wanted on Wednesday. Hopefully, I won't see him before the party next Saturday. It will be easier to meet him when there are plenty of other people around.

So, I'm surprised when he wanders in after lunch and greets me as though nothing has happened. 'Hi, Olivia. How's it going?'

'I'm fine, thanks,' I say cautiously, aware of Isabella's eyes on me.

'Great,' he says. 'I'm after half a dozen currant buns for my landlady, if Abby's made any?'

'You're in luck,' says Isabella. 'She made a fresh batch this morning. Can I make you a coffee while you're here?'

I shoot her an annoyed glance. It's one thing being polite to a customer. It's quite another to invite them to stay for a second longer than they have to.

'Sounds good,' says Will, dropping into a chair.

'It's time for your break, Olivia,' says Isabella. 'I'll make you a coffee too. You can sit and chat with Will while you drink it.'

'Great idea,' says Will easily. 'I need to talk to you about the photographs you want for the party.'

'Are you still doing that?' I say.

'Why not? Were you planning to do them yourself after yesterday's triumph?'

'What triumph?' says Isabella.

'Olivia has discovered a promising new career taking action photos of badly behaved dogs,' says Will.

I open my phone and show Isabella the shot of Bernie leaping for the squirrel.

'That's incredible!' she says. 'Will's right. You should think about becoming a professional photographer.'

'I'm perfectly happy looking after animals,' I say. 'I'll leave the artistic stuff to Will.'

'Why did you think I might not take the photographs?' he asks me.

Isabella looks from me to Will. 'I'll take my coffee to the office. I can drink it when I'm doing the accounts. Keep an eye on the customers for me, Olivia.'

'I'm glad you're still doing the photographs,' I tell Will. 'I thought you might find it a little awkward, that's all.'

'Because I kissed you?'

I flush. 'I suppose so.'

'Does that make things awkward for you?'

'Not at all!' I say with forced breeziness. 'Forget it.'

'I won't do that,' he says in an unusually serious tone. 'But it has nothing to do with whether or not I take photos at the party.'

I fix my gaze on my mug. 'Thanks.'

Neither of us speaks for a moment. The tension is broken when the doorbell jangles. I jump to my feet in relief. Any customer is better than this awkward silence.

The door opens wider, and Bernie rushes in. He gives an excited bark when he sees me, then sits by the counter and looks hopefully at the basket of biscuits.

'Good morning, Mrs Ogilvie,' says Will, pushing back his chair. 'I'm afraid I've taken your table. I'll move our drinks to another one.'

'Not at all,' she says. 'There's plenty of room for the three of us. I'm pleased to have found you here. Bernie and I have had such exciting news. We had to come to the bakery at once to tell you.'

Bernie gives another excited bark.

'He's trying to tell us your news before you can,' I say.

'Is it something about a cat having fallen down a well?' suggests Will.

I catch his eye and grin. The tension between snaps, and I feel as though everything has returned to normal. Perhaps not exactly the same as it was, but something I can live with.

'Can I get you a pot of tea?' I suggest to Mrs Ogilvie. 'If Bernie can keep his news to himself for two more minutes.'

'A cup of tea would be very welcome,' she says. 'It's a warm day, and we were in a hurry to get here. Would you mind finding a biscuit for Bernie too? He likes the ones with the green speckles.'

She waits until I return with the tray of tea things. Bernie has given up trying to tell us the news and is lying by the counter, pretending his biscuit is a rat he's determined to corner.

Mrs Ogilvie beams at us. 'When I went to the Silver Surfers last week, Mavis showed me how to send an email. She helped me to create my own account.'

Will gives a low whistle. 'I'm impressed. It took me weeks to teach my mother how to email.'

'Mrs Carson told me you're a quick learner,' I tell Mrs Ogilvie, who looks pleased.

'I wrote down everything Mavis said, so I wouldn't forget it once I got home. It was far less complicated than I thought.'

'You'll have to give us your email address,' says Will. 'Then we can send you messages.'

Mrs Ogilvie reaches into her bag and pulls out a piece of paper. She peers at it. 'Mavis says it's important to choose one you can remember. Mine is BernieAtTheSugarloaf@gmail.com.'

Will gives a shout of laughter. 'That's wonderful. I'll write to him tonight and send him a picture of a bone!'

'Is that what you came in to tell us today?' I ask.

'Not exactly,' she says. 'I sent an email to my sister!'

'How did you know her email address?'

She looks even more pleased with herself. 'Mavis helped me to look her up online. We did a search!'

'You searched her name and location?' says Will.

She nods. 'I typed her name and the suburb she lives in. The people who do the internet searches told me all about her. They said she runs a yoga class each week, and they told me her email address if I wanted to join it.'

'It's a heck of a way to travel for a yoga class,' says Will.

I give him a reproving look. 'It's a wonderful idea. So, you contacted her?'

'I did,' says Mrs Ogilvie proudly. 'I told her I was now on the line, and I told her my email address.'

'In case the people who do the internet searches forgot to mention it,' Will murmurs in my ear.

I ignore him. 'How long did she take to answer?'

'I got a reply today,' she says. 'I came straight up here to tell you all about it. Mabel didn't want to write to me until she'd made all the arrangements.'

She sounds so delighted I can't help smiling. 'Arrangements?'

'That's what I came to tell you,' she says. 'Mabel is coming over to England! Isn't it exciting?'

Will is the first to speak. 'That is exciting. When is she arriving?'

'Friday,' she says. 'She says she'll take the weekend to get over the jetlag, and then she'll come to see me.'

I almost mention her birthday, but I stop myself in time. I don't want to let Mrs Ogilvie know I've remembered the date. It could lead to a complicated discussion and even, heaven forbid, her realising something is up.

'I'm so pleased for you,' I say. 'You'll both have a lot of catching up to do.'

'We will,' she says. 'She hasn't met Bernie yet.'

It's typical of Mrs Ogilvie that when she receives this news, the first thing that comes to mind is Bernie.

'I'm not sure exactly when she's coming down to Honeywell,' she says. 'But I expect she'll call me sometime over the weekend.'

Will and I exchange glances, but neither of us speaks. Mrs Ogilvie doesn't notice. She's too busy fussing over Bernie and making sure his bowl of water has been freshly filled.

She stays for about an hour. I have to work, but Will sits and chats with Mrs Ogilvie until she leaves. He's such a nice man. Not everyone would have the patience to spend an afternoon talking about the history of a village they barely know and the imaginary ailments of a spoiled dog.

As soon as she and Bernie have left, I join Will again. 'What do you think of this news?'

'I think it's great,' he says. 'It's a pity her sister isn't arriving a day or two earlier or she could have come to the party.'

'That occurred to me too. It's bad timing. But she may not even have remembered it's her sister's birthday. Mrs Ogilvie doesn't seem to think much about birthdays. Perhaps this Mabel is the same.'

Isabella appears from the kitchen, and we fill her in with the news.

'That's wonderful!' she says when we've finished. 'We have to get hold of her and persuade her to come down for the party.'

'I thought about that,' I say. 'But it's no good. We won't be able to find her without letting Mrs Ogilvie know something's up.'

'Don't be so defeatist,' she says. 'Of course, she's coming to the party. It's perfect! I'll find out which hotel she's staying at and call her there.'

'It would be wonderful if you could,' I say. 'Mrs Ogilvie would love it. She was so excited when she came in to tell us.'

Will says goodbye, and I spend the rest of the afternoon filling out the orders for our suppliers. Isabella trusts me to do some of the paperwork now, and it makes a nice change from making tea and coffee.

I leave at five thirty and walk home. It's a beautiful afternoon, and I decide to walk down to the water meadow after dinner. It's become one of my favourite Honeywell walks. It's so calm and peaceful, and I always return from it feeling less stressed.

My phone rings, and I look at the screen. To my surprise, I see it's Allie, the other nurse from my veterinary practice. Is she calling to tell me the place is falling apart without me and begging me to come back?

'Hello,' I say cautiously.

'Olivia? I didn't think you'd answer.'

'Did you think I'd changed my number?'

'I thought it was possible, she says. 'Charlie says he hasn't been able to reach you.'

My heart gives a sickening swoop. 'You've seen Charlie?'

'He came in this morning,' she says. 'He said you left London a while ago, and he hasn't been able to get in touch with you. Are you all right? Is something going on?'

'I'm fine,' I say. 'I needed a break. I didn't expect Charlie to contact you.'

'He seemed really worried,' she says. 'I didn't realise you'd left London. I've been meaning to call you, but you know how it is. Where are you?'

'I'm staying with friends,' I say. I'm not sure what makes me say that, but I don't want to get into a long explanation with Allie. We were friendly enough as co-workers, but I never saw her outside the office.

There's a long pause before she speaks again. 'Look, Olivia, this is none of my business, but I told Charlie I'd try to get in touch with you. And now I have.'

'And now you have,' I agree.

She sounds confused. 'Should I give him a message?'

I relent. This is nothing to do with her. It's my problem, not hers.

'There's no need,' I say. 'I'll give him a call myself. I appreciate you taking the trouble to call and let me know what's going on.'

'No trouble,' she says. 'Are you sure you're ok? Is there anything I can do for you?'

I force myself to speak in a light tone. 'I'm absolutely fine. Thanks for calling. Perhaps I'll see you the next time I'm in London.'

We say goodbye and ring off. I look at my phone, not sure what to do next. I'll have to unblock Charlie. I can't have him going around all my friends, telling them goodness knows what about why I left. It's time I dealt with this myself.

I look at my screen, my finger hovering over the button. Charlie has every right to be upset that I've blocked him. It wasn't the most mature thing to do. But it's given me the break I needed. He's still been there on my phone, waiting, but I've been able to put him on hold for a few weeks.

Hearing Allie's voice has jerked me back to reality. I've been living in a bubble in Honeywell for the past several weeks. I haven't had to think about real life and what I'm going to do next. That's over now. I could keep Charlie blocked for a while longer, but the bubble has burst. My London life has discovered my Honeywell life, and my two worlds have collided. It's time I stopped running away. I have to speak to him some time, and the longer I leave it, the worse it will be when I finally do.

I scroll through my contacts and unblock him. I look at his name on the screen. This isn't a lifelong enemy. This is the man with whom I've spent several years of my life. It's ridiculous to feel scared of talking to him. Without allowing myself to think further, I click on his name and wait. The phone rings several times. If it goes to answerphone, I'm hanging up. This isn't a conversation I can have with the machine. I almost hope it does. It would give me an excuse not to talk to him tonight. But I don't want the prospect of an unpleasant phone call hanging over me all evening.

The ringing stops, and his voice makes me jump. 'Hello?'

I take a deep breath. 'Hi, Charlie. It's Olivia.'

Chapter Twenty-Eight

Thankfully, the train is waiting when I arrive at the station on Friday. I find my seat and stare of the window, wondering what the day will bring. Will it end with things smoothed over with Charlie or with me more confused than ever? Not for the first time, I wonder what's wrong with me. Everyone else seems to navigate their lives with perfect ease, whereas I stumble from disaster to disaster, hurting people as I go, without even the satisfaction of seeing my life move forward.

The problem is that I don't know in which direction I want to go. I never have. I'm so busy thinking about this that I barely notice the train moving away from the station.

'Olivia?'

I jump before realising it's Will. 'What are you doing here?'

He sits in the seat facing me. 'The same as you, I assume. I'm going to London.'

'Oh.'

I don't know what else to say. Why is he going back to London? For work, or for something else? Maybe he's doing what I'm doing. I may not be the only one with unfinished relationship business. He hasn't told me much about the girlfriend who left him for someone else. He didn't speak about her bitterly when he told me how their relationship ended. That may mean he still holds out hope for the future. Good luck to him, if so. It's better to make very sure the past is dealt with before moving on. If it becomes apparent you've made a mistake and you wish you'd done things differently, all well and good.

'Isabella tells me you have urgent business in London,' he says when I don't speak.

'That's right. I'm meeting someone. Why are you going to London?'

'I have to pick up a few things from the office and give my boss an update. Does Isabella know where you're going?'

'Yes. I had to ask for the day off. She was very nice about it. She told me this was the best train.'

'She told me the same thing when I said I was going up to London,' he says. 'She didn't mention you were going too. I could have given you a ride to the station.'

'She didn't mention you'd be on the train,' I say. 'Which train will you be coming back on?'

'The six o'clock,' he says. 'I means killing time in London, but she mentioned the earlier trains involve several changes. Which one are you taking?'

'The same one. She told me the same thing.'

'Perhaps we could get together this afternoon?' he says. 'How long will your meeting take?'

'I have no idea.'

'Can you give me a ballpark figure?'

'No.'

He sees my expression and shrugs. 'Fine. Why don't you call me when you're finished with whatever you're doing, and maybe we can meet up.'

'I didn't mean to bite your head off,' I say. 'But I didn't know how to mention it.'

'Mention what?'

I pleat my fingers in my lap. 'I'm meeting Charlie.'

'Oh.'

He doesn't say anything more. It's better if I leave it there, but for some reason I don't want to.

'I called him a couple of days ago, and we talked,' I say. 'He wants to meet me and see whether we can work this thing out.'

'I see.'

'We were together for nearly six years,' I say. 'That's a long time. I owe it to him to talk about it. I walked out on him without warning. That's an awful thing to do to anyone.'

'Maybe,' he says.

'There's no maybe about it. Imagine if Melissa had done that to you – just disappeared one day without making the slightest attempt to explain what was going on in her head. How would you feel about that?'

'It depends,' he says. 'I agree it was a pretty drastic thing to do. But you had your reasons, or you wouldn't have done it.'

'That's the point. I didn't have a reason. It would have been much easier if I'd decided there was something specific that wasn't working for me. But I didn't. I ran away on an impulse. That's a fairly immature thing to do.'

'Or a desperate one,' he says.

'I wasn't desperate. You may have got the wrong idea about Charlie. He didn't hit me or anything like that.'

'I should hope not!' he says. 'That's a pretty low bar for a relationship – he didn't hit me!'

I give an impatient sigh. 'That's not how I mean it. I'm saying I had no particular reason to leave.'

He raises an eyebrow. 'Do you need a particular reason to leave a relationship?'

'Of course, you do. Otherwise, no one would ever stay with anyone long term. Anyway, I didn't have a reason.'

'Except that you didn't want to be there.'

'But that wasn't Charlie's fault. That was mine. He didn't change. I did.'

He shrugs. 'You're entitled to change.'

'But I ran away. I shouldn't have done that. No wonder Charlie was hurt. And now I need to do the adult thing and deal with it properly.'

'I see,' he says. 'And what does that involve? Do you plan to get back together with him?'

His tone is neutral, but his eyes are anxious. I feel a pang of guilt. I didn't set out to hurt people, but I've done it anyway. When will I learn to behave like an adult and think through the consequences of my decisions?

'I don't know what I'm going to do,' I say in a low tone. 'Our time together wasn't all bad. In fact, most of it was good. I don't want to wake up one morning and realise I've thrown away something valuable. I've been with him for most of my adult life.'

'The fallacy of sunk costs,' he says. 'It isn't a good yardstick by which to live your life.'

'Neither is throwing away something which may be as good as it gets,' I say.

He gives me a half smile. 'We're all encouraged to recycle these days. But we can take it too far.'

'I'm talking about a relationship, not an empty baked bean tin!' I snap.

'I was only teasing.'

There's nothing I can say to this. He may find the whole thing amusing, but I don't.

He seems to read my thoughts. 'I'm sorry, Olivia. I was trying to lighten the mood. Where are you meeting him? At your flat?'

'No. He wanted to, but I didn't.'

When Charlie mentioned meeting at the flat, I felt the same impulse to flee I felt on that fateful morning I left London. Can it only be a couple of months? It seems like years ago.

'He suggested meeting at an ice cream bar I like,' I say. 'It was nice of him. I didn't realise he knew about it.'

'Haven't you been there together?' he says.

'Not very often. Charlie isn't keen on ice cream, which makes it even more thoughtful that he wants to meet me there today. And it shows he isn't angry with me, which is a relief.'

'It would be strange if he was,' says Will. 'No one does what you did without an excellent reason. He wouldn't be much of a partner if his first reaction was to feel angry.'

'I've already told you he wasn't. But he sounded upset on the phone. It made me realise how badly I've treated him.'

He doesn't look convinced. 'Be careful, Olivia. You aren't responsible for anyone else's emotions.'

'I never said I was.'

He looks as though he'd like to say more, but he refrains. 'We'll be in London by eleven o'clock. When are you meeting him?'

'Half past eleven. I'll take a taxi. As long as the train arrives on time, I'll be fine.'

I don't add that Charlie hates it when I'm late. There's no point in giving Will any more ammunition. He seems eager to criticise Charlie. Possibly it's hurt pride on his part or male insecurity. Whatever it is, there's nothing I can do about it, and it won't help us to discuss it further.

The rest of the journey passes uncomfortably. We seem to have lost the easy camaraderie that's characterised the past few weeks. I don't want to be standoffish and cold, but I can't think of anything to say that won't lead to the increasingly long list of forbidden subjects between us.

The train starts to slow, and he reaches into the overhead locker for his backpack. 'We'll arrive in a few minutes. Do you have everything?'

I indicate my handbag. 'I didn't bring much with me. I thought I might pick up a few things from the flat before I leave, depending on how things go.'

'Will Charlie be coming back to Honeywell with you?'

'What?'

'I thought you might invite him to the party,' he says. 'You've worked so hard to arrange it. He'll be pleased to see how well you've done. He'll be proud of you.'

I don't know why the thought of inviting Charlie is such a shock. If Charlie and I get back together, it would be only natural for him to come to Honeywell and see where I've spent the past couple of months and what I've been doing.

I'm not so sure he'll be proud of me. Charlie isn't one for surprise parties, which is fine. Lots of people aren't. And he isn't good with strangers. He lacks

Will's easy touch with people. It's not that he doesn't get along with people. He does. But he prefers people with whom he shares common interests.

I can't imagine him talking to Isabella about the bakery business or chatting about the history of Honeywell with Mrs Ogilvie. Why should he? They're only interesting to me because I've ended up living there. If I'd read about them in a book, I might not bother to finish it.

'I expect he'll be busy,' I say. 'He works most weekends.'

'Too bad. Well, here we are.'

We walk across the concourse to the taxi rank.

'Would you like to share a taxi?' I ask, not sure whether I want him to say yes or no. Now that the time has come to face Charlie, my confidence is evaporating. It's a good thing Will is here. If not, I might be tempted to jump back on the train and return to Honeywell. But I can't do that with him watching me. There's nothing for it but to go through with it.

'My office is in Canary Wharf,' he says. 'Where are you headed?'

'The Meltdown is in Wimbledon,' I say. 'So, that won't work.'

I climb into the nearest taxi and open the window. 'I'll call you and let you know what I'm doing this afternoon if you like.

'Sounds good,' he says. 'Good luck, Olivia.'

He waves and climbs into the taxi behind me.

'Where to?' says my driver.

I'm so busy watching Will's taxi disappear down the street that it takes me a moment to remember where I'm meeting Charlie. I resist the urge to command the driver to 'follow that taxi' and focus on reality.

'The Meltdown, please,' I say. 'It's in Mayfield Street.'

'You've got it.' He noses away from the kerb.

He pulls up outside The Meltdown far too quickly. I've barely got my thoughts in order and prepared myself for this meeting. Perhaps it's better this way. No good comes of overthinking this sort of thing. And I'm not meeting a stranger for a job interview. I'm meeting Charlie, the man with whom I've been in a relationship for six years, and with whom I was living until very recently. I don't know why I've allowed myself to get so wound up.

I straighten my skirt and smooth down my hair before pushing open the shop door. The jangle of the bell is alien, although I've been here a hundred times over the years. I've become accustomed to the Sugarloaf doorbell, that's all. But it makes me feel like a stranger, and I don't like it.

I spot Charlie at once, sitting at a table in the far corner, studying a menu. He hasn't noticed my arrival. His dark hair is brushed smoothly back from his forehead, and his expression is serious. He looks exactly the same as the first day we met. He's even wearing a similar pale blue sweater.

He looks up and sees me and lifts a hand in greeting.

I take a deep breath and walk over to meet him, pleased to find my legs have stopped shaking. 'Hi Charlie!'

Chapter Twenty-Nine

He stands and kisses my cheek. 'You came! I wasn't sure you would.'

I can't help glancing at my watch to make sure I'm not late, although I know I'm not.

He pulls out a chair for me, but I point to my usual booth. 'Do you mind if we sit there? I prefer it.'

He doesn't comment as he sits down. I pick up a menu and study it. I have no idea why. I always have the same thing when I come here.

I lay it down again when the silence threatens to become awkward. 'How are you?'

'How do you think?' he says.

I resume the study of my menu. Thankfully, we're interrupted by the server.

'Hi, I'm Gavin,' he says. 'Welcome to The Meltdown! What can I get you today?'

'Just a coffee,' says Charlie.

'Don't you want an ice cream?' I ask him.

'I'm fine with a coffee. Double espresso, no milk.'

Is it my imagination, or does Gavin look disappointed? I resolve to tip him as though we've both had an ice cream. It's a reasonable expectation that people coming to a place called The Meltdown are here to eat some of the product.

'I'll have a Frostbite Delight,' I say.

'Great choice!' says Gavin. 'That's my favourite too.'

'Do you know him?' says Charlie when Gavin has left.

'I don't think so. Do you?'

He gives an impatient shrug. 'Of course not. But the pair of you seem extremely friendly. And I know you come in here often. I wondered, that's all.'

'I'm not good with faces,' I say. 'But I don't think so.'

Gavin returns with Charlie's coffee.

'The chef's making your Frostbite Delight,' he tells me. 'I told him to put extra crushed candy canes on top.'

'They're my favourite bit!' I say.

'They're everyone's favourite bit.' He looks at Charlie. 'Are you sure you won't change your mind?'

Charlie shakes his head. 'Can you bring me a clean saucer? You've splashed coffee in this one.'

'It's only a drop,' I say. 'Use one of these napkins.'

'I'd rather have a clean saucer,' he says.

I wait until Gavin returns to the kitchen. 'You weren't very nice to him. He's probably working for minimum wage.'

'Lots of people work for minimum wage,' says Charlie. 'It's no reason for poor service. But I didn't come here to talk about coffee.'

'I don't suppose you did. Why don't you go first? I'm feeling a little awkward.'

'Which is hardly surprising,' he says. 'This entire situation is awkward.'

'I know. I'm sorry, Charlie. I'm not sure why I left the way I did.'

'Neither am I,' he says. 'But I'd like to hear what you have to say.'

'I've already said I'm sorry.'

'But you haven't told me what made you do it.' He takes my hand. 'If you could give some more explanation, help me understand.'

I don't pull my hand away, but neither do I return his pressure. This isn't going how I expected. I thought he wanted to see me so he could explain what I did wrong. That's how it usually goes. I upset him, and he tells me how he feels about it. I'm not used to him asking me for an explanation.

'You owe me that,' he says. 'I left for work a couple of months ago, thinking everything was good, thinking we were planning a future together. I arrived home to find you'd left without an explanation. All I got was a scribbled note saying you were fine and not to worry about you. How do you think that made me feel?'

'It wasn't ideal,' I say.

'Ideal? Is that really how you want to play this?'

I try again. 'It must have been upsetting for you.'

He rolls his eyes. 'That's rather an understatement. But let's go with that and say yes, it was upsetting for me. As far as I was aware, I hadn't done anything to justify being treated like that. I couldn't understand it. I tried to call you, but your phone was turned off.'

'I didn't have any phone connection for most of that day,' I say. 'It was terrible timing. My car broke down, and –'

He stops me. 'Eventually, I stopped trying to call you. I thought you might need some space, so I decided to call again the next day. You still didn't answer, so I texted you. That's when I found you'd blocked me.'

'One Frostbite, with extra peppermint candy,' says Gavin, plonking a large glass plate in front of me.

Charlie looks at my ice cream in disbelief. 'Is that what you usually order?'

I dig my spoon into the fudge sauce. 'Long experience has taught me it's the best thing on the menu. Would you like to try some? There's plenty here for both of us.'

'I'm fine with my coffee.'

'All the more for me.' I take a bite of the peppermint ice cream.

'What's happened to you, Olivia?' he says.

'What do you mean?'

He considers. 'You've changed. I can't put my finger on what it is, but something's different. Are you planning to tell me what it is?'

I stir the cookie crumbs into the fudge sauce. 'It's only been a few weeks. How much can I have changed?'

'Where have you been?' he asks abruptly.

'In the countryside.'

'Is that it? Aren't you going to give me any details?'

'Not right now. It isn't relevant.'

'What have you been doing?'

'Also not relevant,' I say.

His face darkens. 'I think it is. But that isn't the most important question.'

'What's that?' I say, my mouth full of ice cream.

'Don't play games, Olivia. You know I hate that. Who were you with?'

'No one!' I say, startled. 'Who would I have been with?'

'You tell me! I was left to imagine all sorts.'

I feel a surge of contrition. 'You thought something terrible had happened to me? Like an accident?'

'I'd have heard from the hospital or the police if you'd had an accident,' he says. 'I assume I'm still listed as your next of kin?'

He's right. It hasn't occurred to me to change that. I don't know who else I'd put. Mrs Ogilvie? Bernie? I stifle a grin at this thought.

'Is something amusing?' he says.

'Not at all. So, what terrible thing did you imagine happening to me?'

'I assumed you'd met someone,' he says curtly.

'I've met lots of people,' I say, not taking his meaning.

'You know perfectly well that's not what I mean.'

Light dawns. 'You mean a man?'

'It's the obvious conclusion to draw.'

I lay down my spoon. 'Do you think I met someone while I was away, or that I ran off with someone?'

'How should I know? All I know is that you disappeared one day without warning and didn't come back. What was I supposed to think?'

'Plenty of things,' I say. 'You could have thought that maybe I wasn't happy with my life, and I didn't know how to talk to you about it. You could have thought things had got too much for me, and I'd snapped. You could have thought I was so overwhelmed by everything that I wasn't thinking straight, but I couldn't keep living a life I hadn't chosen.'

'Are you saying it wasn't a man?' he says, looking confused.

I sigh. 'I don't want to dignify that question with an answer. But if I don't, I know you'll assume the worst. So, no, I didn't run away with a man.'

For the first time since we met, he looks unsure of himself. 'I don't understand. Are saying you left for all those other reasons?'

'All I know is that I couldn't do it anymore. I couldn't keep living the life I'd been living. I had to get away.'

'Why didn't you talk to me about any of this?' he says.

'You wouldn't have listened.'

'Yes, I would.'

'Not properly. You'd have told me I was being ridiculous. You'd have said we'd made plans together, and I was ditching them because of some silly emotional reason. You'd have told me why I was wrong to have felt the way I did, and I'd have ended up agreeing with you.'

'That's not true,' he says.

'Yes, it is, Charlie. It's my fault. I should have realised a long time ago we weren't right for each other.'

He reaches over and takes my hand again. 'But we are! I had no idea you felt like that. Now that I do, things can change. I can change.'

I stare at him, confused. Is this really all I needed to do – to be honest with him about my feelings and my dreams? Could all of this have been avoided if I'd been different? More importantly, could we make it work better this time around? He seems to think so. He hasn't told me I'm wrong to feel the way I do. He hasn't argued with me.

Charlie leans forward, his tone urgent. 'Come home, Olivia. We can work this out. You left without giving me a chance to change.'

I hesitate. He's quite right. I didn't try to talk to him. I told myself there was no point. But maybe I was wrong. I've spent this entire time thinking about myself and how unhappy I was. I haven't given a single thought to how Charlie has been feeling. I feel a huge wave of guilt.

'Charlie –' I begin.

But he isn't listening. He's staring over my shoulder, and his lips have tightened.

'What's wrong now?' I say.

'There's a man over there trying to attract your attention.'

'Don't be ridiculous. You always think –'

I turn my head and break off. Will is standing in the doorway, pointing me out to Gavin and handing him a slip of paper.

He grins when he sees me looking at him. 'Sorry to disturb you, but you aren't answering your phone.'

I looked down at my screen and realise there are several messages. I turned my phone to silent when I got out of the taxi. Charlie hates me taking calls or looking at texts when I'm with him. He says it's only basic politeness to focus on the person you're with.

'Why were you messaging me?' I say, and Will grins again.

'To let you know we need to go to the zoo!'

Chapter Thirty

I stare at him in confusion. 'Did you just say the zoo?'

'That's right,' he says. 'London Zoo, to be exact.'

'Olivia?' says Charlie. 'What's going on?'

I remember his presence for the first time. 'Will, this is Charlie. Charlie, this is Will. He's a friend of mine from Hon … from the place where I've been staying.'

'Nice to meet you,' says Will.

Charlie's face darkens as he looks from me to Will. 'So, that's what's been going on!'

'No, it isn't!' I say. 'Will is just a friend, aren't you, Will?'

Will doesn't answer, and Charlie's face grows grimmer. 'Don't lie to me, Olivia. I can always tell.'

'I'm not lying!' I burst out.

'It all makes sense now,' he says, hardly seeming to hear me. 'All that nonsense you've been giving me about not knowing who you are and not feeling listened to. That was all just a pretence, wasn't it?'

He points to Will. 'He's the reason you left me!'

'No, he isn't,' I insist. 'I didn't meet Will until after I'd left London.'

'How long after? Don't lie to me.'

'I'm not lying!' I almost shout. 'I *did* leave you for all the reasons I said. And I didn't meet Will until after I'd left you.'

'How long after?' he repeats.

'About five hours, wasn't it?' says Will.

Why does he think that was a good thing to say? Can't he see how upset Charlie is? This is a time for pouring oil on troubled waters, not for throwing a lighted match at the oil can.

Will takes a couple of steps towards us, and Charlie jumps up to face him. 'Do you think this is funny?'

'Not in the sense of being amusing,' says Will. 'Funny weird, maybe.'

I touch his arm. 'Don't, Will.'

Charlie glares at me, and I drop my hand.

'Olivia?' he says again. 'I want the truth. I think I deserve it, don't you?'

'You do. And I've told you what happened. I left you because I felt as though I'd lost myself. I took a train out of London, picked up a car, and it broke down. Will happened to come along and rescue me. That's all. It was a complete coincidence that he and I met.'

I turned to Will despairingly. 'Can't you see this isn't a time for jokes?'

He looks at Charlie. 'I imagine there's never a good time for jokes with this one.'

Charlie takes a step towards him. I expect Will to take a step back, but he doesn't. He doesn't seem remotely bothered by Charlie's aggressive demeanour.

'What Olivia says is quite true,' he adds calmly. 'She left London for reasons of her own, and she and I happened to meet later that day. I'm not sure why you need me to tell you that. Isn't Olivia's word good enough for you?'

I'm surprised to see Charlie flush. 'Of course, it is,' he says stiffly. 'This whole thing is rather odd, that's all.'

'It *is* odd,' I break in hastily. 'I can see why you might have thought so.'

'I can't,' says Will.

Charlie almost audibly grinds his teeth. 'You stay out of this! If what you say is true, you've only known Olivia for a few weeks. She and I have been together for more than six years.'

'So she tells me,' says Will. 'You'd think you might know her a little better after all this time.'

'Will –' I begin, but Charlie interrupts me.

'I know her a lot better than you do. You've known her for a few weeks, and you have the audacity to think you know all about her. You don't. I'm the one who's looked after her and protected her all these years, not you.'

'Very commendable,' says Will. 'Did you ever stop to ask yourself whether that was what she wanted?'

'Of course, it was!' snaps Charlie. 'She was a mess when I met her. She had no idea what she wanted to do with her life. She still doesn't. She's impulsive and a dreamer, and she needs someone in her life to keep her on track.'

'No, I don't!' I break in. 'I may be impulsive and unfocused and all those things you say. But what's so wrong with that?'

'Nothing,' says Will.

'You were perfectly happy with me before you met this idiot,' says Charlie. 'I don't know what nonsense he's been filling your head with, but you're a fool if you listen to him. Look at everything you've thrown away – a good job, a nice flat, a great relationship. And for what? Some idiot you meet on the side of the road who happens to have a towbar?'

'Not even that,' says Will, his eyes alight with laughter. 'Sports cars don't usually come with a towbar.'

'Sports cars!' says Charlie contemptuously.

'Can you both stop this?' I say. 'Charlie, for the last time, I didn't leave you for Will. I left because you don't want to be with me. You want to be with the version of me you've created in your head. I thought I wanted to be that person, but I don't. You want someone who's content to stay at home and clean your house and look after you and never have an opinion of their own. That's not me, and it never will be. I left you because I almost disappeared when I was with you. I didn't realise it at the time, but I do now. I needed some time alone to think about who I want to be and what I want to do.'

'Suit yourself,' he says resentfully. 'But don't expect me to be waiting around for you when you come to your senses.'

'I've never expected you to wait around for me,' I say.

'Whatever. See you, Olivia. Good luck with your new man!'

He pushes past Will and strides out of the ice cream parlour without even looking at me.

I sit down abruptly, and Will slides into the booth opposite me. 'I'm sorry, Olivia. Are you ok?'

'I'm not sure. What just happened?'

He picks up Charlie's discarded menu. 'Don't hold me to this, but my impression is that you two just broke up.'

'I'm not talking about that,' I say. 'I came here today trying to get some closure. And now he's stormed out without even listening to me.'

He considers me carefully. 'Do you mind?'

I think about this. I ought to mind. I've just thrown away six years of my life. But somehow, I don't.

'No,' I say. 'In fact, I'm relieved.'

He waves to Gavin. 'I'm not surprised. The guy's a jerk.'

'You don't know him,' I say out of a sense of fairness to Charlie.

'I don't have to. Two minutes was more than enough.'

He looks at Gavin. 'What do you recommend?'

'You're ordering ice cream?' I say, surprised.

'Isn't that what you're supposed to do in a place like this?'

Gavin looks pleased. 'It is, indeed. I can recommend the Tropical Bite and the Frostbite Delight.'

'Is that the Frostbite?' Will asks me.

I survey my plate ruefully. 'It was, but it seems to have melted. Never mind. It will taste almost as good.'

'Can you bring her another of those?' he asks Gavin. 'And I'll try that Tropical thing.'

'That isn't necessary,' I say, but Gavin has already picked up our menus and left.

'Don't worry,' says Will. 'I'm paying.'

Gavin returns a few minutes later with the two plates. 'Enjoy!'

Will picks up his spoon. 'How can we not? This looks amazing. Do you want to try mine, Olivia?'

'No, thanks. I won't have room for mine if I do.'

He takes an enormous mouthful of coconut ice cream and mango sauce.

'Was I hallucinating earlier, or did you say something about the zoo?' I say.

He swallows his mouthful. 'I'd almost forgotten that in all the excit … I mean the upset.'

I can't help smiling. 'Really? Is that what you meant?'

'I don't remember. Anyway, we need to go to the zoo as soon as we finish our ice cream.'

I lay down my spoon. 'Have you been seized with a sudden overwhelming urge to feed some tigers?'

'Penguins are more my style,' he says. 'They're less bitey.'

'Unless you're a fish.'

'Which I'm not. Perhaps I should start at the beginning.'

'It isn't your usual style,' I say, 'but it might be best.'

He considers. 'To cut a long story short, I set off for my office when I left you. I was halfway there when Isabella called and told me she'd managed to track down Mabel. She's been calling the hotel all morning. When she finally got through, the receptionist told her Mabel had just checked out.'

'How annoying!' I say. 'So, we've missed her?'

'We would have missed her,' he says. 'But Mabel mentioned to the woman on reception she was going to the zoo after lunch. That's where she's headed now. Apparently, she's wearing a bright pink jacket. Isabella is certain we'll find her there.'

'That's rather vague,' I say. 'What are we supposed to do – run around all afternoon, shouting her name?'

'I'm not sure. Isabella couldn't talk for long. She said she knew she could trust to our ingenuity.'

I push away my plate. 'That's all very well, but London Zoo is massive. Have you been there?'

'Not since I was a child. But Isabella seems to think it's our last chance. Who knows where Mabel is staying tonight?'

I pick up my bag. 'Have you finished?'

'Almost.' He shovels in the last couple of mouthfuls. 'I'll pay the bill while you call a taxi.'

'We can take the underground,' I say.

'No time,' he says. 'It's nearly one o'clock. That counts as after lunch. She may be there already, wandering around the kangaroo enclosure, marvelling at how similar everything is to back home.'

I put a large tip underneath my plate. 'Fine. I'll get us a taxi.'

Five minutes later, we're driving towards the zoo. Will looks at his watch. 'We'll be there in about twenty minutes. We should make a plan.'

'You mean Isabella hasn't already made one for us?'

'Not that I'm aware of,' he says. 'Here's what I think we should do. As soon as we arrive, we'll get ourselves a couple of maps and mark them into sectors. That way, we can cover twice as much ground.'

'But we don't know what she looks like,' I object. 'We can't walk up to every woman wearing a pink jacket and ask her whether she's Mabel.'

'It may come to that,' he says. 'But hopefully not. It's a pity we don't have a photograph of her, but there's bound to be a family resemblance. That should narrow it down a bit. We'll focus on any woman who appears to be in her seventies and looks even vaguely like Mrs Ogilvie.'

'Are you enjoying this?' I say as the taxi pulls up outside the main entrance of the zoo.

He leans over and opens my door for me. 'Immensely! Aren't you?'

'Absolutely not!'

'Your face says differently. Come on, let's find ourselves some maps.'

Chapter Thirty-One

I'd forgotten how large this zoo is. To make it worse, the taxi has pulled up behind a coach marked *Camden Holiday Club*. Children are pouring out of it and running towards the main entrance.

Will grabs my hand. 'If we wait for this lot to go in, we'll be here for hours. Come on, let's make a run for it.'

We dodge around a knot of children standing next to the turnstiles.

'Coming through!' shouts Will, dragging me behind him. 'Two adults, please.'

'Hey, wait your turn!' shouts one of the boys.

Will looks back over his shoulder. 'It's an emergency. One of the giraffes has got itself tangled in … er … I mean, it's escaped from its cage and is …'

'Giraffes don't live in cages!' says a small girl indignantly.

'You're quite right,' I say. 'This gentleman has got confused. He meant to say gorilla. One of the gorillas has escaped, and we have to persuade it to go back inside its cage before any of you are allowed in.'

'Nice one!' says Will. 'Hurry up before we discover all the gorillas have gone on holiday.'

One of the holiday club helpers strides towards the kiosk. 'Is this true? I've just been told one of your leopards has escaped and is roaming around the zoo.'

'It's a gorilla,' the small girl corrects him. 'That man over there is going to catch it.'

She points to Will, who pulls me through the turnstile at top speed. With a wave of his hand to the group of children, he starts running. I run as fast as I can to keep up with him, but his legs are considerably longer than mine, and I'm quickly out of breath.

He notices me lagging behind and stops running. 'Sorry, I was just trying to get away from those children. Let's start with the African animals.'

We walk past the hippos and giraffes until we reach the giraffe enclosure. I'm pleased to see the giraffes seem to be safely inside. Hopefully, the gorillas are all in their enclosure too.

'How do you want to do this?' I ask Will. 'Should we split up so we can cover more ground?'

'Why don't we spend an hour or two looking for her together?' he says. 'We can split up later if we get desperate.'

I look at my map. 'Time to search the rainforest.'

'They have rainforests in Australia,' says Will. 'We're quite likely to find her there.'

The moment we enter the building, Will gives a grasp and grabs my arm.

'What is it?' I say. 'Have you found her already?'

He pulls his camera out of his bag. 'No, but I've found something even better. Look at that sloth on the branch!'

'It's very nice,' I say. 'I heard the zoo had a baby sloth recently.'

He screws a lens onto his camera. 'You don't understand. I'm talking about the soft drink commercial our company is bidding for. This would be absolutely perfect!'

'What would?'

He points. 'The sloth! It would be a great concept for this new line of drinks. It's a range of sparkling fruit juices called Slo-Mo. The producers have decided the market is saturated with energy drinks filled with caffeine and sugar and goodness knows what, designed to give people a boost. This product line is all about slowing down, appreciating life, that sort of thing. As soon as I saw that sloth hanging on the tree, watching the world go by, I knew we had it! I have to get some shots of him to show my boss what I'm talking about.'

'It's a great idea,' I say. 'But won't you need permission from the zoo if you want to do something like this?'

'This is just to give my company a rough idea of what we have in mind. You'll have to be in it too.'

'Oh no!' I take a step backwards and raise my hand to cover my face.

'Please, Olivia. It's no good unless you do.'

'Yes, it is. Show them a really good picture of the sloth, and they'll get the idea.'

'That's not how it works,' he says. 'The bidding closes tonight. This is a surefire winner.'

'If I agree to do this, can you blur out my face?' I say.

'I suppose I could. It would be rather unusual. Most people are dying to get their faces into ads.'

'Not me,' I say. 'But that's a good idea. There must be plenty of people here today who would love to help you out.'

I point to a group of teenagers looking at the flying foxes. 'Why don't you ask one of them?'

'Because I know you,' he says. 'I'll get a much better picture if I use you. It will only take five minutes.'

'We're supposed to be searching for Mabel, not making me the star of Britain's funniest home videos.'

'I just need a few still shots,' he says. 'It's lucky you're wearing that coral dress. It will show up beautifully against the greenery. If you stand over there, the light will be perfect. And you need something to drink.'

'I'm fine,' I say. 'We can stop at the cafe later if we're thirsty.'

'I don't mean that,' he says. 'I need you to be holding a bottle. We're advertising a drink, remember? Do you have a bottle of water in your bag?'

'I drank it on the train.'

He thinks for a moment. 'Stay here!'

He strides over to the group of teenagers and returns a moment later with a bottle half full of a revolting-looking bright orange drink. He hands it to me. 'It only cost me ten pounds!'

'I don't care how much it cost you,' I say. 'I'm not drinking this.'

He adjusts my arm. 'You'd better not. We need it for the photo. That's perfect. Can you turn your head and look at the sloth? Keep your arm exactly in that position.'

He moves slowly around me, snapping away, while I stand there, increasingly embarrassed. The teenagers have walked over to join us and are watching me with frank interest, which makes me even more embarrassed.

'Just a couple more,' says Will. 'I need you to pretend to drink whatever that is.'

'I want a huge bonus for this,' I grumble.

'I'll have you on the front page of every magazine in the country,' he promises, taking several more photographs.

He puts his camera back into his bag. 'We have to get going.'

'Thanks for the drink,' I say to the teenagers. 'Do you want it back?'

One of the boys takes the bottle. 'I'm not giving you the money back. He said I could keep it.'

'No one's asking for the money,' says Will. 'You can use it buy yourself a few more disgustingly flavoured drinks.'

He looks intensely pleased with himself as we leave the building. 'I'll send these pictures to Marcus, and he can include them in the pitch. I'd be willing to bet we win the contract. And it's all thanks to you, Olivia.'

'I let the drink do most of the work,' I say. 'The sloth did the rest of it.'

His face lights up. 'Look over there!'

'The outback?' I say. 'Do you think Mabel is homesick already?'

'Very possibly,' says Will. 'Look at all those kangaroos and wallabies and other bouncy creatures. We'll probably discover Mabel leaning over the fence, feeding them whatever it is they eat. Chocolate raisins, or cheese slices, I expect.'

'She'll be thrown out at the zoo if she tries anything like that,' I say. 'And quite right too.'

I point to the emus. 'There's a woman in a pink jacket over there. Do you think that's her?'

'Could be,' he says. 'Shall we go and talk to her?'

We make our way towards the woman, who is watching the animals with interest.

'Excuse me,' I say. 'Could I have a quick word with you?'

She doesn't seem to hear me. I try again. 'Are you by any chance Mabel?'

She turns and studies me without speaking. It's a simple enough question. She must know whether or not she's Mabel.

'We're looking for Mabel,' says Will slowly and clearly. I can see he's wondering whether the elderly woman is hard of hearing.

'Is there a problem?' says a man, walking towards us.

'No problem,' I say. 'It's just that we're trying to locate a woman called Mabel. We have a message for her.'

I sound as though I might be from a government agency, but I can't help it.

'This is not the woman you are looking for,' says the man.

I suppress an urge to demand the woman's identification papers. We aren't in an Orson Welles film.

'That's a pity,' says Will. 'The woman we're looking for has just arrived from Australia.'

'And the woman you are speaking to is here on holiday from Slovenia,' says the man. 'She does not speak much English.'

Will and I make our escape as quickly as possible.

'So much for the siren call of the kangaroos,' I say.

'It was worth a try,' says Will. 'Where to next?'

I look at my map and laugh. 'You may want to sit this one out. It's the reptile house!'

He gives an involuntary shudder. 'You don't really think she'd be in there?'

'It's as likely as anything. I'll check it out while you go and hunt for Mabel around the tiger enclosure. Unless you're terrified of big cats too? In which case, you can go to the petting zoo.'

'I'm perfectly all right with lions and tigers,' he says with dignity. 'I'll meet you back here in ten minutes.'

I enter the reptile house and walk up and down, squinting into the darkness. There's no sign of Mabel here. As I turn to come back out, I see the group of teenagers who sold us the drink. I give them a friendly wave as I pass.

'Excuse me,' says one of the girls. 'Could you sign my T-shirt for me?'

'And mine!' says another girl eagerly.

'Why do you want me to sign your T-shirt?' I say, confused. Is this some teenage rite of passage – walking up to a complete stranger and persuading them to write all over your clothes? Will they video it and put it on TikTok to embarrass me?

The first girl pulls off her jacket. 'I can't believe you're here at the zoo today, and we bumped into you!'

This is getting weirder by the minute. 'It was very nice to meet you all,' I say. 'But I have to get going.'

The girl looks devastated. 'Please! Everyone will be so jealous. Chantelle Briggs is always saying what a loser I am. This will show her.'

'And it will shut my sister up,' agrees the other girl. She produces a pen from her pocket and hands it to me.

'You really want me to sign your T-shirt?' I say. 'But why?'

All the girls burst out laughing.

'You're funny!' says one of them. 'She's really funny, isn't she?' she asks the others, and they agree I am.

'Can you write your name and a personal message?' says the girl. 'I'm Sophia.'

'I think you have me mixed up with someone else,' I say politely.

'No, we haven't,' she says. 'That man you were with told us who you are.'

Light begins to dawn. 'The man with the camera? What exactly did he tell you?'

She gives me a starstruck look. 'That you're Olivia Sullivan! The famous supermodel and influencer.'

'Is that right?' I say. 'Had you heard of me before?'

She shakes her head. 'I'm sorry. I hadn't. But he says you're really famous.'

'I'm afraid he was teasing you,' I say. 'I'm not famous at all.'

She looks confused. 'But he was taking pictures of you.'

'He does that. He isn't very good, but no one likes to tell him that. He'd be devastated.'

I take the cap off the pen. 'I can still sign your T-shirt for you, if you like.'

She snatches it off me. 'No way! My mum would kill me.'

'I can't believe you pretended you were famous,' says one of the boys in a disgusted tone as they walk off.

I catch up with Will outside the reptile house. 'You'll never believe what just happened to me in there! Those teenagers we met all asked me to sign their T-shirts. It must be some new craze.'

His eyes widen. 'Did you agree?'

'Of course! I thought it was sweet. I signed all their T-shirts, and a few of them asked me to write messages on their jeans too. Luckily, they had a permanent marker with them, so it won't wash out. We'll probably see them again soon. They were just going to show their parents.'

He gives me a horrified look. 'I don't think you should have done that.'

'Why not?' I say airily. 'It's just a bit of fun. They'll probably ask you too if they see you. Not that I left much room, but maybe you could sign their bags or something.'

He looks even more anguished. 'Are you sure the pen was permanent?'

'Absolutely,' I assure him. 'It won't wash out. The only way to remove it would be with specialist dry-cleaning, and that would be extremely expensive. But they won't want to do that.'

I bite the inside of my cheek to keep myself from laughing. That will teach him to tell random groups of teenagers I'm a supermodel. I have no idea why any of them would have believed it. I'm at least six inches too short. Maybe there are no height restrictions for influencers.

I give him my brightest smile. 'Shall we go and check out the gorillas?'

'Olivia –' He breaks off as the group of teenagers emerge from the bird safari and start walking towards us. He studies them closely, then looks at me. I'm unable to hide my grin.

'I suppose I asked for that,' he says.

'You did indeed.'

The teenagers give us a disgusted look as they walk past.

'We knew all along she wasn't a model,' says one of the girls. 'She isn't nearly skinny enough.'

'And your photographs are rubbish!' one of the boys tells Will.

They give us one last contemptuous look and disappear towards the cafe.

'How do they know what my photographs are like?' says Will.

'I may have mentioned your lack of talent,' I say. 'I felt it was the least I could do.'

'It was,' he agrees. 'Shall we agree to call it quits?'

'Maybe that's best. At least they didn't comment on your physique.'

'That had to hurt,' he says. 'Imagine being told by a random teenager you aren't underweight.'

'They can be very harsh,' I say. 'But I'll try to deal with it.'

He looks at his watch. 'I need to call the office and let them know I'll be sending over these pictures as soon as possible. Will you check the next place, and I'll meet you there when I'm done?'

I set off for Penguin Beach. I'm pretty sure they have penguins in Australia. If Will's theory is correct, I may find Mabel hurling chunks of haddock into the water. I suspect I won't. This whole idea is nonsensical. How likely are we to find one woman in all these crowds? She may not even have come to the zoo today.

She could have mentioned it as one of several options to fill her afternoon, and the receptionist passed it on to Isabella as fact.

Even if Mabel is here, it's just as likely that Will and I are several steps behind her everywhere we go. We need to split up and go around the zoo in opposite directions. We stand far more chance of finding our quarry that way. If it gets towards closing time and we still haven't found her, Will can try to persuade someone to allow us to use the Tannoy system. I hope it doesn't come to that. The embarrassment would be too much for me.

I suspect we'll have to admit defeat and return to Honeywell without having made contact with Mabel at all. It would be a shame to fail at the very last minute, but I don't know what else we can do.

As I expected, there's no sign of a woman in a pink jacket admiring the penguins. I pull out my phone to text Will and tell him I'm moving on to the butterfly house when it rings.

'Hi Will,' I say, without looking at the screen. 'I'm heading over to the butterflies.'

'It's not Will. It's me!' says Isabella's voice. 'I'm so glad I've got hold of you. It's an emergency.'

'What now?' I say. 'Have the koalas gone on strike for more eucalyptus leaves? Have the elephants escaped?'

'Not that I've heard,' she says. 'But wouldn't that be exciting? It's Will. I called him just now to see how you're getting on, and he told me he's hurt his ankle. He's in the Terrace Restaurant. Do you know where that is?'

'I'm right next to it,' I say. 'Is he badly hurt? What happened?'

'I don't know. His battery was almost out of power. He can tell you when you get there. Let me know what's going on.'

I'm already running down the path towards the terrace restaurant. What can have happened to Will? Did the group of teenagers catch up with him? Even if they did, they would hardly have started a fight with him. Did they insult his photography skills, and he chased after them, spraining his ankle in the process? That's also unlikely. Knowing Will, he would just have laughed.

I burst through the door and look around for him. There's no sign of him at any of the tables near the counter. Did Isabella get the wrong restaurant? There are several cafes dotted around the zoo.

'Olivia?' says a voice behind me, and I spin around to find Will standing there, looking worried.

'Thank goodness!' I gasp. 'I was about to run around to all the cafes to find you.'

'With a sprained ankle?' he says.

'You're the one with the sprained ankle,' I say. 'Do you need to sit down?'

His face crumples into laughter. 'Did you by any chance receive a call from Mission Control?'

Did he hit his head when hurt his ankle? Is he convinced we're touring NASA rather than London Zoo?

'You should sit down,' I say again. 'I'll ask someone for help.'

'I'm referring to Isabella,' he says. 'Did she call you?'

'She did. She said you were hurt, and I should meet you here.'

'What a coincidence,' he says. 'She told me the same thing about you. I raced over here at top speed, only to find you standing here with both legs obviously in perfect working order.'

I drop into the nearest chair. 'I should have known she was up to something. Is she worried we won't have eaten, and this is her way of making sure we do?'

'I wouldn't put it past her,' he says. 'But I don't think it was that. I think –'

He breaks off and grasps my shoulder. 'Is that –?'

I look in the direction he's pointing. 'I don't believe it! What's Mrs Ogilvie doing here?'

I watch the woman as she moves along the counter. I've never seen Mrs Ogilvie wearing magenta. She usually sticks to browns and greys.

Will gives me an incredulous look. 'Do you think there's a chance that woman isn't actually Mrs Ogilvie?'

'You mean she has a doppelganger?'

'I don't mean anything of the sort.' He takes my arm and leads me over to the counter where the woman is selecting a slice of carrot cake.

'Excuse me,' he says very politely, tapping her on the shoulder. 'But would you by any chance …?'

She turns and surveys us, and her face breaks into a beaming smile.

'You must be Will and Olivia! How lovely to meet you both.'

Chapter Thirty-Two

Will and I look at each other in astonishment.

'You *are* Will and Olivia, aren't you?' says the woman.

It's bizarre. She looks exactly like Mrs Ogilvie. She even sounds like her.

'We are,' I say. 'But I don't understand. Are you really Mabel? This isn't some elaborate prank of Isabella's?'

She laughs. 'I'm Mabel. If you know Edie, you must have recognised me at once.'

'Edie?' I say. 'Oh, you mean Mrs Ogilvie. We do know her, and we knew she had a sister. What we didn't know was that she had a twin sister. An identical twin sister, at that!'

She looks surprised. 'She never mentioned we were twins? I can't think why not.'

The woman behind us in the queue clears her throat irritably. Mabel stares her down. 'You can go around me if you're so impatient.'

She sounds so like Mrs Ogilvie that I laugh.

'I need something to drink,' says Will.

'I could do with a coffee,' I admit.

He takes Mabel's tray from her. 'I'll get this. What would you like to drink?'

'I was going to get myself a nice pot of tea,' she says. 'The more British, the better.'

Mabel and I go upstairs and find ourselves a table on the terrace. I can't stop staring at her. Now that I observe her more closely, I can see her hair is styled differently to Mrs Ogilvie's. She's also wearing bright pink lipstick, which I can't imagine Mrs Ogilvie doing. But the resemblance is uncanny.

Mabel notices me examining her and laughs. 'Don't worry, dear. I'm quite used to it. People have been doing it since we were tiny. I always tell them I'm the good-looking one, but they never seem to believe me.'

'I wonder why Mrs Ogilvie didn't mention it,' I say. 'She's talked about you several times. You'd have thought it would have come up at some point.'

She stops laughing. 'Perhaps she doesn't like to remember how close we once were.'

'I'm sorry,' I apologise. 'I'd forgotten things were strained between you.'

'It's all so silly,' she says. 'Did she tell you that she and I and Edward planned to move to Australia?'

'She did. And then he had a heart attack.'

Her face clouds. 'That's right. Poor Edie. She and Edward were inseparable. I wanted her to come out to Melbourne after the funeral, but she wouldn't because of her dog.'

'She was worried about him,' I say. 'She still has him, you know. He's a gorgeous dog.'

Will arrives carrying a tray laden with plates of cakes, a teapot, and several mugs. 'What have I missed? Have you solved the mystery of Isabella's obsession with our ankles?'

'We were waiting for you,' I tell him.

'This Isabella sounds a bit of a live wire,' says Mabel. 'I spoke to her on the phone today. She wanted to ask me to come down for this party tomorrow. I told her I was already planning on coming down to Honeywell to surprise Edie. We had a good laugh about that. I mentioned I was coming to the zoo this afternoon, and she said that was a coincidence. Her two friends would be at the zoo, and they'd love to meet me and talk about the arrangements for the party. We agreed I'd meet you here at the cafe.'

'She didn't mention any of that to us,' I say, accepting the slice of coffee and walnut cake Will hands me. 'She told us you'd checked out of your hotel before she could talk to you and invite you down to Honeywell. But the receptionist told her you'd be at the zoo, so she said we should get over here as quickly as possible and look for a woman in a pink jacket.'

'All I know is that I got Edie's email recently,' says Mabel. 'I was so pleased to hear from her after all this time. It may sound silly, but I decided on the spur of the moment to come over and celebrate our birthday together.'

'I've just realised!' says Will. 'You two must share a birthday.'

I roll my eyes. 'Well done, Einstein.'

Mabel smiles. 'I booked myself a hotel in London for a week. Then I wrote and told Edie I was coming to England, and I'd come down to see her as soon as I'd recovered from the jetlag.'

'Will and I rushed over here as soon as we got Isabella's message,' I say. 'And we've spent the afternoon running around looking for you.'

Her mouth twitches. 'I wish I'd seen you at it. But I expect she had her reasons.'

She looks so unconcerned that I burst out laughing. 'You and Isabella will get along very well when you meet. When are you arriving in Honeywell?'

'She's booked me a train ticket for tomorrow morning,' she says. 'First class! She refused to allow me to pay. It was very generous of her.'

'Maybe Olivia and I should upgrade to first class on our way home,' says Will. 'We can charge it to the bank of Isabella.'

Mabel pours herself another cup of tea. 'Now we're all here, why don't we get to know each other?'

We spent the next hour chatting and laughing. Mabel tells us all about her life in Melbourne and entertains us with anecdotes of her and Mrs Ogilvie's childhood.

'Don't mention I've told you any of this,' she warns us at one point. 'She'd never forgive me. Particularly that story about the goat and her winter underwear.'

She's very interested in what Will does for a living. He goes into far more detail about his work than he's ever done with me. I listen with interest as he tells her about some of the trips he's taken in pursuit of once-in-a-lifetime shots.

'And then Olivia went and eclipsed me with a barely functioning mobile phone!' he says.

He tells her about the advertising campaign his firm is hoping to secure, and Mabel laughs. 'You have the wrong person in your photographs. You should have used me. Nothing says slow motion more than an eighty-year-old woman on a hot day.'

'Seventy-nine,' he corrects her. 'And you seem pretty active to me. You dropped everything on a whim and flew halfway across the world. Then, instead of putting your feet up and enjoying the hotel spa, you set off across London to visit a place knows for its tigers and wolves and snakes.'

'No worries, mate!' she says in a comical Australian accent. 'We're used to dangerous wildlife in Australia – and that's just the cities!'

She laughs heartily at her own joke, and Will and I join in. It's impossible not to like this woman. She's so friendly and genuine. I wonder if she was anything like Isabella when she was younger.

It isn't until past five o'clock that Will and I remember we have a train to catch.

'Will you be all right getting back to your hotel?' I ask Mabel.

'I'll be fine,' she assures me. 'It's been a long time since I've been in a London taxi. I'm rather enjoying the experience. I'll see you both on Saturday.'

We walk as quickly as possible to the exit and jump into a taxi.

'That was quite a day,' says Will.

'I still don't know what Isabella was playing at,' I say. 'I know she has a tortuous mind, but this seems unnecessarily complicated, even for her.'

'No doubt she'll have an explanation when we see her,' says Will. 'Not necessarily a good one, but an explanation.'

I yawn. 'I'm exhausted. It feels as though I left Honeywell weeks ago.'

'It's been a busy day,' he agrees. 'But I must say I've enjoyed it. And I got those pictures for the campaign, so I can't feel too annoyed with Isabella. How about you?'

I think back over the day. The first part is a blur. I barely remember meeting with Charlie, which is a good thing. He's a part of my past and growing more so by the minute. And this afternoon was fun. It was almost as good as our day at the mediaeval fair, which until now has been my favourite Honeywell memory.

Even better, the distance between me and Will has completely disappeared. It would be difficult to maintain an awkward coolness after racing around searching for an elusive, pink-clad Australian woman, conning teenagers into thinking I was famous, and both of us enduring imaginary sprained ankles. Maybe this is what Isabella had in mind when she sent us off on this ridiculous expedition.

Will is looking at me, a faint question in his eyes.

I smile back at him. 'Yes, it was fun. I'm glad I came today.'

His face relaxes. 'Me too. Here's the station. I hope your ankle has recovered from its fake sprain because we have exactly three and a half minutes to catch our train!'

Chapter Thirty-Three

We race across the concourse and jump onto the train, ignoring the disapproving look the guard gives us, before making our way to our carriage.

I collapse into my seat. 'I'm exhausted. We must have walked miles today. I'll have a lot to say to Isabella when I see her.'

He leans back in his seat and yawns. 'Like you said, it was a busy day.'

'It was more fun than I expected.'

'Which bit?' he says.

'All of it! Running around the zoo. Being mistaken for an influencer. The usual sort of thing.'

'How about the part before that?' he says.

'You mean Charlie?'

'He was the reason you came up to London,' he reminds me.

'I know. But it all seems so long ago now.'

'How do you feel about what happened?'

'Surprisingly good,' I say. 'I knew I was doing the right thing when I left London. I didn't know why, but I knew I couldn't stay with him any longer. I have no idea why I stayed as long as I did.'

'Why did you?' he says, and I'm surprised by the intent look on his face.

'I've asked myself that same question a hundred times, and the answer is I don't know. It felt as though it was my fault when things didn't go well. I thought if I could discover the one thing about myself I needed to change, everything would be perfect.'

'That's the definition of insanity,' he says. 'Doing the same thing over and over again and expecting a different result.'

'I thought the definition of insanity was leaving freshly baked doughnuts alone with Isabella.'

'I'm serious,' he says. 'Don't you see how useless it is to try to fix things by changing yourself? That's never the answer.'

'I must have known it subconsciously or I wouldn't have left the way I did. I'll always feel bad about that.'

'I don't see why,' he says. 'Do you think Charlie ever thought about your relationship and decided he needed to change something about himself?'

'Probably not. Anyway, it's finished now, so what does it matter?'

He sits up straighter. 'Are you serious? Of course, it matters.'

'Why? It happened, it's over, and that's that. There's no point in rehashing the past.'

'There's every point,' he says. 'How can you prevent yourself from making the same mistake next time if you don't know what went wrong?'

I'm starting to feel annoyed. This is none of Will's business. I don't want to argue with him. I'm too tired, for one thing. But neither do I want to delve into the details of my failed relationship.

I decide that the best form of defence is attack. 'Did you do that after you broke up with Melissa? Did you go back over every gory detail and ask yourself why it all went wrong and what you should have done differently?'

'I thought about what happened,' he says.

'And what conclusions did you draw?'

'That I had no chance unless I started bodybuilding and found myself a plastic surgeon who specialised in the Greek god package.'

'He was better looking than you?' I say.

'In the same way a Rembrandt is better than a finger painting. He was an underwear model, if that helps you to imagine?'

'You're right,' I say. 'How could a troll like you compete?'

He smiles. 'I can always rely on you to make me feel better about myself.'

'Are you telling me your relationship breakdown had nothing to do with you? It was sheer bad luck?'

'That's just what I told myself to soothe my injured pride,' he says. 'The truth was that Melissa and I had almost nothing in common. We met at a sports club, and we kept bumping into each other. I thought we were compatible because we had a shared interest, but that wasn't the case.'

'Isn't that the predictor of success in a relationship?' I say. 'All the magazines say you should enjoy doing the same things.'

'They also say you should drink hideous green smoothies in order to live an extra decade,' he says. 'I don't think we should base our life choices on what any magazine says. In our case, it didn't work out that way. In fact, it kept us together for far too long. We were so busy playing tennis and squash together that we never stopped to ask ourselves whether we wanted the same things for our lives.'

'You'll have to marry a photographer,' I say. 'It's the only way to ensure you're compatible with someone.'

'I could marry ten photographers without being compatible with any of them,' he says. 'That's my point. It doesn't matter what you do. It's all about how you see the world and what your goals are outside work.'

'There wouldn't be any outside work if you married ten photographers,' I say. 'You'd be in jail for bigamy.'

'Must you be so literal?' he says. 'But you get my point?'

'I'm not sure I do.'

He looks surprised. 'It's not about what you do in life. It's about what you want – what's important to you.'

'Like how many children you want?' I say.

'Maybe, for some people. For others, it might be about making a difference. Leaving the world in a better state than you found it or protecting the environment. It's different for everyone.'

'What do you want for yourself?' I ask.

'Lots of things. I want to travel as much as possible. It's a big world, and I'd like to see a lot more of it. I love the idea of using my photographic skills to bring places to people who can't visit them, and to show them in a new light to those who've visited them a thousand times.'

'I like that,' I say. 'But it isn't wholly unrelated to your work. What else?'

'You're embarrassing me,' he complains.

'I'm sorry, but I'm interested.'

'I want to become the best person I can be,' he says. 'I can't say what that entails, but I don't want to be static. I'd like to keep learning new skills and developing meaningful relationships. I'd like a family one day. I don't know what that looks like, but it doesn't matter. I'll know it when I see it. And I hope to be part of a community – not necessarily in a single place, but a group of connected people.'

This is a side of him I haven't seen before. It's somewhat unexpected.

'I hope it all happens for you,' I say.

'Thanks. What about you? What do you want out of life?'

I don't answer. Not because I don't want to, but because I can't. I have no idea what to say. I'm horrified to find my eyes filling with tears.

'Olivia?' he says.

I wipe my eyes on my sleeve. 'I'm sorry. I don't know what's wrong with me.'

'You're tired. It's been quite a day! It isn't the greatest time for these metaphysical discussions.'

I sniff. 'It isn't that. I'm upset because I can't answer your question. I've always thought of my life in terms of steps and plans. What am I going to do next? Where am I going to work? Where are we going to live? I've never thought about any of the rest of it, and now I'm wondering why.'

'I could make a suggestion why you haven't,' he says. 'But I'm not sure you'd like it.'

'Charlie?'

He nods. 'He seems to have done most of the thinking in your relationship. Whenever you talk about your life with him, you always say, "Charlie wants," or, "Charlie says." You don't seem to figure at all in your own life.'

'I can't put all the responsibility on him. I'm an adult. I should have seen that that myself and done something about it.'

He shrugs. 'Maybe. Anyway, that part of your life is over now. At least, I assume it is? Is there a chance you'll go back to him?'

'Not even the tiniest one. As soon as I saw him today, I knew it was no good. I kept telling myself I was being unreasonable, but I knew I wasn't.'

He looks uncomfortable. 'It wasn't because I arrived? I didn't mean to. I was trying to give that server a note for you, and unfortunately Charlie caught sight of me.'

'It wasn't you,' I say. 'It was all me. I may not know what I want, but I finally know what I don't want.'

He looks relieved. 'I'm glad. I didn't like the guy, but I'd hate to be the reason you two broke up.'

'You weren't.'

Surely, this would be the perfect opportunity for him to raise the subject of what he said to me in Mrs Carson's garden. But he doesn't. He picks up a magazine someone has left lying on a nearby table and starts to flick through it.

It's a good thing, really. I don't need any more complications in my life. Will has obviously forgotten about what he said that afternoon, or he's thankful it didn't come to anything. He was carried away by the excitement of the afternoon and almost created a very sticky situation for himself.

He and I can go back to being friends, with none of the awkwardness of the past few days. We won't be seeing each other for much longer anyway. Lily is returning to work next week, which means I'll be moving on. He and I will probably never see each other again.

I remember one of my high school teachers telling me that some friends are there for a reason and a season. That's the case with Will and Isabella. They both came into my life when I needed them, and I'm thankful for them. But it's time for me to move on and create my own future.

It looks very different from the one I planned with Charlie, but that isn't a bad thing. Now that I'm free again, there's almost nothing I can't do if I choose. I can create myself a whole new life. I just wish I knew where to start.

Chapter Thirty-Four

I arrive at the bakery early the following morning. As I expected, Abby is already there. As I also expected, Isabella isn't. She arrives twenty minutes later, looking cheerfully apologetic.

'My car wouldn't start this morning, so I had to wait for Georgia to give me a lift. She said she was almost ready, but I reckoned without her needing breakfast first.'

'She takes after you,' says Abby, emerging from the kitchen covered with flour to make herself a coffee.

'She's nothing like me!' says Isabella. 'I'm able to skip breakfast if it's in a good cause. I mentioned that to Georgia, but she said so could she if she worked in a bakery. There's no reasoning with that girl sometimes.'

'Perhaps you could help me in the kitchen,' says Abby. 'I'm on top of most things, but I still need to fill the sandwiches and ice the cake.'

'No problem,' says Isabella. 'But first, I want to hear all about your day in London, Olivia. Well done on locating Mabel, by the way.'

I give her an exasperated look. 'Well done? We wouldn't have needed to look for her at all if you'd told us the truth. Why did you send us on a wild goose chase?'

She gives me an unrepentant smile. 'I thought it would be fun for you.'

'Racing around London in the heat, trying to find an unknown woman, before discovering you knew where she was all along and there was no need for any of it?'

'That's one way of putting it,' she says. 'The other is that I was giving you and Will a chance to have some fun together and work through whatever's gone wrong between you.'

I grope for the appropriate words, but I can't find them.

She smiles again. 'Did it work? Are you two ok now?'

'I went to see Charlie,' I remind her.

Her face falls. 'Did you and he get back together?'

I'm tempted to tell her we did, just to see her expression change. She ought to realise that tampering in people's lives like this is a dangerous activity. But she looks so eager and friendly that I don't have the heart to. Besides, she's always been so kind to me. I can let this one slide.

'We didn't,' I say. 'But you couldn't have known that when you sent Will up to London on the same train as me. The whole thing could have been extremely awkward.'

'I know,' she says. 'But I couldn't think of any other way to get you two talking again. You are talking, aren't you?'

'We are.'

'And you're not angry with me?'

She looks so much like an excited pre-schooler that I laugh. 'I'm not angry with you. We had a fun afternoon. It's been a while since I've been to the zoo.'

'Good,' she says. 'Now we've got that out of the way, we have another crisis. I heard last night that Mrs Ogilvie won't be here for the party!'

'What?' I almost shriek. 'Do you mean she's managed to leave the village without anyone realising?'

Isabella gives me a pitying look. 'Do you think this is my first rodeo? I've been meddling in people's lives for years. I considered that possibility ages ago. Mrs Ogilvie has been under twenty-four-hour surveillance for the past three days.'

'She's been …?' Words fail me, and I sit down at the nearest table.

'That's right,' she says. 'I didn't want to risk our quarry disappearing at the last moment. I mentioned it to Angela Carson, who suggested I talk to Mavis Sotherby. Say what you like about Mavis, but she takes her work seriously.'

'I'm almost afraid to ask,' I say. 'Have you had a group of women in disguise hanging around Mrs Ogilvie's house, pretending to read her water meter?'

'I thought about that,' she says. 'But Mavis said that kind of activity is strictly against the law. She was most emphatic about it. I wondered how she could be so sure, but she wouldn't say.'

'What a shame,' says Abby. 'What did you come up with instead?'

Isabella looks even more pleased with herself. 'Lots of things. Mrs Carson asked Mrs Ogilvie over for tea on Thursday afternoon. She kept her there until early evening. And Mavis took care of yesterday. She contacted the Silver Surfers and told them she was setting them homework, and she expected everyone to take part. They had to log on every two hours and complete assignments like downloading an image or sending her an email. She said there would be a prize for the competitors who completed all the assignments.'

'And Mrs Ogilvie fell for it?' I say, amused.

'Like a ton of bricks. It turns out she's very competitive. Mavis says she was the first one to log on and do each of her tasks. It helped that they were tailored to her interests. First, the class was told to download a picture of a cavoodle and add it to their photo album. Then they were asked to send Mavis an email describing the funniest thing their pet has ever done. After that, there was an online questionnaire about the history of Honeywell. Things like that.'

'I'm impressed Mrs Ogilvie managed all that by herself,' I say. 'She's only been to a couple of classes.'

'So am I,' says Isabella. 'But she's picking it up surprisingly quickly. Mavis says she's as sharp as a tack, and she doesn't like being told she can't do anything.'

'That figures,' says Abby. 'Remember when we closed the bakery for the first round of the competition last year? She was furious. She was standing on the doorstep with Bernie on the stroke of noon, glaring at the judges until they left.'

'So, what's the problem today?' I ask.

'She called Nigel Farrow last night,' says Isabella. 'He's retired, but he runs a sort of unofficial taxi service for the village. Mrs Ogilvie told him she was going up to London this afternoon, and would he please pick her up at one o'clock?'

'To London?' I say. 'To see Mabel?'

'That's right,' says Isabella. 'We should have thought of that possibility. But we didn't realise until yesterday it was Mabel's birthday too. Mrs Ogilvie told Nigel her sister had just arrived in the country, and she planned to surprise her at her hotel and take her out for dinner to celebrate their joint birthdays.'

'He didn't give the game away?' I say.

'Not at all. Luckily, he's one of the Silver Surfers, so he knew all about the party. He took the booking, then immediately called Mavis, who called me.'

'So, what's the plan?' says Abby. 'Will you tell Mrs Ogilvie about the party and stop her from leaving the village? You've done pretty well to keep everything under wraps so far. Maybe it's time to tell her what's going on.'

Isabella looks disgusted. 'I will not! We said this was a surprise party, and so it is. We only have to prevent her from finding out for a few more hours. If we can't manage that, we aren't worthy of the name of co-conspirators. We have a much better plan. Nigel will pick her up, as planned, and set off for London. Halfway up the motorway, he'll develop engine trouble and have to turn back to Honeywell. He'll bring her back exactly in time for the party.'

'I don't think that's a good idea,' I say. 'You know it's all fake, but Mrs Ogilvie doesn't. She could be quite upset.'

'Oh, ye of little faith!' says Isabella. 'That thought crossed my mind too. Mrs Carson will be with her. She's told Mrs Ogilvie she's going up to London today and suggested they share the cost. When Nigel develops car trouble, Mrs Carson will tell him to take them both back to her house so that Martin can run them up to London.'

'You're wasted running a bakery,' I say. 'Why aren't you working for MI5? I'm sure they could use someone with your devious abilities.'

'Creative abilities,' she corrects me. 'Let's see how this plan works out first. I can send them the details later and offer myself on a consultancy basis.'

Abby finishes her drink. 'I have to get back to the kitchen. We don't want Mrs Ogilvie to arrive at the party and find there's no food.'

'Quite right!' says Isabella. 'I'll help you. Are you ok by yourself, Olivia?'

'I'm fine,' I assure her. 'We don't get many customers on a Saturday morning. And I have something of my own to work on.'

'That sounds exciting,' says Isabella, preparing to sit down again.

'Not now,' I say. 'Off you go and make yourself useful. I'll see you at lunchtime.'

I spend the next few hours serving customers and making coffees. I'm pretty good at this now. I've mastered the art of perfect foam. I haven't attempted any more complicated pattern than an acorn, but they're almost always recognisable. It should serve us in good stead if the bakery is ever attacked by a gang of rambunctious squirrels.

In my spare few minutes, I study the list I've been making and think about the conversation Will and I had on the train. It helped me to see more clearly what's wrong with my life. I don't know why I didn't see it before, but that's often the way things turn out. Something obvious stares us in the face for years without us realising. Then someone new comes along, and it's like a lightbulb going off in our head. That's what happened with Will yesterday. And whatever happens in the future, I'll always be grateful to him for that.

Chapter Thirty-Five

Abby and Isabella emerge from the kitchen at lunchtime, carrying Mrs Ogilvie's cake. They set it down on the nearest table, and we all step back to admire it.

'I can't believe you made that yourself,' I tell Abby. 'I knew you were a talented baker, but this is amazing!'

She looks pleased. 'It came out well, didn't it? I made the cake yesterday, but I didn't want to ice it until today. The buttercream needs to be fresh.'

Isabella checks her phone. 'Two hours to go. Mrs Ogilvie will be finishing packing her bags, and Mavis will have a couple of her best operatives lurking at the end of the street to let us know if she shows signs of making an early getaway.'

'What about Bernie?' I say. 'I'd forgotten him!'

'Tsk,' says Isabella. 'It's lucky you're surrounded by so many older and wiser heads. He's going to Will for the weekend.'

'To Will?' I say.

'That's right. As soon as Nigel told us what was happening last night, I dropped around to Mrs Ogilvie's house with some biscuits for Bernie. She told me about her plans for today and said she was about to call you and ask you to look after Bernie. So, I told her you were going away this weekend. I suggested she ask Will instead and gave her his number. She called him last night, and he agreed.'

'Why did you say I couldn't do it?' I say.

'Because I need you here. Will isn't really looking after Bernie. It's all for show. He'll pick Bernie up from her house at one o'clock, take him for a long walk to shake the fidgets out of him, then bring him to the party. I can't spare you until then. Who knows what might go wrong here at the last minute? So, I dumped the job onto Will.'

I relax. It's true that Bernie will need a walk before he arrives at the Carsons' house. Even with a walk, he'll be bouncing off the walls. Without one, I don't like to think what havoc he might wreak.

Abby turns the shop sign to closed. 'We'd better transport this food to the party. Isabella is taking the savoury things in her car, and I'm taking the sweet.'

'Good plan,' I say. 'It's like the fox, the chicken, and the grain. We can't leave Isabella alone with the cakes, but we need to get all the food there in one piece. Who's taking the birthday cake?'

'That's going on your lap,' says Isabella. 'Unless there's any more rudeness from you. In which case, you can walk through the village with it.'

'Fine,' I say. 'But I'm sitting in the back seat.'

'Don't you trust my driving?'

'I don't trust you not to get hungry halfway there,' I say, and Abby laughs.

We pack the food into the two cars, and I climb into the back seat with the cake.

'Are you sure you wouldn't be better off sitting in the front?' says Isabella. 'It has air bags.'

'It's very nice of you to worry about my safety,' I say. 'But as long as you drive slowly, I should be fine.'

'I was thinking about the cake!' she says.

We drive to the Carsons' house by a circuitous route. Isabella explains she doesn't want to go near Mrs Ogilvie's house in case Nigel drives past and Mrs Ogilvie guesses what's going on. I'm unconvinced, but Isabella is having so much fun with her spy games that I don't want to burst her bubble.

We pass Will walking towards the high street with Bernie. He waves when he sees us but looks preoccupied. I'm not surprised. Bernie is running in alternate circles around a lamp post and Will's legs, creating a figure of eight. Will obviously doesn't know about keeping an excitable dog on a short leash.

'I hope they make it to the party,' says Isabella. 'The way Bernie's carrying on, he'll soon have Will tied to that lamppost, and Bernie will be able to make his escape. Maybe you should go back and help.'

'I have one job, and it isn't rescuing Will,' I say. 'I plan to deliver this cake in one piece or die trying.'

'That's mean,' she says. 'Will rescued you when you first arrived, and you're refusing to return the favour.'

'He'll figure it out,' I say. 'And from now on, I plan to rescue myself.'

She raises an eyebrow but doesn't say anything more as we pull up outside the Carsons' house.

Martin opens the car door and picks up the cake. 'Doesn't this look marvellous? Abby's outdone herself this time.'

We carry the plates of sandwiches and quiches to the back garden. I can't believe the change since I was last here. There's a large pink and white marquee in the centre of the lawn. There are about fifteen small tables dotted around the garden, each with its own umbrella. Each table is decorated with a floral centrepiece, and someone has arranged lanterns in all the trees. The Carsons must have spent days on this.

By the time, we've organised the food, people have started to arrive. I recognise a few of our regular customers, but Isabella seems to know them all. She greets them by name and ushers them into the marquee.

'Mrs Ogilvie mustn't see you too soon,' she explains.

'Were you planning for everyone to jump out and shout *Surprise*!' I say.

'I wanted to,' she says. 'But Abby talked me out of it. She said we don't need Mrs Ogilvie spending her birthday afternoon in the cardiac ward.'

'So, what's the plan?'

'Mrs Carson will take her into the house until I give the signal. Then she'll bring her into the garden to find Martin. I hope Mabel arrives in time.'

'I expect she'll be here,' I say. 'I've only met her once, but she struck me as a competent woman. Just like her sister.'

'It's in the lap of the gods,' says Isabella. 'We've done everything we can, and the rest is up to fate. In the meantime, I'll make sure everyone has something to drink.'

'Soft drinks, I hope. We don't want half the guests to be drunk before the guest of honour arrives.'

'Most of the elderly people I know can drink me under the table,' she says. 'But I'm way ahead of you. Mrs Carson has left several jugs of iced elderflower juice in the kitchen. I'll bring them out.'

I look around the garden at the people chatting and laughing in the sunshine. When I first suggested this party, I assumed we would just be offering tea and cake. I had no idea it would spiral into something like this. This must be what Will meant when he talked about community. An entire village coming together to support someone who needs it. I hope Mrs Ogilvie feels the same. It would be awful if she took one look at our arrangements and ran away.

A sharp yap rouses me from these musings, and I turn to see Will has arrived with Bernie. Will looks exhausted, but Bernie is as perky as ever. He gives an excited yelp when he sees me and tears across the lawn to greet me, with Will barely clinging to his lead.

'This is wonderful!' I say, bending to hug Bernie. 'Have you taken him on a nice long walk to tire him out?'

'About an hour,' says Will. 'I didn't want to be late for the party.'

'I was talking to Bernie,' I say. 'Remind me to show you how to shorten his lead. It will prevent you from being tied to stray lamp posts.'

He laughs. 'I hoped you wouldn't notice that.'

Lily comes out of the house, carrying Daisy. She waves when she sees me. 'Isn't this incredible?'

'It's amazing,' I say. 'Your parents must have worked so hard on all this.'

'They've had a lot of help,' she says. 'Mavis and the Silver Surfers have done most of the organising. They've loaned tables and chairs and plates. One of them knows someone who rents marquees, so they managed to get a huge discount. And they've talked all the local suppliers into donating things. Mr Peters told me it's one of the joys of getting older. You don't care what people think of you, and you have plenty of time to make them see your point of view.'

'Do you think Mrs Ogilvie will like it?' I say.

Will gives me a reassuring smile. 'You worry too much. She'll love it.'

Isabella appears around the side of the house. 'Mabel's here! Just in time. Angela has texted me to say they're almost back in Honeywell. Apparently, Mrs Ogilvie is most unimpressed with Nigel's car maintenance skills.'

'Whizzy!' shrieks Daisy, struggling out of Lily's arms and setting off at a determined crawl towards Isabella.

Isabella scoops her up and gestures to us all to join her in the marquee.

'We should all stay as quiet as possible,' she instructs us. 'Angela and Mrs Ogilvie will be out at any moment.'

'Whizzy!' shouts Daisy again.

Isabella lays a finger on her lips. 'Let's play a game to see who can be the quietest.'

Daisy gives a squawk of laughter and Isabella picks up an iced cookie. 'Don't talk until you've finished that.'

Daisy beams at her and crams the cookie into her mouth.

'You could have given her a piece of cheese,' murmurs Lily.

'Cheese!' says Isabella contemptuously. She lifts a finger. 'I can hear them.'

The marquee has fallen silent. Everyone is staring at the doorway. There's a murmur of voices, which grows louder.

'Let's see where Martin is, shall we?' says Mrs Carson's voice.

They appear a moment later. Mrs Ogilvie takes in the inside of the tent – the tables of food, the crowd of people, the bunches of balloons. She looks around without speaking.

Mabel has been standing at the back of the tent until now. She steps forward when she sees her sister. 'Happy birthday, Edith!'

Chapter Thirty-Six

For a moment, Mrs Ogilvie doesn't move. She looks at Mabel as though she's seen a ghost. Mabel looks back at her, an enquiring smile on her lips. It feels as though the entire crowd is holding its breath. Then Mrs Ogilvie throws her arms around Mabel and bursts into tears.

'Oh dear,' says Mrs Carson uncertainly.

Neither Mabel nor Edith takes any notice. They hug each other as though they never want to let each other go.

There's a chorus of happy birthdays, which seems to bring them back to reality.

Mrs Ogilvie lets go of her sister and looks around, dazed. 'I don't understand.'

'Of course, you do!' says Mabel, wiping her eyes. 'It's your birthday.'

'But you're in London,' says Mrs Ogilvie.

'I was in London,' says Mabel. 'You didn't think I'd miss your party, did you?'

'Both your parties,' says Isabella. 'Once I discovered you were identical twins, it didn't take me more than four or five hours to work out that you must share the same birthday. I'm quick like that.'

'Go on with you!' says Mabel. 'I don't need a party. I'm just happy to see Edith again.'

'Too late,' says Lily, reaching up and pulling a red ribbon hanging down from the top of the tent.

A rolled up banner unfurls itself and opens out. It reads *Happy Birthday, Edith and Mabel!*

'I made that,' says Isabella. 'You wouldn't believe how long it took me. I spelled the first one wrong.'

'Birthday is a tricky word for anyone to spell,' says Will, looking amused.

'I've known how to spell that one for ages,' says Isabella. 'But the first time I made the banner, I put two bs in Mabel. I didn't think anyone would notice, but Lily made me do it again. She's such a perfectionist.'

Mrs Carson has been handing out glasses of champagne to all the guests. She clinks her fork on a plate. 'We should drink a toast! I'd like to thank all of you who have so generously contributed to this party in various ways. We couldn't have done it without you. Also, many thanks to The Sugarloaf Bakery for providing this lovely food. Abby, you've surpassed yourself.'

'Don't forget Olivia,' interjects Isabella. 'This was all her idea in the first place.'

'I was getting to that,' says Mrs Carson. 'We're grateful to everyone who's contributed in whatever way. And last, but not least, the birthday girls! Thank goodness we managed to get you in the same place at the same time. I hope you enjoy your party!'

She raises her glass to Mrs Ogilvie and Mabel and drinks. We all follow suit.

'Help yourselves to this lovely food,' says Mrs Carson. 'We don't have room for it in the freezer, so it all has to go.'

People fill their plates and wander out into the garden. Mrs Ogilvie still looks dazed. 'I don't understand what's happened.'

Mabel takes her arm. 'I'll explain it to you later. In the meantime, you and I have a lot of catching up to do.' She leads Mrs Ogilvie out of the tent, and they disappear towards the house.

'Thank goodness for that,' I say. 'It was touch and go there for a while. There were so many things that could have gone wrong.'

'It was bound to turn out all right in the end,' says Mrs Carson. 'These things always do.'

'Where's Daisy?' says Lily suddenly.

I notice that Isabella is no longer holding her goddaughter. 'Have you lost her already?'

'She's over there.' Isabella points to where Daisy is sitting on the grass underneath a table, sharing a cookie with Bernie.

'Stop that!' exclaims Lily, making a dart for her daughter. Bernie takes advantage of the commotion to snatch the rest of the cookie, and Daisy gives a wail.

Isabella picks her up. 'Don't worry. We're cutting the cake soon, and you shall have the biggest slice!'

Lily groans. 'Don't say that. She'll understand you.'

'Of course, she understands me,' says Isabella. 'She's the cleverest girl in the whole, wide world. Come on, Daisy. We'd better get you something else to eat before we cut the cake. Your mother seems to have a cheese obsession. Let's start with that.'

Lily brushes the grass off her skirt. 'I sometimes wonder what was going through my mind when I made her Daisy's godmother.'

'It was an excellent decision,' I say. 'I wish I'd had a godmother like Isabella.'

It's late afternoon by the time Mrs Ogilvie and Mabel reappear. Their eyes are suspiciously red, but they're both smiling.

Bernie jumps up at Mabel, who pats his head. 'I see what you mean, Edith. He is precious.'

'He's all I have,' says Mrs Ogilvie, her eyes moist.

'That isn't true,' says Mabel.

Mrs Ogilvie gives one of her rare smiles. 'I suppose not.'

Mabel catches my eye. 'You and Will went to so much trouble to find me. You should be the first to know. I'm moving back to Honeywell!'

'Permanently?' I say, astonished.

'That's right. Australia is all very well and good, but I've found myself missing home more and more.'

'What a great idea!' says Will. 'Where will you live?'

'With Edith,' she says. 'I was planning to buy myself a small house in the village, but she won't hear of it.'

'I have two extra bedrooms,' says Mrs Ogilvie. 'There's plenty of room for us both. And Bernie will enjoy the company. He's quite taken to Mabel.'

Bernie has positioned himself under the nearest table in case anyone drops any food. He grins up at me and thumps his tail.

'He'll love it,' I say. 'Bernie is an extremely sociable dog, even for a cavoodle. He'll adore all the extra fuss.'

Mrs Carson bustles up, holding a bottle of champagne. 'Can I fill anyone's glass?'

'Good idea,' says Will. 'We have plenty to celebrate. Mabel is moving to Honeywell.'

Mrs Carson almost drops the bottle. 'That's lovely news! I'm so glad for you both. Will you be living in Honeysuckle Cottage together?'

'That's the plan,' says Mabel. 'But not immediately. Edie and I are going to London tomorrow for a few days. It's high time we spent some time together.'

She turns to me. 'We were hoping you might agree to look after Bernie? It's a lot to ask, but Edie tells me you're so good with him, and he loves you.'

'I'd be honoured,' I say. 'Bernie and I will have lots of fun together. If my landlady isn't keen on the idea, maybe I could stay at the cottage while you're gone?'

'Better still!' she says. 'Edie's always had a thing about burglars.'

Mrs Carson fills the rest of our glasses. 'This seems to be an afternoon for toasts. To the newest member of our village. Welcome home!'

'I'd better fetch another bottle of champagne,' she says when we've drunk the toast. 'In case anyone else has something to celebrate.'

'I'm happy to toast anything you like,' says Isabella, appearing in the doorway with Daisy in her arms. 'But I doubt anything will top that. I never dreamed this party would be such a success. That's all thanks to you, Olivia.'

'I hardly did anything,' I say.

'It was your idea,' she says. 'Without you, there wouldn't have been a party at all. And look what a great time everyone's having.'

Lily appears behind her. 'There you are! I couldn't find Daisy anywhere. She's supposed to be having a nap.'

'She can have a nap any time,' says Isabella. 'It would be a shame to miss this afternoon. She's been having so much fun. She's a party girl, just like her godmother.'

'What are you all talking about?' says Lily.

'The future,' says Will. 'Mabel is moving to Honeywell, and Bernie is getting himself a new servant.'

'I'm so pleased,' Lily tells Mabel. 'I hope you'll be very happy here. Honeywell has probably changed since you last visited. You'll have to get Bernie to show you our bakery. We have a cafe now, and he's one of our most regular customers. We're thinking of putting up a plaque.'

'Speaking of change,' says Isabella. 'Plenty of other things are happening. Lily is starting work back at the bakery on Monday.'

'Is that right?' says Will, shooting me a quick glance.

'It is,' I say. 'She and Isabella told me last week.'

Mrs Ogilvie looks concerned. 'Does that mean Honeywell will be losing you, my dear?'

'I'm afraid so. It's time I moved on. I've had the most amazing summer here, and I'll never forget it. But I don't think it's the place I'm supposed to be – at least not for now.'

She nods. 'You must do what's best for you. But Bernie and I will miss you.'

Will still hasn't spoken. I half expect him to ask me what I'm doing next, but he doesn't.

Isabella breaks the silence. 'Have you made any definite plans, Olivia?'

Everyone's eyes are on me. I hadn't expected to do this now, but why not? It's time I stopped caring what everyone thinks about me and the choices I make.

I reach into my pocket and pull out a crumpled piece of paper, which I clutch like a talisman. 'As a matter of fact, I have.'

Chapter Thirty-Seven

I turn to face the assembled group. Isabella looks amused, while Lily looks anxious. I can't quite read Will's expression.

I unfold the piece of paper. 'I realised something while I was racing around London yesterday. Somewhere along the line, I've lost the ability to say, "I want." I'm not sure when that happened, but it did. I spent a long time thinking about it last night, and I made this list. It isn't complete, but it's a start.'

I take a deep breath and start to read. 'I like mountains, but I'm not too keen on the beach. I love handwritten letters with real wax seals. I like rock music, but I hate jazz. I like thrillers, but I find romance films boring. I prefer plain apple pie and ice cream to Tiramisu. I hate flavoured coffees. I love rainy days and splashing through puddles. I like yellow, but I don't like red. I prefer the autumn to the spring. I hate the idea of going in a helicopter, but I've always wanted to take a trip in a hot air balloon. I love the idea of buying the first plane ticket to anywhere and seeing where I end up. I hate planning my life down to the last second. I'd rather chew my arm off than go to a nightclub. I want to swim with dolphins one day.'

'You can do that in Australia!' says Mabel. 'I'll send you a link.'

Mrs Ogilvie taps her sister's arm. 'This isn't the time.'

'Sorry,' says Mabel. 'I thought she wanted to know where she could find some dolphins.'

'No, she doesn't. Stop talking and listen!'

I resume my list. 'I don't want to be a general veterinary nurse forever. I want to take a post grad course and specialise. I want to travel and see the world. I want to go to California and see the sun rise over the Pacific Ocean. I want to sleep in a tree house in Kenya. I want to learn to cook Mexican food and make a proper margarita. I want to adopt a rescue dog and have my own garden.'

I'm so engrossed in my list that I've almost forgotten everyone is standing there, watching me. I look up and see Mrs Carson's encouraging smile. Isabella gives me a thumbs up, but no one else speaks.

Will breaks the silence at last. 'Is that all you want?'

I force myself to meet his eyes, aware of my heart beating uncomfortably fast. 'No, it isn't. I added one more thing to the list this morning. I want you.'

He doesn't move. 'Are you sure?'

'Yes. I want to do all the things I just said. But it won't be half as much fun doing them by myself. I'd far rather do them with you. It's fine if you don't want the same things I do. But I couldn't leave Honeywell without telling you.'

'I should point out the sun actually sets over the Pacific Ocean,' he says. 'Also, I prefer Italian food to Mexican. But if we're both willing to make a couple of compromises, I think we could make this work.'

'You do?' I say.

'The only thing on your list I care about is the last one,' he says. 'I want you too, Olivia. I've wanted you ever since the first day we met, when we argued about ping pong balls and giant omelettes. I even wanted you when you made fun of me at the quintain.'

'The what?' says Mabel, but Mrs Ogilvie shushes her again.

'So, the only question left unanswered,' says Will, his eyes fixed on mine, 'is whether I'm going to kiss you in front of this crowd of interested observers, or whether we're going to find somewhere more private.'

'Don't you dare!' says Isabella in such an indignant tone I can't help laughing.

Will smiles down at me, his eyes full of amusement. But there's something else there, something that makes my heart beat faster.

'The crowd has spoken,' he says, putting his hands on my shoulders and bending his head to mine.

It's nothing like our last kiss. This isn't a result of the adrenaline fuelled chase across the lawn and my successful picture of Bernie. It feels soft and sweet and familiar, as though I've been kissing him all my life. It's also unfamiliar and exciting, a promise of things to come – things I never knew I wanted, yet I now realise I can't live without.

Will suddenly staggers and slips, letting go of me just in time before he falls.

'Bernie, you naughty boy!' says Mrs Ogilvie. 'What are you doing?'

I look down to see Bernie's lead wrapped around my legs and Will lying in a heap at my feet. I drop to my knees next to him. 'Are you all right?'

He slips an arm around my shoulders and pulls me towards him. 'I've never been better!'

I sit back on my heels. 'Now isn't the time!'

'I disagree,' he says. 'I've been waiting for this for a long time.'

'Don't mind us!' says Isabella. 'Pretend we're not here.'

'You see?' says Will.

I untangle the lead from around his legs. 'I think the moment has passed.'

I help him to his feet, and he hands the lead back to Mrs Ogilvie. 'This is yours, I believe?'

'I'm so sorry,' she says. 'I can't imagine what came over him. He's usually such a well-behaved dog.'

'He's perfect,' I say, holding his paws as he jumps up to lick me. 'He's had an exciting day, that's all. Even the best-behaved dogs forget themselves at times.'

I turn to Will. 'Which reminds me. Where did you put that parcel?'

'In the hall.'

'I'll fetch it!' says Mrs Carson. 'Lily, can you pour some more champagne? It seems we have another toast to drink.'

She returns a minute later, carrying not one but two parcels. 'Are these both yours, Will?'

'That's right.' He hands the first one to Mrs Ogilvie. 'This one is from me. The other is from Olivia.'

She tears open the paper, and her eyes fill with tears. 'Oh, Bernie!'

Everyone crowds around to look at the picture she's holding. Will has framed it beautifully. I smile as I see Bernie sitting in the middle of the flowers, looking up at the butterfly and grinning. That was quite an afternoon.

Mrs Ogilvie wipes her eyes. 'It's so like him!'

'I should hope so,' says Will. 'It's what I do for a living. Open the other one.'

Mrs Ogilvie tears off the wrapping paper. 'However did you manage to take this?'

'I didn't,' says Will. 'Olivia did.'

'I'm impressed!' says Lily. 'I didn't know you were a photographer too, Olivia.'

'My girlfriend is multi-talented,' says Will proudly.

'Aren't you getting a bit ahead of yourself?' I say.

'I don't think so. If we were living in mediaeval times, you'd have to marry me after kissing me like that before all these witnesses.'

'If we were living in mediaeval times,' I retort, 'you'd have had to win me a lot more ribbons before I let you kiss me at all.'

His arm tightens around my shoulders. 'Isn't it lucky we're living in the twenty-first century?'

'They didn't have cameras back then,' says Lily. 'You'd have had to paint Bernie instead.'

'He wouldn't have sat still for long enough,' I say. 'All you'd have seen was a blur of oil paint.'

Mrs Ogilvie lays the pictures on the table next to her. 'I shall hang these over the fireplace as soon as I get home. Bernie will enjoy seeing them each evening as he lies in front of the fire.'

'Good idea,' says Mabel. 'And I'll put up some pictures of Melbourne. It will remind me of all the fun I've had over the past few years.'

'You'll have lots more fun over the next few years,' says Isabella. 'Both of you together.'

'I hope so,' says Mrs Ogilvie.

'Of course, we will,' says Mabel. 'The three of us will make a great team.'

Lily fills everyone's glasses. 'That's the last of the champagne. There's enough for one final toast. We'd better make it a good one.'

Mrs Ogilvie surprises me by speaking first. 'I'd like to propose this one, if no one minds. First of all, Mabel and I would like to say thank you to everyone who has worked so hard to make this wonderful party happen. I haven't enjoyed myself so much since our fifth birthday, which we also celebrated in a garden in Honeywell.'

'That was a corker!' says Mabel. 'You made yourself sick on blancmange, and I fell into the stream at the bottom of the garden.'

Mrs Ogilvie ignores this. 'I'd like to say a special thank you to Olivia. She may not be staying in Honeywell forever, but I'm so pleased she came to visit. I'm even more delighted she found what she was looking for.'

'Hear, hear!' says Will.

'There's something very special about Honeywell,' she goes on. 'I knew that when I was younger, but I've rather lost sight of it. I'm glad both your paths converged in this place so we could all be here to see you start off on your journey together.'

She lifts her glass. 'To Will and Olivia – may your lives be filled with adventure and love.'

Bernie gives an excited yap and tries to knock Mabel's glass out of her hand.

'Steady on, old fellow,' she says, moving it out of his reach. 'You and I will be setting some guidelines before we move in together. The first rule will be that you never, ever touch my drink.'

'He's excited,' says Mrs Ogilvie. 'You'll find he's as good as gold once you come to know him better.'

'He's lovely,' says Isabella. 'But he doesn't enjoy being left out. We've drunk to everything else this afternoon, but we shouldn't forget it's his birthday too. There's enough champagne left in everyone's glasses for one more toast. And I know the very one. To Bernie – may your paws always remain free from thorns, and may you keep The Sugarloaf Bakery in profit for many years to come!'

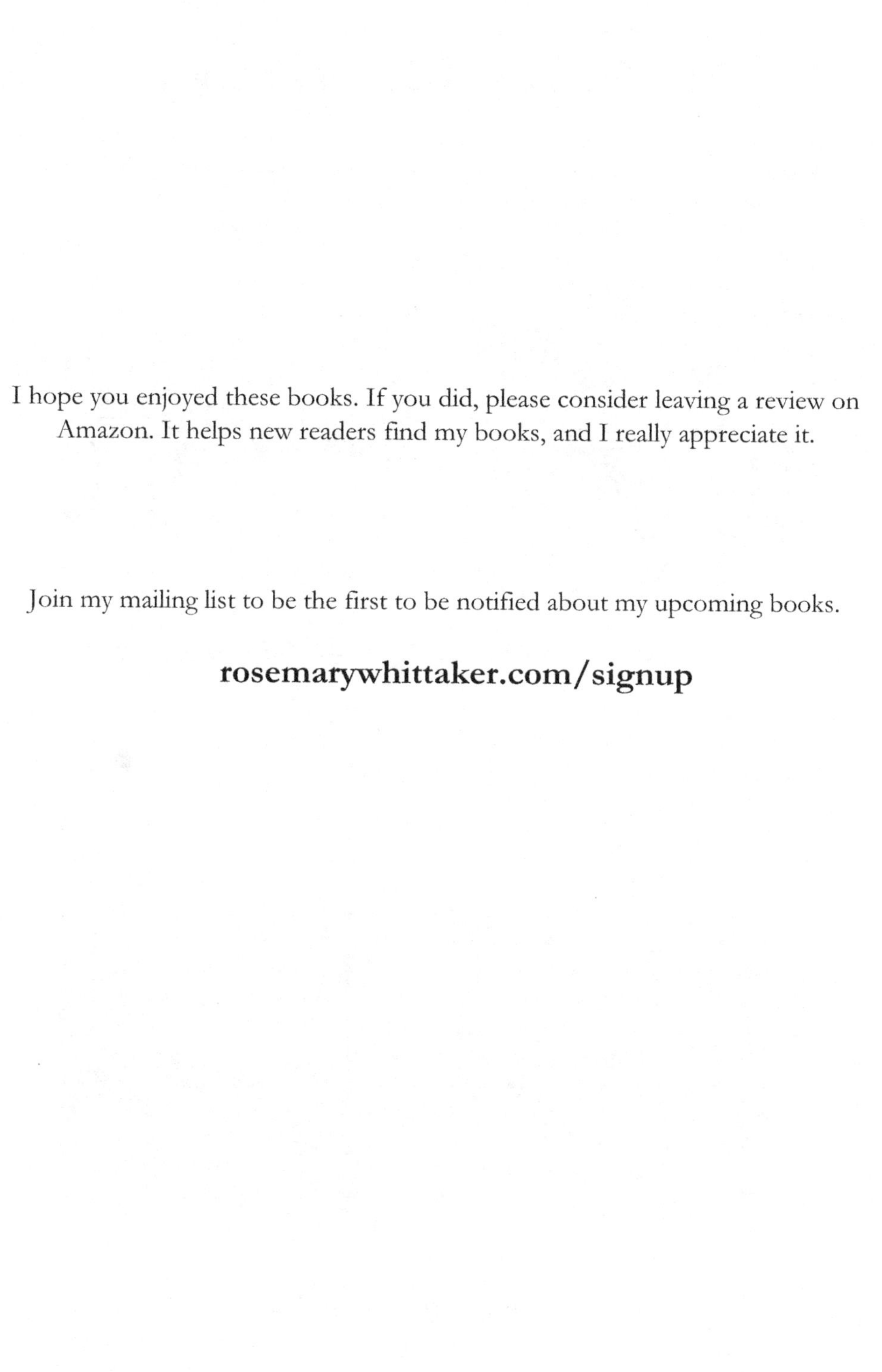

I hope you enjoyed these books. If you did, please consider leaving a review on Amazon. It helps new readers find my books, and I really appreciate it.

Join my mailing list to be the first to be notified about my upcoming books.

rosemarywhittaker.com/signup

The Sugarloaf Bakery Series

Available now in paperback and Kindle ebook

A Tale of Two Christmases

Annie never comes home for Christmas. There's too much chance of running into Alex. He broke her heart, and she never wants to speak to him again.

Alex always comes home for Christmas. He's desperate to talk to Annie about what went wrong between them.

Faced with a family crisis, Annie reluctantly agrees to spend the holidays with her parents. It shouldn't be too difficult to avoid Alex for just one week.

But she didn't expect to arrive in the middle of the wedding of the year. The entire village will be there, and no one will be able to avoid anyone else.

It's a battle of two Christmases, and only one can win.

Snuggle up in front of a roaring fire with a mug of hot chocolate and enjoy this sparkling Christmas romance.

Available now in paperback and Kindle ebook

The Cinnamon Snail

She's found the love of her life. He just hasn't realised it …

When Christian moves from Copenhagen to London, Kate quickly tumbles into love. He's the most handsome and charismatic man she's ever met, and she's all set for her Happily Ever After.

Until he announces that he's returning to Copenhagen, and he doesn't want her to go with him. Nothing Kate can say will change his mind. All she can do is plan a new future without him. And if that future happens to be in Denmark, that's entirely her own business.

She gets a job at The Cinnamon Snail Cafe and sets out to win Christian back. His new girlfriend is a slight problem – but when true love is on the line, anything goes.

Kate has a year to prove she can settle into a new country and persuade the love of her life she means business. A piece of cake!

A delightful new story of Danish pastries, romance, and lots and lots of hygge.

Available now in paperback and Kindle ebook

About the author

Rosemary Whittaker wanted to be an author as soon as she was old enough to hold a book the right way up. From that moment on, she was the despair of her teachers, who attempted to impart the basics of an education while she stared out of the window, making up characters and situations.

Having accidentally absorbed enough to graduate and become a teacher, she spent the next few decades moving around the world with her husband, children, and menagerie of unexpected pets.

She accidentally found herself in Australia some years back and intends to stay there for a very long time. She currently spends her time writing, sourcing English marmite and salad cream and wrangling her two determinedly destructive house bunnies – Pumpkin and Midway.

Rosemary has written several light-hearted romance novels set in the different countries in which she has lived. She also writes children's books as R J Whittaker – in particular a series of books about a recalcitrant monkey named Pom Pom, who is not in any way, shape or form based on her experience of raising her own four boys.

Made in the USA
Monee, IL
28 September 2025